PRAISE FOR *THE CELLAR*

"[A] ripped-from-the-headlines novel."

—*School Library Journal*

"Fans of realistic horror like *Living Dead Girl* (2008) may appreciate this."

—*Booklist Online*

"A well-written, completely absorbing nail-biter of a book...[with] a powerful, suffocating atmosphere of dread and uncertainty."

—*Bookish*

"Like watching an episode of *Law & Order: SVU*... I honestly could not tear myself away."

—*Chapter by Chapter* blog

"A real treat for avid mystery and thriller fans; the story line pulls you inside the world of a madman and the women he preys on... never a dull moment."

—*Teen Reads* blog

ALSO BY NATASHA PRESTON

The Cellar

The Cabin

You Will Be Mine

AWAKE

Natasha Preston

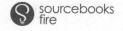

sourcebooks
fire

Published by Sourcebooks Fire, an imprint of Sourcebooks, Inc.
P.O. Box 4410, Naperville, Illinois 60567-4410
(630) 961-3900
Fax: (630) 961-2168
sourcebooks.com

Library of Congress Cataloging-in-Publication Data

Preston, Natasha.
   Awake / Natasha Preston.
      pages cm
   Summary: "A car accident causes Scarlett to start remembering pieces of an unfamil-
iar past. When a new guy moves into town, Scarlett feels an instant spark. But Noah
knows the truth of Scarlett's past, and he's determined to shield her from it...because
Scarlett grew up in a cult called Eternal Light, controlled by her biological parents.
And they want her back"-- Provided by publisher.
   (13 : alk. paper) [1. Cults--Fiction. 2. Memory--Fiction. 3. Love--Fiction. 4. Fami-
lies--Fiction.] I. Title.
   PZ7.P9234Aw 2015
   [Fic]--dc23
                                    2015007493

Printed and bound in the United States of America.
VP 11

I'd like to dedicate this book to my readers.
Thank you for making my dreams come true.

1

SCARLETT

Imogen nudged my arm, nodding toward the classroom door. "Finally, some talent," she whispered.

She wasn't wrong. The guy standing by Mrs. Wells's door was gorgeous—like, *shouldn't even be at our school* gorgeous.

"Welcome to Fordham High, Noah," Mrs. Wells said. "Take a seat over there." She pointed to the empty space next to me, and Imogen gripped my forearm. "Scarlett and Imogen, you have most of the same classes as Noah this year, so please show him around and make him feel welcome."

Im's face lit up. "Absolutely."

Good luck, Noah.

He walked to our desk at the back of the classroom, demanding everyone's attention and owning the room, but his focus was on me. I squirmed in my seat, heat flooding my face. He looked older, the way he carried himself with an air of *I don't give a crap.*

"Hi," he said, still staring just at me.

"Hey. I'm Scarlett, and that's Imogen," I said, pointing to my best friend beside me. "I guess we're your tour guides."

"Thank you," he replied. He even sounded older—he pronounced a lot more of each word than most of the kids here did. "Although this school is so small, I doubt anyone could get lost here."

"So true!" Imogen said, leaning over the desk so Noah could see her past me.

Bobby turned around in his seat. "You like wrestling, Noah?"

Noah's forehead creased.

I held up my hand. "Bobby's a WWE freak; he's not offering you a fight."

"Definitely not," Bobby confirmed. "You look like you can handle yourself."

Noah grinned. "Handling myself is what got me expelled from my last school."

He didn't seem like the fighting type, but then again, I'd known him for five seconds. Maybe he was repeating a grade.

"How old are you?" I asked. "You look older than fifteen or sixteen."

"Sixteen," he replied. "What about you?"

"Same."

"She's *just* sixteen," Imogen cut in, clearly annoyed at being ignored. "I am too."

I wanted to roll my eyes. As if he were going to take her over the desk right now just because she'd been the same age as him that little bit longer.

"Yeah, it was my birthday last month," I explained.

Still ignoring Imogen, Noah said, "It was my brother's birthday last month too. What date was yours?"

"Thirteenth. Thank God it wasn't a Friday this year."

He laughed. "Are you superstitious?"

I nodded once. "Big-time. I won't walk under a ladder or cross paths with a black cat. I wave to magpies, depending on how many there are, of course, and throw salt over my shoulder." He cocked his eyebrow. I shrugged. "My parents are kinda superstitious too. And suspicious."

"Wow," he said. "Well, you never know what's out there in the big, bad world."

Out there in the big, bad world. Déjà vu. I'd heard that somewhere before, but I couldn't place it.

The bell rang, making me jump. "Ready for English lit?" I asked Noah, ignoring the odd feeling inside.

"Not really. You are sitting next to me, right? You're my tour guide, after all."

Imogen stalked off ahead, in a foul mood because she didn't have Noah eating out of her hand.

I smiled. "Sure."

"So where did you move from?" I asked Noah as we walked to our next class.

Throughout our fifty-minute English class, Noah had quizzed me relentlessly. It was as if he was trying to learn every last thing there was to know. New kids weren't usually this chatty. But I liked it and wanted to know all about him too.

"Hayling Island."

"Cool. What's it like there?"

"Small," he replied.

I'd learned about it in geography when we briefly covered the British Isles. It really was small.

"What made you move to Bath?"

"My dad's job. Hayling wasn't much fun, so it's nice to be here."

We reached the science block, and I turned to him. "Well, I'm glad you're here." My eyes widened to the point of pain. *Why on earth did I say that out loud?* I cringed. You didn't tell a guy you kind of liked him right away—especially when you'd only known him an hour.

He shoved a hand through his fair hair, moving it out of the way of his forehead, and smiled. His light-blue eyes sparkled. Actually freakin' sparkled. I used to think I was more of a tall, dark, and handsome type of girl, but it was *definitely* tall, blond, and handsome for me now. His jaw looked like it had been carved from stone, and his lips... Well, those things would have any girl gaping.

He stared down, a full head taller than me. "I'm glad that you're glad."

Sucking my lips between my teeth, I took a small step back. I liked him. There was no question of that, but he looked dangerously close to kissing me, and I was in no way ready for that.

We were called into the classroom, and Noah took a seat next to me. The Bunsen burners were out, which meant I was going to have to really listen because it looked like we were doing an experiment. I hated experiments.

"You good at chemistry?" I asked.

He chuckled. "There is a bad joke in there somewhere. I'm okay, yeah."

"Good, because I suck. I'm failing so badly, I don't know why they continue to make me attend. I think my presence alone dumbs down the rest of the class."

He chuckled. "You can't be that bad."

"Oh, wait and see."

"Settle down," Mr. Gregor said. "Welcome, Noah. Have you covered—"

And that was where I switched off. I couldn't be any less interested in chemistry if I tried. I'd learned more watching *The Big Bang Theory* than I had at school.

I switched back on when Noah poured something into a test tube.

"What's the point of this then?" I asked, nodding to the Bunsen burner.

"You really don't like science, do you?"

"No."

"Me neither, actually. There is too much unexplained that science doesn't have an answer to."

"What do you believe in?"

He shrugged. "I'm not sure yet. Anyway, I might not like all this, but I do understand it, so I'll explain while I work, and you can make notes. Let's see if I can help you pass this class."

Yeah, again, good luck, Noah.

I popped the lid off my pen, trying to concentrate on what he was saying rather than his deep voice and the way his crooked smile made me swoon. There was no way he was going to be able to help me with chemistry—the subject anyway.

As he worked, his eyes kept flicking back to watch me like I was the most interesting thing on the planet, like he was scared if he took his eyes off me, I'd be assassinated.

He turned to me once everything was set up. "Tell me something about yourself."

"We're supposed to be making those chemicals…do something." *And there's not a whole lot to tell.*

He shrugged. "We've got a minute. Come on."

There *was* one thing. I didn't like to bring it up much because it was weird and I always got the same *how can it not drive you crazy* question. Sighing, I replied, "I remember nothing before the age of four."

His eyebrows shot up. "What?"

"There was a house fire and we lost everything. My parents got me and my brother, Jeremy, out, but we were hospitalized for smoke inhalation. When I woke up, I couldn't remember anything."

"Nothing?"

"Nope. All I remember is waking up in a yellow room. I didn't even know my family."

"When did you start remembering?"

I frowned. "I didn't. They filled in the blanks with stories of stuff we'd done, but I don't actually remember any of it."

"That's crazy. Hey, they could've told you anything."

I laughed. "Yeah, they could've had fun with that one. 'We're a normal family and you and your brother fight like cats and dogs' is pretty boring."

"They could have made you a princess. Or you could really be a princess and they stole you away to—"

"Okay," I said, cutting him off, "you have an overactive imagination."

Smiling, he replied, "Sorry. It's just a bit weird."

"Totally weird. I repressed everything because of the traumatic experience, apparently."

"Think you'll ever get your memory back?"

I shrugged. "Probably not. Doesn't matter though."

"I suppose not. I would just hate to have lost *four years* and a lot of experiences I couldn't remember."

"It bugged me before but not now. Lots of people don't remember much of their childhood. I just don't remember the first four years."

"Did you try therapy or get hypnotized?"

I laughed. "Nope. It's really not that big of a deal. I tried remembering, but there's nothing there."

He smiled. "One day you will remember."

I gave up believing that about four years ago.

2

SCARLETT

One hundred and eleven. That was how many texts had gone back and forth between me and Noah in the *six* days we'd known each other. It was a ridiculous amount of texts to send a virtual stranger. But he didn't feel like a stranger. We'd talked about almost everything—our likes and dislikes, family, friends, funniest moments, darkest moments. Although there was a lot more to learn about each other, I felt that I knew him pretty well already. He seemed determined to know everything there was to know about plain old me.

After a full school week of flirting our butts off, I had fully entered the obsessive realm, and now my every thought pretty much involved Noah. I annoyed myself and was sure my family now hated me.

"I'm leaving in a minute," I said to my parents.

"Who's meeting you?"

"No one. I'm walking to Noah's; then we're heading to town together."

One of Dad's dark eyebrows lifted. "We'll take you to this Noah kid's house. It's about time we meet him."

"What?" No, that was not happening.

"Honey, you don't expect us to let you go to the house of

someone you barely know and we've never met, do you?" Mum said.

"Yes! That is *exactly* what I expect. Noah's fine."

"I'm sure he is, but if you're going to be hanging out with him outside of school, then we need to know him," Dad added. "I'll just get the keys."

"You can't be serious. Why're you doing this to me? Do you have *any* idea how embarrassing it's going to be when I show up with my parents?" Did they skip being teenagers altogether?

Jeremy laughed. "I'm really enjoying this."

Glaring at him, I said, "I hate you."

"All right, drama queen," Mum said. "Get your jacket and we'll go now."

"Can you at least wait in the car?"

"That defeats the objective of meeting Noah."

Following her, I grumbled, "I know."

Ten minutes later, I knocked on Noah's door and took a deep breath. He hadn't told me if his parents were home or not; mine were standing behind me. A guy that looked like Noah opened the door. His brother.

"Are you Scarlett?" he asked.

"Yep. You're Finn, right?" He nodded and stepped aside. "This is my mum and dad, Marissa and Jonathan."

"It is nice to meet you all. Come in. He is around somewhere. Can I get you anything? You thirsty?"

I shook my head. "I'm good, thanks."

"No, thank you, Finn," Dad said. "Are your parents home?"

"Yes, in the kitchen. Come through."

I followed Finn into a glossy, white kitchen. He sat on a stool at the counter, so I followed, wishing Noah would hurry up. Why hadn't Finn called for him?

Noah's parents turned around. They were both effortlessly beautiful, just like their sons.

"Marissa and Jonathan, these are my parents, Bethan and Shaun."

Bethan's eyes lit up. "Scarlett! It is so lovely to finally meet you. And I am so glad your parents came too. Jonathan, Marissa, how do you do?"

"So, what are you going to see?" Noah's carbon-copy big brother asked me.

"No idea. We just go and see whatever's on. It's kind of a thing my friends and I do."

"Really? Have you seen many awful movies?"

"Tons," I replied.

Finn smiled, and it made him look even more handsome, though not as much as Noah—but then, I was pretty much obsessed with his younger brother.

"Do I need to ask what your intentions with Noah are?" he asked, fighting another smile.

Laughing, I swiveled on my stool and rested my arms on the counter. "I promise my intentions are good."

"He will be so disappointed," he replied, winking. "Tell me about yourself, Scarlett."

"Not much to tell really."

"So you are the average teenager? No skeletons in your closet?"

I held my finger up. "I stole a chocolate bar from a sweet shop when I was ten. But I felt so bad that I couldn't eat it."

He laughed. "A regular little rebel, aren't you?"

"Totally bad*ass*," I replied, killing the American accent with one syllable.

"I thought I heard the door," Noah said, eyes widening when he saw my parents chatting to his. "Why didn't you call me, Finn?"

"If you weren't too busy doing your hair, you would have been down here to let her in, *girlie*."

Ah, brotherly love.

"Sorry about my brother," Noah said. "And these are your parents?"

Mum and Dad turned around, and another round of introductions started.

I watched my dad closely. His shoulders relaxed, and he smiled as he spoke to Noah. *Yes!* Clearly he didn't think Noah was about to murder me.

"I guess we should get going and let these kids get to the theater," Mum said. "It was lovely to meet you all; we'll have to get together sometime."

Bethan touched Mum's arm. "That would be fantastic. We don't know very many people here."

"Ready?" I asked Noah. "Or do you need more time to do your hair?"

Finn laughed, offering his hand for a high five. I slapped it, earning a glare from the guy I couldn't seem to get out of my head.

"Okay, you are never meeting my brother again," Noah said, pulling me off the stool. I swooned inwardly at the feel of his soft-yet-firm hand covering mine.

We made a quick exit, leaving my parents to continue talking to his, and set out for the shortcut to town. I was so looking forward to spending time with him outside school, I was practically skipping.

"Favorite holiday?"

"Hmm," I murmured. "It's between Christmas and Easter. Probably Easter."

"Why Easter?"

"We go to visit my grandparents, and they put on a massive Easter egg hunt. They own a farm, so it literally takes all day to find the eggs. Then we light a fire in their living room, drink hot chocolate, and eat our eggs. Sugar coma central, but I love it. Three months to go!"

Noah grinned down at me.

"What about you?"

He frowned. "Holidays aren't that big in my family. Christmas, I suppose. So you will be away over Easter?"

"Yep. In Cornwall, so we'll be there Thursday night until Monday afternoon. My friends usually do something Monday night if you want to come too?"

"What do you do?" he asked.

I shrugged. "Just hang out. Imogen has an outdoor pool, so we spend the day in the water. The guys burn barbecue food."

"You go in an outdoor swimming pool in April?"

"Yeah. Last year was okay, but the year before, the English weather was not kind to us."

"You still did it?"

"Yep, it's tradition."

"Crazy tradition," he muttered, making me laugh. "What about your birthday? Anything planned yet?"

"I'm trying to convince my dad to let me have it at an all-ages club."

"He doesn't want to?"

"He thinks people will sneak drinks in and would rather it be at our house."

"They could sneak drinks in there too."

I threw my hands up. "Thank you! He'll give in soon though. I'm sure."

"He's not good at saying no to you?"

We approached the theater, and I saw my friends standing outside. I wanted longer alone time with him.

"He's crap at telling me no." We reached everyone else. "And here we are. Hey, guys."

"Hey," Imogen said, immediately taking a not-so-subtle step closer to Noah. "We can't decide between scary or romantic."

"Yes, we can," Bobby said. "I ain't watchin' nothin' lovey, so we're going for the slasher."

Imogen rolled her eyes. "Fine! Whatever."

"Slasher is cool with me," I said. "Noah?"

He raised his eyebrow as if to say, "Or romance, really?"

Bobby clapped his hands together. "Settled then. It's showin' in half an hour, so should we go to the arcade first?"

With previews, it'd be an hour before the film actually started.

Without answering Bobby's question, we set off toward the arcade opposite the movie theater. Imogen stormed ahead. Since they'd broken up last year, Imogen had been cold with Bobby—because *he* had broken up with her. She didn't like that. Imogen Forest wasn't supposed to be dumped.

"I think I'm going kick your butt at air hockey," Noah said, nudging me with his elbow.

"Probably. I suck."

Chris gave me a disapproving look. He knew I didn't suck. I was actually champ of our group, but that didn't mean I could beat Noah. I had no idea how he played, so I didn't want him to know I was good.

"Yep, Scar-Scar couldn't hit it straight if her life was on the line."

"Thanks, *Chrissie*!"

When I had first arrived at school, Chris had been the one to show me around, and he had taken me in to his group of friends, who I quickly adopted as mine too.

We got in the arcade, and the guys went to change some money into tokens. Chris grabbed my arm and took me aside. "What's going on with you and the new boy?"

Trying not to grin like a moron, I shrugged. "Not much."

"Not much? You two are all flirty, flirty, gonna suck each other's faces off any minute. He's watching us right now, trying to work out if there's anything going on. Should I kiss you?" His face lit up with mischief.

I whacked his arm. "Don't you dare, Christopher."

"Fine, Miss Boring. Has he not tried anything yet?"

"I've known him two minutes."

Imogen slotted beside us and raised her perfectly plucked eyebrows. "Maybe he's gay."

"So what if he is?" I replied, secretly hoping he wasn't.

Chris rolled his eyes. "He's not gay! Clearly he just knows *you're* not easy."

He was having a dig at Imogen, because Im wasn't playing along with the best-friend thing. If she hadn't been attracted to Noah, she would have been as supportive as Chris.

We all looked over to Noah, who was watching me, talking to someone on his phone, and frowning. He looked away as I made eye contact.

"What's that about?" Chris said.

Imogen smirked and shrugged. "Probably his girlfriend."

"Shut up, Im," I said.

Noah hung up, slipped the phone in his pocket, and jogged back to us.

"Everything okay?" I asked. *Please don't have a girlfriend!* It would be pretty crappy of him if he had. We'd been flirting and texting constantly.

"Everything is fine," he said, casually throwing his arm over my shoulder. It was a friendly move, but it made my insides turn to mush. Imogen rolled her eyes and turned away. I didn't really care what she thought.

We walked to the air hockey table with Noah's arm around me and Chris winking over my shoulder. I wasn't complaining.

3
NOAH

I sat through another uninsightful English literature lesson, bored out of my mind. We had yet to leave the classroom in my two weeks in mainstream school. Learning wasn't just about reading from textbooks.

Scarlett sat beside me. I'd made sure to sit next to her enough that now her friends left a space open for me if I didn't make it to class first. She didn't seem to have any issue with it.

Unsurprisingly, we were reading Shakespeare. What I really didn't understand was once we'd finished *Romeo and Juliet,* we'd be watching the film. It was as if the teachers had given up.

Imogen turned around and said, "Movies and arcade tonight?"

"I do hope your interruption to the class has something to do with the Montagues and Capulets," Mr. Stevenson said.

Imogen turned back, scowling, and muttered, "Sorry, sir."

"You want to come tonight too?" Scarlett whispered when Mr. Stevenson went back to whatever he was doing at his desk.

"I thought that maybe we could do something together instead."

She blinked three times before replying. "We went together last time."

"I know, but everyone was there too."

Scarlett was awful at concealing how she felt. Her eyes widened a fraction and her posture lifted. "What do you want to do?"

"I'd like to take you on a walk."

"A walk?"

"Yes," I replied, smiling. So far, we'd not spent time alone; her friends were always with us. I needed to get her alone. "I promise you'll enjoy it."

She turned her nose up. "Doubt it but I'll go."

Of course she would. "Great, I'll pick you up at four to give you time to change after school."

Nodding her head, she went back to reading. It was obvious she didn't want to walk, but she did want to spend time with me. I needed to be able to get her to do things.

The bell rang, signaling lunchtime. I closed the book, which I'd already read when I was nine, and put it in my bag. "You hungry?" I asked Scarlett as we left the classroom.

"Starving. I'm getting fries today for sure."

"You know they're cooked in a lot of oil, don't you?"

"Yep," she replied.

That was another thing I didn't understand. Far too many people didn't care about what they put *inside* their body. They even ate things they *knew* were bad for them.

"What're you having? Another salad?"

"Probably," I replied. It was about the only thing I knew wasn't crawling with chemicals and additives. "It's nice. You should try it."

She halted. "You think I need to swap fries for salad?"

"What the hell, Noah?" Imogen snapped. "How dare you call her fat!"

"What? I never called her fat." I turned to Scarlett. "You know that's not what I meant." She frowned, and I panicked. Touching her arm, I smiled. "Come on, you don't think that's what I was saying. There's not one part of you that needs to change. I was just talking on a health level, not weight loss."

"Scarlett, come with me," Imogen said, glaring at me.

"Why does she need to take you away? I've explained the mis-understanding," I said, stroking Scarlett's forearm with my thumb.

"It's fine, Im. I know what he meant."

"Seriously? I know you're not used to a lot of attention from boys, but this is ridiculous."

Scarlett shrank and bit the inside of her lip. I wanted to bite back and tell Imogen exactly what I thought of her, but that probably wouldn't do me any favors with Scarlett.

"I think maybe you should go and find Bobby and Chris before you hurt your *best friend's* feelings any more," I said.

"This is a joke. Why are you letting him walk all over you?" Imogen said.

"I'm not walking over her, Imogen. You are."

She held her hands up. "Whatever."

I waited until she left to say, "Are you all right?"

"I'm fine," she replied. "Think she'll talk to me again anytime soon?"

"Honestly, I think she's the one that should be worrying about that. She had no right to talk to you that way."

Scarlett shrugged. "She gets like that sometimes."

I gritted my teeth and let go of her arm. Why didn't she stand up for herself more?

"Well, I'm sorry for my part in it," I said, sidestepping so I was in front of her.

She gazed up and bit her lip. Her dark-blue eyes shone. She really was incredibly beautiful. The longer I stared at her, the harder my heart beat. "It wasn't your fault," she whispered, her eyes flicking to my lips and then back up to my eyes.

Heat flooded through my body. I wanted to kiss her too. She was so alluring, so sweet and pure. I couldn't kiss her though. Not yet. I had to remember what I was doing here.

I exhaled hard. "Let's get you those fries."

Grinning, she replied, "Nah, I might try a salad, since I have it on good authority that they don't suck."

Laughing, I put my hand on her back and led her into the cafeteria toward the salad bar. "They definitely don't *suck.*"

After school, I went home to change into some warmer clothes and my walking boots, then left to get Scarlett.

She opened her front door and pouted. "Is this appropriate walking wear?"

"Yes, you look great." She had on a fleece zip-up jacket, slim jeans, and boots.

"Okay, let's go walking then."

"Are your parents in? Shouldn't I talk to them about where we're going first?"

Giggling, she shook her head. "They're both at work still. I've told Jeremy though."

"All right, let's go."

"Where exactly are we going?"

"You have a great countryside here, so we're going to explore it a little. I promise to have you back before dark."

As we walked along the path, I took her hand. She was warm and inviting and so unable to hide her smile that it almost made me laugh. I liked the feel of her hand in mine.

"Okay. I've not really explored where I live before."

"Why not?"

"Well, we moved around a lot when I was growing up. We've been here about three years now, and it's the longest we've stayed in the same place."

"Really? Why do you move so often?"

"Dad's work."

"Oh," I replied, looking away. I wondered if they would ever give her the true reason. "Do you think you'll move again?"

"Not sure. They seem settled so hopefully not. I have friends now."

"You didn't before?"

"No, there was no point. We'd move on and lose contact, so I stopped trying to get to know people."

That sounded so painfully lonely. If she had never been taken, she wouldn't have ever had to know what loneliness felt like.

"The people I'm friends with back home I've known since I was little. We're a close community. I can't imagine what it was like to grow up with just your brother."

She lazily lifted a shoulder in a shrug. "I didn't know any different, so it was fine."

"You may have. Did you move a lot before the fire?"

"I…I don't think so, but I'm not sure. We could have."

"Do you not know much about that time?"

"I remember nothing," she said.

"But your parents must have told you all about it."

"I guess."

Why doesn't she want to remember? I wanted her to—*needed* her to.

"Perhaps you'll get those memories back one day."

She would. I was determined to push gently and often to get her to try to remember.

We took a public footpath and followed it though fields and past forests. The familiarity of it settled something inside. I missed my community so much, but when I was outside, I felt a connection to them through nature and being among the elements.

Soon, Scarlett would understand how that felt too.

4

NOAH

I had never been excited to see a girl before, but after knowing Scarlett just three weeks, she made me feel things I thought I wouldn't experience until I was a lot older. I wasn't supposed to feel *anything* for her. It wasn't even supposed to be possible to have feelings for her.

The doorbell rang and I wiped my hands on my jeans. That would be Scarlett. My parents were sitting and reading on the sofa opposite. They looked up and smiled.

"Are you ready, Noah?" Dad asked.

I nodded once and stood. "I'm always ready."

There was a lot riding on my ability to win over Scarlett. I had to make this work. Taking a look in the mirror in the hallway, I took a deep breath and gave myself a silent pep talk. Thinking of home gave me strength. There was a lot of distance between me and my people, but knowing they were all behind me spurred me on.

I opened the door and she was standing holding a shopping bag and grinning as much as I probably was. Being around her was euphoric.

April had rolled around quickly. I loved spring; everything was coming to life again, and the air was considerably warmer.

"Ready for our movie night? I can't believe you've never had a movie night in with friends before."

I shrugged and moved to let her inside. "I prefer to be outside."

"Well, you've been missing out on something great."

"Hello, Scarlett," Mum said, conveniently walking out of the living room as Scarlett came in. They were going to have to stop popping up everywhere quite as often as they did, or it was going to look weird.

"Hi, Mrs. York."

"Call me Bethan, remember?" Mum said.

Scarlett nodded. "Right."

"What do you two have planned for today?"

Holding up the bag, she replied, "Snacks and movies."

"That sounds fun. Keep your bedroom door open, please, Noah."

I frowned. Supposedly, they trusted me, but every time I was told to leave my door open or not to rush things, I felt like I was being judged, that my loyalty was in question. I knew the proper way to handle this. I wasn't going to mess it up.

I liked her, yes. I could fool my family, but I couldn't fool myself. That didn't mean I was going to throw everything away over a teenage crush.

"I will," I replied a little harder than I usually spoke to my parents. *Trust me.* With a curt nod, Mum retreated back to the living room. "Come on then, show me how much fun a movie night is."

Smiling, she walked past me, heading up the stairs to my bedroom. I couldn't help watching her. She was petite, but her slim

24

legs and slight frame made her look taller. Her dusty brunette hair cascaded down her back in loose, messy waves.

"Okay," she said, turning to me once we were in my room. "Which one do you want to watch first? *Batman Begins* or *Spider-Man*?"

I shrugged. "I haven't seen either so it's your choice."

"What? You've *never* seen the Batman or Spider-Man movies?"

"No."

"Noah, where have you been living for the last sixteen years?"

I forced out a laugh and took *Batman Begins* from her outstretched hand. "This one first."

"Well, I know you've at least had popcorn, but please tell me you've also had Oreos before."

Grinning, I replied, "I was raised on a pretty remote farm on a tiny island, but I am not *that* sheltered." I was. Until she held the packet up, I had no idea what an Oreo was.

"I don't know, you've not watched much TV, never had movie nights, you don't eat a whole lot of junk, and you've never had a girlfriend before."

"Funny how I meet you, and three weeks later, I've corrected all of that." My heart jumped as I realized what I'd said. I knew I needed the girlfriend/boyfriend title but that wasn't exactly how I had envisioned it happening. She had to feel special. It had to be romantic. And not just because that's what I needed to get her to put every ounce of her trust in me.

Unfortunately, Scarlett didn't miss it either. She watched me carefully, silently. "*Have* you done all of them now?"

"Is that what you want?"

She frowned. "No way, I asked you first!"

Laughing, I put the DVD down on the bed, followed by the bag she was still clutching, and bent my head level with hers. "Well, I think it's a pretty good idea."

"We've not known each other long," she replied. Her voice was low, almost a whisper.

"I know, but I like what I've seen so far. I'm not proposing, Scarlett. You're not forced to be with me forever. Look, this is new to me, but I like you, and I'd like to see what happens."

She broke into a heart-stopping smile that did nothing to help me control my feelings for her. "In that case, I'm in," she replied.

We stared at each other like morons as the air thickened. I was supposed to kiss her. I'd never kissed a girl before. She had an ex-boyfriend, so the likelihood of her having kissed someone before was high. I didn't want to look like an inexperienced fool.

Now was the time though. I'd let things go on for far too long with very little physical contact. She wanted to take things further, had for a while now, but I couldn't rush anything with her and risk it burning out.

Reaching out, I gently grabbed her hips and brought her closer. Her hands fell on my chest and she splayed her fingers, running them over my shoulders. Yes, she had definitely done this before.

I leaned in and my heart went wild as I felt her breath across my lips. This was uncharted territory, but being this close to her, having my hands on her and hers on me, felt so natural it scared me. The feelings I had for her were almost so overwhelming I wanted to run and hide from them. I understood love. I felt it for a multitude of people, but this was different. This was confusing, exciting, terrifying, and so, *so* strong.

I closed the inch between us when I couldn't stand it anymore. Her lips were smooth and soft and melded to mine perfectly. Scarlett was warm and felt like home. It was more than I had ever imagined.

Her hands found their way into my hair, and I pulled her tighter against my body. I grazed her bottom lip with my tongue, and she twisted her fingers through the light strands at the back of my head. My heart hammered every second I kissed her. We pulled away at the same time.

I saw, for the first time, that she *was* the light.

"So...*Batman Begins* then?" I asked, clearing my throat and holding on to her. I tried to control my breathing and my erratic heart rate, so she wouldn't know just how much she had affected me.

Nodding with a showstopping smile, she replied, "Good film."

I gave her a chaste kiss and let go. "Get comfortable. I'll put it on."

Scarlett sat closer to me when I got on the bed. Before, we had left a small gap between us, but now her arm was firmly pressed against mine. I wanted her closer and farther away at the same time.

"Ready to experience a movie night?" she asked as the film started.

My arm was itching to be around her. I could smell her berry shampoo; it was as confusing as it was comforting.

"I'm ready," I replied, lying. Whatever was going on between us was real, and I was definitely not ready for that.

It was almost Easter, and I found out just how much she loved the holiday. Her room was full of decorative eggs, chicks, and rabbits. Light-blue and yellow banners hung twisted around each other on the wall above her bed.

Her enthusiasm was both cute and addictive. Since we had gotten together officially, my parents had kept an eye on us from afar and hers had been…well, less far. As much as I wanted to spend time with her completely alone and uninterrupted, I understood why her parents had a *door wide-open* rule.

She lay against my side as we watched *Transformers*. Movie days had sort of become our tradition. I grew up without TV, so Scarlett was determined to show me what I had missed out on. I still preferred to be outside, but I did love spending time with her—whatever we were doing.

"I remember playing with Transformers when I was little. Me and Finn used to fight over who got the yellow one. At least I think it was those."

She looked up from where she was resting on my shoulder. "I can't imagine you and Finn fighting; you're so close."

"Believe me, we used to. What about you and Jeremy?"

"We got along better when we were little. I'm not sure if we fought before the fire. We probably did."

I watched her for a minute, taking in the darkness of her midnight-blue eyes. They were unusual, beautiful.

"What? You still think I'm weird for not remembering, don't you?" she asked.

"No, of course not. I find it strange that you don't *want* to remember but not that you can't."

Sitting up, her posture became defensive. "I do want to, but I can't do it. I've tried a few times over the years, and it just ends up with me getting so frustrated I feel like I'm going crazy. It hurts to try, Noah. Physically too. It gives me headaches."

"All right," I said. "I'm sorry. But if it is something you want to do, I can help. Maybe I can take the pressure off you somewhat. I don't like you wanting something but being too afraid to go and get it."

She pursed her lips. "If I ever decide to try again, I'll let you know."

Holding both hands up, I replied, "All right. I'm sorry. I didn't mean to upset you."

"Can we just watch the movie now?"

I leaned back against the headboard and held my arm out for her. Reluctantly, she lay down with me and tucked herself back into my side again. Something felt wrong, and I realized that I didn't like her being angry with me, even if it didn't last long.

"I'm sorry," I whispered again and kissed the top of her head. This needed to be fixed. I didn't feel right, and I knew I wouldn't until we were okay again.

"It's okay," she replied, holding me tighter and breathing me in. I closed my eyes, enjoying seeing and feeling how she felt about me.

That was our first real disagreement, the first time she'd shied away from me and gotten angry. I wanted to do everything in my power to make sure that never happened again, even though I knew that was impossible.

5

SCARLETT

I was on a total high. It was the last day of school before Easter. Noah and I walked along the corridor hand in hand, trailing behind Imogen, Chris, and Bobby.

In two days I was going to my grandparents' for the weekend, and although I would miss Noah, I couldn't wait. The Easter egg hunt was at the front of my mind. We'd even probably find a few from last year. No matter how old any of us got, we still had a basket and we still went searching.

"I'll see you at lunch," Noah said as we parted ways to go to our one different class.

Imogen pulled me through the door and we took our seats. She was still a little sour about me being with Noah and him not paying her one bit of attention. I tried not to let it bother me, but it was annoying that she couldn't just be happy for me. If she'd had a boyfriend right now, I was sure it would have been a different story.

"Have you slept with him yet?" she asked.

I was taken aback. Imogen was a little too open with things like that, but I hadn't expected her to come right out and ask that, especially since we'd only been officially together four weeks, and it'd be my first time.

"No, but thank you for asking."

She rolled her eyes. "Don't be such a prude. Do you think guys like Noah are going to hang around forever?"

"I'm pretty sure I wouldn't make him wait forever, and Noah's not like that." He really wasn't. He didn't make constant sexual innuendos and talk to girls' breasts. He'd shown me nothing but respect and hadn't even mentioned us having sex yet. I wasn't sure where his head was, although when he kissed me, I had a pretty good idea—but he wasn't the type to push.

"Of course he's not. You're too naive."

"That's the kind of guy you're used to, Imogen. They're not all like that."

"Wow, thanks so much, Scarlett."

"Come on! You can't tell me my boyfriend is going to dump me if I don't put out and then be offended when I come back with the truth. You're my friend, Imogen, so I'm going to be honest and tell you when you're being a cow. You get your heart broken because you go for guys that you *know* are only after one thing. Sorry, but that doesn't really leave you much room to complain or judge."

Mr. Waters started the class, and I'd never been so happy to begin a math lesson before. Imogen pretended to be engrossed in the equations we were given, but I knew she was only doing it to ignore me. I didn't like hurting my friend, but I wasn't going to take her crap.

My phone vibrated once in my pocket and thankfully Mr. Waters was over on the other side of the room helping someone, so he hadn't heard it. I slid the phone halfway out of my pocket and opened the message. It was from Noah, of course, and said "My place after school. Everyone is out."

It wasn't often that we got time alone, so I sent back an immediate reply of "yes" and shoved my phone back away.

School passed far too slowly but that was only because it was the last day. Noah and I walked back to his place after I'd gotten the okay and a "back by nine o'clock" reminder from my mum. I hadn't told Imogen about Noah's text because she would only give me that I-told-you-so expression that I could do without. It wasn't her business anyway.

"So where are your parents and Finn?" I asked.

"Mum and Dad are visiting friends and won't be back until the early hours of the morning, and Finn is taking a girl from work out on a date. Hopefully he won't be back before I have to get you home."

"I'm sure he won't, unless the date is really bad."

He squeezed my hand. "Let's hope they like each other then."

We got back to his house, and he went straight in the kitchen, knowing I needed a post-school snack. He and his family were all health freaks though, so I knew I wouldn't be getting chips or chocolate. That didn't matter; their food was amazing *and* healthy.

Noah fixed us some carrot and cucumber sticks; fresh, home-made bread; cheese; and dip. We sat down in the living room to eat and watch their TV that looked like it belonged in a museum. They weren't big on TV.

We ate snuggled up on the sofa. It was perfect.

"So, what're you cooking for dinner to top this?" I asked, taking a bite of carrot.

"I thought you might cook for me. You know, since you are the one leaving me for four days."

Shrugging one shoulder, I leaned further into him. "Sure, if you don't mind oven french fries and a frozen pizza."

Like I thought, he turned his nose up. "No, thanks. I'll teach you to cook something decent."

"Pizza is decent."

"Freshly made pizza is decent," he countered.

"You're teaching me to make fresh pizza? Like, the dough too?"

"Yes."

This could end badly, but I was surprisingly excited. We weren't completely alone much, and this was likely to be the only time before I went away. I was glad we weren't just spending the afternoon watching the TV. "All right. Don't let me ruin it though."

"You won't ruin it."

We went up to his room to chill before starting dinner. I sat on his bed and Noah stood by his desk, tapping his fingers on his sketchpad. He was incredible and could draw pictures that looked like photographs—it was breathtaking. He'd only just let me see them, and I seriously hated him for how much artistic talent he had. I had none.

I could tell he was considering showing me something but was nervous and maybe a little unsure of it. Suppressing the urge to beg him to show me, I pretended to look around his room. The decision had to come from him.

He bit his lip, picked the pad up, and held it close to his chest. "I've been working on something."

My eyes lit up. "I know. You've been keeping it hidden. Are you ready to share?" He would absolutely not let me see anything that was unfinished.

"I am, but I'm worried."

"Why?"

"You have to promise me it won't scare you. It's something I have been thinking about recently."

"I won't freak, I promise. What is it?"

"Well, even though we have only been together a month, I do think about our future, and I'm not saying I want to rush into anything, but it *is* on my mind."

I held my hands out, on cloud nine. "Show me!"

Taking a deep breath, he gave me the pad and turned away. He hated watching someone looking through his work. It was really personal to him, and I loved that he shared it with me.

I flipped the pad over and the picture made my heart stop. It was me and him, probably about four years older than we were now, standing outside a beautiful wooden house, surrounded by a meadow.

"You said you wanted to live in the city, in a posh apartment, but I couldn't see it. I hope you don't hate this," he said.

"Are you kidding? This is incredible." It brought tears to my eyes. I loved him and our mapped-out future so much I thought

I might burst. How could he think I would freak out? This was perfect. I was fairly certain that unless he cheated or killed someone, he was with the one I wanted to spend my life with.

There was no way anything could be as beautiful or peaceful in the city. Everything changed as I stared at the drawing of us, arms around each other, happy as a person could be, surrounded by nature. I wanted that. I wanted to live a life with Noah where we'd have more time to enjoy things, rather than rushing around a busy city, taking hours to get anywhere, and bumping into people every second. I wanted our house to be surrounded by land we could enjoy and fresh air.

"I want this too, Noah. I have even less idea of what I'd do if we lived in the country like this, but I want it more than a built-up city. I don't care if I don't earn as much money."

He finally looked at me, and his smile melted me. "You have no idea how much I want it too."

"Well, it's done," I said, my voice thick with emotion. "After university, we'll move to the country and live the simple life. I want goats and those cute little micro pigs."

Laughing, he sat beside me and stroked my jaw, stealing my breath. "You want a farm?"

"If I'm living in the country like this, I want animals."

I spent the next hour watching him draw pictures of my animals. He laughed through the whole thing, even adding chicks, rabbits, a cow, and a llama. I added a stick sheep with a bad woolly body. It was stupid fun.

At six we went downstairs to make the pizzas. Noah got the

ingredients, and I got a wooden bowl and spoon. He didn't bother measuring anything out, so I left him to put everything in and I just stirred it until it was thick enough to knead.

Noah slapped the dough down on the countertop and smirked. "Go on, get kneading!"

It was gross. I hated when things stuck to my hands and it greatly amused him, but I was having fun cooking with him.

I pushed the dough down with the palm of my hand and froze.

Noah, sensing something was wrong, asked, "You okay?"

I shook my head, clearing my thoughts. "Yeah, just had a major sense of déjà vu."

"Really? With what?"

"Kneading this with my palm. I've never done it before, so it must be from when I attempted chocolate chip Christmas tree cookies with Mum a few years ago."

"Strange," he said with a shrug. "Hey, perhaps you have done this before, you just don't remember it."

I looked down. "Noah, please."

"No." He lifted my chin and bent down to look right into my eyes. "I'm sorry. I'm not bringing it up again, and I don't want to upset you."

"No, I overreacted. You're allowed to talk about it. Wow, I really am different, aren't I?"

"Yes, you are." Ouch. "You are completely different to everyone else because there is no one else that is perfect to me or for me. Different *is not* a bad thing."

He was still at the same height as me, so I leaned forward and kissed him. His arms quickly wound around my back, and I was pulled onto my tiptoes, flush with his chest. My hands were still gross and sticky from the dough, but that didn't seem to worry him as I gripped his hair.

Noah pushed me against the countertop and ran his hands down my back. When I felt my insides burst into flames, I pulled back. I had the desire to be with him, but I wasn't ready. Why couldn't my body and mind be more in sync?

He kissed my forehead, breathing just a little too fast. "We should get the dough kneaded and rested soon, or this pizza is going to be awful."

I took a deep breath and tried to get my body under control. "Sounds good. I'm getting hungry."

We spent the rest of the evening relaxing together. We didn't mention my loss of memory again because it always turned things tense between us. I hoped he would get past the oddness of it or I would remember already, because I didn't want anything causing friction between us.

I spent the next couple days—supervised—with Noah, and then it was time to go to my grandparents'. I wasn't sad that I wouldn't see him, although I'd miss him, because we were keeping in touch and, as he'd said, we had our whole lives ahead of us, so what was four little days? I seriously loved him.

6
SCARLETT

I waited, impatiently, in the car with Jeremy as our parents had yet another conversation *after* they'd said bye. "Seriously, we shouldn't even get off the sofa until they're in the car," I said, pressing my forehead against the window.

Mum and her parents could talk solidly until the end of time. Getting together had always been a huge deal as far back as I could remember—which was actually only ten years.

"Yep," Jeremy agreed, and I looked over at him. He didn't even glance up from his phone, which had been glued to his hand the entire weekend. "It was really annoying when you were a whiny baby and I had to try amusing you while they were still talkin'."

"Still texting Amie? You so *lurve* her."

"How's Noah?"

"Touché, Big Bro." I looked back out of the window and expected him to make another comment, but he was too engrossed in reading her new text. Well, at least *she* was still talking to him; I hadn't heard anything from Noah all day.

Mum and Dad finally got in the car, and Mum wound down her window, ready to talk more. "You two ready?" she asked over her shoulder.

Jeremy looked up then. "You for real? We've been sitting in here for fifteen bloody minutes."

"Language, Jeremy," Dad scolded, frowning at him in the mirror.

"Can we just go please, Jonathan?" Mum said to Dad, and waved out of the window. "See you soon. Bye! Love you!"

"You kids wanna stop off at McDonald's for lunch?" Dad asked. "We won't be home until after two."

"KFC and you've got a deal," Jeremy replied.

I rolled my eyes. "I don't think they're trying to make a deal, idiot."

Mum sighed. "Jon, just stop at whichever one you see in an hour."

This was going to be a long drive. I pressed the home button on my phone—again—to check if I'd missed a text from Noah—again. Nothing. I was being stupid. It was only one day that I hadn't heard from him, but I was used to waking up with a text and then shooting messages back and forth all day. I loved that we could talk so much and never get tired. We never ran out of things to say, but if we weren't talking, we'd just enjoy unawkward silence together. We'd only been together a little over a month, but I already felt so much more for him than I had for Jack in the eight months we were going out.

Slipping my phone in my pocket, I reasoned with myself. I did not need to text him every waking minute of the day—it was nice, but I didn't need to. We were seeing each other when I got home, so I'd message him later to confirm that we were still on and ask if he was okay.

Feeling better about my decision not to go stalker on him, I lay back against the seat and closed my eyes. I was settled, the steady hum and movement of the car threatening to send me to sleep any second. I welcomed it. Easter was amazing but exhausting.

"No!" Dad snapped, suddenly tugging on the steering wheel. The car jolted to the left. My eyes flew open, and I gasped as I was thrown against Jeremy's side. A scream ripped its way up my throat.

"Jonathan," Mum shouted at the same time Jeremy and Dad swore.

I heard loud horns beeping from several cars as Dad tried to steady the car. He slammed the brakes on as a minibus swerved in front of us.

I screamed again as we were hit from behind. My body flew forward before it was caught by the seat belt. The sound of crunching steel and smashing glass pierced my ears. My heart raced, and I gripped Jeremy's hand as someone else smashed into us from the side, making our car hurtle toward the hard shoulder on the motorway—then a ditch. And trees!

Oh God. I squeezed my eyes closed and everything moved in slow motion. We hit a large tree trunk, but I was out before the car even stopped.

7

SCARLETT

I tried to open my eyes, but they felt like they had been glued shut. My mind was in overdrive, trying to piece everything together. We were in the car. There was screaming, and we must have crashed, but I couldn't remember.

Did we hit something, or did something hit us? Was everyone okay?

Glass. I remember smashing glass and a big gray building. But we couldn't have been in a building. Did we hit a building? No, a tree. Where was the building then? My head throbbed and I wasn't sure if it was because I'd hit it or because I was trying too hard to remember. And then I was drifting—no, it was more like being pulled under.

Mummy brushed my hair and I closed my eyes, smiling. I loved it when she played with my hair. "Can I have pigtails, please?"

"Of course," she replied. "You can have anything you want, my special girl."

"Mummy, can I do your hair too?" I asked.

"You can, but Mummy's hair won't look as pretty as yours. Mine is too short." She sat down and handed me the brush. I combed it through her short, blond hair, pretending to be the mum.

"I want to be a hairdresser when I'm older."

"Oh, sweetheart, you are destined for greater things."

My eyes finally flickered open but only for a second. The light slid through the gap, and I winced, closing them immediately.

"Scarlett," I heard Jeremy say. "Hey, can you do that again? Scarlett, open your eyes." I tried to, but his voice sounded farther away, and then I was gone again.

I sat with David, Gregory, Linda, and Freya, waiting for Mummy and Daddy to get back. The house was crowded today, but we were the only ones still and reading. Jeremy ran through the room and out the other door, chasing Evelyn. I wanted to join in their game but I had to read.

"Auntie Linda, how many days until I'm four?" I knew my birthday was coming up and reading about it made it more exciting.

She didn't look up from her book but replied, "Twenty-one days to go."

"I can't wait!"

"Neither can we," Gregory said, stroking my hair.

"Is my daughter going to be okay?" Mum said. She sounded tired, like she'd not slept in weeks.

I tried to remember my dreams, but I all I could picture was Jeremy running after a little girl I'd never seen before. I didn't usually dream. Well, I didn't remember dreaming anyway. There were things I remembered—Mum combing my hair but she looked different. No one I saw was the same. I didn't recognize anyone but Jere.

"She opened her eyes," Jeremy said. "She's going to be fine."

Another voice I didn't recognize replied, "It's a very good sign that she opened them, but there's still some way to go yet. Let's allow her to rest."

I didn't want to rest anymore. I wanted to wake up properly. I hadn't heard Dad's voice yet, and I needed to know he's okay. I tried my hardest, willing my eyes to open, but it was useless. The darkness was back for me.

The big room was the prettiest room I'd ever seen, especially because it was in a big, ugly gray warehouse. The floor was covered in leaves and pretty red flowers, and Mummy said that's because I was so special. My party was going to be the best party ever. Candles were everywhere, making the room really hot. "Wow," I said, clutching my teddy in my hand.

Daddy held his hand out. He was standing in the middle of the room, in front of a circle of rocks filled with green leaves. "Come, sweetheart."

I walked over to him and looked around. Everyone was here, and they were all dressed in white—just like I was. "Where's Mummy?" I asked.

"Here I am, my special girl," she said, walking into the room. Everyone moved to stand in a big circle around me, Mummy, and Daddy.

Jeremy tugged on someone's arm, but I couldn't see who it was because Aunty Linda was blocking them. He looked scared and had tears running down his face. Jeremy was tough, and I'd never seen him cry before. It made me want to cry. I didn't like this anymore. Everyone looked down at me. They were so tall. I was scared. This was scary.

I looked up at Mummy and Daddy. "Can we go home now?" I asked, my bottom lip trembling.

Mummy shook her head. "No, sweetheart. It is now time."

Everyone was screaming. The flames were taller than Daddy. I started to cry and my body was shaking. "Mummy! Mummy!" I didn't know where she was. I was too hot and dropped to the floor. I wanted Mummy and Daddy to get me, but I didn't see where they went when the fire started.

Someone picked me up, but I was falling asleep.

I jolted awake, but I was still in the dark. What was that? I had a horrible, horrible feeling in the pit of my stomach.

"Can you hear me?" Mum asked, stroking my hair. "I can see your eyes moving. Try opening them, honey." That was all I'd been doing while I was conscious. *Come on.* I forced them open, and this time they responded. "Oh, Scarlett." A tear ran down her cheek. "Thank God you're awake. Everything's going to be okay now."

I nodded slowly and smiled. My head felt like it was being bashed from the inside and my throat was as dry as the desert. "Water?" I croaked.

Jeremy was beside me with a cup of water and straw in an instant. "You sure like to be the center of attention, don't ya?" he joked, but behind it I could see the relief in his eyes. I sipped from the straw until the water slid down easily and it no longer hurt to swallow.

"Dad?" I asked when I'd finished.

"He's fine, being kept for observation as he had a mild concussion, but he's okay. We brought him to see you earlier today, and the doctor says if his latest results come back normal, he'll be discharged this morning."

Thank God he was okay. "What happened?"

"Some arsehole fell asleep at the wheel and caused a six-car pileup," Jeremy replied. I remembered the sounds of the crash and the screams but nothing else.

Mum ignored his colorful language. "There were no fatalities, by some miracle. You came off worst."

"She always was a drama queen."

Mum gave him a stern look. "Jeremy, go fetch a doctor please." My brother saluted and left the room. "You feeling okay?"

"Head hurts, but I'm fine. I had strange dreams when I was out of it."

"Oh? What about?"

I frowned. "Um, a hot building, everyone in white, Jeremy chasing someone. I can't really remember." My brain felt fried. "Were you and Jeremy hurt?"

Mum's lips thinned for a second, and then she stroked my hair. "Only a few cuts and bruises. I'll just go see where Jeremy's got to, hurry that doctor up," she said, standing up and dashing out of the room.

8
NOAH

"Want some, Noah?" Chris asked, holding a forty out to me. And I thought my parents had exaggerated about teenagers. My life before had been fairly sheltered. I'd spent most of my time with a small group of friends walking, hiking, fishing, camping, and building. I wasn't at all prepared for getting drunk at the park.

"Thanks," I said, taking a sip and passing it on. The idea was for me to fit in and make friends, and I had a feeling asking to put the alcohol down and go exploring would do the exact opposite of that.

"When's Scarlett back?" he asked.

Great, going out with Chris and Bobby was supposed to take my mind off her. I was anxious for her to get home. My phone had died and been repaired, but when I finally got it back on, there was nothing on there from her. She'd be home soon though.

"This afternoon. I would've thought they'd be back already, but I've not heard yet," I replied. She was originally going to text me when she got home and I was going over. That should've been around two in the afternoon, but it was now six and still nothing. But Scarlett told me they all liked to talk, so it was entirely plausible that they'd stayed the day and were coming home in the evening. I didn't want to pester.

"Missed her?" he asked, smirking. I had no idea why they felt the need to tease over things like that. Yes, I missed my girlfriend, and I wasn't afraid to admit it to them.

"A lot," I replied. They backed down when they knew it didn't bother me what they thought.

My phone rang an hour later as a second forty was pulled out of Bobby's bag. I didn't care who it was as long as it got me out of drinking that vile stuff again.

"Hello?" I said, answering a number I didn't recognize.

"Noah, this is Marissa."

Her eerily calm voice sent chills down my spine. I stood up and walked a few steps away so I could hear her properly. "Marissa? Is everything okay?"

"We're in the hospital. There was an accident on the way home. Scarlett… She's doing okay, stable, in and out now, but I think you should come," she said, her voice finally giving away how scared she was.

I couldn't go. I could barely function. My muscles tightened, locking up. I felt cold. "Stable and in and out?" That meant something serious had happened. "Stable" was only used when it was touch and go but you were doing all right at that particular time.

Chris and Bobby stood up and moved closer, both now giving me their full, undivided attention.

"Scarlett and Jonathan were on the side of the car that hit the trees. They're okay, but they need rest and monitoring."

I could feel my heart pounding. She'd said Scarlett was "stable."
"She's not awake?"

"No, she's not right now, but she has been."

That wasn't good enough. I needed her awake, properly awake,
and chatting to believe she would be all right. I had to get to her.

"I'm on my way. Is there anything you need?"

"No, thank you. She's on the children's floor. Jeremy and I will
be there too."

"Okay, see you soon," I said, and hung up.

"What's going on? It's Scarlett. Is she okay?" Bobby asked.

"Yes, they were in an accident. She's fine, apparently, but I need
to go."

Chris followed as I jogged toward the gate. "Wait, Noah,
should we come too?"

"I don't think they will even let me in." I stopped when I reached
my bike. "Look, I'll call you when I get there and know more. Think
you can let Imogen know?" *Just stop talking to me so I can get to her!*

"Yeah, 'course," Bobby replied. "Let us know how she's doin'
and tell her we'll visit when we're allowed."

"I will," I said, getting on the bike. "See you later."

I rode home, pedaling as fast as I could. I had never felt so
scared before in my life. Throwing the front door open, I called,
"Mum, Dad, Finn?" I was desperate to get to her, more desperate
than I thought I could ever be. I didn't like how much she was
starting to mean to me.

"Noah, what's wrong?" Mum said, grabbing my arm. Dad and
Finn followed her out of the kitchen.

"Scarlett's been in an accident. She's in the hospital."

Mum's face fell. "Oh God. How is she? Do you know?"

"Stable is all I really know. She's been awake." I felt the prickle of tears rush up my spine. I wasn't going to cry. "We need to go."

"Absolutely," Dad said, face ashen. "Get in the car everyone."

I didn't question them when they all decided to come. Of course they were going too. Dad grabbed the keys, and we rushed to the car.

"Who called you?" Mum asked when we were on the road.

"Marissa."

"What did she say?"

"Just that. She said they hit trees so, I don't know, they lost control or something hit them. Scarlett and Jonathan were hurt, but he's awake and she isn't right now." I didn't want to admit how scared I was.

"She has been awake though. That's a good sign," Finn said. "She is going to be fine."

She has to be.

"Of course she is," Dad said. "Now, no negative thoughts. Positivity is key." He switched the radio on and sound drifted through the car. It didn't make me feel any better. I knew I should stay positive, and I was usually so good at it, but I'd never cared for anything the way I did for her. There was just something about Scarlett—so pure, fun, and innocent—that reached into my very being and attached itself to my soul.

I had never stood a chance.

The hospital was eerily quiet, and the stench of chemicals

attacked my nose. Back home we made our own cleaning products and none of them made my eyes water or stomach turn. We were given directions to a waiting room near where she was. I wanted to see her, to make sure that she was going to be okay, but I wasn't permitted to enter her room.

We were told that she was doing just fine and had been awake. Even though she'd been awake, my concern was increasing. Her mind was resting after a knock to the head, but so far today, all of her tests had come back normal. She would wake up when she was ready, but the wait was excruciating. Scarlett had to heal soon.

We needed her more than she knew.

9

SCARLETT

I woke up to sunlight streaming through the window and Mum looking at me. "Hey," she whispered.

"Hi. How are you? Dad? Jeremy?"

"We're all okay. What about you?"

"I'm good. What time is it?"

"Almost nine. Dad's going to be released soon."

"Good." I wished I would be too. "Mum...did Noah come?" I bit on the inside of my bottom lip anxiously as I waited for her reply.

"Of course. Said he'll be back for visiting hours."

The relief I felt scared me. I *really* liked him. Most of my friends had boyfriends and all the boy drama that came with it. I'd decided I wasn't going to worry about relationships until I was out of school, possibly even university, but then Noah crept his way in. Now I had boy drama.

"He's been beside himself, worrying that he'd never get to see you again."

"He'll definitely be here at visiting time?"

"Absolutely," she replied.

Jeremy came in, followed by a new doctor.

"Scarlett, I'm Dr. Thorn. How're you feeling?" he asked in

a thick Scottish accent. His bulging belly touched the bed as he leaned down and raised a penlight, no doubt to shine in my eyes.

"Head hurts, but I feel fine."

"Okay, I'll sort something for the pain. It's good to see you back with us. We were worried."

"I can't believe I slept for so long."

"It's not unusual when there has been head trauma," Dr. Thorn replied. "I'm just going to check you over and give you some Tylenol."

Once I'd been poked and had a light shone in my eyes, the doctor left to get me something that would hopefully stop the hit-by-a-bus feeling.

"Can I see Dad, please?" I asked. Last night I'd fallen back asleep before I'd seen him or Noah.

"Let's wait until the Tylenol kicks in, and then I'll go and see if he's awake yet," Mum replied.

"What time does he get to leave?"

"After lunch."

"What about me?"

She smiled and took my hand. "As soon as you're feeling better."

That meant forever. I didn't like to be still for long, especially not in the same place. Never had in any situation. I was even feeling bored from staying in one house for the three years we'd been there. We'd always traveled and moved around.

"I feel fine."

Mum laughed. "Oh, do you really? Relax, Scarlett. You need

to give your body time to heal. You were lucky, sweetheart. We almost lost you."

"I'm sorry."

"Don't apologize! Just rest and get better."

"Okay. Can you see if Dad will come now, *please*?"

When the pain meds kicked in, I fell asleep, waking up every now and then. I'd had hours and hours of sleep but felt like I'd had none at all. Dad was fine, and it was good to see him. He exchanged his room for mine, refusing to go home until they were kicked out at night.

At two o'clock in the afternoon, it was visiting hours, and I sat up in bed waiting for Noah. My parents and Jeremy had gone to the café to get some lunch and to give me and Noah some time alone.

"Scarlett, you're awake!" He rushed over, sitting on the bed and wrapping his arms around me. "You okay? I was so scared."

"I'm fine," I replied, burying my head against his neck.

He pulled back, looking me over to make sure I wasn't lying. He checked everywhere with his eyes and fingertips. I closed my eyes as his fingers trailed over my cheek, jaw, chin, neck. His touch made me feel more alive and more awake than ever.

"You're really okay," he said once he'd finished his examination.

"Yep, I'm really okay. I had some weird dreams when I was coming around though. I don't know what they mean."

He raised an eyebrow. "They probably don't mean anything. They're dreams."

"But it was so weird and *so* real."

Smiling, he said, "All right. Tell me what happened?"

"I don't remember all of them, just pieces. Mum—but she looked different—brushing my hair. Jeremy chasing a girl. Candles everywhere. Being in some old building with lots of flowers and everyone was wearing white; then there was some sort of fire. I'm not sure. Wow, okay, maybe that does mean nothing." What I could remember just sounded stupid when I said it aloud.

He took my hand, squeezing a little harder than usual. "Don't worry about it. Perhaps they are memories or nothing at all, but right now we should focus on you healing. I thought you would want something 'decent' to eat," he said, handing me a packet of Oreos.

I took them and stroked the pack. "Thank you! Do you have any idea how much hospital oatmeal, lasagna, and carrot cake sucks?"

He turned his nose up. "I can imagine. Do you know when you will be discharged yet?"

"No, but it'll probably be a day or two. Bet I'm all better right for the start of the school term," I said, turning my nose up. "Evelyn!"

Noah looked at me like I was crazy. "What?"

"Evelyn. That's what the girl in my dream was called. The one Jeremy was chasing."

"Are you sure you feel all right?"

"Yeah. That has to mean something, right?"

"Not really, Scarlett."

"You don't know that."

"All right, you've just been knocked out a day. I don't think it's a good idea to be stressing yourself out over a dream."

58

"Dream*s*. There were a few and apart from the one where Mum was brushing my hair Jeremy was in most. Who's Evelyn though?"

He shrugged.

"She was younger than Jeremy, probably younger than me too."

"They were dreams."

But were they? They seemed like more. I wasn't fully asleep when I'd had them but not fully awake either. Something wasn't right.

"They seemed more like memories." One of his eyebrows rose subtly. "Look, I know you think I'm crazy right now, but what if I'm not?"

"About what, Scarlett? About Jeremy chasing a girl? He probably did. You've probably seen a room full of candles and had your mum brush your hair. I'm not doubting you, but you've had head trauma, and as you were waking up, you were piecing back together who you are and what happened. Things got muddled and you're confused."

"Right, but these things were from before I lost my memory."

"How old were you in the dreams?"

"I don't know. Young. No, three. I was three, and it was almost my birthday. I think."

"You think? So you could have been four, and half dreaming, half trying to remember what was going on."

I frowned. That was a possibility but I thought I remembered my fourth birthday coming up. Was it a birthday? "I wish you weren't so cynical."

Turning more toward me, he grabbed my hand. "I'm sorry. I don't mean to be. It's just that…Scarlett, you almost *died*. You're hurt, and right now you're stressing over dreams. I would rather you focus on figuring out what your dreams mean once you're better." He swallowed. "I thought I'd never see you again, and I just want you to be okay."

He was right. Even if they were memories of before the fire, they were still silly little memories that didn't mean much. Nothing out of the ordinary happened, not really. Not that I could remember now anyway. With all of my focus was on Jeremy and Evelyn, the other dreams had faded.

"Yeah, sorry. I just thought it might be the start of getting those years back."

He groaned. "No, I'm sorry. I don't mean to be insensitive. I just need you to be all right."

"I'm okay." I zipped my mouth. "No more dream talk. What have you been up to while I was out of it?"

"Waiting for you to wake up. Worrying that you wouldn't. Snapping at everyone. Then there was more waiting and more worrying."

"Sorry."

"Don't apologize for being in an accident."

"Right, sorry."

We both laughed at the same time, and he leaned back against my pillows. "My dad was released?"

"Yes, I saw them on the way up. That's good news. It's just you that scared everyone to death."

"I know. Jeremy barely has a scratch on him, thankfully. Guess I'm a good pillow, huh!"

Noah frowned.

"Too soon?" I asked, and he nodded.

I was glad that I was able to save my brother from the impact. I didn't want him to be hurt.

"What're we doing for the rest of break, then?"

He shrugged. "What do you want to do?"

"Movies? Hanging out with the guys. The usual."

"Sounds good. When you're better though."

I saluted, and he smiled so wide it made me laugh.

Noah held his hand up and shook his head. "All right, that's it. You need to sleep."

"You think I'll dream more if I do?"

He leaned forward and placed a kiss on my lips. "Sleep, Scarlett."

Once Noah left, I drifted in and out of a very light sleep. Just when I would nod off, I'd see the flicker of the flames, *feel* the heat, hear a woman's voice that wasn't my mum's, and I would see Evelyn. She was so young and so pretty. I felt her eyes on me. As she ran past with Jeremy, she watched me; it was only for the briefest second, but that one small glance stirred familiarity and it wasn't something I could just forget.

10

NOAH

"How is she?" Jeremy asked the second I closed the door to her room. Scarlett had fallen asleep soon after I told her to rest. Her recovery was far more important than anything else. She was starting to remember pieces, which scared him and excited me. But I was concerned that she would remember suddenly. We didn't want that. There was too much time left. If she found out the truth now, she would never come with me.

"Acting strange," I replied.

"She's always weird."

I sat down next to him on the seats opposite Scarlett's room. "All right then, more strange. She kept talking about some dreams she had. Apparently in Scarlett's head, you chase girls." I smirked at him. "I won't tell Amie." He rolled his eyes. "Do you know someone called Evelyn?"

Jeremy froze. "Evelyn?"

He knew her.

"Yes, that's the name Scarlett gave. Do you know her?"

After a pause, he replied, "Not really. Scarlett had a doll called Evelyn when she was really little. I think that was its name anyway. It was lost in the fire."

I laughed on cue. "So you chase girl dolls in her dreams."

"Yeah, I guess."

"She was talking about her like she's a person though."

"You said yourself that she's strange."

"Right," I replied, nodding. "She just seemed upset over it, so I thought I should ask. She must remember the doll and her mind created a person."

"Yep," he replied, his posture visibly stiffening in front of me. He was worried.

"She okay in there alone?"

"Yes. She's sleeping."

"Good. Look, I'm going back down to meet the folks. They're getting even more magazines for her."

I stood up. "Sure. I need to get home anyway. I'll see you tomorrow morning. Tell her I'll call later."

"Will do. Later, Noah."

"Bye, Jeremy."

I walked out of the hospital feeling about twenty pounds lighter now that I knew she was all right. But I was left with an uneasy sense of relief that she was remembering.

My dad was waiting for me in the parking lot. "Hi," I said as I got in.

"Is she all right?"

"Yes, she's fine. She's awake and her usual self."

I should tell him about her memories. It was a big deal and something Eternal Light would *need* to know, but the image of her eyes fluttering up at me and her face breaking into a smile stopped me. I told myself that it didn't really matter because she was confused and remembered very little. They could be passed off as dreams for now.

"Thank goodness," he said and breathed a sigh of relief. "We wanted to stay all day with you but thought that might look strange."

"Yes, that's fine. I was all right, and it gave me plenty of opportunity to watch Jonathan and Marissa." They played the concerned parents so well. Of course, I understood that they'd brought her up since she was four and, as far as they were concerned, they were her parents, but they knew better. They were lying to hospital staff, giving false information and fake identification for Scarlett, yet they were still so calm.

"And?"

I shrugged. "Nothing out of the ordinary. You would never know they weren't her parents. They seem to love her the same as Jeremy."

"They are not her parents," Dad said.

"I know."

He shook his head, frowning. "I'm sorry, Noah. Being out here puts me on edge. I don't like it."

"Neither do I. It's hard to keep up the pretense every single day, but it will be worth it."

"It will, Son. I'm proud of you, you know? I was unsure to begin with. Not that I didn't think you could do this, but it is a big task and I know you are a good person. You hate dishonesty and Jonathan, Marissa, and Jeremy are lying to Scarlett every day. But you have really come through, and it won't be long until we are home with her and can get back to normal. Nothing about the way people live out here is normal. Absolutely nothing."

I'd started to doubt that. But I couldn't say that to my father. "You're right," I replied, only half lying.

There were certain things, sure. People called themselves free when they were governed and bound by so many laws. They worked forty-plus hours a week, and most still struggled, gave up a portion of their money, and followed what society expected. That was the furthest thing from being free, but they still went on fooling themselves. They believed they had a voice, but they didn't use it past voting for someone they knew was lying to them anyway. It made absolutely no sense. Democracy. Freedom. Bullshit.

It was beyond stupid, the amount of rubbish people fed *themselves*, but they valued human life in a way that Eternal Life did not. Scarlett would be protected out here. I couldn't help question my own attitude toward human life. If I was successful, Scarlett wouldn't be safe. I would be hurting her, allowing Eternal Light to hurt her.

How was I going to watch Donald drive a knife through her chest?

11

SCARLETT

After just two days in the hospital, I was allowed to go home. Besides feeling tired and having a lingering headache, I felt fine. Dad and I had been on the sofa since, lying under fluffy blankets and under strict orders not to move. Throughout the morning I'd been drifting in and out of short naps, resting my tired body.

Startled, I woke abruptly, the explosion thundered through my unconscious mind. My heart raced. I was hot all over, and sweat beaded at the back of my neck. The dream was so real that I expected the house to be in flames.

Mum and Dad were talking to each other, unaware that I'd woke. I gulped and pushed myself up. They looked up as I forced myself to calm down.

"Hey, are you okay?"

I nodded.

"Missa," Dad said, using his pet name for Mum.

"Yes, honey," she replied, smirking.

"Can you pass the remote, please? I'd get it myself but…"

"Of course."

I shook my head. He was loving being the patient. I was climbing the walls. Dad was completely fine now, and I gave it a day before Mum refused to do anything for him anymore. Lying around and sleeping would have suited me just fine before the nightmares started.

"Do you need anything, Scarlett?" Mum asked once she'd given Dad the remote.

All I needed was my heart to return to its normal rate. "I'm good. Think I can go out tomorrow? Just to Noah's."

She tilted her head to the side, and I knew the answer was no. "Sweetheart, you've just gotten home from the *hospital*. You were in and out of unconsciousness for a whole day."

"So that's a no, huh?"

"It's a no," she confirmed. "Noah's welcome here. You know that."

It wasn't just seeing Noah; it was getting out for a bit. I'd been cooped up inside a hospital room and now my house. I missed the outside. I wanted to sit in the new hammock in Noah's garden and get some fresh air. They were outdoorsy people, and I wanted that for a while.

My eyes slid over a photo of Jeremy when he was about seven or eight. He had a big smile that showed his missing front teeth. My mind instantly conjured the image of Evelyn. I saw them in my head, running around together. I blinked and looked away, but her eyes followed me, looking directly into mine as she whizzed past me with Jere.

"Yeah. Thanks," I said, trying to shove thoughts of Evelyn out of my mind. "I'll text him now." I fired off a message asking if Noah wanted to come over and turned back to Mum. My skin still felt itchy hot, like it had when the explosion in my dream went off. "Can I talk to you about my dreams?"

Mum pursed her lips the way she always did when she was tired of a subject. It was the look she gave Jeremy when he was ten and absolutely needed a cell phone. It was the look that she gave me when I absolutely needed to go to Disneyland. Both times.

Dad stayed still, silent and looked on, waiting.

"Okay," she said.

Her hesitance gave me second thoughts. I hated that talking about it was so hard for her. I opened my mouth but quickly closed it again and shook my head. "Never mind. They're just stupid dreams."

"They are just dreams, but if they're bothering you, they're not stupid," Mum said. She may have said the words, but the stiffness in her posture and moisture in her eyes told me she didn't want to have this conversation at all. I watched her lick her lips twice and clench her hands around her knees so hard, her tendons popped up.

Her fear and Dad's indifference frightened me. How could I make her relive that when it hurts her so much? "Thanks, but I'm okay actually. It just freaked me out, especially since I have a four-year gap in my memory, that's all."

"Are you sure you don't want to talk about it?" Dad asked, finally saying something.

"Yeah, I'm sure. I made a decision to leave my memory thing in the past, so that's what I'm going to do. I just want to be better and get on with my life." I said the words, but I didn't believe them, not completely. After remembering—or thinking

I remembered—snippets from my childhood, I really wanted to know it all. But my parents weren't the most approachable on the subject, and I didn't know how to talk to them.

"We're glad to hear you say that, sweetheart. We just want you to be happy," Dad said. They both looked relieved.

"Thanks. I'm going to lie down in bed for a while. Send Noah up when he gets here, please," I said.

"Of course," Mum replied faintly.

I smiled and walked out, going to my bedroom. They only made me feel guilty for wanting answers, and it was exhausting. Plus, Noah had replied saying he was on his way, and I would have much rather focused on that instead.

I'd just changed into an oversized knitted top and leggings when he walked in. He wouldn't care about seeing me in my pajamas, but I felt more human in clothes.

He sat down beside me on my bed and gave me a chaste kiss. "Hey," he said, flashing me his cute smile I loved so much.

"Hi."

"How're you feeling?"

"Cramped. Want to get out but…"

"Where do you want to go?"

"I'd settle for anywhere outside right now."

He stood and held his hand out. "Your wish is my command." Noah helped me up, still worried about my lightly bruised ribs. Honestly, they were fine now, as long as I didn't start doing somersaults. "Thanks. I need to tell Mum where we go." Where were we going?

"Already done. She said you were plotting your escape when she let me in. I'm allowed to take you into the garden."

I wanted to pout and whine, *We don't have a hammock.* But I really wanted light that didn't come from a bulb.

We went out and sat on the bench. I curled my legs, leaning against his side as he wrapped his arm around my back. "Oh God, I'll never take fresh air for granted again."

"You really have been going crazy in bed, haven't you?"

"Yeah. Normally I'd love to lay in bed all day, but when I *have* to it stops being fun."

"You are a child," he teased.

"A child? You looking for an argument there?" I teased.

He frowned and tapped the side of his leg. "No, I don't enjoy arguing with you."

"Oh, come on, it was once and you could barely call that an argument. People do fight though, Noah." His frown deepened, and I realized he was so not used to people arguing. "Come on, your parents never fight?"

"No, actually. They sit down and discuss things a lot, but they have never shouted."

My parents didn't scream at each other, but I'd heard them bicker. Everyone did it…or so I thought. "Wow, we really did have different upbringings." Noah and his family were organic vegetarians, and although we didn't eat a whole lot of unhealthy things in my house, I definitely liked junk food and fast food.

"Opposites attract though, right?" He smiled but I could tell his mind was off somewhere else.

"Definitely, look at Penny and Leonard."

He frowned. "Who?"

"Never mind, just remind me to make you watch *The Big Bang Theory* sometime. All that matters is that we're fine, me and my dad are getting better, and we have another week before school starts again."

"All right. What do you want to do this week?"

"Movies? Theme park?"

"Yes to the first, no to the second. You can't seriously be thinking about riding roller coasters when you've just been in a car accident."

"Well, I wouldn't do the roller coasters, but maybe we can save that until summer break."

He did that *going far away* thing again. I hated that. It was obvious something was on his mind, but he never said anything.

"You okay?" I asked.

"I'm fine."

"You're not moving, are you?" I felt my world slow down a little. He couldn't just leave.

"What? No, I'm not going anywhere. What made you ask that?"

"I don't know. You went all spaced out."

"Sorry, it's nothing. Finn is missing home. Him visiting my aunt in Ireland last week didn't help, and I'm not sure what to do to make it better. Things here are a lot different."

"Does he want to go back?"

Finn was nineteen, plenty old enough to live by himself, so he could go if he didn't like it here. But I didn't think he'd leave his family because they were all really close. Selfishly I didn't want Noah to leave, but I also didn't want his family to be unhappy.

"He wants to but he wouldn't. I think my parents are considering going home when I've finished school."

There it was, the panic. That was far away enough to have my life and happiness completely linked and wound around him, even more than it already was.

He laughed and kissed me. "Don't look so scared, although it's nice to know how you feel. I won't be going with them. I'll be old enough to live alone, and I'll stay for university here." He smiled shyly and added, "Well, I'll stay for you."

I bit my lip and then kissed him because I wasn't sure what to say or how to express how much I loved him. I almost blurted the words out, but we hadn't said that yet. He would stay with me when his family left. I *should* have just told him what he made me feel.

Confiding in my parents about my memories wasn't an option, but I could with Noah. I trusted him. Evelyn's big, innocent eyes seemed to watch me constantly. Every picture of Jeremy I saw, she was there.

"You were right," I said when we pulled away. "I know this is a total conversation changer, but I do need to try to face whatever happened to me when I was a kid. After my dreams, I'm so ready to." *I need to know who Evelyn is and why I feel like I know her.*

He winced and lowered his head. "No, I'm sorry about that. I pushed and I shouldn't have. Things like that happen, and just because I thought it was strange, it didn't give me the right to make you question your decision to let it go. I was wrong, Scarlett. Maybe you *should* leave it for now."

"I don't want to, and even if I did, I couldn't. It's not a bad thing that you got me thinking about it again. I always would've liked to know. It's just, now, I *need* to. Will you help me?" He hesitated before dipping his chin in agreement. "Thank you."

"So, what are you going to do exactly?"

"I'm not sure yet. I'm going to write the dreams down. Every time I have one, I remember a tiny bit more, although nothing extra really happens, I don't think. Maybe the more I write it, the more will come back to me about my past?"

"All right. You could also try talking to me or your parents though."

"I don't think I can. They're clearly uncomfortable talking about it."

"I'm sure it's difficult for them, but surely they'll do it if it's best for you."

"Probably, but I don't like making them feel bad. If I can remember without hurting my parents, then that's what I'll do."

"Fair enough."

"I can't get Evelyn off my mind. I still see her so clearly as she ran past me with Jere."

"You're convinced she's a person and not a doll."

There was no doubt in my mind. "One hundred percent. But that means my family is lying to me, and I don't like that."

"Understandable. Perhaps there's a good reason."

"Such as?"

"I don't know. Something horrible could have happened to her, maybe in the fire, and they don't want to upset you."

Perhaps, but that couldn't possibly be a strong enough reason to lie to me my whole life. "I don't mean to sound like a terrible person here, but I don't remember her. I don't know if we were friends, and they could tell me if a stranger died."

"What if you two were close?"

A cold shudder ran the length of my spine. *No!* She was playing with Jeremy. A sister? My pulse started thumping in my ears. What if she was a sister and she died in the fire? They wouldn't talk about the fire because it was too painful—maybe that was why.

"Hey, you okay?"

I shook my head slowly, eyes filling with tears. "What if she was? Oh God, what if she was my sister? What if I'm pushing my parents and Jeremy to talk about something as horrific as their daughter, our sister, dying in a fire? They managed to get me and Jeremy out, but perhaps they couldn't get to Evelyn."

His eyes widened. "Shh, don't do that. I didn't mean closer than a friend. It's just one possibility that, right now, is completely unfounded. Please don't beat yourself up and feel guilty over something that is probably untrue."

"You're right, but what if she was my sister?"

"I don't know, Scarlett. I really think you should talk to your parents."

I shook my head. "No. No way they would hold that back. I know them, and they would never pretend a child they had didn't exist. Also, Jeremy would have asked about her growing up, and he didn't."

"Exactly. She couldn't have been their daughter. You need to speak to your parents."

I nodded. "I know." It just wasn't that easy.

12

SCARLETT

"Hi, Scarlett," Bethan said, pushing a plate of cookies toward us.

"Hey. Thanks," I replied, taking one with a big cluster of chocolate chips on top and trying not to yawn. Since I started dreaming—always the same ones—I'd been tired almost all the time. Every night I'd wake up in the early hours, sweating from seeing flames and feeling emotionally drained from worrying who Evelyn was and why Mum was never herself.

This morning, I'd jumped awake when flames encased Evelyn; she'd still looked at me and then followed Jeremy through the fire until I couldn't see either of them anymore. I was terrified and panting and knew there was no way I would get back to sleep, whether it was five in the morning or not.

No matter where I was or what I was doing, something brought me back to her. Any little girl with a similar shade of light hair and big eyes would shoot her to the forefront of my mind for the rest of the day. It was too irrational to feel...close to someone I couldn't remember. I had no idea who Evelyn was, but I knew she was important. I cared about her.

Noah sat on the stool beside me, leaning over so our arms were touching. I loved it when he did that.

I was completely healed, and just in time for school to start up again, like I thought I would be. I was still going crazy over not remembering, but Noah wanted to wait a little longer after the accident and then he'd help me. Right now I was just enjoying spending time with him and seeing my friends again. I wanted to be normal for a while and not let Evelyn consume my thoughts.

"How was school?" Bethan asked.

"It was all right," Noah replied. "What's for dinner?"

"Casserole. Are you staying, Scarlett?"

"If that's okay?"

Bethan smiled, leaning on the counter. "Of course it is. It's strange when you're not here."

Yeah, me and Noah were pretty much joined at the hip lately, but I was pretty sure he was my future husband, so I wanted to spend as much time with him as possible.

"You should let her stay over then," Noah said.

Bethan smirked. "Nice try."

I wondered how long before they would let us stay over at each other's houses. It would be so cool to wake up and at least be in the same house as him. But I doubted that was happening before I was eighteen.

"Anyway, we have to go," Noah said.

"Shopping, right?" Bethan asked.

"Yes," he replied. "We'll try to be back for dinner, unless Scarlett can't find the right shade of lipstick; then we'll be late."

I narrowed my eyes at him as he winked. He knew I didn't even wear lipstick. What he didn't know though, was that we weren't going shopping. I was taking control of my memory problem and trying something that wouldn't hurt my parents. They were a last resort. After the sleepless nights had rolled on, I had known writing my dreams down wasn't helping. I never saw anything new when I was asleep. I had the same dreams over and over. What I needed was professional help, so I'd made an appointment.

"All right, that's fine. I'll save you some if you're not back. Whatever happens, remember to have Scarlett home by nine, even if you're later."

He nodded. "Always." We wouldn't be back that late though. Noah was strict when it came to getting me home on time. He was determined to respect my parents' rules and not lose their trust. It was sweet and a lot easier than Imogen and her ex; her parents had hated him.

Noah took my hand as we walked to the bus stop, rubbing his thumb over my knuckles. "Are you feeling better?" he asked.

"Yeah, all that hurts is my ribs if I twist suddenly or lift something too heavy. The rest of me is fine."

"That's good. And don't lift anything heavy."

"You sound like my dad. I won't."

Noah looked at the timetable and frowned. "I thought you said the bus was at three forty-five?"

"It is."

"Not one that goes into town."

"Yeah, we're not actually getting that one."

One of his eyebrows arched. "Which one are we getting?"

"Can you just get on it and not ask until we're there? Trust me."

He bent forward and kissed me. "All right."

The fact that Noah trusted me so completely and wholeheartedly was one of the things I loved most about him.

"Thank you."

He wrapped me in his arms as we waited. I felt so safe when I was with him. The rest of my life and the people in it were messy, and I didn't know who or what to trust. But when it came to him, I was sure.

The bus turned up five minutes later and we got on, sitting near the back. Noah picked my legs up and put them over his, rubbing circles on my knee the way he did with my knuckles.

"You know for someone that's never had a girlfriend before, you're pretty pro at it."

He smiled. "You make it so easy."

I think my heart actually melted into a puddle. For the rest of the ride, we sat in perfect, comfortable silence.

"So why are we here?" he asked as we got off the bus on the opposite side of the high streets and shops.

"I have an appointment."

"I'm not a mind reader, babe. I'm going to need more than that." He slung his arm over my shoulder as we walked along the outskirts of town.

It was mid-May and it'd just started to warm up. Fresh green leaves blossomed on the trees and colorful flowers popped out of the ground. I loved spring. But then, I found at least five things I loved about every season. Noah still held me as close to him as he had through the end of winter.

"Well, my plan to write down what I see when I'm asleep isn't working."

He gave me a sympathetic smile. "I didn't think so. You've not mentioned it at all."

"It was frustrating. But I think I've found someone who can help. She's a therapist, Dr. Pain."

"Come on!" He laughed.

"It would be funnier if she were a doctor and not a therapist."

She was more of a hypnotist actually, but I thought telling Noah that would make him think I was totally crazy. I wasn't crazy. I was desperate.

"Ah, your therapist. Do I drive you insane?"

"Yes, but that's not why I'm going to see her. I'm trying to get my memory back, as I might've mentioned once or twice before, so I can figure out if those weird dreams are real or not."

"I know. I'm only joking. Do you think she's going to tell you if they're real or not?"

"I don't know. That's what I'm hoping she can help with." At this point, I knew the fire and Evelyn were real. I dreamed of them most. The rest I wasn't sure about.

"Well, it seems like a good idea. I think you should do whatever it takes to remember, if that's what you want, but why the secrecy?"

I stopped walking, forcing Noah to as well. The warm breeze blew his short, blond hair. His eyes looked even bluer in the direct sunlight. I was lucky to have him. We'd not been together all that long, but I trusted him, relied on him, and he never let me down.

I should've told him last week when I'd made the appointment. I owed him that.

"I'm sorry. My parents and Jeremy don't like talking about it. I can understand that. It's a tough time for them to revisit. I didn't want to tell anyone and have them talk me out of it."

Frowning deeply, he wrapped his arms around me, pulling me to his chest. "You never have to keep anything from me. No matter what you want to do—even if it's bathing in baked beans—I'll be right behind you. On the outside of the bath, but I'll be there. I don't want any secrets, Scarlett. I want to know everything about you."

"Every couple has secrets."

He blinked twice before replying, "Not us."

"You have secrets."

"You can ask me anything and I'll tell you," he said.

"Why haven't you tried getting in my pants yet?"

It bothered me. Now, I so wasn't ready for that yet, but I still wanted him to want me in that way. It was stupid and a bit irrational. He knew I didn't want to yet, but here I was questioning why he hadn't tried.

He arched an eyebrow. "This isn't temporary for me, so I want to do this right. We're a big deal. Sex means something. It means a lot, actually."

I felt like I was floating. Smirking, I said, "You still haven't answered my question."

His eyes glittered with humor. "You really know how to kill a moment. I haven't tried anything because you're not ready. But please let me know the *second* you are." He slapped my butt, grabbed my hand, and pulled me in the direction I had been leading us.

I gave Noah the address, and we followed the street until we came to 7D.

"Her office is next to KFC," I said. "Perfect."

He turned his nose up, not liking the idea of fast food. "You'll regret eating that rubbish one day."

"I really doubt it, Mr. Health Kick."

Noah pushed the door open and we walked inside. The building was tiny, wedged between KFC and a post office. A gold-coated plaque beside the door saying "Dr. Pain" was all that gave away what was inside.

"Hello, can I help you?" a plump woman behind a small mahogany desk asked.

"Um, yeah. I'm Scarlett Garner. I have an appointment with Dr. Pain at four thirty."

She looked at her screen and smiled. "Have a seat, fill out this form, and I'll let her know you're here."

I took the sheet of paper and a pen. "Thank you."

Noah led me to the leather seats in the corner of the room. "Do you want me to come in with you or wait out here?" he asked as I filled the paperwork in.

"I don't know," I replied, rapidly ticking boxes and giving a brief description of what was wrong in the tiny space they'd allowed.

Part of me wanted him there. I was nervous, and he always made that better, but I also wanted to talk without anyone else around. I didn't want Noah's opinions swaying Dr. Pain. Not that I thought a professional would side with a teenage boy and tell me I was just having normal dreams like everyone else, but I wanted her to hear only my side before she made up her mind.

"I'll do whatever you want, Scarlett," he said, squeezing my knee.

"Why do I feel so nervous?"

He shrugged. "Don't be. Should I wait here, and if you need me, you can come and get me?"

"Yeah, thanks."

"Miss Garner," a super-tall lady said from beside the reception desk just as I'd signed the bottom of the form. Noah and I were the only ones in here. I gave his hand a squeeze before letting go and standing up. "Hello, I'm Dr. Pamela Pain. Please, come through."

"Thank you," I said, giving Noah a fleeting smile over my shoulder.

I sat down on a massive, high-backed leather sofa as instructed and Pamela sat on a smaller chair beside me.

"What brings you here today?" she asked.

"Well," I said, shifting in my seat. "When I was four I lost my memory and it never came back."

"And you want it back?"

I nodded. "I was recently in a car accident, and as I was waking up, I remembered things. I'm not really sure what it all was—just parts, like broken memories. But it could just have been weird dreams. I guess I want your help to try and figure out what it was."

She nodded once, her chin-length bob falling in her face. Tucking her hair behind her ears, only to have it fall in front of them again, she replied, "We can certainly try, but first can you

84

tell me a little more about how you lost your memory and what you saw when you were waking?"

I told her everything I remembered in detail. She said very little, only stopping me occasionally to ask for additional information.

"Okay, well, we can certainly try to tap into the lost memories, but there is no guarantee, Scarlett. I have to make you aware of that. The brain is a very complex thing and occasionally pieces of information are lost forever. There is a possibility that this is one of those instances, especially since it has been so long."

I sat on my hands, too eager despite what she said. "But there's a chance it might work, and I'm willing to try. If you are, of course."

"Absolutely," she said, holding her hands out. "Lay back against the seat, and we'll get to work."

"Right now?"

"Unless you'd like to do something else for the last fifteen minutes?"

I shook my head and laid back. "This could really only take fifteen minutes?"

"Potentially. Usually it takes longer, but we should get something, a glimmer of hope for future sessions. Are you ready, Scarlett?"

"Yes," I replied with a weak voice.

"Okay, please close your eyes and relax your muscles."

I felt stupid but I did what she said. Her voice was soft and soothing, just what you'd expect, and I felt almost instantly sleepy.

"I want you to imagine yourself as a three-year-old child. You know nothing of the fire that took your memory."

I did that, picturing myself just a little bit younger than I looked in the photos we had at home.

"You're playing with your brother Jeremy," she said.

I instantly aged in my head, to a five-year-old playing the Hungry Hungry Hippos board game.

"I can't see that far back with him. There's nothing there."

"Okay, shh," she said, placing her hand over mine as I scrunched my eyes and tried to force myself to think further back. "Relax, Scarlett. Leave Jeremy and go back to the start. You're three, a full year before the fire. Where are you?"

"I'm nowhere. There's just white around me, like those models in photo frames."

"All right. Take that girl and put her in the park with Evelyn." I did that. I was in the park with Evelyn, but the image was blurry, flickering, and unreliable. It didn't happen.

"What're you doing in the park?"

"Nothing, I'm watching her run with Jeremy."

"No, you're seeing your dream, Scarlett. Take Jeremy away. You and Evelyn are on the swings. You're laughing and having fun. Keep that image in your head. Keep playing with her and tell me when there's a change."

There wasn't a change. Not one that happened naturally that would help. The only change was Evelyn getting up and running off with Jeremy. I kept seeing that one image play over and over. It was the only memory that I knew happened; the rest was what Dr. Pain was planting, but it couldn't fool me into linking it to something real.

Pamela ended our session when my time was up, and I could tell she was as deflated as I was. She clearly didn't like when she couldn't do *anything*. It wasn't going to work. There was nothing there. Maybe if I remembered more, she might be able to help me piece everything back together, but right now, all I had was a three-second snippet of Evelyn running with my brother.

"Why don't you see how things go, and if you want to try again, give me a call?"

I nodded and fake smiled. "Thank you."

Noah stood up as I walked back into reception. He saw my expression and his face fell. "It didn't go well, then?"

Shaking my head, I took his hand and led him outside, thanking the receptionist as we left. "Didn't work. Nothing happened. I don't know where to go from here, so why don't we forget it and walk for a little while before we catch the bus?"

"Of course," he replied, pulling me tight against his side and kissing the top of my head.

13

NOAH

I shoved the thought out of my head before I did the same thing Jonathan and Marissa had done ten years ago and decided to just take her away. Since Scarlett got home from the hospital, Dad had been agonizing over whether to tell Donald and Fiona about the accident or not.

Dad tapped his fingertips on his desk and peered up at me. "Do you know what you are going to do yet?" I asked.

"I believe so. When Donald calls tonight, I plan to tell them about the car accident. I do wonder if this will make them move faster though."

I swallowed audibly. "Right."

"She could have been killed and if she had... Well, I'm just saying I think they will want to get her to Ireland as soon as they can, fearing something else could happen at any minute."

I rubbed my jaw and closed my eyes. I needed longer. It couldn't happen soon. She had so much left to do. It was unfair. Even though we'd spent almost all of our free time together, texting or on the phone, I didn't know her enough. I didn't know what it was like to wake up beside her, and I didn't expect to be allowed to sleep beside her with the short time we'd have together, but I still wanted it.

"They can't," I said. "Not by too much anyway."

"Noah, they can do what they want if they think it is in our best interest."

"Yes, I know that, but I mean that her parents probably aren't going to let her out of their sight for a while. She's recovering, and I don't know if she would willingly come with me yet. I don't think risking taking her without her permission would be a good idea. How would we get her on the ferry? She would cause a scene."

I watched Dad's frown subside as he absorbed what I'd said. *Come on, Dad, side with me.*

"I agree," he finally said. "When I speak to them, I will let them know our fears, but you know as well as I that the decision on this one is theirs. Being her parents grants them a much larger claim over her than the rest of us."

"I'm sure they will see continuing with the original plan is the best idea. They don't want this to go wrong either, and it's already so dangerous."

He nodded once. "I'm sure you are right."

Thank you.

"Do you need me any longer?"

"Are you planning on visiting Scarlett?" he asked.

"I am."

He tilted his head toward the door. "Send our well wishes."

"Will do," I replied, leaving his office and heading straight out the door.

Walking to Scarlett's, I rubbed the ache between my eyes. I felt like I was living with a constant headache and I hated it. My mind was constantly buzzing. I didn't know what to do, what was right. I just wanted it to stop.

My breathing was heavy, but I couldn't get enough oxygen and felt like I was going to collapse. I wasn't too proud to admit that I was lost, scared, and needed help. There was no one to help or guide me though. I had no one to talk to, so I just had to fight my way through it.

Scarlett was on my mind constantly. The relief I felt when I found out she was all right was stronger than anything I'd felt before. She had gotten beneath my skin already. I was terrified that she was the one for me. We were taught there is one person, the other half of yourself, out there. Scarlett was mine. How could she not be when I already felt this strongly about her?

But what it came down to was this: I couldn't turn my back on everything I had ever known. Eternal Light was my whole life. It flowed through my veins; it was what made me who I was, and every member was *family*. I couldn't betray that. I didn't even know how to.

When I fell asleep every night, it was restless, and I had a hard time keeping Scarlett off my mind for very long. I hated every single part of being away from the safety of my community, and I loved and hated falling for Scarlett in equal measures.

Scarlett was in a bad mood when I got to her house. I had absolutely no experience with a moody teenage girl; everyone back home was disciplined and could deal with disappointment well. I wanted to go home and wait for her spirits to lift, but I didn't want to leave her upset.

I felt like I was constantly battling between what was expected of me and what I wanted. We were in her room because she refused to go downstairs and be anywhere near her parents. The atmosphere in her house was uncomfortable and tense. Since the therapist, things had gotten worse. She blamed her parents for not giving her the answers she wouldn't ask them for.

Every day I struggled, and every day I fell in love with her that little bit more.

She sat at the end of her bed, absentmindedly looking at the TV. I could tell her mind was elsewhere. She'd really believed the therapist would be able to help, but when she came out of that room looking defeated, I knew it hadn't gone her way.

But she was close to remembering. I watched her look at her parents differently. She might not even need to remember; soon, she would probably just put two and two together and realize her parents weren't Jonathan and Marissa.

It was still a bit too soon. I wanted to hold her off, to steer her from the truth a little longer. But I wouldn't mess with that. She had a right to the truth, and it wasn't something I was willing to sabotage too heavily.

"Hey, you okay?" I asked.

She looked up and bit her lip. "I guess. I'm just disappointed that she couldn't help."

"Come here," I said, holding my hands out.

Usually she would curl into my side, but today she climbed on my lap and laid her head on my shoulder. I was momentarily stunned. We hadn't been quite that close before. I liked it far too much. Everything about her felt right, natural, and she fit against me perfectly.

"I'm so glad I have you, Noah. You're the only one I can trust."

I bit my tongue. The stress and guilt was going to give me an ulcer. Weaving my fingers through her long hair, I replied, "It's okay. Try not to let it get to you so much. The mind is a complicated thing. The fact that you've remembered this much is a huge step."

"But is it a memory?" She groaned. "It's driving me crazy, whirling around in my head *all* the time. Make me forget it, Noah."

This was it. We were alone in her house apart from Jeremy, who was in his room with Amie. I had never had sex before and I was sure I wanted my first time to be with Scarlett, but I didn't want to do this if it was just to take her mind off everything.

"Not like this," I said, leaning my forehead against hers. She frowned, and I ran my thumb along her jaw. "You mean so much to me, but I want our first time to be because you want me, not because you want me to help you forget."

"That's not what I meant." Her arms tightened around my neck. "If you're not ready that's fine."

Not ready. I wanted to laugh. Just because my experience with women was a list of one person didn't mean I didn't have those feelings. I wanted her, but I could see the indecision in her eyes. It wasn't the right time, her mind was too all over the place, and I wasn't going to give her something else to regret about us.

"Scarlett, I love you."

Her dark eyes widened a fraction before they glowed. "I love you too."

"I can wait." A part of me hoped she wouldn't be ready. I was betraying her and soon she would find out. Could I let our relationship turn physical? I shouldn't, but I knew it wouldn't be easy once she wanted to.

Tipping her head up, she offered her mouth. I kissed her long and slow, unable to resist. She melted against me until her whole weight was pressing me against the wall. I wanted more.

Her fingers dug into my neck as I nipped her bottom lip. She invaded all of my senses, threatening to drive me insane. Everything was Scarlett, Scarlett, Scarlett, and I *never* wanted that to stop.

Was this what it was like to be completely in love? No one back home showed the *can't keep your hands off each other* stage. We didn't want to be part of the oversexed nation where no one gave a second thought to displaying anything and everything. But I wasn't so sure I wanted what they wanted. I understood it now—it was the best feeling in the world to be so in the moment with someone, so absorbed in them, that you could explode from being so happy.

She was the first one to break the kiss, when she felt something that I thought would make my face burn with embarrassment. But I wasn't embarrassed with her. It was a physical action *showing* how much I wanted her.

"Okay," she said, breathing deeply. "Um…"

I ran my hands up her back, smiling. "I know and it's fine. Really. You can stop me whenever you need to. No pressure, remember?"

Nodding, she beamed.

"Anyway, I should go soon."

"Really?" she asked, pouting.

I was sure my pupils dilated when she pouted, remembering biting her lip in our kiss that had been much more frantic and needy than before.

"I'll see if I can come back after dinner."

"You could eat here."

"And I wish I'd asked my parents before, so I could stay."

She tilted her head in a nod. "But you didn't, so your mum's cooked for you."

"Exactly."

"Okay. Let me know if you can come back, and I'll pick a movie."

"Sounds perfect."

And I hated how perfect it did sound.

When I got home, I could hear Finn's music upstairs, Dad's office door was shut, so he was locked away in there, and I had no idea where Mum was. There was a vegetable stew in the slow cooker, making the kitchen smell incredible.

I walked outside and saw Mum kneeling in the mud, planting something.

"Hey," I said, lowering myself to the ground beside her. "Need help?"

Her hands and knees were muddy, but she always had the biggest smile when she was outside. She was the true embodiment of Eternal Light. The text might as well have been written about her. When I saw her like that, the way I did every morning back home, I missed my community that much more.

"Always," she replied. "The soil isn't as good as back home, but we are getting good produce. I do miss corn though. Can you pick the ripe tomatoes and strawberries for me?"

"Sure." I took a bowl and went to the greenhouse beside where she was digging the ground.

"How is Scarlett?" she asked.

"She's fine." She wasn't fine, but I didn't feel like discussing Scarlett's private life, even though I should. "I might go back over later, if that's okay?"

"Of course. Are things between you going well?"

Now I wasn't sure what to answer. Things between us were going really well; the more I saw her the more I wanted to be around her. When it was just her and I, I felt free. I thought of nothing but us. It was addictive.

"Things are going according to plan. She's a nice girl, very sweet."

"Do you think she's in love with you yet?"

I swallowed razor blades. Yes, and that both thrilled and sickened me. "I'm not sure. Maybe. It's still early days." My face burned, and I had to busy myself, unable to look my mother in the eye as I lied to her.

"I've seen how she looks at you, Noah."

So had I.

"Even if she's not, we have a couple of months," I said, picking the red tomatoes off the vines.

"I don't think that's going to be an issue. She adores you. I know she'll go with you without incident."

My heart sank. Mum had said it to make me feel better, but it made me feel worthless. I loved Scarlett's feelings for me; they were as plain to see when she stared into my eyes as they were when she said the words. I shouldn't have felt anything back, but I loved her too.

It'll be fine. I'll get an eternity with her afterward.

"Can I ask you something, Mum?"

"You know you can. Anything, anytime."

I licked my lips, gripping the bowl with both hands. "Do you think it will hurt her?"

Silence stretched on for too long.

"Do you mean when she finds out you have lied or the final ritual?"

Which one did I mean? Well, I didn't want to know the answer to the first, even though I already did. "The ritual," I replied.

"No, I don't. It will be over too soon."

I clawed the plastic bowl, fingertips turning white. "And do you think sixteen is the right age?"

She appeared in front of the door, tilting her head to the side. "Noah…"

I raised my hands. "No, that's not what I mean. No second thoughts. You know how committed I am to Eternal Light. I agreed to five months in the pit that is *civilization*. I am in this one hundred percent. I just wondered if it would be better when she's twenty or twenty-four. She'd be an adult; we could talk to her adult to adult, get her to come with us voluntarily when there's no chance of being arrested for kidnapping."

Mum's body visibly relaxed, the stress in her eyes evaporating. "I understand where you are coming from, but there is no guarantee that she would come even then. It is dangerous to wait. She is out here, where anything could happen to her. Death is an occurrence that happens every second out here. All you hear about on the news is death. If she dies before the rituals, it is over for all of us, including Scarlett."

"Right." I scratched my forehead. "I know. Sorry, I do know that. I was just thinking aloud."

"You are entitled to ask questions, Noah. As you know, it is encouraged; you should never hold a doubt in. Is it still a doubt?"

"No," I replied, lying to my mother's face for the first second time today alone. It was the first time in my eighteen years that I had lied. What had I become?

She smiled, proving she believed me and making me feel worse. "Good. You know you can come to me if you ever need confirmation on anything?"

"I do. Thank you."

"Would you like to go over some literature tonight?"

No. "That sounds good."

"Noah," Dad called from inside.

"Yes?"

"Can you come into my office for a minute, please?"

"Sure. I'll be there in a second."

Mum smiled. "All right, you are officially let off gardening duty."

"Thanks."

His door was open, and he was sitting back on his chair behind the desk. "Come in," he said.

I closed the door behind me and sat on the armchair in the corner. "What's up?"

"How is Scarlett doing?"

She was starting to remember. That was huge and I should tell him but something stopped me every time I opened my mouth to.

"She's okay. Now that she's home, she's back to normal."

Dad smiled. "Good. That's good. I was very concerned for a while there."

Me too, but I think for completely different reasons.

"If she'd have died, what would have happened?" I asked.

"Nothing. Nothing can happen without her. We need to keep her safe and well."

I nodded, crossing my legs at the ankle. Evelyn was already gone; we needed to protect Scarlett's life until we got her to Ireland. "I know that."

"How are you doing? The pressure isn't getting to you, is it?"

"No. Hanging out with her isn't stressful. She's a great girl."

"She is," Dad agreed. "Jonathan and Marissa have done a good job raising her, I'll give them that. I had visions of a teenage brat, but she's polite and kind."

And beautiful, funny, trusting, considerate, and loving.

"You care for her?" Dad asked.

"We all do. You have just listed some of the reasons why."

He laughed. "Yes, you are right about that."

After talking to Mum, I felt like I was on trial. They trusted me. Trust was a huge part of Eternal Light. We didn't betray. There had been just one case: Jonathan and Marissa. I wouldn't let them down. They were what made me *me*. I didn't exist without them. I just had to get Scarlett out of my head and remind myself that I was doing the right thing for everyone here. *I'm doing the right thing.*

14
SCARLETT

Jeremy was out with friends, so it was the perfect time to finally speak to my parents about what was going on. Only I was terrified to. They didn't like going over the past and discussing the fire. I understood why. It must've been awful, but I had questions that were just getting louder and louder until I wanted to scream.

They were sitting on the sofa watching a house renovation show when I walked in the living room. *Here goes.* "Mum, Dad, can I talk to you about something?"

Looking up, they both smiled. "Of course, sweetheart," Mum said. They looked happy, like I was about to tell them something great. I felt worse.

Sitting down, I avoided eye contact. "When I was waking up from the accident, I had dreams, as you know. They seemed so real that it made me wonder about before."

"About before?" Dad said, prompting me to elaborate. He knew what I meant; he just didn't want to be the first one to say it.

"Before the fire."

I was met with silence and finally had to look up. They watched me carefully.

"I'm sorry. I know you don't like talking about it, but there are things that I think I remember."

"Like what?" Mum asked.

"Like a girl named Evelyn. Who is she?"

"Darling, we've told you before, that was your doll."

Yeah, they'd all said that, but the "doll" I remembered was running around. "I remember a girl; this wasn't a doll."

"I don't know what to tell you, Scarlett. Evelyn was your doll. This was a dream, not a memory."

"It felt like a memory. Everything was so familiar that I…"

Dad sat forward, straightening his back, and asked, "That you what?"

"I went to see a hypnotist."

"What? Why didn't you tell us? Why is this the first we're hearing about it?" Mum asked, sitting up far too straight.

"Because I know how you feel when we talk about the fire."

"Hey," Dad said softly. "It's hard. I won't deny that, but I don't ever want you to feel like you can't come to us. Nothing is off limits, Scarlett, no matter how difficult the conversation may be."

"Okay," I replied, dipping my head. "Then will you tell me about it again?"

Dad took Mum's hand. "The hypnotist couldn't help?" he asked. I shook my head. "Right. Well, it was just after two in the morning when we were woken by the smoke alarm. We ran out of our room and grabbed you and Jeremy. You were hysterical, screaming and crying on your bed. You were so scared. Your mum picked you up and covered you with a blanket, to try to limit how much smoke you inhaled. I got Jere, and we made our way downstairs."

They obviously had a hard time reliving what'd happened. Mum's knuckles had turned white around Dad's hand and her eyes had glossed over.

"The smoke was so thick, and when I think back, I can still feel how suffocating it was. The whole of the ground floor was in flames. We made it out the back door. Your grandparents made it out the back window, from where they were sleeping on a sofa bed in the dining room. I think if we had been just minutes later, we'd have been trapped there. Your mum collapsed to the ground when we got out. Neighbors had come to help. You screamed the entire time, Scarlett. By the time we got you on the lawn to check you over, you had passed out and didn't come to until a few hours later in the hospital. When you woke, you remembered nothing."

"Why was I the only one in the hospital?"

"We all went, sweetheart," Mum said. "We all had inhaled smoke and needed to see a doctor, but because you were in such a state, you inhaled a lot more and you were very young."

"Okay. Then what happened?"

"Then we had to start again. We tried everything we could to get you to remember. We were told that familiar things might jog your memory, but we lost everything to the fire. I'm sorry, sweetheart. We tried therapy, and we spent every night for a long time telling you stories of your past but nothing helped."

I remembered them telling me stories. But not being in the hospital. The earliest thing I could recall was being curled up on a sofa with them while Jeremy told me about a hamster we'd had. There was one thing that bugged me: if Evelyn was a doll I had, why was now the first I was hearing of it? Surely they would have mentioned her if they went through everything in my past to try to help me remember.

Something was definitely off, and I couldn't help thinking that my parents were lying to me.

"What did the doll look like?" I asked.

"Um," Mum said, "she wore a dress and had fair hair, I think."

So did the girl I saw when I was waking up. Either my fuzzy mind made her a human, or I was remembering a girl I'd known before and they weren't telling the truth. At this point, I had no idea.

"Why didn't you tell me about it before?"

Dad frowned. "We did, but it was clear that talking about your toys wasn't helping you remember, so I guess we just concentrated on the more important things like family and things we'd done together."

"Did you take me back to the house?"

"No, by the time you had calmed down enough to talk and interact with us again, the house was gone. There was too much damage, so the landlord had it torn down and built three houses on the land."

Completely possible, but I wasn't sure I believed it.

"Why do you think your dreams were of something that happened?" Mum asked. "You've had plenty of dreams and nightmares over the years. Why this one?"

That was true. I did dream a lot, and there was some pretty odd stuff in them, but it was because this one wasn't like the others. I didn't walk through my bedroom door and go into the public swimming pool or get chased by a heard of sheep one minute and fly in a plane the next. This was real, normal stuff that just wasn't dreamlike.

"It feels different," I replied.

"So you don't just think, because Noah has said a few things about how strange it is to have no recollection of almost four years of your life, that you're slotting perfectly normal things into something that makes sense, or no sense, of that time you lost?" Dad said.

I understood what he meant, and it was possible. It'd been a long time since I had given up letting it bug me, but since Noah, I *was* trying to remember again.

"Honey, I know it is strange and frustrating, but it doesn't make you different from anyone else," Mum said.

"This isn't about fitting in. Noah hasn't said anything horrible about it or me."

"Good," Dad said, raising his eyebrows and sitting back in his seat. "So, the hypnotherapy didn't work. Is there anything else you'd like to try?"

Sighing, I ran my hands through my unruly hair. "I don't know. I don't want to obsess about it anymore. It's tiring, but it does bother me that I don't know."

"Would you like to work on seeing if you can remember or learning how to let it go again?" Dad asked.

I'd let it go before. When I was eleven and determined to remember. It had been useless and Mum and Dad had spent a lot of time helping me come to terms with the fact that I probably wouldn't ever get it back. It was a difficult time when I argued with my parents a lot, even though it wasn't their fault. I had no desire to thrust us back to that.

"Let it go," I said with a defeated sigh. "I want to let it go again."

Mum smiled. "I think that's a wise choice. And you never know. You may remember one day. You're most likely to when you're not stressing over it."

"Yeah, maybe."

I didn't feel like I would remember though. I wished I could let it go like I had before. This time was different; I had *something* to hold on to. The memories as I had awoken from the accident had created real hope.

"What do you need from us?" Mum asked.

I need you to tell the truth.

"Nothing," I said. "Can we just forget this happened and I'll stop letting some stupid dreams eat away at me?"

Mum smiled, swallowing hard. "Of course we can."

"Good," I replied, standing up. "I'm going to get ready to go over to Noah's."

I didn't look back, but I knew they were watching me as I left the living room. I hadn't let it go, but they needed to believe I had. They weren't going to tell me anything, if there even was anything else to tell. Whatever happened before my fourth birthday, it was up to me to unlock it, because no one else was going to tell me the bloody truth.

15

SCARLETT

I walked along the backstreets of town toward the industrial areas after not going to Noah's. It was stupid and irrational, but the disappointment of my failed conversations with Mum and Dad left me desperate and determined.

So here I was, trawling the nearest industrial estate, looking for anything familiar to what I'd seen in my dreams. I wasn't even in the same town, that I knew for sure, but I hoped that something would look similar. How different were warehouses anyway?

I wrapped my arms around myself as I walked. The cold wind nipped at my skin, and I wished I had worn a thicker coat. It was supposed to warm up in May, but the weather had turned again. Going back wasn't an option. As crazy as I was right now, at least I was doing something.

Images of what I'd seen when I was coming around plagued me twenty-four seven. They were more than dreams, and my family wasn't talking. I *had* to know what was going on—or what had gone on. I still didn't understand how the information could just get lost. It didn't make any sense.

My phone rang in my jeans pocket. I answered the call from Noah and took shelter in the doorway of a UPS warehouse. "Hey," I said.

"Hey. Where are you?"

"At home," I replied, wincing as I lied to him. I had been hoping he wouldn't call until after I'd gotten back. Noah was the only person I could actually talk to about it. Imogen thought I was just being a drama queen and told me there were things that she didn't remember but it didn't stress her out. It was different; mine was four years and not just a few occasions.

"Right," he said, his tone telling me he was obviously upset. "Shall we try that again, Scarlett?"

"What?"

"You're lying. You're not at home."

Blood rushed to my face. "I'm sorry."

"You're lucky I called before I came over. Your parents told me you were on your way to my house, but when you didn't show… What's going on?"

"I'll go home now," I said.

"Where are you? Who're you with?"

"No one. I'm just walking."

"You're just walking," he repeated, sounding like the least-convinced person in the world.

I started making my way home, walking with long strides, so I'd make it back quickly.

"Yeah. Things have been crazy recently, you know they have. I feel like my head's going to explode. The stress is too much. You think I'm obsessing for no reason because I'll remember eventually, and my family refuses to talk about it. No one stops to think about what I need. I just wanted some fresh air and to think for a while."

"Without telling anyone where you were going?"

"Yes!" I stopped walking. He was irritating me, and I knew it was only because he was worried, but I was tired of not doing what I needed because of other people's opinions.

"I'm not coming back yet. I need time."

"Scarlett—"

"I'll speak to you tomorrow. Bye, Noah."

Hanging up and turning around, I headed back to the industrial park. I didn't want to sneak around and lie to my parents and Noah, but none of them understood how badly I needed to figure out what was going on in my head. Every time I thought about it, ice settled in my stomach. I couldn't help feeling that something was very, very wrong.

My phone rang in my pocket, and as soon as it stopped, it started again. Noah was persistent. I switched it to silent.

Back at UPS, where I'd answered the call to Noah, I looked around. Warehouses all looked the same, right? Big and gray. I took it all in and...nothing. Closing my eyes, I tried to put myself back there. Walking into the building with someone holding my hand. There was mud and rubble under my feet. The warehouse was abandoned. My white dress skimmed the ground as I walked.

I squeezed my eyes shut and pinched the top of my nose, feeling a banging headache coming on. *Remember.* It shouldn't have been that hard. I'd lived through those four years; I should have been able to remember them. My head constantly hurt while I desperately tried to fix the broken link in my mind.

Evelyn. Focus on her. She was the only name I knew of the strange faces I saw. I wished I knew who she was. I didn't see much of her face, but she was pretty and had long, dark-blond hair that fell down to her waist and curled at the ends. That was all I knew about her, but it was still a lot more than the others.

She was running with Jeremy. Where? What were they doing? The soft glow of candlelight made them seem dreamlike, but I knew better than that. They were in the room that was hot too. I couldn't remember if I was playing with anyone, but at the time, I was just standing and watching them. Why wouldn't I have joined in? Jeremy and I played all the time when we were younger.

I leaned back against the metal wall and gripped my hair. I was back there, playing the same memory over and over in my mind, desperately trying to extend it past the few short seconds it lasted. What happened next? I imagined a broken link and fixed it in my head, hoping, praying that it'd somehow trick my mind into mending whatever went wrong after the accident.

It happened.

I was there.

I could do this.

Gripping my hair, I whimpered as my head started to throb. *Stay with it. Don't give up.* Everything was inside my head; I just had to let it out. *Think. Remember. Please.* I tried to do what Dr. Pain got me to do and manipulate the memory. I paused it, keeping Evelyn still in my mind. All I could see was the side of her face, her rosy cheek, button nose, and the corner of her eye that had no color right now but I thought it was dark.

I imagined I was with her, standing by her side, slightly taller because back then I was only a few inches shorter than Jeremy and she only came up to his shoulder. She wore a white dress like the one I'd been wearing. I didn't feel anything when she was there. The memories of me crying and feeling hot from the candles made my heart race in the worst way. Evelyn brought on nothing.

But the candles might. The smell, warmth, and *feel* of having candles alight may do something. I'd been around them before, of course, but I hadn't been focused on them before. I turned around yet again and jogged home, hoping this latest direction would work. I had to know what had happened to me. The more they avoided it and the more I listened to what my mind was telling me while I was asleep, the more I *knew* it wasn't just a simple case of a PTSD from a house fire.

Mum and Dad were watching a movie in the living room when I got home. Jeremy's car wasn't in the driveway, so he was probably off with Amie. "Is that you, Scarlett?" Dad called.

"Yeah."

"Do you want to watch *The Man with the Golden Gun* with us? It's just starting."

"No, thanks, I'm going to have a bath."

"Okay," he replied, and I headed upstairs, stopping in the hall to grab Mum's box of candles from the dresser. If I didn't remember tonight, I didn't know what I was going to do. I was close to tears and so frustrated, I felt like slamming my fist into the mirror. *Something is wrong and they won't tell me!*

I locked the bathroom door, took a deep breath, and started

running the water. I was going to have to actually have a bath now I'd said it.

I set two tea lights on the windowsill and a candlestick in a holder on the side of the bath, and struck a match against the side of the box. Staring at the flame, I said a quiet prayer for this to work and lit the wicks.

Sitting on the edge of the bath, I stared at the tall, white candle on the side of the bath. That one was the closest to the one I'd seen, and I just wanted the others to give the illusion of there being more flames around without the danger of them falling out of their silver holders.

I felt the warmth and calm that staring at a flame brought; it was like cuddling up indoors on a cold, winter day. I loved fire, had always been drawn to it. Ironic really, as it was fire that stole four years from me.

Stripping out of my clothes, I got into the bath and sat closer, making sure to leave enough distance so if the candle did fall, I wouldn't get burnt. I breathed in and out slowly for five seconds, closed my eyes, and felt myself being drawn toward the heat.

I gasped and was a child again, in the room that was too hot. Jeremy and Evelyn were running, and this time I made them run around and around, coming in and out of my view. And I didn't focus on them now. I left them and walked to the candles. I felt the heat from the one in front of me and smelled the smoke as the small flame flickered, creating light and dark patches behind my eyelids.

I didn't realize I was breathing hard until my chest started to hurt.

I should've stopped, but I felt closer than I ever had before. The heat and smell made me feel something. Fear. My skin may have felt hot, but inside I was cold. Frozen still. I gagged, swallowing bile as I *felt* betrayal and loneliness, even though I didn't understand it.

My eyes flew open and I clung to the handles on the bath. Tears streamed down my face as I tried to make sense of what'd just happened. I wanted to curl up and sob until my throat was raw because of the feeling of pure fear I'd just experienced. And I didn't even know why I was afraid. Something really bad had happened to me, something that my memory was protecting me from, and even though I could feel how scared I was back then, it still refused to let me relive it.

"Scarlett?" Mum called, knocking on the door.

I jumped and spun around, making water swoosh up the side of the wall. My head and heart hurt so much, I felt like I was going to pass out. "Yeah?" I replied as calmly as I could.

"Are you okay in there? Are you crying? Did something happen with Noah?"

Hearing her concern suddenly made me furious. How dare she ask if I was okay when this was all her fault?

"I'm fine," I replied. "We argued but we've made up already."

"Are you sure you're okay? Why don't you come out and we can talk?"

I gripped the handles tighter. "No, thanks. Really, I'm okay, just want to relax for a while." I honestly did want to relax—not that I could.

"All right. I'm downstairs if you need me."

"Thanks." I think I managed to keep the seething anger out of my words. She was my mum. How could she keep something that was obviously a huge deal from me? They demanded honesty from me but were lying themselves. I never thought my parents would turn out to be hypocrites. I was so disappointed in them and frustrated with myself.

The truth was all I wanted. Why wouldn't anyone just give me that?

16

NOAH

"Hello, Donald," I said, as I took the phone from Dad and walked to my room for privacy. My nerves were all over the place after getting off the phone with Scarlett. I wanted to know where she was so I could go and get her. I felt like I was losing my grip on everything.

This was the absolute worst time to speak to Donald.

"Noah," he said smoothly. "How are you?"

"I'm fine."

"Staying strong?"

"Of course," I replied. I was trying to anyway.

"Good. We knew you would be. You ascended long ago. Your mind is strong and sharp."

Hearing those words from him now sounded...odd. "Thank you."

"No need to thank me, Noah. You are responsible for all that you have achieved."

Silence hung in the air.

He cleared his throat. "I'll get to the point, shall I?" he said, chuckling under his breath. "Scarlett. How is my daughter?"

I gripped the phone tight, something twisting in the pit of my stomach. "She's fine." She was out there somewhere.

"Good. I expect you are keeping a close eye on her."

"I am."

"We are almost there. Just six weeks to go now."

They—*we*—needed her six days prior to the ceremony day to perform the rituals necessary for the sacrifice to be accepted, so we had seven days in total that she had to be with us. Her parents and the police could easily find her in that time.

"Are you worried about being caught?" I asked.

"No," he replied. "Jonathan and Marissa will expect us to have stayed in England, where we have other land. They will not suspect we bought land in Ireland and merged our commune with Eternal Light in Bournemouth."

Bournemouth had been my home until we'd heard that the Light was going to be sacrificed, when we'd moved to Ireland where we waited for the other commune to join us. Donald had bought land in the woods in Ireland so we could all relocate and live together as one larger united community. A few weeks later, they turned up ten people lighter and without Scarlett.

My directions were clear: make her love and trust me, then take her to Dublin on a day trip and hand her over.

The more time I spent with her, the more my instructions bothered me. I didn't want to hurt her, and I didn't want her to lose faith in me. But this was bigger than my feelings or what I wanted.

"All right, good. I'm looking forward to coming home," I said.

"And we are looking forward to being complete once again. If you need anything, please call," Donald said. "I need to make my way back now. You know how I don't like being away from the community, even if it is to make a quick call."

No one did. We had to make runs into the nearest town every month for supplies and drive to the edge of the forest to make any phone calls. We all hated going.

"I will. Bye, Donald."

"Noah," he said, and hung up.

Closing my eyes, I took a deep breath and dropped my phone onto my bed.

I rubbed my forehead, downing a glass of water. Scarlett's parents and Eternal Light couldn't both be telling the truth about what would happen to her after the sacrifice. They took her because they didn't believe anymore, but could it not be true? It was my entire life. My community, my beliefs made me the person I was. One of them was lying, and I had no idea who that was anymore.

"How is it going?" Finn asked from behind me.

I lowered the glass and turned around. "Fine."

"Everything going according to the plan?"

My scalp prickled. "Yes, why?"

He shrugged. "You are spending a lot of time with her."

"That was the whole point, you idiot!" I was harsher than I planned to be. It was getting harder and harder to control my feelings and pretend this was all business. I trusted my family, but what if Eternal Light was wrong? What if we were just killing the funniest, most loving, passionate, annoying, and beautiful girl I'd ever met?

What if she wasn't the Light, the key to the next life, to eternal life?

But what if she was, and I could spend an eternity with her?

I wanted to ask Finn if he'd ever have doubts, but I didn't know whom to trust anymore. If he told anyone that I did, I could get sent back to the others and where would that leave Scarlett?

Finn held his hands up. "All right, just asking. What crawled up your arse and died?"

"Nothing. I'm tired, that's all."

"Is she keeping you up?"

I ground my teeth. "Nothing's happened between us."

"Whoa, Noah, calm down. I know it hasn't."

I turned back around, scared that he'd see the guilt in my eyes. Kissing was as far as I was supposed to go. Our relationship had to look real; Scarlett had to believe it.

I'd built a wall around myself the first day we'd met, but she used a sledgehammer to smash it down and made me care for her.

"You know exactly when Donald and Fiona want to do this thing?" I asked. *Do this thing.* It was a crappy way to say *sacrifice Scarlett.* I knew six weeks but not a specific date.

"When they're ready," he replied. "Are you ready?" *I used to be.* We'd been working toward this forever. Everything we did was in preparation of the ritual. Now I wasn't so sure. They'd chosen me because they said I was strong and could keep the poison of the outside world out of my mind. The outside world I could do. What I couldn't do was keep a fifteen-year-old girl out.

I was either the weakest member of Eternal Light or the strongest.

"I'm ready," I replied.

"Good. Me too." He slapped my shoulder. "I can't wait."

Smiling, I tried to dig through my mind to a time when I thought the same as Finn, when everything was easier and my life was clear. I didn't like how clouded it had become.

"I'm going to Scarlett's. I'll see you later."

He nodded, already engrossed in the contents of the fridge.

Walking to Scarlett's at a faster pace than I usually did, I contemplated what she would do when she found out. Would she believe Eternal Light, like Fiona and Donald said? She was their daughter after all. Or would she hate us all, especially me?

Marissa answered the door and sent me up to Scarlett's room, telling me yet again to leave the door open. We always did, but she insisted on relaying the rule every time.

Her door was open and she was lying on her stomach on her bed, facing away, reading a new book. Her chin was resting on her hands and her legs were in the air. Her hair was still damp from a shower. She'd not even taken the time to dry it before delving into another fictional land.

I watched her for a minute; she was carefree, with everything ahead of her. Was eternal life worth sacrificing this girl for? Even if we waited another four years, gave her one more cycle before performing the sacrifice, it still wasn't enough time for her to properly live this life.

I sighed, and she looked over her shoulder, smiling as her eyes landed on mine. "Hey," she said, sitting up. "I didn't think you were coming until later...or at all."

Walking in, I sat on the bed and replied, "Couldn't wait, and of course I was coming. I'm sorry."

She smiled. "I'm sorry too."

"Did you get done what you wanted?"

"No. Can we just relax, please?"

"That sounds perfect. I don't want to argue. I just want to spend time with the girl I love."

"That's sweet," she replied, leaning over for a kiss. "I'll put a movie on."

We got into our usual film-watching position—me lying against the pillows and cushions and her lying against my chest with her legs between mine. It was sitting like this that had started the doubt.

17

SCARLETT

There was nothing left to try. What else could I do? It was so frustrating and hurtful knowing that my parents had the answers, but I didn't feel like I could go to them. All I had were fractured memories and parents who were lying to me.

I could hear them talking in the kitchen. Jeremy was telling them something about extra football practice now he'd made the university team. Jere taught me to kick a ball before I could walk, apparently. Was that a lie too?

Then I heard Noah laugh. No one had told me he was here. I walked in and he immediately looked up and smiled. I didn't return it. How could Mum and Dad carry on as normal, laughing and joking around, when they were so obviously lying to me? I didn't understand how they could look me in the eye, but they did every single day and that hurt more than anything.

Neither of them cared that I was having a hard time dealing with my flashbacks or dreams or whatever they were. They didn't put aside how difficult it was to help me. Wasn't that what you were supposed to do for your child?

Something inside me snapped and boiled over. I couldn't stand pretending anymore. They were telling me now, or I was getting on the first bus to my grandparents' house.

"Are you all right?" Mum asked.

I shook my head. "No. What's going on? I'm sick of not knowing what happened, and I'm sick of you lying to me. I know that Evelyn isn't a bloody doll, so tell me the truth." Mum grabbed Dad's hand, her face ashen as if she'd seen a ghost. Fear gripped me. "Stop hiding things and tell me what's going on."

"Sweetheart…" Mum said.

"No! Don't do that anymore. I deserve the truth and you know I do. This isn't fair."

"She's right," Dad said, eyes glazed with tears. "It's time she knew the truth. We can't continue doing this, Marissa. We always said if she remembered, we would help her through. It shouldn't be different for partial memories. Sit down, Scarlett."

I did as he said and carried myself to a chair with shaking legs. Noah sat too, his face ashen. Mum and Jeremy looked downright terrified.

"Before we tell you this, I need you to know we did what we did to protect you."

Gulping, I replied, "Okay."

"Your dreams are memories. You're right. You're remembering what you repressed after the fire," Dad said, and sat forward in his seat.

The fire was true?

Out of the corner of my eye, I saw Mum and Jeremy exchange a worried glance. Did Jeremy know everything? *Of course he does.*

I shook my head, trying to put everything together, but it was like trying to complete a puzzle with pieces missing. "Tell me," I demanded.

Mum pursed her lips, blinking back tears.

"Sweetheart," Dad started, "twenty years ago, we were involved with a cult, although at the time we didn't see that."

My head hurt more. Was he joking? It didn't make sense. A cult. "What...?"

"Eternal Light was a group of people who believed in inner well-being, living off the land, and harmony. Our faith was put in nature and its ability to regenerate and adapt. We believed in an afterlife, one with no pain or loss, just peace and happiness. One night, there was a fire in the old warehouse building we used for our weekly meetings. A few made it out and we scattered, to later meet up back at the commune. It wasn't long until we realized how misplaced our faith had been."

That wasn't it. They could've told me that. "You're holding something back. You said you kept it secret to protect me. Where's the danger in what you just told me?"

"Honey, I don't think—"

"No, Dad, tell me *everything*." How dare he still try to cover things up?

His knuckles and Mum's turned white around each other. "The leaders, Donald and Fiona Mapel, convinced us that the only way we would *all* find eternal peace in the beyond is by human sacrifice."

My pulse roared in my ears. I stood up, steadying myself on the arm of the sofa. Noah was up with me, checking I was okay, but Mum, Dad, and Jeremy sat dead still.

"Human sacrifice?" Noah said, his complexion paling in front of my face.

"Please sit down, love," Mum said.

Noah helped me sit. But I wasn't sure if I wanted to hear any more. Did they actually murder someone? Were my parents murderers?

"I don't understand. You killed someone? You were all going to kill yourselves?"

"No, that's not it," Dad said.

"Then what is it?"

He took a deep breath and licked his bottom lip. "That night was the night we were supposed to perform the sacrifice. For the months previous, your mum and I had been having severe doubts. How could you find peace after murdering someone? Things Donald and Fiona said stopped making sense to us. We told no one of our doubt, of course. We feared being thrown out and unable to intervene."

"What happened that night? That's what I was remembering, right? I remember candles. It was hot—and white. Everyone was in white."

"The sacrifice was going ahead, and we knew then and there that Donald and Fiona were off their bloody rockers. They were going to go through with it. I stepped in," Dad said.

"An argument," I said, suddenly seeing an image of Dad shouting and wrestling with someone. It made my head pound, but I didn't care because it was another memory. Was he fighting with Donald? People joined in, limbs flailing around as they tried to throw Mum and Dad out of the door.

"Yes," he said. "In the scuffle, candles were knocked over and the room was quickly engulfed in flames."

"I remember the heat."

Mum nodded. "I grabbed Jeremy's arm and Dad picked you up. We made a run for it. One half of the building was already falling down, so we knew it wouldn't be long before the room buckled under the pressure."

"I barely remember anything. Why didn't you tell me before?"

"On our way out, the building started collapsing, timber from the roof fell, and we were hit. Not badly. You had a small cut on your forehead. We're not sure if that caused memory loss or if you repressed it. Either way, when you woke, you remembered nothing at all."

I knew that I had no memories before the age of four because of a fire, but I had been lead to believe it was a house fire, not a derelict building because of a cult.

"And you never filled in the blanks?" It still didn't make sense. They'd had years to tell me the truth and yet they chose to fill my head with fake memories of a childhood I'd never had. Neither looked at me. "No, that's not all, is it? What're you not telling me?"

"We love you, Scarlett. Never forget that," Mum said.

My heart stuttered. "What are you not telling me?" I repeated.

Dad closed his eyes and said, "Donald and Fiona are your biological parents." The air left my lungs in a rush. "And the sacrifice was you."

18

SCARLETT

"No!" I sprung to my feet, tears welling in my eyes. Everything I thought I knew was a lie. I wanted to rewind ten minutes because the lie was better than the truth. "I... How could you...? Shit, I was..." I didn't know what I wanted to say. There were too many questions whizzing through my mind to pick one to concentrate on. *They were going to kill me.*

"Please, Scarlett," Mum said, standing and holding her hands up. "We're sorry. It was never going to happen. We'd never have let them go through with it. We love you so much. It doesn't matter where you came from. You're our daughter."

She took a step closer and I backed up, the backs of my legs hitting the sofa. I held my hand up. Over the last few months, my head had hurt from trying to remember everything but that paled in comparison to how I felt now. I felt like I'd just had my whole world tipped upside down.

"I need to leave," I said and rushed out of the room.

My parents shouted my name, but Jeremy told them to let me go. Noah followed and I was glad. I didn't want to be alone, but I didn't want to be around someone who had betrayed me.

I collapsed on my bed in a daze. It couldn't be true. It was too... A cult. How could they have been in a cult? One that I was going to be killed in? Surely things like that didn't actually happen? But they wouldn't have made that up. It was far too much.

"Are you okay?" Noah asked, lying down behind me and bundling me up in his arms.

"No," I replied. "I'm not dreaming, right?" I muttered, staring at my wall as I tried to make sense of something that was so senseless.

He shook his head against mine. He'd barely said a word. He was probably thinking of the best way to break up with me and get the hell out.

"You're not dreaming. I wish you were."

"It doesn't make sense."

"No," he replied.

"I think I would've believed them more if they'd told me we were vampires."

"You can go out in the sunlight," he said, trying to lighten the atmosphere.

"What am I going to do?"

Shrugging, he replied, "I don't know. I can't get my head around what they said. What do you want to do?"

"I've no idea. No, actually I do. I want to rewind time to before the car accident and leave my grandparents' house later. I want for it not to be true. I want to go back to a time when everything was simple. I hate this, Noah," I said and started to sob. "I hate this and I just want to be normal."

He held me tighter and let me cry. I completely lost it, sobbing until I could barely breathe. He'd been too quiet and distracted since we found out my whole life had been a complete messed-up lie. I was scared of what I'd been told, scared of what it meant now, and scared that Noah would leave and I wouldn't have any normality in my life.

"Are you going to run? I wouldn't blame you at all," I asked once I'd calmed down enough that I wasn't gasping for breath anymore.

"No, I'm not going to run. I love you, Scarlett, no matter what. I'm not going anywhere," he whispered into my hair.

I turned around and clung to him, his words setting me off again, and I cried until I literally couldn't shed another tear. My heart was breaking. My parents weren't my parents, my whole life was one big lie, and I was almost murdered before I turned four.

Noah stayed with me until I'd calmed down. He looked stressed and tired but he'd been amazing, everything I needed. We lay side by side on my bed, with him playing with and stroking my fingers. It was calming.

"How are you feeling now?" he asked.

"I don't know if there's a word to describe it. Shocked, betrayed, hurt, confused all come close."

"You're going to be all right."

I sure didn't feel like I was going to be all right. I didn't know how to even process what they'd told me, let alone come to terms with it. "Yeah, how do you know that?"

"Because I won't give you another option. I won't pretend to understand how you are feeling, but I know that there is nothing I wouldn't do to make things better."

Closing my eyes, I turned on my side and snuggled closer to

him. "I'm going to miss you this weekend. You always manage to put things into perspective for me."

"Do you want me to stay?"

"No, you're excited to see your friends again. Besides, I've got a lot to get my head around."

"I know, but if you need me to help you get your head around it…"

He was so sweet, always thinking about me first, but now I had the chance to do something for him, and letting him go home without guilt was exactly what he needed.

"I do, but this isn't going to get better in a weekend, Noah. Maybe time alone will help me, and when you're back, things might be clearer and then you can help me move on." It all sounded so simple. I didn't even buy my own words, so there was no way he would either.

"I still don't like to leave you when you're upset."

"That's exactly why I love you so much. You spend time with your family, and I'll work on talking things through with mine."

He rolled to his side so we were facing each other. When his fingertips brushed my chin, I took a deep breath. He made me feel so many things all at once, and even though sometimes the intensity of those feelings scared me, I wouldn't have changed it for the world.

"*I love you*, Scarlett," he whispered, and claimed my lips.

19

NOAH

It'd been months since I'd been home, and I missed everything and everyone. We were such a close community and I hated how distant everyone was here. I had no idea who our neighbors were. The most contact we'd had were grumbled hellos over the fence.

But we were finally going back to visit for the weekend and I couldn't wait. Dad loaded up our bags while Mum made food for the long journey. We were leaving in an hour, but I wanted to spend some time with Scarlett before I left.

"I'll be back soon," I said to Dad as I walked down the path.

"All right, send our regards to Scarlett."

"I will." Stuffing my hands in my pockets, I made my way to her house, not even bothering to try to convince myself I wasn't overeager to see her anymore. I felt what I felt, and I couldn't change it any more than I could control it.

I arrived minutes later and Jeremy answered the door. He rolled his eyes and told me she was upstairs. I'd become a regular at their house as me and Scarlett went through that *needing to be around each other all the time* stage that really didn't need to be faked by me anymore. I honestly didn't think I ever needed to fake it. Even before she consumed most of my thoughts, I had enjoyed spending time with her.

They shouldn't have chosen me.

Scarlett was lying on her back on the bed when I walked in, just staring up at the ceiling.

"You okay?" I asked.

She didn't look over, but she did smile. "I'm *really* good." She wasn't but she was dealing. Having me there helped because she thought I hadn't betrayed her. And I hadn't. Yet.

I sat on the bed and started playing with her fingers. "Yeah, why is that?"

Looking over, she arched an eyebrow and replied, "Why do you think?"

Of course I knew, but every time she said something like that, she made me feel a hundred feet tall. Hell, every time she looked at me the way she always did.

"But I'm also sad." She pouted adorably. "Two days is a long time."

"It's not that long."

"No," she said, sitting up. "You're supposed to agree with me here because you'll miss me too."

"I will miss you too, but it's okay."

"How is it okay?"

"Because there are people out there, living and working so far away from the people they love for months, years even. Time doesn't mean anything, Scarlett, not when you really care about someone."

"Okay, that just made me feel a hundred times better about this weekend."

"Good, because I don't think I'll be able to speak to you much. I'll try going to town a couple times though."

She shook her head. "No, it's actually okay. Time doesn't mean anything, right? Just enjoy your time with your family and don't worry about leaving your stupid limited service and no Internet village and checking in. I'll see you when you get back."

It didn't really feel like checking in, not when I wanted to talk to her. I wasn't going out of my way because I wanted that contact. But she was right, and I needed to reconnect with everyone back home because I could feel myself losing touch.

"I'll still try to call. I want to," I said, making her smile.

"Okay, it's not like I'd ignore the call or anything."

I knew she wouldn't, and I loved that she wanted me just as much as I wanted her.

"What do you have planned?"

"Sleepover at Imogen's. I've been a bit of a crap friend since you came along."

"No, you haven't. You still spend time with your friends." She'd made sure she spent time with Imogen and Chris. She wasn't going to Imogen's because she felt like a bad friend; she was going because she didn't want to stay home all weekend.

She shrugged. "I do but not as much as I used to. A girls' night will be good, especially after everything that's been going on."

"Yeah, you deserve some time away from the tension." There was still a *lot* of tension; Jonathan and Marissa tiptoed around her and she barely spoke to them. She still had a lot of questions and still didn't know who Evelyn was, but she could barely look at them to ask.

I wanted to tell her, but of course I couldn't. Even if I could have, I wouldn't have. After everything, she deserved the truth when she asked for it, when she was ready.

"Think one weekend I can come with you to visit your family?" she asked. "I want to see where you grew up."

"You want to see my tiny, technology-neglected island or my aunt's in Dublin? Both are home." I couldn't show her the island. I'd never even been there and only knew enough to answer any general questions. Ireland, where I grew up from the age of seven, she would see soon enough.

"I'd love to see both."

I would love to show her around too. I would love for us to be normal and be able to live out the life I'd started to fantasize about. She deserved that. I deserved that.

"Do you think your parents would let you go away with me? They look like they want to run away with you when you mention leaving the house to go in the garden," I said.

She shrugged. "I don't know. They can't stop me from doing everything. It's so weird. A part of me wants to meet my biological parents, even after everything they've done. I don't know how to speak to my parents anymore. I still have so many questions and I'm pretty sure I'm either still in shock or dead inside. How stupid is that?"

"It's not stupid. It's going to take a while to get your head around everything—it would for *anyone*. You're not dead inside for needing time to process what you've been told or for not being ready to have another conversation with your parents about it. And it's natural to want to know where you come from, Scarlett. But how would you even find them?"

"I've no idea. I wouldn't actually do it. Believe me, I get the danger of being anywhere near them, and I'd be lying if I said I hadn't considered running too."

That was news to me. "You have?"

"At first, yeah. When they told me who they are, I was so scared. But we've moved around a lot, and they obviously have no idea where I am. And, you know, if they ever tried to contact us, we'd call the police."

"You're going to be fine here."

"I know. Besides, I don't want to have to start all over again and I don't want to leave you."

"What do your parents think?"

"They don't think I'm in any danger just because I know the truth. In fact, they agree that it's safer I do, so I can be more cautious. We love where we live and the friends we've made and don't want some crazy cult to ruin that. I need the familiarity of here and my friends when everything else has changed so much."

I swallowed hard, an uneasy feeling settling down. I still felt loyal and didn't like her calling my family crazy. But I could see it from her point of view—a point of view I was leaning more and more toward sharing. I'd never needed to go home so much before. I had to be back in my community, so I hoped I could set everything straight in my head.

"Look, I've got to go or my parents are going to be angry. I'll try calling, but if I can't I'll see you in just two days." I kissed her, cupping her cheeks in my hands. When I was with her like this, nothing else but her made sense. If she was the only thing that gave me clarity after this weekend, I would know Eternal Light was wrong and everything I'd been led to believe my whole life was built on poor judgment and twisted truths.

I was petrified.

20

NOAH

We arrived at the commune hours later, and I felt like I could breathe easily again. Everything was right here. I didn't have so many difficult choices. We had a clear path and followed clear rules.

We were immediately jumped on by the community and led to the communal table, which I'd helped to carve from fallen trees in the forest. They had so many dishes laid out, I couldn't count them. It was real food and I knew exactly where it'd come from and what it was going to—or not going to—do to my body.

I couldn't keep the elation off my face as I sat on the wooden bench and tucked into Bernadette's famous asparagus fettuccine. I sat at the end of the table with Finn and a couple friends: Skye, Zeke, and Willow. They were the only ones around my age, with Skye and Willow the closest. I wished they were guys, so one of them could've gone to betray Scarlett instead.

Everyone started passing dishes around, filling their plates, wide smiles on their faces. The atmosphere was electric. We were all happy to be back together again.

"Thank you," I said to Bernadette as she passed me the basket of homemade rolls. The only things that were different were the sunflowers—they were bigger, taller, brighter than when we'd left. A feeling of belonging settled in my heart, and I properly relaxed for the first time since we moved.

Our laughter filled the air, and there were animated conversations along the stretched table.

"So what's she like?" Willow asked. She and Skye were identical twins, and if it wasn't for Willow's love of short hair and Skye's of long, you'd never have been able to tell them apart. They sat side by side, directly opposite me.

"She is everything we've been told," I replied. We'd grown up loving Scarlett, only now I think I loved her in a completely different way.

Skye rolled her dark green eyes. "Oh, come on, Noah!"

"Fine. She's beautiful, funny, compassionate, a little bit crazy, stubborn, and smart. She never has a bad thing to say about anyone." *And she deserves a chance to go to university and live off cheap noodles like she wants.* But that couldn't happen. The next life she has will be perfect, much more than this one. She'll be happier and I'll join her eventually.

"I can't wait to meet her," Zeke said. He spoke of her with such admiration it made my throat thicken. There wasn't one person here who wouldn't give their life to protect her for as long as it took to get her here. "Do you think she will hate us though?"

Yes, absolutely.

I shrugged. "I'm sure once Donald and Fiona explain, she'll understand. She challenges society's ideas already, so I don't think it'll take her long to come around." She didn't really challenge anything. Or I hadn't had a conversation about anything like that with her, but she was a good person, always looking to do the right thing. But in the end it didn't matter.

"What is it like living out there?" Willow asked, making it sound like we'd moved to the moon, which didn't feel too far off actually.

"It's horrible," Finn said. "I can't wait until she's back here and I never have to step foot outside the commune again."

"You'll still have to do the food runs," Willow pointed out.

"You know what I mean."

"I'm with Finn," I said. "Although I'm not having quite as hard time adjusting. It'll be good to be home permanently." When that happened, it'd mean Scarlett would be dead. I didn't like "civilization" much, but I'd stay there if it meant I could stay with her. I wished Donald would give me four years with her.

I took a deep breath and pushed all of that stuff away. I wasn't home long and I was determined to enjoy it. Whatever I was feeling would sort itself out. We all loved her, but I knew her in a way no one else did, and that was bound to throw up some issues and emotions. It didn't mean I wasn't still just as devoted to Eternal Light.

After our meal, I helped to clean up, and we gathered goblets of water. The year of water was coming to an end in a short few months. The year of earth would start again, and Scarlett would be safe for a while—if it wasn't for the fact that we already had her within our grasp.

Fiona gathered us around a lake I had helped to build six years ago. It was between the edge of the forest and our wooden houses.

We'd dug it wide and somewhat narrow, so it was a rectangle with curved edges. It was the length of forty people with their arms stretched out to their sides.

I held my goblet up in one hand, mirroring what everyone else was doing. Donald walked along the line, touching each goblet and bowing his head.

"You give us life, give us the means to sustain ourselves," Fiona said. "Water cleanses the earth. It allows people to drink, to wash, and to grow crops. You give us all we need to live now and beyond."

Donald reached the end of the line and took his offering from Fiona.

"We will not forget to be thankful every day for what the earth provides us. We will not take it for granted nor will we be selfish with it. We will take only what we need and make sure we are able to replenish what we use." He tilted the goblet, and the water poured over lip of the glass into the lake, adding to the water we'd blessed and built up over the last six years.

Once Donald's was empty, he bowed his head, giving the cue for us to follow. I tipped mine slowly and watched it trickle into the water. There wasn't a day that passed that I wasn't grateful for life. People abused the earth we lived on, most without any realization of what they were doing. I wouldn't turn into that.

That day and the next, I fell back into my old life, but there was something missing. Or someone. I couldn't stop thinking about her, wondering what she was doing, if she was hoping I'd call. There was no way I'd get a signal out here, and they'd already done a run into town to get supplies the week before.

When it was time to leave, I felt an even mixture of dread and longing. I'd missed Scarlett, but my community was everything, and it was hard to be without them.

"Not long now," Bernadette said, handing me a paper bag that would be filled with snacks for the journey back.

"Thank you. I cannot wait until we're back here for good."

Our good-byes took a while; everyone hugged me and my family for longer than usual, trying to shorten the time we would be apart, even if by precious seconds. We knew what it was like to be separated now, whereas the first time we left, we knew it would be difficult but didn't know how much.

Donald and Fiona approached, saving their good-bye with me until last.

"Noah," Donald said. "I cannot even begin to express how proud of you we are and how grateful."

"You are doing a wonderful job of keeping Scarlett safe," Fiona added. "But I know that it is not easy, so remember why we are doing this. Keep that in your heart and you will be fine."

I felt like she could read my doubts and see that what I felt for Scarlett had evolved. Would they have said that anyway, or were they concerned that I was falling in love so felt they had to back up our beliefs?

"It isn't easy, but I know what I have to do, and I know it's the right thing for us all."

Donald smiled and put his hand on my shoulder. "You are wise beyond your years, Son."

Sometimes I didn't feel it. Coming home for a while was

exactly what I'd needed, but that didn't stop me wanting more for Scarlett before she made the ultimate sacrifice for our community. If I thought they would consider my request and let me go back to her, I would have asked them for those four years. I could stay with her, see that she did everything she wanted to, and then in four years' time, bring her here. But I knew if I asked, they would question my loyalty and I couldn't risk that.

"Thank you," I replied.

"Are you ready, Noah?" Dad asked. My tearful mum was already in the car, and Finn was saying a last good-bye to Zeke, Willow, and Skye.

With an uncertain nod of my head, I replied, "I'm ready."

As we got in the car, people shouted things like "bye," "see you soon," "take care," and "remember we love you." I took a deep breath and waved good-bye to my home. Knowing I would see Scarlett soon made me miss her more. I was anxious to get back to her. My heart beat faster knowing I would see her soon.

I felt sad to leave, but that was quickly replaced with a contented smile at the thought of holding her again. The whole way home, I was silently counting down the minutes until I could go and see her. I was hopelessly in love with her—and our love was hopeless.

21

SCARLETT

I was counting down the seconds until Noah got there. Two days without him around was awful. I didn't know how to look my parents or Jeremy in the eye. They'd told so many lies that I didn't even know who they were anymore. I wanted to know more, but I couldn't handle them dressing up the truth again. Noah was right; I needed time.

"Scarlett, good morning, honey," Mum said, pouring boiling water into four mugs as I came downstairs and ignored them.

I grumbled a "morning" and sat at the table.

"Come on, please talk to us. You have to understand why we made the choices we made," she said.

"I understand them, I really do. If you hadn't stopped me from being murdered, then you wouldn't be the people I know, deep down, you are, but you lied to me for years. You moved us around so much and told me it was because of Dad's work. You had your parents and son lie. That's the part I can't get past. You didn't have to make some elaborate story up; you could've told me the truth."

She looked at me like I was insane. "You were a *child*. We thought about it, believe me, but we couldn't risk you saying something. We had to keep you safe—all of us safe. This was the easiest way to do that, and I'm sorry that you feel betrayed, but keeping you alive meant more to us than you being upset about us lying."

"Is Evelyn your daughter?"

"No," she said."

"She's not a doll?"

Shaking her head, she replied, "No."

"She was a friend of Jeremy's?"

"She was, yes."

"Is she dead?"

"I don't know." Lowering her head, she wiped her eyes. "I think so."

"Why couldn't you tell me that?"

Sighing, Dad said, "We were trying to protect you."

We could go over it and over it, but it would never get us anywhere. I would never think they were right for letting me believe something that wasn't true for so long. While I was younger, sure, but I was fifteen, and they could've told me a few years ago, when we'd moved here. They should have told me when I started remembering.

"This isn't getting us anywhere," Jeremy said. "We're not sorry, Scarlett. If we'd have done things differently, you could be dead now."

"Jeremy!" Dad scolded.

"No, Dad, I'm tired of tiptoeing around her. We lied, but we did it for good reason. Now stop being a brat and get over it. You're my sister whether we share genes or not." He pointed to

Mum and Dad. "They brought you up and love you the same as me. You're theirs, so enough now."

My eyes narrowed. He was right and that only made me angrier. How could he tell me to just get over it? He hadn't just been told that his biological parents would've murdered him if no one had stepped in.

"Okay, we all need to calm down," Mum said. "Coffee is ready, so let's try to have breakfast like a normal family."

That was all well and good, but we were nothing like a normal family. I almost laughed.

Hurry up, Noah.

Breakfast wasn't normal; it couldn't be. I sat beside my brother and focused solely on the pastries and coffee. They watched me the whole time, making everything ten times more awkward. Did they think I didn't love them anymore? Did they think I would feel out of place knowing I didn't share their genes? I didn't. I loved them. No matter what, they still felt like family. But they'd hurt me so badly by keeping the truth from me.

We ate mostly in silence, with Jeremy occasionally saying something about football, the present he got Amie for her birthday, or a trip he and his friends were going on. I picked at my croissant, only having managed a few bites.

"What time is Noah home?" Dad asked. I think he was just as eager to get him here as I was, hoping he'd be able to help.

I looked up at the clock and back to him, meeting eyes that I once thought were the same shape as mine, even if they were a different color. Everything looked different now. "Around now.

He's dropping his bags off and coming straight here. I'm finished. Can I go to my room?"

Mum's dark eyebrows pulled together. "You've not eaten much." Neither had she.

"I'm not hungry."

With a sober smile, she nodded, and I left the table.

I wasn't back in my room long before Noah's confident knock echoed through my room. "Come in," I said, immediately brightening.

His smile for me was wide and light, and I didn't realize how much I'd missed him until I saw how happy he was to see me. "Hey," he said, flopping down on the bed beside me and pulling me in for a kiss.

I held on to his upper arms and kissed him back, feeling more whole by the second. He was someone linked to the me I knew, someone who hadn't changed almost beyond recognition. His lips were soft but the kiss was much firmer than usual.

"Hey back," I whispered when he broke the kiss and leaned against my forehead.

"I missed you, Scarlett. It's stupid. It was only two days, but not seeing you just felt wrong."

"I missed you too," I replied, grinning like a fool. "Things here have sucked, but knowing you were coming back made it bearable."

He winced. "I'm sorry."

"No, don't be. I didn't mean to make you feel bad. You're allowed to have a life outside of me, you know."

"I know. Not that sure if I want to." Frowning, he shook his head. "All right, that sounded less codependent in my head."

I laughed and replied, "I know what you mean."

"So tell me the truth. Are you okay?" he asked.

I wrapped my arms around my legs. I was so not okay, but I felt better now that he was back. It was stupid. He wasn't gone long, but I really needed him to stay for a while now.

"Not really. It's still hard even trying to get my head around what they told me, you know? They had Mum's parents in on it too. What a burden their lie must've been on everyone." And they did it all for me. I felt horrible for being angry and angry for feeling horrible all at the same, mind-screwing time.

He pulled my hands apart, untangling my body, and wrapped me tightly in his arms. "Yes, it's…" His foot tapped on the bed, and I was so sure he was about to run off.

"Screwed up?"

The corner of his mouth kicked up. "That is one way of putting it."

"If you want to leave, Noah, I'll understand." We hadn't been together that long really and add that to the fact that we found out my biological parents are crazy cult leaders, I wouldn't have blamed him if he'd wanted to run for the hills.

"No." Taking my hand, he turned to me. "I know things are… strained right now and you have been told something that's hard to understand and hard to believe, but I'm not going anywhere. When I told you I love you, I meant it. We'll get through this together. You need to decide what you want to do."

"Thank you," I whispered, squeezing his hand. "I have no idea what I want to do. I don't even know what to think right now. It's so surreal. Cults and human sacrifice…"

Me as the sacrifice.

"I know," he whispered.

"This stuff only happens on TV."

"I'm so sorry, Scarlett."

I shrugged. "It's not your fault."

"Still," he said, "I hate that you're upset. Is there anything I can do?"

"You can tell me about visiting your family and how your aunt is doing."

"Come on, you don't want to be talking about that stuff right now."

"No, I really do, Noah. Please." I would've talked about football if it meant it would stop me watching the memories of my childhood rip apart. None of it was real.

"Okay. They're all good. My aunt overfed us all and my cousins are going through a pirate phase. They spent the two days running around with patches on their eyes. Lottie had both on for a while, and I had to guide her around the house for an hour."

A face flashed through my mind, giving me an instant headache. I rubbed my forehead, trying to get the fog in my mind to lift.

You will guide us.

I scrunched my eyes closed and shook my head. What did that mean and who had said it? I felt familiarity, comfort, and fear at the same time.

Noah's voice pierced through the haze and pulled me back to reality. He was sitting on his knees right in front of me, eyes wide with worry.

"I. Um." Licking my lips, I slouched forward and into his arms. "I think I remembered something else."

"What was it?"

"A face of a lady. She was pretty and had long, light-brown hair. She said, 'You will guide us,' and…" I closed my eyes again, trying to go back there, repeating the phrase over and over to try to get my brain to latch on to the memory and give me more. I hated that it was so out of my control. Why couldn't I just get my brain to work properly?

"Who do you think she was?" he asked.

"I don't know. Could be anyone. I don't recognize her at all."

"Do you remember her eye color? Think you could try to draw her? That might help."

I shook my head. "She would just look like a stick person. I don't remember her eye color. She had a kind face though, and she was smiling as she spoke."

"Do you think it could be…"

My biological mother. That was what he couldn't finish saying.

I shrugged, and he immediately wrapped his arms around me. "I don't know. She didn't look like me, but then maybe I look like him…my dad. Anyway, I'm tired of this. Can we do something else? Why don't you put a DVD on while I go and get some snacks?"

His face lit up. "All right." Before he got up he added, "Hey, you know I love you, right?"

"I do know. I love you too."

"It'll be all right. You'll see," he said and kissed my forehead before going to find something for us to watch. I hoped it would, because I missed feeling close to my family. If I could have fast-forwarded to a time when we were past this and had healed, I would have.

22

NOAH

"Is she okay?" Marissa asked, wiping her eyes as I got down-stairs. Scarlett had fallen asleep and I didn't want to wake her, so I'd left a note telling her I loved her and would see her later. I wasn't sure where Jonathan and Jeremy were, but I couldn't hear them in the house.

"She will be," I replied.

"This is such a mess. I never wanted her to find out. We only ever wanted to protect her."

"She'll understand that. She just needs time to process every-thing and adjust. I mean, that was some confession."

This was the first time since Scarlett had found out the truth that I was talking to them about it. But everything they'd said was exactly what Donald told me they'd say. Jonathan and Marissa had completely lost sight of what our *community* was trying to achieve. They'd let their doubt grow into something toxic that clouded their judgment and caused them to make snap decisions that affected everyone. In their heads, they'd turned Eternal Light into something it wasn't.

When I finally got my chance, Scarlett would see the truth behind her parents' tale.

Marissa managed a smile. "Yes, it was. We had to get her out of there, and when she woke up and couldn't remember a thing, it was so easy. It was as if fate had given us this chance to start over and make it up to her. What we almost sat back and allowed happen…" She paused, shaking her head. "Finally, we could give Scarlett and Jeremy a normal, safe childhood, so we took it."

"Did you ever worry about her remembering?"

"At first, yes. As time went on, we assumed it wasn't going to happen. Perhaps we shouldn't have been so complacent."

"Do you think you should have told her?"

"No," she replied. "We had to protect her and this was the best way to do it. Those people were going to murder her, Noah."

I pursed my lips and nodded. That wasn't right. *I don't think.* Going home hadn't given me the clarity I'd hoped for. I was still just as confused.

"I'm terrified she's going to hate us and even more terrified that she'll try looking for them. If they knew where she was…" Scrunching her eyes closed, she took a deep breath. "She may not have my blood running through her veins, but she's my daughter and I love her. There's nothing I wouldn't do to keep her safe."

"You mean leaving town?" I asked. The thought of not seeing her hurt, but at the same time, I wanted to tell them to take her and get as far away as possible.

"I don't know what I mean. I don't believe there's any danger to her here. If they knew where she was, they would have tried to take her already. We're safe here; I'm more concerned about Scarlett right now."

"She'll be all right."

"I hope so," she replied.

"I've got to head home for a bit, but I'll be back tonight, if that's okay?"

"Of course," she said. "It helps her, you being here."

"I won't be long. See you later."

I had to get out of there. I couldn't think straight. The walls were closing in, air thinning to the point where I could barely take a breath. My head hurt, and I was mentally exhausted from trying to work out what I believed and what I was going to do.

This was exactly what they'd talked about. They'd said that the outside world could get to you, make you believe whatever they wanted you to. The government fed you little pieces of information that made you think things were okay.

I didn't want to be one of them. I wanted to think for myself, but what if Donald and Fiona were the equivalent of a government? The tug-of-war between Eternal Light and Scarlett was going to ruin me.

Home wasn't even a break from it. The second I got in, Dad told me I needed to call Donald. I just wanted a break from everything, some time where I could be left alone to think independently.

Scarlett occupied ninety percent of my thoughts, but that could just be because of the attraction I felt toward her. I liked her, loved her, fancied her like crazy, but I shouldn't have let that come between me and what I'd known my whole life. Everyone back home was family and you put your family first.

I went to my room to call him, knowing my dad would allow me privacy to speak to Donald. We held trust very highly, something that made me feel even worse about doubting Eternal Light.

"Noah," Don said. His smooth voice calmed me, made me remember what I was part of. I wanted it to be over already. I wanted to be home again, where everything was simple and I didn't have to constantly struggle and fight to find my way.

"Hello, Donald. How is everyone?"

"We are doing just fine. And you? I trust the journey home was pleasant?"

"Yes, it was all right," I replied, rubbing vigorously between my eyebrows. Headaches were coming all too often now. I never got ill back home, where we had little to stress about.

"Noah, I am going to have to call you back another time, tomorrow perhaps. Fiona needs assistance with something rather urgently."

I opened my mouth to protest. *I should tell him about Scarlett knowing the truth.* Nothing was more urgent than that, but nothing came out. I'd spent two days pretending everything was all right with her, and I still couldn't tell him what was really going on.

I should've told him. It should've been the first thing out of my mouth when we'd arrived home.

"All right, was there something you wanted me for though?"

"No, it was just to check in and see how everything is. But we will talk later. I have to get back."

"Speak to you soon," I said, and he hung up.

I put my phone down and looked up to the ceiling. *What am I going to do?*

"Everything all right?" Finn asked. I snapped back to reality to see my brother leaning up against the door frame.

"Yes. Why?"

He shrugged. "You look tired."

That was an understatement.

"I am. Nothing a good night's sleep won't cure."

"All right." He pushed away, and I was left with my obsessive thoughts again.

Scarlett or Eternal Light? It shouldn't have even been a choice.

Before I could think anymore, I dialed Donald's number back. Family first. My community had to stay my number-one priority. *Please don't let him be far enough back to the commune to not get signal.*

My heart was in my throat as I called. Part of me wanted to take Scarlett to the other side of the world, away from her family who had broken her heart, and away from Eternal Light who valued their eternal life over her human one. Either way, someone was going to suffer. And either way *I* was going to.

I understood why they wanted to do it—Scarlett was our salvation—and we'd be reunited with her afterward, but she deserved to get everything she wanted out of life.

"Noah," Donald said. "Is everything all right?"

Closing my eyes, I replied, "No. Sorry, you didn't give me the chance before, but Scarlett knows. Jonathan and Marissa told her everything."

A minute's silence stretched out in front of us until he finally replied, "I see. When did this happen?"

Swallowing, I replied with more lies. "Today. What do you want to do?"

Call it all off. Please.

"Act," he replied, and I closed my eyes, temples throbbing. "We move this forward. It's not ideal, but perhaps it will work in our favor."

"How so?"

"Right now, she will be confused. It will be easier to get through to her with the truth."

What was the truth?

"Are you sure, Donald? We're still weeks off."

"I understand that, Noah, but we do not have a choice. We cannot risk them running."

"With all due respect, I don't think they are going to run. They have nothing to run from."

"We can't risk the fear that Scarlett will now undoubtedly feel forcing Jonathan and Marissa's hand. You know they moved every few years in the past. They don't know what to do, so they run; it is their answer to everything. We need Scarlett here, Noah. The longer we leave it, the higher the risk of something happening to her. We have worked so hard for this. Scarlett will be sacrificed so that we may all live on. She is the one, our salvation, our *everything*. My daughter is the light that will lead us to eternal life. I am not willing to wait, not another four years, not even another three weeks."

Ignoring the distaste on my tongue and twist in my gut, I replied, "Yes, Donald. When do you want to do this?"

"I'll call you tomorrow to finalize the details, but we move on Saturday."

"Saturday? That's only six days away." *I should have weeks. I need weeks.*

"I know. Can you do this, Son?" he asked. He often called me and the other guys "son," but this was the first time it bothered me. That alone left me with an uneasy feeling. I used to rely on him for answers. He always had answers, but they just didn't make as much sense anymore.

"I can," I replied.

"Good. You are strong, Noah. Do not let the outside world make you crumble."

Donald hung up, and I dropped the phone on my bed. I wasn't sure that hadn't already happened.

What have I done?

"Dad," I called. My heart was stuttering and my palms began to sweat. "Donald wants it done on Saturday."

The next thing I heard were three sets of footsteps thudding up the stairs.

My final week with Scarlett was passing too quickly. She tried to act as though nothing had happened, but she still hadn't sat down with her parents and sorted their situation out. I wanted them to now more than ever. I didn't want their last memories of each other to be tense.

It was Wednesday, just three days before we would be in Ireland. And I still hadn't asked her to come with me. We sat on the bench at school during lunch hour, while our friends laid on the grass listening to music.

I was putting off the inevitable. Turning to her, I blurted out in a low voice, "Let's go to Dublin this weekend."

"Dublin?" Scarlett said, eyes widening in surprise. "You want to take me to Dublin? This weekend?"

I shrugged, swallowing the acidic taste of bile, and took a look around to make sure no one was listening. Chris and Imogen were engrossed in what they were doing and Bobby was serving detention. If either of them had heard, they would have questioned it or at least looked up. "You said you wanted to."

"I know, but it's a bit sudden, isn't it?"

"I suppose, but you could probably do with the break, and it would be nice to fall off the face of the earth with you for a while. We could do something that's just for us. I'll tell my parents I'm staying with Chris and you tell yours you're staying with Imogen."

"Dublin?" she repeated, a slow smile spreading across her face.

"Yeah, why not? It's no different than going to London for the day. We'd just take the ferry rather than a train."

"I suppose. I do like it when it's just me and you. We don't get that enough."

Bending my head, I kissed her and replied, "Me too. I want us to be alone."

She gulped, biting the inside of her cheek. "Like…that?"

"I love you."

Her breathing came out a little harder; then she smiled. "Yeah, I think I really want that. No, I know I do because I love you too, so much."

Her words sucked the air out of my lungs until I felt like I was suffocating. Keeping my calm, I said, "I'm *so* glad you said that. I would also like us to have fun, and I can show you some of the places I visited a lot growing up."

"And try Guinness?" she asked, giggling.

"If we can get served!"

"You look older than sixteen. You'll get served."

"Then yes, we will try Guinness."

She watched me for a minute. I didn't want to push it and have her get suspicious, but I think I wanted her to say no. When she agreed, my stomach churned. She looked at me with big, trusting eyes. Her expression for me was different than her expression for everyone else—softer, happier. I didn't deserve it.

She placed the palm of her hand on my chest as she stared at me.

My throat started to close. A weight crushed my body until I felt like I was going to break. *No.* She looked at me with such adoration that it made me feel physically sick.

"What's up?" she asked, her voice so low I barely heard her.

Gulping, I replied, "Nothing."

"There is. All of a sudden you tensed up and you're looking at me like… Well, I don't know what like."

"Nothing is wrong. I just *really* love you, Scarlett."

Her eyes filled with tears. "I just *really* love you too."

I kissed her. "Right."

Biting her lip, she did a surveillance of our surroundings. "I want to be with you, Noah. Today."

My body went rigid. I wasn't supposed to do that. But would it be so wrong to give us that? After what we would both have to sacrifice very soon, was it wrong to want something perfect first?

"Tonight," I repeated, and kissed her.

She loved me, trusted me, and I was about to throw her to the lions.

23

SCARLETT

I felt a rush of adrenaline as we got off the bus at the port. It had been a four-and-a-half-hour bus ride and now we had a three-and-a-half-hour ferry ride, but I didn't care because we were free until tomorrow morning.

Imogen was covering for me if my mum called her. Noah said he'd asked Chris to do the same for him. Neither of them knew where we were. We'd just told them we were spending time together and they had to cover.

Im was too busy telling me all about how I was going to lose my virginity to bother with any other details anyway. Little did she know I'd lost it on Wednesday. It had been perfect. Noah had been perfect, and I felt even closer to him than I did before.

Mum didn't take long before she'd agreed to let me stay at Imogen's for the night, but she never did. I was pretty sure both my parents would be glad to have me out of the house. Dad had said the space would do us good and he was right. We needed to not be under each other's feet for a day, and then maybe, when I got home, we could talk and sort everything out. I was ready for things to be normal with them now.

We'd get the ferry back at two in the morning and be home by eleven, when I could claim to have come from Im's. It was going to be a long two days, but I needed to get away for a while, and spending time with Noah—alone time—was an added bonus.

Noah had our passports—I'd snuck mine out of the drawer last night—and led us through the port. It was obvious he'd done this quite a few times before; he knew exactly where to go. It didn't take long, and we were soon sitting in the café. After the long drive, I needed a coffee. Noah had caffeine-free green tea. I had no idea how he coped without caffeine.

"You okay?" I asked.

He stared at his mug and nodded. "I'm fine, just tired."

"Me too. Are you excited to see your aunt again?" It wasn't that long ago that he was there, but this time he was bringing his girlfriend home. It was a lot different.

Smiling, he nodded and sipped his tea. "I am. You excited to meet her?"

"Excited and nervous. You're sure she won't call your parents?"

"Everyone will love you. I promise. And no, she won't. I'll get told to never go behind their back again, but she will be fine."

"Wait, everyone? Wow, how many people am I meeting?"

"Just a few cousins and my aunt's boyfriend. They are all nice, so you'll be fine. She can't wait to see you."

"You told her much about me?"

"Maybe."

"Like what?"

"Like how amazing you are and how much I love you."

Yeah, that'd do. I grinned and was pretty sure I blushed as well. Noah was so sweet. Some of the lads at school would never say things like that to their girlfriends in front of people. Noah said it no matter who was around.

We got off the ferry and were officially in *Ireland*. If my parents found out, they were going to freak and probably ground me until I was thirty. "We'll definitely be home in time, right?"

He nodded, not meeting my eye. The closer we got to Ireland, the more distant he'd become. He usually held my hand, but he'd dropped that an hour into the ferry ride.

"You okay?" I asked.

"Let's get a taxi," he said, taking my hand and ignoring my question.

Frowning, I followed. Something wasn't right. He was never off with me, and I was worried he was having second thoughts about me meeting his aunt. Maybe it was a too big a step for him and he hadn't realized until now?

"Noah, have you changed your mind? If you're not sure about this, we can do it another time. I don't mind."

Shaking his head, he opened the back door of a black taxi. "Get in, babe."

I did as he said and he climbed in beside me. I looked at the driver and froze. Shaun. What was his dad doing here? Noah hadn't told me he was coming too, and why wouldn't he have taken the same ferry? Were we being busted? My heart sank. If Shaun told my parents, I would be in so much trouble.

"What's going on?" I asked, gulping and looking between the two men. They watched each other through the mirror. He wasn't here to bust us?

Noah took a deep breath, clenched his fists, and looked out of the window as Shaun locked the doors and sped off. I gripped the seat in front of me as Shaun's erratic driving had me falling to the side. He leveled off and started to drive properly. My heart was rattling in my chest. *This isn't right.*

"Noah!" I said. "Look at me! What's going on?"

He refused to face me, but I could make out him squeezing his eyes closed as he leaned against the window. I started to feel sick. Noah had never made me feel anything but safe and loved before, but right now, it was like I was sitting next to a different person—one who scared me.

"Shaun, what's going on?"

"We are taking you home, sweetheart."

Beside me, Noah's body tensed.

"Home? What do you mean 'home'?" We weren't getting back on the ferry. "Shaun, what do you mean?"

"Eternal Light, Scarlett. We are taking you home."

My eyes widened. *What?* "I don't…"

Suddenly everything slotted into place and my world spun off its axis. *They are part of it.* Whimpering, I pressed my fist to my mouth as bile shot up my throat. No, no, no. He *lied*. All that time, Noah had been lying to me.

I couldn't believe he was taking me back to them. After everything my parents said, after everything he *knew* about them, he was taking me to them. They were part of that cult and had come to England to get me.

"Noah," I whispered, tears rolling down my face. "How could you?"

His jaw tightened. "Hurry up, Dad."

"I can't speed, Son, you know that."

"Shaun, please," I said, poking my head between the seats, desperate to get him to listen to me. "They're going to kill me. You know they are. Just let me go and I promise I won't tell anyone. Please, I just want to go home. You don't have to do this."

"Sit tight, Scarlett. It won't be long until we are back."

I shook my head, hair flying around my face, sticking to my tears. Neither of them cared that I was going to die for no reason. Falling back in the seat, I looked at Noah. Had everything he said been a lie? He told me he loved me, but he couldn't.

"Why did you pretend to love me?" I asked, sobbing. It hurt so, so bad. He might as well have been stomping my heart into the ground. "You didn't have to take it that far. Did you want to hurt me before they murdered me?"

He stared out of his window, clenching his fist against his forehead.

"Noah!" I snapped. "You at least owe me an explanation. You didn't have to take it that far! Why? Answer me, damn it!"

"Settle down, Scarlett," Shaun said. "Noah had his instructions."

"Instructions!"

"Shut up!" Noah shouted. "Both of you. Please, just stop talking." He rubbed his forehead roughly.

"Did you ever live on that island?"

He shook his head.

"Always in Ireland?" He didn't have the Irish accent.

"Since I was seven."

Wow. He made up a whole life. *Just like my parents.* Was there anyone in my life who didn't lie?

"Was any of it real?"

He turned back away, and I wasn't sure if that was a yes or no. As much as it broke me, I wanted to believe no; it was easier than thinking he loved me but was doing this anyway.

"You're going to be fine, Scarlett. Your parents will explain better than we can, so just sit quietly until we get there," he said.

"But I'm not going to be fine. You know I'm not. My *parents* told you what those people are going to do." He blinked a few times, looking down at his feet. The blood drained from my face. He knew before that. "No," I whispered, and his eyes closed again.

Noah knew they were going to kill me all along and he still brought me here. I pulled my legs up, curling into a ball and cried. My heart was splitting, pieces breaking off. Everything he'd said, we'd done, we had, was set on fire and burned to ashes. None of it was real.

He'd played me, and I'd fallen for it.

I held myself tighter, holding my body together. How could he? Did he even care about me at all, or was it all one big, fat lie to get me to his cult?

"Scarlett," he whispered. "I'm sorry."

Sorry would never be good enough. I would never forgive him for what he'd done. He always seemed so mature and levelheaded. How was Noah in a cult?

"Don't talk to me ever again," I said, sobbing around each word. I was done. No matter if he felt guilt or not, we were done. Sighing, he looked away and I cowered back inside myself, burying my head between my knees and wrapping my arms as tightly as they'd go around my legs.

I didn't know what I was going to do or how I was going to get home. How stupid was I to go off somewhere without my parents knowing, even if it was with someone I trusted? I was so upset with them for lying to me that I'd compromised my own safety.

All I wanted was to be home. I wanted to forget Noah ever existed. It was too good to be true. I should've known I wasn't going to be lucky enough to find *the one* in school and be childhood sweethearts. Noah's betrayal was already killing me.

I had no one to blame but myself.

24

NOAH

Dad pulled up to the commune and Scarlett froze. For thirty minutes, she'd said nothing to either of us and stared out of the window in a daze. I was worried that she was in shock—of course she was in shock. Before she turned into stone, she'd cried non-stop from the second she found out. Every sob was like a deep cut to my skin. I felt her pain like we were one person.

I wanted to ask if she was okay, but I knew I was the last person in the world she wanted to talk to. Her eyes that were usually so full of light and happiness were cold and empty. She hadn't looked at me much, but when she had, it was with hate and contempt. That wasn't the girl I knew and loved. But it was nothing I didn't deserve.

"Here we are," Dad said. "Are you ready to be reunited with your parents, Scarlett?"

She glared at him. Her skin was pale, but around her eyes was red and blotchy. She looked like she was going to be sick. I wanted to take her and run again.

"Scarlett," I said softly, "it's going to be all right."

"How?" she spat, finally looking at me. I was momentarily stunned by how much darker her eyes looked. It was like a punch to the gut. She may well be the Light, but it'd definitely gone from her eyes.

I felt as sick as she looked.

People started to gather and walk toward the car, led by Donald and Fiona. They all looked so excited; our savior was here. Only I wasn't sure she was—not for Eternal Light anyway, but perhaps she was mine.

Scarlett saw everyone walking, and her eyes widened in alarm. "Please take me back. Please. I swear I won't say anything, just take me back to town, and I'll find my own way home. Shaun, please."

"Shh, it's all right now. You are home," Dad said.

She shook her head, eyes filling with more tears that took my breath away. I wasn't at all ready for how I felt seeing her upset.

Turning to me, she whispered, "Noah, *please*."

I'd never felt so low in all my life. Even after everything I'd done, she still turned to me. I knew it was only out of desperation, but she still relied on me.

"I promise you, it'll be fine," I said. I didn't know how yet, but there had to be a way. She didn't believe my words. I wasn't sure if I believed them either.

"Don't do this. You told me you love me, and I *loved* you. Please don't let them hurt me."

That was out of my control entirely. I didn't get to make decisions for the community. We did that as a whole and there was no way I'd be able to convince them to postpone. They'd wanted this for years. It would be like asking a child to wait a week after Christmas to open his presents.

Her door was opened by Donald, and she shouted *no* and leaped into the middle of the backseat, wedging me against my door.

"Scarlett, it's okay," Donald said, staring at her in amazement. No one could quite believe she was finally with us again.

"Hey," I said. "I'm going to get out my side, and I want you to follow me. It's going to be all right, just come with me."

She laughed without humor. "Why would I trust you ever again? Get away from me. All of you freaks, just leave me alone!"

"Scarlett." Donald's tone was sterner. "You have nothing to fear. We are not going to hurt you. Please do as Noah asked or take my hand."

She pressed back against my side, and I opened the door, grabbing her hand and taking her with me. Malcolm and Drew grabbed her, so she wouldn't get the chance to run. We were out in the middle of nowhere, and she didn't even know which way was north; there was no way running would do her any good.

"Get off," she yelled, thrashing in their grip. "Noah! Get them off. Let me go. Get off! Get off!"

I couldn't stand there and watch her like that. I took off, going back to my house, leaving her to be carried into Donald and Fiona's kicking and screaming. I hated myself and had never felt lower.

Flopping down on my bed, I growled into the pillow, pulling my hair. Everything felt hopeless now. What was I going to do when Scarlett wasn't walking around on this planet anymore? Her happiness was my happiness.

It took me ten minutes to compose myself. I knew I didn't have long. I was supposed to be over the moon about her being back. When I stepped outside the house having changed, I was greeted like a king. Friends came up and hugged me. My community thanked me and told me how incredible I was for pulling it off and getting her home.

I had a hero's welcome but I didn't feel like a hero.

I felt like the devil.

Scarlett had struggled in Donald and Fiona's grip, but they'd managed to get her in their house. I knew they took her inside straightaway to prevent her running and so that they could explain. They'd want to do that alone, but I didn't like being separated. As much as she hated me right now, I was one of the only people she knew here.

"Noah, well done. Didn't I tell you you're the best man for the job?" Zeke said, slapping me on the shoulder. Zeke was a year older than me and it had either been me or him going to England to get Scarlett. I was closest to Scarlett's age though, and Zeke did look older than he was. I had a better chance at blending in with fifteen- and sixteen-year-olds.

Smiling, I nodded and replied, "You did. At least she's here now." I half wished it had been him that did it, so I wouldn't have to carry around as much guilt as I was. She deserved better than how I'd treated her.

"I know you were nervous, but I never had any doubt. This is it, Noah. This is what we have been waiting for."

He was absolutely correct; this was everything we'd worked for, everything we believed. But it didn't feel right anymore.

"I know. Hard to believe it's finally happening after years and years of planning."

I remembered it all. The planning and discussions. When was the best time to get her? Some thought right away, but Donald and Fiona wanted her to understand what was going on. But we couldn't leave it another four years for the next cycle to be complete. It was easier to get her away from her parents, but if we'd have waited until she was twenty, she could've had a boyfriend.

Logically, I knew I wasn't her boyfriend anymore; she hadn't said anything but I knew the second she found out she'd ended our relationship, but I still felt like it. The whole thing was only supposed to be for show, but I couldn't fool myself. It was much, much more than that.

Ironic how she started out being the only one really into us as a couple and now that was me.

"You all right?" he asked. "You don't look very pleased."

I wasn't rejoicing like they were, that's what he was questioning. I couldn't let anyone know I was having doubts. Well, I could—everyone would be there for me and help me through it, but I didn't feel like Eternal Light lessons right now.

"Yes, I'm fine. Sorry, it's just been a very long day. I've missed home, and honestly, lying to so many people, even strangers, didn't feel great."

He winced. "Sorry. I should have thought. It couldn't have been easy being away and everything else you had to do. You weren't lying for selfish reasons though, Noah. You were doing good."

"I was. It feels good to have her here, be home, and not have to lie anymore." So why was I still lying?

"Do you want to grab a drink? My dad made another batch of pear cider yesterday and it's his best yet."

No, I wanted to go and check on Scarlett, but I knew I couldn't do that yet. I smiled, making it as genuine as I could. "You have no idea how good that sounds. The mass-produced stuff is nothing like Kian's."

"I'll bet."

Kian and his wife, Marley, were over on their porch, handing out the cider. Zeke strolled up and grabbed two that his mum handed him.

"We're so proud of you, Noah," Marley said. Her sentiments were echoed again by everyone who was around us.

"Thank you," I replied, taking a sip. "Do you know when my mum and Finn will arrive?"

"We spoke to them about half an hour ago and their ferry had just arrived. They're going a different route though, to make it look like they're headed for Shannon airport."

My dad was doing that as well. After dropping us off, he was going to head to Cork airport in the hope that the car would be spotted on a security camera and lead police to think we'd left Ireland.

We weren't stupid. Once Jonathan and Marissa discovered Scarlett wasn't at Imogen's, they would call the police. Eventually the police would find out where we'd taken her. I had no doubt that they'd call the police, despite what it would do to them. They loved Scarlett and put her life before theirs. They were nothing like Eternal Light.

An hour later, Fiona came out of her house looking as calm and composed as ever. Scarlett's clear distress hadn't bothered her at all. For me, it felt like taking a knife.

I held my hand up, leaped to my feet, and jogged over to her.

"How is she?" I asked.

"She is doing well, Noah."

"Can I see her?"

I hoped she didn't pick up on how desperate I was. Scarlett had every right to hate me, and when we met again, I knew it wouldn't go how I wanted it to, but I had to see her.

"I don't think that is a good idea," Donald said, shutting his front door behind him. My parents had stopped beside me too. Why did I get the feeling that I was being kept away from her?

"Why not?"

"Noah," Dad said, "I know you've formed a friendship with her, but it's unlikely that she will want to see you until Donald and Fiona have had a chance to explain and educate her."

Well, how long would that take? Once the rituals started, she had just seven days. Would I get the chance to talk to her at all before she was gone? The thought filled me with dread. I hated that I might not get to hear her voice again.

"I understand that she's angry with me, but she really doesn't know anyone here. She knows me and surely we don't want her to feel alone?"

"Absolutely," Donald said, smiling. "We all want exactly that, Noah, but she's not even been here three hours yet. It is too soon. Give us today to talk to her, and tomorrow we will bring her out in the community before the rituals start. All right?"

I didn't like it. Donald's words used to be gospel. I believed everything he said, but now he didn't satisfy the questions I had. And there were a lot of questions.

"All right, I respect that. I just want this to be as easy on her as possible. She's a good person."

Fiona touched my arm. "We understand how you feel and know your intentions are good. You will get to see her and spend time together before the ceremony. We promise."

Now I was confused. In my community, you never made a promise you couldn't keep. Never. Even though I was questioning Eternal Light, I knew that Fiona would not break that promise. Were they telling the truth when they said no for now?

25

SCARLETT

I sat motionless on the sofa, same thing I'd been doing for what could've been minutes or days. But it'd only been two and a half hours. I still couldn't believe it'd all happened. Noah was someone I trusted. I'd never thought he would betray me. I'd never thought he'd be involved in a damn cult. He hurt me more than my parents.

His lie wasn't to protect me; it was to hurt me. *Kill* me.

Fiona had left me with Donald and he looked clueless as to what to do with me. They tried talking, but I didn't want to talk. They didn't listen when I shouted, screamed, and pleaded with them to let me go, so why should I do anything for them? All they kept saying was "let us explain" and "if you'll allow us, we can show you the truth." I didn't want to hear it.

The sun was starting to disappear, and I felt my heart go with it. My parents thought I was staying at Imogen's and Imogen would cover for me. Donald and Fiona had taken my phone, which I was positive Noah would use to text Mum, telling her I was at Im's.

I was *so* stupid.

Fiona came back after about half an hour and knelt in front of me. "How are you doing, Scarlett?"

What a stupid question.

"Awful," I replied. "What are you going to do to me?" I wanted to hear her say the words. What part of killing your own child made sense to her?

"We are not here to hurt you. This is where you belong. We have brought you home. We are going to protect you, and you are going to save us."

But it wasn't real. Their idea of how I would save them was all in their mind. I rubbed my hands over my face and shook my head. "That's not what will happen. How can you not see that?"

"Scarlett, you have only heard the version Jonathan and Marissa have told you. They took you and poisoned your mind. I ask that you open it and allow us to show you the truth."

"I have questions," I said.

"You may ask us anything," Donald said.

I didn't want to talk about the sacrifice right now. That could absolutely wait for a time when I wasn't wound so tight, wasn't so angry, scared, and heartbroken. I wanted them to acknowledge it, but I sure as hell wasn't ready for it.

"Who is Evelyn?"

"They told you about her?"

"No." *They tried to pass her off as a doll and then told me she was Jere's friend.* "I remember her name and face."

Fiona straightened her legs, stretched, and sat beside me. "Scarlett, Evelyn is your sister."

The air in the room thinned. "I have a sister?"

Donald leaned forward. "You do."

"Just one?"

"Yes. Just you and Evelyn. You used to call her Evie."

Evie. *Evie.* I still couldn't remember her.

"Once the ceremony is over and the sacrifice has been made, you will be reunited with her," Donald added.

Two things took my breath away; how casually and callously he spoke of killing me, and the fact that my sister was dead.

"When did she…?"

"Not long after you were taken," Fiona replied. "But please do not be sad. She is not lost forever."

Their youngest child died, and they were talking about her like she was a bloody shoe.

They didn't seem that cut up over her death, and I wasn't sure if that was because they believed they would see her again or because they didn't believe she was the one that could save them. Either way, I knew they were selfish and didn't deserve to have children.

Noah had led me to think Evelyn was someone close to me. I didn't understand how he could lie so well for so long, drip-feeding me information in the sneakiest ways. He was so convincing. I had believed he loved me. That hurt the most.

"They did tell me one thing," I said.

"Oh?" Fiona said.

"That you're all brainwashed lunatics who are going to murder me in cold blood which will end up with your sorry arses in prison. My parents will look, which means the police will look. Do you really think you're going to get away with it?"

I had no idea what'd come over me. I hated confrontation, but here I was, completely out of character, telling things exactly how they were. As scared as I was, I also felt liberated. The Scarlett before the betrayal let so many things go.

I wasn't weak. I could be strong. I wasn't going to take anything lightly anymore, and I was going to fight. One way or another, I was going to make sure they didn't take my life. My teeth clenched together, and a burning fire inside me roared to life, willing me on.

Fiona shook her head lightly. Even when challenged, she was calm and smiling. Evil cow. "We are not the brainwashed ones, Scarlett. We want love, peace, and happiness. We do not live in a place where war, discrimination, and hate occur. We live with nature; we do not rip it down. We do not eat once-living creatures."

"Right, you only murder your offspring."

"You will see. I promise you that."

"I already see everything for what it is. Do you honestly think I believe life outside here is perfect? Grow up. I've watched the news. I know what evil shit is out there and I don't think it's right, but I will *never* believe taking someone's life is okay. No matter what you *think* is going to happen after. You're monsters dressing up belief as something else to justify what you *want* to do."

"If you would rather not eat with the community tonight, Scarlett, you may eat in your room. Perhaps you may benefit from an early night," Donald said, totally changing the subject.

"I think I'd rather skip dinner and just sleep."

Fiona tilted her head as she looked at Donald. Getting his permission? Was he the one who led her to believe killing her child was a fabulous idea? I didn't understand what made them think I was anything other than just a girl. Who decided I was the one to save them all? *Him.* My guess was him.

Donald dipped his chin. "As you wish. Fiona, would you like to show our daughter to her room?"

"Of course," Fiona said, rising to her feet. She stared down at me, her dark-blue eyes that matched mine glowing with happiness. I looked a lot like her, but my hair was a light ash-brown like Donald's. Seeing them made me realize how much I didn't look like my parents or brother. It was another hard kick to the stomach.

The thought of my family waiting for me to come home was like having a knife rip through my heart. How would they react when they found out? I regretted ever being moody and angry with them. They had saved me from this. I had never had so much love, respect, and admiration for them as I did right then.

I followed Fiona through the short corridor to the room at the end. Everywhere was clad in a light wood, giving it a cabin feel. I didn't want to think it was pretty but it was. She opened the door and there was my room—cream-painted wooden walls, a slightly darker painted built-in wardrobe with matching bed and bedside tables.

In the corner of the room was a mint-green fabric chair and small bookcase. It looked like there was a lot of Eternal Light literature on there and I was undecided if I wanted to read it.

Knowledge was power after all, and if I stood a chance of stopping the sacrifice or getting away, I needed to know them. On the wall above the bed was a photo of what looked like all of them. It was relatively recent; Noah didn't look much younger than he did now. I *hated* that he was in this room, even in photo form.

"There are clothes in the wardrobe. If you would like something to eat or drink, please come and let me know. Donald and I will be in the living room tonight."

I stared back at this older version of me and felt nothing. "I won't want anything." Besides them taking that picture down, which I didn't think they would. It looked like an everyone-has-one kind of thing.

"Very well," she said, closing the door behind her.

As soon as I heard her footsteps getting farther away I tried the window, shoving the glass to see if it would budge. It didn't, of course. Dropping my hands, I leaned my forehead against the glass and tried to hold it together. I was close to crying. I hurt physically and emotionally. I missed my family and, damn it, I missed Noah. My heart ached for the person I thought he was, the one I loved and thought I had a future with.

Breathing deeply through my nose, I tried to compose myself to think of a plan. I refused to believe there wasn't a way. Appeal to the mother in Fiona—if she even had anything maternal inside her. Run for it and hope I found someone to help? Try to find a phone or computer to contact my parents and the police

Knowledge is power.

That was it. I was going to learn about them, be one of them until I found a way out. They hadn't told me when the first ceremony was going to start, but there would be seven days of rituals. I could do this. It was live or die, and I wasn't dying without one hell of a fight.

I grabbed the first hand-bound book off the shelf and flicked it open. With a deep breath, I started to read, mumbling words aloud. "Nature regenerates, should live in harmony with what naturally grows on the earth, eat well, blah blah blah." I rolled my eyes until I came to a part about the Light. Me.

It was hard reading. "The Light will be born in human form. It will provide a link between this life and eternity." Closing the book, I closed my eyes. It spoke of me like I wasn't real. But I had to do this. I opened it back up and continued. *Seven rituals must take place before the sacrificing of the Light.*

Nope. Slamming it shut, I shoved it back on the bookshelf. I wasn't ready to know it. Jumping on the bed, I buried myself under the layers of blankets and closed my eyes, thinking of anything else other than what Noah had done and where I was.

26
SCARLETT

I woke up to the two crazy people—who were my *parents*—watching over me. They looked perfectly normal, well dressed, and friendly. It was only when they opened their mouths that you realized how batshit they were.

"Good morning, Scarlett," Donald said. "Did you sleep well?"

"You kidnapped me yesterday. Didn't sleep too well, no."

"You are our daughter. We are not the ones who took you from where you belong. But that doesn't matter now because you are home," Fiona said.

"I'm not your daughter. You don't *murder* your daughter."

She shook her head. "No, Scarlett, you don't understand." *Damn right I don't.* "You are the Light. You are going to lead us to a higher plane, a better existence. It is not death; it is eternal life in a much better place than this."

"But I'll be dead."

Donald covered Fiona's hand with his giant one. "Perhaps we should show our daughter around and explain properly."

I didn't want to go anywhere with them, but I did want to look around and try to find a way to escape. I also wanted to scream and shout at Noah. His betrayal stung deep. I felt sick whenever I thought about what he'd done. Not only had he brought me here to be killed, but he'd also made me love him first. He was evil.

"That is a good idea, love," Fiona said to Donald, returning his sickening smile. "We'll give you ten minutes to get dressed, Scarlett."

I watched them stand in sync and leave my prison cell of a room. They were my parents. They made me and they wanted to kill me. The door closed and was locked. My room was nice, I'd give them that much. They gave me nice things to…what? Soften the blow for when they stuck a knife through my heart?

Ignoring the hysteria building, I got out of bed and opened the wardrobe. Everything in there was pretty. Lots of long dresses. I dressed in a floor-length white-and-yellow sundress and brushed my hair. It felt pointless, but I had to keep it together.

If I had a chance at escaping, I had to get out of this room as much as possible. Maybe I could pretend that I'd converted to whatever crap it was they believed. If they trusted me, I could get out. I'd glanced through the *She Is the Light* book last night but on page one, where it basically referred to me as a door that needed opening—not a person—I threw it back on the bookshelf.

Taking a deep breath, I slipped on a pair of sandals, knocked on the door, and waited. The lock clicked and then my *mother* was standing before me. I couldn't just go from telling them all to get lost to being a converted Eternal Light member because they'd know it was fake, so I scowled.

"You look beautiful, Scarlett."

"Where're you taking me?" I asked coldly.

"We will meet your father outside and show you around."

"Will Noah be there?"

She looked at me out of the corner of her eye. "He is around, yes."

I wanted to refuse to go. He was the last person on the planet I wanted to see.

"Well, he can go to hell."

Wisely, she said nothing and just pursed her lips. In her eyes, he was a damn hero. To me he was the enemy. He was the worst one, pretending to love me.

Arsehole.

I followed her out of the cute, log-cabin style house and stood on the deck. All the other houses were the same, and I had a feeling they'd built them all themselves. A large meadow to the left of the settlement stretched on as far as the eye could see and to the right was thick forest. I had no idea where I was or where the nearest town was.

A sense of hopelessness knocked the air from my lungs and I fought to stay positive. It wasn't over yet. I had to focus on that. I wasn't doomed yet.

Gulping, I took another step, following Fiona. *I can do this.* The forest was probably my best bet. If I ran across the meadow, they would see me straightaway. But I wasn't sure when I'd be left alone long enough to make my escape. And I had no idea how big the forest was.

I was getting ahead of myself. First I had to work out how I would escape and then I could worry about where I would escape to. *For now, just fall in line.*

"How many people live here?" I asked emotionlessly. I wanted to sound bored for a while longer. I had to remain angry for another day or so before slowly starting to fit in. There was a danger that they'd see through it, but my options were limited to two: fight or die.

"Thirty-nine," she replied.

That was what I was dying for—thirty-nine people who could supposedly live for eternity in some magical world Donald and Fiona cooked up. Still, people had been killed for less.

"Wow, that's a lot of people you've brainwashed. Nice one."

She stopped and turned to me. I worried that I'd overstepped. If she thought I believed they'd been completely brainwashed, then she wouldn't trust me when I started to listen. Had I gone too far?

"It is not brainwashing, Scarlett. From the age of four you have had your mind trapped within society's walls. Free it now. Let me help you, and you *will* see the truth. You are the Light."

I wanted to laugh in her face. I was human. *Who does she think she is?* I wondered if she'd always been like that—crazy—or if someone made her believe the things she lived by. Eternal Light was older than me. They were going to kill me when I was four and you didn't just decide to do that five minutes after creating a cult or religion—or whatever they wanted to call it.

Half of me wanted to appeal to her as her biological daughter. I thought it was just ingrained in you when you gave birth: protect child at all cost. That was how it was supposed to be. Parents were meant to die for their children, not be the ones hurting them.

"We'll see," I replied, walking down the stairs.

Three people stood on high alert, spinning to face me, thinking I was going to run, ready to pounce. They didn't give me much credit if they thought I would run in broad daylight with everyone around.

Fiona held her hand up and they immediately relaxed. "Do not be alarmed. I am just showing Scarlett around."

One of them, a plump lady wearing a long skirt and apron, nodded. She looked maternal. Surely she wouldn't stand by as someone drove a knife into me...or however they were going to do it?

"Welcome, Scarlett. I am Judith," the plump lady said. "This is my husband, Bill, and son, Terry. Oh, it is lovely to see you again. It has been so long, sweetheart."

She knew me before, when I was just a little child. My heart sank with the realization that she wouldn't help; if she had been willing to stand back and let a four-year-old be killed, then she wouldn't help me at sixteen.

I gritted my teeth and stared. *What's wrong with you?*

"Ah, there are my two girls," Donald said, coming out of one of the houses.

"And there you are," Fiona replied. "Are you joining us on the tour?"

"I wish I could, but I have business to attend to. Will you be all right on your own?"

Fiona nodded. "Of course."

What did he think I was going to do? Could I even do anything?

Could I hurt her to get away? I'd never even squished a spider, even though I was scared of them. What a stupid, irrational fear. I was scared of a small bug with eight legs when there were people like this in the world.

"Mother-daughter bonding time, huh?" I muttered dryly. "Perhaps after the tour we could drown a litter of bunnies. Or do you only do that to your child?" I was now definitely going too far, but I couldn't hold back when my stomach tied in knots and I wanted to scream.

Everyone fell silent. Fiona and Donald watched me cautiously. "I can explain everything, Scarlett, but please keep an open mind," Fiona said. Hilarious that she would tell me—repeatedly—to keep an open mind when hers was so closed.

"It's all right," Donald said to Judith and her family, who just stood there openmouthed. "Her mind has been closed off. We have discussed that. This is not a surprise, and we are here to help and not to judge, remember?"

Judith's husband nodded. "Right, of course. Despite what you may have heard, Scarlett, we are not bad people. You will see that soon."

I smiled sarcastically and turned to Fiona. "Can we go now?" Standing around listening to that garbage spout out of their mouths was just making me feel ill. I wouldn't see the "light" or anything else, so talking about it was pointless.

Fiona took me past the ten wooden houses and past a field before the meadow that was home to different kinds of crops. No wonder Noah only ate "real" and organic food; it was all he'd ever had.

No, don't think of him.

Ridiculously, I still loved who I thought he was, and every time I thought about what he'd done, it sent sharp, stabbing pains through my heart. He could've just befriended me; he didn't have to make me fall for him first.

In the distance, I saw Bethan and Finn picking what looked like potatoes. I didn't know where Shaun or Noah were and I didn't care.

Ahead of us was a larger wooden building and beside that a small lake that looked out of place for the location. "What's that?" I asked, lifting my chin to the place in front of us.

"That is our community hall, where we meet most nights, where we will celebrate being reunited with you."

"Will you kill me in there too?"

I wanted to say it as plainly and bluntly as I could in the hope that it would register something in her. She was killing her child. She *had* to understand that.

"I will show you where the rituals will take place and explain everything fully, so you won't still believe we are taking your life."

"You do know how death works, right? And how many rituals?" I swallowed glass. What were they going to do to me?

"There are seven in total," she said as we reached the heavy, wooden double doors. "Please, come inside." I weighed my options and took a look over my shoulder. There were too many people about for me to run. One against thirty-nine was not good odds. I couldn't be reckless.

With trembling hands, I stepped inside. Chairs were stacked along one side, but the room was relatively bare; a few tables were dotted around holding large jugs of fresh wildflowers. Paintings of nature—the meadow, flowers, trees, water—hung on the walls, and glass lanterns hung from the vaulted ceiling.

Everything they'd done was beautifully simple. They were just insane.

"So you come in here to do what?"

"This is where we hold meetings and celebrations if the weather isn't nice. This is where we give thanks for you on your birthday, my beautiful daughter. Our savior."

"Savior? Who's threatening you? As long as you're not off sacrificing people, no one's gonna care that you're here."

"If they hadn't taken you, I would've raised you and you wouldn't be so disrespectful."

"If they hadn't taken me, I'd be dead."

"You would be at peace, waiting for us to join you. We have the chance to live another life. This is not the only one we can have, Scarlett."

She believed that totally. She stared straight into my eyes and said it with so much conviction.

"How can you be so sure?" I whispered, purposefully widening my eyes.

The corner of her mouth twitched. She thought that was the first crack: that my mind was beginning to *open*. Good.

"Faith, my darling. I would not risk my daughter for something I was not completely sure of."

There it was. My *appeal to the mother in her* plan vanished with her words. Not that I had had much hope for it.

I stood in their pretty barn and knew that my only option was running.

"But what if you're wrong?"

I felt the tingle of tears and blinked rapidly. She wasn't going to see me cry. I wouldn't crumble in front of them.

"I am not. That I can promise you. Now, let me show you the outdoor communal eating area before dinner is served."

"Will you tell me more about the rituals?"

"Of course. I can tell you some," she replied, smiling. *Some.*

I couldn't work her out. One minute she was cautious of me, suspicious even, and the next, she was grinning like I'd just converted to her church of crazy.

"So?" I pressed, not totally sure if I even wanted to know.

"Most involve us calling upon nature, chanting, if you will. The first one is a cleansing and the call will be for nature to accept you and accept us. Ritual two," she started, closing the doors behind us, "links us to you. We have to become one entity to follow you into eternity."

I gritted my teeth. "And how long will I be in eternity alone until you all follow? You killing yourselves after or waiting out your cozy, little lives here until you die old, fat, and happy?"

"It is not what you think, Scarlett. You will be happy. You will be at peace."

"So you are living out your lives here. Lovely. And I was perfectly peaceful back home."

"You will understand if you allow yourself to open your mind to us."

"Perhaps you'll understand if you open your mind to what's really going on," I said. "What're the other rituals?"

"They are much alike. There is a binding that will then bind us as a whole."

"I thought I'd already be linked to you all with that first one?"

"That is slightly different. We need a piece of you, so we are physically linked, each one of us to you, and then we need to be spiritually bound as a community."

That made absolutely no sense. But then, what did here?

"Right. Lots of chanting, cleansing, and binding."

She smiled and it looked a lot like mine. She may have looked like my mum, but she certainly wasn't. "Ritual one that will take place tomorrow will be in the lake. But don't worry. The water is clean."

She was murdering me in seven days' time but thought I'd worry about a little dirty water.

I was speechless for a second before replying, "Great."

"You will be dressed in a white gown and stand in the middle of the lake. It is not too deep, perhaps waist height on you. Donald and I will bless you, and then we will leave. For ten minutes, we will stand near the lake and say a few words."

"Where will I be?"

"In the water still. To be cleansed you need to be alone. We don't want to contaminate the blessed area by staying. You are the key to everything, Scarlett. We don't want to get in the way of your light."

Then let me go.

"What time are you doing this cleansing?"

"Tomorrow at noon. The water should have warmed up a little."

I found myself almost thanking her, but fortunately I caught myself. I had *nothing* to thank her for. I turned away, unable to look at her anymore.

27

SCARLETT

The more I knew about them, the more terrified I became. There wasn't going to be any getting through to them. They genuinely believed all the crap about my "crossing over" and "opening the door" for all of our eternal life. In-freaking-sane.

Today marked day one of the ritual and my second full day at the commune. It was too soon for me to jump in the water and cry with happiness because I was the Light, but I also didn't want to put up too much fight.

I was told to wear one of my white gowns; they hung to the left of the wardrobe. Not giving a crap what I wore, I ripped the first white one off the hanger and threw it on. Tonight was the first "ritual." We were going to be "joined" or some crap like that. We weren't going to be joined; I was just going to be terrified while they did whatever they felt they had to. Then I'd die.

"Are you ready?" Bethan asked.

The last time I spoke to her, she had been offering me cake in her kitchen. I straightened my back and stared at the traitorous bitch. How could she have had me over at her house so many times knowing what was going to happen?

"Yes," I replied sharply.

"Don't look afraid, Scarlett. This is just the beginning."

Yeah, that was what I was afraid of.

"Can't wait," I said sarcastically.

Smiling, she reached up and placed a headband made from daisies on my head. I almost asked the significance of it but then I realized I didn't care.

Fiona and Donald walked me out of their house and toward the lake. The rest of them followed. I didn't falter one step as we walked past the houses and stopped in front of the water.

"The Light has returned," Donald said. "She and she alone will lead us into eternal peace and harmony. We will become at one with nature. We accept the Light as our salvation. Cleanse her and let her lead."

Fiona took my arm and walked me into the water. My bare toes slipped beneath the cool surface and I wanted to bolt. Donald's words were insane. This was all insane. Fiona took another step forward and extended her arm, making me go it alone the rest of the way.

Looking back over my shoulder and purposefully avoiding Noah's eyes, I took a step closer to the center. The water stung for a second before I became accustomed to the temperature. Fiona was right about one thing; it wasn't too cold.

I shook with fear as I reached the middle, flattening the dress to my side so it didn't puff up and float to the surface. Turning around, I saw them all standing much farther back, watching me. They were in a single row, and although I couldn't hear them, I knew they were speaking. Their mouths moved in perfect synchrony.

Leaves rustled in the light wind, making it even harder to hear. I managed to lip read the Light a few times. The dress, now plastered to my legs, felt like it weighed a ton. I might as well be wearing an anchor.

I could run now. They were far enough away that I could get a head start, but it would probably just be a few seconds. And I had no idea where I would go.

Gulping, I closed my eyes, as I couldn't hold in the fear and uncertainty anymore. I cried in the middle of the lake while thirty-nine people watched.

I hoped ritual day two was going to be better. Yesterday had been horrendous. Ten minutes after I was sent into the water I was taken out, carried back to Fiona and Donald's, and put in a bath. I tried to be strong but I was exhausted in every sense. I curled up in bed, refusing to talk to anyone or eat anything, and cried until I fell asleep.

That was the one weak moment I'd allowed myself, and I put it down to the shock of it all actually happening. From now on, I would hide my feelings. I would be strong. Whatever they had in store for over the next few days, I would be ready and I would deal with it.

All forty of us sat around the communal outdoor dining table eating dinner. I knew the second ritual was coming this evening, but I didn't know exactly when and that had me on edge. I didn't want to ask because then I'd be able to count down the minutes.

At the end of the table was Noah. I could feel his gaze burning a hole in the side of my head. Hell would freeze over before I acknowledged him.

I picked at, annoyingly, one of the most delicious homemade bread rolls I had ever eaten. We had vegetable soup, bread, and salad for dinner. I was starving, but I knew something was happening to me again soon, and that made my stomach churn too much to accept food. It looked like I was missing another dinner.

If I wasn't careful, I wouldn't have enough energy to bloody escape.

"Are we all ready?" Donald asked once Judith and her sister, Mary-Elizabeth, had cleared the table so fast I almost missed it.

Everyone stood and walked off without answering. Noah too. He was ready. I wasn't, but then I didn't get a choice.

Where were they going? I craned my neck to try and see, but they disappeared around the houses, lost to the night. My eyes darted toward the people that gave me life. What was going on?

"It is time," Fiona said after five minutes of nail-biting silence.

Like with the last ritual, they led me to what felt like my death already. I hated having no idea what they were going to do to me almost as much as I would have hated knowing what was coming. This time we went to their community hall. I bit my lip. It was eerily quiet tonight and the sky was a moody gray. I walked slower, placing my gladiator sandal–clad feet hard on the grass as if I could make them stick.

As we approached the barn, I started to feel cold and wanted to bolt in the opposite direction. Whatever was waiting for me in there I knew I didn't want it. Every step took every ounce of courage I had.

"Do not be afraid, Scarlett," Fiona said.

I wanted to ask her why I shouldn't be afraid. I pursed my lips and stared ahead at the closed double doors. It didn't really matter what was going on; they could have had me cuddle a puppy for an hour and I'd still be scared.

"Okay," Donald said, stopping and grabbing the handle. "I can't tell you how elated I am that we have been reunited, Scarlett." He already had.

He opened one of the doors, and I stopped breathing altogether. Everyone was in the hall, dressed only in white, standing in a circle. They'd done all that in five minutes?

Candles were alight everywhere. I closed my eyes as my mind forced a few missing puzzle pieces together. I remembered this before, a few times it'd happened.

My head throbbed. I saw a sea of white, smiles on everyone's face, and blood. Why blood? Shit, why blood? My mind felt like it was cracking, fizzing, bursting. It *hurt*.

"Are you okay?" Fiona asked.

There was no point in telling her that I was remembering before. She wouldn't care anyway. "Fine," I whispered, balling my hands into fists as the throbbing escalated so quickly I felt sharp pain behind my eyes.

"Good evening," Donald said. "I know how exciting tonight is, believe me, but Scarlett is still new to this again, so I ask that we try to keep things as calm as possible." He was met with a sea of nods. "Thank you. Scarlett, please step into the circle."

I looked down, and on the floor was a ring of wildflowers and sticks. "Are you bloody kidding?"

"Please step into the circle," he repeated, completely ignoring how rude I was.

As I stepped forward, I caught Noah's eye. No, I hadn't wanted to do that. He didn't deserve anything from me at all.

He watched me carefully, regret plastered across his face. Seeing him brought his betrayal back and it stung just as much as it had three days ago. I wanted to stop loving him. Turning away, I looked down at the floor. I couldn't do it. I couldn't be around him. He made me feel claustrophobic, like the walls were closing in, ceiling collapsing. I hated him.

"Does Noah have to be in here?" I asked, not bothering to lower my voice. I didn't check if he'd heard. I hoped he did, so he knew I hated him as much as I still loved him.

"He does, yes," Fiona replied. "Please don't be too hard on him. He was only doing what was right for Eternal Light. And for you."

I turned away from her too. There was no point in saying anything else. They were all too far into their stupid cult to understand what Noah had done was wrong and to see what they were doing was just plain crazy—not to mention illegal and something they'd be imprisoned for.

"If we are ready, we can begin," Donald said.

Everyone took one step forward. They were so obedient. He'd really done a good job in convincing them he was the leader and could take them—by sacrificing his firstborn child—into eternal life. And no one questioned that. No one.

Evelyn. My heart ached for a sister I didn't even know. I wondered if she cried when she saw what they'd done to me? Was she as scared as I felt? I wished my parents could have taken her too.

"The Light was given to us so that our souls may be reborn and we may be reunited upon our human death. Through her, we will live on. Through her, we will be with loved ones passed. We offer her. She is the one; she is the Light," Donald said. He spoke slowly, quietly, believing every word as much as the rest of them.

"She is the one; she is the Light," Fiona repeated and then so did the rest of them. Their voices, although low, carried through the room, making it deafening. Or it could just be deafening because they were basically chanting about murdering me.

I was so scared I wanted to run away and hide somewhere until my parents found me. That wasn't an option. I was all I had. *Stay calm.* If I could just switch off while they did the rituals, I would be able to hold everything together until I found a way out. I could do that.

Donald took a knife and my eyes widened. I turned cold and spun around to face the door. Behind me, now in front of me, were Shaun and Bill. They were obviously there to stop me running. They each grabbed an arm and kept me in place.

I shook my head. "No! What're you going to do? No, please don't." This wasn't supposed to happen, not yet. Ice traveled through my veins. I stepped forward as much I could, putting as much distance between me and Donald as I could. He had a bloody knife! "Don't. Please, please, don't."

"It is okay, Scarlett," Donald said.

"It's not," I wailed, thrashing in their arms, spilling tears all over the floor. My heart beat so fast I felt light-headed. "Please don't do this. Noah, help me! Please help me." This couldn't be happening. Did they lie about the other rituals? I started to hyperventilate, completely unable to get enough oxygen. This couldn't be happening.

I screamed, knees buckling as another memory smashed its way back into my mind. Burning hot fire. A throbbing in my arm. People yelling. Panic. I could taste the panic. I was crying, but it was different to now; it was a petrified *child's* cry. I was scared of my parents for the first time. Now I was scared of them again.

I came to again as a pain sliced through my arm. I screamed so loud it left a ringing in my ears. He'd cut my inner forearm. The gash was about four inches long and deep enough for blood to steadily pour out.

I watched, frozen, wide-eyed, and in horror as the man that half created me held a white goblet under my arm to catch the blood. I think I was in shock. Would I know if I was? I couldn't move. I was too stunned that he'd cut me, even though I knew what their end plan for me was. Before it was all talk, but now he'd physically hurt me and I knew there would be no convincing him to let me go. My breathing was far too fast, but my rapidly rising and falling chest was the only part of me capable of moving at all right now.

"Shh," Fiona said in a soothing voice while the rest of the cult chanted, but in whispers this time.

I did what she said but not through choice. I latched on to her calm aura and kept my eyes glued on hers. Surely she couldn't actually let her husband murder her daughter?

"I...I don't... Why?" I rambled, trying to make sense of something that was senseless.

"It is all right, Scarlett, but you need to calm down and breathe."

Breathe. I took breaths as evenly as I could while I was still crying and a little dazed. My entire body shook violently. They'd opened up the light scar that I was told I got from a bike riding accident when I was four. The scar wasn't from an accident.

Fiona hugged me awkwardly as Shaun kept hold of the arm that wasn't bleeding. But he didn't have to; I couldn't move anyway. I saw Noah over Fiona's shoulder, watching me with such pain and sadness in his eyes that it made me cry harder.

How could you?

Bethan brought forward a large, deep bowl made from bamboo. Donald poured my blood into it and I watched threads of blood sink into the water. My eyes flicked back to Noah. He was still watching me, still looked in pain.

"We will become one. We will share her light," Donald said, prompting the rest to switch their chant.

Noah's mouth moved in time with the words, but it didn't look like he was making a sound, but that could have just been wishful thinking.

Taking the bowl from Bethan, Fiona held it to her lips and

took a sip. I wanted to throw up and felt very close to losing what little I ate at dinner. They were all going to drink my blood. Noah. I looked to him, but this time he didn't meet my eye.

2 8

NOAH

I unlocked Scarlett's door, so grateful that I was allowed to see her again. I needed to see her, especially after today. Irrationally, I could still taste her blood on my tongue, long after I'd eaten and brushed my teeth.

Today would go down as the worst day of my life to date. When Donald cut her, I wanted to kill him. When she looked at me, tears streaming down her face, I wanted to kill myself. He'd hurt her and every instinct screamed at me to fight them all and take her away.

I had never felt emotion as strongly as I did then. Standing there and watching it was the hardest thing I had ever done. But the veil covering Eternal Light lifted as I sipped her blood. What we were doing was wrong. I loved her more than anything else in the world and I wouldn't stand by and let anyone hurt her.

I *had* to make it right. Today was also a turning point for me. I realized that without a shadow of a doubt, Scarlett came first. I was turning my back on Eternal Light, and as soon as I'd made that decision, everything became clear. All I saw after that was waves of long, ash hair and dark-blue eyes.

She was sitting on the bed, staring out the window and holding her bandaged arm. Her posture was tense and she was trying to ignore whoever came in. I had a plate of dinner for her. Fiona wasn't going to make her socialize after what'd happened, but she let me be the one to give it her. Maybe because I was a more consistent face? Who knows? I wasn't complaining.

"Scarlett," I whispered, closing the door behind me.

She stiffened and clenched her jaw.

"Please, I need to explain."

I took a step closer and she snapped out of it, pushing herself to her knees and holding her hand up, warning me not to come closer. "Don't," she hissed. "There's *nothing* you can say to make this okay. Just get the hell out, Noah. If that's even your name."

Ignoring her, I moved closer to the room. "That's my name. I didn't lie about that."

"Well, thanks so much for that tiny piece of honesty," she spat bitterly. "Now get out."

Rubbing a hand over my face, I blurted, "I love you."

"You can stop lying now."

"I didn't lie about that either."

"You murder everyone you *love*?"

"You have five days of ceremonies left."

"Yeah, believe me, I'm counting too."

Closing my eyes, I took a deep breath. Her icy reception was no shock, but it did hurt. "Look, there is nothing I can do until the morning of the sacrifice." I paused, expecting her to say something. "It's the only time you will be far enough away from everyone. You will be cleansed in the lake again, and you'll do it alone for thirty minutes."

Hope widened her eyes and she stepped off the bed. "They think I'm actually going to stay there? I knew I had to go in again, but for that long? They'll stay away for half an hour the day they try to kill me?"

"Yes. They will be there but back far enough that we'll have a good head start. No one is permitted to be within fifty feet of you." I winced as it all sounded so ridiculous now. "They don't want your cleansing to be...contaminated."

She raised her eyebrow.

"I know, Scarlett. I know...now." I put her plate down on the table. "That," I said, tipping my chin in the direction of her bandaged arm, "was an eye-opener for me. I felt sick seeing you hurt and all I wanted to do was leap in and stop it all from happening. I can't change what they just did to you and I will have to live with that for the rest of my life, but I can help you now. The final ceremony, I'll be on the other side of the lake, hiding. When I say, you run to me and we'll be gone."

Her eyebrow rose yet again. "How can I trust you?"

I was waiting for that. "I have made a *huge* mistake—many huge mistakes actually. But you have to understand, Scarlett, my whole life I have believed what I was told. It is all I've ever known. I never questioned it, just like you never questioned your parents until you started remembering."

Her eyes narrowed a fraction at the mention of her parents. "I need you to answer my questions *honestly*." I nodded. "How did you meet them?"

"Your parents?"

"No, Donald and Fiona."

"Right. Sorry. They arrived at our commune when I was a kid, had similar beliefs, but, like I said, theirs made more sense." Scarlett snorted, and I couldn't fault her for it, not now I saw everything so clearly. "And it wasn't long before they were running the place, maybe a week. They told us about the fire in the warehouse and how you were kidnapped."

"How did they find me?"

Gripping the post at the end of the bed, I looked down and replied, "Scarlett, you were never lost." I didn't look up to see her reaction; I felt it. "Every four years, once the cycle of elements have been complete, they get a chance to...you know. When you were eight, you were living in a flat and being homeschooled, we couldn't get near. Then you moved a couple of times and settled down."

"You all knew where I was the whole time?" she whispered.

"Yes. I'm sorry."

She took an uneven breath. "Why you?"

"I'm closest to your age. My family was to move to your town, and I was to enroll in high school. Then I had to get close to you, make you love me, and take you to Ireland."

"Well," she said, "you did that just fine."

"I wasn't supposed to fall in love with you. I tried so hard not to, but the more I did, the less I believed what I'd been taught my whole life. My dad always said that you know you are in love when someone comes along that makes you question everything. You did that, and at first I hated it."

She didn't react at all, just stared at me with empty eyes.

"Things used to be so clear and so easy. Eternal Light came first, like any other religion. Being on the outside made me realize that religion is flawed. People twist things to suit themselves and their needs. It makes normal people fight and kill and hate. It's supposed to be pure, but people make it the most tainted thing on the planet. I didn't see it until I saw the outside world…until I fell in love with you. Even if it was all true, I still wouldn't let them touch you again."

"Why?" she whispered, standing up.

I made the two steps to her, our chests almost touching. Reaching out, I tucked her hair behind her face. Just touching her again made everything fall into place. She where I was supposed to be. We were made for each other. I was born to love and protect her, and that was exactly what I was going to do. "Because your human life means more to me than my eternal one."

Gulping, she lowered her eyes and replied, "Don't, Noah."

"I am so sorry. I know I've let you down so badly, but I won't let them take your life. I *will* make it right, Scarlett. I promise. I understand that you can't forgive me. I don't deserve your forgiveness. Hell, I don't deserve anything from you. But *please* trust me one last time, just so I can get you out of here."

"Why can't you just call my parents or the police?"

"No phone," I said. "I ditched it, and we don't get reception out here anyway. If I leave and they put two and two together… Scarlett, this is *so* dangerous. I don't want to risk raising their suspicion. I'm terrified that they will take you and that will be it.

We get one chance and this is the only way I can think of that actually stands a shot at working."

"I don't know…" she said, trailing off and frowning. "This could be a test. You could be lying."

"Why else would I get you to run, Scarlett?"

She gripped her hair and sighed sharply. "I don't know! I don't know anything anymore. Everything is so screwed up and I…" She burst into tears and fell against my chest.

I hadn't expected that. I didn't think she would ever want to be near me again.

For the first time in days, I held her again, and I felt complete. I needed her away from here. I needed her to live a full life the way everyone was supposed to. Sacrificing someone for your own sake was selfish, no matter how it was dressed up. No human is worth more than another. Scarlett deserved to have the life she wanted; she didn't owe us her life. We had no right to take hers.

I held her close, burying my head in her shoulder, breathing her in. It was very likely to be the last time I'd have my arms around her. I memorized everything—the way she clung to me, the way she fit perfectly against me, the softness of her hair, the perfect scent of her skin.

"Shh, it's okay. Everything is going to be okay. Trust me, beautiful girl, *trust me*."

She pulled away first, and I resisted the urge to grab her back.

"I don't have a choice anymore."

"I promise you I won't let you down, not again. Now you need to eat that," I said, nodding to the food on the side. "And every-thing else you're offered, okay?"

Stubbornly, she folded her arms over her chest, ready to argue.

"I mean it, Scarlett. We are going to be *running* from these people, and I need you to have all the strength you can."

"Fine," she replied. "Where do we go?"

"Through the forest and into town. There are two police sta-tions there. Which one we go to depends on where we come out. We will maybe have a one- or two-minute head start. We run as fast as we can without looking back. I will get you to safety and back to your parents."

"What happens to you?"

Gulping, I shrugged, genuinely not knowing. "Don't worry about me. I'll leave, and you will never see me again."

Her eyes hardened. "If they find you?"

"I'll go to a city. They won't look there. With any hope, the police will pick them up anyway."

"Your parents?"

"Are dangerous. I love them, I can't help that, and as much as it kills me to hand them over—because they're victims too—they won't stand by and let me help you. I will tell the police every-thing. I know it's the right thing to do. If they killed someone because I didn't give them up…"

She nodded once and sat back down. "Don't make me hate you all over again."

That hurt. "I won't. Never again, Scarlett. I have to go. Try to calm down the attitude. We don't want them to be on high alert."

"I know," she replied.

"I'll see you later."

Fiona was reading in the living room when I left Scarlett's room. She looked up and smiled. "How is she?"

"Hungry. She seems to be doing well, doesn't she?"

"I think so. I had hoped she would have understood when I explained on the first night, but I think she is now. I am grateful for that. This is so much easier now she is beginning to believe."

"Beginning to?"

"I think there is a little way to go. There are things she still doesn't understand, but we haven't had a chance to go through everything yet. She is reading, but there is a lot."

I nodded. "There is. We have had years and she only gets eight days. I think she's extraordinary for coming this far."

"I completely agree, Noah."

"I'll see you at lunch tomorrow, Fiona."

Smiling, she nodded and then went back to her reading. It was dark when I left. Thick gray clouds coated the sky. I used to find beauty in all seasons, but this bleak weather summed up how I felt right now. I wanted to get her out and I would try, but that didn't mean I'd be able to do it.

When I left my house the next morning, Donald and Fiona were outside with Scarlett. They were showing her the gardens where we grow crops. She looked so uninterested, but she watched everything they did and listened to everything they said.

Her long hair blew in the light wind and she wrapped it in her hand, throwing it over one shoulder. She was beautiful, full of life and passion. It had to work; I had to get her out. Whatever it cost me, I had to get her away.

I slowly walked over to them. Yesterday had been the first time I'd been allowed to see her one-on-one, and I didn't want to push it, but I still couldn't stop myself from going to her.

"Morning," I said as I approached.

Donald and Fiona stood; Scarlett already was. She wasn't sure how to play things, whether she should ignore me or reply. I needed her to act angry but still respond, as that's what was expected of her.

"Good morning, Noah. Would you like to help pick tomatoes?" Fiona said.

Scarlett gripped the wicker basket with both hands, and I wasn't sure if she was trying to tell me something. "I would, if that's okay with you, Scarlett?"

Shrugging as if she didn't give a damn, she turned around and started wrenching red tomatoes from the vine. She was good— almost too good. Of course she would still be angry with me, but I hated the extent of her anger. I was doing everything I could to make it right.

"Well, grab a basket then," Donald said.

Donald and Fiona gave us a little space once we started picking. I think they liked that I was friends with her. If she wasn't the key to our eternity, then I had no doubt that they'd be happy for us to be together.

I slowed my picking down so I could have more time with her. Donald and Fiona didn't seem to notice or they didn't care. If they didn't care that I wanted more time with her, then getting her out might be a little bit easier.

"How are you finding it here?" I asked when they moved a little closer.

She glanced at them before answering, probably wondering why I'd asked her that and understanding when she saw where they now were. "Um…it's different."

"Yes, it is definitely different."

"It's confusing."

I nodded. "It's an adjustment. I remember my first few weeks out of the commune; it was pretty horrible. You're home now though, and that's all that matters."

Donald and Fiona smiled at each other. They were so sure of Eternal Light and their ability to convince everyone else that they didn't even consider that Scarlett could've changed me completely.

"Okay, I think we have enough for lunch," Donald said, raising his basket. "Let's get these to Mildred, Bernard, and Kathy, and then I need to help Hank and Bill finish Hank's veranda."

That was one thing I loved about my community; everyone worked together. If you needed something, everyone was willing to help. I liked some of the core values of Eternal Light and the way we lived, but there was a dangerous side to our beliefs that had to stop. Only I knew I would never be able to convince anyone that Donald and Fiona were wrong and we shouldn't sacrifice their daughter.

"All right," I said, taking Donald's basket so he could get straight off.

"Thank you, Noah. I'll see you all at lunch then."

He left me with Fiona and Scarlett. "Fiona, do you think once we drop these things off I could show Scarlett the chapel?"

"What chapel?" Scarlett asked.

Thank God she hadn't seen it yet. I didn't think she had, since they were keeping her close to the commune and the chapel was a minute's walk into the meadow.

"I think that is a lovely idea, Noah," she replied.

Scarlett looked hopeful, wondering if we were running now. There was no way. The meadow would maybe hide us up to our knees but we needed the cover the thick forest offered. We dropped the tomatoes for the lunchtime salad off, and I led Scarlett past the houses and hall.

"Are we doing it now?" she asked once we were safely away.

"No, I just wanted to be able to talk to you in private. We won't get many opportunities between now and the…day."

"Why aren't we going now?"

"Look around, Scarlett. There's nothing but the meadow and open fields on this side." Sure, we were slightly downhill, and that was why the chapel wasn't visible from the commune, but we'd have to run uphill to get away and we'd be seen immediately. "They can drive over the fields. We'd be seen until we hit the

217

forest at the farside, and by that time, they would've caught up. I'm just as desperate to get you away but we have to be smart about it. I promise you the way I have chosen to do this gives us the best possible chance."

"I just want to leave."

"I know, and I do too."

Sighing, she folded her arms over her stomach. "Sorry. Are you really showing me this chapel then?"

"Yes, it's where we get married. Well, not *we* but you know what I mean."

She smiled as I squirmed in embarrassment. If things had been different, if Eternal Light were just a simple way of living off the land and not about living forever, then maybe we could've been married here one day. I wished that were true. I wanted so bad for Eternal Light to be an innocent alternative to the *normal* way of living and for Scarlett to stay here with us. I wasn't going to get much more time with her, but I desperately wanted it.

"Yeah, I know what you mean."

"How is your arm?"

Her hand immediately went to the wound. "It's okay. Fiona gave me ginger tea."

"It is a good natural painkiller."

She smiled tightly. "So she said. It just tasted gross."

I pushed the door to the chapel open and ignored where our conversation was headed. I knew it relieved pain. I'd used it when I broke my wrist a few years back, but Scarlett was used to pills and modern medicine.

"It's nice," she said, looking around. It was a fairly simple hexagon-shaped wooden building with a steeple roof and exposed, chunky beams that had wildflowers and vines wrapped around them for a wedding. I wished there were one on before the rituals; I would've loved for Scarlett to witness a wedding Eternal Light style.

"It's better when it's decorated."

"You love it here." It wasn't a question; she knew I did and I wasn't ever going to hide that from her.

"I do. I won't lie. But I understand what they want to do is very wrong and I don't believe, for one second, that what they think is going to happen after is actually going to happen. Please don't doubt me, Scarlett. There is nothing that will change my mind, no matter how much I love my home and my community."

"Promise me," she whispered.

I didn't hesitate when I said, "I promise. I love you so much more."

29

SCARLETT

Fiona led me into the meadow, smiling warmly as if everything were completely normal. Her cult was there already, standing in a circle. They each held a white candle in a cup, even though it was daylight. It was hot today, much too hot. I had the only spaghetti strap dress in white on because I woke up melting, but it wasn't doing much to keep me cool. That could also be because of Noah's confession last night and the fact that my "father" had cut me.

Noah was there, eyes burning into me. I refused to look at him out of fear of giving away our plan—his plan. I wasn't even sure if I believed him, but he was all I had right now. I'd contemplated not running off to the side Noah would be waiting on but in another direction and going it alone, but that was probably just stupid. It was hard to know who to trust when every single person important to me had lied.

We walked slowly. Fiona kept breathing in and out deeply, and I wanted to laugh but I was too scared. They all looked absolutely ridiculous, dressed only in white, lips moving with whispered words.

Without a word, Fiona took me to the center of the circle and went to stand between Donald and Shaun-the-Traitor. I licked my lips. What was about to happen? On the floor in front of their feet were vines of what looked like ivy. I didn't even want to know what they were going to do with them, but no doubt I would very soon.

The only comfort I had was in knowing that they wouldn't kill me before the final ritual in a few days' time. But would they hurt me again? Would Noah stand by and let that happen for a second time? Probably. If he intervened, they'd know he was—possibly—on my side and that would be it.

I hated placing my faith in a guy who had betrayed me and crushed my heart.

Donald picked up a vine and closed in. I braced myself, clenching my fists and breathing heavily. *Don't hurt me, don't hurt me.*

He stopped and knelt down, winding the vine around my ankles. They were tying me up? My breathing came out in thick pants as he wrapped around and around until my ankle was covered.

With wide eyes, I looked at Fiona. She had at least half explained what was going to happen. I knew we were going to a field and there would be chanting, but I hadn't known about being tied up.

He stood and with a warm smile said, "What are we but part of nature? Like trees breathing new life in spring, we will be born again. Into eternal light, you shall lead us, wind around our souls, and take us with you, my love. The Light, our savior, my daughter."

If I could have moved, I would've run right then. My fists

trembled, digging into my legs as I tried to stop people from seeing how scared I was. I didn't want to give them the satisfaction, not that I thought they'd get any out of it anyway.

My eyes flicked to Noah. He looked like the rest of them, calm and happy. He looked like he didn't care about me in the way he'd said, but I'd learned the hard way that the guy had the best damn poker face, so I hoped he was pretending to still fit in. I was counting on him completely.

Fiona was the next to move. She picked up her vine and made her way over. She looked at me like she loved me but she didn't, not in any real way. If she did, she wouldn't have let this happen. I held myself tighter, arm throbbing as it pushed against my side. I couldn't worry about the cut right now.

Smiling, she bent her knees and wound the vine around my legs, starting where Donald left off. How long was this going to go on for? "You are the one who will lead us, Scarlett. Your gift grants us eternity."

You're bloody welcome.

Biting my lip, I nodded and stopped myself blinking, so I could make my eyes tear up. I didn't need them to trust me or think I was all for their cult now Noah was getting me out, but it'd help them relax, and I wanted to catch them off guard when I ran. It was thirty-eight against two. We didn't stand much chance, but I was determined to do everything I could to get away. All I wanted was to be back with my family. I had a few apologies to make too.

I closed my eyes as one by one they tied vines around my body.

I hated not being able to move. There was about half a centimeter leeway where I could move and that felt tighter with every second. The vines bound me to the elbow and there was still one person left to go. Noah.

He stepped forward and I held my breath. This was the hardest one. I could push away the panic of being trapped, but Noah having a hand in it was awful. When he was right in front of me, far enough from the others that he could show his true emotions, his face fell. His eyes looked haunted, pained. He didn't want to do this. That meant something. Actually, that meant a lot.

"It's okay," I said under my breath, trying not to move my lips.

He reached around my back, feeding the vine to his other hand. I didn't take my eyes off him. He worked slowly, eyes tight, jaw clenched, and it didn't bother me as much. As stupid as it was to allow him to be my comfort, he was. We were in it together right now. He was following their orders, but I knew he was with me.

His breath blew across my neck as he leaned around to wrap the vine around me. I closed my eyes, and it was almost like we were back in my room, cuddled up on my bed with him kissing my neck and behind my ear.

"Don't," he said.

Stepping back, he turned and walked away, leaving the last knot as loose as he could get away with. He hadn't elaborated on his "don't," but he didn't need to. He knew I was thinking about the way things were before all this happened and I knew he wanted it back as much as I did.

When Noah stood back, I noticed that they'd all closed in,

standing in front of me in a crowd rather than a circle. I stood my ground, lifting my chin to appear unaffected.

They can't kill me. Yet.

"Let these vines bind her with nature; let her lead us into forever." Their chant chilled me. It was repeated over and over until I wanted to scream. Even with the crazy chanting, they still looked kind, like they would give you their last bloody piece of candy.

I couldn't move at all without hurting my arm more and it made me panic.

Closing my eyes, I tried to imagine I was somewhere else. I wanted to get out of the vines and be free, but I didn't know how long they were going to keep me tied up. I had to think of something else because I was so close to struggling and I was trying to get them to think I was coming around.

I refused to think of my parents or Jeremy because I wouldn't be able to hold it together. Even though I missed them and just wanted to be home, I couldn't cry over my family right then. I looked up at the bright sky and wondered how people like this could exist in such a beautiful place. They had the perfect location; everything was peaceful and pretty, but they'd ruined it.

Evelyn's pretty face drifted into my head. My sister. I smiled, finally being able to picture her doing something other than running with Jeremy for three seconds. I could still only see her profile, but she was standing next to me, holding my hand. I felt love for her even though I didn't remember it.

I will remember you, Evie.

I felt someone pull the vine behind me, and slowly they were removed. I flexed my hands when they were free, noticing blood beginning to seep through the bandage. It came as no surprise that it'd started bleeding again. I didn't care.

"How do you feel?" Fiona asked as the last vine was removed.

I couldn't tell her the truth, but I couldn't come right out and lie. "It was okay, I suppose. I don't like not being able to move." There, that wasn't too bad but not so positive that she would question why I was completely okay with them so suddenly. I honestly had no idea if she would suspect anything if I told her right now that I loved her and couldn't wait to be the sacrifice. It wasn't a risk I was willing to take.

"I can imagine that wasn't pleasant. It is done now though, and it means we are one step closer."

I smiled tightly but didn't reply. She could take that however she wanted.

"Let's head back," Donald said. "We have a communal dinner tonight, so let's make it a special one for Scarlett."

A special dinner with all of the psychos. Daddy really knew what I wanted.

The sky was now light orange where the sun had begun to set, but it was still really warm out. Everyone was outside, around the large, dug-out seating area. Two small pit fires in the middle kept us warm. I was sitting with Donald and Fiona, and Shaun and Bethan were beside Fiona.

Noah was here too, but I ignored him as much as I could. We needed everyone to believe that he was just with me to get me here and I was still half-angry with him. I had to thaw with everyone else the longer I stayed, but I wasn't sure if forgiving Noah would be realistic, so I'd opted for pretending he didn't exist.

Dinner was large, stone-baked pizzas with vegetarian toppings—of course. I hated to like anything about this place and these people, but they could cook. Living a life the way they did could be amazing if it wasn't for the added insanity.

No one spoke about the fact that they'd tied me up just a few short hours ago, but I preferred it that way. I couldn't pretend that I didn't hate them if they spoke about one of the most terrifying things I'd ever been through.

Noah avoided me just enough but not too much that it looked wrong. He made an effort to speak to me a couple times. I'd overheard him telling his mum that he didn't try too much because he wanted to give me space to realize what Eternal Light were about before we had the inevitable conversation about what he'd done. He was almost too good at lying; it made me question who his allegiance was to—again.

"Scarlett, would you like pepper and mushroom or spring onion and sweet corn?" Fiona asked. "Or a little of both."

"Onion and corn, please. I don't like mushrooms."

"Really? You used to like them."

Did I? "I don't now."

"Okay, I will be right back."

Finn planted himself in Fiona's seat and smiled over his shoulder. I couldn't help the less-than-warm reception I gave him. Tightening my jaw, I made a show of looking away, as far away as I could.

"Come on, Scarlett, don't be like that."

I turned back. "Don't be like that? Are you serious right now?"

"We didn't do any of this to hurt you."

Sacrificing didn't fall under the category of hurting?

"Think about that for a second, Finn."

"Donald and Fiona have explained. Haven't they?"

My eyes widened. He was questioning me with the obvious goal of finding out just how anti–Eternal Light I was. I had been doing so well gradually coming around and I didn't want to let anything ruin that, especially not Noah's brother, the only one who seemed to look deeper than the show I was putting on. I'd barely said anything, but I could already feel my shot at freedom slipping, and it made me feel like breaking down and crying.

I just want to go home.

"They have," I replied, swallowing my emotions. "But that doesn't mean I'm not still scared."

"I suppose that is understandable. You've not been here long. By the time of the seventh ritual, you will be sure. All you need to do is keep an open mind and let the truth in."

Wow, they all sounded the same. That could've been Finn, Donald, Shaun, or any one of them speaking just then; there was no difference. You could tell they were singing from the same crazy song sheet.

"Right," I replied.

"Are you sure?" His eyes were too questioning, too searching.

"Finn, a couple of weeks ago I didn't even know you all existed. I thought two other people were my parents. Forgive me for feeling a little scared and confused right now. I'm human. I need time."

He looked down, wincing. "You're right. I'm sorry. We want the reunion to be a happy one for us all and sometimes overlook what a huge adjustment it is for you. Just remember that you are back with your family now. This is where you belong."

For the next few days…

"I'm trying to."

"It's all we can ask," he said, getting up as Fiona walked back over with two plates of pizza.

"Have you had anything to eat yet, Finn?" Fiona asked.

He shook his head. "Noah's gone for us both."

I hated how casually everyone spoke about Noah in front of me. There was no consideration for the fact that I loved him and he had betrayed me. But then, they didn't view it as a betrayal. He was doing his duty the way I would have to at the sacrifice.

Human life didn't mean anything to them—well, not mine anyway.

30
NOAH

Today marked the final full day Eternal Light had planned for Scarlett. At lunch she was expected to give element offerings, and tomorrow those elements would guide her into the next stage of her eternal life.

It was only hearing it when you'd turned your back on them that you really *heard* it. I had an ice-cold shower, not wanting to be comfortable. My muscles locked, my skin tightened, and it stung. It hurt, but I welcomed the pain, the distraction. Tomorrow weighed heavily on my mind.

I shut off the shower when I shook so violently that I felt ill. My skin had lost its color—I was pale and looked lifeless. Wrapping the towel around myself, I stood still until I'd dried enough to put clothes on.

I had to pull myself together. If I couldn't, Scarlett wouldn't have a chance and she was all that mattered to me. I dressed quickly, feeling the sting as warmth seeped into my icy skin. Since getting home with her, I looked tired all the time. Everything that I'd done haunted me.

Even though I was now doing the right thing, I still couldn't forgive myself.

"Noah, are you ready?" Finn asked, knocking once on the door with what sounded like his palm.

"Almost. I'll meet you there."

Communal lunch, offerings, communal dinner, then early night before tomorrow. That was what Donald had ordered for all of us today. He didn't usually try to tell us what to do when—we sort of all did that together, but he was completely running the show now.

"All right, don't take too long."

I wanted to take all the time in the world. My nerves were running wild. Although I hadn't had second thoughts about helping her escape, I did question how we were going to do it. Was there a better way? Could I have snuck out of the commune, got help, and returned unnoticed before anyone realized I was missing?

Stretching my muscles, I mentally prepared to lie to everyone again and pretend I was excited as them. In a way, I was glad this day was here—I couldn't do this for much longer. Soon I wouldn't have to pretend anymore. Everyone would know where my loyalties lie, and I hoped Scarlett would be safely away.

As soon as the front door closed behind my family, I went to my bedroom. They would be distracted for a while before anyone came to look for me, so I knew I had at least five minutes to find the bag for tomorrow.

There would be a few things that we needed, and while I didn't have time to pack everything with everyone milling around outside, I at least needed the bag under my bed, ready for me to pack a few things in while everyone was distracted later.

The bags were in the storage closet beside the bathroom. I

opened the long door and reached up on the top shelf to get it, looking over my shoulder to make sure no one had come back in. I didn't want to use the one I had brought here because that was still on the chair in my room, unpacked, and it would look suspicious if it suddenly disappeared.

I grabbed the lone bag at the back and headed back to my room. I hated lying and sneaking around, but they'd left me with no option.

"Noah," Finn called.

I jumped, my heart slamming against my chest, and looked around. He wasn't near me. Yet. But I was in the middle of the hallway holding a bag. Opening the bathroom door as quietly as I could, I stepped inside and carefully slid the lock in place.

I stopped breathing and pressed my ear to the door so I could try to hear where he was. His footsteps thudded lightly on the wooden floor, but they were getting louder.

"Noah, are you in here?"

I flexed the hand that didn't have the bag in a death grip. "In the bathroom," I called.

"You all right?"

"Fine, just needed the toilet. I'll be back out soon."

"Sure? You want me to wait?"

No, please just go.

"I'm all right, thank you. See you outside in a minute."

"Sure," he replied.

I forced my ear against the door harder, but it was difficult to hear. I felt sick at the thought of being caught. What would I tell him if I walked out there with the bag, and he'd decided to wait for me anyway?

Giving him enough time to leave, I placed the bag on the floor where it would be hidden when I opened the door, flushed the toilet, and washed my hands.

My nerves were shot as I unlocked the door and pulled it open. I was met with complete silence. Finn would have surely talked to me if he were here. Poking my head around the corner, I did a quick sweep down the hall. Empty.

I swiped the bag, dashed to my room, and shoved it deep under the bed.

"Where have you gone now?" Finn asked.

I froze, crouched on the floor by my bed. He'd been waiting there? Straightening my legs, I turned to face the door a second before he walked through it.

"All right?"

"I was just contemplating getting a jacket, but I think I'll be too hot."

"Yes, it's warm out. You ready now?"

"I am," I replied. "You didn't have to wait."

He shrugged. "I was worried when you didn't come out."

I smiled as I left my room, closing the door behind me. "Let's do this," I said.

"All right!" Finn didn't hide his excitement. I used to feel the same when we spoke about what was going to happen and what Scarlett was leading us to.

When we left the house, the last few people were making their way to our outdoor dining area. They carried vases of water and bright-green leaves.

Scarlett stood in a long, white dress that made me think about marrying her one day. She was undeniably beautiful, naturally beautiful. She had no makeup on and nothing had been done to her hair, but she took my breath away.

"Finally," Zeke said, handing me and Finn a lantern.

Donald was, as usual, the first to approach Scarlett. He carried soil and rocks in one hand and placed them by her feet. Earth.

Fiona stepped forward next, placing a small, freshly dug-up plant next to Donald's offering. Air.

Judith was up next, laying down a lantern. The orange flame flickered in the glass. Fire.

Lastly, Bill laid a vase of water by Scarlett.

Gulping, I held my lantern at arm's length, the same as everyone else, and closed my eyes. I couldn't watch.

"By the four elements we live. By the four elements you shall ascend. By the four elements we shall live on, be reborn upon death, so that we shall be joined in eternity," Donald said.

"By the four elements we shall live on," I said in tune with the rest of the community, a piece of me dying because, technically, I was still taking part in this.

That night was also the last time we'd eat together as a community before Scarlett was supposed to be sacrificed. There was a buzz in the air that was slightly infectious. Everyone was elated that we'd finally reached the point we'd been striving for all these years.

It felt a bit surreal to be living something we'd spoke about almost on a daily basis. But I now knew the dangerous truth behind Eternal Light's teachings.

Under her perfected act, Scarlett looked rightfully terrified, and I had an even harder time tonight pretending that I couldn't wait until tomorrow. Things were about to get very real, and I still wasn't convinced we'd be able to pull it off and get away. It *had* to work. If we didn't get out, the girl I was in love with was going to die.

"Are you okay, Noah?" Mum asked, frowning, questioning why I didn't have a big, fat smile on my face.

"Yes, I'm fine. Just can't believe it's finally here, you know?" *Please know.*

She smiled. "I do. I know exactly what you mean. But it is here, so please try to enjoy it."

Damn. "I am, Mum. I'm just taking everything in. This is the night you've been talking about since I was little. You told me to step back and take everything in because it'll go by in a flash. That's what I'm trying to do."

Her eyes filled with tears. "I remember that. I am so proud of you, Noah. You really have grown into a wonderful man." She kissed me on the cheek and then looked around, sighing in contentment.

I wasn't a wonderful man, but I was hoping tomorrow might correct that, even a little. I was going to do the right thing. It was the right thing by Scarlett, myself, and Eternal Light. Not only was I going to do everything I could to save her life, but I was stopping us from becoming murderers.

Scarlett stood with her parents as people came forward and kissed both of her cheeks. She played it so well. She was withdrawn enough to play the nervous card but smiled and interacted enough to make people believe she was with us all the way. She wasn't the only one who was nervous—we all were, but for different reasons.

I managed to get a minute with her out of earshot of everyone else when we both went back for more food. Donald watched us; I didn't even need to look around to know that. I kept smiling.

"How are you feeling?" I asked. It was an innocent question and one that everyone had asked her, but I was referring to our escape, not the ritual.

She nodded, giving me a reserved smile. To everyone else she'd not quite forgiven me yet and still acted cooler to me. She probably didn't have to pretend that much.

"I'm okay," she replied. "Nervous."

"I think we all are a little. Don't worry though. Tomorrow is going to run smoothly and then everything will be all right."

"Yeah, everyone has been reassuring me all day."

"They all love you and just want you to feel at ease with what's going to happen."

I knew she was talking about the same thing I was, but I hoped everyone else thought it was about the ritual.

"I know that. It's just been a huge change, and I've only just had time to stop and think about what's coming, and I'm a little scared."

"That's natural, Scarlett, but trust me when I tell you that it will be all right." I had no right to tell her to trust me, not after what I'd done, but I was all she had now. The responsibility was overwhelming, but I made a promise not to let her down again.

"Do you really think so?" she asked.

I didn't want to lie to her. The odds were heavily stacked against us, but the only choice was to try.

"I know so. Stop worrying and enjoy tonight. This is all for you, Scarlett."

Donald stepped behind her and smiled at us both. "Noah is right. Come and enjoy the evening. Everything will be fine tomorrow."

Scarlett smiled up at Donald and followed him back to their seats. I wasn't sure how I felt about her being able to lie and manipulate so easily, but then she was facing death, so I couldn't question her character too hard. And what I was doing was no better. I was lying to everyone I loved—everyone but her.

"Tell Finn not to eat everything. I'm just running home for a second," I said to Mum.

Her eyes immediately filled with concern. "Are you all right?"

"I think I have a headache coming on, and I want to make a tea in case. I won't be long."

She nodded. "Do you want me to make it?"

"No, you stay here and enjoy. I'll bring it back when it's made," I said, walking off.

I had our bag and needed to pack and stash it. The only chance to plant it in the forest would be now, while they were all distracted with the festivities. Scarlett watched me go back to my house, but I didn't look at her. I didn't want anyone to see me looking at her and become suspicious, not that they would. You didn't turn your back on Eternal Light, your family, and the community. Jonathan and Marissa had. They'd lost their chance at eternal peace, tranquillity, and happiness. They would get nothing when they died.

I closed the front door and ran to the kitchen, boiling a pan of water to make tea. Then I went to my room and pulled the rucksack from under my bed, filling it with some clothes and fleece jackets that I'd set aside in my drawer, water and food that I'd stashed right at the back, and a pair of shoes for Scarlett. There wasn't a lot in it really, enough for one day. I didn't want to be weighed down when we had to run as fast as we could.

I made the tea and left it on the counter while I went outside to creep into the forest. I could hear everyone talking and laughing, but I was far enough out that I couldn't be seen in the dark. I hoped.

I felt every thud of my heart as I crept past the lake. If I was caught, that would be it—I'd be out and Scarlett would die. There was so much riding on this that I felt sick.

Letting Scarlett down was the last thing I ever wanted to do, but it was a huge possibility.

I walked slowly, being careful not to make too much noise as I stepped on fallen branches. It was stupid; they wouldn't hear a stick breaking over the sound of the fire and everyone's talking, but I was scared and paranoid.

There was a collection of bushes relatively close to the edge of the forest and the lake Scarlett would be in before she was taken to the barn and sacrificed. It was my chosen hiding place for the bag now and me tomorrow.

I shoved the bag under the bush, covering it with leaves and whatever else I could find on the ground, all while scanning the area to see if anyone had broken away from the group. The houses farthest away from the fire were just silhouettes, so I was confident that I couldn't be seen from where they were. Still, I stood up and crept back as fast as I could.

It'd been cold in the forest, and I was glad I'd packed the fleece jackets and a change of clothes and shoes for Scarlett; she'd be running straight after getting out of water and would be freezing.

31

SCARLETT

I woke with the strongest urge to throw up. My stomach rolled and flipped. Today was *the* day. The day with only two outcomes: Noah and I escaped, or I died. Apparently, there was going to be a day of celebration, and lots of big meals and well-wishing to send me on a safe journey where I would wait to be reunited with each of them when they died.

I literally couldn't understand why it didn't sound ridiculous to them too.

Laid out on the chair beside my bed was a soft-mint color sundress and new underwear. The only time I was told what to wear was when I had to be in something white for the rituals. This was green but clearly laid out for me to wear. I hadn't been there long, but it was long enough to establish a routine and to be scared when it was broken. They ran the community so smoothly, I would nominate them to run the world if it wasn't for the fact that they were all insane.

"Good morning," Fiona said after I'd gotten dressed and made me way into the small kitchen.

"Morning," I replied, wishing for a cup of coffee to settle my nerves. Green tea was about as good as it got.

"Breakfast is in ten minutes. Would you like some tea before we go?" she asked.

I shook my head. "No, thanks."

"Please don't look so nervous, Scarlett."

Please don't kill me.

"I'm trying," I replied, forcing myself to smile at her. "I know the pain will only last a few seconds but…"

Tilting her head, she held the tops of my arms. "It is understandable, of course. Don't fear it though; revel in the knowledge that you are destined for something much greater than this world can offer. You are a miracle."

I need a miracle.

Gulping, I replied, "Okay. Thank you."

Every single time I had to pretend to agree, I felt my heart sink further. It was wrong and I hated having to act like I was fine being sacrificed. Talking about the ending of my life wasn't an easy thing to do, and I had to do it with bloody cheer.

"Good. Now, are you sure about that tea?"

"I'm sure." It tasted like pee. "What's for breakfast?"

"Ah, we're having fruit, freshly made bread, and pastries."

Their food was incredible, but I could've killed for a bacon sandwich. It was my last breakfast. Shouldn't it be what I want?

"Sounds great. Should we go and help prepare?"

"No need," Donald said, walking into the room and leaning against the table. "It is all in hand and they want to give us a few moments alone before the day starts. I just want to thank you, Scarlett. I know it couldn't have been easy, especially after what you have lived through with Jonathan and Marissa."

The sound of my parents' names made me ache. I missed them

so much it hurt. But I was doing everything I could to get back to them, and I was sure they were doing everything they could to find me.

He smiled. "None of that matters now because you are here and you have made us so proud. We have always known you are an inspiration, and nothing gives me more pleasure than seeing you have grown into a beautiful young woman who is willing to take her destiny with such grace and elegance. It will be with a heavy heart that we let you go, but I know it won't be long before we are reunited again. Fifty years, or whatever we may have left, is nothing compared to the eternity awaiting us."

I wondered if he actually listened to himself.

"Thank you," I said. "I know my transition hasn't been easy on anyone, but I didn't know the truth."

"Oh, we know," Fiona said, "and we all understand. No one has ever thought badly of you."

I couldn't have cared less if they thought badly of me.

"Okay, good. I don't want them to," I lied and smiled.

I wanted to throw myself in the lake now, so we could get this thing started and over with. Glancing at the clock, I counted down. *Five hours.*

After eating breakfast together, we had to set up the hall. "Are you coming with us, Scarlett?" Willow asked, linking arms with Skye. She and her twin sister were the only teen girls here. There were four children, but they were the only ones around my age. I tried my best not to remember names or make much of an effort with anyone that wasn't Donald and Fiona. It would be too tragic to hear children talk like the rest of them.

"Yeah," I replied, and then turned back to Fiona. "Is that okay?"

She smiled brightly. "Of course, it is. We are headed to the barn, so we'll see you there in a few minutes."

"We won't be long," Willow said. "We just want to talk to Scarlett a bit. We haven't had much chance to yet."

And this was the only chance they were going to get. One way or another, I wouldn't be here in *two hours*.

"It has been a strange and busy week, hasn't it?" Skye said.

"Understatement," I muttered. I didn't want to talk to these girls or be their friend. It was pointless.

"Right. Yes, obviously," Willow said. "I'm sorry we didn't get to spend much time together. Noah told us you are an amazing person."

Skye grinned and added, "Not that we didn't know that already."

How often did Noah talk to them about me? Were there weekly reports? I fisted my hands. *No, don't think about that.* I couldn't look back, not now. It had to be in the past. I had to trust him.

"Well, thanks." We started to walk toward the barn at a leisurely pace, the same pace that Imogen and I walked to math class.

"What's high school like?" Skye asked, completely taking me by surprise.

I frowned. "Um, it's okay, I guess."

"Sorry," Willow said, "we just haven't been to a public school. Obviously."

"No, you never got the chance to experience that. Noah hadn't even had a movie night before…" I stopped myself. What the hell was I doing? Why was I talking about this? It was sick. We weren't friends and never would be. And I couldn't talk about what happened with Noah so casually when it still burned.

"He said he will miss that. I know he is a lover of the outdoors, but he did enjoy the films," Willow said.

I wanted to hit her. I knew he enjoyed it. He may have lied about everything, but he reacted to the movies and you couldn't fake laughter like that. I hated that she was trying to make me feel better about Noah. I didn't want to talk about him with anyone. It was private and it still *hurt*.

Skye touched my arm, and I fought hard not to whack it away. "We are very glad you're here, Scarlett."

Through gritted teeth, I replied, "Thanks."

They walked in ahead of me, and I stopped to look up at the brass clock above the barn door. *One hour and forty minutes.*

I stepped into the building and something that felt like an explosion went off in my head. I cried out and gripped my forehead. Everything slotted into place, and I felt dizzy. Memories came flooding back all at once, making my head pound.

The barn inside looked identical to the warehouse. I saw the final ceremony, the one after the cleansing.

I was little. I started to cry when they laid the leaves and red tulips on the ground inside the stone circle. They held me down. Dad had a knife. I was screaming. There was fire. The curtains were alight. Hot. Too hot. People ran, trying to find something to put the flames out with. Chaos. Terror. Pain.

Then Mum—Marissa—grabbed me. Darkness.

I couldn't breathe. Turning, I ran out of the barn and leaned against the wall outside. Oh God, *that's* what they were hiding. I was scared before, but now that I remembered, everything was a million times worse.

Don't cry. I didn't want them to know something was really wrong. I wasn't supposed to not want this.

"Scarlett!" Fiona said, hot on my heels. She bent down to meet me eye to eye. "What happened?"

Gulping, I replied, "I was remembering, but I couldn't really see anything. It gives me headaches, that's all. I just had to get some fresh air."

I wanted to scream at her. I remembered her hovering over her young child—me—watching and not caring how worked up and scared I was. How could she?

"Are you all right now?"

No! "I'm fine," I replied, straightening up and smiling. It took everything I had. "Like I said, I just needed some air."

"Why don't you go with Bethan and Noah?" She pointed to where they were in the field. "I'm sure they could use some help harvesting the potatoes."

They were having a feast after I was slaughtered, and she wanted me to help prepare for that. She was beyond sick.

Trying to keep the sarcasm from my voice, I said, "Good idea."

I left her as quickly as I could and made my way over to the field beside the meadow. They were both happy to see me, for completely different reasons.

"Fiona asked me to come and help," I said.

Bethan smiled. "We love having you. The potatoes aren't buried too far down, so you should get them up easily."

There were about five other people digging up potatoes too. How much were they going to eat? They would all eat together, celebrating for fifteen nights after I was gone. It was disgusting.

Harvesting gave me the opportunity to be alone with Noah and even then we weren't really alone. We still had people everywhere, watching me in case I took off. If I thought I could make it alone, I would go in a heartbeat. Noah was risking a lot to help me.

We were on our hands and knees, picking potatoes from the ground and putting them in a basket. It was warm but I felt freezing. I focused on my task and realized this could be one of the last things I ever did. My heart raced with nerves. I felt cornered, and I fought to keep playing along until the time was right.

Once the potatoes were picked and everything was ready, it was time to get dressed for the ceremony. Fiona took me back to the house, and I was instructed to have a bath and get ready in the dress she would set out on my bed.

I did as I was told because there was little else I could do right then. After soaking in a bath, using most of the bubble bath up as my own little screw you, I got out, dried, and went back to my room.

Unsurprisingly, the dress I was to wear was full-length and white. It was pretty and thankfully not a slim fit, so I would be able to run properly in it. I held it up—*this is what I'm supposed to die in.* Not many people knew what their last outfit would be. I instantly hated it.

I pulled it over my head. It fit me perfectly. It had long, loose-fitting sleeves, a modest neckline, and waves of material on the skirt. I pulled it and was satisfied when I could stretch both arms out to the sides.

There were no shoes, and I was afraid I'd have to run through the forest barefoot, but there wasn't a lot I could do about that. I couldn't ask for shoes and have Fiona question why I'd need them if I was getting in a lake. Besides, I'd run barefoot over a bed of nails or hot coals to get away.

I looked in the mirror and took deep breaths to calm my nerves. I could do this. I was strong.

"Scarlett, are you ready?" Donald called.

Time to fight for my life.

32

SCARLETT

Two things entered my mind as every member of Eternal Light stared at me from the meadow. One, no matter how hot it was outside, it never warmed the water enough for it to not be cold. And two, if this didn't go according to plan, I would be dead in *forty minutes*.

Noah wasn't there. He walked out with them but soon disappeared around the back of the houses. I didn't watch where he went from there out of fear of it gaining the attention of someone else. Obviously he'd positioned himself right at the back, and when they'd said whatever crap they were saying while kneeling down with their eyes closed, he'd slinked off.

Since they'd stood up and opened their eyes, they hadn't stopped staring at me.

I pretended to look around, turning my body so I could take a few unnoticed steps back toward the other side. Running in water wasn't easy, and I would be slow to get out, giving them plenty of time to make it around the lake. I had to give myself as much time as I could. At least they would be farther away as they called upon nature to accept and cleanse me for the final time.

Idiots.

Soon I had to run for my life in a cold, wet dress. Noah said he was packing me some clothes, but we couldn't stop to change until we knew we'd lost them. I had no idea how long it would be before I could change, or how cold it was going to get in the forest at night.

In the distance, I could just about see their lips moving, but I had to strain. Some of them had their eyes closed again. Why couldn't they all do that? My heart started to pound. How long would they chant for, and why hadn't Noah called me yet? Had someone realized that he'd slipped away? He said they'd be so focused on what they had to do to that he didn't see a problem with getting away. I couldn't be so confident—this was *my* life on the line.

Where was he? Gulping as my stomach churned with petrified nerves, I glanced around, still trying to make it look like I was just moving to get more comfortable and flattening the floating skirt of the dress.

When their chant felt like it'd entered the third minute, I started to panic. I didn't know how many more opportunities I was going to get to escape. My hands shook and I felt like crying. I clenched my trembling lip.

I should just go now. This was my last chance and Noah wasn't here. I officially had nothing to lose. Just when I was about to go it alone, I heard him. His voice was like an answered prayer.

Looking over my shoulder, I twisted my body in the direction of his voice. It took a minute, but after another whisper and rustling of a bush, I saw him.

"Now!" he hissed.

I took off, wading through the water as fast as I could. It

was difficult, and I burst into tears as the water fought against me, determined to keep me there. I pushed myself harder and it was when the water reached the bottom of my knees that I heard shouting. Noah stood up, dashing forward with his hand outstretched.

I whimpered, terrified that they would catch up with me. We were stupid; they were going to get us. It felt like ages before I was out and Noah was tugging me forward. My ankle-length dress weighed a ton, and I was instantly freezing as the wind nipped at my skin. But none of that mattered because I was free and had a chance.

"Faster, Scarlett," Noah said.

They were behind us, but there was no way I was turning around to see how far. Their footsteps and voices were quiet, so I hoped we still had a good head start. Noah didn't seem to care about where they were; he ran with sheer determination, half dragging me behind him.

Loose branches snapped under my bare feet, and I knew it was only a matter of time before they broke my skin. I pushed myself, ignoring the burn as my calf muscles screamed in protest. There was no time to care about anything but reaching safety.

"How far behind us do you think they are?" I asked, holding on to his hand so tight I could feel myself crushing his bones together.

There were so many of them and just two of us. *They're going to catch us!* My heart hurt it was beating so fast, so hard. Adrenaline and fear coursed through my veins.

They couldn't be too far back.

I tensed as much as I could, terrified that I'd feel a hand grip my shoulder at any second.

I wanted to be home.

"Probably not far. Keep going." He didn't sound as out of breath as me, but he was close, and it had only been a few minutes.

Five minutes in and I was completely overwhelmed and already exhausted. I felt tears stab my eyes like I was being pricked with hundreds of needles and then my vision was blurred. My side stung, my lungs burned, my legs hurt, and my feet throbbed, and I was chilled to the bone, but the worst part was the fear of being chased down, caught, and taken back.

"You okay?" he puffed after we'd run another ten or fifteen minutes, going deeper into the woods.

I blinked rapidly and replied, "Yeah." Not being able to see wasn't helping with the panic, but it was dark under the trees anyway, and we were running fast, so there wasn't really a lot to see. "We're going to be okay, aren't we?" I asked, wheezing.

I'd forgotten how my PE teacher had told me to breathe when running. It was either breathe in through your nose and out through your mouth or the other way around. I tried both, and my lungs and throat still burned.

Everything *burned* and ached.

"We'll be fine. Don't slow down."

Not once while we were sprinting toward the unknown did he let go of my hand. He would never know how much I appreciated that. I forgave him, right then and there, while he risked everything and turned his back on all he'd ever known to save my life. I forgave him.

One agonizing hour later, I couldn't do it anymore. "Noah, I need a break," I said, doubling over. I gagged.

He stopped immediately and dropped to his knees as I slumped to the ground. My legs were now completely unable to support my weight. We'd been slowing for some time now, but I'd run faster and for longer than I ever had before.

"I'm sorry, but I can't." Red spots danced in front of my face and felt like I was going to be sick.

"Okay, we'll take two." He tugged open the backpack. He pulled out two bottles of water and a pair of socks and trainers. We downed the water, breathing heavily between long swigs, and I put on the shoes. My feet were swollen and sore, but it felt good to have some protection again. Noah winced as he saw the blood seeping from my feet, instantly turning patches of the white socks red.

"Sorry," I said. *We need to go. We can't stop.*

"Don't. You have nothing to be sorry for. I should've made you put them on sooner, but we really didn't have time."

"It's not your fault. We couldn't stop too soon. Cut feet are a small price to pay for my life."

He stroked my hair and tucked it behind my ear like he had dozens of times before. I wanted to close my eyes at the contact; it felt so real and still so natural. He sighed. "We have to get up, Scarlett. We need to keep moving. They would've closed the gap considerably by now."

His words made me get up. I didn't want to; the thought of moving even an inch brought me to tears, but I didn't have a choice.

Stuffing the empty bottles back in the bag, he stood and then helped me up. My legs almost gave out again.

Clenching my teeth, I breathed through the throbbing pain. "Do you know where we're going?" I bit out.

"I know a general direction, but I've not been this deep into the forest before. There are miles before the nearest town—it's the reason Donald bought the land."

Great, we were going in a "general" direction, and I couldn't complain or let myself get disheartened. I had less of an idea than he did. We were in this together and we'd find a way out together.

"Let's go then," I said, looking back to check if anyone was coming. I wasn't nearly ready to run again, but then again, I wasn't nearly ready to die, so I had no choice.

Noah threw the bag on his back and held his hand out. I took it without hesitation and we started off in the direction we were headed before. The first few steps were the hardest; my muscles had seized from our few short minutes' stop but I ignored the pain.

The stitch in my side slowed us down considerably. Sweat dampened my clothes. I swallowed metallic bile from overexerting myself, and exhaustion threatened to collapse my legs again. But we pushed on, much, much slower than before but still heading away from Eternal Light.

"Your parents are in Ireland, you know," he said.

My heart ached to be reunited with them. "How do you know that?"

"It's all over the news. My dad drove the car eighty miles to try to put the police off, make it look like we were heading to an airport, but they quickly realized. Your parents are here."

It was a huge comfort just knowing they were in the same country. I didn't have time to dwell on the fact that they'd probably told the truth about who we all are and why they took me because Noah upped the pace and had us sprinting through the forest again. The thought of getting to safety and telling everyone that my parents were heroes for taking me that day gave me the added boost I needed.

After weaving between tall trees and jumping a few fallen ones, Noah pulled us to an abrupt stop and slapped his hand over my mouth. My eyes widened. What could he hear? I swallowed glass and pressed my body into his side. They were close—close enough for Noah to hear them, so that meant there was a strong possibility that they'd heard us.

"Noah," I whispered behind his palm.

He mouthed "it's okay" and led us to one of the fallen trees. We were going to have to hide.

We made it behind the large tree before the footsteps and voices got too loud. Noah had me pinned to his chest. We both tried to control our breathing so we were barely making a noise. Both of my hands covered my mouth and I forced myself to suck air in slowly and quietly.

My heart thumped hard when they sounded like they were

practically on top of us. Their feet broke sticks and squelched damp moss. They had to be right near us. I closed my eyes and prayed, pushing back into Noah, trying to melt into his body. I was so, so scared.

"Where would he take her?" Donald seethed.

"I don't know," Shaun replied, sounding just as angry with his son. "We will find them both though. Noah doesn't know this forest as well as he obviously thinks. We'll pick them up soon."

Noah's arms tightened around me and he buried his head in my hair. What was Noah thinking? I'd not been around them long, but they'd always spoken to each other and about each other with respect. When Noah was telling me he wanted to get me out, he still never spoke ill about his community. It had to hurt that they could speak about him with such hatred in their voices.

Despite what he'd done, I wanted to comfort him. I hated that he could be in pain and I wanted to fix it. I loved him completely, whether he was an ex–cult member or not. I loved who I thought he was and I adored that he'd grown into that person.

We didn't move for a long time and my body started to seize up again. When we finally moved, I wanted to ask him if he was okay, what he was thinking, but fear prevented me.

"Ready?" he said, after a few more minutes.

"Yes. Which way?" I asked.

He did another scan of the area and stood up, taking my hand. "Not the direction they went in. We'll go farther west."

I had no idea how he knew which way was west, but I gripped his hand and ran beside him.

33

NOAH

I was exhausted. Completely and utterly exhausted. Sweat ran down my forehead and my lungs burned. Scarlett was tired too, but we still kept moving. Before they'd caught up with us, I knew the direction we were going, but now we could have been heading back to the commune for all I knew.

"Noah," she said through ragged, struggling breaths.

We'd slowed down a lot, going at a pace somewhere between a walk and a jog. The sun was beginning to set, slowly cloaking the forest into darkness. Soon we would lose all light and the temperature would drop dramatically.

"I know," I replied, pulling her to a stop. Her legs buckled, and she fell to the ground as soon as I stopped her, and I doubled over, leaning against a tree.

"What're we going to do?" she asked.

It was all on me, but then it was my fault for promising to get her out. "Right now we should concentrate on finding shelter. I've seen a few dirt roads and I know there are houses in the forest. Rather than trying to find town, I think we should find somewhere to stay the night and head back out at first light."

Her dark-blue, fear-filled eyes widened. "Isn't that dangerous? What if they come for us?"

That I wasn't sure of. Eternal Light usually avoided outside interaction at all cost. We didn't want to be known, and knocking at someone's door asking for two runaway teens wouldn't help. They had nothing to lose now so I wasn't sure if they'd just go for it, or if because of what they were going to do they would lay low and try to find us alone.

At this point, it was anyone's guess.

"We have to be smart about this. As soon as that sun's gone, it's going to get really cold. Add complete darkness to that and it's not looking good for us. We'll find somewhere to stay the night. I think someone's house is the best bet. I have a story."

"You really think that'll work?"

I stood up straight and scrubbed my face with my hands. "I don't know, Scarlett. It's all I have right now. I wish I could wave a magic wand and get us out of this, but I can't."

"It's okay," she said softly. "I know you're doing all you can, and I understand what you risked."

We jogged for what seemed like hours and finally came across an old bike and gardening tools. Scarlett looked at me, afraid. "Whose do you think those are?" she asked.

"I don't know, but it probably means we have stumbled onto private property and a house is nearby. This is good." Finally.

"Is it good? We don't know who is going to be there."

"It will be fine, Scarlett. No one can be as dangerous to us as them right now. You know that we have no choice."

She nodded. "I'm with you. Can we just walk now, no running? I feel like I'm going to collapse." I was finally able to let her slow even more. We were very quickly losing light, and it was getting harder to see her right in front of me.

"Yes, let's take two minutes first, so you can get finally changed now that we're farther away. We don't want this look any more suspicious than it already does." I dropped the bag and she bent down, taking the clothes out of it. I had just a pair of jeans and T-shirt for her, but it was better than the dress. "Put the fleece on too. You're freezing."

I could just about see her rosy cheeks with the last of the light, but that didn't fool me. She was cold to the touch and we'd been steadily slowing our pace for the last couple of hours. I slipped my fleece on as well and turned around, giving her some privacy even though I'd seen her naked before.

It only took her a minute to get changed, probably because she was cold. "I'm done, Noah," she said. I turned back to see her shoving the dress in the bag and gripping the front of the fleece against her in an attempt to warm up quicker. "We should take this so they don't find it and know we've been here, right?"

I smiled and took the bag. "Yes, good thinking."

When I stood up from bending down to get the bag, we were closer than before. I could smell her hair, her skin, and it drove me crazy. I missed her so much. Everything was entirely my fault. I'd lost the best thing that had ever happened to me and I had no one to blame but myself.

Her eyes locked me in, preventing me from moving or even speaking. She was so beautiful, inside and out. "Noah," she whispered, and the softness in her voice made me ache. Even if it was only for a moment, she remembered how we were, how she loved me. It might not have been much, but that tender look was enough for me. I didn't deserve more. I didn't even deserve that.

"I know," I replied. "Let's try to find this house."

She stepped back first and the warmth I felt when I was near her subsided. I put my hand on the small of her back to guide her in what I hoped was the right direction. I didn't need to, but the urge to have some physical contact with her was overwhelming.

She tried not to look at me when I touched her, but I caught the glance in my direction. I took it as a good sign that she didn't push me away. We only had each other right now, and I desperately wanted her to, at the very least, not hate me.

"Are you feeling warmer?" I asked as we power walked ahead, being careful to watch the ground as well as the surroundings since we couldn't see that well anymore.

"Yeah, thank you."

"Sorry we couldn't have stopped longer for you to change earlier."

"It's okay. I wasn't that cold back then anyway. Not sure if it was because it was warmer or if the shock has just worn off now."

"You're not going to faint on me, are you?"

She smiled, looking out into the distance and then in front of her feet. "No, I'm pretty sure I'm saving that for when we get to town."

"Noted," I replied. "I'll remember that for when we step into the police station."

"That's where we're going first?"

"Of course."

"You're turning them in?" she asked, genuinely surprised. I could just take her home, let her parents run away with her, and go somewhere myself, but I could never think of doing that anymore. Eternal Light was dangerous and had to be stopped. Besides, the police were looking for her.

I pulled her to a stop and spun her around. "I understand that I have no right to ask anything of you, but I need you to believe me when I tell you I love you. They would have killed you, Scarlett, and I have never felt fear like that. I felt physically sick from the moment I woke, worrying that something would go wrong with the escape. Nothing matters but you and maybe I'm blinded but I don't care. Bottom line is, you come first and there's not one person in this world I wouldn't betray to keep you safe. So, yeah, I'm turning them in. I'm keeping you safe."

She looked like she was going to cry, but not in a bad way. I loved that I could still affect her.

"We need to keep moving. They could be anywhere." There was a dirt track road to our left and it had to lead somewhere. I led her down it.

Ten minutes later, we found a small cottage. An old Ford Mondeo was parked outside. Eternal Light had Jeeps because of how deep into the forest we lived. I was confident we'd be safe here.

Scarlett's hand slipped into mine and she squeezed. She was afraid.

"It's all right. Just let me do the talking."

With a little nod she replied, "Okay."

I hated the next words out of my mouth. "We can't be holding hands for this. I'm going to tell them you're my sister."

She let go and I wanted to punch myself. That may well have been the last time I got to hold her hand. I shouldn't have said anything until we had gotten closer. I needed more time.

"What will you tell them?"

"We've lost our camp." We couldn't tell them the truth; it was too dangerous. I wouldn't put their lives at risk if they knew about Eternal Light.

Frowning adorably, she said, "Huh?"

"Don't worry, just follow my lead," I said, knocking on the faded red door. When it opened, an elderly man smiled at us. "Hello, my name is Jacob, and this is my sister, Amelia. We got lost in the woods with the loss of light and wondered if we could stay until morning, please? We won't be any trouble, but we're cold and just need a floor to sleep on."

"You're lost? Where are you parents?" he asked.

"We know our way around here but ventured farther than usual and I would prefer not to have my sister walking through the woods in the dark. And our parents will be at home, drunk, sir. We camp out a lot. They know about it. I'm eighteen, old enough to take care of us both, but right now I just need a little help."

"Who is it, dear?" the man's wife said, leaning around his shoulder.

"Kids here lost in the woods," he replied.

"I was just explaining to your husband that my sister and I

walked farther than usual and didn't think about the time. Before we knew it, the sun had set and we couldn't find our way back. We just need somewhere to sleep until sunlight, when we can see our way home."

"Of course, of course, dear things," she said, shoving her husband to the side and taking Scarlett's hand. "Come on in. Let's get you warm and fed. Through there, dear, that's right." She showed Scarlett into the living room and me and her husband followed.

"Thank you for this. We really appreciate it. We'll be out of your hair at first light."

"Nonsense," he said. "You're no trouble. We don't get too many folk knocking on our door anymore."

That, I believed. I just hoped we'd be the only ones knocking on the door that night.

34

SCARLETT

Bridget had me and Noah sitting on the sofa, wedged under a thick tartan blanket and drinking hot chocolate with mini marshmallows on top. It was so unbelievably nice to have freshened up a little and be somewhere warm and dry.

I felt human again, but my nerves were still raging. They were still out there looking for me, and any minute they could knock on the door. Noah didn't seem to think they would in case anyone asked questions, but they didn't have anything to lose anymore. If I disappeared, they wouldn't get their chance at eternal life.

"So, you two live in town? You don't sound like you're from around here," Seamus said.

"We moved here from England two years ago. I imagine the accent will catch eventually," I replied.

I hated lying to them. They were so sweet and so kind, but we couldn't exactly tell them the truth. It was too unbelievable anyway. Eternal Light was well hidden and although they had electricity and running water I doubted many locals knew they were even there.

"Ah, I thought as much."

Noah smiled. "We camp through most of the summer. We've

always loved the great outdoors and wish our parents had bought one of the houses in the forest."

"They don't come along too often, I'm afraid."

"No, I don't expect they would."

"We've been here forty years now," Bridget said.

I was waiting for her to say something about a cult or weird group of people living in self-made shacks in the woods, but she didn't. She didn't know about them, which wasn't surprising.

"Wow, I bet you know everything about this forest then," I said. "We've only been exploring for a couple of years."

Noah looked at me out of the corner of my eye, but I didn't care about his warning to stop. I wanted to know if they at least suspected something odd was happening around here.

"We like to think so," Seamus said. "We were young explorers like yourselves back in our youth. We've always loved it out here, the peace and tranquillity it has to offer, so when this house came on the market shortly after we married, we snapped it up. There are seven houses in total. Ours is about the deepest into the woods."

Noah watched him with curiosity. I could tell he was thinking, *There's a lot more in the woods than seven houses.*

"Any horror stories?" I asked.

"Amelia!" Noah said, and it took me a minute to realize he was talking to me and that was the name he'd given me when we knocked. "I'm sorry. She's really into ghost stories."

"No, no, it's fine," Bridget said. "I was too at your age."

"You still are, dear," Seamus added. "Not much happens

here. Most exciting thing that's happened is a little girl being seen running in the woods. There was talk of a young girl haunting the forest. Best thing that story ever did was stopping so many teenagers partying until all hours by that clearing a half a mile west."

A rush of adrenaline sat me forward. Evelyn? Was it my little sister they saw, running scared and alone? Did no one stop to help because they'd assumed she was a ghost?

I felt such empathy for her. I'd experienced a similar thing but I was sixteen, not a toddler and I wasn't alone. She must've been petrified. They should've gone after her. I didn't understand why she ran.

"Wow," Noah said. "That is crazy. We'll be sure to look out for child ghosts."

Him making a joke out of it made me feel sick, even if I did understand why he was doing it. I suddenly felt even more tired and I couldn't take another sip of the hot chocolate.

Noah and I were given a guest bedroom at the side of the house. Shortly after the ghost story, Bridget told Seamus to let us get some rest. The room was small and only had a tiny single bed and a sofa bed, but it was perfect. I wasn't sure if either of them had ever been used before. They really didn't have many visitors and no family, which was sad because they obviously wanted the company and were so lovely.

I sat on the bed while Noah paced the room, my mind half on Evelyn and half on what the plan for morning was. Noah had acted relaxed when we were in the living room with them, but I could tell he was listening for every outside noise. He'd scanned the room, checking out the windows and positions of the doors. Although he told me he didn't think they'd come knocking, his actions showed me he wasn't so sure.

"Are you okay?" I asked. I'd never seen anyone look so stressed before. I knew he felt responsible for what happened and for getting me away, but the situation wasn't all down to him.

"Fine," he said, not paying any attention to me at all.

"We're in this together now, Noah. You can tell me your thoughts and fears. Maybe I can help."

He stopped his pacing to look at me. "I think my fears are obvious, Scarlett. I don't want you to worry."

"What are you doing?"

"Thinking," he replied. "Trying to work out where we are and which way we should go."

"Maybe you should sit down for a while?"

"Can't," he said and started the pacing again. "I'm sorry about before."

"What about before?" He was talking about Evelyn. Raising his eyebrow, he cocked his head as if to say *don't act stupid.* "It hurts to think about what happened to her."

"I know and I'm sorry. She was only with us a day when your commune joined mine in here in Ireland after the fire. Evelyn ran into the forest."

"No one went after her?" He licked his lips and closed his eyes. There was more to this. "Noah!" I hissed, feeling my body go cold. What wasn't he telling me?

"Donald and Fiona let her go. She wasn't supposed to make it out of the forest. Evelyn was a trade. Let her go and nature would find a way to bring you back. One sister for another."

I was falling into a deep, dark pit of despair. It kept getting worse. Every new thing I learned made less sense then the last.

"Evelyn was born as insurance, just like a second child to a royal couple, or so we were told. She was loved in the way you were, but she wasn't worshipped. There was always a risk that something could happen to you. No one is immune to death or disease. That's why you're so close in age—there's barely eleven months between you. You were born to save us all; she was born to trade her life for yours should anything happen to you first."

I wanted to reject what he'd told me, but why would he lie about that?

"I'm sorry," he said when he saw the tears in my eyes. I hated them so much. They let her go to die cold, hungry, and alone in the woods.

"You didn't do anything then?"

"I was seven, and I was told she was going to bring you back to save us all. I didn't really understand."

I couldn't blame him. It was wrong to, but it was still hard to believe he sat by while that happened, even though he was just a child himself. "I know," I said, not wanting to make him feel worse about something that was out of his control.

"I really am though, Scarlett. I wish I'd been strong enough to see through what they were doing this whole time."

"You couldn't. We believe what we've been taught, right? Especially by the people we trust the most."

He turned quiet again, like he'd slipped into his own world.

"Do you think we should split up?" I asked.

"Are you…" He trailed off, looking at me like I'd said the most stupid thing in the world. I knew it wasn't the best idea, but I was worried about him. I didn't trust any of them and I knew they took loyalty very seriously. What Noah had done was unheard of. He knew the woods and the cult better than me, so he had a better chance. "We're not even talking about that."

"I'm worried about you. Betraying them wasn't easy, was it?"

"When I finish talking, we'll pretend this conversation never happened and perhaps you'll finally believe how much I would sacrifice for you and stop asking stupid questions." He'd turned deadly serious, posture stiffening, jaw hardening. "You above *everything*. In the end, turning my back on the people that were going to drive a knife through your heart was almost as easy as falling in love with you."

He turned away again, and that was the abrupt end of that conversation. He made my heart swell, made me want to be with him again. I didn't know how we could be, but it hurt to think that we could never have a chance to be together. We had a chance at a normal relationship if we got away. We'd both been through something horrific and both made mistakes.

"Noah," I whispered. "I love you too."

AWAKE

He sucked in his breath but didn't look back at me. I didn't need him to though; he felt it just as much as I did. He wanted what I wanted, but neither of us was sure if we could ever have it.

35

NOAH

"How long do you think we should stay here?" Scarlett asked, peering out of the window for the hundredth time.

"Come away," I said, tugging on her hand. "We don't want to be seen."

"I'm scared."

"I am too," I replied. "We have to keep our heads down until light. If we keep going now, we'll only get lost in the forest."

"But isn't it more dangerous to stay? They'll expect us to be staying somewhere."

"We don't have many options, Scarlett. You agreed this is our best chance. Why don't you try to get some sleep?"

She shook her head. "There's no way I can sleep."

"We are leaving at first light and we'll probably have a whole day of running and hiding. You're going to need all the strength you can get."

"What about you?"

"No."

I could see in her eyes that she didn't completely trust me. She wanted to, but she couldn't. I was determined to get her to safety and earn that trust back.

"So you don't think I'm the key to eternal life now?"

I started to pace again. "No. I think you're the key to my happiness. As long as you're okay, I'm okay. There's nothing in this world I wouldn't fight against to make sure you're still breathing."

"Do you think we're going to make it out of this?"

"Yes, I do." They'd be looking, and they wouldn't stop until they found her, but there was no way I was letting anything happen to her. She was getting out of here. "I need you to think positively." I ran my hands through my hair. I was starting to sound like my dad. "We're going to be fine, Scarlett. I need you to trust me."

"I'm trying but it's hard."

I left my post and knelt down in front of her, pulling her arms from around her legs. "I won't betray you again. I love you, Scarlett."

Her eyes filled with tears and she opened her mouth to reply, but a knock on the front door had me covering her mouth with my hand.

She looked as terrified as I felt. "Shh," I whispered. "Get off the bed and follow me."

Her hand trembled in mine as I led her to the door. The knock, this time harder, echoed through the tiny cottage.

"I'm coming, I'm coming," Seamus said, heading to the door in his slippers and a threadbare dressing gown.

I picked up the bag and yanked Scarlett's arm. "Put this on," I said, putting the strap over her head. "Remember we run straight and don't stop. In the morning, we'll see where we are, listen for sounds that we're near town."

We made it into the kitchen when Seamus's guttural scream

stopped me in my tracks. Scarlett froze. What was going on? I turned around, heart racing. "Noah!" my dad shouted.

"What's going on? Who're you?" Bridget asked. "Seamus!" she screamed next. "No, Seamus. What did you do? What did you do?"

"Go now, Scarlett!" I shoved her toward the door. They were already coming. Their footsteps thudded between Bridget's wailing. It was so much worse than I could have imagined. I expected a fight, but I never dreamed they'd hurt someone else. What had they done to him?

Scarlett grabbed my arm when I opened the door.

"Go now," I said, pushing her.

"No, what're you doing?"

"There's not enough time. I'll hold them off. Run, Scarlett, let me do this one thing right. I love you. Run." I kissed her hard and shoved her out the door.

Her eyes were wild. I closed the door and turned around. They were searching the rooms. I heard doors being opened and lights being switched on. There weren't too many rooms, so it wasn't long before the kitchen door was slammed open. Dad and Donald stood in before me.

I straightened my back, having no clue what was about to happen or what to do other than stall them so Scarlett had as much time to get away as possible.

"Where is she?" Dad asked.

"Gone," I replied.

My dad had never looked disappointed or angry because of me before. But then, I had never done anything to disagree with or disobey him before. Sacrificing—*murdering*—Scarlett would have been a mistake, one that we could never right.

"I'm sorry," I said, "but you are wrong about this."

Donald took a step beyond my dad and held his hands up as if I were dangerous and he had to calm me down. "It is all right, Noah. We don't blame you. This was a risk, having you on the outside for so long. But you know the truth. Everything we have taught you is the truth, and deep down you still know that."

I shook my head. "No. You're just going to kill her. Nothing will happen; she will just be *dead*."

"That isn't true, Noah. Everything *they* are told is a lie, one to make them conform and fit perfectly into society. I used to be there too, until I realized the truth, until I had my mind unlocked. You're making a huge mistake here, Noah, but it's not too late to rectify it. None of us are angry with you. We can help."

I gripped my hair, closing my eyes. No, he was lying. I thought about Scarlett, her smile, her soft, musical voice, the way her hair naturally curled just a little bit, her bright eyes. Opening my eyes again, I said, "But she'll be dead."

"Only in this life, Noah. There is so much beyond this," Donald replied.

"Why now? Why not when she's sixty or sixty-five?"

Donald tilted his head. "If we want our community as it is now to achieve eternal life, then it has to be now. You know that if we waited that long I, Fiona, your parents, the rest of the elders would be dead and it would be over for us."

Selfish. That was all this was. He was willing to sacrifice his own daughter so he could live in eternal happiness while he was still fit and healthy. Never mind Scarlett wanting to grow up and have a family of her own.

"What about what Scarlett wants?" I asked. "Does it not matter that she has things she wants to achieve?"

"This life won't matter in the next," Dad said. "We'll be reunited. We'll see Scarlett again for eternity. Now, stop this, Noah, you know what is true."

I stood taller. "I won't give her up."

Dad took a step closer. "You either step aside right now so we can find her and you can return home, or this is it. Either way, we'll get her back, but this the only chance you'll get to make the right choice."

"I won't give her up," I repeated.

Dad's face sobered. "All right. Remember that you have made your choice, Noah. There is nothing we can do for you now."

Fear clawed its way up my throat. His eyes hollowed. There was nothing that looked at me like I was his son, his blood. He was choosing Eternal Light. He pulled a blade out of his pocket.

I looked between him and the knife, too shocked that my *dad* had pulled a knife on me.

"Dad, what're you doing?"

"Shh," he said, moving closer. Donald stood behind him, watching. The order would have come from Donald, but the fact that my own father could go ahead with stabbing his child made me sick.

"Dad, don't." I backed up again, taking a sweeping look around the room to see if there was anything I could use to fight him off—an umbrella and an old wooden walking stick that looked like it would break if I picked it up. "You'll regret this for the rest of your life. I'm your *son*. Think about it for a second. How can you believe in Eternal Light and everything Donald's told you if he's asking you to kill? Love, peace, respect, and harmony. Does that sound like what's happening right now?"

My heart thumped against my chest, beating too fast and too hard.

"Dad, please. You know this isn't right."

"Stop talking, Noah. You made your choice, and *you* have to live with the consequences. You are a loose cannon now, a risk to us all and one we are not willing to leave."

I lurched forward, grabbing the arm that held the blade and shoving it away from me. Dad cried out and spun around, trying to shake me off. I held on, fighting for my life, knowing that if I gave him the chance, it could be all over for me.

He stopped being my dad in that moment. When I knew I had to fight against my father to keep him from murdering me, he became nothing but an enemy.

He flung us forward, and my back cracked against the concrete wall, knocking the air from my lungs. Gritting my teeth, I tightened my grip on his wrist and tried to turn the knife back on him.

Donald did nothing but stand and watch. I had expected him to dart after Scarlett.

He must have had other people out there looking for her.

The muscles in my arms ached from the struggle, and I didn't know how much longer I could hold him off. I kicked my leg out, and he grunted as it came in contact with his shin.

"What will Mum think?" I said. "Or Finn?"

"They'll understand because they haven't been poisoned," he said through clenched teeth, straining to get the upper hand. Growling, he slammed me back again, and my head hit the wall with a loud thud. My vision blurred, and I saw black dots float in front of my face.

Dad used it to his full advantage, punching me in the stomach hard enough that I doubled over and felt like I was going to throw up all over the floor. He pushed his whole body weight against me, forcing me to stand up straight. I was pinned against the wall, my abdomen in agony, and I could barely see properly from hitting my head so hard. But I didn't need sight to feel the pinch of the knife against my skin and then the hot, blistering pain as he shoved it into my gut.

I was frozen, suspended in time as he stepped back, retracting the knife. It hurt so badly, but the shock kept me from crumbling to the floor and screaming.

"Likeliness is she went out that door," Donald said. "Let's go."

Neither of them looked back at me as I slowly slid down the wall. I tried to breathe evenly, but I couldn't. I was cold, shivering, and already felt dead.

36

SCARLETT

I couldn't stop running. The stitch in my side slowed me down, but I wasn't going to stop until I found a town. I promised Noah I would keep running, and that was exactly what I was going to do. But I also wanted to go back for him. I was scared about what they'd do after he turned his back on their sick cult.

My feet hit the ground, crunching the crisp leaves beneath them as I went. Sunrise was just around the corner. Between the trees, I could see a glow of orange starting to appear. I had to have been running for two or three hours at least. I hadn't stopped at all, just slowed down to grab a bottle of water from the bag.

I was hungry, thirsty, and tired, but I wasn't going to stop. They could be anywhere in the woods. I was terrified that I'd run into one of them. As far as I knew, I'd been running straight, but without being able to see, I could have easily veered off to the left or right. I just wanted to find someone who could help and get me back to my parents.

I wanted to be safely in my mum's arms. Before I was taken, I had been so angry with them for lying to me. Now I understood what they were protecting me from. I just hoped I got the chance to tell them how much they all meant to me—even Jeremy.

Noah was nowhere to be seen. I half expected him to pop up and tell me to run faster. They loved him, so I wanted to believe that they would never hurt him, but I wasn't so sure. They'd done something to Seamus and Bridget at the house and they were completely innocent. That wasn't supposed to happen. If we'd have known they would do something like that, we'd never have gone there.

Tears leaked from my eyes, rolling down my face. I felt awful for them. They were nice, decent people who had taken us in, and they didn't deserve anything bad. When was it going to end? Who else was going to be hurt over me?

Continuing to run became increasingly difficult. I could feel the fear and heartache slowly start to pull me under, digging its ugly claws into my skin. If I'd just handled my parents telling me the truth better, I wouldn't be here now. If I hadn't fallen in love with Noah, then it never would have happened.

Then I lost my footing on damp, slippery leaves and crashed to the ground. I threw my arms out and pain shot through my wrist. "Ahh," I cried out, instantly stopping myself by slapping my good hand over my mouth.

Sitting on the damp floor of the forest, holding my screaming wrist, I had never felt so alone.

Get up. Keep moving.

I took a few deep breaths and battled the urge to cry. I'd done something to my wrist and while I was at it stretched the cut on my forearm too. Everything seemed hopeless. I forced myself up, crying silently as I hobbled forward again, trying to work up to a jog. My muscles and bones screamed at me to give in, and I almost listened.

But from somewhere, I found the strength to keep going.

Every step sent sharp pains the full length of my legs. I didn't know how much I had left inside before I gave in to the need to curl up and for it all to be over one way or another. But then I heard something. I froze, gripping a dead tree for stability.

Road traffic. I had never been so happy to hear cars before, but I wasn't so stupid to go straight out in case one of the Eternal Light was in it. A shimmer of hope was all I needed to keep going.

I stumbled forward, barely having the energy to move anymore. I saw houses first, on the other side of a road, and burst into tears. The area was built up, and to the right of the housing estate were shops. *There must be a police station nearby. Please.* Sobbing, I ran faster, stopping briefly to make sure there were no cars coming.

I ran along the street, probably going no faster than a walk, desperately trying to see through tear-filled eyes. People stopped and looked, a few pointed, and at the end of the road, two police officers did a double take and then ran toward me. They knew who I was. *Oh thank God.*

"Scarlett Garner?" one of them said as they approached.

I cried harder and collapsed into his arms, nodding my head. He scooped me up and turned around, walking back the way they'd come. "It's all right," he said. "You're safe now."

They had me bundled in the police car within seconds. I rambled about everything—the cult, almost dying, but mostly about Noah. Where was Noah? Even I knew I wasn't making sense, but I couldn't stop the jumbled words flowing out of my mouth.

The officer that sat in the back with me placed his hand on my upper arm. "Scarlett," he said.

I looked over my knees from where I was huddled against the door and finally spoke my only legible word, "Yeah?"

"I need you to calm down so we can find out what happened and help you. Can you do that for me?" I nodded. "Where are they?"

"I-In the forest. Noah's still out there. You have to find him."

"Noah? The one who took you to Ireland?"

I knew how it looked. "Yeah, he was the one who helped me escape in the end. He turned his back on them, and now he's out there, and if he didn't get away in time…" I took a deep, shaky breath. "They found us in a house, and I don't know what they did to the people living there, but Bridget screamed for Seamus and then Noah made me run. Please. *Please* go back to that house, check that the old couple is okay, and find Noah."

"Okay, shh, calm down. We'll have people check that out. Don't worry. Are you hurt?"

I shook my head, even though I was. My feet ached and stung from running barefoot for ages, pain throbbed through my wrist, and the cut to my arm had started to hurt too. But I didn't want to go to the hospital first. They would make it all about me. I needed to go to the police station and tell them what happened so they could find Noah and arrest every crazy member of Eternal Light.

"No, I just need you to find Noah and that house."

He nodded once. "All right."

When we got to the station, I was helped to freshen up in the bathroom, given a hot drink and biscuits, and provided with a blanket to wrap around myself. I sat in a room with my hands hugging a steaming mug of coffee, trying to keep it together long enough so that I could go over everything—again.

"Hello, Scarlett. I'm Detective Crossby but you can call me Adele, and this is my colleague Detective Long. We need to speak to you and ask you a few questions if that's all right?"

I nodded and sat up in the seat. "Do you know where my parents are?"

"They're here in Ireland. We want to have a chat with you first."

Thank God. It was a good sign that they were free to go wherever they wanted. "What do you want to know?"

She scratched the back of her neck, probably not knowing where to start either. There was so much. "Your family said you've no memory before the age of four. Is that correct?"

At least she was still referring to them as my family and not making them out to be child-snatching criminals. "That's right. Want to start from the beginning?"

Detective Crossby smiled and tilted her head in a nod, making her short, black hair slide into her eyes, and I went right back to where I could remember—waking up a scared and confused four-year-old girl.

When I'd told my story, every detail, right up to escaping, two hours had passed. It was the same story I'd already told the police, but they had been lucky enough to only need the condensed version. Naturally, she had a lot of questions.

"So, you were never told where you were really from? You knew nothing of Eternal Light?" Detective Crossby asked.

"No, I only found out…um, a few weeks ago, I think. It was recent anyway, not long before Noah brought me to Dublin. Listen, I know in the eyes of the law my parents did wrong taking me, but the Eternal Light was going to kill me. They saved my life, and I just want to see my family again."

"We understand, Scarlett, but we need to establish all of the facts and make sure you're protected."

"Everything I told you is true, and my parents protect me. They could've left me and lived a normal, lie-free life, but instead they risked everything to keep me safe. No one else out there is going to go to those lengths for me. You have to believe me."

"We do, Scarlett. We just need to hear your side of things, that's all," Detective Crossby said.

"Now you have, can I please see my family? Please?"

She smiled. "Absolutely, in a little while. I promise. We need to take you to the hospital and get you checked out first though."

"Why? I'm fine." *I want my parents.*

"You've been through a terrible ordeal. You're exhausted and probably in dire need of some pain medication, especially for that wrist," she said, lifting an eyebrow.

How did she know my wrist hurt? I'd thought it would have gotten better after a while, but it hadn't; it was throbbing.

I pursed my lips. "But what about—"

She held her hand up. "We're taking you to the hospital to get checked out and then we will call your parents and get them to meet you there. Okay."

It was an order not a question.

Nodding, I replied, "Yeah, okay."

Detective Crossby drove me to the hospital and had me checked out. I had a sprained wrist from the fall and minor cuts and bruises on my arms. The cuts to my feet stung now and walking was slow, but it wasn't too bad.

I was finally given a bed, had an IV for pain relief, a drink, and toast. It was now just after six in the morning, and I'd been awake for twenty-four hours. I felt like putting toothpicks in my eyes just to keep them open.

"Thank you, Adele," I said as she handed me another cup of coffee.

She'd stayed with me, asking the occasional question, while I waited for my parents and Jeremy to arrive. I'd asked for an update on Noah every five seconds, but they hadn't found him or the rest of them yet. It'd been hours. He should've been found by now.

"Are they here yet? Has Noah been found?" I asked, feeling my eyes getting heavy. I yawned and blinked hard. There was no way I was going to sleep until I knew how he was. If I found my way out, then he should've done it by now. I didn't want to think of any reason why he wouldn't be able to find his way out.

"You're exhausted, Scarlett. Please try to relax. Your parents are due here any minute now, and I promise you as soon as we find

Noah, we'll tell you. Now drink your coffee if you won't sleep. I'll wait outside your room until your parents get here."

I waited until she got outside before I collapsed against the pillows. *Please hurry up. All of you.*

37

SCARLETT

I had been in the hospital almost two hours when my parents and brother burst into the room.

"Scarlett!" Mum sobbed. I started crying the instant I saw them. It was over. They were here, and I was safe.

"Mum, I'm so sorry," I said, crying on her shoulder as she held me tighter than she ever had before. She smelled like home, and it made me grip hold of her and never want to let go.

"Shh, it's okay. Everything's going to be okay now, sweetheart."

We sat together crying for a good ten minutes. Dad and Jeremy joined in, huddling together on my bed.

"Are you okay?" Dad asked for the millionth time.

"I am now. Just worried about Noah."

"He'll be fine. They'll find him," Mum said, stroking my hair. "Does your wrist hurt? We can get you some more pain relief."

"I had some not long ago. Stop fussing. I'm fine." Jeremy stared out of the window, at the police officers outside my room. "What's up, Jere?"

He turned back and spoke more to Dad when he replied, "I think we should leave, like right now. If they're all in Ireland and the police feel the need to have two people guarding Scarlett, maybe we should go."

Mum squeezed my hand and looked up at Dad. "He has a point. The police in England can work with the police here. There's no need for us to stay longer then necessary."

"I'm not going anywhere," I said, causing a stunned silence. "I mean it. Noah is out there somewhere and I'm not just leaving." Besides, could they just go somewhere with me? I was still sixteen and a minor in the eyes of the law, they didn't have me or adopt me, so they weren't legally my parents.

"What?" Jeremy said. "These *people* almost killed you and you're worried about one of them?"

"No. He's not one of them; he's one of us. I would be dead now if it wasn't for him."

"None of it would've happened if it wasn't for him," Jeremy said.

I didn't like how Jeremy spoke about him, even though it was understandable. I felt loyalty to Noah and I wasn't going to let him down. "I know that, but it wasn't his fault, not really. He realized the truth and put things right. Sound familiar?"

Jeremy's mouth set into a hard line. "Fine."

"Calm down," Mum said. "Jeremy's just worried. We all are, but we know exactly what you mean. Hopefully Noah will be found soon and then we can go home."

"Can we go home? Are you allowed to do that?"

Dad smiled. "We've been speaking to a very good lawyer and a solicitor, and both seem to think given the unique situation and circumstances, we'll be able to adopt you. It's going to be a long process, but we'll fight through it."

"So, I can't go home with you yet?" I asked, panicking. Where would I go? I didn't want to be in some facility, I wanted my room in the house I shared with my *family*.

"We've already applied for a Residence Order, which will basically mean we'll be fostering you. After that, we'll go for adoption. Our case is a little more complicated than most, but we're hoping that might go in our favor," Dad said.

"And if it doesn't? What happened anyway? Were you arrested?"

"Shh," Mum said. "We were all questioned for hours when we reported you missing, but we're thankful that they believed us. Your father had two leaflets on Eternal Light and our stories matched, of course, so that helped. We've been told that no charges will be brought against us for taking you, as your life was literally on the line and we were fearful of what the cult would do if we were found, which is why we never told anyone, not even you."

"So, you won't go to prison and I can still live with you?"

Mum squeezed my hand again. "We're not going to prison and there is no battle we won't take on to have you with us."

That wasn't quite what I wanted to hear, but I realized it was probably the best I was going to get right now.

"Okay. When will we know if I can go home with you?"

"We're hoping in the next few days. The doctors want to keep you here until tomorrow anyway."

Right. After everything I'd been through, and my family had been through, you'd have thought I'd just have been allowed to go home with them. They saved my damn life. It wasn't like they'd taken me because they just felt like having a daughter that day.

"Don't worry, love, there is no way we're not going home as a family," she said, brushing my hair from my face.

I nodded, wishing I could be as optimistic as her. It would be cruel and wrong if they tried to split us up, but it wasn't like those things didn't happen every day.

"Will you tell me about Fiona and Donald? They treated you well?"

"Yeah. Well, besides the obvious."

Smiling sadly, she brushed my hair again. "I'm glad they weren't cruel." She frowned. "You know what I mean."

"I do. How were you and Dad part of that, Mum? I don't understand how it could have ever made sense."

"Neither do we now. At first, Eternal Light was just about living off the land. It was such a simple and beautiful way to live. We did believe that there was someone who would take us into eternal peace, much like any other god in any other religion. But then you were born and Donald announced that you were 'the one.' He said he could feel it the second he held you. For hundreds of years, animals and humans had been offered as sacrifices. We knew that; we studied it and already celebrated the elements and nature with rituals and food offerings. When Donald talked about sacrificing you on your fourth birthday we felt joy…" She cleared her throat and blinked to stop her tears falling. "We felt joy because it wasn't the end, not for you and not for us."

"Right." I couldn't dwell on that, it'd happened, and the main thing was they had taken me away. "How did you and Dad start questioning it?"

"We asked Donald why when you were four and not older, so you could experience growing up and falling in love. He said it was because he couldn't risk our community being found and broken up or something happening to you. It all made sense and we accepted it, but the more we saw you, the more unfair it seemed. We had many late-night talks when Jeremy was in bed, and the more we spoke, the less sense any of it made."

"Do you know what happened to Evelyn?"

Mum gulped but wasn't surprised that I knew about her. "No, honey, I don't. When we settled down, we tried to find out. There were no reports of a child being found, so we assumed Eternal Light had her. She wouldn't be in any danger if she was back with them; she wasn't the one. She wasn't there, huh?"

"No. They let her go."

Mum gasped.

"They sent her into the woods as some sort of messed-up exchange—her life for my return. How terrible is that?" My heart hurt for a little sister I didn't even know. "Didn't you know about that?"

Dad's face paled. "We knew that she was born to protect you; we thought they meant spiritually. God, how stupid we were."

"I'm so sorry, Scarlett." I could tell what Mum was thinking, and I guessed she was right: Evelyn probably died out in the forest. But what if she hadn't? Either way, she deserved to be found. I wasn't sure how much resources the police would put into looking for a girl who had gone missing ten years ago. They would have to look. They were legally required to look, surely.

"Why haven't they found him yet?" I asked, changing one painful conversation for another. At least I knew he was definitely still out there. For now, I had to concentrate on him. "I need to go and help look."

"No, honey. We just got you back and you need rest. You need to stay right here. They'll find him," Mum said.

"But I don't understand why they haven't found him. What did they do to him, Mum? I shouldn't have gone. I should've stayed and helped him."

"Shh," she whispered, stroking my hair again. "You did the right thing, and Noah did the right thing by making you run."

Logically I knew getting as far away from them as possible was the right thing, but they were insane and I didn't, for one second, think that they wouldn't hurt Noah. He'd disobeyed them, gone against everything they believe and everything they'd taught him to save me. I'd hated him at first, but he'd done the right thing and that was what mattered.

"Can you take me for a walk please? I'm tired of sitting in this bed, worrying."

Dad stood up. "I think that will do you good. Do you need a wheelchair?"

"Yeah, thanks, Dad." My cut feet made walking very, very difficult.

"I'll go with you to find a chair," Jeremy said.

"How're you feeling?" Mum asked when they left the room. "And I don't mean physically."

I took a deep breath. That, I didn't know. "Right now it all seems like a really bad dream. I know what happened. I know how scared

I was and then how relieved I was to escape, but I don't know. I feel disconnected. Do you think there's something wrong with me?"

"No, I don't. I know *exactly* what you mean, Scarlett. You're safe, thank God, but it's not over yet, is it?"

I shook my head. "Not until Noah's found. He was part of it."

"Yes," she said. "He had us all fooled, but that's something I can identify with. For years your father and I, even you and Jeremy, believed the same things Noah was taught, and like us, he realized the truth and turned his back on it."

"What if he never gets a chance at a normal life?"

"I have faith that he will."

We didn't even know if he was alive.

Jeremy held the door open as Dad wheeled in a chair. "Your chariot awaits. We're only allowed down the corridors on the ground floor, but it's better than these four walls, right?"

"Definitely. I'll take anything right now," I replied.

Swinging my legs off the bed, I stood carefully and winced as my tender feet screamed at me for putting weight on them. "Here," Jeremy said, leaping forward and taking my weight with his arm around my waist.

"Thanks."

Dad pushed the wheelchair because I couldn't get it to go in a straight line. It felt good to be out of bed. We rounded the corner with Mum and Dad behind and Jeremy walking next to me. I even managed to ignore the police officer behind us.

We went through the double doors to go through the Accident and Emergency waiting room when paramedics and doctors came jogging toward us, gripping the sides of a gurney and talking rapidly.

Dad moved me to the side of the corridor so they had plenty of room to get through. The first thing I saw was blood, and then my whole world came to an abrupt stop. "No!" I pushed to my feet as Noah's pale, sleeping face cut my heart.

38

SCARLETT

"Oh God, no, no, no."

"Scarlett," Mum said, rushing to me but it was too late. I was up and hobbling along toward them.

"Noah! Noah!"

One of the nurses looked back and held her hand up. "You know him?"

I nodded frantically and collapsed to the floor, consumed with grief. "Is he dead?" I asked, sobbing on the floor.

Mum knelt down and wrapped me in her arms.

"He's dead, isn't he? They killed him. He's gone."

The same nurse had a quick conversation with someone else and then came rushing toward us as they took Noah through another door.

"Scarlett, sweetheart, you need to get up," Dad said. I could barely understand what he'd said. My mind was stuck on seeing Noah like that. He couldn't die. After everything we'd been through and what he'd done to get me away from Eternal Light, he couldn't just be gone.

"I can't. It hurts so much," I sobbed, trying to catch my breath. He was gone and I had never felt anything hurt so badly.

"Are you all right?" the nurse said, keeling in front of me.

"No. Is he okay? You need to make him okay," I said, gripping her arm.

"Shh, we're doing everything we can for him, but I need you to help. Can you do that?"

I nodded. "Whatever you need just, *please*, don't let him die." Tears burned my cheeks and made everything blurry.

"Do you know his name?"

"Noah. It's Noah."

She smiled and nodded her head. "We thought so."

"How do you know?"

"He was found about thirty minutes ago in the forest."

The police had found him.

"Why is he bleeding? What's wrong with him."

"Let's get you back to your room and then—"

"No. I'm not going anywhere until I know he's okay."

"All right. Maybe we can get you back in your chair and you can go to a room up the corridor to wait."

I looked longingly at the door they'd taken him through. They wouldn't let me in there, so I didn't even bother asking.

"That would be great," Dad said, picking me up and carrying me to the room. Jeremy wheeled the chair in too. After lowering me onto one of the chairs, Dad kneeled on the floor, probably worried that I would take off.

"What happened to him?" I asked.

The nurse smiled but her eyes didn't. "He's received a stab wound to his abdomen and lost a lot of blood."

Stabbed. I coughed, sobbing at the same time. "What?"

"He'll be all right," Mum said, stroking my hair from the seat beside mine.

What if he wasn't?

I cried harder. I'd lost him once but we'd found each other. I couldn't lose him forever. We'd been through too much for it to end like this. We deserved a chance, a proper chance.

"Mum," I said, leaning over and crying on her shoulder. My body shook with every painful sob. "He can't die, he can't die," I chanted. It was too much. I wanted to retreat back into myself and stop the pain, but Noah was a part of me now. There was no way to stop it hurting so much.

"Shh, honey, it's okay," Mum soothed. "I'm *sure* he's going to be all right." She was crying too. That didn't look good. Noah wasn't her favorite person right now, but she was still upset over what was happening to him.

"I'll go and check on him and let you know when we have an update," the nurse said.

"Thank you," Dad replied.

The update could be *he's fine* or *I'm sorry, there's nothing more we can do.*

"I need him, Mum."

"I know you do. Jonathan, Jeremy, can you follow and see if there is any immediate news you can find out rather than waiting?"

"You've forgiven him completely?" Mum asked when Dad left, Jeremy following.

I curled up against her side. "Yes. Have you?"

She was silent for a minute. "I think so. I understand what it's like to be completely controlled by someone or something else. Don't get me wrong. I'm angry. You could've died. But I don't blame Noah. He was merely a pawn in their game. They would sacrifice his life to get what they want. They make you feel part of the best thing on earth. I could never judge Noah for something I would've done when I was still under their influence."

"Do you think Jeremy will come around?"

"Of course. It's a little more difficult for him. He was so young and never knew the level of control people like that have over you. Noah believed he was doing what was best for everyone, you included. His love for you was able to help him override and question what he was taught, just like us. Then he was able to think freely and form his own opinion."

"Thank you," I said, wiping my wet cheeks with my hands only for them to be damp again the next second. "It means so much that you don't hate him. I knew you'd understand." How could she not though, really?

"Of course, honey. He's going to need a lot of support. Living outside the commune, knowing what a fool you'd been for so long, isn't easy."

"I'll be there for him."

She smiled and kissed the side of my head. "I had a feeling you might."

"What do you think is going to happen to him now? I mean after he's better, because he will get better." There was no way he couldn't.

"He'll be fine, and I guess that's up to him. He is in charge of his life now. For the first time ever, he can do what he wants, go where he wants, and believe what he wants."

"Yeah," I replied. He deserved that, and I thought he'd want to be with me. I took a deep breath and threaded my fingers together, nervously tapping the backs of my hands. Now I was sitting down and a little calmer than before I'd felt the consequences of standing up. My feet hurt, but it was nothing compared to the feeling of possibly losing Noah.

I loved him so much still—probably more now than before he'd betrayed me. It hadn't been easy for him to turn his back on everything he'd known and risk his life to save me. Now it was my turn to help him and *when* he was better and out of hospital, I was determined to do just that.

39

SCARLETT

Dad and Jeremy had come back shortly after leaving, having heard nothing new. It was another thirty minutes before I found out what was going on. Adele turned up and tilted her head to the side.

"You okay, Scarlett?"

"I'm fine. Have you heard anything?"

"I've just spoken to the doctor and he'll be in soon. Noah's out of surgery and doing fine."

I closed my eyes as the relief took my breath away. Mum squeezed my hand. "Thank God. Do you know when I can see him?"

"A nurse will come and get you...from *your* room, so let's get you back up there. They're just getting him settled first."

I nodded and accepted Dad's help into the wheelchair. "Okay, let's go, so we don't miss her."

Dad laughed and started pushing me toward the door.

Adele waited until I was back in my room and then said, "Thirty-seven members of Eternal Light have been picked up. There was a massive raid on the commune and most of them were still there. Donald and Shaun were found on the edge of the woods, still looking for you. The couple from the house is okay.

They're in the hospital with stab wounds but nothing as serious as Noah's injuries."

"Oh my God," I whispered. They were only trying to help us and that was what they got because of it. Guilt burned in my chest. I wiped yet another round of tears and replied, "Okay, thank you."

"I'll be outside if you need me," Adele said. "Nurse shouldn't be too long now."

I practically leaped out of bed when the nurse came for me. Mum, Dad, and Jeremy trailed behind. I hadn't had a chance to speak to my brother about Noah yet, but his clear concern meant he'd forgiven him too—or at the very least, was willing to work on it. There was no doubt that Noah saved my life, and in the end, that was the part that mattered.

"Slow down, Scarlett," Jeremy said. "I'm not carrying your arse when you collapse on the floor."

He was right. I should slow down. I was still beyond tired and every single part of my body ached beyond belief, especially my legs, but Noah was alive and wanting to see me as much as I wanted to see him. A normal walking pace was not an option.

"I won't collapse." Well, I would, but not until I saw he was okay and was back in my bed.

I reached his room with a lot of help from Dad, who was practically holding me up the entire way, and turned to my family.

"You want a few minutes first?" Mum asked.

"Yeah, thanks."

There was a police officer outside his room, but he gestured with a nod for me to go in. I recognized him from the station, but he hadn't been one of the ones questioning me.

"Noah," I said, slowly peeking around the door. He was pale and looked exhausted, but he was sitting against his pillows *alive*. "Can I come in?"

He half smiled and nodded once. "You all right?" He even sounded tired.

"I'm fine, just worried about you," I said, taking very slow, careful steps toward him.

"Why?"

"Um, because you were stabbed."

"Wasn't too bad. Good thing my dad has bad aim."

I stopped dead, eyes filling with tears. *No.* I had assumed it was Donald. "Your *dad* did that?"

"Don't be surprised, Scarlett. Your parents were going to do the same to you."

I guess I shouldn't have been surprised, but his parents had raised him for sixteen years. How could his own dad turn around and try to kill him?

"I know, but I'm still sorry."

Sighing, he replied, "Yeah, me too. Scarlett, why are you even talking to me?"

"Because of what happened."

"That's exactly why you shouldn't be talking to me. I know what you said when we were out in the forest, but we're safe now. The danger is over. You don't have to forgive what I did to you…"

"You saved my life, Noah. I'm not going to pretend that I

understand Eternal Light, but I do know that when it came down to it, you put me before what you'd believed your whole life. And that matters." I sat on the bed. "Seeing you like that, being wheeled into the hospital…" Taking a deep breath, I continued, "It changed me. I was terrified that you wouldn't make it. You chose me and you almost died because of it."

He gulped. "Yeah, well, I love you. I always knew it, but I didn't know how strong it was. I love you more than everything I've ever known, and I didn't care if the prophecy was true and you were the key to eternal life because you deserve this life. Every dream or goal you have you deserve a chance of achieving."

"You're pretty amazing," I said, swallowing what was likely to turn into an ugly cry. My heart swelled at his words. "And I love you too. I tried to stop when I found out who you were but I couldn't turn it off. That actually made me even angrier with you. But I do *really* love you."

He held his hand out. "Come and lie with me for a bit."

"I don't want to hurt you."

"You won't. Just stay on the side that wasn't stabbed."

I dropped my head. He was stabbed saving me. I lay on the bed against his pillows, keeping a little distance so I didn't put any pressure on his body at all.

"I won't break, Scarlett." He pulled me closer and I laid my head on his shoulder, keeping my arms and legs away from him.

"You were stabbed, and I don't want to do anything to hurt you more." He'd lost a lot of blood.

"Believe me, you lying with me won't hurt. How are you feeling?"

"Tired, sore, and achy but nothing a really, *really* long sleep won't fix."

There was a lot more than that to fix, but I couldn't even think about the emotional stuff right now. If I stopped to admit how scared I still was and much I just wanted to hide away, I wasn't sure if I'd be able to make it through another minute.

"It's going to be all right now," he whispered.

Now was the start of the hard work to be okay, but that was fine. I didn't have to fight for my life now; I just had to fight to come to terms with having to do it.

"My parents and Jeremy are outside," I said, tracing the letter *S* and *N* on his chest with my finger.

"They didn't want to come in." He said it as a statement, not a question.

"That's not it at all. They just wanted to give us some time first."

He looked away in shame. "I'm surprised they let you near me again."

"They've been you, Noah. Don't forget that."

He raised his head and looked me in the eye. "They don't hate me?"

"No one hates you." Except probably every member of Eternal Light. "I want to help you."

His smile was unconvincing, and I wasn't sure if he didn't think I should help because he felt guilty or if he wanted a clean break and was worried about ditching me. A clean break would probably be the most sensible thing to do; we had a lot to work through, but it wasn't what we both wanted, and if we left each other, then Eternal Light would win.

Mum, Dad, and Jeremy gave us ten minutes before coming in. They had nothing but sympathy and understanding for Noah. It made him uncomfortable. He didn't think he deserved it. But you shouldn't just forgive and help someone when they feel worthy; you should do it just because.

"What's your next move?" Jeremy asked. He was still mad at Noah, but he was trying, and I couldn't ask for more than that.

"I don't know. I don't have a plan yet," he said. "I'm eighteen next month but—"

"What?" I asked, cutting him off. He wasn't that old.

"Almost eighteen?" Dad said. "Noah, we thought you were sixteen."

"That's what I was told to be. My birthday is the same, Scarlett. I just lied about my age." He closed his eyes and sighed. "I'm so, so sorry."

I nodded. After everything that'd happened, him being a year older wasn't that big of a deal. "Okay," I said, wondering just how much more there was that he'd lied about. I was nearly sixteen, and he was nearly eighteen; that wasn't too bad. I was fine about it and understood he was just following instructions, but I wanted to know the real him. I doubted even Noah knew who the real him was right now though.

Even if he didn't know what his next move should be, I did. "I want Noah to come home with us," I said.

The atmosphere thickened. Mum and Dad, although clearly not thrilled, couldn't really say no. They were in the same position as Noah when they'd left the cult.

Noah shook his head. "No. After everything, Scarlett, you can't ask your parents to do that."

"She's not asking," Dad said. "We're offering."

Jeremy's eyebrows shot up in shock, and I think mine did the same. I expected to have to chew Dad's ear off before I got him to agree.

"Jonathan, you've done more than enough for me already."

Dad held his hand up. "You saved my daughter's life. I almost stood by and let her be sacrificed too."

I licked my lips. I hated hearing about myself like that. I was nothing to my birth parents but the key to an imaginary door. It wasn't a great feeling.

"There are going to be rules. You and Scarlett will *not* share a room, you will not be around each other without being fully dressed, and the door will remain open. We will figure out what's next for you, be that education or work, and we'll do it together."

Noah breathed deeply and squeezed my hand. "I don't know what to say."

"You don't need to say anything," Mum said. "You deserve a life the same as me, my husband, and my children. It won't be easy. Believe me, it's a huge adjustment, but if you're willing to put in the work, then we're willing to help you."

Smiling, Noah replied, "Thank you. I'll do whatever it takes. I *want* a normal life like everyone else. I feel like I've lost seventeen years; my whole childhood was a lie. I want to be a better person, to deserve Scarlett."

I wasn't even going to waste my breath commenting on that stupid remark.

"It's okay. Your life starts now, and I promise it's going to be pretty great from now on," I said.

"Not too great though, Scar, yeah?" Jeremy said.

My face caught on fire. I wasn't ashamed that I'd been with Noah. I loved him, but I sure didn't want my parents to know anything about it. Ever.

"Ignore him," Noah said, fighting a smile.

Twenty minutes later, Noah and I were left alone again while my family went to get something to eat. "Are you really okay?" I asked.

He smiled from his bed. "Never better. I get the chance at a normal life with the girl I'm crazy about. That is, if you'll have me?"

I shrugged. "Suppose. You did take a knife for me and all."

He sighed, content. "So, I get out of here in a couple days and we'll be living under the same roof." *Same roof but not living together*. Rules, rules, rules. I loved my parents so much. "You've got to finish school, and I have to do something to get some sort of qualification. Life is going to be good, Scarlett."

I took his hand, not knowing how this would go down. "It is," I replied. Man, I could not wait to get out of the hospital, go home to England, and help Noah adjust to normal life.

"When we get back, what do you want to do first?" he asked, probably thinking I'd say a movie night. I had other plans.

Licking my lips, I replied, "I have a sister out there, Noah, and I'm going to find her."

EPILOGUE

SCARLETT

Today marked the two-year anniversary of my almost-death. Last year, Noah barely said a word to me, too caught up in his continued guilt. This year was going to be different. We'd worked through a lot of issues, fought each other and others to stay together. It had taken a lot, but we were there. We were secure and solid, and everyone around us now accepted that.

Noah had gotten himself a job after taking exams. Eternal Light educated their children, but they had no formal education. He'd been working for a small marketing company for almost a year and loved his job. It paid well enough for him to rent a flat while he saved to eventually buy a house.

My parents had offered to let him stay until he had a down payment, but he was keen to get out and do it for himself. I think my dad respected him a whole lot more for that. And in a month's time, I would be eighteen and planned to move in with him. I told my parents I was thinking logically, because his house was closer to my university and that would mean I didn't need to pay to stay in their dorms. We all knew it was because I wanted to be with him all the time.

I sat on Noah's sofa, studying for my last final exam while he cooked us dinner. It was these results that would determine if I had a shot at getting into the university I wanted, so my stress levels were through the roof.

But something else was weighing on my mind, something that rarely left.

"Noah, have you spoken to Chad recently?"

"No, I'll call him tomorrow if you want?"

"Yeah, thanks."

Chad was a guy Noah worked with. He was kind of a geek in the sense that he could hack into anything. He'd been helping me try to find out what happened to Evelyn. The police had looked, but with miles and miles of forest and ten years passing, they couldn't put the resources into it.

He poked his head around the door and smiled down at me sitting cross-legged on his living room floor surrounded by books. "I love that you won't give up on her."

"I hope that I find her and tell her that at least one member of her family cares. If she's…dead, then she deserves a proper burial. She deserves justice and peace."

After Eternal Light had been found, they'd been rehabilitated in psychiatric units. Fiona and Donald were in prison, along with Noah's dad. The day Shaun was sent down for kidnapping and attempted murder was incredible.

Noah walked into the room when he saw me drifting off to darker places. It'd taken me a long time to get past what had happened, but I'd done it. Forgetting Evelyn would help—thinking about her brought so many memories of Eternal Light back—but I couldn't forget.

Our parents had left her in the middle of the forest, scared and alone. I would not let her down.

Sitting down in front of me, he pulled me onto his lap and held me. I wasn't going to cry, but I was close. Thinking about what they did to her made every part of me ache. She was just a little girl. There was no humanity in them at all.

"Hey, come back to me."

"Sorry," I said, tucking my head under his chin. "I promised myself I would get through these notes before I asked you about Chad."

"Do you want me to call him now? I can if it will take your mind off Evelyn long enough to allow you to focus."

"No, it's fine. I don't want to disturb him now. He would call if he had news. We can check in tomorrow."

Chad had only been looking for a month. Before that, it had been just me contacting everyone I could around the area. No one knew anything. No one outside Eternal Light even knew of her existence. It seemed hopeless, but she was somewhere.

"All right, I'll contact him before work. I'm proud of you."

I wrapped my arms around his back and snuggled closer. "I'm proud of you too."

Laughing quietly, he kissed the top of my head. "I'm going to get back to making dinner. You need to eat if you're planning on studying late again."

I untangled myself from him but he didn't get up. He sat on his knees, lifted my chin with his finger, and kissed me. "I love you, Scarlett," he murmured into the kiss.

When he pulled away, I replied, "I love you more."

Kicking his eyebrow up in the way he did whenever I said that, he stood. "She's alive, sweetheart, and we'll find her," he said, and went back to cooking.

He always said that, and I had hope too. I wouldn't give up on her. She was my little sister and I loved her. Whatever happened, I would find out. *I'm coming, Evie.*

ACKNOWLEDGMENTS

I would first like to say thank you to my editor, Aubrey, for helping me develop this book, and to the design team for creating the perfect cover.

Second, I need to thank fellow Sourcebooks author Ali Novak, for always being on the end of the Facebook PM while I was writing and editing *Awake*. Ali, thank you for all of your support through this process.

Lastly, thank you to my family. To my husband, Joe, for never complaining when I wrote into the early hours and neglected him, and to my mum, Sharon, and mother-in-law, Vicky, for babysitting my son when I needed to meet a deadline.

NOT ALL FLOWERS GROW WEAK IN THE DARK...

Don't miss

THE
CELLAR

Natasha Preston

1

SUMMER

Saturday, July 24th (Present)

Looking out my bedroom window, I'm faced with yet another dull English summer day. The heavy clouds made it look way too dark for July, but not even that was going to faze me. Tonight I was going to celebrate the end of the school year at a gig by a school band, and I was determined to have some fun.

"Hey, what time are you leaving?" Lewis asked. He let himself into my room—as usual—and sat down on the bed. We'd been together over a year, so we were more than comfortable with each other now. Sometimes I missed the time when Lewis didn't tell me he was getting off the phone because he needed to pee or when he would pick up his dirty underwear *before* I came over. My mum was right: the longer you were with a man, the grosser they became. Still, I wouldn't change him. You're supposed to accept someone you love for who they were, so I accepted his messiness.

I shrugged and studied my reflection in the mirror. My hair was boring, flat, and never looked right. I couldn't even pull off the messy look. No matter how "easy" the steps to the perfect bedhead look were in a magazine, I never could make it work. "In a minute. Do I look okay?"

Apparently the most attractive thing was confidence. But what did you do if you weren't confident? That couldn't be faked without it being obvious. I wasn't model pretty or *Playboy* sexy, and I didn't have bucket loads of confidence. Basically, I was screwed and downright lucky that Lewis was so blind.

He smirked and rolled his eyes—his *here she goes again* look. It used to annoy him at first, but now I think it just amused him. "You know I can see you in the mirror, right?" I said, glaring at his reflection.

"You look beautiful. As always," he replied. "Are you sure you don't want me to drop you off tonight?"

I sighed. *This again.* The club where the gig was being held was barely a two-minute walk from my house. It was a walk that I had done so many times I could make it there blindfolded. "No thanks. I'm fine walking. What time are you leaving?"

He shrugged and pursed his lips. I loved it when he did that. "Whenever your lazy brother's ready. Are you sure? We can give you a lift on the way."

"It's fine, seriously! I'm leaving right now, and if you're waiting for Henry to get ready, you'll be a while."

"You shouldn't walk alone at night, Sum."

I sighed again, deeper, and slammed my brush down on the wooden dresser. "Lewis, I've been walking around on my own for *years*. I used to walk to and from school every day, and I'll do it again next year. These"—I slapped my legs for emphasis—"work perfectly fine."

His eyes trailed down to my legs and lit up. "Hmm, I can see that."

Grinning, I pushed him back on the bed and sat on his lap. "Can you take your overprotective boyfriend hat off and kiss me?" Lewis chuckled, and his blue eyes lit up as his lips met mine.

Even after eighteen months, his kisses still made my heart skip a beat. I started liking him when I was eleven. He would come home with Henry after football practice every week while his mum was at work. I thought it was just a silly crush—like the one I also had on Usher at the time—and didn't think anything of it. But when he still gave me butterflies four years later, I knew it had to be something more.

"You two are disgusting." I jumped back at the sound of my brother's deep, annoying voice.

I rolled my eyes. "Shut up, Henry."

"Shut up, Summer," he shot back.

"It's impossible to believe you're eighteen."

"Shut up, Summer," he repeated.

"Whatever. I'm going," I said and pushed myself off Lewis. I gave him one last kiss and slipped out of the room.

"Idiot," Henry muttered. *Immature idiot*, I thought. We did get along—sometimes—and he was the best big brother I could ask for, but he drove me crazy. I had no doubt we would bicker until we died.

"Summer, are you now leaving?" Mum called from the kitchen. *No, I'm walking out the door for fun!*

"Yeah."

"Sweetheart, be careful," Dad said.

"I will. Bye," I replied quickly and walked out the door before they could stop me. They still treated me like I was in elementary school and couldn't go out alone. Our town was probably—actually definitely—the most boring place on earth; nothing even remotely interesting ever happened.

The most excitement we'd ever had was two years ago when old Mrs. Hellmann—yeah, like the mayonnaise—went missing and was found hours later wondering the sheep field looking for her late husband. The whole town was looking for her. I still remember the buzz of something finally happening.

I started walking along the familiar pavement toward the pathway next to the graveyard. That was the only part of walking alone that I didn't like. Graveyards. They were scary—fact—and especially when you were alone. I subtly glanced around while I walked along the footpath. I felt uneasy, even after passing the graveyard. We had moved to this neighborhood when I was five, and I had always felt safe here. My childhood had been spent playing out in the street with my friends, and as I got older, I hung out at the park or club. I knew this town and the people in it like the back of my hand, but the graveyard *always* creeped me out.

I pulled my jacket tightly around myself and picked up the pace. The club was almost in view, just around the next corner. I glanced over my shoulder again and gasped as a dark figure stepped out from behind a hedge.

"Sorry, dear, did I frighten you?"

I sighed in relief as old Harold Dane came into view. I shook my head. "I'm fine."

He lifted up a heavy-looking black bag and threw it into his garbage can with a deep grunt as if he had been lifting weights. His skinny frame was covered in wrinkled, saggy skin. He looked like he'd snap in half if he bent over. "Are you going to the disco?"

I grinned at choice of word. *Disco.* Ha! That's probably what they called it back when he was a teenager. "Yep. I'm meeting my friends there."

"Well, you have a good night, but watch your drinks. You don't know what the boys today slip in pretty young girls' drinks," he warned, shaking his head as if it were the scandal of the year and every teenage boy was out to date-rape everyone.

Laughing, I raised my hand and waved. "I'll be careful. Night."

"Good night, dear."

The club was visible from Harold's house, and I relaxed as I approached the entrance. My family and Lewis had made me jumpy; it was ridiculous. As I got to the door, my friend Kerri grabbed my arm from beside me, making me jump. She laughed, her eyes alight with humor. *Hilarious.* "Sorry. Have you seen Rachel?"

My heart slowed to its normal pace as my brain processed my friend's face and not the face of the *Scream* dude or Freddy Kruger. "Not seen anyone. Just got here."

"Damn it. She ran off after another argument with the idiot, and her phone's turned off!" Ah, the idiot. Rachel had a very on/off relationship with her boyfriend, Jack. I never understood that—if you pissed each other off 90 percent of the time, then just call it a day. "We should find her."

Why? I had hoped for a fun evening with friends, not chasing after a girl who should have just dumped her loser boyfriend's arse already. Sighing, I resigned myself to the inevitable. "Okay, which direction did she go?"

Kerri gave me a flat look. "If I knew that, Summer..."

Rolling my eyes, I pulled her hand, and we started walking back toward the road. "Fine. I'll go left, you go right." Kerri saluted and marched off to the right. I laughed at her and then went my way. Rachel had better be close.

I walked across the middle of the playing field near the club, heading toward the gate at the back to see if she had taken the shortcut through to her house. The air turned colder, and I rubbed my arms. Kerri said Rachel's phone was off, but I tried calling it anyway and, of course, it went straight to voice mail. If she didn't want to speak to anyone, then why were we trying to find her?

I left an awkward message on her phone—I hated leaving messages—and walked through the gate toward the skate ramp at the back of the park. The clouds shifted, creating a gray swirling effect across the sky. It looked moody, creepy but pretty at the same times. A light, cool breeze whipped across my face, making my light honey-blond hair—according to hairdresser wannabe Rachel—blow in my face and a shudder ripple through my body.

"Lily?" a deep voice called from behind me. I didn't recognize it. I spun around and backed up as a tall, dark-haired man stepped into view. My stomach dropped. Had he been hiding between the trees? What the heck? He was close enough that I could see the satisfied grin on his face and neat hair not affected by the wind. How much hairspray must he have used? If I weren't freaked out, I would have asked what product he used because my hair never played fair. "Lily," he repeated.

"No. Sorry." Gulping, I took another step back and scanned the area in the vain hope that one of my friends would be nearby. "I'm not Lily," I mumbled, straightening my back and looking up at him in an attempt to appear confident. He towered over me, glaring down at me with creepily dark eyes.

He shook his head. "No. You are Lily."

"I'm *Summer*. You have the wrong person." *You utter freak!*

I could hear my pulse crashing in my ears. How stupid to give him my real name. He continued to stare at me, smiling. It made me feel sick. Why did he think I was Lily? I hoped that I just looked like his daughter or something and he wasn't some crazy weirdo.

I took another step back and searched around to find a place that I could escape if needed. The park was big, and I was still near the back, just in front of the trees. There was no way anyone would be able to see me from here. That thought alone made my eyes sting. Why did I come here alone? I wanted to scream at myself for being so stupid.

"You are Lily," he repeated.

Before I could blink, he threw his arms forward and grabbed me. I tried to shout, but he clasped his hand over my mouth, muffling my screams. What the heck was he doing? I thrashed my arms, frantically trying to get out of his grip. *Oh God, he's going to kill me.* Tears poured from my eyes. My heart raced. My fingertips tingled and my stomach knotted with fear. *I'm going to die. He's going to kill me.*

The Lily man pulled me toward him with such force the air left my lungs in a rush as I slammed against him. He spun me around so my back pressed tightly against his chest. And with his hand sealed over my mouth and nose, I struggled to breathe. I couldn't move, and I didn't know if it was because he had such a strong iron grip or if I was too stunned. He had me, and he could do whatever he wanted because I couldn't bloody move a muscle.

He pushed me through the gate at the back of the park and then through the field. I tried again to scream for help, but against his palm, I hardly made a sound. He whispered "Lily" over and over while he dragged me toward a white van. I watched trees pass me by and birds fly over us, landing on branches. Everything carried on as normal. Oh God, I needed to get away now. I dug my feet into the ground and screamed so hard that my throat instantly started to hurt. It was useless though; no one was around to hear me but the birds.

He tugged his arm back, pressing it into my stomach. I cried out in pain. As soon as he let go to open the van's back door, I screamed for help. "Shut up!" he shouted as he pushed me inside the vehicle. My head smashed into the side of the van while I struggled.

"Please let me go. Please. I'm *not* Lily. Please," I begged and gripped the side of my throbbing head. My whole body shook with fear and I gasped for breath, desperate to get some air into my lungs.

His nostrils flared and his eyes widened. "You're bleeding. Clean it. Now," he growled in a menacing tone that made me tremble. He handed me a tissue and sanitizer. *What?* I was so scared and confused that I could barely move. "Clean it now!" he screamed, making me flinch.

I lifted the tissue to my head and wiped away the blood. My hands shook so much that I almost spilled the sanitizer as I squirted it onto my palm and rubbed it into the cut. The stinging caused me to clench my jaw. I winced at how much it hurt. The man watched me carefully, breathing heavily and appearing repulsed. What the heck was wrong with him?

My vision quickly blurred as fresh tears spilled over and rolled down my cheeks. He grabbed the tissue, careful not to touch the bloody part, threw it into a plastic bag, and shoved it into his pocket. He then cleaned his hands with the sanitizer. I watched in horror. My heart slamming against my chest. Was this really happening?

"Give me your phone, Lily," he said calmly, holding his hand out. I cried harder as I reached into my own pocket, took my phone out, and handed it to him. "Good girl." He slammed the back door shut, immersing me in darkness. No! I screamed and banged against the door. A moment later, I heard the unmistakable roar of the engine and felt a rocking sensation as the van began moving. He was driving. Driving me somewhere. To do what?

"Please help me!" I shouted and repeatedly slammed my fists

down on the back door. It was useless; there was no way the door was going to move, but I had to try. Every time he turned a corner, I fell against the side of the van, but I got up and continued shouting for help and banging on the door. My breathing turned to panting, and I gasped for breath. I didn't feel as if air was getting into my lungs.

He continued driving, and with every passing second, I started to give up hope. I was going to die. The van finally came to a stop and my body froze. *This is it. This is where he kills me.*

After a few painful seconds of waiting and listening to his footsteps crunch on the ground outside, the door flew open and I whimpered. I wanted to say something, but I couldn't find my voice. He smiled and reached in, grabbing my arm before I had chance to jump back. We were in the middle of nowhere. There was a large redbrick house sitting at the end of a stone path; tall bushes and trees surrounded the house. Who could ever find me here? There was nothing around I recognized; it looked the same as every other country lane surrounding my town. I had no idea where he'd brought me.

I tried to resist as he pulled me from the van and pushed me toward the house, but he was too strong. I screamed loudly in one final attempt to get help, and this time he allowed it, which was so much scarier—it meant that he didn't think anyone would be able to hear me.

I repeated over and over in my head *I love you, Lewis* as I prepared to die—and for whatever he had planned for me before that. My heart sunk. What did he plan? He pushed me through the front door and along a long hallway. I tried to take it all in, the color of the walls, where the doors were, in the hope I could escape, but the shock of what was happening stopped anything sticking. From what I could tell the hall was bright, and it was warm, not what I expected at all. My blood turned to ice in my veins, and the pinch in my arms as his fingers dug into my skin stung. I looked down and saw his fingertips sink into my arm, making four craters in my skin.

My body came into sharp, hard contact with a mint-green wall as he shoved me forward. I pressed myself into the corner of the room, shaking violently and praying he would miraculously have a change of heart and let me go. *Just do what he says*, I told myself. If I stayed calm and maybe got talking to him, I could convince him to let me go, or I could somehow escape.

With a small grunt, he pushed a shoulder-height bookcase out of the way, revealing a door handle. He pushed the hidden door open and I gasped as my eyes landed on a wooden staircase inside. My head swam. Down there was where he was going to do whatever he planned on doing to me. I pictured a dirty, dingy room with a wooden operating table, trays of sharp equipment, and a mold-covered sink.

I found my voice and screamed again, this time not stopping when my throat burned. "No, no," I shouted over and over at the top of my lungs. My chest heaved as I gasped for air. *I'm dreaming. I'm dreaming. I'm dreaming. I'm dreaming.*

With his strong grip, he dragged me with ease even though I thrashed around as hard as I could. It was like I weighed nothing to him. I was pushed to the narrow, exposed-brick wall opposite the door. He gripped my arm again, harder, and pushed me halfway down the stairs. I stood still, frozen in shock and not fully registering what was happening.

My eyes widened as I looked around. I was in a large room painted in a surprisingly pretty light blue—too pretty for a crazy man's torture cellar. There was a small kitchen along one end, two brown leather sofas, and a chair in the corner that faced a small television in the middle of the room, and three wooden doors opposite the kitchen. I was almost as shocked by what was actually down here than I was relieved.

It didn't look like a cellar. It was too clean and tidy, everything tucked away neatly. The smell of lemon hit me, making my nose tingle. Four vases sat proudly on the side table behind the dining table and chairs; one held roses, one violets, one poppies. The fourth was empty.

I collapsed on the step, grasping the wall to stop myself from falling down the stairs. The door slammed shut, sending a shiver down my spine. Now I was trapped. I let out a startled cry and jumped into the hard wall as three women stepped into view at the bottom of the stairs. One of them, a pretty brunette who reminded me a little of my mum in her early twenties, smiled warmly but sadly and held her hand out. "Come, Lily."

ABOUT THE AUTHOR

UK native Natasha Preston grew up in small villages and towns. She discovered her love of writing when she stumbled across an amateur writing site and uploaded her first story and hasn't looked back since. She enjoys writing NA romance, thrillers, gritty YA, and the occasional serial killer.

THE ONE YEAR®
BIBLE
FOR KIDS
CHALLENGE EDITION

Greatest Bible passages arranged
in 365 daily readings from
the New Living Translation

NLT.

Tyndale House Publishers, Inc.
Carol Stream, Illinois

contents

february 14
Exodus 19:3-19
Ephesians 1:4

february 15
Exodus 20:1-21
Colossians 2:13

february 16
Exodus 32:1-14
Ephesians 1:7

february 17
Exodus 40:1-2, 33-38
John 14:16-17

february 18
Numbers 12:1-15
Romans 13:1

february 19
Numbers 13:17-20,
25-33
Romans 10:11

february 20
Numbers 14:1-23
Romans 12:2

february 21
Numbers 21:4-9
Hebrews 12:2

february 22
Numbers 22:21-38
Ephesians 5:6

february 23
Deuteronomy 29:1-6,
9-18
2 Corinthians 3:5-6

february 24
Deuteronomy 30:11-
20
Luke 14:33

february 25
Deuteronomy 31:1-8
Matthew 28:20

february 26
Deuteronomy 32:1-14
Ephesians 1:3

february 27
Joshua 1:1-11
2 Timothy 3:16-17

february 28
Joshua 2:3-16, 22-24
2 Timothy 4:18

march 1
Joshua 3:5-8, 14–4:7
Hebrews 13:8

march 2
Joshua 6:1-20
1 Corinthians 15:57

march 3
Joshua 7:10-22
1 John 1:8-10

march 4
Joshua 10:7-14
2 Peter 1:3

march 5
Joshua 23:1-11
Matthew 5:19

march 6
Joshua 24:1-18
Matthew 6:24

march 7
Judges 4:1-16
Psalm 103:12-14

march 8
Judges 6:1-16
2 Corinthians 12:9

march 9
Judges 7:2-8
1 Corinthians 1:31

march 10
Judges 7:9-21
Philippians 4:6-7

march 11
Judges 13:2-24
James 1:5

march 12
Judges 15:9-19
Romans 12:6-7

march 13
Judges 16:4-22
Romans 12:2

march 14
Judges 16:23-30
Hebrews 6:10

march 15
Ruth 1:3-19
John 15:12-13

march 16
Ruth 2:2-16
Matthew 5:42

march 17
1 Samuel 1:6-20
Psalm 116:1-2

march 18
1 Samuel 1:24–2:2, 11
1 Peter 4:10

march 19
1 Samuel 3:1-10
John 10:27

march 20
1 Samuel 7:3-10
Acts 3:19

march 21
1 Samuel 8:1-5
Proverbs 28:2

march 22
1 Samuel 8:6-20
Psalm 119:4-5

march 23
1 Samuel 9:3-17
Romans 8:28

march 24
1 Samuel 10:1-11
2 Corinthians 5:17

march 25
1 Samuel 10:17-26
1 Peter 5:7

march 26
1 Samuel 13:5-14
1 Corinthians 10:13

march 27
1 Samuel 14:1-15
Psalm 62:1-2

march 28
1 Samuel 14:24-30,
36-45
James 5:12

march 29
1 Samuel 16:1-13
Proverbs 27:19

march 30
1 Samuel 17:4-11,
17-30
Matthew 17:20

march 31
1 Samuel 17:32-50
1 Corinthians 1:27

april 1
1 Samuel 18:5-16
Proverbs 27:4

april 2
1 Samuel 20:1-4,
24-42
Proverbs 27:17

april 3
1 Samuel 24:2-17
1 Peter 3:9

april 4
1 Samuel 25:10-28,
32-33
Ephesians 4:29

april 5
2 Samuel 5:17-25
Psalm 73:24

april 6
2 Samuel 9:1-13
Proverbs 27:10

april 7
2 Samuel 12:1-14
Luke 6:41-42

April 8
2 Samuel 13:23-38
Psalm 133:1

April 9
2 Samuel 15:13-36
Romans 12:12

April 10
2 Samuel 16:5-13
Luke 6:28

April 11
2 Samuel 18:1-14, 33
Psalm 145:9

April 12
2 Samuel 24:2-4, 10-25
Hebrews 12:5-6

April 13
1 Kings 1:16-20, 32-50
Psalm 33:10-11

April 14
1 Kings 3:5-14
James 1:5

April 15
1 Kings 3:17-28
1 Corinthians 12:7

April 16
1 Kings 10:1-10
1 Corinthians 10:31

April 17
1 Kings 12:4-19
Proverbs 6:20-22

April 18
1 Kings 17:1-16
Luke 12:29, 31

April 19
1 Kings 18:20-39
Jeremiah 10:12

April 20
1 Kings 19:1-8
Philippians 4:13

April 21
1 Kings 19:9-21
Psalm 46:10

April 22
1 Kings 21:1-19
Galatians 5:16-17

April 23
2 Kings 2:1-15
1 John 5:14-15

April 24
2 Kings 4:1-7
Matthew 6:26

April 25
2 Kings 5:1-14
John 14:21

April 26
2 Kings 11:1-8, 12-21
John 17:15

April 27
2 Chronicles 34:14-33
Psalm 38:18

April 28
Ezra 3:7-13
1 Thessalonians 5:18

April 29
Nehemiah 4:1-21
1 Thessalonians 5:15

April 30
Nehemiah 5:1-11
Proverbs 28:27

may 1
Nehemiah 8:2-6, 8-12
2 Timothy 3:16

may 2
Esther 2:5-11, 15-20
Proverbs 20:11

may 3
Esther 3:2-14
Romans 12:2

may 4
Esther 4:1–5:2
Mark 8:35

may 5
Esther 5:9–6:13
Galatians 6:14

may 6
Esther 7:1-10
Romans 13:1

may 7
Job 1:6-22
James 1:2-3

may 8
Job 2:1-10
Romans 8:35, 37

may 9
Job 2:11–3:7
Jeremiah 8:21

may 10
Job 38:1-18; 40:1-5
James 4:10

may 11
Job 42:1-17
Psalm 30:5

may 12
Psalm 1:1-6
Deuteronomy 30:20

may 13
Psalm 8:1-9
Ephesians 2:10

may 14
Psalm 23:1-6
John 10:14-15

may 15
Psalm 51:1-17
1 John 1:9

may 16
Psalm 103:1-22
1 John 4:16

may 17
Psalm 119:97-106
John 17:17

may 18
Psalm 139:1-18
Matthew 6:8

may 19
Psalm 145:1-21
Acts 4:20

may 20
Proverbs 4:1-27
James 1:5

may 21
Ecclesiastes
    11:7–12:2, 9-14
1 Timothy 4:12

may 22
Isaiah 6:1-8
1 Peter 5:6

may 23
Isaiah 53:1-12
1 Peter 2:24-25

may 24
Jeremiah 1:4-12,
    17-19
Acts 18:9-10

may 25
Jeremiah 36:1-4,
    21-31
Luke 9:35

may 26
Ezekiel 37:1-14
Ephesians 2:5

may 27
Daniel 1:3-5, 8-17
James 1:25

may 28
Daniel 2:1-19
Matthew 7:7

may 29
Daniel 3:1-18
Exodus 20:3-5

may 30
Daniel 3:19-28
John 14:1

vi

november 11
Acts 28:16-31
Colossians 4:3

november 12
Romans 3:9-26
Psalm 14:3

november 13
Romans 5:1-11
Psalm 86:5

november 14
Romans 6:6-23
John 8:32

november 15
Romans 8:1-17
Hebrews 3:6

november 16
Romans 8:28-39
1 John 4:16

november 17
Romans 12:1-21
1 Samuel 24:17

november 18
Romans 13:1-10
Colossians 2:10

november 19
1 Corinthians 13:1-13
John 13:34-35

november 20
1 Corinthians 15:35-58
Revelation 21:3-4

november 21
2 Corinthians 4:7-18
Romans 8:17

november 22
2 Corinthians 9:6-15
Isaiah 32:8

november 23
Galatians 5:13-26
Ezekiel 36:26

november 24
Ephesians 1:15-23
Philippians 1:9

november 25
Ephesians 2:1-10
Romans 5:8

november 26
Ephesians 4:17–5:2
Leviticus 19:1-2

november 27
Ephesians 6:1-9
Proverbs 1:8-9

november 28
Ephesians 6:10-20
Romans 13:12

november 29
Philippians 2:1-15
Psalm 25:9

november 30
Philippians 3:12–4:9
Isaiah 26:3

december 1
Colossians 1:28–2:15
John 15:5

december 2
Colossians 3:1-17
Romans 12:2

december 3
1 Thessalonians 1:1-10
Titus 2:7

december 4
1 Thessalonians 5:5-24
Mark 13:33

december 5
2 Thessalonians 1:1-12
Psalm 9:8

december 6
2 Thessalonians 3:1-18
Proverbs 14:23

december 7
1 Timothy 4:4-16
Joshua 1:8

december 8
1 Timothy 6:6-21
Philippians 4:12-13

december 9
2 Timothy 2:1-24
Psalm 119:33

december 10
2 Timothy 3:10–4:5
Psalm 119:9

december 11
Titus 2:1-15
James 1:25

december 12
Titus 3:1-11
Proverbs 12:2

december 13
Hebrews 4:12–5:9
Psalm 130:1-2

december 14
Hebrews 11:1-16
Proverbs 3:5-6

december 15
Hebrews 12:1-13
Psalm 18:32-33

december 16
Hebrews 12:14-29
Psalm 147:5

december 17
Hebrews 13:1-21
2 Corinthians 11:4

december 18
James 1:2-18
Psalm 34:17

december 19
James 2:1-17
Proverbs 14:21

december 20
James 3:1-18
Proverbs 17:20

december 21
1 Peter 2:13-25
Romans 12:19

december 22
1 Peter 4:7-19
1 Corinthians 12:7

december 23
2 Peter 1:2-21
Psalm 119:97-98

december 24
1 John 1:1-10
Psalm 79:9

december 25
1 John 3:1-18
Mark 12:31

december 26
1 John 5:1-15
Psalm 5:2

december 27
2 John 1:1-11
James 1:27

december 28
Jude 1:14-25
Psalm 97:10

december 29
Revelation 1:1-19
Psalm 102:21-22

december 30
Revelation 21:1-12, 22-27
Psalm 140:13

december 31
Revelation 22:1-20
Psalm 23:6

June 2008

Dear Gavin,

This book you hold in your hands is one of the greatest gifts you'll ever receive. I'm not kidding. ☺ Throughout your life you may get some gifts that are more fun and might be more exciting, but none will last longer and be more beneficial than this book. I'm still not kidding! ☺ Between the covers of this book are words that will be with you the rest of your life. Think about that. This gift can be with you for the rest of your life.

I'm thrilled to give you this Bible. We, the church, hope and pray that this book, the Word of God, becomes your guide, your friend, and the place you turn to again and again through-out your life. We love you and wish God's blessings upon you.

In Christ's Love,

Jamie

Jamie Crook
Senior Pastor

"All scripture is given by God and is useful for teaching, for showing people what is wrong in their lives, for correcting faults, and for teaching us how to live right. Using the scriptures, the person who serves God will be capable, having all that is needed to do every good work." 2 Timothy 3:16-17
New Century Version

introduction
to The One Year Bible For Kids Challenge Edition

So what's a challenge?
A challenge is anything that seems difficult or different or daring—or maybe all three! It might be trying a new trick on your skateboard or learning a new song on your instrument. Maybe it's trying to better your time in swimming or score more goals in soccer. It might be walking into a new classroom for the very first time. Challenges come in many different shapes and sizes.

Reading the Bible is a challenge. After all, it has sixty-six books and more than one thousand pages! That's a lot to read. Maybe you have tried to read through the Bible before. But it's hard to know how much to read each day. And sometimes it's hard to understand what's going on in a passage. So you get discouraged and stop reading. And your Bible sits on the shelf (or under the bed) collecting dust.

But don't give up. There is a way for you to read through the Bible in *one year* and understand what God is saying to you. Keep reading!

So how can I read the Bible?
The One Year Bible for Kids Challenge Edition is designed so that day by day, week by week, you will be reading a bit of the Bible. Think of it like learning a new sport or practicing your instrument. You don't just pick up your instrument and play a new song. You have to practice the song each day, working on it section by section. The same is true with a sport. You don't just go out and play the game—you have to practice and do drills to improve your skills. It's no different with reading your Bible. Each daily reading adds up until you have reached your goal!

So how do I get started?
Here's what you do. Set a goal of reading this Bible each day. Find a good time—maybe it's right before you go to bed or right after dinner before you do your homework. The more you can make your Bible reading part of your day-to-day routine, the more successful you will be. Next, tell someone you are taking this challenge. Tell your mom or dad, a friend, or your youth group leader. You may even want to challenge a friend or your Sunday school class to read with you.

It doesn't matter if it's January 1 or July 15. You can begin this adventure any time you want. Just check today's date and find the same date in *The One Year Bible for Kids Challenge Edition*. That's all there is to it! Follow the reading plan through the months ahead until you have read all the passages.

So why take the challenge?
Good question! How do you get to know someone? Probably by spending time with the person and talking with him or her, right? The same is true with getting to know God. If

you want to know what God is like and what he wants you to do, you have to spend time with him. One of the best ways to do that is by reading his special message to you—the Bible. And the cool truth is that as you spend time with God, you will see how he works in your life and helps you change in ways you never thought possible!

It may not be obvious from day one. But as you keep at the challenge with *The One Year Bible for Kids Challenge Edition*, you will become more and more aware that God is right there beside you. You'll discover that he can help you with your problems, give you a peaceful feeling, and show you how to really enjoy the life he has given you. Bite-size amounts of God's Word, taken each day, can lead to big changes—good, important changes—for the rest of your life!

Are you ready for that challenge? Sure you are. And now is the time to start!

A Note to Parents from the Publishers of the New Living Translation

The *Holy Bible,* New Living Translation, was first published in 1996. It quickly became one of the most popular Bible translations in the English-speaking world. While the NLT's influence was rapidly growing, the Bible Translation Committee determined that an additional investment in scholarly review and text refinement could make it even better. So shortly after its initial publication, the committee began an eight-year process with the purpose of increasing the level of the NLT's precision without sacrificing its easy-to-understand quality. This second-generation text was completed in 2004 and is reflected in this edition of the New Living Translation.

The goal of any Bible translation is to convey the meaning and content of the ancient Hebrew and Greek texts as accurately as possible to contemporary readers. The challenge for our translators was to create a text that would communicate as clearly and powerfully to today's readers as the original texts did to readers and listeners in the ancient biblical world. The resulting translation is easy to read and understand, while also accurately communicating the meaning and content of the original biblical texts. The NLT is a general-purpose text especially good for study, devotional reading, and to be read aloud in public worship.

We believe that the New Living Translation—which combines the latest biblical scholarship with a clear, dynamic writing style—will communicate God's Word powerfully to all who read it. We publish it with the prayer that God will use it to speak his timeless truth to the church and the world in a fresh, new way.

The Publishers
July 2004

JANUARY 1

How It All Started

God created the entire universe—everything! He even created you.

Genesis 1:1–2:3

In the beginning God created the heavens and the earth.* ²The earth was formless and empty, and darkness covered the deep waters. And the Spirit of God was hovering over the surface of the waters.

³Then God said, "Let there be light," and there was light. ⁴And God saw that the light was good. Then he separated the light from the darkness. ⁵God called the light "day" and the darkness "night."

And evening passed and morning came, marking the first day.

⁶Then God said, "Let there be a space between the waters, to separate the waters of the heavens from the waters of the earth." ⁷And that is what happened. God made this space to separate the waters of the earth from the waters of the heavens. ⁸God called the space "sky."

And evening passed and morning came, marking the second day.

⁹Then God said, "Let the waters beneath the sky flow together into one place, so dry ground may appear." And that is what happened. ¹⁰God called the dry ground "land" and the waters "seas." And God saw that it was good. ¹¹Then God said, "Let the land sprout with vegetation—every sort of seed-bearing plant, and trees that grow seed-bearing fruit. These seeds will then produce the kinds of plants and trees from which they came." And that is what happened. ¹²The land produced vegetation—all sorts of seed-bearing plants, and trees with seed-bearing fruit. Their seeds produced plants and trees of the same kind. And God saw that it was good.

¹³And evening passed and morning came, marking the third day.

¹⁴Then God said, "Let great lights appear in the sky to separate the day from the night. Let them mark off the seasons, days, and years. ¹⁵Let these lights in the sky shine down on the earth." And that is what happened. ¹⁶God made two great lights, the sun and the moon—the larger one to govern the day, and the smaller one to govern the night. He also made the stars. ¹⁷God set these lights in the sky to light the earth, ¹⁸to govern the day and night, and to separate the light from the darkness. And God saw that it was good.

¹⁹And evening passed and morning came, marking the fourth day.

²⁰Then God said, "Let the waters swarm

with fish and other life. Let the skies be filled with birds of every kind." ²¹So God created great sea creatures and every living thing that scurries and swarms in the water, and every sort of bird—each producing offspring of the same kind. And God saw that it was good. ²²Then God blessed them, saying, "Be fruitful and multiply. Let the fish fill the seas, and let the birds multiply on the earth."

²³And evening passed and morning came, marking the fifth day.

²⁴Then God said, "Let the earth produce every sort of animal, each producing offspring of the same kind—livestock, small animals that scurry along the ground, and wild animals." And that is what happened. ²⁵God made all sorts of wild animals, livestock, and small animals, each able to produce offspring of the same kind. And God saw that it was good.

²⁶Then God said, "Let us make human beings* in our image, to be like ourselves. They will reign over the fish in the sea, the birds in the sky, the livestock, all the wild animals on the earth, and the small animals that scurry along the ground."

²⁷So God created human beings* in his own image.

In the image of God he created
   them;
male and female he created them.

²⁸Then God blessed them and said, "Be fruitful and multiply. Fill the earth and govern it. Reign over the fish in the sea, the birds in the sky, and all the animals that scurry along the ground."

²⁹Then God said, "Look! I have given you every seed-bearing plant throughout the earth and all the fruit trees for your food. ³⁰And I have given every green plant as food for all the wild animals, the birds in the sky, and the small animals that scurry along the ground—everything that has life." And that is what happened.

³¹Then God looked over all he had made, and he saw that it was very good!

And evening passed and morning came, marking the sixth day.

²:¹So the creation of the heavens and the earth and everything in them was completed. ²On the seventh day God had finished his work of creation, so he rested* from all his work. ³And God blessed the seventh day and declared it holy, because it was the day when he rested from all his work of creation.

1:1 Or *In the beginning when God created the heavens and the earth, . . .* Or *When God began to create the heavens and the earth, . . .* 1:26 Or *man;* Hebrew reads *adam.* 1:27 Or *the man;* Hebrew reads *ha-adam.* 2:2 Or *ceased;* also in 2:3.

Look around you. God created everything you see! He created the sun and the moon. He created all the plants and animals. He created all people— even you! But do you know the best part? God thought that everything— and everyone—he made was very good. That means *you* are God's specially made creation.

Since everything God created is good, we should not reject any of it but receive it with thanks. I TIMOTHY 4:4

JANUARY 2

Adam and Eve

When God created Adam and Eve, he gave them a beautiful place to live and plenty to eat. The only rule they had to keep was not to eat from the tree at the center of the garden. Read what happened.

Genesis 3:1-19, 22-23

The serpent was the shrewdest of all the wild animals the LORD God had made. One day he asked the woman, "Did God really say you must not eat the fruit from any of the trees in the garden?"

²"Of course we may eat fruit from the trees in the garden," the woman replied. ³"It's only the fruit from the tree in the middle of the garden that we are not allowed to eat. God said, 'You must not eat it or even touch it; if you do, you will die.'"

⁴"You won't die!" the serpent replied to the woman. ⁵"God knows that your eyes will be opened as soon as you eat it, and you will be like God, knowing both good and evil."

⁶The woman was convinced. She saw that the tree was beautiful and its fruit looked delicious, and she wanted the wisdom it would give her. So she took some of the fruit and ate it. Then she gave some to her husband, who was with her, and he ate it, too. ⁷At that moment their eyes were opened, and they suddenly felt shame at their nakedness. So they sewed fig leaves together to cover themselves.

⁸When the cool evening breezes were blowing, the man* and his wife heard the LORD God walking about in the garden. So they hid from the LORD God among the trees. ⁹Then the LORD God called to the man, "Where are you?"

¹⁰He replied, "I heard you walking in the garden, so I hid. I was afraid because I was naked."

¹¹"Who told you that you were naked?" the LORD God asked. "Have you eaten from the tree whose fruit I commanded you not to eat?"

¹²The man replied, "It was the woman you gave me who gave me the fruit, and I ate it."

¹³Then the LORD God asked the woman, "What have you done?"

"The serpent deceived me," she replied. "That's why I ate it."

¹⁴Then the LORD God said to the serpent,

"Because you have done this, you
    are cursed
      more than all animals, domestic and
      wild.
You will crawl on your belly,
    groveling in the dust as long as
    you live.
¹⁵And I will cause hostility between you
    and the woman,
    and between your offspring and her
    offspring.
He will strike* your head,
    and you will strike his heel."

¹⁶Then he said to the woman,

"I will sharpen the pain of your
    pregnancy,
    and in pain you will give birth.

And you will desire to control your
husband,
but he will rule over you.*"

¹⁷And to the man he said,

"Since you listened to your wife and ate
from the tree
whose fruit I commanded you
not to eat,
the ground is cursed because of you.
All your life you will struggle to
scratch a living from it.
¹⁸It will grow thorns and thistles
for you,
though you will eat of its grains.
¹⁹By the sweat of your brow

will you have food to eat
until you return to the ground
from which you were made.
For you were made from dust,
and to dust you will return."

²²Then the LORD God said, "Look, the human beings* have become like us, knowing both good and evil. What if they reach out, take fruit from the tree of life, and eat it? Then they will live forever!" ²³So the LORD God banished them from the Garden of Eden, and he sent Adam out to cultivate the ground from which he had been made.

3:8 Or *Adam*, and so throughout the chapter.   3:15 Or *bruise;* also in 3:15b.   3:16 Or *And though you will have desire for your husband, / he will rule over you.*   3:22 Or *the man;* Hebrew reads *ha-adam.*

After the serpent persuaded Eve to disobey God, Eve then convinced Adam to disobey. Sometimes doing the wrong thing seems to feel better if other people are doing it too. That's why people who do wrong often ask you to join them. But you can always say "NO!" God promises he will give you the strength to do the right thing. Just ask him.

The temptations in your life are no different from what others experience. And God is faithful. He will not allow the temptation to be more than you can stand. When you are tempted, he will show you a way out so that you can endure.
I CORINTHIANS 10:13

JANUARY 3

Cain and Abel

After they left Eden, Adam and Eve had two sons, Cain and Abel. Look what happened when one brother became jealous of the other one.

Genesis 4:3-16

When it was time for the harvest, Cain presented some of his crops as a gift to the LORD. ⁴Abel also brought a gift—the best of the firstborn lambs from his flock. The LORD accepted Abel and his gift, ⁵but he did not accept Cain and his gift. This made Cain very angry, and he looked dejected.

⁶"Why are you so angry?" the LORD asked Cain. "Why do you look so dejected? ⁷You will be accepted if you do what is right. But if you refuse to do what is right, then watch out! Sin is crouching at the door, eager to control you. But you must subdue it and be its master."

⁸One day Cain suggested to his brother, "Let's go out into the fields."* And while they were in the field, Cain attacked his brother, Abel, and killed him.

⁹Afterward the LORD asked Cain, "Where is your brother? Where is Abel?"

"I don't know," Cain responded. "Am I my brother's guardian?"

¹⁰But the LORD said, "What have you done? Listen! Your brother's blood cries out to me from the ground! ¹¹Now you are cursed and banished from the ground, which has swallowed your brother's blood. ¹²No longer will the ground yield good crops for you, no matter how hard you work! From now on you will be a homeless wanderer on the earth."

¹³Cain replied to the LORD, "My punishment* is too great for me to bear! ¹⁴You have banished me from the land and from your presence; you have made me a homeless wanderer. Anyone who finds me will kill me!"

¹⁵The LORD replied, "No, for I will give a sevenfold punishment to anyone who kills you." Then the LORD put a mark on Cain to warn anyone who might try to kill him. ¹⁶So Cain left the LORD's presence and settled in the land of Nod,* east of Eden.

4:8 As in Samaritan Pentateuch, Greek and Syriac versions, and Latin Vulgate; Masoretic Text lacks *"Let's go out into the fields."* 4:13 Or *My sin.* 4:16 *Nod* means "wandering."

Cain and Abel didn't get along well, did they? Cain was extremely jealous of Abel when God accepted his sacrifice. Cain was so jealous that he killed his brother. Your brothers and sisters probably bother you at times. But God wants you to love them because he loved you first. When your brothers or sisters annoy you, ask God to help you treat them as he does—with love.

If someone says, "I love God," but hates a Christian brother or sister, that person is a liar; for if we don't love people we can see, how can we love God, whom we cannot see?* I JOHN 4:20

4:20 Greek *hates his brother.*

JANUARY 4

noah Builds a Boat

People had become so bad by Noah's time that God decided to punish them with a terrible flood. But he kept Noah and his family safe. Watch how Noah obeyed God.

Genesis 6:9-22

This is the account of Noah and his family. Noah was a righteous man, the only blameless person living on earth at the time, and he walked in close fellowship with God. ¹⁰Noah was the father of three sons: Shem, Ham, and Japheth.

¹¹Now God saw that the earth had become corrupt and was filled with violence. ¹²God observed all this corruption in the world, for everyone on earth was corrupt. ¹³So God said to Noah, "I have decided to destroy all living creatures, for they have filled the earth with violence. Yes, I will wipe them all out along with the earth!

¹⁴"Build a large boat* from cypress wood* and waterproof it with tar, inside and out. Then construct decks and stalls throughout its interior. ¹⁵Make the boat 450 feet long, 75 feet wide, and 45 feet high.* ¹⁶Leave an 18-inch opening* below the roof all the way around the boat. Put the door on the side, and build three decks inside the boat—lower, middle, and upper.

¹⁷"Look! I am about to cover the earth with a flood that will destroy every living thing that breathes. Everything on earth will die. ¹⁸But I will confirm my covenant with you. So enter the boat—you and your wife and your sons and their wives. ¹⁹Bring a pair of every kind of animal—a male and a female—into the boat with you to keep them alive during the flood. ²⁰Pairs of every kind of bird, and every kind of animal, and every kind of small animal that scurries along the ground, will come to you to be kept alive. ²¹And be sure to take on board enough food for your family and for all the animals."

²²So Noah did everything exactly as God had commanded him.

6:14a Traditionally rendered *an ark.* **6:14b** Or *gopher wood.* **6:15** Hebrew *300 cubits* [138 meters] *long, 50 cubits* [23 meters] *wide, and 30 cubits* [13.8 meters] *high.* **6:16** Hebrew *an opening of 1 cubit* [46 centimeters].

God told Noah to build a boat so that he would be ready for the coming flood. Then God said to take *tons* of animals on board. That probably sounded like a wild idea—especially since the people had never seen a flood before. But Noah believed God and did just what God said. That's called faith. How does your faith stack up against Noah's?

It was by faith that Noah built a large boat to save his family from the flood. He obeyed God, who warned him about things that had never happened before. By his faith Noah condemned the rest of the world, and he received the righteousness that comes by faith. HEBREWS 11:7

JANUARY 5

All Aboard!

Once Noah and the animals got on the boat, it started pouring rain! As the floodwaters rose, Noah and his family must have been afraid of what would happen to them. Read and find out what did happen.

Genesis 7:1-23

When everything was ready, the LORD said to Noah, "Go into the boat with all your family, for among all the people of the earth, I can see that you alone are righteous. ²Take with you seven pairs—male and female—of each animal I have approved for eating and for sacrifice,* and take one pair of each of the others. ³Also take seven pairs of every kind of bird. There must be a male and a female in each pair to ensure that all life will survive on the earth after the flood. ⁴Seven days from now I will make the rains pour down on the earth. And it will rain for forty days and forty nights, until I have wiped from the earth all the living things I have created."

⁵So Noah did everything as the LORD commanded him.

⁶Noah was 600 years old when the flood covered the earth. ⁷He went on board the boat to escape the flood—he and his wife and his sons and their wives. ⁸With them were all the various kinds of animals—those approved for eating and for sacrifice and those that were not—along with all the birds and the small animals that scurry along the ground. ⁹They entered the boat in pairs, male and female, just as God had commanded Noah. ¹⁰After seven days, the waters of the flood came and covered the earth.

¹¹When Noah was 600 years old, on the seventeenth day of the second month, all the underground waters erupted from the earth, and the rain fell in mighty torrents from the sky. ¹²The rain continued to fall for forty days and forty nights.

¹³That very day Noah had gone into the boat with his wife and his sons—Shem, Ham, and Japheth—and their wives. ¹⁴With them in the boat were pairs of every kind of animal—domestic and wild, large and small—along with birds of every kind. ¹⁵Two by two they came into the boat, representing every living thing that breathes. ¹⁶A male and female of each kind entered, just as God had commanded Noah. Then the LORD closed the door behind them.

¹⁷For forty days the floodwaters grew deeper, covering the ground and lifting the boat high above the earth. ¹⁸As the waters rose higher and higher above the ground, the boat floated safely on the surface. ¹⁹Finally, the water covered even the highest mountains on the earth, ²⁰rising more than twenty-two feet* above the highest peaks. ²¹All the living things on earth died—birds, domestic animals, wild animals, small animals that scurry along the ground, and all the people. ²²Everything that breathed and lived on dry land died. ²³God wiped out every living thing on the earth—people, livestock, small

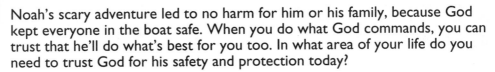

animals that scurry along the ground, and the birds of the sky. All were destroyed.

The only people who survived were Noah and those with him in the boat.

7:2 Hebrew *of each clean animal;* similarly in 7:8.　7:20 Hebrew *15 cubits* [6.9 meters].

Noah's scary adventure led to no harm for him or his family, because God kept everyone in the boat safe. When you do what God commands, you can trust that he'll do what's best for you too. In what area of your life do you need to trust God for his safety and protection today?

[God] will not let you stumble; the one who watches over you will not slumber. PSALM 121:3

JANUARY 6

A Long Wait

Noah stayed in the boat for a long time! Look how long Noah waited until it was safe to leave the boat.

Genesis 8:1-16

God remembered Noah and all the wild animals and livestock with him in the boat. He sent a wind to blow across the earth, and the floodwaters began to recede. [2]The underground waters stopped flowing, and the torrential rains from the sky were stopped. [3]So the floodwaters gradually receded from the earth. After 150 days, [4]exactly five months from the time the flood began,* the boat came to rest on the mountains of Ararat. [5]Two and a half months later,* as the waters continued to go down, other mountain peaks became visible.

[6]After another forty days, Noah opened the window he had made in the boat [7]and released a raven. The bird flew back and forth until the floodwaters on the earth had dried up. [8]He also released a dove to see if the water had receded and it could find dry ground. [9]But the dove could find no place to land because the water still covered the ground. So it returned to the boat, and Noah held out his hand and drew the dove back inside. [10]After waiting another seven days, Noah released the dove again. [11]This time the dove returned to him in the evening with a fresh olive leaf in its beak. Then Noah knew that the floodwaters were almost gone. [12]He waited another seven days and then released the dove again. This time it did not come back.

[13]Noah was now 601 years old. On the first day of the new year, ten and a half months after the flood began,* the floodwaters had almost dried up from the earth. Noah lifted back the covering of the boat and saw that the surface of the ground was drying. [14]Two more months went by,* and at last the earth was dry! [15]Then God said to Noah, [16]"Leave the boat, all of you—you and your wife, and your sons and their wives."

8:4 Hebrew *on the seventeenth day of the seventh month;* see 7:11.　8:5 Hebrew *On the first day of the tenth month;* see 7:11 and note on 8:4.　8:13 Hebrew *On the first day of the first month;* see 7:11.　8:14 Hebrew *The twenty-seventh day of the second month arrived;* see note on 8:13.

It was a year before Noah and the animals could leave the boat. When have you waited that long for something? You will have times when God wants you to wait. That's when you have to learn to be patient and trust that God is at work in your life. Just wait . . . you'll see the amazing things he will do!

You, too, must be patient. Take courage, for the coming of the Lord is near. JAMES 5:8

JANUARY 7

Rules and Rainbows

Do you know why God made rainbows? Read this story to find out what the rainbow tells us about God.

Genesis 9:1-17

Then God blessed Noah and his sons and told them, "Be fruitful and multiply. Fill the earth. [2]All the animals of the earth, all the birds of the sky, all the small animals that scurry along the ground, and all the fish in the sea will look on you with fear and terror. I have placed them in your power. [3]I have given them to you for food, just as I have given you grain and vegetables. [4]But you must never eat any meat that still has the lifeblood in it.

[5]"And I will require the blood of anyone who takes another person's life. If a wild animal kills a person, it must die. And anyone who murders a fellow human must die. [6]If anyone takes a human life, that person's life will also be taken by human hands. For God made human beings* in his own image. [7]Now be fruitful and multiply, and repopulate the earth."

[8]Then God told Noah and his sons, [9]"I hereby confirm my covenant with you and your descendants, [10]and with all the ani-

9:6 Or *man;* Hebrew reads *ha-adam.*

mals that were on the boat with you—the birds, the livestock, and all the wild animals—every living creature on earth. [11]Yes, I am confirming my covenant with you. Never again will floodwaters kill all living creatures; never again will a flood destroy the earth."

[12]Then God said, "I am giving you a sign of my covenant with you and with all living creatures, for all generations to come. [13]I have placed my rainbow in the clouds. It is the sign of my covenant with you and with all the earth. [14]When I send clouds over the earth, the rainbow will appear in the clouds, [15]and I will remember my covenant with you and with all living creatures. Never again will the floodwaters destroy all life. [16]When I see the rainbow in the clouds, I will remember the eternal covenant between God and every living creature on earth." [17]Then God said to Noah, "Yes, this rainbow is the sign of the covenant I am confirming with all the creatures on earth."

Rainbows are beautiful to look at, but they are also a sign of God's promise to us. Every time you see a rainbow, remember it is God's never-ending promise not to destroy the earth with a flood again. For thousands of years, rainbows have been a wonderful symbol of God's love for us.

We know how much God loves us, and we have put our trust in his love. God is love, and all who live in love live in God, and God lives in them. 1 JOHN 4:16

JANUARY 8

The Tower of Babel

God isn't happy when people act as if they don't need his help. Look what happened when these people built a tower to show off how great they thought they were.

Genesis 11:1-9

At one time all the people of the world spoke the same language and used the same words. ²As the people migrated to the east, they found a plain in the land of Babylonia* and settled there.

³They began saying to each other, "Let's make bricks and harden them with fire." (In this region bricks were used instead of stone, and tar was used for mortar.) ⁴Then they said, "Come, let's build a great city for ourselves with a tower that reaches into the sky. This will make us famous and keep us from being scattered all over the world."

⁵But the LORD came down to look at the city and the tower the people were building. ⁶"Look!" he said. "The people are united, and they all speak the same language. After this, nothing they set out to do will be impossible for them! ⁷Come, let's go down and confuse the people with different languages. Then they won't be able to understand each other."

⁸In that way, the LORD scattered them all over the world, and they stopped building the city. ⁹That is why the city was called Babel,* because that is where the LORD confused the people with different languages. In this way he scattered them all over the world.

11:2 Hebrew *Shinar*.   11:9 Or *Babylon. Babel* sounds like a Hebrew term that means "confusion."

These people wanted their tall tower to make them really famous. They wanted everyone to say, "Look at how smart and strong the builders of this tower are!" Instead of praising God, the people wanted everyone to notice and praise them. We act the same way when we brag and take the credit for our abilities without thanking God. Next time you're tempted to boast about yourself, remember to thank God instead. He loves a humble heart.

Those who exalt themselves will be humbled, and those who humble themselves will be exalted. MATTHEW 23:12

JANUARY 9

God's Promises to Abram

When God told Abram to leave his country, Abram did it. Look for the fabulous promise God gave to him.

Genesis 12:1-9

The LORD had said to Abram, "Leave your native country, your relatives, and your father's family, and go to the land that I will show you. ²I will make you into a great nation. I will bless you and make you famous, and you will be a blessing to others. ³I will bless those who bless you and curse those who treat you with contempt. All the families on earth will be blessed through you."

⁴So Abram departed as the LORD had instructed, and Lot went with him. Abram was seventy-five years old when he left Haran. ⁵He took his wife, Sarai, his nephew Lot, and all his wealth—his livestock and all the people he had taken into his household at Haran—and headed for the land of Canaan. When they arrived in Canaan, ⁶Abram traveled through the land as far as Shechem. There he set up camp beside the oak of Moreh. At that time, the area was inhabited by Canaanites.

⁷Then the LORD appeared to Abram and said, "I will give this land to your descendants.*" And Abram built an altar there and dedicated it to the LORD, who had appeared to him. ⁸After that, Abram traveled south and set up camp in the hill country, with Bethel to the west and Ai to the east. There he built another altar and dedicated it to the LORD, and he worshiped the LORD. ⁹Then Abram continued traveling south by stages toward the Negev.

12:7 Hebrew *seed.*

God promised to make Abram's family grow into a great nation of people. They would be God's chosen nation—Israel. God made another promise to all people, including you: Anyone who believes in his Son, Jesus Christ, will have eternal life. Through Jesus, you can become part of God's chosen family that he promised so long ago to Abram. Aren't you glad that you can be part of the family?

For God loved the world so much that he gave his one and only Son, so that everyone who believes in him will not perish but have eternal life. JOHN 3:16

JANUARY 10

Hard to Believe

Abraham and Sarah (originally named Abram and Sarai) were really old—beyond the time when they could have children. But God promised them that they would have a son. Check out Sarah's reaction.

Genesis 18:1-15

The LORD appeared again to Abraham near the oak grove belonging to Mamre. One day Abraham was sitting at the entrance to his tent during the hottest part of the day. ²He looked up and noticed three men standing nearby. When he saw them, he ran to meet them and welcomed them, bowing low to the ground.

³"My lord," he said, "if it pleases you, stop here for a while. ⁴Rest in the shade of this tree while water is brought to wash your feet. ⁵And since you've honored your servant with this visit, let me prepare some food to refresh you before you continue on your journey."

"All right," they said. "Do as you have said."

⁶So Abraham ran back to the tent and said to Sarah, "Hurry! Get three large mea-sures* of your best flour, knead it into dough, and bake some bread." ⁷Then Abraham ran out to the herd and chose a tender calf and gave it to his servant, who quickly prepared it. ⁸When the food was ready, Abraham took some yogurt and milk and the roasted meat, and he served it to the men. As they ate, Abraham waited on them in the shade of the trees.

⁹"Where is Sarah, your wife?" the visitors asked.

"She's inside the tent," Abraham replied.

¹⁰Then one of them said, "I will return to you about this time next year, and your wife, Sarah, will have a son!"

Sarah was listening to this conversation from the tent. ¹¹Abraham and Sarah were both very old by this time, and Sarah was long past the age of having children. ¹²So she laughed silently to herself and said,

"How could a worn-out woman like me enjoy such pleasure, especially when my master—my husband—is also so old?"

¹³Then the LORD said to Abraham, "Why did Sarah laugh? Why did she say, 'Can an old woman like me have a baby?' ¹⁴Is any-

18:6 Hebrew *3 seahs*, about 15 quarts or 18 liters.

thing too hard for the LORD? I will return about this time next year, and Sarah will have a son."

¹⁵Sarah was afraid, so she denied it, saying, "I didn't laugh."

But the LORD said, "No, you did laugh."

Sarah laughed to herself because she couldn't believe it. *No way!* she thought. But it did happen, and Sarah learned that God can do anything—nothing is impossible for him! When you follow God and trust in him, you can expect amazing things to happen. Get ready to see the impossible come true!

What is impossible for people is possible with God. LUKE 18:27

JANUARY 11

Sodom and Gomorrah

God was going to punish the cities of Sodom and Gomorrah because of the horrible things they were doing. But first he sent two angels to warn Lot of the coming doom. Would Lot listen?

Genesis 19:12-29

Meanwhile, the angels questioned Lot. "Do you have any other relatives here in the city?" they asked. "Get them out of this place—your sons-in-law, sons, daughters, or anyone else. ¹³For we are about to destroy this city completely. The outcry against this place is so great it has reached the LORD, and he has sent us to destroy it."

¹⁴So Lot rushed out to tell his daughters' fiancés, "Quick, get out of the city! The LORD is about to destroy it." But the young men thought he was only joking.

¹⁵At dawn the next morning the angels became insistent. "Hurry," they said to Lot. "Take your wife and your two daughters who are here. Get out right now, or you will be swept away in the destruction of the city!"

¹⁶When Lot still hesitated, the angels seized his hand and the hands of his wife and two daughters and rushed them to safety outside the city, for the LORD was merciful. ¹⁷When they were safely out of the city, one of the angels ordered, "Run for your lives! And don't look back or stop anywhere in the valley! Escape to the mountains, or you will be swept away!"

¹⁸"Oh no, my lord!" Lot begged. ¹⁹"You have been so gracious to me and saved my life, and you have shown such great kindness. But I cannot go to the mountains. Disaster would catch up to me there, and I would soon die. ²⁰See, there is a small village nearby. Please let me go there instead; don't you see how small it is? Then my life will be saved."

²¹"All right," the angel said, "I will grant your request. I will not destroy the little

village. ²²But hurry! Escape to it, for I can do nothing until you arrive there." (This explains why that village was known as Zoar, which means "little place.")

²³Lot reached the village just as the sun was rising over the horizon. ²⁴Then the LORD rained down fire and burning sulfur from the sky on Sodom and Gomorrah. ²⁵He utterly destroyed them, along with the other cities and villages of the plain, wiping out all the people and every bit of vegetation. ²⁶But Lot's wife looked back as she was following behind him, and she turned into a pillar of salt.

²⁷Abraham got up early that morning and hurried out to the place where he had stood in the LORD's presence. ²⁸He looked out across the plain toward Sodom and Gomorrah and watched as columns of smoke rose from the cities like smoke from a furnace.

²⁹But God had listened to Abraham's request and kept Lot safe, removing him from the disaster that engulfed the cities on the plain.

Lot was pretty comfortable living in Sodom. He couldn't imagine life being any different from the way it was. So Lot didn't want to obey the angels' warnings right away. He made it out of the city just at the last minute. God warns people today to turn from their sins—to stop doing wrong. When God tells you to do something, don't wait! The best time to choose to follow and obey God is *right now.*

Jesus began to preach, "Repent of your sins and turn to God, for the Kingdom of Heaven is near."* MATTHEW 4:17
4:17 Or *has come,* or *is coming soon.*

JANUARY 12

Hagar and Ishmael

When Abraham sent Hagar and her son out into the desert, Hagar was very upset. She didn't know what was going to happen to her and her boy, so she started to cry. Do you think her cries went unanswered?

Genesis 21:8-21
When Isaac grew up and was about to be weaned, Abraham prepared a huge feast to celebrate the occasion. ⁹But Sarah saw Ishmael—the son of Abraham and her Egyptian servant Hagar—making fun of her son, Isaac.* ¹⁰So she turned to Abraham and demanded, "Get rid of that slave-woman and her son. He is not going to share the inheritance with my son, Isaac. I won't have it!"

¹¹This upset Abraham very much because Ishmael was his son. ¹²But God told Abraham, "Do not be upset over the boy and your servant. Do whatever Sarah tells you, for Isaac is the son through whom your descendants will be counted. ¹³But I will also make a nation of the descendants of Hagar's son because he is your son, too."

¹⁴So Abraham got up early the next morning, prepared food and a container of water, and strapped them on Hagar's

shoulders. Then he sent her away with their son, and she wandered aimlessly in the wilderness of Beersheba.

¹⁵When the water was gone, she put the boy in the shade of a bush. ¹⁶Then she went and sat down by herself about a hundred yards* away. "I don't want to watch the boy die," she said, as she burst into tears.

¹⁷But God heard the boy crying, and the angel of God called to Hagar from heaven, "Hagar, what's wrong? Do not be afraid! God has heard the boy crying as he lies there. ¹⁸Go to him and comfort him, for I will make a great nation from his descendants."

¹⁹Then God opened Hagar's eyes, and she saw a well full of water. She quickly filled her water container and gave the boy a drink.

²⁰And God was with the boy as he grew up in the wilderness. He became a skillful archer, ²¹and he settled in the wilderness of Paran. His mother arranged for him to marry a woman from the land of Egypt.

21:9 As in Greek version and Latin Vulgate; Hebrew omits *of her son, Isaac.*   21:16 Hebrew *a bowshot.*

God saw that Hagar was in trouble and needed his help. God heard her cries, and he took care of her. God promises to take care of us as well. Jesus tells us not to worry about food or clothing because God cares about us and knows what we need. He promises to provide for us. How can you trust God to care for you?

Don't worry about these things, saying, "What will we eat? What will we drink? What will we wear?" These things dominate the thoughts of unbelievers, but your heavenly Father already knows all your needs. Seek the Kingdom of God above all else, and live righteously, and he will give you everything you need.* MATTHEW 6:31-33

6:33 Some manuscripts do not include *of God.*

JANUARY 13

Abraham's Painful Decision

God gave Abraham and Sarah a miracle baby. Then God tested Abraham's love for him by giving him a very difficult task. Read on to see what God told Abraham to do and what Abraham did.

Genesis 22:1-18

Some time later, God tested Abraham's faith. "Abraham!" God called.

"Yes," he replied. "Here I am."

²"Take your son, your only son—yes, Isaac, whom you love so much—and go to the land of Moriah. Go and sacrifice him as a burnt offering on one of the mountains, which I will show you."

³The next morning Abraham got up early. He saddled his donkey and took two of his servants with him, along with his son, Isaac. Then he chopped wood for a fire for a burnt offering and set out for the place

God had told him about. ⁴On the third day of their journey, Abraham looked up and saw the place in the distance. ⁵"Stay here with the donkey," Abraham told the servants. "The boy and I will travel a little farther. We will worship there, and then we will come right back."

⁶So Abraham placed the wood for the burnt offering on Isaac's shoulders, while he himself carried the fire and the knife. As the two of them walked on together, ⁷Isaac turned to Abraham and said, "Father?"

"Yes, my son?" Abraham replied.

"We have the fire and the wood," the boy said, "but where is the sheep for the burnt offering?"

⁸"God will provide a sheep for the burnt offering, my son," Abraham answered. And they both walked on together.

⁹When they arrived at the place where God had told him to go, Abraham built an altar and arranged the wood on it. Then he tied his son, Isaac, and laid him on the altar on top of the wood. ¹⁰And Abraham picked up the knife to kill his son as a sacrifice. ¹¹At that moment the angel of the LORD called to him from heaven, "Abraham! Abraham!"

"Yes," Abraham replied. "Here I am!"

¹²"Don't lay a hand on the boy!" the angel said. "Do not hurt him in any way, for now I know that you truly fear God. You have not withheld from me even your son, your only son."

¹³Then Abraham looked up and saw a ram caught by its horns in a thicket. So he took the ram and sacrificed it as a burnt offering in place of his son. ¹⁴Abraham named the place Yahweh-Yireh (which means "the LORD will provide"). To this day, people still use that name as a proverb: "On the mountain of the LORD it will be provided."

¹⁵Then the angel of the LORD called again to Abraham from heaven. ¹⁶"This is what the LORD says: Because you have obeyed me and have not withheld even your son, your only son, I swear by my own name that ¹⁷I will certainly bless you. I will multiply your descendants beyond number, like the stars in the sky and the sand on the seashore. Your descendants will conquer the cities of their enemies. ¹⁸And through your descendants all the nations of the earth will be blessed—all because you have obeyed me."

Abraham must have been totally confused when God told him to sacrifice his only son. How could Abraham become the father of a great nation if his only son were killed? Even though Abraham did not understand what was happening, he believed that God would bring Isaac back to life (Hebrews 11:17-19). And he knew one thing: He had to obey God. When Abraham obeyed, God blessed him even more. Obeying God is always your best choice, even when you don't completely understand his commands.

Blessed are all who hear the word of God and put it into practice. LUKE 11:28

show me the way

Abraham's servant was on a mission. He had to find a wife for Abraham's son, Isaac. Look at how the servant got the job done.

Genesis 24:34-48

"I am Abraham's servant," he explained. 35"And the LORD has greatly blessed my master; he has become a wealthy man. The LORD has given him flocks of sheep and goats, herds of cattle, a fortune in silver and gold, and many male and female servants and camels and donkeys.

36"When Sarah, my master's wife, was very old, she gave birth to my master's son, and my master has given him everything he owns. 37And my master made me take an oath. He said, 'Do not allow my son to marry one of these local Canaanite women. 38Go instead to my father's house, to my relatives, and find a wife there for my son.'

39"But I said to my master, 'What if I can't find a young woman who is willing to go back with me?' 40He responded, 'The LORD, in whose presence I have lived, will send his angel with you and will make your mission successful. Yes, you must find a wife for my son from among my relatives, from my father's family. 41Then you will have fulfilled your obligation. But if you go to my relatives and they refuse to let her go with you, you will be free from my oath.'

42"So today when I came to the spring, I prayed this prayer: 'O LORD, God of my master, Abraham, please give me success on this mission. 43See, I am standing here beside this spring. This is my request. When a young woman comes to draw water, I will say to her, "Please give me a little drink of water from your jug." 44If she says, "Yes, have a drink, and I will draw water for your camels, too," let her be the one you have selected to be the wife of my master's son.'

45"Before I had finished praying in my heart, I saw Rebekah coming out with her water jug on her shoulder. She went down to the spring and drew water. So I said to her, 'Please give me a drink.' 46She quickly lowered her jug from her shoulder and said, 'Yes, have a drink, and I will water your camels, too!' So I drank, and then she watered the camels.

47"Then I asked, 'Whose daughter are you?' She replied, 'I am the daughter of Bethuel, and my grandparents are Nahor and Milcah.' So I put the ring on her nose, and the bracelets on her wrists.

48"Then I bowed low and worshiped the LORD. I praised the LORD, the God of my master, Abraham, because he had led me straight to my master's niece to be his son's wife."

Abraham's servant had a difficult job to do. But do you notice what he did first? He asked God for guidance, and God answered him. When you have a tough assignment or problem to solve, your first step should be to ask God for his help. You'll be amazed at how God will answer you. Trust him!

If you need wisdom, ask our generous God, and he will give it to you. He will not rebuke you for asking. JAMES 1:5

JANUARY 15

Rebekah's Response

It was obvious to Rebekah's family that God had guided Abraham's servant to Rebekah. Still, she had never met Isaac. Would Rebekah leave her family and marry him? Read and find out.

Genesis 24:50-67

Then Laban and Bethuel replied, "The LORD has obviously brought you here, so there is nothing we can say. ⁵¹Here is Rebekah; take her and go. Yes, let her be the wife of your master's son, as the LORD has directed."

⁵²When Abraham's servant heard their answer, he bowed down to the ground and worshiped the LORD. ⁵³Then he brought out silver and gold jewelry and clothing and presented them to Rebekah. He also gave expensive presents to her brother and mother. ⁵⁴Then they ate their meal, and the servant and the men with him stayed there overnight.

But early the next morning, Abraham's servant said, "Send me back to my master."

⁵⁵"But we want Rebekah to stay with us at least ten days," her brother and mother said. "Then she can go."

⁵⁶But he said, "Don't delay me. The LORD has made my mission successful; now send me back so I can return to my master."

⁵⁷"Well," they said, "we'll call Rebekah and ask her what she thinks." ⁵⁸So they called Rebekah. "Are you willing to go with this man?" they asked her.

And she replied, "Yes, I will go."

⁵⁹So they said good-bye to Rebekah and sent her away with Abraham's servant and his men. The woman who had been Rebekah's childhood nurse went along with her. ⁶⁰They gave her this blessing as she parted:

"Our sister, may you become
the mother of many millions!
May your descendants be strong
and conquer the cities of their
enemies."

⁶¹Then Rebekah and her servant girls mounted the camels and followed the man. So Abraham's servant took Rebekah and went on his way.

⁶²Meanwhile, Isaac, whose home was in the Negev, had returned from Beer-lahai-roi. ⁶³One evening as he was walking and meditating in the fields, he looked up and

saw the camels coming. ⁶⁴When Rebekah looked up and saw Isaac, she quickly dismounted from her camel. ⁶⁵"Who is that man walking through the fields to meet us?" she asked the servant.

And he replied, "It is my master." So Rebekah covered her face with her veil.

⁶⁶Then the servant told Isaac everything he had done.

⁶⁷And Isaac brought Rebekah into his mother Sarah's tent, and she became his wife. He loved her deeply, and she was a special comfort to him after the death of his mother.

Rebekah had a tough decision to make. She had never met her husband-to-be, and her family wanted her to stay with them longer. But Rebekah knew that God wanted her to go, so she put her faith in him and went with Abraham's servant. When you step out in faith and follow God, you never know what he may call you to do. But you can always trust that he will be with you wherever you go.

[Jesus said,] "Teach these new disciples to obey all the commands I have given you. And be sure of this: I am with you always, even to the end of the age." MATTHEW 28:20

JANUARY 16

Jacob Versus Esau

Jacob and Esau were twin brothers who fought a lot. Read about how nasty they were to each other. Does this story remind you of two other brothers? (Remember Genesis 4:3-16, which you read on January 3?)

Genesis 25:21-34

Isaac pleaded with the LORD on behalf of his wife, because she was unable to have children. The LORD answered Isaac's prayer, and Rebekah became pregnant with twins. ²²But the two children struggled with each other in her womb. So she went to ask the LORD about it. "Why is this happening to me?" she asked.

²³And the LORD told her, "The sons in your womb will become two nations. From the very beginning, the two nations will be rivals. One nation will be stronger than the other; and your older son will serve your younger son."

²⁴And when the time came to give birth, Rebekah discovered that she did indeed have twins! ²⁵The first one was very red at birth and covered with thick hair like a fur coat. So they named him Esau.* ²⁶Then the other twin was born with his hand grasping Esau's heel. So they named him Jacob.* Isaac was sixty years old when the twins were born.

²⁷As the boys grew up, Esau became a skillful hunter. He was an outdoorsman, but Jacob had a quiet temperament,

preferring to stay at home. ²⁸Isaac loved Esau because he enjoyed eating the wild game Esau brought home, but Rebekah loved Jacob.

²⁹One day when Jacob was cooking some stew, Esau arrived home from the wilderness exhausted and hungry. ³⁰Esau said to Jacob, "I'm starved! Give me some of that red stew!" (This is how Esau got his other name, Edom, which means "red.")

³¹"All right," Jacob replied, "but trade me your rights as the firstborn son."

³²"Look, I'm dying of starvation!" said Esau. "What good is my birthright to me now?"

³³But Jacob said, "First you must swear that your birthright is mine." So Esau swore an oath, thereby selling all his rights as the firstborn to his brother, Jacob.

³⁴Then Jacob gave Esau some bread and lentil stew. Esau ate the meal, then got up and left. He showed contempt for his rights as the firstborn.

25:25 *Esau* sounds like a Hebrew term that means "hair." 25:26 *Jacob* sounds like the Hebrew words for "heel" and "deceiver."

Jacob cheated Esau out of his inheritance. He shouldn't have done that. But it was also wrong for Esau to trade in his privileges as the firstborn son for a bowl of stew. God wants you to know what's most valuable—your faith, your family, and your friends. Don't trade away these important blessings for anything else!

Store your treasures in heaven, where moths and rust cannot destroy, and thieves do not break in and steal. Wherever your treasure is, there the desires of your heart will also be. MATTHEW 6:20-21

JANUARY 17

Jacob Tricks His Father

Isaac was about to give his older son, Esau, a final blessing. This meant Isaac would ask for God's special favor upon Esau. But Jacob, the younger son, wanted this special blessing. Read what he did to trick his father to get it.

Genesis 27:5-30

Rebekah overheard what Isaac had said to his son Esau. So when Esau left to hunt for the wild game, ⁶she said to her son Jacob, "Listen. I overheard your father say to Esau, ⁷'Bring me some wild game and prepare me a delicious meal. Then I will bless you in the LORD's presence before I die.'

⁸Now, my son, listen to me. Do exactly as I tell you. ⁹Go out to the flocks, and bring me two fine young goats. I'll use them to prepare your father's favorite dish. ¹⁰Then take the food to your father so he can eat it and bless you before he dies."

¹¹"But look," Jacob replied to Rebekah, "my brother, Esau, is a hairy man, and my

skin is smooth. ¹²What if my father touches me? He'll see that I'm trying to trick him, and then he'll curse me instead of blessing me."

¹³But his mother replied, "Then let the curse fall on me, my son! Just do what I tell you. Go out and get the goats for me!"

¹⁴So Jacob went out and got the young goats for his mother. Rebekah took them and prepared a delicious meal, just the way Isaac liked it. ¹⁵Then she took Esau's favorite clothes, which were there in the house, and gave them to her younger son, Jacob. ¹⁶She covered his arms and the smooth part of his neck with the skin of the young goats. ¹⁷Then she gave Jacob the delicious meal, including freshly baked bread.

¹⁸So Jacob took the food to his father. "My father?" he said.

"Yes, my son," Isaac answered. "Who are you—Esau or Jacob?"

¹⁹Jacob replied, "It's Esau, your firstborn son. I've done as you told me. Here is the wild game. Now sit up and eat it so you can give me your blessing."

²⁰Isaac asked, "How did you find it so quickly, my son?"

"The LORD your God put it in my path!" Jacob replied.

²¹Then Isaac said to Jacob, "Come closer so I can touch you and make sure that you really are Esau." ²²So Jacob went closer to his father, and Isaac touched him. "The voice is Jacob's, but the hands are Esau's," Isaac said. ²³But he did not recognize Jacob, because Jacob's hands felt hairy just like Esau's. So Isaac prepared to bless Jacob. ²⁴"But are you really my son Esau?" he asked.

"Yes, I am," Jacob replied.

²⁵Then Isaac said, "Now, my son, bring me the wild game. Let me eat it, and then I will give you my blessing." So Jacob took the food to his father, and Isaac ate it. He also drank the wine that Jacob served him. Then Isaac said to Jacob, ²⁶"Please come a little closer and kiss me, my son."

²⁷So Jacob went over and kissed him. And when Isaac caught the smell of his clothes, he was finally convinced, and he blessed his son. He said, "Ah! The smell of my son is like the smell of the outdoors, which the LORD has blessed!

²⁸"From the dew of heaven
    and the richness of the earth,
may God always give you abundant
        harvests of grain
    and bountiful new wine.
²⁹May many nations become your
        servants,
    and may they bow down to you.
May you be the master over your
        brothers,
    and may your mother's sons bow
        down to you.
All who curse you will be cursed,
    and all who bless you will be
        blessed."

³⁰As soon as Isaac had finished blessing Jacob, and almost before Jacob had left his father, Esau returned from his hunt.

Jacob wanted his father's blessing so badly that he lied to get it. His lie worked, but Jacob's actions led to future problems with his family. God wants us to be honest with other people—especially our family. Lying may seem like an easy way out, but in the long run, telling the truth is always the best choice.

If you are faithful in little things, you will be faithful in large ones. But if you are dishonest in little things, you won't be honest with greater responsibilities. LUKE 16:10

JANUARY 18

stairway to Heaven

To get away from his brother Esau, Jacob went to the land of his uncle Laban. On the way, Jacob had an unusual meeting. See who spoke to Jacob and what he had to say.

Genesis 28:10-22

Meanwhile, Jacob left Beersheba and traveled toward Haran. ¹¹At sundown he arrived at a good place to set up camp and stopped there for the night. Jacob found a stone to rest his head against and lay down to sleep. ¹²As he slept, he dreamed of a stairway that reached from the earth up to heaven. And he saw the angels of God going up and down the stairway.

¹³At the top of the stairway stood the LORD, and he said, "I am the LORD, the God of your grandfather Abraham, and the God of your father, Isaac. The ground you are lying on belongs to you. I am giving it to you and your descendants. ¹⁴Your descendants will be as numerous as the dust of the earth! They will spread out in all directions—to the west and the east, to the north and the south. And all the families of the earth will be blessed through you and your descendants. ¹⁵What's more, I am with you, and I will protect you wherever you go. One day I will bring you back to this land. I will not leave you until I have finished giving you everything I have promised you."

¹⁶Then Jacob awoke from his sleep and said, "Surely the LORD is in this place, and I wasn't even aware of it!" ¹⁷But he was also afraid and said, "What an awesome place this is! It is none other than the house of God, the very gateway to heaven!"

¹⁸The next morning Jacob got up very early. He took the stone he had rested his head against, and he set it upright as a memorial pillar. Then he poured olive oil over it. ¹⁹He named that place Bethel (which means "house of God"), although the name of the nearby village was Luz.

²⁰Then Jacob made this vow: "If God will indeed be with me and protect me on this journey, and if he will provide me with food and clothing, ²¹and if I return safely to my father's home, then the LORD will certainly be my God. ²²And this memorial pillar I have set up will become a place for worshiping God, and I will present to God a tenth of everything he gives me."

God's promise that had been given to Abraham and Isaac was now offered to Jacob. But it was not enough to be Abraham's grandson and Isaac's son. Jacob needed to form his own relationship with God. In the same way, it is not enough for you to rely on the faith of your parents or grandparents. You need to become part of God's family on your own. Have you made that decision?

To all who believed [Jesus] and accepted him, he gave the right to become children of God. JOHN 1:12

Jacob Returns Home

Jacob hadn't seen Esau in a really long time, and he was scared. Would Esau still be angry about the birthright and the blessing that Jacob had stolen? Read and find out.

Genesis 32:3-21; 33:1-4

Then Jacob sent messengers ahead to his brother, Esau, who was living in the region of Seir in the land of Edom. ⁴He told them, "Give this message to my master Esau: 'Humble greetings from your servant Jacob. Until now I have been living with Uncle Laban, ⁵and now I own cattle, donkeys, flocks of sheep and goats, and many servants, both men and women. I have sent these messengers to inform my lord of my coming, hoping that you will be friendly to me.'"

⁶After delivering the message, the messengers returned to Jacob and reported, "We met your brother, Esau, and he is already on his way to meet you—with an army of 400 men!" ⁷Jacob was terrified at the news. He divided his household, along with the flocks and herds and camels, into two groups. ⁸He thought, "If Esau meets one group and attacks it, perhaps the other group can escape."

⁹Then Jacob prayed, "O God of my grandfather Abraham, and God of my father, Isaac—O LORD, you told me, 'Return to your own land and to your relatives.' And you promised me, 'I will treat you kindly.' ¹⁰I am not worthy of all the unfailing love and faithfulness you have shown to me, your servant. When I left home and crossed the Jordan River, I owned nothing except a walking stick. Now my household fills two large camps! ¹¹O LORD, please rescue me

from the hand of my brother, Esau. I am afraid that he is coming to attack me, along with my wives and children. ¹²But you promised me, 'I will surely treat you kindly, and I will multiply your descendants until they become as numerous as the sands along the seashore—too many to count.'"

¹³Jacob stayed where he was for the night. Then he selected these gifts from his possessions to present to his brother, Esau: ¹⁴200 female goats, 20 male goats, 200 ewes, 20 rams, ¹⁵30 female camels with their young, 40 cows, 10 bulls, 20 female donkeys, and 10 male donkeys. ¹⁶He divided these animals into herds and assigned each to different servants. Then he told his servants, "Go ahead of me with the animals, but keep some distance between the herds."

¹⁷He gave these instructions to the men leading the first group: "When my brother, Esau, meets you, he will ask, 'Whose servants are you? Where are you going? Who owns these animals?' ¹⁸You must reply, 'They belong to your servant Jacob, but they are a gift for his master Esau. Look, he is coming right behind us.'"

¹⁹Jacob gave the same instructions to the second and third herdsmen and to all who followed behind the herds: "You must say the same thing to Esau when you meet him. ²⁰And be sure to say, 'Look, your servant Jacob is right behind us.'"

Jacob thought, "I will try to appease him

by sending gifts ahead of me. When I see him in person, perhaps he will be friendly to me." ²¹So the gifts were sent on ahead, while Jacob himself spent that night in the camp.

⊙

³³:¹Then Jacob looked up and saw Esau coming with his 400 men. So he divided the children among Leah, Rachel, and his two servant wives. ²He put the servant wives and their children at the front, Leah and her children next, and Rachel and Joseph last. ³Then Jacob went on ahead. As he approached his brother, he bowed to the ground seven times before him. ⁴Then Esau ran to meet him and embraced him, threw his arms around his neck, and kissed him. And they both wept.

Knowing that Esau had a right to be mad, Jacob was afraid of what Esau would do to him and his family. To deal with his fears, Jacob prayed for protection, and God answered him. God kept Jacob and his entire family safe. When we are fearful of someone or something, we need to pray and ask God to keep us safe. God protected Jacob, and he will protect you, too.

[Jesus said,] "I am leaving you with a gift—peace of mind and heart. And the peace I give is a gift the world cannot give. So don't be troubled or afraid." JOHN 14:27

JANUARY 20
Joseph and His Brothers
Joseph's brothers were jealous of him, and they let it get out of control. Look what they did to Joseph!

Genesis 37:3-4, 12-34
Jacob* loved Joseph more than any of his other children because Joseph had been born to him in his old age. So one day Jacob had a special gift made for Joseph—a beautiful robe.* ⁴But his brothers hated Joseph because their father loved him more than the rest of them. They couldn't say a kind word to him.

⊙

¹²Soon after this, Joseph's brothers went to pasture their father's flocks at Shechem. ¹³When they had been gone for some time, Jacob said to Joseph, "Your brothers are pasturing the sheep at Shechem. Get ready, and I will send you to them."

"I'm ready to go," Joseph replied.

¹⁴"Go and see how your brothers and the flocks are getting along," Jacob said. "Then come back and bring me a report." So Jacob sent him on his way, and Joseph traveled to Shechem from their home in the valley of Hebron.

¹⁵When he arrived there, a man from the area noticed him wandering around

the countryside. "What are you looking for?" he asked.

¹⁶"I'm looking for my brothers," Joseph replied. "Do you know where they are pasturing their sheep?"

¹⁷"Yes," the man told him. "They have moved on from here, but I heard them say, 'Let's go on to Dothan.'" So Joseph followed his brothers to Dothan and found them there.

¹⁸When Joseph's brothers saw him coming, they recognized him in the distance. As he approached, they made plans to kill him. ¹⁹"Here comes the dreamer!" they said. ²⁰"Come on, let's kill him and throw him into one of these cisterns. We can tell our father, 'A wild animal has eaten him.' Then we'll see what becomes of his dreams!"

²¹But when Reuben heard of their scheme, he came to Joseph's rescue. "Let's not kill him," he said. ²²"Why should we shed any blood? Let's just throw him into this empty cistern here in the wilderness. Then he'll die without our laying a hand on him." Reuben was secretly planning to rescue Joseph and return him to his father.

²³So when Joseph arrived, his brothers ripped off the beautiful robe he was wearing. ²⁴Then they grabbed him and threw him into the cistern. Now the cistern was empty; there was no water in it. ²⁵Then, just as they were sitting down to eat, they looked up and saw a caravan of camels in the distance coming toward them. It was a group of Ishmaelite traders taking a load of gum, balm, and aromatic resin from Gilead down to Egypt.

²⁶Judah said to his brothers, "What will we gain by killing our brother? His blood would just give us a guilty conscience. ²⁷Instead of hurting him, let's sell him to those Ishmaelite traders. After all, he is our brother—our own flesh and blood!" And his brothers agreed. ²⁸So when the Ishmaelites, who were Midianite traders, came by, Joseph's brothers pulled him out of the cistern and sold him to them for twenty pieces* of silver. And the traders took him to Egypt.

²⁹Some time later, Reuben returned to get Joseph out of the cistern. When he discovered that Joseph was missing, he tore his clothes in grief. ³⁰Then he went back to his brothers and lamented, "The boy is gone! What will I do now?"

³¹Then the brothers killed a young goat and dipped Joseph's robe in its blood. ³²They sent the beautiful robe to their father with this message: "Look at what we found. Doesn't this robe belong to your son?"

³³Their father recognized it immediately. "Yes," he said, "it is my son's robe. A wild animal must have eaten him. Joseph has clearly been torn to pieces!" ³⁴Then Jacob tore his clothes and dressed himself in burlap. He mourned deeply for his son for a long time.

37:3a Hebrew *Israel;* also in 37:13. The names "Jacob" and "Israel" are interchanged throughout the Old Testament, referring sometimes to the individual patriarch and sometimes to the nation. 37:3b Traditionally rendered *a coat of many colors.* The exact meaning of the Hebrew is uncertain. 37:28 Hebrew *20 shekels,* about 8 ounces or 228 grams in weight.

Joseph was obviously Jacob's favorite out of all his sons. And Joseph's brothers did not like that at all. The situation got out of hand, though, when his brothers let their jealousy grow into hatred, and they nearly killed Joseph. Everyone struggles with jealousy at times. But it's important not to let those feelings grow into wrong actions or feelings. Ask God to help you when you feel jealous.

Love is patient and kind. Love is not jealous or boastful or proud.
I CORINTHIANS 13:4

JANUARY 21

Joseph in Trouble

Joseph was working as a slave in Egypt. He was such a good worker that his master put him in charge of the whole house. Check out the problem he had even though he was doing nothing wrong.

Genesis 39:1-21

When Joseph was taken to Egypt by the Ishmaelite traders, he was purchased by Potiphar, an Egyptian officer. Potiphar was captain of the guard for Pharaoh, the king of Egypt.

²The LORD was with Joseph, so he succeeded in everything he did as he served in the home of his Egyptian master. ³Potiphar noticed this and realized that the LORD was with Joseph, giving him success in everything he did. ⁴This pleased Potiphar, so he soon made Joseph his personal attendant. He put him in charge of his entire household and everything he owned. ⁵From the day Joseph was put in charge of his master's household and property, the LORD began to bless Potiphar's household for Joseph's sake. All his household affairs ran smoothly, and his crops and livestock flourished. ⁶So Potiphar gave Joseph complete administrative responsibility over everything he

owned. With Joseph there, he didn't worry about a thing—except what kind of food to eat!

Joseph was a very handsome and well-built young man, ⁷and Potiphar's wife soon began to look at him lustfully. "Come and sleep with me," she demanded.

⁸But Joseph refused. "Look," he told her, "my master trusts me with everything in his entire household. ⁹No one here has more authority than I do. He has held back nothing from me except you, because you are his wife. How could I do such a wicked thing? It would be a great sin against God."

¹⁰She kept putting pressure on Joseph day after day, but he refused to sleep with her, and he kept out of her way as much as possible. ¹¹One day, however, no one else was around when he went in to do his work. ¹²She came and grabbed him by his cloak, demanding, "Come on, sleep with me!" Joseph tore himself away, but he left

his cloak in her hand as he ran from the house.

¹³When she saw that she was holding his cloak and he had fled, ¹⁴she called out to her servants. Soon all the men came running. "Look!" she said. "My husband has brought this Hebrew slave here to make fools of us! He came into my room to rape me, but I screamed. ¹⁵When he heard me scream, he ran outside and got away, but he left his cloak behind with me."

¹⁶She kept the cloak with her until her husband came home. ¹⁷Then she told him her story. "That Hebrew slave you've brought into our house tried to come in and fool around with me," she said. ¹⁸"But when I screamed, he ran outside, leaving his cloak with me!"

¹⁹Potiphar was furious when he heard his wife's story about how Joseph had treated her. ²⁰So he took Joseph and threw him into the prison where the king's prisoners were held, and there he remained. ²¹But the LORD was with Joseph in the prison and showed him his faithful love. And the LORD made Joseph a favorite with the prison warden.

What a tough situation for Joseph! It would have been so easy for him to give in to temptation when Potiphar's wife cornered him. But it was more important to Joseph to obey God, so he ran from temptation. That's a good lesson for us. When a temptation is really strong, the best course of action is to get away from it fast. What tempts you? Follow Joseph's example and run!

Run from anything that stimulates youthful lusts. Instead, pursue righteous living, faithfulness, love, and peace. Enjoy the companionship of those who call on the Lord with pure hearts. 2 TIMOTHY 2:22

JANUARY 22

A Dream in Prison

Although Joseph was in prison, he kept a good attitude and remained useful to God. Read to see how God used Joseph while in prison.

Genesis 40:1-15

Some time later, Pharaoh's chief cup-bearer and chief baker offended their royal master. ²Pharaoh became angry with these two officials, ³and he put them in the prison where Joseph was, in the palace of the captain of the guard. ⁴They remained in prison for quite some time, and the captain of the guard assigned them to Joseph, who looked after them.

⁵While they were in prison, Pharaoh's cup-bearer and baker each had a dream one night, and each dream had its own meaning. ⁶When Joseph saw them the next morning, he noticed that they both looked upset. ⁷"Why do you look so worried today?" he asked them.

⁸And they replied, "We both had dreams last night, but no one can tell us what they mean."

"Interpreting dreams is God's business," Joseph replied. "Go ahead and tell me your dreams."

⁹So the chief cup-bearer told Joseph his dream first. "In my dream," he said, "I saw a grapevine in front of me. ¹⁰The vine had three branches that began to bud and blossom, and soon it produced clusters of ripe grapes. ¹¹I was holding Pharaoh's wine cup in my hand, so I took a cluster of grapes and squeezed the juice into the cup. Then I placed the cup in Pharaoh's hand."

¹²"This is what the dream means," Joseph said. "The three branches represent three days. ¹³Within three days Pharaoh will lift you up and restore you to your position as his chief cup-bearer. ¹⁴And please remember me and do me a favor when things go well for you. Mention me to Pharaoh, so he might let me out of this place. ¹⁵For I was kidnapped from my homeland, the land of the Hebrews, and now I'm here in prison, but I did nothing to deserve it."

Joseph was in jail for doing the right thing. He had every reason to complain and become bitter. Instead, Joseph chose to work hard and do his best. He was put in charge of the other prisoners, and that's how Joseph learned about the dream of the cup-bearer (and later, a baker). When life is not going your way, you can complain. Or you can choose to have a good attitude and do your best. Which do you think is more pleasing to God?

Dear brothers and sisters,* when troubles come your way, consider it an opportunity for great joy. For you know that when your faith is tested, your endurance has a chance to grow. JAMES 1:2-3
1:2 Greek *brothers.*

JANUARY 23

A Dream in the Palace

Pharaoh had a dream that none of his magicians could interpret; in other words, they were unable to tell Pharaoh what the dream meant. At that moment, the cup-bearer remembered who had interpreted his dream in prison. So Joseph was called to come before Pharaoh. See what happened next.

Genesis 41:15-32
Then Pharaoh said to Joseph, "I had a dream last night, and no one here can tell me what it means. But I have heard that when you hear about a dream you can interpret it."

¹⁶"It is beyond my power to do this,"
Joseph replied. "But God can tell you what it means and set you at ease."

¹⁷So Pharaoh told Joseph his dream. "In my dream," he said, "I was standing on the bank of the Nile River, ¹⁸and I saw seven fat, healthy cows come up out of the river and begin grazing in the marsh grass.

¹⁹But then I saw seven sick-looking cows, scrawny and thin, come up after them. I've never seen such sorry-looking animals in all the land of Egypt. ²⁰These thin, scrawny cows ate the seven fat cows. ²¹But afterward you wouldn't have known it, for they were still as thin and scrawny as before! Then I woke up.

²²"Then I fell asleep again, and I had another dream. This time I saw seven heads of grain, full and beautiful, growing on a single stalk. ²³Then seven more heads of grain appeared, but these were blighted, shriveled, and withered by the east wind. ²⁴And the shriveled heads swallowed the seven healthy heads. I told these dreams to the magicians, but no one could tell me what they mean."

²⁵Joseph responded, "Both of Pharaoh's dreams mean the same thing. God is telling Pharaoh in advance what he is about to do. ²⁶The seven healthy cows and the seven healthy heads of grain both represent seven years of prosperity. ²⁷The seven thin, scrawny cows that came up later and the seven thin heads of grain, withered by the east wind, represent seven years of famine.

²⁸"This will happen just as I have described it, for God has revealed to Pharaoh in advance what he is about to do. ²⁹The next seven years will be a period of great prosperity throughout the land of Egypt. ³⁰But afterward there will be seven years of famine so great that all the prosperity will be forgotten in Egypt. Famine will destroy the land. ³¹This famine will be so severe that even the memory of the good years will be erased. ³²As for having two similar dreams, it means that these events have been decreed by God, and he will soon make them happen."

As Joseph stood before Pharaoh, he could have taken all the credit for explaining what the king's dream meant. But Joseph did not. Instead, he gave credit where it was due—to God. When God gives you success in the things you do, be sure to thank him for what he has accomplished through you.

Everything comes from [God] and exists by his power and is intended for his glory. All glory to him forever! Amen. ROMANS 11:36

JANUARY 24

Joseph in charge

It was obvious to Pharaoh that God had given Joseph great wisdom. Not only did he tell Pharaoh what his dream meant, but Joseph also gave Pharaoh excellent advice. Check out what happened to Joseph next.

Genesis 41:33-43, 46-49

[Joseph said,] "Pharaoh should find an intelligent and wise man and put him in charge of the entire land of Egypt. ³⁴Then Pharaoh should appoint supervisors over the land and let them collect one-fifth of

29

all the crops during the seven good years. ³⁵Have them gather all the food produced in the good years that are just ahead and bring it to Pharaoh's storehouses. Store it away, and guard it so there will be food in the cities. ³⁶That way there will be enough to eat when the seven years of famine come to the land of Egypt. Otherwise this famine will destroy the land."

³⁷Joseph's suggestions were well received by Pharaoh and his officials. ³⁸So Pharaoh asked his officials, "Can we find anyone else like this man so obviously filled with the spirit of God?" ³⁹Then Pharaoh said to Joseph, "Since God has revealed the meaning of the dreams to you, clearly no one else is as intelligent or wise as you are. ⁴⁰You will be in charge of my court, and all my people will take orders from you. Only I, sitting on my throne, will have a rank higher than yours."

⁴¹Pharaoh said to Joseph, "I hereby put you in charge of the entire land of Egypt." ⁴²Then Pharaoh removed his signet ring from his hand and placed it on Joseph's finger. He dressed him in fine linen clothing and hung a gold chain around his neck. ⁴³Then he had Joseph ride in the chariot reserved for his second-in-command. And wherever Joseph went, the command was shouted, "Kneel down!" So Pharaoh put Joseph in charge of all Egypt.

⁴⁶He was thirty years old when he began serving in the court of Pharaoh, the king of Egypt. And when Joseph left Pharaoh's presence, he inspected the entire land of Egypt.

⁴⁷As predicted, for seven years the land produced bumper crops. ⁴⁸During those years, Joseph gathered all the crops grown in Egypt and stored the grain from the surrounding fields in the cities. ⁴⁹He piled up huge amounts of grain like sand on the seashore. Finally, he stopped keeping records because there was too much to measure.

After listening to Joseph's advice, Pharaoh put Joseph in charge of all of Egypt. Why? He realized that Joseph was a man "filled with the spirit of God." When we are faithful and live by God's commands, others should see God in us. How much of God do your friends and family see in you? It may be in your encouraging words, your kind actions, or your wise advice.

The Holy Spirit produces this kind of fruit in our lives: love, joy, peace, patience, kindness, goodness, faithfulness, gentleness, and self-control. There is no law against these things! GALATIANS 5:22-23

JANUARY 25

JOSEPH SEES HIS BROTHERS AGAIN

Joseph's brothers hadn't seen him since the day they sold him as a slave. When they went to Egypt to buy food, they got an unexpected "welcome." Check it out.

Genesis 42:1-21

When Jacob heard that grain was available in Egypt, he said to his sons, "Why are you standing around looking at one another? [2]I have heard there is grain in Egypt. Go down there, and buy enough grain to keep us alive. Otherwise we'll die."

[3]So Joseph's ten older brothers went down to Egypt to buy grain. [4]But Jacob wouldn't let Joseph's younger brother, Benjamin, go with them, for fear some harm might come to him. [5]So Jacob's* sons arrived in Egypt along with others to buy food, for the famine was in Canaan as well.

[6]Since Joseph was governor of all Egypt and in charge of selling grain to all the people, it was to him that his brothers came. When they arrived, they bowed before him with their faces to the ground. [7]Joseph recognized his brothers instantly, but he pretended to be a stranger and spoke harshly to them. "Where are you from?" he demanded.

"From the land of Canaan," they replied. "We have come to buy food."

[8]Although Joseph recognized his brothers, they didn't recognize him. [9]And he remembered the dreams he'd had about them many years before. He said to them, "You are spies! You have come to see how vulnerable our land has become."

[10]"No, my lord!" they exclaimed. "Your servants have simply come to buy food.

[11]We are all brothers—members of the same family. We are honest men, sir! We are not spies!"

[12]"Yes, you are!" Joseph insisted. "You have come to see how vulnerable our land has become."

[13]"Sir," they said, "there are actually twelve of us. We, your servants, are all brothers, sons of a man living in the land of Canaan. Our youngest brother is back there with our father right now, and one of our brothers is no longer with us."

[14]But Joseph insisted, "As I said, you are spies! [15]This is how I will test your story. I swear by the life of Pharaoh that you will never leave Egypt unless your youngest brother comes here! [16]One of you must go and get your brother. I'll keep the rest of you here in prison. Then we'll find out whether or not your story is true. By the life of Pharaoh, if it turns out that you don't have a younger brother, then I'll know you are spies."

[17]So Joseph put them all in prison for three days. [18]On the third day Joseph said to them, "I am a God-fearing man. If you do as I say, you will live. [19]If you really are honest men, choose one of your brothers to remain in prison. The rest of you may go home with grain for your starving families. [20]But you must bring your youngest brother back to me. This will prove that you are telling the truth, and you will not die." To this they agreed.

²¹Speaking among themselves, they said, "Clearly we are being punished because of what we did to Joseph long ago. We saw his anguish when he pleaded for his life, but we wouldn't listen. That's why we're in this trouble."

42:5 Hebrew *Israel's.*

Joseph's brothers knew they had sinned. So when Joseph demanded that they bring their youngest brother to him, the brothers immediately thought God was punishing them for what they had done. There's no doubt that God punishes sin, but he also offers us forgiveness. That can happen, though, only when we confess our sins to him and tell him we are sorry. Is there anything you need to confess to God today?

If we confess our sins to [God], he is faithful and just to forgive us our sins and to cleanse us from all wickedness. I JOHN 1:9

JANUARY 26

Joseph Tests His Brothers

To discover if his brothers had truly changed, Joseph decided to test them and watch how they treated each other. Read and see what happened.

Genesis 44:3-18, 32-34

The brothers were up at dawn and were sent on their journey with their loaded donkeys. ⁴But when they had gone only a short distance and were barely out of the city, Joseph said to his palace manager, "Chase after them and stop them. When you catch up with them, ask them, 'Why have you repaid my kindness with such evil? ⁵Why have you stolen my master's silver cup,* which he uses to predict the future? What a wicked thing you have done!'"

⁶When the palace manager caught up with the men, he spoke to them as he had been instructed.

⁷"What are you talking about?" the brothers responded. "We are your servants and would never do such a thing! ⁸Didn't we return the money we found in our sacks? We brought it back all the way from the land of Canaan. Why would we steal silver or gold from your master's house? ⁹If you find his cup with any one of us, let that man die. And all the rest of us, my lord, will be your slaves."

¹⁰"That's fair," the man replied. "But only the one who stole the cup will be my slave. The rest of you may go free."

¹¹They all quickly took their sacks from the backs of their donkeys and opened them. ¹²The palace manager searched the brothers' sacks, from the oldest to the youngest. And the cup was found in Benjamin's sack! ¹³When the brothers saw this, they tore their clothing in despair. Then they loaded their donkeys again and returned to the city.

[14]Joseph was still in his palace when Judah and his brothers arrived, and they fell to the ground before him. [15]"What have you done?" Joseph demanded. "Don't you know that a man like me can predict the future?"

[16]Judah answered, "Oh, my lord, what can we say to you? How can we explain this? How can we prove our innocence? God is punishing us for our sins. My lord, we have all returned to be your slaves—all of us, not just our brother who had your cup in his sack."

[17]"No," Joseph said. "I would never do such a thing! Only the man who stole the cup will be my slave. The rest of you may go back to your father in peace."

44:5 As in Greek version; Hebrew lacks this phrase.

[18]Then Judah stepped forward and said, "Please, my lord, let your servant say just one word to you. Please, do not be angry with me, even though you are as powerful as Pharaoh himself.

[32]"My lord, I guaranteed to my father that I would take care of the boy. I told him, 'If I don't bring him back to you, I will bear the blame forever.'

[33]"So please, my lord, let me stay here as a slave instead of the boy, and let the boy return with his brothers. [34]For how can I return to my father if the boy is not with me? I couldn't bear to see the anguish this would cause my father!"

Joseph tested his brothers by putting his silver cup in Benjamin's sack. Joseph wanted to see if they would stand up for Benjamin or allow him to be punished for something he didn't do. Judah passed the test when he stood up for his youngest brother and offered to take Benjamin's punishment. When your character is tested, follow Judah's example. Stand up for what you know is right.

God blesses those who patiently endure testing and temptation. Afterward they will receive the crown of life that God has promised to those who love him.
JAMES 1:12

JANUARY 27

surprise!

Joseph's brothers were in for the surprise of their lives. Check out their reactions as Joseph tells them who he really is.

Genesis 45:1-15
Joseph could stand it no longer. There were many people in the room, and he said to his attendants, "Out, all of you!" So he was alone with his brothers when he told

them who he was. [2]Then he broke down and wept. He wept so loudly the Egyptians could hear him, and word of it quickly carried to Pharaoh's palace.

[3]"I am Joseph!" he said to his brothers. "Is

33

my father still alive?" But his brothers were speechless! They were stunned to realize that Joseph was standing there in front of them. ⁴"Please, come closer," he said to them. So they came closer. And he said again, "I am Joseph, your brother, whom you sold into slavery in Egypt. ⁵But don't be upset, and don't be angry with yourselves for selling me to this place. It was God who sent me here ahead of you to preserve your lives. ⁶This famine that has ravaged the land for two years will last five more years, and there will be neither plowing nor harvesting. ⁷God has sent me ahead of you to keep you and your families alive and to preserve many survivors.* ⁸So it was God who sent me here, not you! And he is the one who made me an adviser* to Pharaoh—the manager of his entire palace and the governor of all Egypt.

⁹"Now hurry back to my father and tell him, 'This is what your son Joseph says: God has made me master over all the land of Egypt. So come down to me immediately! ¹⁰You can live in the region of Goshen, where you can be near me with all your children and grandchildren, your flocks and herds, and everything you own. ¹¹I will take care of you there, for there are still five years of famine ahead of us. Otherwise you, your household, and all your animals will starve.'"

¹²Then Joseph added, "Look! You can see for yourselves, and so can my brother Benjamin, that I really am Joseph! ¹³Go tell my father of my honored position here in Egypt. Describe for him everything you have seen, and then bring my father here quickly." ¹⁴Weeping with joy, he embraced Benjamin, and Benjamin did the same. ¹⁵Then Joseph kissed each of his brothers and wept over them, and after that they began talking freely with him.

45:7 Or *and to save you with an extraordinary rescue.* The meaning of the Hebrew is uncertain.   45:8 Hebrew *a father.*

Why was Joseph sold into slavery? Why was he thrown into prison? Did you catch it? God had a good plan for Joseph, even during those hard times. God was saving Joseph and his family from the famine, a time when there was no food. God can bring great things out of really hard times—just as he did for Joseph. When you go through bad times, remember God's goodness. Wait to see what he will do.

We know that God causes everything to work together* for the good of those who love God and are called according to his purpose for them. ROMANS 8:28

8:28 Some manuscripts read *And we know that everything works together.*

JANUARY 28

Past wrongs

Years later, Joseph's brothers still couldn't believe that Joseph wasn't angry with them. When their father died, they were afraid of Joseph again. Would Joseph take revenge on his brothers now?

Genesis 50:15-21

But now that their father was dead, Joseph's brothers became fearful. "Now Joseph will show his anger and pay us back for all the wrong we did to him," they said.

[16]So they sent this message to Joseph: "Before your father died, he instructed us [17]to say to you: 'Please forgive your brothers for the great wrong they did to you—for their sin in treating you so cruelly.' So we, the servants of the God of your father, beg you to forgive our sin." When Joseph received the message, he broke down and wept. [18]Then his brothers came and threw themselves down before Joseph. "Look, we are your slaves!" they said.

[19]But Joseph replied, "Don't be afraid of me. Am I God, that I can punish you? [20]You intended to harm me, but God intended it all for good. He brought me to this position so I could save the lives of many people. [21]No, don't be afraid. I will continue to take care of you and your children." So he reassured them by speaking kindly to them.

Joseph's brothers were so amazed by his forgiveness that they had a hard time believing it. But it was true. Even when Joseph had the power to get even with his brothers, he chose forgiveness instead. God wants you to forgive others when they hurt you, just as Joseph forgave his brothers. Don't try to get even—forgive instead.

If you forgive those who sin against you, your heavenly Father will forgive you. But if you refuse to forgive others, your Father will not forgive your sins.
MATTHEW 6:14-15

JANUARY 29

moses in the nile

Pharaoh had made a terrible law. He said that all the Israelite baby boys had to be drowned in the Nile River. But read about how God protected baby Moses during that time.

Exodus 2:1-10

A man and woman from the tribe of Levi got married. ²The woman became pregnant and gave birth to a son. She saw that he was a special baby and kept him hidden for three months. ³But when she could no longer hide him, she got a basket made of papyrus reeds and waterproofed it with tar and pitch. She put the baby in the basket and laid it among the reeds along the bank of the Nile River. ⁴The baby's sister then stood at a distance, watching to see what would happen to him.

⁵Soon Pharaoh's daughter came down to bathe in the river, and her attendants walked along the riverbank. When the princess saw the basket among the reeds, she sent her maid to get it for her. ⁶When the princess opened it, she saw the baby. The little boy was crying, and she felt sorry for him. "This must be one of the Hebrew children," she said.

⁷Then the baby's sister approached the princess. "Should I go and find one of the Hebrew women to nurse the baby for you?" she asked.

⁸"Yes, do!" the princess replied. So the girl went and called the baby's mother.

⁹"Take this baby and nurse him for me," the princess told the baby's mother. "I will pay you for your help." So the woman took her baby home and nursed him.

¹⁰Later, when the boy was older, his mother brought him back to Pharaoh's daughter, who adopted him as her own son. The princess named him Moses,* for she explained, "I lifted him out of the water."

2:10 *Moses* sounds like a Hebrew term that means "to lift out."

God's power is much greater than Pharaoh's. God kept Moses safe from Pharaoh's horrible plan. When you are in danger, remember that God sees you and cares about you. He can keep you safe from evil. Just as God protected Moses, he will watch over you as well.

*The Lord is faithful; he will strengthen you and guard you from the evil one.** 2 THESSALONIANS 3:3

3:3 Or *from evil.*

JANUARY 30

moses on the run

Moses really messed up in this story when he tried to take matters into his own hands. Look what his anger caused him to do.

Exodus 2:11-21

Many years later, when Moses had grown up, he went out to visit his own people, the Hebrews, and he saw how hard they were forced to work. During his visit, he saw an Egyptian beating one of his fellow Hebrews. [12]After looking in all directions to make sure no one was watching, Moses killed the Egyptian and hid the body in the sand.

[13]The next day, when Moses went out to visit his people again, he saw two Hebrew men fighting. "Why are you beating up your friend?" Moses said to the one who had started the fight.

[14]The man replied, "Who appointed you to be our prince and judge? Are you going to kill me as you killed that Egyptian yesterday?"

Then Moses was afraid, thinking, "Everyone knows what I did." [15]And sure enough, Pharaoh heard what had happened, and he tried to kill Moses. But Moses fled from Pharaoh and went to live in the land of Midian.

When Moses arrived in Midian, he sat down beside a well. [16]Now the priest of Midian had seven daughters who came as usual to draw water and fill the water troughs for their father's flocks. [17]But some other shepherds came and chased them away. So Moses jumped up and rescued the girls from the shepherds. Then he drew water for their flocks.

[18]When the girls returned to Reuel, their father, he asked, "Why are you back so soon today?"

[19]"An Egyptian rescued us from the shepherds," they answered. "And then he drew water for us and watered our flocks."

[20]"Then where is he?" their father asked. "Why did you leave him there? Invite him to come and eat with us."

[21]Moses accepted the invitation, and he settled there with him. In time, Reuel gave Moses his daughter Zipporah to be his wife.

Sometimes life just isn't fair, and that can make us really angry! But when Moses tried to take revenge, he wound up killing someone and getting in a mess of trouble. His angry actions were not a good solution. When you are tempted to get revenge, stop and think about Moses. Trust God to make things right rather than trying to do it yourself by paying back evil for evil.

Never pay back evil with more evil. Do things in such a way that everyone can see you are honorable. ROMANS 12:17

JANUARY 31

The Burning Bush

While Moses was doing his normal, everyday job, God spoke to him in an incredible way. Read on to see Moses' reaction.

Exodus 3:1-15

One day Moses was tending the flock of his father-in-law, Jethro,* the priest of Midian. He led the flock far into the wilderness and came to Sinai,* the mountain of God. ²There the angel of the LORD appeared to him in a blazing fire from the middle of a bush. Moses stared in amazement. Though the bush was engulfed in flames, it didn't burn up. ³"This is amazing," Moses said to himself. "Why isn't that bush burning up? I must go see it."

⁴When the LORD saw Moses coming to take a closer look, God called to him from the middle of the bush, "Moses! Moses!"

"Here I am!" Moses replied.

⁵"Do not come any closer," the LORD warned. "Take off your sandals, for you are standing on holy ground. ⁶I am the God of your father*—the God of Abraham, the God of Isaac, and the God of Jacob." When Moses heard this, he covered his face because he was afraid to look at God.

⁷Then the LORD told him, "I have certainly seen the oppression of my people in Egypt. I have heard their cries of distress because of their harsh slave drivers. Yes, I am aware of their suffering. ⁸So I have come down to rescue them from the power of the Egyptians and lead them out of Egypt into their own fertile and spacious land. It is a land flowing with milk and honey—the land where the Canaanites, Hittites, Amorites, Perizzites, Hivites, and Jebusites now live. ⁹Look! The cry of the people of Israel has reached me, and I have seen how harshly the Egyptians abuse them. ¹⁰Now go, for I am sending you to Pharaoh. You must lead my people Israel out of Egypt."

¹¹But Moses protested to God, "Who am I to appear before Pharaoh? Who am I to lead the people of Israel out of Egypt?"

¹²God answered, "I will be with you. And this is your sign that I am the one who has sent you: When you have brought the people out of Egypt, you will worship God at this very mountain."

¹³But Moses protested, "If I go to the people of Israel and tell them, 'The God of your ancestors has sent me to you,' they will ask me, 'What is his name?' Then what should I tell them?"

¹⁴God replied to Moses, "I AM WHO I AM.* Say this to the people of Israel: I AM has sent me to you." ¹⁵God also said to Moses, "Say this to the people of Israel: Yahweh,* the God of your ancestors—the God of Abraham, the God of Isaac, and the God of Jacob—has sent me to you.

This is my eternal name,
my name to remember for all
generations."

3:1a Moses' father-in-law went by two names, Jethro and Reuel.   3:1b Hebrew *Horeb*, another name for Sinai.   3:6 Greek version reads *your fathers*.   3:14 Or *I WILL BE WHAT I WILL BE*.   3:15 *Yahweh* is a transliteration of the proper name YHWH that is sometimes rendered "Jehovah"; in this translation it is usually rendered "the LORD."

No doubt Moses was shocked to see a bush on fire that did not burn up. But he was even more surprised to hear God's job assignment for him. And scared! Even though Moses was afraid that he wouldn't be able to do it, God promised to be with him. God has a job for you to do too. God helped Moses; he will also help you.

I can do everything through Christ,* who gives me strength. PHILIPPIANS 4:13
4:13 Greek *through the one.*

congratulations!

You've made it all the way through the month of January! Way to go!

Each month you'll be climbing one level on your way to the top of Challenge Mountain. You can use a marker or a highlighter to fill in one level for each month of readings that you complete. At the end of a year of reading, you'll be at the peak of the mountain. And not only that, you'll feel closer to God than ever before. Know why? You'll have read all the way through the Bible, and you'll have learned many things about God—who he is, how much he loves you, and how you can please him every day.

Now it's time to take a rest, think back on what you read, and have some fun. Write down three things you learned about God this month.

1.

2.

3.

IMPORTANT STUFF TO REMEMBER FROM JANUARY

❑ God created everything!

❑ God punishes sin.

❑ God promised to bless all people through Abraham's descendants.

❑ God takes care of his people.

Time for Some Word Fun!

From the story of Noah and the Flood, find the following words in the puzzle.

Word Bank

ANIMALS	DOVE	FORTY	RAINBOW	SUMMER
BIRDS	EARTH	GOD	REMEMBER	WATER
BOAT	ETERNAL	LIFE	SEND	WINDOW
CLOUDS	FLOATED	NEVER	SIGN	WINTER
COVENANT	FLOOD	NOAH	SONS	WOOD
DESTROY				

```
R  A  I  L  B  W  I  N  D  O  W  O  W
G  E  A  N  I  M  A  L  S  B  E  N  S
O  V  C  O  U  F  R  T  D  A  T  F  A
D  Y  O  R  T  S  E  D  R  P  E  O  R
N  E  S  T  W  O  B  N  I  A  R  R  E
F  L  O  O  D  F  M  A  B  I  N  T  V
I  L  O  G  S  M  E  V  O  D  A  Y  E
V  D  E  N  G  O  M  A  R  S  L  I  N
C  E  H  C  O  V  E  N  A  N  T  G  S
A  T  U  L  T  A  R  A  K  O  I  M  U
W  A  B  O  A  T  H  E  R  S  L  A  M
B  O  W  U  S  E  N  D  A  T  A  Y  M
E  L  A  D  A  R  E  T  A  W  H  O  E
A  F  R  S  P  S  I  W  I  N  T  E  R
```

41

FEBRUARY 1

This is Impossible!

God told Moses to lead the Israelites out of Egypt. But Moses didn't think he would be able to do what God wanted. See what God had to say about that.

Exodus 4:1-17

But Moses protested again, "What if they won't believe me or listen to me? What if they say, 'The LORD never appeared to you'?"

²Then the LORD asked him, "What is that in your hand?"

"A shepherd's staff," Moses replied.

³"Throw it down on the ground," the LORD told him. So Moses threw down the staff, and it turned into a snake! Moses jumped back.

⁴Then the LORD told him, "Reach out and grab its tail." So Moses reached out and grabbed it, and it turned back into a shepherd's staff in his hand.

⁵"Perform this sign," the LORD told him. "Then they will believe that the LORD, the God of their ancestors—the God of Abraham, the God of Isaac, and the God of Jacob—really has appeared to you."

⁶Then the LORD said to Moses, "Now put your hand inside your cloak." So Moses put his hand inside his cloak, and when he took it out again, his hand was white as snow with a severe skin disease.* ⁷"Now put your hand back into your cloak," the LORD said. So Moses put his hand back in, and when he took it out again, it was as healthy as the rest of his body.

⁸The LORD said to Moses, "If they do not believe you and are not convinced by the first miraculous sign, they will be convinced by the second sign. ⁹And if they don't believe you or listen to you even after these two signs, then take some water from the Nile River and pour it out on the dry ground. When you do, the water from the Nile will turn to blood on the ground."

¹⁰But Moses pleaded with the LORD, "O Lord, I'm not very good with words. I never have been, and I'm not now, even though you have spoken to me. I get tongue-tied, and my words get tangled."

¹¹Then the LORD asked Moses, "Who makes a person's mouth? Who decides whether people speak or do not speak, hear or do not hear, see or do not see? Is it not I, the LORD? ¹²Now go! I will be with you as you speak, and I will instruct you in what to say."

¹³But Moses again pleaded, "Lord, please! Send anyone else."

¹⁴Then the LORD became angry with

Moses. "All right," he said. "What about your brother, Aaron the Levite? I know he speaks well. And look! He is on his way to meet you now. He will be delighted to see you. [15]Talk to him, and put the WORDS in his mouth. I will be with both of you as you speak, and I will instruct you both in what to do. [16]Aaron will be your spokesman to the people. He will be your mouthpiece, and you will stand in the place of God for him, telling him what to say. [17]And take your shepherd's staff with you, and use it to perform the miraculous signs I have shown you."

4:6 Or *with leprosy*. The Hebrew word used here can describe various skin diseases.

"I can't do it." Have you ever felt that way when facing something new or a tough assignment at school? Moses sure did. But God promised to be with Moses and help him. In fact, God would do all the hard work. If God tells you to do something hard, he will help you get it done. Do any of God's commandments seem impossible to you? Trust him and he will help you do what he wants you to.

Let us come boldly to the throne of our gracious God. There we will receive his mercy, and we will find grace to help us when we need it most. HEBREWS 4:16

FEBRUARY 2

Pharaoh says no

Pharaoh was not going to give up his slaves easily. In fact, rather than let the Israelites go free, he made things even harder for them. Read and find out what Pharaoh did.

Exodus 5:1-21

Moses and Aaron went and spoke to Pharaoh. They told him, "This is what the LORD, the God of Israel, says: Let my people go so they may hold a festival in my honor in the wilderness."

[2]"Is that so?" retorted Pharaoh. "And who is the LORD? Why should I listen to him and let Israel go? I don't know the LORD, and I will not let Israel go."

[3]But Aaron and Moses persisted. "The God of the Hebrews has met with us," they declared. "So let us take a three-day journey into the wilderness so we can offer sacri-fices to the LORD our God. If we don't, he will kill us with a plague or with the sword."

[4]Pharaoh replied, "Moses and Aaron, why are you distracting the people from their tasks? Get back to work! [5]Look, there are many of your people in the land, and you are stopping them from their work."

[6]That same day Pharaoh sent this order to the Egyptian slave drivers and the Israel-ite foremen: [7]"Do not supply any more straw for making bricks. Make the people get it themselves! [8]But still require them to make the same number of bricks as before. Don't reduce the quota. They are lazy.

44

That's why they are crying out, 'Let us go and offer sacrifices to our God.' ⁹Load them down with more work. Make them sweat! That will teach them to listen to lies!"

¹⁰So the slave drivers and foremen went out and told the people: "This is what Pharaoh says: I will not provide any more straw for you. ¹¹Go and get it yourselves. Find it wherever you can. But you must produce just as many bricks as before!" ¹²So the people scattered throughout the land of Egypt in search of stubble to use as straw.

¹³Meanwhile, the Egyptian slave drivers continued to push hard. "Meet your daily quota of bricks, just as you did when we provided you with straw!" they demanded. ¹⁴Then they whipped the Israelite foremen they had put in charge of the work crews. "Why haven't you met your quotas either yesterday or today?" they demanded.

¹⁵So the Israelite foremen went to Pharaoh and pleaded with him. "Please don't treat your servants like this," they begged. ¹⁶"We are given no straw, but the slave drivers still demand, 'Make bricks!' We are being beaten, but it isn't our fault! Your own people are to blame!"

¹⁷But Pharaoh shouted, "You're just lazy! Lazy! That's why you're saying, 'Let us go and offer sacrifices to the LORD.' ¹⁸Now get back to work! No straw will be given to you, but you must still produce the full quota of bricks."

¹⁹The Israelite foremen could see that they were in serious trouble when they were told, "You must not reduce the number of bricks you make each day." ²⁰As they left Pharaoh's court, they confronted Moses and Aaron, who were waiting outside for them. ²¹The foremen said to them, "May the LORD judge and punish you for making us stink before Pharaoh and his officials. You have put a sword into their hands, an excuse to kill us!"

Pharaoh was making life hard for the Israelites even though they hadn't done anything to deserve it. Sometimes people try to cause problems for you, even when you haven't done anything to deserve it. If that happens, don't get discouraged. God will help you hang in there until he rescues you from the problems. How will you react when someone makes fun of you for no reason?

God blesses those who patiently endure testing and temptation. Afterward they will receive the crown of life that God has promised to those who love him. JAMES 1:12

FEBRUARY 3

Down and out

The tougher Pharaoh got on the Israelites, the more discouraged they became. God promised to free the Israelites, but they felt like just giving up! They couldn't figure out what was going to happen to them.

Exodus 6:1-12

Then the LORD told Moses, "Now you will see what I will do to Pharaoh. When he feels the force of my strong hand, he will let the people go. In fact, he will force them to leave his land!"

²And God said to Moses, "I am Yahweh—'the LORD.'* ³I appeared to Abraham, to Isaac, and to Jacob as El-Shaddai—'God Almighty'*—but I did not reveal my name, Yahweh, to them. ⁴And I reaffirmed my covenant with them. Under its terms, I promised to give them the land of Canaan, where they were living as foreigners. ⁵You can be sure that I have heard the groans of the people of Israel, who are now slaves to the Egyptians. And I am well aware of my covenant with them.

⁶"Therefore, say to the people of Israel: 'I am the LORD. I will free you from your oppression and will rescue you from your slavery in Egypt. I will redeem you with a powerful arm and great acts of judgment. ⁷I will claim you as my own people, and I will be your God. Then you will know that I am the LORD your God who has freed you from your oppression in Egypt. ⁸I will bring you into the land I swore to give to Abraham, Isaac, and Jacob. I will give it to you as your very own possession. I am the LORD!'"

⁹So Moses told the people of Israel what the LORD had said, but they refused to listen anymore. They had become too discouraged by the brutality of their slavery.

¹⁰Then the LORD said to Moses, ¹¹"Go back to Pharaoh, the king of Egypt, and tell him to let the people of Israel leave his country."

¹²"But LORD!" Moses objected. "My own people won't listen to me anymore. How can I expect Pharaoh to listen? I'm such a clumsy speaker!*"

6:2 *Yahweh* is a transliteration of the proper name *YHWH* that is sometimes rendered "Jehovah"; in this translation it is usually rendered "the LORD." **6:3** *El-Shaddai* means "God Almighty." **6:12** Hebrew *I have uncircumcised lips.*

God had promised to free the Israelites from slavery, but they still wanted to give up. They had a hard time believing that their situation would ever change. Following God was just too hard. Sometimes following God can be difficult for us, too. But rather than quitting, look to God, who will give you strength.

I can do everything through Christ, who gives me strength.* PHILIPPIANS 4:13
4:13 Greek *through the one.*

FEBRUARY 4

A Stubborn Ruler

God had a message for Pharaoh. Would Pharaoh listen? Read and see.

Exodus 7:1-13

Then the LORD said to Moses, "Pay close attention to this. I will make you seem like God to Pharaoh, and your brother, Aaron, will be your prophet. ²Tell Aaron everything I command you, and Aaron must command Pharaoh to let the people of Israel leave his country. ³But I will make Pharaoh's heart stubborn so I can multiply my miraculous signs and wonders in the land of Egypt. ⁴Even then Pharaoh will refuse to listen to you. So I will bring down my fist on Egypt. Then I will rescue my forces—my people, the Israelites—from the land of Egypt with great acts of judgment. ⁵When I raise my powerful hand and bring out the Israelites, the Egyptians will know that I am the LORD."

⁶So Moses and Aaron did just as the LORD had commanded them. ⁷Moses was eighty years old, and Aaron was eighty-three when they made their demands to Pharaoh.

⁸Then the LORD said to Moses and Aaron, ⁹"Pharaoh will demand, 'Show me a miracle.' When he does this, say to Aaron, 'Take your staff and throw it down in front of Pharaoh, and it will become a serpent.*'"

¹⁰So Moses and Aaron went to Pharaoh and did what the LORD had commanded them. Aaron threw down his staff before Pharaoh and his officials, and it became a serpent! ¹¹Then Pharaoh called in his own wise men and sorcerers, and these Egyptian magicians did the same thing with their magic. ¹²They threw down their staffs, which also became serpents! But then Aaron's staff swallowed up their staffs. ¹³Pharaoh's heart, however, remained hard. He still refused to listen, just as the LORD had predicted.

7:9 Hebrew *tannin*, which elsewhere refers to a sea monster. Greek version translates it "dragon."

Moses gave Pharaoh an important message from God. But Pharaoh wanted to have his own way. He didn't care who sent the message—Pharaoh wasn't going to listen. When have you had a hard time listening to God? Learn from what happened to Pharaoh. It's always wiser to listen to God and obey than to insist on having your own way.

Come and listen to [Wisdom's] counsel. I'll share my heart with you and make you wise. PROVERBS 1:23

FEBRUARY 5

The Plagues Begin

Pharaoh didn't get it. He wouldn't let the Israelites go. What would God do to make him change his mind?

Exodus 7:19–8:4, 8-19

Then the LORD said to Moses: "Tell Aaron, 'Take your staff and raise your hand over the waters of Egypt—all its rivers, canals, ponds, and all the reservoirs. Turn all the water to blood. Everywhere in Egypt the water will turn to blood, even the water stored in wooden bowls and stone pots.'"

²⁰So Moses and Aaron did just as the LORD commanded them. As Pharaoh and all of his officials watched, Aaron raised his staff and struck the water of the Nile. Suddenly, the whole river turned to blood! ²¹The fish in the river died, and the water became so foul that the Egyptians couldn't drink it. There was blood everywhere throughout the land of Egypt. ²²But again the magicians of Egypt used their magic, and they, too, turned water into blood. So Pharaoh's heart remained hard. He refused to listen to Moses and Aaron, just as the LORD had predicted. ²³Pharaoh returned to his palace and put the whole thing out of his mind. ²⁴Then all the Egyptians dug along the riverbank to find drinking water, for they couldn't drink the water from the Nile.

²⁵Seven days passed from the time the LORD struck the Nile.

⁸:¹*Then the LORD said to Moses, "Go back to Pharaoh and announce to him, 'This is what the LORD says: Let my people go, so they can worship me. ²If you refuse to let them go, I will send a plague of frogs across your entire land. ³The Nile River will swarm with frogs. They will come up out of the river and into your palace, even into your bedroom and onto your bed! They will enter the houses of your officials and your people. They will even jump into your ovens and your kneading bowls. ⁴Frogs will jump on you, your people, and all your officials.'"

◉

⁸Then Pharaoh summoned Moses and Aaron and begged, "Plead with the LORD to take the frogs away from me and my people. I will let your people go, so they can offer sacrifices to the LORD."

⁹"You set the time!" Moses replied. "Tell me when you want me to pray for you, your officials, and your people. Then you and your houses will be rid of the frogs. They will remain only in the Nile River."

¹⁰"Do it tomorrow," Pharaoh said.

"All right," Moses replied, "it will be as you have said. Then you will know that there is no one like the LORD our God. ¹¹The frogs will leave you and your houses, your officials, and your people. They will remain only in the Nile River."

¹²So Moses and Aaron left Pharaoh's palace, and Moses cried out to the LORD about the frogs he had inflicted on Pharaoh. ¹³And the LORD did just what Moses had predicted. The frogs in the houses, the courtyards, and the fields all died. ¹⁴The Egyptians piled them into great heaps, and a terrible stench filled the land. ¹⁵But when

Pharaoh saw that relief had come, he became stubborn.* He refused to listen to Moses and Aaron, just as the LORD had predicted.

¹⁶So the LORD said to Moses, "Tell Aaron, 'Raise your staff and strike the ground. The dust will turn into swarms of gnats throughout the land of Egypt.'" ¹⁷So Moses and Aaron did just as the LORD had commanded them. When Aaron raised his hand and struck the ground with his staff, gnats infested the entire land, covering the Egyptians and their animals. All the dust in the land of Egypt turned into gnats. ¹⁸Pharaoh's magicians tried to do the same thing with their secret arts, but this time they failed. And the gnats covered everyone, people and animals alike.

¹⁹"This is the finger of God!" the magicians exclaimed to Pharaoh. But Pharaoh's heart remained hard. He wouldn't listen to them, just as the LORD had predicted.

8:1 Verses 8:1-4 are numbered 7:26-29 in Hebrew text.   8:15 Hebrew *made his heart heavy;* also in 8:32.

Since Pharaoh was not cooperating with God's plan, God sent frogs and gnats to bother him. Sometimes God uses the little, annoying things in our life to remind us that he is in charge. What does it take for God to get your attention? Remember that God is in charge of everything.

Our earthly fathers disciplined us for a few years, doing the best they knew how. But God's discipline is always good for us, so that we might share in his holiness. HEBREWS 12:10

FEBRUARY 6
The Trouble Continues
Although God sent plagues to Egypt, he protected his people.

Exodus 8:20–9:7

Then the LORD told Moses, "Get up early in the morning and stand in Pharaoh's way as he goes down to the river. Say to him, 'This is what the LORD says: Let my people go, so they can worship me. ²¹If you refuse, then I will send swarms of flies on you, your officials, your people, and all the houses. The Egyptian homes will be filled with flies, and the ground will be covered with them. ²²But this time I will spare the region of Goshen, where my people live. No flies will be found there. Then you will know that I am the LORD and that I am present even in the heart of your land. ²³I will make a clear distinction between* my people and your people. This miraculous sign will happen tomorrow.'"

²⁴And the LORD did just as he had said. A thick swarm of flies filled Pharaoh's palace and the houses of his officials. The whole land of Egypt was thrown into chaos by the flies.

²⁵Pharaoh called for Moses and Aaron. "All right! Go ahead and offer sacrifices to

your God," he said. "But do it here in this land."

²⁶But Moses replied, "That wouldn't be right. The Egyptians detest the sacrifices that we offer to the Lᴏʀᴅ our God. Look, if we offer our sacrifices here where the Egyptians can see us, they will stone us. ²⁷We must take a three-day trip into the wilderness to offer sacrifices to the Lᴏʀᴅ our God, just as he has commanded us."

²⁸"All right, go ahead," Pharaoh replied. "I will let you go into the wilderness to offer sacrifices to the Lᴏʀᴅ your God. But don't go too far away. Now hurry and pray for me."

²⁹Moses answered, "As soon as I leave you, I will pray to the Lᴏʀᴅ, and tomorrow the swarms of flies will disappear from you and your officials and all your people. But I am warning you, Pharaoh, don't lie to us again and refuse to let the people go to sacrifice to the Lᴏʀᴅ."

³⁰So Moses left Pharaoh's palace and pleaded with the Lᴏʀᴅ to remove all the flies. ³¹And the Lᴏʀᴅ did as Moses asked and caused the swarms of flies to disappear from Pharaoh, his officials, and his people. Not a single fly remained. ³²But Pharaoh again became stubborn and refused to let the people go.

⁹:¹"Go back to Pharaoh," the Lᴏʀᴅ commanded Moses. "Tell him, 'This is what the Lᴏʀᴅ, the God of the Hebrews, says: Let my people go, so they can worship me. ²If you continue to hold them and refuse to let them go, ³the hand of the Lᴏʀᴅ will strike all your livestock—your horses, donkeys, camels, cattle, sheep, and goats—with a deadly plague. ⁴But the Lᴏʀᴅ will again make a distinction between the livestock of the Israelites and that of the Egyptians. Not a single one of Israel's animals will die! ⁵The Lᴏʀᴅ has already set the time for the plague to begin. He has declared that he will strike the land tomorrow.'"

⁶And the Lᴏʀᴅ did just as he had said. The next morning all the livestock of the Egyptians died, but the Israelites didn't lose a single animal. ⁷Pharaoh sent his officials to investigate, and they discovered that the Israelites had not lost a single animal! But even so, Pharaoh's heart remained stubborn,* and he still refused to let the people go.

8:23 As in Greek and Latin versions; Hebrew reads *I will set redemption between.*   9:7 Hebrew *heavy.*

Even though some pretty bad stuff was happening to the Egyptians, God kept the Israelites safe. Not a single cow died, not a single fly landed where the Israelites lived. God still lovingly protects his people. When you love God, you can trust that he will always be with you and watch over you.

*The Lord is faithful; he will strengthen you and guard you from the evil one.**
2 Tʜᴇssᴀʟᴏɴɪᴀɴs 3:3

3:3 Or *from evil.*

FEBRUARY 7

Obedience or Consequences?

God kept punishing Pharaoh and his kingdom. But Pharaoh was not getting the point. He just kept disobeying God.

Exodus 9:8-12, 22-34

Then the LORD said to Moses and Aaron, "Take handfuls of soot from a brick kiln, and have Moses toss it into the air while Pharaoh watches. ⁹The ashes will spread like fine dust over the whole land of Egypt, causing festering boils to break out on people and animals throughout the land."

¹⁰So they took soot from a brick kiln and went and stood before Pharaoh. As Pharaoh watched, Moses threw the soot into the air, and boils broke out on people and animals alike. ¹¹Even the magicians were unable to stand before Moses, because the boils had broken out on them and all the Egyptians. ¹²But the LORD hardened Pharaoh's heart, and just as the LORD had predicted to Moses, Pharaoh refused to listen.

◉

²²Then the LORD said to Moses, "Lift your hand toward the sky so hail may fall on the people, the livestock, and all the plants throughout the land of Egypt."

²³So Moses lifted his staff toward the sky, and the LORD sent thunder and hail, and lightning flashed toward the earth. The LORD sent a tremendous hailstorm against all the land of Egypt. ²⁴Never in all the history of Egypt had there been a storm like that, with such devastating hail and continuous lightning. ²⁵It left all of Egypt in ruins. The hail struck down every-

9:34 Hebrew *made his heart heavy.*

thing in the open field—people, animals, and plants alike. Even the trees were destroyed. ²⁶The only place without hail was the region of Goshen, where the people of Israel lived.

²⁷Then Pharaoh quickly summoned Moses and Aaron. "This time I have sinned," he confessed. "The LORD is the righteous one, and my people and I are wrong. ²⁸Please beg the LORD to end this terrifying thunder and hail. We've had enough. I will let you go; you don't need to stay any longer."

²⁹"All right," Moses replied. "As soon as I leave the city, I will lift my hands and pray to the LORD. Then the thunder and hail will stop, and you will know that the earth belongs to the LORD. ³⁰But I know that you and your officials still do not fear the LORD God."

³¹(All the flax and barley were ruined by the hail, because the barley had formed heads and the flax was budding. ³²But the wheat and the emmer wheat were spared, because they had not yet sprouted from the ground.)

³³So Moses left Pharaoh's court and went out of the city. When he lifted his hands to the LORD, the thunder and hail stopped, and the downpour ceased. ³⁴But when Pharaoh saw that the rain, hail, and thunder had stopped, he and his officials sinned again, and Pharaoh again became stubborn.*

Pharaoh was determined to get his own way—even if it meant certain punishment. He knew what God wanted, but still he chose to disobey. As a result, Pharaoh and his people suffered terrible consequences. There are always consequences when we choose to disobey. Pray that God will help you choose the best way—listening to him and obeying him.

Dear friends, if we deliberately continue sinning after we have received knowledge of the truth, there is no longer any sacrifice that will cover these sins.
HEBREWS 10:26

FEBRUARY 8

Enough Already!

Pharaoh finally had enough. But he still didn't want to do exactly what God said. Would he get his way?

Exodus 10:8-27

So Moses and Aaron were brought back to Pharaoh. "All right," he told them, "go and worship the LORD your God. But who exactly will be going with you?"

⁹Moses replied. "We will all go—young and old, our sons and daughters, and our flocks and herds. We must all join together in celebrating a festival to the LORD."

¹⁰Pharaoh retorted, "The LORD will certainly need to be with you if I let you take your little ones! I can see through your evil plan. ¹¹Never! Only the men may go and worship the LORD, since that is what you requested." And Pharaoh threw them out of the palace.

¹²Then the LORD said to Moses, "Raise your hand over the land of Egypt to bring on the locusts. Let them cover the land and devour every plant that survived the hailstorm."

¹³So Moses raised his staff over Egypt, and the LORD caused an east wind to blow over the land all that day and through the night. When morning arrived, the east wind had brought the locusts. ¹⁴And the locusts swarmed over the whole land of Egypt, settling in dense swarms from one end of the country to the other. It was the worst locust plague in Egyptian history, and there has never been another one like it. ¹⁵For the locusts covered the whole country and darkened the land. They devoured every plant in the fields and all the fruit on the trees that had survived the hailstorm. Not a single leaf was left on the trees and plants throughout the land of Egypt.

¹⁶Pharaoh quickly summoned Moses and Aaron. "I have sinned against the LORD your God and against you," he confessed. ¹⁷"Forgive my sin, just this once, and plead with the LORD your God to take away this death from me."

¹⁸So Moses left Pharaoh's court and pleaded with the LORD. ¹⁹The LORD responded by shifting the wind, and the

strong west wind blew the locusts into the Red Sea.* Not a single locust remained in all the land of Egypt. [20]But the LORD hardened Pharaoh's heart again, so he refused to let the people go.

[21]Then the LORD said to Moses, "Lift your hand toward heaven, and the land of Egypt will be covered with a darkness so thick you can feel it." [22]So Moses lifted his hand to the sky, and a deep darkness covered the entire land of Egypt for three days. [23]During all that time the people could not see each other, and no one moved. But there was light as usual where the people of Israel lived.

10:19 Hebrew *sea of reeds.*

[24]Finally, Pharaoh called for Moses. "Go and worship the LORD," he said. "But leave your flocks and herds here. You may even take your little ones with you."

[25]"No," Moses said, "you must provide us with animals for sacrifices and burnt offerings to the LORD our God. [26]All our livestock must go with us, too; not a hoof can be left behind. We must choose our sacrifices for the LORD our God from among these animals. And we won't know how we are to worship the LORD until we get there."

[27]But the LORD hardened Pharaoh's heart once more, and he would not let them go.

Pharaoh wanted God to stop punishing him, but he tried to bargain with God. Obedience is not about bargaining. It's about doing *exactly* what God says. Following God means we please him by doing what he wants in *all* situations. Are you willing to obey God all the time, in every way?

Jesus said to his disciples, "If any of you wants to be my follower, you must turn from your selfish ways, take up your cross, and follow me." MATTHEW 16:24

FEBRUARY 9

The Last Plague

After nine plagues, Pharaoh still would not let the Israelites go. What would it take to make Pharaoh free the Hebrew slaves? Check out what finally changed Pharaoh's mind.

Exodus 12:1-8, 21-36
While the Israelites were still in the land of Egypt, the LORD gave the following instructions to Moses and Aaron: [2]"From now on, this month will be the first month of the year for you. [3]Announce to the whole community of Israel that on the tenth day of this month each family must choose a lamb or a young goat for a sacri-fice, one animal for each household. [4]If a family is too small to eat a whole animal, let them share with another family in the neighborhood. Divide the animal according to the size of each family and how much they can eat. [5]The animal you select must be a one-year-old male, either a sheep or a goat, with no defects.

[6]"Take special care of this chosen animal

until the evening of the fourteenth day of this first month. Then the whole assembly of the community of Israel must slaughter their lamb or young goat at twilight. [7]They are to take some of the blood and smear it on the sides and top of the doorframes of the houses where they eat the animal. [8]That same night they must roast the meat over a fire and eat it along with bitter salad greens and bread made without yeast.

[21]Then Moses called all the elders of Israel together and said to them, "Go, pick out a lamb or young goat for each of your families, and slaughter the Passover animal. [22]Drain the blood into a basin. Then take a bundle of hyssop branches and dip it into the blood. Brush the hyssop across the top and sides of the doorframes of your houses. And no one may go out through the door until morning. [23]For the Lord will pass through the land to strike down the Egyptians. But when he sees the blood on the top and sides of the doorframe, the Lord will pass over your home. He will not permit his death angel to enter your house and strike you down.

[24]"Remember, these instructions are a permanent law that you and your descendants must observe forever. [25]When you enter the land the Lord has promised to give you, you will continue to observe this ceremony. [26]Then your children will ask, 'What does this ceremony mean?' [27]And you will reply, 'It is the Passover sacrifice to the Lord, for he passed over the houses of the Israelites in Egypt. And though he struck the Egyptians, he spared our families.'" When Moses had finished speaking, all the people bowed down to the ground and worshiped.

[28]So the people of Israel did just as the Lord had commanded through Moses and Aaron. [29]And that night at midnight, the Lord struck down all the firstborn sons in the land of Egypt, from the firstborn son of Pharaoh, who sat on his throne, to the firstborn son of the prisoner in the dungeon. Even the firstborn of their livestock were killed. [30]Pharaoh and all his officials and all the people of Egypt woke up during the night, and loud wailing was heard throughout the land of Egypt. There was not a single house where someone had not died.

[31]Pharaoh sent for Moses and Aaron during the night. "Get out!" he ordered. "Leave my people—and take the rest of the Israelites with you! Go and worship the Lord as you have requested. [32]Take your flocks and herds, as you said, and be gone. Go, but bless me as you leave." [33]All the Egyptians urged the people of Israel to get out of the land as quickly as possible, for they thought, "We will all die!"

[34]The Israelites took their bread dough before yeast was added. They wrapped their kneading boards in their cloaks and carried them on their shoulders. [35]And the people of Israel did as Moses had instructed; they asked the Egyptians for clothing and articles of silver and gold. [36]The Lord caused the Egyptians to look favorably on the Israelites, and they gave the Israelites whatever they asked for. So they stripped the Egyptians of their wealth!

In the same way that God freed the Israelites from slavery, he has freed us from our sins. Because God's firstborn Son, Jesus, died, all people can be forgiven and set free from sin. While the ten plagues occurred many years before Jesus actually came to earth, isn't it remarkable how God gave his people a hint so far ahead of time about how they could be saved?

If the Son sets you free, you are truly free. JOHN **8:36**

FEBRUARY 10

A narrow Escape

The Israelites were finally leaving Egypt, but now they were stuck between Pharaoh's army and the Red Sea! How would they get away? This story shows how God saved them.

Exodus 14:10-31

As Pharaoh approached, the people of Israel looked up and panicked when they saw the Egyptians overtaking them. They cried out to the LORD, ¹¹and they said to Moses, "Why did you bring us out here to die in the wilderness? Weren't there enough graves for us in Egypt? What have you done to us? Why did you make us leave Egypt? ¹²Didn't we tell you this would happen while we were still in Egypt? We said, 'Leave us alone! Let us be slaves to the Egyptians. It's better to be a slave in Egypt than a corpse in the wilderness!'"

¹³But Moses told the people, "Don't be afraid. Just stand still and watch the LORD rescue you today. The Egyptians you see today will never be seen again. ¹⁴The LORD himself will fight for you. Just stay calm."

¹⁵Then the LORD said to Moses, "Why are you crying out to me? Tell the people to get moving! ¹⁶Pick up your staff and raise your hand over the sea. Divide the water so the Israelites can walk through the middle of the sea on dry ground. ¹⁷And I will harden the hearts of the Egyptians, and they will charge in after the Israelites. My great glory will be displayed through Pharaoh and his troops, his chariots, and his charioteers. ¹⁸When my glory is displayed through them, all Egypt will see my glory and know that I am the LORD!"

¹⁹Then the angel of God, who had been leading the people of Israel, moved to the rear of the camp. The pillar of cloud also moved from the front and stood behind them. ²⁰The cloud settled between the Egyptian and Israelite camps. As darkness fell, the cloud turned to fire, lighting up the night. But the Egyptians and Israelites did not approach each other all night.

²¹Then Moses raised his hand over the sea, and the LORD opened up a path through the water with a strong east wind. The wind blew all that night, turning the seabed into dry land. ²²So the people of Israel walked through the middle of the sea on dry ground, with walls of water on each side!

²³Then the Egyptians—all of Pharaoh's horses, chariots, and charioteers—chased them into the middle of the sea. ²⁴But just before dawn the LORD looked down on the Egyptian army from the pillar of fire and cloud, and he threw their forces into total confusion. ²⁵He twisted* their chariot wheels, making their chariots difficult to drive. "Let's get out of here—away from these Israelites!" the Egyptians shouted. "The LORD is fighting for them against Egypt!"

²⁶When all the Israelites had reached the other side, the LORD said to Moses, "Raise your hand over the sea again. Then the waters will rush back and cover the Egyptians and their chariots and charioteers." ²⁷So as the sun began to rise, Moses raised his hand

over the sea, and the water rushed back into its usual place. The Egyptians tried to escape, but the LORD swept them into the sea. 28Then the waters returned and covered all the chariots and charioteers—the entire army of Pharaoh. Of all the Egyptians who had chased the Israelites into the sea, not a single one survived.

29But the people of Israel had walked through the middle of the sea on dry ground, as the water stood up like a wall on both sides. 30That is how the LORD rescued Israel from the hand of the Egyptians that day. And the Israelites saw the bodies of the Egyptians washed up on the seashore. 31When the people of Israel saw the mighty power that the LORD had unleashed against the Egyptians, they were filled with awe before him. They put their faith in the LORD and in his servant Moses.

14:25 As in Greek version, Samaritan Pentateuch, and Syriac version; Hebrew reads *He removed.*

The Israelites thought there was no way out. The entire Egyptian army was on one side, the Red Sea on the other. Dead end. But God had a surprise rescue planned for them. Whenever you're feeling afraid because you think there is no way out of a problem, stop and ask God for help. He'll help you in amazing ways that you can't even imagine!

The LORD hears his people when they call to him for help. He rescues them from all their troubles. PSALM 34:17

FEBRUARY 11

WE'RE THIRSTY!

The Israelites were hiking around in the desert, and they were getting really thirsty. Check out how they finally found something to drink.

Exodus 15:22-27

Then Moses led the people of Israel away from the Red Sea, and they moved out into the desert of Shur. They traveled in this desert for three days without finding any water. 23When they came to the oasis of Marah, the water was too bitter to drink. So they called the place Marah (which means "bitter").

24Then the people complained and turned against Moses. "What are we going to drink?" they demanded. 25So Moses cried out to the LORD for help, and the LORD showed him a piece of wood. Moses threw it into the water, and this made the water good to drink.

It was there at Marah that the LORD set before them the following decree as a standard to test their faithfulness to him. 26He said, "If you will listen carefully to the voice of the LORD your God and do what is right in his sight, obeying his commands and keeping all his decrees, then I will not make you suffer any of the diseases I sent on the Egyptians; for I am the LORD who heals you."

²⁷After leaving Marah, the Israelites traveled on to the oasis of Elim, where they found twelve springs and seventy palm trees. They camped there beside the water.

Just when the situation looked bleakest, God took care of the Israelites. He used a piece of wood to make the water good! Once again, God did the unexpected to provide for his people. Whenever you don't know how you will possibly get what you need, remember this story. If God can do this, he certainly will be able to give you what you need too.

Look at the birds. They don't plant or harvest or store food in barns, for your heavenly Father feeds them. And aren't you far more valuable to him than they are? MATTHEW 6:26

FEBRUARY 12

It's Raining Bread

The Israelites couldn't find food in the desert. But God would take care of them in another surprising way.

Exodus 16:2-5, 13-28

There, too, the whole community of Israel complained about Moses and Aaron.

³"If only the LORD had killed us back in Egypt," they moaned. "There we sat around pots filled with meat and ate all the bread we wanted. But now you have brought us into this wilderness to starve us all to death."

⁴Then the LORD said to Moses, "Look, I'm going to rain down food from heaven for you. Each day the people can go out and pick up as much food as they need for that day. I will test them in this to see whether or not they will follow my instructions. ⁵On the sixth day they will gather food, and when they prepare it, there will be twice as much as usual."

¹³That evening vast numbers of quail flew in and covered the camp. And the next morning the area around the camp was wet with dew. ¹⁴When the dew evaporated, a flaky substance as fine as frost blanketed the ground. ¹⁵The Israelites were puzzled when they saw it. "What is it?" they asked each other. They had no idea what it was.

And Moses told them, "It is the food the LORD has given you to eat. ¹⁶These are the LORD's instructions: Each household should gather as much as it needs. Pick up two quarts* for each person in your tent."

¹⁷So the people of Israel did as they were told. Some gathered a lot, some only a little. ¹⁸But when they measured it out,* everyone had just enough. Those who gathered a lot had nothing left over, and those who gathered only a little had enough. Each family had just what it needed.

¹⁹Then Moses told them, "Do not keep any of it until morning." ²⁰But some of

57

them didn't listen and kept some of it until morning. But by then it was full of maggots and had a terrible smell. Moses was very angry with them.

²¹After this the people gathered the food morning by morning, each family according to its need. And as the sun became hot, the flakes they had not picked up melted and disappeared. ²²On the sixth day, they gathered twice as much as usual—four quarts* for each person instead of two. Then all the leaders of the community came and asked Moses for an explanation. ²³He told them, "This is what the LORD commanded: Tomorrow will be a day of complete rest, a holy Sabbath day set apart for the LORD. So bake or boil as much as you want today, and set aside what is left for tomorrow."

²⁴So they put some aside until morning, just as Moses had commanded. And in the morning the leftover food was wholesome and good, without maggots or odor. ²⁵Moses said, "Eat this food today, for today is a Sabbath day dedicated to the LORD. There will be no food on the ground today. ²⁶You may gather the food for six days, but the seventh day is the Sabbath. There will be no food on the ground that day."

²⁷Some of the people went out anyway on the seventh day, but they found no food. ²⁸The LORD asked Moses, "How long will these people refuse to obey my commands and instructions?"

16:16 Hebrew *1 omer* [2 liters].   16:18 Hebrew *measured it with an omer.*   16:22 Hebrew *2 omers* [4 liters].

Making water come from a rock is one thing. But making bread fall from the sky is even more extraordinary. The Israelites must have wondered what God would think of next! Not only is God powerful and loving enough to take care of us, he is also exciting to follow. He gets things done in ways we never would have thought possible. If you are a follower of God, get ready for plenty of surprises!

[Jesus said,] "I am the living bread that came down from heaven. Anyone who eats this bread will live forever; and this bread, which I will offer so the world may live, is my flesh." JOHN 6:51

FEBRUARY 13

TOO much to DO

Moses had too much to do! Look at the great advice his father-in-law gave him.

Exodus 18:5-26

Jethro, Moses' father-in-law, now came to visit Moses in the wilderness. He brought Moses' wife and two sons with him, and they arrived while Moses and the people were camped near the mountain of God. ⁶Jethro had sent a message to Moses, saying, "I, Jethro, your father-in-law, am coming to see you with your wife and your two sons."

[7]So Moses went out to meet his father-in-law. He bowed low and kissed him. They asked about each other's welfare and then went into Moses' tent. [8]Moses told his father-in-law everything the LORD had done to Pharaoh and Egypt on behalf of Israel. He also told about all the hardships they had experienced along the way and how the LORD had rescued his people from all their troubles. [9]Jethro was delighted when he heard about all the good things the LORD had done for Israel as he rescued them from the hand of the Egyptians.

[10]"Praise the LORD," Jethro said, "for he has rescued you from the Egyptians and from Pharaoh. Yes, he has rescued Israel from the powerful hand of Egypt! [11]I know now that the LORD is greater than all other gods, because he rescued his people from the oppression of the proud Egyptians."

[12]Then Jethro, Moses' father-in-law, brought a burnt offering and sacrifices to God. Aaron and all the elders of Israel came out and joined him in a sacrificial meal in God's presence.

[13]The next day, Moses took his seat to hear the people's disputes against each other. They waited before him from morning till evening.

[14]When Moses' father-in-law saw all that Moses was doing for the people, he asked, "What are you really accomplishing here? Why are you trying to do all this alone while everyone stands around you from morning till evening?"

[15]Moses replied, "Because the people come to me to get a ruling from God. [16]When a dispute arises, they come to me, and I am the one who settles the case between the quarreling parties. I inform the people of God's decrees and give them his instructions."

[17]"This is not good!" Moses' father-in-law exclaimed. [18]"You're going to wear yourself out—and the people, too. This job is too heavy a burden for you to handle all by yourself. [19]Now listen to me, and let me give you a word of advice, and may God be with you. You should continue to be the people's representative before God, bringing their disputes to him. [20]Teach them God's decrees, and give them his instructions. Show them how to conduct their lives. [21]But select from all the people some capable, honest men who fear God and hate bribes. Appoint them as leaders over groups of one thousand, one hundred, fifty, and ten. [22]They should always be available to solve the people's common disputes, but have them bring the major cases to you. Let the leaders decide the smaller matters themselves. They will help you carry the load, making the task easier for you. [23]If you follow this advice, and if God commands you to do so, then you will be able to endure the pressures, and all these people will go home in peace."

[24]Moses listened to his father-in-law's advice and followed his suggestions. [25]He chose capable men from all over Israel and appointed them as leaders over the people. He put them in charge of groups of one thousand, one hundred, fifty, and ten. [26]These men were always available to solve the people's common disputes. They brought the major cases to Moses, but they took care of the smaller matters themselves.

It is really important to have older and wiser people help us figure out what to do. Do you have someone you can ask for advice? Parents are great for giving advice. So are teachers, Sunday school teachers, and other trusted adults. When you feel confused or overwhelmed, ask someone older and wiser to help you know what to do. It's a great way to solve a problem.

Get all the advice and instruction you can, so you will be wise the rest of your life. PROVERBS 19:20

FEBRUARY 14

An Appointment with God

The Israelites had an appointment to meet God! Read about what they did to get ready to meet him.

Exodus 19:3-19

Then Moses climbed the mountain to appear before God. The LORD called to him from the mountain and said, "Give these instructions to the family of Jacob; announce it to the descendants of Israel: ⁴'You have seen what I did to the Egyptians. You know how I carried you on eagles' wings and brought you to myself. ⁵Now if you will obey me and keep my covenant, you will be my own special treasure from among all the peoples on earth; for all the earth belongs to me. ⁶And you will be my kingdom of priests, my holy nation.' This is the message you must give to the people of Israel."

⁷So Moses returned from the mountain and called together the elders of the people and told them everything the LORD had commanded him. ⁸And all the people responded together, "We will do everything the LORD has commanded." So Moses brought the people's answer back to the LORD.

⁹Then the LORD said to Moses, "I will come to you in a thick cloud, Moses, so the people themselves can hear me when I speak with you. Then they will always trust you."

Moses told the LORD what the people had said. ¹⁰Then the LORD told Moses, "Go down and prepare the people for my arrival. Consecrate them today and tomorrow, and have them wash their clothing. ¹¹Be sure they are ready on the third day, for on that day the LORD will come down on Mount Sinai as all the people watch. ¹²Mark off a boundary all around the mountain. Warn the people, 'Be careful! Do not go up on the mountain or even touch its boundaries. Anyone who touches the mountain will certainly be put to death. ¹³No hand may touch the person or animal that crosses the boundary; instead, stone them or shoot them with arrows. They must be put to death.' However, when the ram's horn sounds a long blast, then the people may go up on the mountain.*"

¹⁴So Moses went down to the people. He consecrated them for worship, and they washed their clothes. ¹⁵He told them, "Get ready for the third day, and until then abstain from having sexual intercourse."

¹⁶On the morning of the third day, thunder roared and lightning flashed, and a dense cloud came down on the mountain. There was a long, loud blast from a ram's horn, and all the people trembled. ¹⁷Moses led them out from the camp to meet with God, and they stood at the foot of the mountain. ¹⁸All of Mount Sinai was covered with smoke because the LORD had descended on it in the form of fire. The smoke billowed into the sky like smoke from a brick kiln, and the whole mountain shook violently. ¹⁹As the blast of the ram's horn grew louder and louder, Moses spoke, and God thundered his reply.

19:13 Or *up to the mountain.*

The Israelites had a lot of cleaning up to do before they were ready to meet God. But God is so perfect and holy that no amount of scrubbing could make us clean enough to meet him. That's why Jesus came. Jesus' death and resurrection were like the bath we needed to cleanse us from our sins. If you believe in Jesus and have asked for forgiveness, you are clean and holy because of what Jesus did. Isn't it wonderful to know that he took care of all that for us?

Even before he made the world, God loved us and chose us in Christ to be holy and without fault in his eyes. Ephesians 1:4

FEBRUARY 15

GOD'S TOP TEN RULES

God spoke to Moses and gave him some very important instructions for how he wanted his people to act. Read what they are.

Exodus 20:1-21
Then God gave the people all these instructions*:

²"I am the LORD your God, who rescued you from the land of Egypt, the place of your slavery.
³"You must not have any other god but me.
⁴"You must not make for yourself an idol of any kind or an image of anything in the heavens or on the earth or in the sea. ⁵You must not bow down to them or worship them, for I, the LORD your God, am a jealous God who will not tolerate your affection for any other gods. I lay the sins of the parents upon their children; the entire family is affected—even children in the third and fourth generations of those who reject me. ⁶But I lavish unfailing love for a thousand generations on those* who love me and obey my commands.
⁷"You must not misuse the name of the LORD your God. The LORD will not let

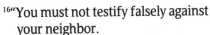

you go unpunished if you misuse his name.

⁸"Remember to observe the Sabbath day by keeping it holy. ⁹You have six days each week for your ordinary work, ¹⁰but the seventh day is a Sabbath day of rest dedicated to the LORD your God. On that day no one in your household may do any work. This includes you, your sons and daughters, your male and female servants, your livestock, and any foreigners living among you. ¹¹For in six days the LORD made the heavens, the earth, the sea, and everything in them; but on the seventh day he rested. That is why the LORD blessed the Sabbath day and set it apart as holy.

¹²"Honor your father and mother. Then you will live a long, full life in the land the LORD your God is giving you.

¹³"You must not murder.

¹⁴"You must not commit adultery.

¹⁵"You must not steal.

¹⁶"You must not testify falsely against your neighbor.

¹⁷"You must not covet your neighbor's house. You must not covet your neighbor's wife, male or female servant, ox or donkey, or anything else that belongs to your neighbor."

¹⁸When the people heard the thunder and the loud blast of the ram's horn, and when they saw the flashes of lightning and the smoke billowing from the mountain, they stood at a distance, trembling with fear.

¹⁹And they said to Moses, "You speak to us, and we will listen. But don't let God speak directly to us, or we will die!"

²⁰"Don't be afraid," Moses answered them, "for God has come in this way to test you, and so that your fear of him will keep you from sinning!"

²¹As the people stood in the distance, Moses approached the dark cloud where God was.

20:1 Hebrew *all these words.*   20:6 Hebrew *for thousands of those.*

God gave the Israelites only ten laws to follow. Do you think you could keep from breaking ten rules? It doesn't sound too hard, does it? But people have a really hard time keeping just those ten rules. Whenever we break one of God's rules, we sin and deserve God's punishment. But God gave our punishment to Jesus so that we could be forgiven. Tell God how thankful you are for what Jesus did for you.

You were dead because of your sins and because your sinful nature was not yet cut away. Then God made you alive with Christ, for he forgave all our sins.
COLOSSIANS 2:13

FEBRUARY 16

The Golden Calf

The Israelites deserved to be punished by God for their disobedience. But Moses asked God to forgive them. Read and see what God did.

Exodus 32:1-14

When the people saw how long it was taking Moses to come back down the mountain, they gathered around Aaron. "Come on," they said, "make us some gods who can lead us. We don't know what happened to this fellow Moses, who brought us here from the land of Egypt."

²So Aaron said, "Take the gold rings from the ears of your wives and sons and daughters, and bring them to me."

³All the people took the gold rings from their ears and brought them to Aaron. ⁴Then Aaron took the gold, melted it down, and molded it into the shape of a calf. When the people saw it, they exclaimed, "O Israel, these are the gods who brought you out of the land of Egypt!"

⁵Aaron saw how excited the people were, so he built an altar in front of the calf. Then he announced, "Tomorrow will be a festival to the LORD!"

⁶The people got up early the next morning to sacrifice burnt offerings and peace offerings. After this, they celebrated with feasting and drinking, and they indulged in pagan revelry.

⁷The LORD told Moses, "Quick! Go down the mountain! Your people whom you brought from the land of Egypt have corrupted themselves. ⁸How quickly they have turned away from the way I commanded them to live! They have melted down gold and made a calf, and they have bowed down and sacrificed to it. They are saying, 'These are your gods, O Israel, who brought you out of the land of Egypt.'"

⁹Then the LORD said, "I have seen how stubborn and rebellious these people are. ¹⁰Now leave me alone so my fierce anger can blaze against them, and I will destroy them. Then I will make you, Moses, into a great nation."

¹¹But Moses tried to pacify the LORD his God. "O LORD!" he said. "Why are you so angry with your own people whom you brought from the land of Egypt with such great power and such a strong hand? ¹²Why let the Egyptians say, 'Their God rescued them with the evil intention of slaughtering them in the mountains and wiping them from the face of the earth'? Turn away from your fierce anger. Change your mind about this terrible disaster you have threatened against your people! ¹³Remember your servants Abraham, Isaac, and Jacob.* You bound yourself with an oath to them, saying, 'I will make your descendants as numerous as the stars of heaven. And I will give them all of this land that I have promised to your descendants, and they will possess it forever.'"

¹⁴So the LORD changed his mind about the terrible disaster he had threatened to bring on his people.

32:13 Hebrew *Israel*. The names "Jacob" and "Israel" are often interchanged throughout the Old Testament, referring sometimes to the individual patriarch and sometimes to the nation.

Can you believe it? After all God had done for the Israelites, they wound up worshiping a false god made with human hands! What were they thinking? God was very angry. But when Moses asked for forgiveness, God forgave the people. The Bible tells us that God forgives sinners again and again. It doesn't matter what you have done or how awful you have been—God will forgive you. Tell him that you're sorry and you want to obey.

[God] is so rich in kindness and grace that he purchased our freedom with the blood of his Son and forgave our sins. EPHESIANS 1:7

FEBRUARY 17

GOD'S PRESENCE

God wanted to live with his people, the Israelites. Read about how he did it.

Exodus 40:1-2, 33-38

Then the LORD said to Moses, ²"Set up the Tabernacle* on the first day of the new year.*"

³³Then [Moses] hung the curtains forming the courtyard around the Tabernacle and the altar. And he set up the curtain at the entrance of the courtyard. So at last Moses finished the work.

³⁴Then the cloud covered the Tabernacle, and the glory of the LORD filled the Tabernacle. ³⁵Moses could no longer enter the Tabernacle because the cloud had settled down over it, and the glory of the LORD filled the Tabernacle.

³⁶Now whenever the cloud lifted from the Tabernacle, the people of Israel would set out on their journey, following it. ³⁷But if the cloud did not rise, they remained where they were until it lifted. ³⁸The cloud of the LORD hovered over the Tabernacle during the day, and at night fire glowed inside the cloud so the whole family of Israel could see it. This continued throughout all their journeys.

40:2a Hebrew *the Tabernacle, the Tent of Meeting.* 40:2b Hebrew *the first day of the first month.* This day of the ancient Hebrew lunar calendar occurred in March or April.

Imagine God staying right in your campground! While the Israelites were living in tents in the desert, God stayed in a tent too. He was right there with his people in the form of a cloud. Does God appear as a cloud today? No, something even better happens. God sends his Spirit to live within all who believe in his Son. We also have his Word to guide and encourage us.

[Jesus said,] "I will ask the Father, and he will give you another Advocate,* who will never leave you. He is the Holy Spirit, who leads into all truth. The world cannot receive him, because it isn't looking for him and doesn't recognize him. But you know him, because he lives with you now and later will be in you.*" JOHN 14:16-17

14:16 Or *Comforter,* or *Encourager,* or *Counselor.* Greek reads *Paraclete.* 14:17 Some manuscripts read *and is in you.*

FEBRUARY 18

Sibling Rivalry

Miriam and Aaron were not being respectful to Moses. They thought they could lead the people just as well as their brother could. Read and see what God had to say to them.

Numbers 12:1-15

While they were at Hazeroth, Miriam and Aaron criticized Moses because he had married a Cushite woman. ²They said, "Has the LORD spoken only through Moses? Hasn't he spoken through us, too?" But the LORD heard them. ³(Now Moses was very humble—more humble than any other person on earth.)

⁴So immediately the LORD called to Moses, Aaron, and Miriam and said, "Go out to the Tabernacle,* all three of you!" So the three of them went to the Tabernacle. ⁵Then the LORD descended in the pillar of cloud and stood at the entrance of the Tabernacle.* "Aaron and Miriam!" he called, and they stepped forward. ⁶And the LORD said to them, "Now listen to what I say:

"If there were prophets among you,
    I, the LORD, would reveal myself in
        visions.
    I would speak to them in dreams.
⁷But not with my servant Moses.
    Of all my house, he is the one I trust.
⁸I speak to him face to face,
    clearly, and not in riddles!

He sees the LORD as he is.
So why were you not afraid
    to criticize my servant
        Moses?"

⁹The LORD was very angry with them, and he departed. ¹⁰As the cloud moved from above the Tabernacle, there stood Miriam, her skin as white as snow from leprosy.* When Aaron saw what had happened to her, ¹¹he cried out to Moses, "Oh, my master! Please don't punish us for this sin we have so foolishly committed. ¹²Don't let her be like a stillborn baby, already decayed at birth."

¹³So Moses cried out to the LORD, "O God, I beg you, please heal her!"

¹⁴But the LORD said to Moses, "If her father had done nothing more than spit in her face, wouldn't she be defiled for seven days? So keep her outside the camp for seven days, and after that she may be accepted back."

¹⁵So Miriam was kept outside the camp for seven days, and the people waited until she was brought back before they traveled again.

12:4 Hebrew *the Tent of Meeting.* 12:5 Hebrew *the tent;* also in 12:10. 12:10 Or *with a skin disease.* The Hebrew word used here can describe various skin diseases.

God had chosen Moses to be the leader. But Miriam and Aaron were not making it easy for him. When God gives us leaders, it's our job to listen to them and to respect them. We shouldn't worry about whether or not we could do a better job. No leader can do a good job if people won't obey. God wasn't happy that Aaron and Miriam challenged Moses. We need to honor God by respecting those in authority over us, including our parents, teachers, pastors, city officials, and the leaders of our country.

Everyone must submit to governing authorities. For all authority comes from God, and those in positions of authority have been placed there by God. ROMANS 13:1

FEBRUARY 19
Spying on the Promised Land
Some spies went to see what the land God had promised was like. They brought back a great report! What do you think the Israelites did when they heard? Read and see.

Numbers 13:17-20, 25-33
¹⁷Moses gave the men these instructions as he sent them out to explore the land: "Go north through the Negev into the hill country. ¹⁸See what the land is like, and find out whether the people living there are strong or weak, few or many. ¹⁹See what kind of land they live in. Is it good or bad? Do their towns have walls, or are they unprotected like open camps? ²⁰Is the soil fertile or poor? Are there many trees? Do your best to bring back samples of the crops you see." (It happened to be the season for harvesting the first ripe grapes.)

²⁵After exploring the land for forty days, the men returned ²⁶to Moses, Aaron, and the whole community of Israel at Kadesh in the wilderness of Paran. They reported to the whole community what they had seen and showed them the fruit they had taken from the land. ²⁷This was their report to Moses: "We entered the land you sent us to explore, and it is indeed a bountiful country—a land flowing with milk and honey. Here is the kind of fruit it produces. ²⁸But the people living there are powerful, and their towns are large and fortified. We even saw giants there, the descendants of Anak! ²⁹The Amalekites live in the Negev, and the Hittites, Jebusites, and Amorites live in the hill country. The Canaanites live along the coast of the Mediterranean Sea* and along the Jordan Valley."

³⁰But Caleb tried to quiet the people as they stood before Moses. "Let's go at once to take the land," he said. "We can certainly conquer it!"

³¹But the other men who had explored the land with him disagreed. "We can't go

up against them! They are stronger than we are!" ³²So they spread this bad report about the land among the Israelites: "The land we traveled through and explored will devour anyone who goes to live there. All the people we saw were huge. ³³We even saw giants* there, the descendants of Anak. Next to them we felt like grasshoppers, and that's what they thought, too!"

13:29 Hebrew *the sea.* 13:33 Hebrew *nephilim.*

The Israelites knew that God was giving them a wonderful place to live. But they were too afraid to go and take it. Sometimes, even when we know that God has a great plan for us, it can be scary to do what he wants. But if we trust God to do what he says, we'll get amazing rewards! Will you trust God enough to take the challenge and follow him?

As the Scriptures tell us, "Anyone who trusts in him will never be disgraced.*"
ROMANS 10:11

10:11 Isa 28:16 (Greek version).

FEBRUARY 20

The Wrong Crowd

Almost none of the Israelites would trust in God. Would Joshua and Caleb be able to make them change their minds?

Numbers 14:1-23

Then the whole community began weeping aloud, and they cried all night. ²Their voices rose in a great chorus of protest against Moses and Aaron. "If only we had died in Egypt, or even here in the wilderness!" they complained. ³"Why is the LORD taking us to this country only to have us die in battle? Our wives and our little ones will be carried off as plunder! Wouldn't it be better for us to return to Egypt?" ⁴Then they plotted among themselves, "Let's choose a new leader and go back to Egypt!"

⁵Then Moses and Aaron fell face down on the ground before the whole community of Israel. ⁶Two of the men who had explored the land, Joshua son of Nun and Caleb son of Jephunneh, tore their clothing. ⁷They said to all the people of Israel,

"The land we traveled through and explored is a wonderful land! ⁸And if the LORD is pleased with us, he will bring us safely into that land and give it to us. It is a rich land flowing with milk and honey. ⁹Do not rebel against the LORD, and don't be afraid of the people of the land. They are only helpless prey to us! They have no protection, but the LORD is with us! Don't be afraid of them!"

¹⁰But the whole community began to talk about stoning Joshua and Caleb. Then the glorious presence of the LORD appeared to all the Israelites at the Tabernacle.* ¹¹And the LORD said to Moses, "How long will these people treat me with contempt? Will they never believe me, even after all the miraculous signs I have done among them? ¹²I will disown them and

destroy them with a plague. Then I will make you into a nation greater and mightier than they are!"

¹³But Moses objected. "What will the Egyptians think when they hear about it?" he asked the Lord. "They know full well the power you displayed in rescuing your people from Egypt. ¹⁴Now if you destroy them, the Egyptians will send a report to the inhabitants of this land, who have already heard that you live among your people. They know, Lord, that you have appeared to your people face to face and that your pillar of cloud hovers over them. They know that you go before them in the pillar of cloud by day and the pillar of fire by night. ¹⁵Now if you slaughter all these people with a single blow, the nations that have heard of your fame will say, ¹⁶'The Lord was not able to bring them into the land he swore to give them, so he killed them in the wilderness.'

¹⁷"Please, Lord, prove that your power is as great as you have claimed. For you said,

¹⁸'The Lord is slow to anger and filled with unfailing love, forgiving every kind of sin and rebellion. But he does not excuse the guilty. He lays the sins of the parents upon their children; the entire family is affected—even children in the third and fourth generations.' ¹⁹In keeping with your magnificent, unfailing love, please pardon the sins of this people, just as you have forgiven them ever since they left Egypt."

²⁰Then the Lord said, "I will pardon them as you have requested. ²¹But as surely as I live, and as surely as the earth is filled with the Lord's glory, ²²not one of these people will ever enter that land. They have all seen my glorious presence and the miraculous signs I performed both in Egypt and in the wilderness, but again and again they have tested me by refusing to listen to my voice. ²³They will never even see the land I swore to give their ancestors. None of those who have treated me with contempt will ever see it."

14:10 Hebrew *the Tent of Meeting.*

Even when no one else would trust God, Joshua and Caleb stood up for what was right. They were the only explorers who had true faith in God. They knew that they had to trust God no matter what everyone else said or did. Sometimes you have to go against the crowd in order to do the right thing. It's not easy, but God will take care of you when you obey.

Don't copy the behavior and customs of this world, but let God transform you into a new person by changing the way you think. Then you will learn to know God's will for you, which is good and pleasing and perfect. ROMANS 12:2

FEBRUARY 21

Keep Your Eyes on the Snake

God was not happy with the way the Israelites were complaining. And he had a harsh punishment for them. But look at the way he still took care of them afterward.

Numbers 21:4-9

Then the people of Israel set out from Mount Hor, taking the road to the Red Sea* to go around the land of Edom. But the people grew impatient with the long journey, ⁵and they began to speak against God and Moses. "Why have you brought us out of Egypt to die here in the wilderness?" they complained. "There is nothing to eat here and nothing to drink. And we hate this horrible manna!"

⁶So the LORD sent poisonous snakes among the people, and many were bitten

21:4 Hebrew *sea of reeds.*

and died. ⁷Then the people came to Moses and cried out, "We have sinned by speaking against the LORD and against you. Pray that the LORD will take away the snakes." So Moses prayed for the people.

⁸Then the LORD told him, "Make a replica of a poisonous snake and attach it to a pole. All who are bitten will live if they simply look at it!" ⁹So Moses made a snake out of bronze and attached it to a pole. Then anyone who was bitten by a snake could look at the bronze snake and be healed!

The Israelites should not have complained about the good food God was giving them. As a result, God sent them a terrible punishment. But God also gave them a way to be healed. The bronze snake was a hint about Jesus. Just as the people had to look at the bronze snake on a pole to be healed, we need to look at Jesus on the cross to be saved from our sins. Keep your eyes on him!

We do this by keeping our eyes on Jesus, the champion who initiates and perfects our faith.* Because of the joy* awaiting him, he endured the cross, disregarding its shame. Now he is seated in the place of honor beside God's throne. HEBREWS 12:2

12:2a Or *Jesus, the originator and perfecter of our faith.*   12:2b Or *Instead of the joy.*

FEBRUARY 22

A Talking Donkey?

Balaam set out to disobey God. But wait till you see the surprise God had waiting for him!

Numbers 22:21-38

So the next morning Balaam got up, saddled his donkey, and started off with the Moabite officials. ²²But God was angry that Balaam was going, so he sent the angel of the LORD to stand in the road to block his way. As Balaam and two servants were riding along, ²³Balaam's donkey saw the angel of the LORD standing in the road with a drawn sword in his hand. The donkey bolted off the road into a field, but Balaam beat it and turned it back onto the road. ²⁴Then the angel of the LORD stood at a place where the road narrowed between two vineyard walls. ²⁵When the donkey saw the angel of the LORD, it tried to squeeze by and crushed Balaam's foot against the wall. So Balaam beat the donkey again. ²⁶Then the angel of the LORD moved farther down the road and stood in a place too narrow for the donkey to get by at all. ²⁷This time when the donkey saw the angel, it lay down under Balaam. In a fit of rage Balaam beat the animal again with his staff.

²⁸Then the LORD gave the donkey the ability to speak. "What have I done to you that deserves your beating me three times?" it asked Balaam.

²⁹"You have made me look like a fool!" Balaam shouted. "If I had a sword with me, I would kill you!"

³⁰"But I am the same donkey you have ridden all your life," the donkey answered. "Have I ever done anything like this before?"

"No," Balaam admitted.

³¹Then the LORD opened Balaam's eyes, and he saw the angel of the LORD standing in the roadway with a drawn sword in his hand. Balaam bowed his head and fell face down on the ground before him.

³²"Why did you beat your donkey those three times?" the angel of the LORD demanded. "Look, I have come to block your way because you are stubbornly resisting me. ³³Three times the donkey saw me and shied away; otherwise, I would certainly have killed you by now and spared the donkey."

³⁴Then Balaam confessed to the angel of the LORD, "I have sinned. I didn't realize you were standing in the road to block my way. I will return home if you are against my going."

³⁵But the angel of the LORD told Balaam, "Go with these men, but say only what I tell you to say." So Balaam went on with Balak's officials. ³⁶When King Balak heard that Balaam was on the way, he went out to meet him at a Moabite town on the Arnon River at the farthest border of his land.

³⁷"Didn't I send you an urgent invitation? Why didn't you come right away?" Balak asked Balaam. "Didn't you believe me when I said I would reward you richly?"

³⁸Balaam replied, "Look, now I have come, but I have no power to say whatever I want. I will speak only the message that God puts in my mouth."

Have you ever wished animals could talk to you? This donkey had some very wise advice for Balaam. He kept Balaam from disobeying God and being punished by the angel. Are you disobeying God in any way? You can't count on an animal to keep you from sinning. That is a pretty rare event! But you will know what God wants you to do as you study his Word and listen to other believers.

Don't be fooled by those who try to excuse these sins, for the anger of God will fall on all who disobey him. Ephesians 5:6

FEBRUARY 23

everything you need

God had given the Israelites everything they needed on their journey through the desert. What did God want the Israelites to do?

Deuteronomy 29:1-6, 9-18

These are the terms of the covenant the LORD commanded Moses to make with the Israelites while they were in the land of Moab, in addition to the covenant he had made with them at Mount Sinai.

²*Moses summoned all the Israelites and said to them, "You have seen with your own eyes everything the LORD did in the land of Egypt to Pharaoh and to all his servants and to his whole country—³all the great tests of strength, the miraculous signs, and the amazing wonders. ⁴But to this day the LORD has not given you minds that understand, nor eyes that see, nor ears that hear! ⁵For forty years I led you through the wilderness, yet your clothes and sandals did not wear out. ⁶You ate no bread and drank no wine or other alcoholic drink, but he gave you food so you would know that he is the LORD your God.

⁹"Therefore, obey the terms of this covenant so that you will prosper in everything you do. ¹⁰All of you—tribal leaders, elders, officers, all the men of Israel—are standing today in the presence of the LORD your God. ¹¹Your little ones and your wives are with you, as well as the foreigners living among you who chop your wood and carry your water. ¹²You are standing here today to enter into the covenant of the LORD your God. The LORD is making this covenant, including the curses. ¹³By entering into the covenant today, he will establish you as his people and confirm that he is your God, just as he promised you and as he swore to your ancestors Abraham, Isaac, and Jacob.

¹⁴"But you are not the only ones with whom I am making this covenant with its curses. ¹⁵I am making this covenant both

with you who stand here today in the presence of the LORD our God, and also with the future generations who are not standing here today.

¹⁶"You remember how we lived in the land of Egypt and how we traveled through the lands of enemy nations as we left. ¹⁷You have seen their detestable practices and their idols* made of wood, stone, silver, and gold. ¹⁸I am making this covenant with you so that no one among you—no man, woman, clan, or tribe—will turn away from the LORD our God to worship these gods of other nations, and so that no root among you bears bitter and poisonous fruit."

29:1a Verse 29:1 is numbered 28:69 in Hebrew text.   29:1b Hebrew *Horeb,* another name for Sinai.   29:2 Verses 29:2-29 are numbered 29:1-28 in Hebrew text.   29:17 The Hebrew term (literally *round things*) probably alludes to dung.

God was making a covenant with Israel. A covenant is a very serious agreement. God would be the Israelites' God and provide for them just as he had been doing. The people needed to agree to worship and serve him as their only God. God wants to have the same kind of covenant with you. Will you worship and serve him with your whole life, trusting him to take care of you?

It is not that we think we are qualified to do anything on our own. Our qualification comes from God. He has enabled us to be ministers of his new covenant. This is a covenant not of written laws, but of the Spirit. 2 CORINTHIANS 3:5-6

FEBRUARY 24

A Life-and-Death Decision

The Israelites had heard the law, and they had found out about God's offer to be their God and take care of them. Now it was time for them to make a decision.

Deuteronomy 30:11-20

"This command I am giving you today is not too difficult for you to understand, and it is not beyond your reach. ¹²It is not kept in heaven, so distant that you must ask, 'Who will go up to heaven and bring it down so we can hear it and obey?' ¹³It is not kept beyond the sea, so far away that you must ask, 'Who will cross the sea to bring it to us so we can hear it and obey?' ¹⁴No, the message is very close at hand; it is on your lips and in your heart so that you can obey it.

¹⁵"Now listen! Today I am giving you a choice between life and death, between prosperity and disaster. ¹⁶For I command you this day to love the LORD your God and to keep his commands, decrees, and regulations by walking in his ways. If you do this, you will live and multiply, and the LORD your God will bless you and the land you are about to enter and occupy.

¹⁷"But if your heart turns away and you refuse to listen, and if you are drawn away to serve and worship other gods, ¹⁸then I

warn you now that you will certainly be destroyed. You will not live a long, good life in the land you are crossing the Jordan to occupy.

[19]"Today I have given you the choice between life and death, between blessings and curses. Now I call on heaven and earth to witness the choice you make. Oh, that you would choose life, so that you and your descendants might live! [20]You can make this choice by loving the LORD your God, obeying him, and committing yourself firmly to him. This* is the key to your life. And if you love and obey the LORD, you will live long in the land the LORD swore to give your ancestors Abraham, Isaac, and Jacob."

30:20 Or *He.*

If people serve and obey God, they get life and the wonderful promises of God's good favor. If they don't, they get punishment and death. Seems like an easy choice to make, doesn't it? We have the same choice. We can either choose to follow Jesus, or we can choose to go our own way. The second choice might sound good, but it brings a lot of trouble and sadness. What will you choose? For the best choice, choose Jesus!

[Jesus said,] "You cannot become my disciple without giving up everything you own." LUKE 14:33

FEBRUARY 25

A NEW LEADER
Moses gave Joshua the scary job of conquering Canaan. Would he have the courage?

Deuteronomy 31:1-8

When Moses had finished giving these instructions* to all the people of Israel, [2]he said, "I am now 120 years old, and I am no longer able to lead you. The LORD has told me, 'You will not cross the Jordan River.' [3]But the LORD your God himself will cross over ahead of you. He will destroy the nations living there, and you will take possession of their land. Joshua will lead you across the river, just as the LORD promised.

[4]"The LORD will destroy the nations living in the land, just as he destroyed Sihon and Og, the kings of the Amorites. [5]The LORD will hand over to you the people who live there, and you must deal with them as I have commanded you. [6]So be strong and courageous! Do not be afraid and do not panic before them. For the LORD your God will personally go ahead of you. He will neither fail you nor abandon you."

[7]Then Moses called for Joshua, and as all Israel watched, he said to him, "Be strong and courageous! For you will lead these people into the land that the LORD swore to their ancestors he would give them. You are the one who will divide it among them as their grants of land. [8]Do

not be afraid or discouraged, for the LORD will personally go ahead of you. He will be with you; he will neither fail you nor abandon you."

31:1 As in Dead Sea Scrolls and Greek version; Masoretic Text reads *Moses went and spoke*.

Joshua was going to take over and be the new leader of the Israelites. It would be a big job! But Moses reminded Joshua that the Lord God would go with him. You can take comfort for the same reason. Jesus promises to be with us always. No matter how big the job you have to do, he will be with you and help you.

[Jesus said,] "Teach these new disciples to obey all the commands I have given you. And be sure of this: I am with you always, even to the end of the age."
MATTHEW 28:20

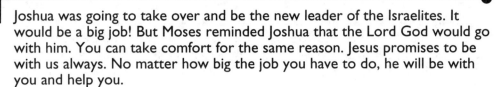

FEBRUARY 26

MOSES' SONG

Moses knew he would not live much longer. But he still wanted to sing about God. Look for all the ways he praised God.

Deuteronomy 32:1-14
Listen, O heavens, and I will speak!
    Hear, O earth, the words that I say!
²Let my teaching fall on you like rain;
    let my speech settle like dew.
Let my words fall like rain on tender
    grass,
    like gentle showers on young plants.
³I will proclaim the name of the LORD;
    how glorious is our God!
⁴He is the Rock; his deeds are perfect.
    Everything he does is just and fair.
He is a faithful God who does no wrong;
    how just and upright he is!

⁵But they have acted corruptly toward
    him;
    when they act so perversely,
are they really his children?*
    They are a deceitful and twisted
    generation.

⁶Is this the way you repay the LORD,
    you foolish and senseless people?
Isn't he your Father who created you?
    Has he not made you and established
    you?
⁷Remember the days of long ago;
    think about the generations past.
Ask your father, and he will
    inform you.
    Inquire of your elders, and they will
    tell you.
⁸When the Most High assigned lands
    to the nations,
    when he divided up the human race,
he established the boundaries of the
    peoples
    according to the number in his
    heavenly court.*

⁹For the people of Israel belong to the
    LORD;

Jacob is his special possession.
¹⁰He found them in a desert land,
in an empty, howling wasteland.
He surrounded them and watched over
them;
he guarded them as he would guard
his own eyes.*
¹¹Like an eagle that rouses her chicks
and hovers over her young,
so he spread his wings to take
them up
and carried them safely on his
pinions.
¹²The Lord alone guided them;

they followed no foreign gods.
¹³He let them ride over the highlands
and feast on the crops of the fields.
He nourished them with honey from
the rock
and olive oil from the stony ground.
¹⁴He fed them yogurt from the herd
and milk from the flock,
together with the fat of lambs.
He gave them choice rams from Bashan,
and goats,
together with the choicest wheat.
You drank the finest wine,
made from the juice of grapes.

32:5 The meaning of the Hebrew is uncertain. **32:8** As in Dead Sea Scrolls, which read *the number of the sons of God,* and Greek version, which reads *the number of the angels of God;* Masoretic Text reads *the number of the sons of Israel.* **32:10** Hebrew *as the pupil of his eye.*

Moses had a lot of reasons to praise God! God loves it when we praise him. What reasons do you have to praise God? You could make up your own song to praise him for being so good to you and for taking care of you.

All praise to God, the Father of our Lord Jesus Christ, who has blessed us with every spiritual blessing in the heavenly realms because we are united with Christ. Ephesians 1:3

FEBRUARY 27

meditate on it

God was giving Joshua advice about how to lead his people. What would God tell him?

Joshua 1:1-11

After the death of Moses the Lord's servant, the Lord spoke to Joshua son of Nun, Moses' assistant. He said, ²"Moses my servant is dead. Therefore, the time has come for you to lead these people, the Israelites, across the Jordan River into the land I am giving them. ³I promise you what I promised Moses: 'Wherever you set foot, you will be on land I have given you—⁴from the Negev wilderness in the south to the Lebanon mountains in the north, from the Euphrates River in the east to the Mediterranean Sea* in the west, including all the land of the Hittites.' ⁵No one will be able to stand against you as long as you live. For I will be with you as I was with Moses. I will not fail you or abandon you.

⁶"Be strong and courageous, for you are the one who will lead these people to possess all the land I swore to their ancestors I would give them. ⁷Be strong and very courageous. Be careful to obey all the instructions Moses gave you. Do not deviate from them, turning either to the right or to the left. Then you will be successful in everything you do. ⁸Study this Book of Instruction continually. Meditate on it day and night so you will be sure to obey every-thing written in it. Only then will you prosper and succeed in all you do. ⁹This is my command—be strong and courageous! Do not be afraid or discouraged. For the LORD your God is with you wherever you go."

¹⁰Joshua then commanded the officers of Israel, ¹¹"Go through the camp and tell the people to get their provisions ready. In three days you will cross the Jordan River and take possession of the land the LORD your God is giving you."

1:4 Hebrew *the Great Sea.*

God told Joshua how important it was to spend a lot of time studying and thinking about the Book of Instruction. This book was all that was written of the Bible back then. Knowing God's Word would bring Joshua success and help him to be strong and courageous. That's good advice for us, too. If you want to know how to have a good life, study God's Word.

All Scripture is inspired by God and is useful to teach us what is true and to make us realize what is wrong in our lives. It corrects us when we are wrong and teaches us to do what is right. God uses it to prepare and equip his people to do every good work. 2 TIMOTHY 3:16-17

FEBRUARY 28
Trapped in Jericho

The Israelites were about to go to war with Jericho. Read about what happened to two Israelite spies when they snuck into the city.

Joshua 2:3-16, 22-24

So the king of Jericho sent orders to Rahab: "Bring out the men who have come into your house, for they have come here to spy out the whole land."

⁴Rahab had hidden the two men, but she replied, "Yes, the men were here earlier, but I didn't know where they were from. ⁵They left the town at dusk, as the gates were about to close. I don't know where they went. If you hurry, you can probably catch up with them." ⁶(Actually, she had taken them up to the roof and hidden them beneath bundles of flax she had laid out.) ⁷So the king's men went looking for the spies along the road leading to the shallow crossings of the Jordan River. And as soon as the king's men had left, the gate of Jericho was shut.

⁸Before the spies went to sleep that night,

Rahab went up on the roof to talk with them. ⁹"I know the LORD has given you this land," she told them. "We are all afraid of you. Everyone in the land is living in terror. ¹⁰For we have heard how the LORD made a dry path for you through the Red Sea* when you left Egypt. And we know what you did to Sihon and Og, the two Amorite kings east of the Jordan River, whose people you completely destroyed.* ¹¹No wonder our hearts have melted in fear! No one has the courage to fight after hearing such things. For the LORD your God is the supreme God of the heavens above and the earth below.

¹²"Now swear to me by the LORD that you will be kind to me and my family since I have helped you. Give me some guarantee that ¹³when Jericho is conquered, you will let me live, along with my father and mother, my brothers and sisters, and all their families."

¹⁴"We offer our own lives as a guarantee for your safety," the men agreed. "If you don't betray us, we will keep our promise and be kind to you when the LORD gives us the land."

¹⁵Then, since Rahab's house was built into the town wall, she let them down by a rope through the window. ¹⁶"Escape to the hill country," she told them. "Hide there for three days from the men searching for you. Then, when they have returned, you can go on your way."

²²The spies went up into the hill country and stayed there three days. The men who were chasing them searched everywhere along the road, but they finally returned without success.

²³Then the two spies came down from the hill country, crossed the Jordan River, and reported to Joshua all that had happened to them. ²⁴"The LORD has given us the whole land," they said, "for all the people in the land are terrified of us."

2:10a Hebrew *sea of reeds.*   2:10b The Hebrew term used here refers to the complete consecration of things or people to the Lord, either by destroying them or by giving them as an offering.

The Israelite spies would have been in real trouble if Rahab hadn't helped them. But God made a way for them to be safe. God also took care of Rahab because of what she did to help them. When you are on God's side, no matter what happens, you can trust that he will take care of you. Knowing that should make you brave enough to do anything for him!

The Lord will deliver me from every evil attack and will bring me safely into his heavenly Kingdom. All glory to God forever and ever! Amen. 2 TIMOTHY 4:18

FEBRUARY CHALLENGE

Bravo!

You are doing an awesome job. Give yourself a pat on the back for completing the readings for February. You can use a marker or a highlighter to show how many levels you've climbed on your way to the top of Challenge Mountain.

What was the most interesting story you read this month? How do you think you might have felt if you had been one of the Israelites crossing the Red Sea? (See the February 10 reading.)

. . . .

. . . .

. . . .

. . . .

. . . .

. . . .

IMPORTANT STUFF TO REMEMBER FROM FEBRUARY

❏ God rescues his people.

❏ God wants his people to be holy.

❏ God provides for his people's needs.

Time for some puzzle fun!

Follow the string from each number to a letter. Write the number on the blank line beside that same letter below. Then you'll see the order of the Ten Commandments. (You can check your answers by looking up the reading for February 15.)

1
2
3
4
5
6
7
8
9
10

A. Honor your father and mother.

B. Don't steal.

C. Don't misuse the name of the Lord.

D. Don't commit adultery.

E. Don't testify falsely against your neighbor.

F. Have no other god but God.

G. Don't covet anything that belongs to your neighbor.

H. Don't make for yourself any idol.

I. Don't murder.

J. Remember to observe the Sabbath day.

MARCH 1

Crossing the Jordan

The Jordan River was flooding, and the Israelites needed to get across. How would they do it?

Joshua 3:5-8, 14–4:7

Then Joshua told the people, "Purify yourselves, for tomorrow the LORD will do great wonders among you."

⁶In the morning Joshua said to the priests, "Lift up the Ark of the Covenant and lead the people across the river." And so they started out and went ahead of the people.

⁷The LORD told Joshua, "Today I will begin to make you a great leader in the eyes of all the Israelites. They will know that I am with you, just as I was with Moses. ⁸Give this command to the priests who carry the Ark of the Covenant: 'When you reach the banks of the Jordan River, take a few steps into the river and stop there.'"

◉

¹⁴So the people left their camp to cross the Jordan, and the priests who were carrying the Ark of the Covenant went ahead of them. ¹⁵It was the harvest season, and the Jordan was overflowing its banks. But as soon as the feet of the priests who were carrying the Ark touched the water at the river's edge, ¹⁶the water above that point began backing up a great distance away at a town called Adam, which is near Zarethan. And the water below that point flowed on to the Dead Sea* until the riverbed was dry. Then all the people crossed over near the town of Jericho.

¹⁷Meanwhile, the priests who were carrying the Ark of the LORD's Covenant stood on dry ground in the middle of the riverbed as the people passed by. They waited there until the whole nation of Israel had crossed the Jordan on dry ground.

⁴:¹When all the people had crossed the Jordan, the LORD said to Joshua, ²"Now choose twelve men, one from each tribe. ³Tell them, 'Take twelve stones from the very place where the priests are standing in the middle of the Jordan. Carry them out and pile them up at the place where you will camp tonight.'"

⁴So Joshua called together the twelve men he had chosen—one from each of the tribes of Israel. ⁵He told them, "Go into the middle of the Jordan, in front of the Ark of the LORD your God. Each of you must pick up one stone and carry it out on your

shoulder—twelve stones in all, one for each of the twelve tribes of Israel. ⁶We will use these stones to build a memorial. In the future your children will ask you, 'What do these stones mean?' ⁷Then you can tell them, 'They remind us that the Jordan River stopped flowing when the Ark of the LORD's Covenant went across.' These stones will stand as a memorial among the people of Israel forever."

3:16 Hebrew *the sea of the Arabah, the Salt Sea.*

Just as God parted the Red Sea so his people could pass through safely, God now stopped the flow of the Jordan River. The Israelites built a stone altar after safely crossing so that no one would ever forget what God had done. God had been with them in the past; he was with them in the present; and he would be with them in the future. What a great thought for us as well. God is the same forever—count on it.

Jesus Christ is the same yesterday, today, and forever. HEBREWS 13:8

MARCH 2

Follow My Instructions

Jericho was a big city with huge walls—they were more than twenty feet thick! How could the Israelites capture this city? What do you think they did? Read and see.

Joshua 6:1-20

The gates of Jericho were tightly shut because the people were afraid of the Israelites. No one was allowed to go out or in. ²But the LORD said to Joshua, "I have given you Jericho, its king, and all its strong warriors. ³You and your fighting men should march around the town once a day for six days. ⁴Seven priests will walk ahead of the Ark, each carrying a ram's horn. On the seventh day you are to march around the town seven times, with the priests blowing the horns. ⁵When you hear the priests give one long blast on the rams' horns, have all the people shout as loud as they can. Then the walls of the town will collapse, and the people can charge straight into the town."

⁶So Joshua called together the priests and said, "Take up the Ark of the LORD's Covenant, and assign seven priests to walk in front of it, each carrying a ram's horn." ⁷Then he gave orders to the people: "March around the town, and the armed men will lead the way in front of the Ark of the LORD."

⁸After Joshua spoke to the people, the seven priests with the rams' horns started marching in the presence of the LORD, blowing the horns as they marched. And the Ark of the LORD's Covenant followed behind them. ⁹Some of the armed men marched in front of the priests with the horns and some behind the Ark, with the priests continually blowing the

horns. ¹⁰"Do not shout; do not even talk," Joshua commanded. "Not a single word from any of you until I tell you to shout. Then shout!" ¹¹So the Ark of the LORD was carried around the town once that day, and then everyone returned to spend the night in the camp.

¹²Joshua got up early the next morning, and the priests again carried the Ark of the LORD. ¹³The seven priests with the rams' horns marched in front of the Ark of the LORD, blowing their horns. Again the armed men marched both in front of the priests with the horns and behind the Ark of the LORD. All this time the priests were blowing their horns. ¹⁴On the second day they again marched around the town once and returned to the camp. They followed this pattern for six days.

¹⁵On the seventh day the Israelites got up at dawn and marched around the town as they had done before. But this time they went around the town seven times. ¹⁶The seventh time around, as the priests sounded the long blast on their horns, Joshua commanded the people, "Shout! For the LORD has given you the town! ¹⁷Jericho and everything in it must be completely destroyed* as an offering to the LORD. Only Rahab the prostitute and the others in her house will be spared, for she protected our spies.

¹⁸"Do not take any of the things set apart for destruction, or you yourselves will be completely destroyed, and you will bring trouble on the camp of Israel. ¹⁹Everything made from silver, gold, bronze, or iron is sacred to the LORD and must be brought into his treasury."

²⁰When the people heard the sound of the rams' horns, they shouted as loud as they could. Suddenly, the walls of Jericho collapsed, and the Israelites charged straight into the town and captured it.

6:17 The Hebrew term used here refers to the complete consecration of things or people to the LORD, either by destroying them or by giving them as an offering; similarly in 6:18.

Does blowing horns seem like a strange way to capture a city? God gave the Israelites some unusual instructions for conquering Jericho. But God worked through these instructions and his people's obedience to bring down Jericho's thick walls. Today we have Jesus' instructions to obey. Sometimes, Jesus' instructions may not make sense to us (like loving our enemies). But when we are obedient, God will give us great victories too.

Thank God! He gives us victory over sin and death through our Lord Jesus Christ.
I CORINTHIANS 15:57

MARCH 3

Who Did It?

In this story, Israel was in big trouble with God. Read to find out who was responsible.

Joshua 7:10-22

The LORD said to Joshua, "Get up! Why are you lying on your face like this? [11]Israel has sinned and broken my covenant! They have stolen some of the things that I commanded must be set apart for me. And they have not only stolen them but have lied about it and hidden the things among their own belongings. [12]That is why the Israelites are running from their enemies in defeat. For now Israel itself has been set apart for destruction. I will not remain with you any longer unless you destroy the things among you that were set apart for destruction.

[13]"Get up! Command the people to purify themselves in preparation for tomorrow. For this is what the LORD, the God of Israel, says: Hidden among you, O Israel, are things set apart for the LORD. You will never defeat your enemies until you remove these things from among you.

[14]"In the morning you must present yourselves by tribes, and the LORD will point out the tribe to which the guilty man belongs. That tribe must come forward with its clans, and the LORD will point out the guilty clan. That clan will then come forward, and the LORD will point out the guilty family. Finally, each member of the guilty family must come forward one by one. [15]The one who has stolen what was set apart for destruction will himself be burned with fire, along with everything he has, for he has broken the covenant of the LORD and has done a horrible thing in Israel."

[16]Early the next morning Joshua brought the tribes of Israel before the LORD, and the tribe of Judah was singled out. [17]Then the clans of Judah came forward, and the clan of Zerah was singled out. Then the families of Zerah came forward, and the family of Zimri was singled out. [18]Every member of Zimri's family was brought forward person by person, and Achan was singled out.

[19]Then Joshua said to Achan, "My son, give glory to the LORD, the God of Israel, by telling the truth. Make your confession and tell me what you have done. Don't hide it from me."

[20]Achan replied, "It is true! I have sinned against the LORD, the God of Israel. [21]Among the plunder I saw a beautiful robe from Babylon,* 200 silver coins,* and a bar of gold weighing more than a pound.* I wanted them so much that I took them. They are hidden in the ground beneath my tent, with the silver buried deeper than the rest."

[22]So Joshua sent some men to make a search. They ran to the tent and found the stolen goods hidden there, just as Achan had said, with the silver buried beneath the rest.

7:21a Hebrew *Shinar*. **7:21b** Hebrew *200 shekels of silver*, about 5 pounds or 2.3 kilograms in weight. **7:21c** Hebrew *50 shekels*, about 20 ounces or 570 grams in weight.

Sometimes we try to hide our sins from other people, but God sees everything. You can't hide *anything* from him. Achan and his family learned this lesson the hard way. The good news is that if we confess our sins, God will forgive us. But if we try to hide them, we won't get away from God's punishment. Do you have something you need to confess to God? He'll forgive you as soon as you ask!

If we claim we have no sin, we are only fooling ourselves and not living in the truth. But if we confess our sins to him, he is faithful and just to forgive us our sins and to cleanse us from all wickedness. If we claim we have not sinned, we are calling God a liar and showing that his word has no place in our hearts.
I JOHN 1:8-10

MARCH 4

The sun stops

It was the battle to end all battles—the armies of Israel against five enemy armies. Joshua and his men were winning the battle, but Joshua needed more time to finish the job. Read what Joshua requested.

Joshua 10:7-14

So Joshua and his entire army, including his best warriors, left Gilgal and set out for Gibeon. ⁸"Do not be afraid of them," the LORD said to Joshua, "for I have given you victory over them. Not a single one of them will be able to stand up to you."

⁹Joshua traveled all night from Gilgal and took the Amorite armies by surprise. ¹⁰The LORD threw them into a panic, and the Israelites slaughtered great numbers of them at Gibeon. Then the Israelites chased the enemy along the road to Beth-horon, killing them all along the way to Azekah and Makkedah. ¹¹As the Amorites retreated down the road from Beth-horon, the LORD destroyed them with a terrible hailstorm from heaven that continued until they reached Azekah. The hail killed more of the enemy than the Israelites killed with the sword.

¹²On the day the LORD gave the Israelites victory over the Amorites, Joshua prayed to the LORD in front of all the people of Israel. He said,

"Let the sun stand still over Gibeon,
  and the moon over the valley of
    Aijalon."

¹³So the sun stood still and the moon stayed in place until the nation of Israel had defeated its enemies.

Is this event not recorded in *The Book of*

Jashar*? The sun stayed in the middle of the sky, and it did not set as on a normal day.* [14]There has never been a day like this one before or since, when the LORD answered such a prayer. Surely the LORD fought for Israel that day!

10:13a Or *The Book of the Upright.* 10:13b Or *did not set for about a whole day.*

When Joshua asked God to make the sun stay up, God did it! Since God made the sun and the earth, he has control over whether or not the earth moves and when the sun rises and sets. We could never do anything like this. In human terms, it is impossible. But when we ask God to help us, things that seem impossible become possible. When you need something impossible to happen, ask God first.

By his divine power, God has given us everything we need for living a godly life. We have received all of this by coming to know him, the one who called us to himself by means of his marvelous glory and excellence.
2 PETER 1:3

MARCH 5
wise words
Joshua was getting older, and he wanted to pass along what he had learned to the Israelites. Read what Joshua told them.

Joshua 23:1-11

The years passed, and the LORD had given the people of Israel rest from all their enemies. Joshua, who was now very old, [2]called together all the elders, leaders, judges, and officers of Israel. He said to them, "I am now a very old man. [3]You have seen everything the LORD your God has done for you during my lifetime. The LORD your God has fought for you against your enemies. [4]I have allotted to you as your homeland all the land of the nations yet unconquered, as well as the land of those we have already conquered—from the Jordan River to the Mediterranean Sea* in the west. [5]This land will be yours, for the LORD your God will himself drive out all the people living there now. You will take possession of their land, just as the LORD your God promised you.

[6]"So be very careful to follow everything Moses wrote in the Book of Instruction. Do not deviate from it, turning either to the right or to the left. [7]Make sure you do not associate with the other people still remaining in the land. Do not even mention the names of their gods, much less swear by them or serve them or worship them. [8]Rather, cling tightly to the LORD your God as you have done until now.

[9]"For the LORD has driven out great and powerful nations for you, and no one has yet been able to defeat you. [10]Each one

of you will put to flight a thousand of the enemy, for the LORD your God fights for you, just as he has promised. ¹¹So be very careful to love the LORD your God."

23:4 Hebrew *the Great Sea.*

Joshua reminded the people of all the ways God had protected them and had fought for them. Land once held by Israel's enemies now belonged to the Israelites. So what should they do next? Joshua told the people that they needed to do three things: keep God's laws, be faithful to him, and love him. Jesus expects us to do the same. When we consider all that Jesus has done for us, can we do anything less?

If you ignore the least commandment and teach others to do the same, you will be called the least in the Kingdom of Heaven. But anyone who obeys God's laws and teaches them will be called great in the Kingdom of Heaven. MATTHEW 5:19

MARCH 6

Choose Today

Joshua had a challenge for the Israelites. Would they choose to serve God or not?

Joshua 24:1-18

Then Joshua summoned all the tribes of Israel to Shechem, including their elders, leaders, judges, and officers. So they came and presented themselves to God.

²Joshua said to the people, "This is what the LORD, the God of Israel, says: Long ago your ancestors, including Terah, the father of Abraham and Nahor, lived beyond the Euphrates River,* and they worshiped other gods. ³But I took your ancestor Abraham from the land beyond the Euphrates and led him into the land of Canaan. I gave him many descendants through his son Isaac. ⁴To Isaac I gave Jacob and Esau. To Esau I gave the mountains of Seir, while Jacob and his children went down into Egypt.

⁵"Then I sent Moses and Aaron, and I brought terrible plagues on Egypt; and afterward I brought you out as a free people. ⁶But when your ancestors arrived at the Red Sea,* the Egyptians chased after you with chariots and charioteers. ⁷When your ancestors cried out to the LORD, I put darkness between you and the Egyptians. I brought the sea crashing down on the Egyptians, drowning them. With your very own eyes you saw what I did. Then you lived in the wilderness for many years.

⁸"Finally, I brought you into the land of the Amorites on the east side of the Jordan. They fought against you, but I destroyed them before you. I gave you victory over them, and you took possession of their land. ⁹Then Balak son of Zippor, king of Moab, started a war against Israel. He summoned Balaam son of Beor to curse you,

¹⁰but I would not listen to him. Instead, I made Balaam bless you, and so I rescued you from Balak.

¹¹"When you crossed the Jordan River and came to Jericho, the men of Jericho fought against you, as did the Amorites, the Perizzites, the Canaanites, the Hittites, the Girgashites, the Hivites, and the Jebusites. But I gave you victory over them. ¹²And I sent terror* ahead of you to drive out the two kings of the Amorites. It was not your swords or bows that brought you victory. ¹³I gave you land you had not worked on, and I gave you towns you did not build— the towns where you are now living. I gave you vineyards and olive groves for food, though you did not plant them.

¹⁴"So fear the LORD and serve him wholeheartedly. Put away forever the idols your ancestors worshiped when they lived be- yond the Euphrates River and in Egypt. Serve the LORD alone. ¹⁵But if you refuse to serve the LORD, then choose today whom you will serve. Would you prefer the gods your ancestors served beyond the Euphrates? Or will it be the gods of the Amorites in whose land you now live? But as for me and my family, we will serve the LORD."

¹⁶The people replied, "We would never abandon the LORD and serve other gods. ¹⁷For the LORD our God is the one who rescued us and our ancestors from slavery in the land of Egypt. He performed mighty miracles before our very eyes. As we traveled through the wilderness among our enemies, he preserved us. ¹⁸It was the LORD who drove out the Amorites and the other nations living here in the land. So we, too, will serve the LORD, for he alone is our God."

24:2 Hebrew *the river;* also in 24:3, 14, 15.   24:6 Hebrew *sea of reeds.*   24:12 Often rendered *the hornet.* The meaning of the Hebrew is uncertain.

God had done so much for the people of Israel. But he would not force them to serve him. The people had to decide if they would allow him to be their God. They made a great choice! They knew about God's power and love, and they wanted to be his people and always worship him. What about you? Will you serve God?

No one can serve two masters. For you will hate one and love the other; you will be devoted to one and despise the other. You cannot serve both God and money. MATTHEW 6:24

MARCH 7

Deborah Predicts Victory

The Israelites had gotten themselves into a bad situation because they were disobeying God. Would God rescue them from the cruel king who was abusing them?

Judges 4:1-16

After Ehud's death, the Israelites again did evil in the LORD's sight. ²So the LORD turned them over to King Jabin of Hazor, a Canaanite king. The commander of his army was Sisera, who lived in Harosheth-haggoyim. ³Sisera, who had 900 iron chariots, ruthlessly oppressed the Israelites for twenty years. Then the people of Israel cried out to the LORD for help.

⁴Deborah, the wife of Lappidoth, was a prophet who was judging Israel at that time. ⁵She would sit under the Palm of Deborah, between Ramah and Bethel in the hill country of Ephraim, and the Israelites would go to her for judgment. ⁶One day she sent for Barak son of Abinoam, who lived in Kedesh in the land of Naphtali. She said to him, "This is what the LORD, the God of Israel, commands you: Call out 10,000 warriors from the tribes of Naphtali and Zebulun at Mount Tabor. ⁷And I will call out Sisera, commander of Jabin's army, along with his chariots and warriors, to the Kishon River. There I will give you victory over him."

⁸Barak told her, "I will go, but only if you go with me."

⁹"Very well," she replied, "I will go with you. But you will receive no honor in this venture, for the LORD's victory over Sisera

4:11 Or *father-in-law*.

will be at the hands of a woman." So Deborah went with Barak to Kedesh. ¹⁰At Kedesh, Barak called together the tribes of Zebulun and Naphtali, and 10,000 warriors went up with him. Deborah also went with him.

¹¹Now Heber the Kenite, a descendant of Moses' brother-in-law* Hobab, had moved away from the other members of his tribe and pitched his tent by the oak of Zaanannim near Kedesh.

¹²When Sisera was told that Barak son of Abinoam had gone up to Mount Tabor, ¹³he called for all 900 of his iron chariots and all of his warriors, and they marched from Harosheth-haggoyim to the Kishon River.

¹⁴Then Deborah said to Barak, "Get ready! This is the day the LORD will give you victory over Sisera, for the LORD is marching ahead of you." So Barak led his 10,000 warriors down the slopes of Mount Tabor into battle. ¹⁵When Barak attacked, the LORD threw Sisera and all his chariots and warriors into a panic. Sisera leaped down from his chariot and escaped on foot. ¹⁶Then Barak chased the chariots and the enemy army all the way to Harosheth-haggoyim, killing all of Sisera's warriors. Not a single one was left alive.

When the Israelites cried out to God for help, he answered them through Deborah and Barak. The people had been sinning and doing wrong things, but God didn't desert them. Sometimes it may feel as if God should turn his back on us because we have messed up too many times. But that's never the case. God is always willing to help and forgive us when we come to him. He is just waiting for us to come back to him and ask!

He has removed our sins as far from us as the east is from the west. The LORD is like a father to his children, tender and compassionate to those who fear him. For he knows how weak we are; he remembers we are only dust. PSALM 103:12-14

MARCH 8

mighty Gideon?

The Israelites were in trouble again. This time God would use Gideon to rescue them. What would Gideon think about the job that God was giving him? Read about it.

Judges 6:1-16

The Israelites did evil in the LORD's sight. So the LORD handed them over to the Midianites for seven years. ²The Midianites were so cruel that the Israelites made hiding places for themselves in the mountains, caves, and strongholds. ³Whenever the Israelites planted their crops, marauders from Midian, Amalek, and the people of the east would attack Israel, ⁴camping in the land and destroying crops as far away as Gaza. They left the Israelites with nothing to eat, taking all the sheep, goats, cattle, and donkeys. ⁵These enemy hordes, coming with their livestock and tents, were as thick as locusts; they arrived on droves of camels too numerous to count. And they stayed until the land was stripped bare. ⁶So Israel was reduced to starvation by the Midianites. Then the Israelites cried out to the LORD for help.

⁷When they cried out to the LORD because of Midian, ⁸the LORD sent a prophet to the Israelites. He said, "This is what the LORD, the God of Israel, says: I brought you up out of slavery in Egypt. ⁹I rescued you from the Egyptians and from all who oppressed you. I drove out your enemies and gave you their land. ¹⁰I told you, 'I am the LORD your God. You must not worship the gods of the Amorites, in whose land you now live.' But you have not listened to me."

¹¹Then the angel of the LORD came and sat beneath the great tree at Ophrah, which belonged to Joash of the clan of Abiezer. Gideon son of Joash was threshing wheat at the bottom of a winepress to hide the grain from the Midianites. ¹²The

angel of the LORD appeared to him and said, "Mighty hero, the LORD is with you!"

¹³"Sir," Gideon replied, "if the LORD is with us, why has all this happened to us? And where are all the miracles our ancestors told us about? Didn't they say, 'The LORD brought us up out of Egypt'? But now the LORD has abandoned us and handed us over to the Midianites."

¹⁴Then the LORD turned to him and said, "Go with the strength you have, and rescue Israel from the Midianites. I am sending you!"

¹⁵"But Lord," Gideon replied, "how can I rescue Israel? My clan is the weakest in the whole tribe of Manasseh, and I am the least in my entire family!"

¹⁶The LORD said to him, "I will be with you. And you will destroy the Midianites as if you were fighting against one man."

Why did God choose Gideon to save Israel? It wasn't because Gideon was strong or wise or even superobedient. (Did you notice how Gideon doubted God?) No, God chose Gideon because he was weak! Through Gideon, God could show the Israelites his power. The Israelites would know it was God, not Gideon, who delivered them from their enemies. Ever feel weak like Gideon? Don't worry. That's when God can work best through you. Just ask him.

Each time [the Lord] said, "My grace is all you need. My power works best in weakness." So now I am glad to boast about my weaknesses, so that the power of Christ can work through me. 2 CORINTHIANS 12:9

MARCH 9

Choosing an Army

God was about to rescue the Israelites in an amazing way that would let everyone know who really had won the battle.

Judges 7:2-8

The LORD said to Gideon, "You have too many warriors with you. If I let all of you fight the Midianites, the Israelites will boast to me that they saved themselves by their own strength. ³Therefore, tell the people, 'Whoever is timid or afraid may leave this mountain* and go home.'" So 22,000 of them went home, leaving only 10,000 who were willing to fight.

⁴But the LORD told Gideon, "There are still too many! Bring them down to the spring, and I will test them to determine who will go with you and who will not." ⁵When Gideon took his warriors down to the water, the LORD told him, "Divide the men into two groups. In one group put all those who cup water in their hands and lap it up with their tongues like dogs. In the other group put all those who kneel down and drink with their mouths in the stream." ⁶Only 300 of the men drank from

their hands. All the others got down on their knees and drank with their mouths in the stream.

⁷The LORD told Gideon, "With these 300 men I will rescue you and give you victory over the Midianites. Send all the others home." ⁸So Gideon collected the provisions and rams' horns of the other warriors and sent them home. But he kept the 300 men with him.

The Midianite camp was in the valley just below Gideon.

7:3 Hebrew *may leave Mount Gilead*. The identity of Mount Gilead is uncertain in this context. It is perhaps used here as another name for Mount Gilboa.

God had promised to help Gideon defeat the Midianites. So why was God sending most of the Israelite army back home? God did this because he didn't want his people to brag about their great strength or mighty army. God wanted the Israelites to praise and thank him for their victory. God wants us to do the same. When we are tempted to brag about how smart we are or how fast or strong, we must remember who gives us our abilities and praise the one who deserves it!

As the Scriptures say, "If you want to boast, boast only about the LORD."*
I CORINTHIANS 1:31

1:31 Jer 9:24.

MARCH 10

Gideon is outnumbered

Gideon was getting ready to fight a huge Midianite army with only three hundred soldiers. How would God calm his fears?

Judges 7:9-21

That night the LORD said, "Get up! Go down into the Midianite camp, for I have given you victory over them! ¹⁰But if you are afraid to attack, go down to the camp with your servant Purah. ¹¹Listen to what the Midianites are saying, and you will be greatly encouraged. Then you will be eager to attack."

So Gideon took Purah and went down to the edge of the enemy camp. ¹²The armies of Midian, Amalek, and the people of the east had settled in the valley like a swarm of locusts. Their camels were like grains of sand on the seashore—too many to count!

¹³Gideon crept up just as a man was telling his companion about a dream. The man said, "I had this dream, and in my dream a loaf of barley bread came tumbling down into the Midianite camp. It hit a tent, turned it over, and knocked it flat!"

¹⁴His companion answered, "Your dream can mean only one thing—God has given Gideon son of Joash, the Israelite, victory over Midian and all its allies!"

¹⁵When Gideon heard the dream and its interpretation, he bowed in worship before the LORD.* Then he returned to the Israelite camp and shouted, "Get up! For the LORD has given you victory over the

Midianite hordes!" [16]He divided the 300 men into three groups and gave each man a ram's horn and a clay jar with a torch in it.

[17]Then he said to them, "Keep your eyes on me. When I come to the edge of the camp, do just as I do. [18]As soon as I and those with me blow the rams' horns, blow your horns, too, all around the entire camp, and shout, 'For the LORD and for Gideon!'"

[19]It was just after midnight,* after the changing of the guard, when Gideon and the 100 men with him reached the edge of the Midianite camp. Suddenly, they blew the rams' horns and broke their clay jars. [20]Then all three groups blew their horns and broke their jars. They held the blazing torches in their left hands and the horns in their right hands, and they all shouted, "A sword for the LORD and for Gideon!"

[21]Each man stood at his position around the camp and watched as all the Midianites rushed around in a panic, shouting as they ran to escape.

7:15 As in Greek version; Hebrew reads *he bowed.*   7:19 Hebrew *at the beginning of the second watch.*

Gideon knew God had promised to help him, but he was getting a little jittery the night before the big battle. So God, who was prepared to give Gideon the victory, also calmed Gideon's fears and gave him the needed confidence to do the job. If you are nervous about a big project or upcoming game, tell God. He can calm your fears and give you the confidence you need to do your best. Trust him with your worries.

Don't worry about anything; instead, pray about everything. Tell God what you need, and thank him for all he has done. Then you will experience God's peace, which exceeds anything we can understand. His peace will guard your hearts and minds as you live in Christ Jesus. PHILIPPIANS 4:6-7

MARCH 11

samson's Birth

God had a message for Manoah, and it would be delivered in a surprising way. Read and see who gave God's message to Manoah and his wife.

Judges 13:2-24

In those days a man named Manoah from the tribe of Dan lived in the town of Zorah. His wife was unable to become pregnant, and they had no children. [3]The angel of the LORD appeared to Manoah's wife and said, "Even though you have been unable to have children, you will soon become pregnant and give birth to a son. [4]So be careful; you must not drink wine or any other alcoholic drink nor eat any forbidden food.* [5]You will become pregnant and give birth to a son, and his hair must never be cut. For he will be dedicated to God as a

Nazirite from birth. He will begin to rescue Israel from the Philistines."

[6] The woman ran and told her husband, "A man of God appeared to me! He looked like one of God's angels, terrifying to see. I didn't ask where he was from, and he didn't tell me his name. [7] But he told me, 'You will become pregnant and give birth to a son. You must not drink wine or any other alcoholic drink nor eat any forbidden food. For your son will be dedicated to God as a Nazirite from the moment of his birth until the day of his death.'"

[8] Then Manoah prayed to the LORD, saying, "Lord, please let the man of God come back to us again and give us more instructions about this son who is to be born."

[9] God answered Manoah's prayer, and the angel of God appeared once again to his wife as she was sitting in the field. But her husband, Manoah, was not with her. [10] So she quickly ran and told her husband, "The man who appeared to me the other day is here again!"

[11] Manoah ran back with his wife and asked, "Are you the man who spoke to my wife the other day?"

"Yes," he replied, "I am."

[12] So Manoah asked him, "When your words come true, what kind of rules should govern the boy's life and work?"

[13] The angel of the LORD replied, "Be sure your wife follows the instructions I gave her. [14] She must not eat grapes or raisins, drink wine or any other alcoholic drink, or eat any forbidden food."

13:4 Hebrew *any unclean thing;* also in 13:7, 14.

[15] Then Manoah said to the angel of the LORD, "Please stay here until we can prepare a young goat for you to eat."

[16] "I will stay," the angel of the LORD replied, "but I will not eat anything. However, you may prepare a burnt offering as a sacrifice to the LORD." (Manoah didn't realize it was the angel of the LORD.)

[17] Then Manoah asked the angel of the LORD, "What is your name? For when all this comes true, we want to honor you."

[18] "Why do you ask my name?" the angel of the LORD replied. "It is too wonderful for you to understand."

[19] Then Manoah took a young goat and a grain offering and offered it on a rock as a sacrifice to the LORD. And as Manoah and his wife watched, the LORD did an amazing thing. [20] As the flames from the altar shot up toward the sky, the angel of the LORD ascended in the fire. When Manoah and his wife saw this, they fell with their faces to the ground.

[21] The angel did not appear again to Manoah and his wife. Manoah finally realized it was the angel of the LORD, [22] and he said to his wife, "We will certainly die, for we have seen God!"

[23] But his wife said, "If the LORD were going to kill us, he wouldn't have accepted our burnt offering and grain offering. He wouldn't have appeared to us and told us this wonderful thing and done these miracles."

[24] When her son was born, she named him Samson. And the LORD blessed him as he grew up.

Even though Manoah believed everything that the angel of God had told his wife, Manoah needed more information. So what did Manoah do? He prayed! Respectfully and prayerfully, Manoah sought God's wisdom. And God answered Manoah's request. When we are confused and don't know what to do, we too can ask God for wisdom.

If you need wisdom, ask our generous God, and he will give it to you. He will not rebuke you for asking. JAMES 1:5

MARCH 12
samson and the Jawbone

Samson was in big trouble—the Philistines were after him. How would he get away?

Judges 15:9-19

The Philistines retaliated by setting up camp in Judah and spreading out near the town of Lehi. ¹⁰The men of Judah asked the Philistines, "Why are you attacking us?"

The Philistines replied, "We've come to capture Samson. We've come to pay him back for what he did to us."

¹¹So 3,000 men of Judah went down to get Samson at the cave in the rock of Etam. They said to Samson, "Don't you realize the Philistines rule over us? What are you doing to us?"

But Samson replied, "I only did to them what they did to me."

¹²But the men of Judah told him, "We have come to tie you up and hand you over to the Philistines."

"All right," Samson said. "But promise that you won't kill me yourselves."

¹³"We will only tie you up and hand you over to the Philistines," they replied. "We won't kill you." So they tied him up with

two new ropes and brought him up from the rock.

¹⁴As Samson arrived at Lehi, the Philistines came shouting in triumph. But the Spirit of the LORD came powerfully upon Samson, and he snapped the ropes on his arms as if they were burnt strands of flax, and they fell from his wrists. ¹⁵Then he found the jawbone of a recently killed donkey. He picked it up and killed 1,000 Philistines with it. ¹⁶Then Samson said,

"With the jawbone of a donkey,
I've piled them in heaps!
With the jawbone of a donkey,
I've killed a thousand men!"

¹⁷When he finished his boasting, he threw away the jawbone; and the place was named Jawbone Hill.*

¹⁸Samson was now very thirsty, and he cried out to the LORD, "You have accomplished this great victory by the strength of your servant. Must I now die of thirst and fall into the hands of these pagans?"

¹⁹So God caused water to gush out of a hollow in the ground at Lehi, and Samson was revived as he drank. Then he named that place "The Spring of the One Who Cried Out,"* and it is still in Lehi to this day.

15:17 Hebrew *Ramath-lehi.* 15:19 Hebrew *En-hakkore.*

God gave Samson the gift of incredible strength. Samson was one of the strongest men ever. God gives everyone special abilities so they can serve him. What are you good at? Thank God for giving you that gift! Then use it to serve God and others.

In his grace, God has given us different gifts for doing certain things well. So if God has given you the ability to prophesy, speak out with as much faith as God has given you. If your gift is serving others, serve them well. If you are a teacher, teach well. ROMANS 12:6-7

MARCH 13

samson and Delilah

Samson's girlfriend, Delilah, was giving him a really hard time. She wanted to know what would make Samson weak, and she wouldn't stop asking until he told her. Would Samson break down and tell her?

Judges 16:4-22

Some time later Samson fell in love with a woman named Delilah, who lived in the valley of Sorek. ⁵The rulers of the Philistines went to her and said, "Entice Samson to tell you what makes him so strong and how he can be overpowered and tied up securely. Then each of us will give you 1,100 pieces* of silver."

⁶So Delilah said to Samson, "Please tell me what makes you so strong and what it would take to tie you up securely."

⁷Samson replied, "If I were tied up with seven new bowstrings that have not yet been dried, I would become as weak as anyone else."

⁸So the Philistine rulers brought Delilah seven new bowstrings, and she tied Samson up with them. ⁹She had hidden some men in one of the inner rooms of her house, and she cried out, "Samson! The Philistines have come to capture you!" But Samson snapped the bowstrings as a piece of string snaps when it is burned by a fire. So the secret of his strength was not discovered.

¹⁰Afterward Delilah said to him, "You've been making fun of me and telling me lies! Now please tell me how you can be tied up securely."

¹¹Samson replied, "If I were tied up with brand-new ropes that had never been used, I would become as weak as anyone else."

¹²So Delilah took new ropes and tied him up with them. The men were hiding in the inner room as before, and again Delilah cried out, "Samson! The Philistines

have come to capture you!" But again Samson snapped the ropes from his arms as if they were thread.

¹³Then Delilah said, "You've been making fun of me and telling me lies! Now tell me how you can be tied up securely."

Samson replied, "If you were to weave the seven braids of my hair into the fabric on your loom and tighten it with the loom shuttle, I would become as weak as anyone else."

So while he slept, Delilah wove the seven braids of his hair into the fabric. ¹⁴Then she tightened it with the loom shuttle.* Again she cried out, "Samson! The Philistines have come to capture you!" But Samson woke up, pulled back the loom shuttle, and yanked his hair away from the loom and the fabric.

¹⁵Then Delilah pouted, "How can you tell me, 'I love you,' when you don't share your secrets with me? You've made fun of me three times now, and you still haven't told me what makes you so strong!" ¹⁶She tormented him with her nagging day after day until he was sick to death of it.

¹⁷Finally, Samson shared his secret with her. "My hair has never been cut," he confessed, "for I was dedicated to God as a Nazirite from birth. If my head were shaved, my strength would leave me, and I would become as weak as anyone else."

¹⁸Delilah realized he had finally told her the truth, so she sent for the Philistine rulers. "Come back one more time," she said, "for he has finally told me his secret." So the Philistine rulers returned with the money in their hands. ¹⁹Delilah lulled Samson to sleep with his head in her lap, and then she called in a man to shave off the seven locks of his hair. In this way she began to bring him down,* and his strength left him.

²⁰Then she cried out, "Samson! The Philistines have come to capture you!"

When he woke up, he thought, "I will do as before and shake myself free." But he didn't realize the Lord had left him. ²¹So the Philistines captured him and gouged out his eyes. They took him to Gaza, where he was bound with bronze chains and forced to grind grain in the prison. ²²But before long, his hair began to grow back.

16:5 Hebrew *1,100 shekels,* about 28 pounds or 12.5 kilograms in weight.   16:13-14 As in Greek version and Latin Vulgate; Hebrew lacks *I would become as weak as anyone else. / So while he slept, Delilah wove the seven braids of his hair into the fabric. Then she tightened it with the loom shuttle.*   16:19 Or *she began to torment him.* Greek version reads *He began to grow weak.*

Samson played with trouble. After being tied up a few times, he should have realized that Delilah was up to no good and he shouldn't tell her his secret. But finally Samson gave in to Delilah's pressure. If a friend tells you to do something you know isn't smart, don't give in. It doesn't matter how much the person bugs you—you need to do the right thing.

Don't copy the behavior and customs of this world, but let God transform you into a new person by changing the way you think. Then you will learn to know God's will for you, which is good and pleasing and perfect. ROMANS 12:2

MARCH 14

SAMSON'S REVENGE

The Philistines had put Samson in prison. He had lost his strength and his freedom. Do you think God forgot about him?

Judges 16:23-30

The Philistine rulers held a great festival, offering sacrifices and praising their god, Dagon. They said, "Our god has given us victory over our enemy Samson!"

²⁴When the people saw him, they praised their god, saying, "Our god has delivered our enemy to us! The one who killed so many of us is now in our power!"

²⁵Half drunk by now, the people demanded, "Bring out Samson so he can amuse us!" So he was brought from the prison to amuse them, and they had him stand between the pillars supporting the roof.

²⁶Samson said to the young servant who was leading him by the hand, "Place my hands against the pillars that hold up the temple. I want to rest against them." ²⁷Now the temple was completely filled with people. All the Philistine rulers were there, and there were about 3,000 men and women on the roof who were watching as Samson amused them.

²⁸Then Samson prayed to the LORD, "Sovereign LORD, remember me again. O God, please strengthen me just one more time. With one blow let me pay back the Philistines for the loss of my two eyes." ²⁹Then Samson put his hands on the two center pillars that held up the temple. Pushing against them with both hands, ³⁰he prayed, "Let me die with the Philistines." And the temple crashed down on the Philistine rulers and all the people. So he killed more people when he died than he had during his entire lifetime.

Samson had to live with a lot of negative consequences because he told his secret to Delilah. Despite Samson's sins, God did not forget about him. When Samson prayed, God heard him and gave Samson what he asked for. No matter what happens in your life, God will *always* love you and will *always* listen when you show your love for him as you pray. Believe it!

God is not unjust. He will not forget how hard you have worked for him and how you have shown your love to him by caring for other believers,* as you still do. HEBREWS 6:10

6:10 Greek *the saints.*

MARCH 15

Ruth and naomi

Naomi was going through difficult times. She and her family had moved to another country when food crops wouldn't grow in Judah. Her husband and her sons had died in the land of Moab. But now the crops were growing in Judah again. So Naomi decided to go back home. Would she have to live the rest of her life all alone there?

Ruth 1:3-19

Then Elimelech died, and Naomi was left with her two sons. ⁴The two sons married Moabite women. One married a woman named Orpah, and the other a woman named Ruth. But about ten years later, ⁵both Mahlon and Kilion died. This left Naomi alone, without her two sons or her husband.

⁶Then Naomi heard in Moab that the LORD had blessed his people in Judah by giving them good crops again. So Naomi and her daughters-in-law got ready to leave Moab to return to her homeland. ⁷With her two daughters-in-law she set out from the place where she had been living, and they took the road that would lead them back to Judah.

⁸But on the way, Naomi said to her two daughters-in-law, "Go back to your mothers' homes. And may the LORD reward you for your kindness to your husbands and to me. ⁹May the LORD bless you with the security of another marriage." Then she kissed them good-bye, and they all broke down and wept.

¹⁰"No," they said. "We want to go with you to your people."

¹¹But Naomi replied, "Why should you go on with me? Can I still give birth to other sons who could grow up to be your husbands? ¹²No, my daughters, return to your parents' homes, for I am too old to marry again. And even if it were possible, and I were to get married tonight and bear sons, then what? ¹³Would you wait for them to grow up and refuse to marry someone else? No, of course not, my daughters! Things are far more bitter for me than for you, because the LORD himself has raised his fist against me."

¹⁴And again they wept together, and Orpah kissed her mother-in-law good-bye. But Ruth clung tightly to Naomi. ¹⁵"Look," Naomi said to her, "your sister-in-law has gone back to her people and to her gods. You should do the same."

¹⁶But Ruth replied, "Don't ask me to leave you and turn back. Wherever you go, I will go; wherever you live, I will live. Your people will be my people, and your God will be my God. ¹⁷Wherever you die, I will die, and there I will be buried. May the LORD punish me severely if I allow anything but death to separate us!" ¹⁸When Naomi saw that Ruth was determined to go with her, she said nothing more.

¹⁹So the two of them continued on their journey. When they came to Bethlehem, the entire town was excited by their arrival. "Is it really Naomi?" the women asked.

Naomi was sure that her daughters-in-law, Ruth and Orpah, would not want to leave their home and move to a strange country. But Ruth loved Naomi so much that she would not leave her. Real love means being loyal—sticking with a family member or friend even when it isn't easy. Ruth is a great example of loyalty. Who do you need to stick with today? Be like Ruth, and be a loyal friend.

This is my commandment: Love each other in the same way I have loved you. There is no greater love than to lay down one's life for one's friends. JOHN 15:12-13

MARCH 16

Ruth and Boaz

Ruth and Naomi were all alone with no money, nothing to eat, and no way to support themselves. What would they do to survive?

Ruth 2:2-16

One day Ruth the Moabite said to Naomi, "Let me go out into the harvest fields to pick up the stalks of grain left behind by anyone who is kind enough to let me do it."

Naomi replied, "All right, my daughter, go ahead." ³So Ruth went out to gather grain behind the harvesters. And as it happened, she found herself working in a field that belonged to Boaz, the relative of her father-in-law, Elimelech.

⁴While she was there, Boaz arrived from Bethlehem and greeted the harvesters. "The LORD be with you!" he said.

"The LORD bless you!" the harvesters replied.

⁵Then Boaz asked his foreman, "Who is that young woman over there? Who does she belong to?"

⁶And the foreman replied, "She is the young woman from Moab who came back with Naomi. ⁷She asked me this morning if she could gather grain behind the harvesters. She has been hard at work ever since, except for a few minutes' rest in the shelter."

⁸Boaz went over and said to Ruth, "Listen, my daughter. Stay right here with us when you gather grain; don't go to any other fields. Stay right behind the young women working in my field. ⁹See which part of the field they are harvesting, and then follow them. I have warned the young men not to treat you roughly. And when you are thirsty, help yourself to the water they have drawn from the well."

¹⁰Ruth fell at his feet and thanked him warmly. "What have I done to deserve such kindness?" she asked. "I am only a foreigner."

¹¹"Yes, I know," Boaz replied. "But I also know about everything you have done for your mother-in-law since the death of

your husband. I have heard how you left your father and mother and your own land to live here among complete strangers. ¹²May the LORD, the God of Israel, under whose wings you have come to take refuge, reward you fully for what you have done."

¹³"I hope I continue to please you, sir," she replied. "You have comforted me by speaking so kindly to me, even though I am not one of your workers."

¹⁴At mealtime Boaz called to her, "Come over here, and help yourself to some food. You can dip your bread in the sour wine." So she sat with his harvesters, and Boaz gave her some roasted grain to eat. She ate all she wanted and still had some left over.

¹⁵When Ruth went back to work again, Boaz ordered his young men, "Let her gather grain right among the sheaves without stopping her. ¹⁶And pull out some heads of barley from the bundles and drop them on purpose for her. Let her pick them up, and don't give her a hard time!"

Boaz took great care of Ruth. He ordered his workers not to bother her, but instead to leave some grain for her to gather. He even fed Ruth lunch. Why was Boaz so kind to a stranger? Boaz did these things because he had heard all about what Ruth had done for Naomi. Because of Ruth's kindness, Boaz wanted to help her. Jesus wants us to do the same—help those who aren't as fortunate as we are. Look around you and find someone you might help today.

Give to those who ask, and don't turn away from those who want to borrow.
MATTHEW 5:42

MARCH 17

ANSWERED PRAYER

Hannah was discouraged because she couldn't have any children. What would Hannah do? Read and see.

1 Samuel 1:6-20

Peninnah would taunt Hannah and make fun of her because the LORD had kept her from having children. ⁷Year after year it was the same—Peninnah would taunt Hannah as they went to the Tabernacle.* Each time, Hannah would be reduced to tears and would not even eat.

⁸"Why are you crying, Hannah?" Elkanah would ask. "Why aren't you eating? Why be downhearted just because you have no children? You have me—isn't that better than having ten sons?"

⁹Once after a sacrificial meal at Shiloh, Hannah got up and went to pray. Eli the priest was sitting at his customary place beside the entrance of the Tabernacle.* ¹⁰Hannah was in deep anguish, crying bitterly as she prayed to the LORD. ¹¹And she made this vow: "O LORD of Heaven's

Armies, if you will look upon my sorrow and answer my prayer and give me a son, then I will give him back to you. He will be yours for his entire lifetime, and as a sign that he has been dedicated to the LORD, his hair will never be cut.*"

¹²As she was praying to the LORD, Eli watched her. ¹³Seeing her lips moving but hearing no sound, he thought she had been drinking. ¹⁴"Must you come here drunk?" he demanded. "Throw away your wine!"

¹⁵"Oh no, sir!" she replied. "I haven't been drinking wine or anything stronger. But I am very discouraged, and I was pouring out my heart to the LORD. ¹⁶Don't think I am a wicked woman! For I have been praying out of great anguish and sorrow."

¹⁷"In that case," Eli said, "go in peace! May the God of Israel grant the request you have asked of him."

¹⁸"Oh, thank you, sir!" she exclaimed. Then she went back and began to eat again, and she was no longer sad.

¹⁹The entire family got up early the next morning and went to worship the LORD once more. Then they returned home to Ramah. When Elkanah slept with Hannah, the LORD remembered her plea, ²⁰and in due time she gave birth to a son. She named him Samuel,* for she said, "I asked the LORD for him."

1:7 Hebrew *the house of the LORD;* also in 1:24.   1:9 Hebrew *the Temple of the LORD.*   1:11 Some manuscripts add *He will drink neither wine nor intoxicants.*   1:20 *Samuel* sounds like the Hebrew term for "asked of God" or "heard by God."

Hannah couldn't have any children. She was teased and made fun of because of her situation. That made her feel discouraged and sad, but no one seemed to understand. Hannah could have given up or tried to get even, but she did neither. Instead, Hannah prayed. When you are feeling picked on or discouraged, remember Hannah. Talk to God. Tell him what's bothering you. God will listen.

I love the LORD because he hears my voice and my prayer for mercy. Because he bends down to listen, I will pray as long as I have breath! PSALM 116:1-2

MARCH 18

Hannah and Samuel

When God gave Hannah her son, Samuel, she was overjoyed! What would she give God in return?

1 Samuel 1:24–2:2, 11

When the child was weaned, Hannah took him to the Tabernacle in Shiloh. They brought along a three-year-old bull* for the sacrifice and a basket* of flour and some wine. ²⁵After sacrificing the bull, they brought the boy to Eli. ²⁶"Sir, do you remember me?" Hannah asked. "I am the woman who stood here several years ago praying to the LORD. ²⁷I asked the LORD to give me this boy, and he has granted my request. ²⁸Now I am giving him to the

Lord, and he will belong to the Lord his whole life." And they* worshiped the Lord there.

²·¹Then Hannah prayed:

"My heart rejoices in the Lord!
The Lord has made me strong.*
Now I have an answer for my enemies;
I rejoice because you rescued me.

²No one is holy like the Lord!
There is no one besides you;
there is no Rock like our God."

¹¹Then Elkanah returned home to Ramah without Samuel. And the boy served the Lord by assisting Eli the priest.

1:24a As in Dead Sea Scrolls, Greek and Syriac versions; Masoretic Text reads *three bulls.*   1:24b Hebrew *and an ephah* [20 quarts or 22 liters].   1:28 Hebrew *he.*   2:1 Hebrew *has exalted my horn.*

God gave Samuel to Hannah, and then she gave him right back to God! Gifts we give to other people or receive from them are different from gifts we give to God or receive from him. Everything we have is a gift from God— whether we asked him for those gifts or not! But God expects us to use all the gifts he gives us. As we use our gifts to serve and help others, we're actually giving those gifts back to God.

God has given each of you a gift from his great variety of spiritual gifts. Use them well to serve one another. I PETER 4:10

MARCH 19

A mysterious voice

Samuel heard a voice calling his name at night. If Eli wasn't calling him, then who was?

1 Samuel 3:1-10

Meanwhile, the boy Samuel served the Lord by assisting Eli. Now in those days messages from the Lord were very rare, and visions were quite uncommon.

²One night Eli, who was almost blind by now, had gone to bed. ³The lamp of God had not yet gone out, and Samuel was sleeping in the Tabernacle* near the Ark of God. ⁴Suddenly the Lord called out, "Samuel!"

"Yes?" Samuel replied. "What is it?" ⁵He got up and ran to Eli. "Here I am. Did you call me?"

"I didn't call you," Eli replied. "Go back to bed." So he did.

⁶Then the Lord called out again, "Samuel!"

Again Samuel got up and went to Eli. "Here I am. Did you call me?"

"I didn't call you, my son," Eli said. "Go back to bed."

⁷Samuel did not yet know the Lord because he had never had a message from the

LORD before. ⁸So the LORD called a third time, and once more Samuel got up and went to Eli. "Here I am. Did you call me?"

Then Eli realized it was the LORD who was calling the boy. ⁹So he said to Samuel, "Go and lie down again, and if someone

3:3 Hebrew *the Temple of the Lord.*

calls again, say, 'Speak, LORD, your servant is listening.'" So Samuel went back to bed.

¹⁰And the LORD came and called as before, "Samuel! Samuel!"

And Samuel replied, "Speak, your servant is listening."

If you heard someone calling your name and had to guess who was calling, how many guesses would it take before you would think of God? Probably a lot! Having God call your name is not an everyday occurrence. But God does speak to us all the time in other ways—through the Bible, through other people, and through the Holy Spirit. Keep your ears and eyes open for messages from God.

[Jesus said,] "My sheep listen to my voice; I know them, and they follow me."
JOHN 10:27

MARCH 20
The Lord Thunders

Because of Israel's sin, the Philistines had been able to conquer the Israelites. What do you think God's people would need to do in order to beat the Philistines?

1 Samuel 7:3-10

Then Samuel said to all the people of Israel, "If you are really serious about wanting to return to the LORD, get rid of your foreign gods and your images of Ashtoreth. Determine to obey only the LORD; then he will rescue you from the Philistines." ⁴So the Israelites got rid of their images of Baal and Ashtoreth and worshiped only the LORD.

⁵Then Samuel told them, "Gather all of Israel to Mizpah, and I will pray to the LORD for you." ⁶So they gathered at Mizpah and, in a great ceremony, drew water from a well and poured it out before the LORD. They also went without food all day and confessed that they had sinned against the LORD. (It was at Mizpah that Samuel became Israel's judge.)

⁷When the Philistine rulers heard that Israel had gathered at Mizpah, they mobilized their army and advanced. The Israelites were badly frightened when they learned that the Philistines were approaching. ⁸"Don't stop pleading with the LORD our God to save us from the Philistines!" they begged Samuel. ⁹So Samuel took a young lamb and offered it

to the LORD as a whole burnt offering. He pleaded with the LORD to help Israel, and the LORD answered him.

¹⁰Just as Samuel was sacrificing the burnt offering, the Philistines arrived to attack Israel. But the LORD spoke with a mighty voice of thunder from heaven that day, and the Philistines were thrown into such confusion that the Israelites defeated them.

The question Samuel had for the Israelites was this: Are you really serious about returning to God? If so, he told them, stop sinning! Once the Israelites turned from their disobedience, God was ready to help them. Samuel's question is a good one for us as well. How serious are we about following Jesus? What habits or attitudes do we need to get rid of if we are *really serious*? Show God today that you are determined to obey.

Now repent of your sins and turn to God, so that your sins may be wiped away. ACTS 3:19

MARCH 21

samuel's sons

Samuel was a good leader of Israel because he followed God. Would his sons serve God the way he had done?

1 Samuel 8:1-5

As Samuel grew old, he appointed his sons to be judges over Israel. ²Joel and Abijah, his oldest sons, held court in Beersheba. ³But they were not like their father, for they were greedy for money. They accepted bribes and perverted justice.

⁴Finally, all the elders of Israel met at Ramah to discuss the matter with Samuel. ⁵"Look," they told him, "you are now old, and your sons are not like you. Give us a king to judge us like all the other nations have."

The people of Israel loved Samuel as their leader because he helped them follow God. But Samuel's sons were selfish and greedy, and nobody wanted to follow them. If you want to be a good leader, be sure you are following God first. Then others will want to follow you.

When there is moral rot within a nation, its government topples easily. But wise and knowledgeable leaders bring stability. PROVERBS 28:2

MARCH 22

Just like the others

All the other nations near Israel had kings, and Israel was starting to want one too. How would they respond to Samuel's advice about whether or not they should have a king?

1 Samuel 8:6-20

Samuel was displeased with their request and went to the LORD for guidance. ⁷"Do everything they say to you," the LORD replied, "for it is me they are rejecting, not you. They don't want me to be their king any longer. ⁸Ever since I brought them from Egypt they have continually abandoned me and followed other gods. And now they are giving you the same treatment. ⁹Do as they ask, but solemnly warn them about the way a king will reign over them."

¹⁰So Samuel passed on the LORD's warning to the people who were asking him for a king. ¹¹"This is how a king will reign over you," Samuel said. "The king will draft your sons and assign them to his chariots and his charioteers, making them run before his chariots. ¹²Some will be generals and captains in his army,* some will be forced to plow in his fields and harvest his crops, and some will make his weapons and chariot equipment. ¹³The king will take your daughters from you and force them to cook and bake and make perfumes for him. ¹⁴He will take away the best of your fields and vineyards and olive groves and give them to his own officials. ¹⁵He will take a tenth of your grain and your grape harvest and distribute it among his officers and attendants. ¹⁶He will take your male and female slaves and demand the finest of your cattle* and donkeys for his own use. ¹⁷He will demand a tenth of your flocks, and you will be his slaves. ¹⁸When that day comes, you will beg for relief from this king you are demanding, but then the LORD will not help you."

¹⁹But the people refused to listen to Samuel's warning. "Even so, we still want a king," they said. ²⁰"We want to be like the nations around us. Our king will judge us and lead us into battle."

8:12 Hebrew *commanders of thousands and commanders of fifties.*   **8:16** As in Greek version; Hebrew reads *young men.*

Samuel warned the Israelites very plainly that they would not like it if they had a king. But the Israelites didn't want to hear it. They wanted to be like everyone else. At times, we all have acted like the Israelites. It's easy to fall into the trap of thinking that because everyone else is doing something, we should too. When you are trying to decide whether to do something, listen to God's instructions and the advice from godly people who love you. Don't just follow the crowd!

You have charged us to keep your commandments carefully. Oh, that my actions would consistently reflect your decrees! PSALM 119:4-5

MARCH 23

The Lost Donkeys

Saul's father had lost his donkeys and sent Saul to find them. But someone found Saul instead!

1 Samuel 9:3-17

One day Kish's donkeys strayed away, and he told Saul, "Take a servant with you, and go look for the donkeys." ⁴So Saul took one of the servants and traveled through the hill country of Ephraim, the land of Shalishah, the Shaalim area, and the entire land of Benjamin, but they couldn't find the donkeys anywhere.

⁵Finally, they entered the region of Zuph, and Saul said to his servant, "Let's go home. By now my father will be more worried about us than about the donkeys!"

⁶But the servant said, "I've just thought of something! There is a man of God who lives here in this town. He is held in high honor by all the people because everything he says comes true. Let's go find him. Perhaps he can tell us which way to go."

⁷"But we don't have anything to offer him," Saul replied. "Even our food is gone, and we don't have a thing to give him."

⁸"Well," the servant said, "I have one small silver piece.* We can at least offer it to the man of God and see what happens!" ⁹(In those days if people wanted a message from God, they would say, "Let's go and ask the seer," for prophets used to be called seers.)

¹⁰"All right," Saul agreed, "let's try it!" So they started into the town where the man of God lived.

¹¹As they were climbing the hill to the town, they met some young women coming out to draw water. So Saul and his servant asked, "Is the seer here today?"

¹²"Yes," they replied. "Stay right on this road. He is at the town gates. He has just arrived to take part in a public sacrifice up at the place of worship. ¹³Hurry and catch him before he goes up there to eat. The guests won't begin eating until he arrives to bless the food."

¹⁴So they entered the town, and as they

passed through the gates, Samuel was coming out toward them to go up to the place of worship.

¹⁵Now the LORD had told Samuel the previous day, ¹⁶"About this time tomorrow I will send you a man from the land of Benjamin. Anoint him to be the leader of

9:8 Hebrew ¼ *shekel of silver*, about 0.1 ounces or 3 grams in weight.

my people, Israel. He will rescue them from the Philistines, for I have looked down on my people in mercy and have heard their cry."

¹⁷When Samuel saw Saul, the LORD said, "That's the man I told you about! He will rule my people."

God had a plan for Saul's life—and it had nothing to do with donkeys! But God used the lost donkeys to bring Saul and Samuel together. Saul's problem was turned into a huge blessing when Samuel eventually anointed Saul king. Sometimes problems are just God's way of preparing us for something better. God has a plan for you. Trust him to use your problems for your good.

We know that God causes everything to work together* for the good of those who love God and are called according to his purpose for them. ROMANS 8:28

8:28 Some manuscripts read *And we know that everything works together.*

MARCH 24
A Changed Man

Samuel had anointed Saul to be the leader of God's people. Read and see what happened when the Holy Spirit changed Saul's heart.

1 Samuel 10:1-11

Then Samuel took a flask of olive oil and poured it over Saul's head. He kissed Saul and said, "I am doing this because the LORD has appointed you to be the ruler over Israel, his special possession.* ²When you leave me today, you will see two men beside Rachel's tomb at Zelzah, on the border of Benjamin. They will tell you that the donkeys have been found and that your father has stopped worrying about them and is now worried about you. He is asking, 'Have you seen my son?'

³"When you get to the oak of Tabor, you will see three men coming toward you who are on their way to worship God at

Bethel. One will be bringing three young goats, another will have three loaves of bread, and the third will be carrying a wineskin full of wine. ⁴They will greet you and offer you two of the loaves, which you are to accept.

⁵"When you arrive at Gibeah of God,* where the garrison of the Philistines is located, you will meet a band of prophets coming down from the place of worship. They will be playing a harp, a tambourine, a flute, and a lyre, and they will be prophesying. ⁶At that time the Spirit of the LORD will come powerfully upon you, and you will prophesy with them. You will be changed into a different person. ⁷After

these signs take place, do what must be done, for God is with you. ⁸Then go down to Gilgal ahead of me. I will join you there to sacrifice burnt offerings and peace offerings. You must wait for seven days until I arrive and give you further instructions."

⁹As Saul turned and started to leave, God gave him a new heart, and all Samuel's signs were fulfilled that day. ¹⁰When Saul and his servant arrived at Gibeah, they saw a group of prophets coming toward them. Then the Spirit of God came powerfully upon Saul, and he, too, began to prophesy. ¹¹When those who knew Saul heard about it, they exclaimed, "What? Is even Saul a prophet? How did the son of Kish become a prophet?"

10:1 Greek version reads *over Israel. And you will rule over the LORD's people and save them from their enemies around them. This will be the sign to you that the Lord has appointed you to be leader over his special possession.* 10:5 Hebrew *Gibeath-elohim.*

God had an important job for Saul—he would be Israel's first king! But Saul's life needed to change before he could do his job. The Holy Spirit can change people's lives to help them serve God. When you become a Christian and the Holy Spirit comes into your life, he can change your life too! He will give you the power to do what God wants.

This means that anyone who belongs to Christ has become a new person. The old life is gone; a new life has begun! 2 CORINTHIANS 5:17

MARCH 25

saul becomes king
Saul knew that God had chosen him to be king. But look what he did when Samuel tried to introduce him to the Israelites for the first time.

1 Samuel 10:17-26
Later Samuel called all the people of Israel to meet before the LORD at Mizpah. ¹⁸And he said, "This is what the LORD, the God of Israel, has declared: I brought you from Egypt and rescued you from the Egyptians and from all of the nations that were oppressing you. ¹⁹But though I have rescued you from your misery and distress, you have rejected your God today and have said, 'No, we want a king instead!' Now, therefore, present yourselves before the LORD by tribes and clans."

²⁰So Samuel brought all the tribes of Israel before the LORD, and the tribe of Benjamin was chosen by lot. ²¹Then he brought each family of the tribe of Benjamin before the LORD, and the family of the Matrites was chosen. And finally Saul son of Kish was chosen from among them. But when they looked for him, he had disappeared! ²²So they asked the LORD, "Where is he?"

And the LORD replied, "He is hiding among the baggage." ²³So they found him and brought him out, and he stood head and shoulders above anyone else.

²⁴Then Samuel said to all the people,

"This is the man the LORD has chosen as your king. No one in all Israel is like him!"

And all the people shouted, "Long live the king!"

²⁵Then Samuel told the people what the rights and duties of a king were. He wrote them down on a scroll and placed it before the LORD. Then Samuel sent the people home again.

²⁶When Saul returned to his home at Gibeah, a group of men whose hearts God had touched went with him.

Why was Saul, the new king of Israel, hiding? Saul was afraid to take his rightful place as the leader of his people. Sometimes, even if we are excited about doing something great and important, we get nervous and anxious. That's when we need to have faith. Faith makes us stick to God and follow him, even when we feel afraid or worried. We can always trust God, even if we don't feel like we can!

Give all your worries and cares to God, for he cares about you. I PETER 5:7

MARCH 26

foolish Actions

The Philistines were about to attack Israel, and Saul was getting worried. Would he trust God or take matters into his own hands?

1 Samuel 13:5-14

The Philistines mustered a mighty army of 3,000* chariots, 6,000 charioteers, and as many warriors as the grains of sand on the seashore! They camped at Micmash east of Beth-aven. ⁶The men of Israel saw what a tight spot they were in; and because they were hard pressed by the enemy, they tried to hide in caves, thickets, rocks, holes, and cisterns. ⁷Some of them crossed the Jordan River and escaped into the land of Gad and Gilead.

Meanwhile, Saul stayed at Gilgal, and his men were trembling with fear. ⁸Saul waited there seven days for Samuel, as Samuel had instructed him earlier, but Samuel still didn't come. Saul realized that his troops were rapidly slipping away. ⁹So

he demanded, "Bring me the burnt offering and the peace offerings!" And Saul sacrificed the burnt offering himself.

¹⁰Just as Saul was finishing with the burnt offering, Samuel arrived. Saul went out to meet and welcome him, ¹¹but Samuel said, "What is this you have done?"

Saul replied, "I saw my men scattering from me, and you didn't arrive when you said you would, and the Philistines are at Micmash ready for battle. ¹²So I said, 'The Philistines are ready to march against us at Gilgal, and I haven't even asked for the LORD's help!' So I felt compelled to offer the burnt offering myself before you came."

¹³"How foolish!" Samuel exclaimed. "You have not kept the command the LORD

your God gave you. Had you kept it, the LORD would have established your kingdom over Israel forever. ¹⁴But now your kingdom must end, for the LORD has

sought out a man after his own heart. The LORD has already appointed him to be the leader of his people, because you have not kept the LORD's command."

13:5 As in Greek and Syriac versions; Hebrew reads *30,000*.

Under pressure, Saul disobeyed God by offering sacrifices without a priest. Because of that, Saul lost his kingdom. Often temptation strikes when we are under pressure. Giving in to that temptation seems like an easy way out. God wants us to obey him no matter how difficult it may seem at the time. It may be easy to disobey, but it is never easy to live with the consequences of disobedience.

The temptations in your life are no different from what others experience. And God is faithful. He will not allow the temptation to be more than you can stand. When you are tempted, he will show you a way out so that you can endure.
I CORINTHIANS 10:13

MARCH 27

Jonathan's courage

Jonathan fought the whole Philistine army by himself! Do you think he made it home safely?

1 Samuel 14:1-15

One day Jonathan said to his armor bearer, "Come on, let's go over to where the Philistines have their outpost." But Jonathan did not tell his father what he was doing.

²Meanwhile, Saul and his 600 men were camped on the outskirts of Gibeah, around the pomegranate tree* at Migron. ³Among Saul's men was Ahijah the priest, who was wearing the ephod, the priestly vest. Ahijah was the son of Ichabod's brother Ahitub, son of Phinehas, son of Eli, the priest of the LORD who had served at Shiloh.

No one realized that Jonathan had left the Israelite camp. ⁴To reach the Philistine outpost, Jonathan had to go down between

two rocky cliffs that were called Bozez and Seneh. ⁵The cliff on the north was in front of Micmash, and the one on the south was in front of Geba. ⁶"Let's go across to the outpost of those pagans," Jonathan said to his armor bearer. "Perhaps the LORD will help us, for nothing can hinder the LORD. He can win a battle whether he has many warriors or only a few!"

⁷"Do what you think is best," the armor bearer replied. "I'm with you completely, whatever you decide."

⁸"All right then," Jonathan told him. "We will cross over and let them see us. ⁹If they say to us, 'Stay where you are or we'll kill you,' then we will stop and not go up to them. ¹⁰But if they say, 'Come on up and

fight,' then we will go up. That will be the LORD's sign that he will help us defeat them."

¹¹When the Philistines saw them coming, they shouted, "Look! The Hebrews are crawling out of their holes!" ¹²Then the men from the outpost shouted to Jonathan, "Come on up here, and we'll teach you a lesson!"

"Come on, climb right behind me," Jonathan said to his armor bearer, "for the LORD will help us defeat them!"

¹³So they climbed up using both hands and feet, and the Philistines fell before Jonathan, and his armor bearer killed those who came behind them. ¹⁴They killed some twenty men in all, and their bodies were scattered over about half an acre.*

¹⁵Suddenly, panic broke out in the Philistine army, both in the camp and in the field, including even the outposts and raiding parties. And just then an earthquake struck, and everyone was terrified.

14:2 Or *around the rock of Rimmon.*   14:14 Hebrew *half a yoke;* a "yoke" was the amount of land plowed by a pair of yoked oxen in one day.

Jonathan's courage might seem incredible. But he was brave because he knew that God was with him and would fight for him. If God is on our side, it doesn't matter how many people are fighting against us. God's power is stronger than anything else in this world. We never have to worry about what other people might do to us if God is with us.

I wait quietly before God, for my victory comes from him. He alone is my rock and my salvation, my fortress where I will never be shaken. PSALM 62:1-2

MARCH 28
Jonathan's snack

Saul was so anxious to destroy the Philistines that he made a very serious vow without thinking. Wait till you see what kind of trouble he got into.

1 Samuel 14:24-30, 36-45

Now the men of Israel were pressed to exhaustion that day, because Saul had placed them under an oath, saying, "Let a curse fall on anyone who eats before evening—before I have full revenge on my enemies." So no one ate anything all day, ²⁵even though they had all found honeycomb on the ground in the forest. ²⁶They didn't dare

touch the honey because they all feared the oath they had taken.

²⁷But Jonathan had not heard his father's command, and he dipped the end of his stick into a piece of honeycomb and ate the honey. After he had eaten it, he felt refreshed.* ²⁸But one of the men saw him and said, "Your father made the army take a strict oath that anyone who eats food to-

day will be cursed. That is why everyone is weary and faint."

²⁹"My father has made trouble for us all!" Jonathan exclaimed. "A command like that only hurts us. See how refreshed I am now that I have eaten this little bit of honey. ³⁰If the men had been allowed to eat freely from the food they found among our enemies, think how many more Philistines we could have killed!"

³⁶Then Saul said, "Let's chase the Philistines all night and plunder them until sunrise. Let's destroy every last one of them."

His men replied, "We'll do whatever you think is best."

But the priest said, "Let's ask God first."

³⁷So Saul asked God, "Should we go after the Philistines? Will you help us defeat them?" But God made no reply that day.

³⁸Then Saul said to the leaders, "Something's wrong! I want all my army commanders to come here. We must find out what sin was committed today. ³⁹I vow by the name of the LORD who rescued Israel that the sinner will surely die, even if it is my own son Jonathan!" But no one would tell him what the trouble was.

⁴⁰Then Saul said, "Jonathan and I will stand over here, and all of you stand over there."

And the people responded to Saul, "Whatever you think is best."

⁴¹Then Saul prayed, "O LORD, God of Israel, please show us who is guilty and who is innocent.*" Then they cast sacred lots, and Jonathan and Saul were chosen as the guilty ones, and the people were declared innocent.

⁴²Then Saul said, "Now cast lots again and choose between me and Jonathan." And Jonathan was shown to be the guilty one.

⁴³"Tell me what you have done," Saul demanded of Jonathan.

"I tasted a little honey," Jonathan admitted. "It was only a little bit on the end of my stick. Does that deserve death?"

⁴⁴"Yes, Jonathan," Saul said, "you must die! May God strike me and even kill me if you do not die for this."

⁴⁵But the people broke in and said to Saul, "Jonathan has won this great victory for Israel. Should he die? Far from it! As surely as the LORD lives, not one hair on his head will be touched, for God helped him do a great deed today." So the people rescued Jonathan, and he was not put to death.

14:27 Or *his eyes brightened;* similarly in 14:29.   14:41 Greek version adds *If the fault is with me or my son Jonathan, respond with Urim; but if the men of Israel are at fault, respond with Thummim.*

This story is a serious reminder for us to think before we speak. It's easy to get carried away by the moment and say something we don't mean. But our words can have tremendous consequences! Saul's reckless vow got him into big trouble. He had to either break his vow or kill his son. Be careful what you say to others and to God.

Most of all, my brothers and sisters, never take an oath, by heaven or earth or anything else. Just say a simple yes or no, so that you will not sin and be condemned. JAMES 5:12

MARCH 29

samuel and David

Samuel was going to pick a new person to be king over Israel. How do you think he decided which person to choose?

1 Samuel 16:1-13

Now the LORD said to Samuel, "You have mourned long enough for Saul. I have rejected him as king of Israel, so fill your flask with olive oil and go to Bethlehem. Find a man named Jesse who lives there, for I have selected one of his sons to be my king."

²But Samuel asked, "How can I do that? If Saul hears about it, he will kill me."

"Take a heifer with you," the LORD replied, "and say that you have come to make a sacrifice to the LORD. ³Invite Jesse to the sacrifice, and I will show you which of his sons to anoint for me."

⁴So Samuel did as the LORD instructed. When he arrived at Bethlehem, the elders of the town came trembling to meet him. "What's wrong?" they asked. "Do you come in peace?"

⁵"Yes," Samuel replied. "I have come to sacrifice to the LORD. Purify yourselves and come with me to the sacrifice." Then Samuel performed the purification rite for Jesse and his sons and invited them to the sacrifice, too.

⁶When they arrived, Samuel took one look at Eliab and thought, "Surely this is the LORD's anointed!"

⁷But the LORD said to Samuel, "Don't judge by his appearance or height, for I

have rejected him. The LORD doesn't see things the way you see them. People judge by outward appearance, but the LORD looks at the heart."

⁸Then Jesse told his son Abinadab to step forward and walk in front of Samuel. But Samuel said, "This is not the one the LORD has chosen." ⁹Next Jesse summoned Shimea,* but Samuel said, "Neither is this the one the LORD has chosen." ¹⁰In the same way all seven of Jesse's sons were presented to Samuel. But Samuel said to Jesse, "The LORD has not chosen any of these." ¹¹Then Samuel asked, "Are these all the sons you have?"

"There is still the youngest," Jesse replied. "But he's out in the fields watching the sheep and goats."

"Send for him at once," Samuel said. "We will not sit down to eat until he arrives."

¹²So Jesse sent for him. He was dark and handsome, with beautiful eyes.

And the LORD said, "This is the one; anoint him."

¹³So as David stood there among his brothers, Samuel took the flask of olive oil he had brought and anointed David with the oil. And the Spirit of the LORD came powerfully upon David from that day on. Then Samuel returned to Ramah.

16:9 Hebrew *Shammah,* a variant spelling of Shimea.

114

Eliab was tall and handsome. Samuel thought he looked like a great king! But God was not paying attention to Eliab's looks. He knew that David's heart would make *him* the best king. Since Samuel was listening to God, he learned that David was God's choice for Israel's next leader. Listening to God helps us understand what people are really like. Don't judge people by how they look. Instead, consider what God would say about each person's heart.

As a face is reflected in water, so the heart reflects the real person.
PROVERBS 27:19

MARCH 30
Goliath's Challenge

Goliath was saying that no one in Israel was strong enough to fight him. Do you think the Israelites would prove him wrong?

1 Samuel 17:4-11, 17-30

Then Goliath, a Philistine champion from Gath, came out of the Philistine ranks to face the forces of Israel. He was over nine feet* tall! ⁵He wore a bronze helmet, and his bronze coat of mail weighed 125 pounds.* ⁶He also wore bronze leg armor, and he carried a bronze javelin on his shoulder. ⁷The shaft of his spear was as heavy and thick as a weaver's beam, tipped with an iron spearhead that weighed 15 pounds.* His armor bearer walked ahead of him carrying a shield.

⁸Goliath stood and shouted a taunt across to the Israelites. "Why are you all coming out to fight?" he called. "I am the Philistine champion, but you are only the servants of Saul. Choose one man to come down here and fight me! ⁹If he kills me, then we will be your slaves. But if I kill him, you will be our slaves! ¹⁰I defy the armies of Israel today! Send me a man who will fight me!" ¹¹When Saul and the Isra-

elites heard this, they were terrified and deeply shaken.

⊙

¹⁷One day Jesse said to David, "Take this basket* of roasted grain and these ten loaves of bread, and carry them quickly to your brothers. ¹⁸And give these ten cuts of cheese to their captain. See how your brothers are getting along, and bring back a report on how they are doing.*" ¹⁹David's brothers were with Saul and the Israelite army at the valley of Elah, fighting against the Philistines.

²⁰So David left the sheep with another shepherd and set out early the next morning with the gifts, as Jesse had directed him. He arrived at the camp just as the Israelite army was leaving for the battlefield with shouts and battle cries. ²¹Soon the Israelite and Philistine forces stood facing each other, army against army. ²²David left his things with the keeper of supplies and

hurried out to the ranks to greet his brothers. [23]As he was talking with them, Goliath, the Philistine champion from Gath, came out from the Philistine ranks. Then David heard him shout his usual taunt to the army of Israel.

[24]As soon as the Israelite army saw him, they began to run away in fright. [25]"Have you seen the giant?" the men asked. "He comes out each day to defy Israel. The king has offered a huge reward to anyone who kills him. He will give that man one of his daughters for a wife, and the man's entire family will be exempted from paying taxes!"

[26]David asked the soldiers standing nearby, "What will a man get for killing this Philistine and ending his defiance of Israel? Who is this pagan Philistine anyway, that he is allowed to defy the armies of the living God?"

[27]And these men gave David the same reply. They said, "Yes, that is the reward for killing him."

[28]But when David's oldest brother, Eliab, heard David talking to the men, he was angry. "What are you doing around here anyway?" he demanded. "What about those few sheep you're supposed to be taking care of? I know about your pride and deceit. You just want to see the battle!"

[29]"What have I done now?" David replied. "I was only asking a question!" [30]He walked over to some others and asked them the same thing and received the same answer.

17:4 Hebrew *6 cubits and 1 span* [which totals about 9.75 feet or 3 meters]; Dead Sea Scrolls and Greek version read *4 cubits and 1 span* [which totals about 6.75 feet or 2 meters].   17:5 Hebrew *5,000 shekels* [57 kilograms].   17:7 Hebrew *600 shekels* [6.8 kilograms].   17:17 Hebrew *ephah* [20 quarts or 22 liters].   17:18 Hebrew *and take their pledge.*

Not one Israelite soldier took up Goliath's challenge. All of them were too afraid to fight him. But David was ready. He was not a soldier, and he wasn't very big. But his faith was! David believed that the God of Israel could and would defeat Goliath. You don't need to be an adult or a strong person to have faith. You only need to do two things: (1) Believe that God is who he says he is; (2) Trust God to do what he says he will do.

"You don't have enough faith," Jesus told them. "I tell you the truth, if you had faith even as small as a mustard seed, you could say to this mountain, 'Move from here to there,' and it would move. Nothing would be impossible."
MATTHEW 17:20

march 31

David and Goliath

Finally David, a young teen, answered Goliath's challenge and went out to fight him. Who do you think won the fight: the youth or the giant?

1 Samuel 17:32-50

"Don't worry about this Philistine," David told Saul. "I'll go fight him!"

³³"Don't be ridiculous!" Saul replied. "There's no way you can fight this Philistine and possibly win! You're only a boy, and he's been a man of war since his youth."

³⁴But David persisted. "I have been taking care of my father's sheep and goats," he said. "When a lion or a bear comes to steal a lamb from the flock, ³⁵I go after it with a club and rescue the lamb from its mouth. If the animal turns on me, I catch it by the jaw and club it to death. ³⁶I have done this to both lions and bears, and I'll do it to this pagan Philistine, too, for he has defied the armies of the living God! ³⁷The LORD who rescued me from the claws of the lion and the bear will rescue me from this Philistine!"

Saul finally consented. "All right, go ahead," he said. "And may the LORD be with you!"

³⁸Then Saul gave David his own armor— a bronze helmet and a coat of mail. ³⁹David put it on, strapped the sword over it, and took a step or two to see what it was like, for he had never worn such things before.

"I can't go in these," he protested to Saul. "I'm not used to them." So David took them off again. ⁴⁰He picked up five smooth stones from a stream and put them into his shepherd's bag. Then, armed only with his shepherd's staff and sling, he started across the valley to fight the Philistine.

⁴¹Goliath walked out toward David with his shield bearer ahead of him, ⁴²sneering in contempt at this ruddy-faced boy. ⁴³"Am I a dog," he roared at David, "that you come at me with a stick?" And he cursed David by the names of his gods. ⁴⁴"Come over here, and I'll give your flesh to the birds and wild animals!" Goliath yelled.

⁴⁵David replied to the Philistine, "You come to me with sword, spear, and javelin, but I come to you in the name of the LORD of Heaven's Armies—the God of the armies of Israel, whom you have defied. ⁴⁶Today the LORD will conquer you, and I will kill you and cut off your head. And then I will give the dead bodies of your men to the birds and wild animals, and the whole world will know that there is a God in Israel! ⁴⁷And everyone assembled here will know that the LORD rescues his people, but not with sword and spear. This is the LORD's battle, and he will give you to us!"

⁴⁸As Goliath moved closer to attack, David quickly ran out to meet him. ⁴⁹Reaching into his shepherd's bag and taking out a stone, he hurled it with his sling and hit the Philistine in the forehead. The stone sank in, and Goliath stumbled and fell face down on the ground.

⁵⁰So David triumphed over the Philistine with only a sling and a stone, for he had no sword.

King Saul thought David was crazy for wanting to fight Goliath. The giant made fun of David when he saw him coming out to fight. But David had the last laugh! Everyone but David was thinking about the size of the people in the fight. But David remembered the size of the God on his side. He trusted in God's strength, and God helped him win. When you face a giant problem, remember that God can help you. Trust in his strength, and you will knock that huge problem right down!

God chose things the world considers foolish in order to shame those who think they are wise. And he chose things that are powerless to shame those who are powerful. I CORINTHIANS 1:27

MARCH CHALLENGE
well done!

You are really flying high! You've just finished the readings for March. Are you going to quit now? Of course not. You're going to make it to the top—you can do it! Don't forget to use a marker or highlighter to fill in the number of levels you've conquered so far.

Which lesson helped you learn the most this month? If you could be one of the Bible characters you read about this month, which one would you most like to be? Why? Which one would you least like to be? Why?

. . . .

. . . .

. . . .

. . . .

. . . .

. . . .

IMPORTANT STUFF TO REMEMBER FROM MARCH

❏ God fights for his people.

❏ God is stronger than any human power.

❏ God wants his people to be strong and courageous.

❏ We can trust God to do what he promises.

Do you remember reading about Ruth and Naomi? Ruth was a great example of a loyal friend. Use the code below to see what Ruth said to Naomi when Naomi told her she could go home. You'll find the answer in the March 15 reading.

A	B	C	D	E	F	G	H	I	J	K	L	M
1	2	3	4	5	6	7	8	9	10	11	12	13

N	O	P	Q	R	S	T	U	V	W	X	Y	Z
14	15	16	17	18	19	20	21	22	23	24	25	26

___ ___ ___ ___ ___ ___ ___ ___ ___   ___ ___ ___   ___ ___,   ___   ___ ___ ___ ___   ___ ___;
23 8 5 18 5 22 5 18   25 15 21   7 15   9   23 9 12 12   7 15

___ ___ ___ ___ ___ ___ ___ ___ ___   ___ ___ ___   ___ ___ ___ ___,   ___   ___ ___ ___ ___
23 8 5 18 5 22 5 18   25 15 21   12 9 22 5   9   23 9 12 12

___ ___ ___ ___.   ___ ___ ___ ___   ___ ___ ___ ___ ___ ___   ___ ___ ___ ___   ___ ___
12 9 22 5   25 15 21 18   16 5 15 16 12 5   23 9 12 12   2 5

___ ___   ___ ___ ___ ___ ___ ___,   ___ ___ ___   ___ ___ ___ ___ ___   ___ ___ ___
13 25   16 5 15 16 12 5   1 14 4   25 15 21 18   7 15 4

___ ___ ___ ___   ___ ___   ___ ___   ___ ___ ___.
23 9 12 12   2 5   13 25   7 15 4

120

APRIL 1

The Trouble with Jealousy

Saul was happy to have David help him, because David always did everything really well. But how do you think Saul felt when the people started praising David more than they praised him?

1 Samuel 18:5-16

Whatever Saul asked David to do, David did it successfully. So Saul made him a commander over the men of war, an appointment that was welcomed by the people and Saul's officers alike.

⁶When the victorious Israelite army was returning home after David had killed the Philistine, women from all the towns of Israel came out to meet King Saul. They sang and danced for joy with tambourines and cymbals.* ⁷This was their song:

"Saul has killed his thousands,
    and David his ten thousands!"

⁸This made Saul very angry. "What's this?" he said. "They credit David with ten thousands and me with only thousands. Next they'll be making him their king!" ⁹So from that time on Saul kept a jealous eye on David.

¹⁰The very next day a tormenting spirit* from God overwhelmed Saul, and he began to rave in his house like a madman. David was playing the harp, as he did each day. But Saul had a spear in his hand, ¹¹and he suddenly hurled it at David, intending to pin him to the wall. But David escaped him twice.

¹²Saul was then afraid of David, for the LORD was with David and had turned away from Saul. ¹³Finally, Saul sent him away and appointed him commander over 1,000 men, and David faithfully led his troops into battle.

¹⁴David continued to succeed in everything he did, for the LORD was with him. ¹⁵When Saul recognized this, he became even more afraid of him. ¹⁶But all Israel and Judah loved David because he was so successful at leading his troops into battle.

18:6 The type of instrument represented by the word *cymbals* is uncertain.   18:10 Or *an evil spirit.*

Saul was so jealous of David that he tried to kill him. Jealousy is dangerous, because it makes us feel angry about things we should be happy about. David was doing great things for Israel, but Saul wasn't happy about it at all. Instead, Saul was worried that he wasn't getting enough attention. The best way to beat jealousy is to focus on others instead of ourselves. If we can be happy for other people, we won't be jealous.

Anger is cruel, and wrath is like a flood, but jealousy is even more dangerous.
PROVERBS 27:4

APRIL 2

Best Friends Forever

David's life was in danger because Saul was determined to kill him. David knew he had to leave, but he was sad to say good-bye to Jonathan, who was his best friend and Saul's son. How would David and Jonathan stay friends?

1 Samuel 20:1-4, 24-42

David now fled from Naioth in Ramah and found Jonathan. "What have I done?" he exclaimed. "What is my crime? How have I offended your father that he is so determined to kill me?"

²"That's not true!" Jonathan protested. "You're not going to die. He always tells me everything he's going to do, even the little things. I know my father wouldn't hide something like this from me. It just isn't so!"

³Then David took an oath before Jonathan and said, "Your father knows perfectly well about our friendship, so he has said to himself, 'I won't tell Jonathan—why should I hurt him?' But I swear to you that I am only a step away from death! I swear it by the LORD and by your own soul!"

⁴"Tell me what I can do to help you," Jonathan exclaimed.

²⁴So David hid himself in the field, and when the new moon festival began, the king sat down to eat. ²⁵He sat at his usual place against the wall, with Jonathan sitting opposite him* and Abner beside him. But David's place was empty. ²⁶Saul didn't say anything about it that day, for he said to himself, "Something must have made David ceremonially unclean." ²⁷But when David's place was empty again the next day, Saul asked Jonathan, "Why hasn't the son of Jesse been here for the meal either yesterday or today?"

²⁸Jonathan replied, "David earnestly asked me if he could go to Bethlehem. ²⁹He said, 'Please let me go, for we are having a family sacrifice. My brother demanded that I be there. So please let me

get away to see my brothers.' That's why he isn't here at the king's table."

³⁰Saul boiled with rage at Jonathan. "You stupid son of a whore!"* he swore at him. "Do you think I don't know that you want him to be king in your place, shaming yourself and your mother? ³¹As long as that son of Jesse is alive, you'll never be king. Now go and get him so I can kill him!"

³²"But why should he be put to death?" Jonathan asked his father. "What has he done?" ³³Then Saul hurled his spear at Jonathan, intending to kill him. So at last Jonathan realized that his father was really determined to kill David.

³⁴Jonathan left the table in fierce anger and refused to eat on that second day of the festival, for he was crushed by his father's shameful behavior toward David.

³⁵The next morning, as agreed, Jonathan went out into the field and took a young boy with him to gather his arrows. ³⁶"Start running," he told the boy, "so you can find the arrows as I shoot them." So the boy ran, and Jonathan shot an arrow beyond him. ³⁷When the boy had almost reached the arrow, Jonathan shouted, "The arrow is still ahead of you. ³⁸Hurry, hurry, don't wait." So the boy quickly gathered up the arrows and ran back to his master. ³⁹He, of course, suspected nothing; only Jonathan and David understood the signal. ⁴⁰Then Jonathan gave his bow and arrows to the boy and told him to take them back to town.

⁴¹As soon as the boy was gone, David came out from where he had been hiding near the stone pile.* Then David bowed three times to Jonathan with his face to the ground. Both of them were in tears as they embraced each other and said good-bye, especially David.

⁴²At last Jonathan said to David, "Go in peace, for we have sworn loyalty to each other in the LORD's name. The LORD is the witness of a bond between us and our children forever." Then David left, and Jonathan returned to the town.*

20:25 As in Greek version; Hebrew reads *with Jonathan standing.*   20:30 Hebrew *You son of a perverse and rebellious woman.*
20:41 As in Greek version; Hebrew reads *near the south edge.*   20:42 This sentence is numbered 21:1 in Hebrew text.

Even though David had to leave, he and Jonathan knew that their friendship would last, because they were committed to God. Friendships that are based on putting God first will last forever! The best way for a friendship to grow and last is for both friends to love God and to help each other love God more. Do you have friends like that? Spend time with your friends and with God.

As iron sharpens iron, so a friend sharpens a friend. PROVERBS 27:17

APRIL 3

TOO CLOSE FOR COMFORT

Saul had been hunting David so that he could kill him. But David was the one who found Saul—when Saul was least expecting it. What do you think David did when he had a chance to get rid of his enemy?

1 Samuel 24:2-17

So Saul chose 3,000 elite troops from all Israel and went to search for David and his men near the rocks of the wild goats.

³At the place where the road passes some sheepfolds, Saul went into a cave to relieve himself. But as it happened, David and his men were hiding farther back in that very cave!

⁴"Now's your opportunity!" David's men whispered to him. "Today the LORD is telling you, 'I will certainly put your enemy into your power, to do with as you wish.'" So David crept forward and cut off a piece of the hem of Saul's robe.

⁵But then David's conscience began bothering him because he had cut Saul's robe. ⁶"The LORD knows I shouldn't have done that to my lord the king," he said to his men. "The LORD forbid that I should do this to my lord the king and attack the LORD's anointed one, for the LORD himself has chosen him." ⁷So David restrained his men and did not let them kill Saul.

After Saul had left the cave and gone on his way, ⁸David came out and shouted after him, "My lord the king!" And when Saul looked around, David bowed low before him.

⁹Then he shouted to Saul, "Why do you listen to the people who say I am trying to harm you? ¹⁰This very day you can see with your own eyes it isn't true. For the LORD placed you at my mercy back there in the cave. Some of my men told me to kill you, but I spared you. For I said, 'I will never harm the king—he is the LORD's anointed one.' ¹¹Look, my father, at what I have in my hand. It is a piece of the hem of your robe! I cut it off, but I didn't kill you. This proves that I am not trying to harm you and that I have not sinned against you, even though you have been hunting for me to kill me.

¹²"May the LORD judge between us. Perhaps the LORD will punish you for what you are trying to do to me, but I will never harm you. ¹³As that old proverb says, 'From evil people come evil deeds.' So you can be sure I will never harm you. ¹⁴Who is the king of Israel trying to catch anyway? Should he spend his time chasing one who is as worthless as a dead dog or a single flea? ¹⁵May the LORD therefore judge which of us is right and punish the guilty one. He is my advocate, and he will rescue me from your power!"

¹⁶When David had finished speaking, Saul called back, "Is that really you, my son David?" Then he began to cry. ¹⁷And he said to David, "You are a better man than I am, for you have repaid me good for evil."

Even David's men thought that David had a good reason to kill Saul. But David wouldn't do it. He knew that it would be wrong to kill the man whom God had chosen to be Israel's king. Jesus tells us to love our enemies. No matter how wrong people's actions are, we don't have the right to act the same way. How can you show Jesus' love to someone who has hurt you?

Don't repay evil for evil. Don't retaliate with insults when people insult you. Instead, pay them back with a blessing. That is what God has called you to do, and he will bless you for it. I PETER 3:9

APRIL 4

David and Abigail

Nabal had been really rude and had insulted David. Would Nabal's wife, Abigail, be able to smooth things out before David's anger got the best of him?

1 Samuel 25:10-28, 32-33

"Who is this fellow David?" Nabal sneered to the young men. "Who does this son of Jesse think he is? There are lots of servants these days who run away from their masters. ¹¹Should I take my bread and my water and my meat that I've slaughtered for my shearers and give it to a band of outlaws who come from who knows where?"

¹²So David's young men returned and told him what Nabal had said. ¹³"Get your swords!" was David's reply as he strapped on his own. Then 400 men started off with David, and 200 remained behind to guard their equipment.

¹⁴Meanwhile, one of Nabal's servants went to Abigail and told her, "David sent messengers from the wilderness to greet our master, but he screamed insults at them. ¹⁵These men have been very good to us, and we never suffered any harm from them. Nothing was stolen from us the whole time they were with us. ¹⁶In fact, day and night they were like a wall of protection to us and the sheep. ¹⁷You need to know this and figure out what to do, for there is going to be trouble for our master and his whole family. He's so ill-tempered that no one can even talk to him!"

¹⁸Abigail wasted no time. She quickly gathered 200 loaves of bread, two wineskins full of wine, five sheep that had been slaughtered, nearly a bushel* of roasted grain, 100 clusters of raisins, and 200 fig cakes. She packed them on donkeys ¹⁹and said to her servants, "Go on ahead. I will follow you shortly." But she didn't tell her husband Nabal what she was doing.

²⁰As she was riding her donkey into a mountain ravine, she saw David and his men coming toward her. ²¹David had just been saying, "A lot of good it did to help this fellow. We protected his flocks in the

wilderness, and nothing he owned was lost or stolen. But he has repaid me evil for good. ²²May God strike me and kill me* if even one man of his household is still alive tomorrow morning!"

²³When Abigail saw David, she quickly got off her donkey and bowed low before him. ²⁴She fell at his feet and said, "I accept all blame in this matter, my lord. Please listen to what I have to say. ²⁵I know Nabal is a wicked and ill-tempered man; please don't pay any attention to him. He is a fool, just as his name suggests.* But I never even saw the young men you sent.

²⁶"Now, my lord, as surely as the LORD lives and you yourself live, since the LORD has kept you from murdering and taking vengeance into your own hands, let all your enemies and those who try to harm you be as cursed as Nabal is. ²⁷And here is a present that I, your servant, have brought to you and your young men. ²⁸Please forgive me if I have offended you in any way. The LORD will surely reward you with a lasting dynasty, for you are fighting the LORD's battles. And you have not done wrong throughout your entire life."

³²David replied to Abigail, "Praise the LORD, the God of Israel, who has sent you to meet me today! ³³Thank God for your good sense! Bless you for keeping me from murder and from carrying out vengeance with my own hands."

25:18 Hebrew *5 seahs* [30 liters].   25:22 As in Greek version; Hebrew reads *May God strike and kill the enemies of David.* 25:25 The name *Nabal* means "fool."

Abigail and Nabal were complete opposites in the way they acted. Nabal was as mean and rude as Abigail was reasonable and kind. Thankfully for Nabal, Abigail's apology was enough to calm David down after her husband's rudeness. Be careful what you say to people. Insulting words are powerful. But words of apology are just as powerful in a positive way—able to make a situation better. If you've made somebody mad by what you've said, tell that person you are sorry.

Don't use foul or abusive language. Let everything you say be good and helpful, so that your words will be an encouragement to those who hear them.
EPHESIANS 4:29

APRIL 5

David and the Philistines

David was facing a big challenge. The Philistine army was coming to fight him, and he didn't know what to do. Who do you think would be the best person to ask for advice?

2 Samuel 5:17-25

When the Philistines heard that David had been anointed king of Israel, they mobilized all their forces to capture him. But David was told they were coming, so he went into the stronghold. [18]The Philistines arrived and spread out across the valley of Rephaim. [19]So David asked the LORD, "Should I go out to fight the Philistines? Will you hand them over to me?"

The LORD replied to David, "Yes, go ahead. I will certainly hand them over to you."

[20]So David went to Baal-perazim and defeated the Philistines there. "The LORD did it!" David exclaimed. "He burst through my enemies like a raging flood!" So he named that place Baal-perazim (which means "the Lord who bursts through"). [21]The Philistines had abandoned their idols there, so David and his men confiscated them.

[22]But after a while the Philistines returned and again spread out across the valley of Rephaim. [23]And again David asked the LORD what to do. "Do not attack them straight on," the LORD replied. "Instead, circle around behind and attack them near the poplar* trees. [24]When you hear a sound like marching feet in the tops of the poplar trees, be on the alert! That will be the signal that the LORD is moving ahead of you to strike down the Philistine army." [25]So David did what the LORD commanded, and he struck down the Philistines all the way from Gibeon* to Gezer.

5:23 Or *aspen,* or *balsam;* also in 5:24. The exact identification of this tree is uncertain.   5:25 As in Greek version (see also 1 Chr 14:16); Hebrew reads *Geba.*

When faced with a tough challenge, David went straight to God—the best source of advice. God told David exactly what to do in order to beat the Philistines. And because David followed God's advice, he was successful. When you have a big question or problem, take it to God. He knows exactly how to guide you, and he *will* help you when you ask him. Is there anything you need to ask him about today?

You [God] guide me with your counsel, leading me to a glorious destiny.
PSALM 73:24

APRIL 6

The King's Kindness

One day David remembered a promise he had made a long time ago. Was it still important for him to keep it?

2 Samuel 9:1-13

One day David asked, "Is anyone in Saul's family still alive—anyone to whom I can show kindness for Jonathan's sake?" ²He summoned a man named Ziba, who had been one of Saul's servants. "Are you Ziba?" the king asked.

"Yes sir, I am," Ziba replied.

³The king then asked him, "Is anyone still alive from Saul's family? If so, I want to show God's kindness to them."

Ziba replied, "Yes, one of Jonathan's sons is still alive. He is crippled in both feet."

⁴"Where is he?" the king asked.

"In Lo-debar," Ziba told him, "at the home of Makir son of Ammiel."

⁵So David sent for him and brought him from Makir's home. ⁶His name was Mephibosheth*; he was Jonathan's son and Saul's grandson. When he came to David, he bowed low to the ground in deep respect. David said, "Greetings, Mephibosheth."

Mephibosheth replied, "I am your servant."

⁷"Don't be afraid!" David said. "I intend to show kindness to you because of my promise to your father, Jonathan. I will give you all the property that once belonged to your grandfather Saul, and you will eat here with me at the king's table!"

⁸Mephibosheth bowed respectfully and exclaimed, "Who is your servant, that you should show such kindness to a dead dog like me?"

⁹Then the king summoned Saul's servant Ziba and said, "I have given your master's grandson everything that belonged to Saul and his family. ¹⁰You and your sons and servants are to farm the land for him to produce food for your master's household.* But Mephibosheth, your master's grandson, will eat here at my table." (Ziba had fifteen sons and twenty servants.)

Ziba replied, ¹¹"Yes, my lord the king; I am your servant, and I will do all that you have commanded." And from that time on, Mephibosheth ate regularly at David's table,* like one of the king's own sons.

¹²Mephibosheth had a young son named Mica. From then on, all the members of Ziba's household were Mephibosheth's servants. ¹³And Mephibosheth, who was crippled in both feet, lived in Jerusalem and ate regularly at the king's table.

9:6 *Mephibosheth* is another name for Merib-baal.   **9:10** As in Greek version; Hebrew reads *your master's grandson.*   **9:11** As in Greek version; Hebrew reads *my table.*

Many years had passed since David had promised Jonathan that he would take care of Jonathan's family. Still, David was determined to keep his word. Imagine how Mephibosheth must have felt when David kept his promise! God considers it a very serious matter that we keep the promises we make. What promises have you made to your family? to your friends? to God? What can you do today to keep those promises?

Never abandon a friend—either yours or your father's. When disaster strikes, you won't have to ask your brother for assistance. PROVERBS 27:10

APRIL 7

The Poor Man's Lamb

Nathan told David a sad story. But the reason Nathan told David the story was even sadder.

2 Samuel 12:1-14

The LORD sent Nathan the prophet to tell David this story: "There were two men in a certain town. One was rich, and one was poor. ²The rich man owned a great many sheep and cattle. ³The poor man owned nothing but one little lamb he had bought. He raised that little lamb, and it grew up with his children. It ate from the man's own plate and drank from his cup. He cuddled it in his arms like a baby daughter. ⁴One day a guest arrived at the home of the rich man. But instead of killing an animal from his own flock or herd, he took the poor man's lamb and killed it and prepared it for his guest."

⁵David was furious. "As surely as the LORD lives," he vowed, "any man who would do such a thing deserves to die! ⁶He must repay four lambs to the poor man for the one he stole and for having no pity."

⁷Then Nathan said to David, "You are that man! The LORD, the God of Israel, says: I anointed you king of Israel and saved you from the power of Saul. ⁸I gave you your master's house and his wives and the kingdoms of Israel and Judah. And if that had not been enough, I would have given you much, much more. ⁹Why, then, have you despised the word of the LORD and done this horrible deed? For you have murdered Uriah the Hittite with the sword of the Ammonites and stolen his wife. ¹⁰From this time on, your family will live by the sword because you have despised me by taking Uriah's wife to be your own.

¹¹"This is what the LORD says: Because of what you have done, I will cause your own household to rebel against you. I will give your wives to another man before your very eyes, and he will go to bed with them

in public view. ¹²You did it secretly, but I will make this happen to you openly in the sight of all Israel."

¹³Then David confessed to Nathan, "I have sinned against the LORD."

Nathan replied, "Yes, but the LORD has forgiven you, and you won't die for this sin. ¹⁴Nevertheless, because you have shown utter contempt for the LORD* by doing this, your child will die."

12:14 As in Dead Sea Scrolls; Masoretic Text reads *the Lord's enemies.*

Sometimes it's easier to point out the mistakes another person has made than to see our own errors. That was true for King David. The king was very upset when Nathan told him the story about a rich man and a lamb. But David had done something in real life that was much worse. Before we point our finger at another person for doing something wrong, we need to stop and think about the things *we* have done. There may be a bigger wrong that we need to confess.

How can you think of saying, "Friend,* let me help you get rid of that speck in your eye," when you can't see past the log in your own eye? Hypocrite! First get rid of the log in your own eye; then you will see well enough to deal with the speck in your friend's eye. LUKE 6:42

6:42 Greek *Brother.*

APRIL 8

Brotherly Love?

David's sons Absalom and Amnon did not get along. Eventually, Absalom let his dislike of his brother get out of control. Look what a mess Absalom made because of his anger and hate.

2 Samuel 13:23-38

Two years later, when Absalom's sheep were being sheared at Baal-hazor near Ephraim, Absalom invited all the king's sons to come to a feast. ²⁴He went to the king and said, "My sheep-shearers are now at work. Would the king and his servants please come to celebrate the occasion with me?"

²⁵The king replied, "No, my son. If we all came, we would be too much of a burden on you." Absalom pressed him, but the king would not come, though he gave Absalom his blessing.

²⁶"Well, then," Absalom said, "if you can't come, how about sending my brother Amnon with us?"

"Why Amnon?" the king asked. ²⁷But Absalom kept on pressing the king until he finally agreed to let all his sons attend, including Amnon. So Absalom prepared a feast fit for a king.*

²⁸Absalom told his men, "Wait until Amnon gets drunk; then at my signal, kill him! Don't be afraid. I'm the one who has given the command. Take courage and do it!" ²⁹So at Absalom's signal they murdered

Amnon. Then the other sons of the king jumped on their mules and fled.

³⁰As they were on the way back to Jerusalem, this report reached David: "Absalom has killed all the king's sons; not one is left alive!" ³¹The king got up, tore his robe, and threw himself on the ground. His advisers also tore their clothes in horror and sorrow.

³²But just then Jonadab, the son of David's brother Shimea, arrived and said, "No, don't believe that all the king's sons have been killed! It was only Amnon! Absalom has been plotting this ever since Amnon raped his sister Tamar. ³³No, my lord the king, your sons aren't all dead! It was only Amnon." ³⁴Meanwhile Absalom escaped.

Then the watchman on the Jerusalem wall saw a great crowd coming toward the city from the west. He ran to tell the king, "I see a crowd of people coming from the Horonaim road* along the side of the hill."

³⁵"Look!" Jonadab told the king. "There they are now! The king's sons are coming, just as I said."

³⁶They soon arrived, weeping and sobbing, and the king and all his servants wept bitterly with them. ³⁷And David mourned many days for his son Amnon.

Absalom fled to his grandfather, Talmai son of Ammihud, the king of Geshur. ³⁸He stayed there in Geshur for three years.

13:27 As in Greek and Latin versions (compare also Dead Sea Scrolls); the Hebrew text omits this sentence.   13:34 As in Greek version; Hebrew reads *from the road behind him.*

Absalom was so angry with his brother that he decided to murder him. Hating someone is a terrible thing. But within a family, hatred is even worse because the entire family is affected. A family should be a safe place where all family members are loved and accepted. God wants us to do all we can to live in peace and love within our families. How can you encourage peace in your family today?

How wonderful and pleasant it is when brothers live together in harmony!
PSALM 133:1

APRIL 9

David in Distress

Absalom had rebelled against his father, King David, and was bringing an army to challenge David. How do you think David responded?

2 Samuel 15:13-36

A messenger soon arrived in Jerusalem to tell David, "All Israel has joined Absalom in a conspiracy against you!"

¹⁴"Then we must flee at once, or it will be too late!" David urged his men. "Hurry!

If we get out of the city before Absalom arrives, both we and the city of Jerusalem will be spared from disaster."

¹⁵"We are with you," his advisers replied. "Do what you think is best."

¹⁶So the king and all his household set

out at once. He left no one behind except ten of his concubines to look after the palace. [17]The king and all his people set out on foot, pausing at the last house [18]to let all the king's men move past to lead the way. There were 600 men from Gath who had come with David, along with the king's bodyguard.*

[19]Then the king turned and said to Ittai, a leader of the men from Gath, "Why are you coming with us? Go on back to King Absalom, for you are a guest in Israel, a foreigner in exile. [20]You arrived only recently, and should I force you today to wander with us? I don't even know where we will go. Go on back and take your kinsmen with you, and may the LORD show you his unfailing love and faithfulness.*"

[21]But Ittai said to the king, "I vow by the LORD and by your own life that I will go wherever my lord the king goes, no matter what happens—whether it means life or death."

[22]David replied, "All right, come with us." So Ittai and all his men and their families went along.

[23]Everyone cried loudly as the king and his followers passed by. They crossed the Kidron Valley and then went out toward the wilderness.

[24]Zadok and all the Levites also came along, carrying the Ark of the Covenant of God. They set down the Ark of God, and Abiathar offered sacrifices* until everyone had passed out of the city.

[25]Then the king instructed Zadok to take the Ark of God back into the city. "If the LORD sees fit," David said, "he will bring me back to see the Ark and the Tabernacle* again. [26]But if he is through with me, then let him do what seems best to him."

[27]The king also told Zadok the priest, "Look,* here is my plan. You and Abiathar* should return quietly to the city with your son Ahimaaz and Abiathar's son Jonathan. [28]I will stop at the shallows of the Jordan River* and wait there for a report from you." [29]So Zadok and Abiathar took the Ark of God back to the city and stayed there.

[30]David walked up the road to the Mount of Olives, weeping as he went. His head was covered and his feet were bare as a sign of mourning. And the people who were with him covered their heads and wept as they climbed the hill. [31]When someone told David that his adviser Ahithophel was now backing Absalom, David prayed, "O LORD, let Ahithophel give Absalom foolish advice!"

[32]When David reached the summit of the Mount of Olives where people worshiped God, Hushai the Arkite was waiting there for him. Hushai had torn his clothing and put dirt on his head as a sign of mourning. [33]But David told him, "If you go with me, you will only be a burden. [34]Return to Jerusalem and tell Absalom, 'I will now be your adviser, O king, just as I was your father's adviser in the past.' Then you can frustrate and counter Ahithophel's advice. [35]Zadok and Abiathar, the priests, will be there. Tell them about the plans being made in the king's palace, [36]and they will send their sons Ahimaaz and Jonathan to tell me what is going on."

15:18 Hebrew *the Kerethites and Pelethites.*　**15:20** As in Greek version; Hebrew reads *and may unfailing love and faithfulness go with you.*　**15:24** Or *Abiathar went up.*　**15:25** Hebrew *and his dwelling place.*　**15:27a** As in Greek version; Hebrew reads *Are you a seer?* or *Do you see?*　**15:27b** Hebrew lacks *and Abiathar;* compare 15:29.　**15:28** Hebrew *at the crossing points of the wilderness.*

David could have stayed and fought, but he chose to flee instead. Rather than trusting in his own strength and ability, David trusted in God's plan for his future. He knew that if God wanted him to remain king, God would work it out. We can be sure that God is at work in our lives too. When you face tough situations, be like David. Trust God to care for you and help you.

Rejoice in our confident hope. Be patient in trouble, and keep on praying.
ROMANS 12:12

APRIL 10

Don't Throw Stones

As David passed Shimei's village east of Jerusalem, Shimei acted very rude. How would David respond?

2 Samuel 16:5-13

As King David came to Bahurim, a man came out of the village cursing them. It was Shimei son of Gera, from the same clan as Saul's family. ⁶He threw stones at the king and the king's officers and all the mighty warriors who surrounded him. ⁷"Get out of here, you murderer, you scoundrel!" he shouted at David. ⁸"The LORD is paying you back for all the bloodshed in Saul's clan. You stole his throne, and now the LORD has given it to your son Absalom. At last you will taste some of your own medicine, for you are a murderer!"

⁹"Why should this dead dog curse my lord the king?" Abishai son of Zeruiah demanded. "Let me go over and cut off his head!"

16:11 Hebrew *this Benjaminite.*

¹⁰"No!" the king said. "Who asked your opinion, you sons of Zeruiah! If the LORD has told him to curse me, who are you to stop him?"

¹¹Then David said to Abishai and to all his servants, "My own son is trying to kill me. Doesn't this relative of Saul* have even more reason to do so? Leave him alone and let him curse, for the LORD has told him to do it. ¹²And perhaps the LORD will see that I am being wronged and will bless me because of these curses today." ¹³So David and his men continued down the road, and Shimei kept pace with them on a nearby hillside, cursing as he went and throwing stones at David and tossing dust into the air.

David didn't let Shimei's insults get the best of him. He just ignored what Shimei was saying and prayed that God would notice what happened. Remember that God sees everything. He knows when people treat you badly. You don't have to pay back anyone who insults you. God sees your suffering and will take care of you.

Bless those who curse you. Pray for those who hurt you. LUKE 6:28

APRIL 11

Absalom's Death

David's army finally beat Absalom's army and killed Absalom. How do you think David felt about this "victory"?

2 Samuel 18:1-14, 33

David now mustered the men who were with him and appointed generals and captains* to lead them. ²He sent the troops out in three groups, placing one group under Joab, one under Joab's brother Abishai son of Zeruiah, and one under Ittai, the man from Gath. The king told his troops, "I am going out with you."

³But his men objected strongly. "You must not go," they urged. "If we have to turn and run—and even if half of us die—it will make no difference to Absalom's troops; they will be looking only for you. You are worth 10,000 of us,* and it is better that you stay here in the town and send help if we need it."

⁴"If you think that's the best plan, I'll do it," the king answered. So he stood alongside the gate of the town as all the troops marched out in groups of hundreds and of thousands.

⁵And the king gave this command to Joab, Abishai, and Ittai: "For my sake, deal gently with young Absalom." And all the troops heard the king give this order to his commanders.

⁶So the battle began in the forest of Ephraim, ⁷and the Israelite troops were beaten back by David's men. There was a great slaughter that day, and 20,000 men laid down their lives. ⁸The battle raged all across the countryside, and more men died because of the forest than were killed by the sword.

⁹During the battle, Absalom happened to come upon some of David's men. He tried to escape on his mule, but as he rode beneath the thick branches of a great tree, his hair* got caught in the tree. His mule kept going and left him dangling in the air. ¹⁰One of David's men saw what had happened and told Joab, "I saw Absalom dangling from a great tree."

¹¹"What?" Joab demanded. "You saw him there and didn't kill him? I would have rewarded you with ten pieces of silver* and a hero's belt!"

[12]"I would not kill the king's son for even a thousand pieces of silver,*" the man replied to Joab. "We all heard the king say to you and Abishai and Ittai, 'For my sake, please spare young Absalom.' [13]And if I had betrayed the king by killing his son—and the king would certainly find out who did it—you yourself would be the first to abandon me."

[14]"Enough of this nonsense," Joab said. Then he took three daggers and plunged them into Absalom's heart as he dangled, still alive, in the great tree.

◉

[33]*The king was overcome with emotion. He went up to the room over the gateway and burst into tears. And as he went, he cried, "O my son Absalom! My son, my son Absalom! If only I had died instead of you! O Absalom, my son, my son."

18:1 Hebrew *appointed commanders of thousands and commanders of hundreds.* 18:3 As in two Hebrew manuscripts and some Greek and Latin manuscripts; most Hebrew manuscripts read *Now there are 10,000 like us.* 18:9 Hebrew *his head.* 18:11 Hebrew *10 shekels of silver,* about 4 ounces or 114 grams in weight. 18:12 Hebrew *1,000 shekels,* about 25 pounds or 11.4 kilograms in weight. 18:33 Verse 18:33 is numbered 19:1 in Hebrew text.

Even though Absalom had acted horribly toward his father, King David, the king did not rejoice at the news that his son had been defeated and killed. David loved his son, although Absalom had done nothing to deserve David's continued love and kindness. God showers us with the same kind of love and undeserved kindness. Even though we sadden God daily whenever we disobey him, God still loves us. Thank God today for his wonderful love and kindness.

The LORD is good to everyone. He showers compassion on all his creation.
PSALM 145:9

APRIL 12

David Counts His Soldiers

David had sinned against God, and God was about to punish him. When David asked for forgiveness, would God forgive him?

2 Samuel 24:2-4, 10-25

The king said to Joab and the commanders* of the army, "Take a census of all the tribes of Israel—from Dan in the north to Beersheba in the south—so I may know how many people there are."

[3]But Joab replied to the king, "May the LORD your God let you live to see a hundred times as many people as there are now! But why, my lord the king, do you want to do this?"

[4]But the king insisted that they take the census, so Joab and the commanders of the army went out to count the people of Israel.

◉

[10]But after he had taken the census, David's conscience began to bother him. And

he said to the Lord, "I have sinned greatly by taking this census. Please forgive my guilt, Lord, for doing this foolish thing."

[11]The next morning the word of the Lord came to the prophet Gad, who was David's seer. This was the message: [12]"Go and say to David, 'This is what the Lord says: I will give you three choices. Choose one of these punishments, and I will inflict it on you.'"

[13]So Gad came to David and asked him, "Will you choose three* years of famine throughout your land, three months of fleeing from your enemies, or three days of severe plague throughout your land? Think this over and decide what answer I should give the Lord who sent me."

[14]"I'm in a desperate situation!" David replied to Gad. "But let us fall into the hands of the Lord, for his mercy is great. Do not let me fall into human hands."

[15]So the Lord sent a plague upon Israel that morning, and it lasted for three days.* A total of 70,000 people died throughout the nation, from Dan in the north to Beersheba in the south. [16]But as the angel was preparing to destroy Jerusalem, the Lord relented and said to the death angel, "Stop! That is enough!" At that moment the angel of the Lord was by the threshing floor of Araunah the Jebusite.

[17]When David saw the angel, he said to the Lord, "I am the one who has sinned and done wrong! But these people are as innocent as sheep—what have they done? Let your anger fall against me and my family."

[18]That day Gad came to David and said to him, "Go up and build an altar to the Lord on the threshing floor of Araunah the Jebusite."

[19]So David went up to do what the Lord had commanded him. [20]When Araunah saw the king and his men coming toward him, he came and bowed before the king with his face to the ground. [21]"Why have you come, my lord the king?" Araunah asked.

David replied, "I have come to buy your threshing floor and to build an altar to the Lord there, so that he will stop the plague."

[22]"Take it, my lord the king, and use it as you wish," Araunah said to David. "Here are oxen for the burnt offering, and you can use the threshing boards and ox yokes for wood to build a fire on the altar. [23]I will give it all to you, Your Majesty, and may the Lord your God accept your sacrifice."

[24]But the king replied to Araunah, "No, I insist on buying it, for I will not present burnt offerings to the Lord my God that have cost me nothing." So David paid him fifty pieces of silver* for the threshing floor and the oxen.

[25]David built an altar there to the Lord and sacrificed burnt offerings and peace offerings. And the Lord answered his prayer for the land, and the plague on Israel was stopped.

24:2 As in Greek version (see also 24:4 and 1 Chr 21:2); Hebrew reads *Joab the commander*. 24:13 As in Greek version (see also 1 Chr 21:12); Hebrew reads *seven*. 24:15 Hebrew *for the designated time*. 24:24 Hebrew *50 shekels of silver*, about 20 ounces or 570 grams in weight.

By counting the people of Israel, David was depending on the big numbers to give him a big army. David had disobeyed God by trusting in people rather than in God. David deserved God's punishment—and he knew it. So David wisely chose to confess his sin and to have God punish him rather than letting other men do it. What sins do you need to confess to God? Follow David's example. Choose to confess your sins and trust God to discipline you out of his love for you.

Have you forgotten the encouraging words God spoke to you as his children? He said, "My child,* don't make light of the LORD's discipline, and don't give up when he corrects you. For the LORD disciplines those he loves, and he punishes each one he accepts as his child."* HEBREWS 12:5-6*

12:5a Greek *sons;* also in 12:7, 8.   12:5b Greek *son;* also in 12:6, 7.   12:5-6 Prov 3:11-12 (Greek version).

APRIL 13

Solomon is King!

King David was getting old, and the Israelites wondered who should be the next king. Would Solomon become king like David had promised, or would Adonijah take over?

1 Kings 1:16-20, 32-50

Bathsheba bowed down before the king.

"What can I do for you?" he asked her.

¹⁷She replied, "My lord, you made a vow before the LORD your God when you said to me, 'Your son Solomon will surely be the next king and will sit on my throne.' ¹⁸But instead, Adonijah has made himself king, and my lord the king does not even know about it. ¹⁹He has sacrificed many cattle, fattened calves, and sheep, and he has invited all the king's sons to attend the celebration. He also invited Abiathar the priest and Joab, the commander of the army. But he did not invite your servant Solomon. ²⁰And now, my lord the king, all Israel is waiting for you to announce who will become king after you."

³²Then King David ordered, "Call Zadok the priest, Nathan the prophet, and Benaiah son of Jehoiada." When they came into the king's presence, ³³the king said to them, "Take Solomon and my officials down to Gihon Spring. Solomon is to ride on my own mule. ³⁴There Zadok the priest and Nathan the prophet are to anoint him king over Israel. Blow the ram's horn and shout, 'Long live King Solomon!' ³⁵Then escort him back here, and he will sit on my throne. He will succeed me as king, for I have appointed him to be ruler over Israel and Judah."

³⁶"Amen!" Benaiah son of Jehoiada replied. "May the LORD, the God of my lord the king, decree that it happen. ³⁷And may the LORD be with Solomon as he has been with you, my lord the king, and may he make Solomon's reign even greater than yours!"

³⁸So Zadok the priest, Nathan the prophet, Benaiah son of Jehoiada, and the king's bodyguard* took Solomon down to Gihon Spring, with Solomon riding on King David's own mule. ³⁹There Zadok the priest took the flask of olive oil from the sacred tent and anointed Solomon with the oil. Then they sounded the ram's horn and all the people shouted, "Long live King Solomon!" ⁴⁰And all the people followed Solomon into Jerusalem, playing flutes and shouting for joy. The celebration was so joyous and noisy that the earth shook with the sound.

⁴¹Adonijah and his guests heard the

celebrating and shouting just as they were finishing their banquet. When Joab heard the sound of the ram's horn, he asked, "What's going on? Why is the city in such an uproar?"

⁴²And while he was still speaking, Jonathan son of Abiathar the priest arrived. "Come in," Adonijah said to him, "for you are a good man. You must have good news."

⁴³"Not at all!" Jonathan replied. "Our lord King David has just declared Solomon king! ⁴⁴The king sent him down to Gihon Spring with Zadok the priest, Nathan the prophet, and Benaiah son of Jehoiada, protected by the king's bodyguard. They had him ride on the king's own mule, ⁴⁵and Zadok and Nathan have anointed him at Gihon Spring as the new king. They have just returned, and the whole city is celebrating and rejoicing. That's what all the noise is about. ⁴⁶What's more, Solomon is now sitting on the royal throne as king. ⁴⁷And all the royal officials have gone to King David and congratulated him, saying, 'May your God make Solomon's fame even greater than your own, and may Solomon's reign be even greater than yours!' Then the king bowed his head in worship as he lay in his bed, ⁴⁸and he said, 'Praise the LORD, the God of Israel, who today has chosen a successor to sit on my throne while I am still alive to see it.'"

⁴⁹Then all of Adonijah's guests jumped up in panic from the banquet table and quickly scattered. ⁵⁰Adonijah was afraid of Solomon, so he rushed to the sacred tent and grabbed onto the horns of the altar.

1:38 Hebrew *the Kerethites and Pelethites;* also in 1:44.

There was a close contest for who would be the next king. Adonijah appointed himself king, but he was neither David's choice nor God's choice. Even though Adonijah had big plans, he couldn't change God's plan to make Solomon king. No matter what people try to do, God's plan will always win. Ask him to show you what he has planned for you.

The LORD frustrates the plans of the nations and thwarts all their schemes.
But the LORD's plans stand firm forever; his intentions can never be shaken.
PSALM 33:10-11

APRIL 14

Anything You Want

If you could have anything you wanted, what would it be? Find out what Solomon asked for when God granted him whatever he wanted.

1 Kings 3:5-14

That night the LORD appeared to Solomon in a dream, and God said, "What do you want? Ask, and I will give it to you!"

⁶Solomon replied, "You showed faithful love to your servant my father, David, because he was honest and true and faithful to you. And you have continued your faithful love to him today by giving him a son to sit on his throne.

138

7"Now, O LORD my God, you have made me king instead of my father, David, but I am like a little child who doesn't know his way around. 8And here I am in the midst of your own chosen people, a nation so great and numerous they cannot be counted! 9Give me an understanding heart so that I can govern your people well and know the difference between right and wrong. For who by himself is able to govern this great people of yours?"

10The Lord was pleased that Solomon had asked for wisdom. 11So God replied, "Because you have asked for wisdom in governing my people with justice and have not asked for a long life or wealth or the death of your enemies—12I will give you what you asked for! I will give you a wise and understanding heart such as no one else has had or ever will have! 13And I will also give you what you did not ask for— riches and fame! No other king in all the world will be compared to you for the rest of your life! 14And if you follow me and obey my decrees and my commands as your father, David, did, I will give you a long life."

Solomon could have had anything he wanted—wealth, fame, power, a long life. But Solomon asked for wisdom. Why wisdom? Having wisdom helps us in every other area of life. If you are wise, you will be able to make good choices that will make you happy and healthy. Ask God to make you wise. He gives wisdom to anyone who asks for it.

If you need wisdom, ask our generous God, and he will give it to you. He will not rebuke you for asking. JAMES 1:5

APRIL 15

TWO WOMEN AND A BABY

God had given Solomon great wisdom. See how his wisdom is put to the test in this story.

1 Kings 3:17-28

"Please, my lord," one of them began, "this woman and I live in the same house. I gave birth to a baby while she was with me in the house. 18Three days later this woman also had a baby. We were alone; there were only two of us in the house.

19"But her baby died during the night when she rolled over on it. 20Then she got up in the night and took my son from beside me while I was asleep. She laid her dead child in my arms and took mine to sleep beside her. 21And in the morning when I tried to nurse my son, he was dead! But when I looked more closely in the morning light, I saw that it wasn't my son at all."

22Then the other woman interrupted, "It certainly was your son, and the living child is mine."

"No," the first woman said, "the living child is mine, and the dead one is yours." And so they argued back and forth before the king.

[23]Then the king said, "Let's get the facts straight. Both of you claim the living child is yours, and each says that the dead one belongs to the other. [24]All right, bring me a sword." So a sword was brought to the king.

[25]Then he said, "Cut the living child in two, and give half to one woman and half to the other!"

[26]Then the woman who was the real mother of the living child, and who loved him very much, cried out, "Oh no, my lord! Give her the child—please do not kill him!"

But the other woman said, "All right, he will be neither yours nor mine; divide him between us!"

[27]Then the king said, "Do not kill the child, but give him to the woman who wants him to live, for she is his mother!"

[28]When all Israel heard the king's decision, the people were in awe of the king, for they saw the wisdom God had given him for rendering justice.

God didn't give Solomon wisdom just so he could show everyone how smart he was. God gave Solomon the gift of wisdom so he could help others. The king used his wisdom to judge these two women fairly. When God gives you a gift, he wants you to use it to help the people around you. What is one gift God has given to you? Maybe it's wisdom or faith or helpfulness. How can you use that gift today to help someone?

A spiritual gift is given to each of us so we can help each other.
I CORINTHIANS 12:7

APRIL 16

A QUEEN'S VISIT

Solomon was so wise that people in other countries came to talk to him and see what he knew. Read about when the queen of Sheba came to visit him.

1 Kings 10:1-10

When the queen of Sheba heard of Solomon's fame, which brought honor to the name of the LORD,* she came to test him with hard questions. [2]She arrived in Jerusalem with a large group of attendants and a great caravan of camels loaded with spices, large quantities of gold, and precious jewels. When she met with Solomon, she talked with him about everything she had on her mind. [3]Solomon had answers for all her questions; nothing was too hard for the king to explain to her. [4]When the queen of Sheba realized how very wise Solomon was, and when she saw the palace he had built, [5]she was overwhelmed. She was also amazed at the food on his tables, the organization of his officials and their splendid clothing, the cup-bearers, and the burnt offerings Solomon made at the Temple of the LORD.

⁶She exclaimed to the king, "Everything I heard in my country about your achievements* and wisdom is true! ⁷I didn't believe what was said until I arrived here and saw it with my own eyes. In fact, I had not heard the half of it! Your wisdom and prosperity are far beyond what I was told. ⁸How happy your people* must be! What a privilege for your officials to stand here day after day, listening to your wisdom! ⁹Praise the LORD your God, who delights in you and has placed you on the throne of Israel. Because of the LORD's eternal love for Israel, he has made you king so you can rule with justice and righteousness."

¹⁰Then she gave the king a gift of 9,000 pounds* of gold, great quantities of spices, and precious jewels. Never again were so many spices brought in as those the queen of Sheba gave to King Solomon.

10:1 Or *which was due to the name of the Lord.* The meaning of the Hebrew is uncertain.   10:6 Hebrew *your words.*
10:8 Greek and Syriac versions and Latin Vulgate read *your wives.*   10:10 Hebrew *120 talents* [4,000 kilograms].

The queen of Sheba was very impressed with Solomon's wisdom. Yet she recognized that God was the one who had blessed Solomon with this gift. The queen praised God for the wisdom he had given Solomon. Our gifts should also make people praise God. How can you use your gifts from God in a way that honors him?

Whether you eat or drink, or whatever you do, do it all for the glory of God.
I CORINTHIANS 10:31

APRIL 17

Good and Bad Advice

Rehoboam was the new king after Solomon. He didn't know how to rule, so he asked lots of people for advice. Whose advice should he have listened to?

1 Kings 12:4-19

"Your father was a hard master," they said. "Lighten the harsh labor demands and heavy taxes that your father imposed on us. Then we will be your loyal subjects."

⁵Rehoboam replied, "Give me three days to think this over. Then come back for my answer." So the people went away.

⁶Then King Rehoboam discussed the matter with the older men who had counseled his father, Solomon. "What is your advice?" he asked. "How should I answer these people?"

⁷The older counselors replied, "If you are willing to be a servant to these people today and give them a favorable answer, they will always be your loyal subjects."

⁸But Rehoboam rejected the advice of the older men and instead asked the opinion of the young men who had grown up with him and were now his advisers. ⁹"What is your advice?" he asked them.

"How should I answer these people who want me to lighten the burdens imposed by my father?"

¹⁰The young men replied, "This is what you should tell those complainers who want a lighter burden: 'My little finger is thicker than my father's waist! ¹¹Yes, my father laid heavy burdens on you, but I'm going to make them even heavier! My father beat you with whips, but I will beat you with scorpions!'"

¹²Three days later Jeroboam and all the people returned to hear Rehoboam's decision, just as the king had ordered. ¹³But Rehoboam spoke harshly to the people, for he rejected the advice of the older counselors ¹⁴and followed the counsel of his younger advisers. He told the people, "My father laid heavy burdens on you, but I'm going to make them even heavier! My father beat you with whips, but I will beat you with scorpions!"

¹⁵So the king paid no attention to the people. This turn of events was the will of the LORD, for it fulfilled the LORD's message to Jeroboam son of Nebat through the prophet Ahijah from Shiloh.

¹⁶When all Israel realized that the king had refused to listen to them, they responded,

"Down with the dynasty of David!
 We have no interest in the son
  of Jesse.
Back to your homes, O Israel!
 Look out for your own house,
  O David!"

So the people of Israel returned home. ¹⁷But Rehoboam continued to rule over the Israelites who lived in the towns of Judah.

¹⁸King Rehoboam sent Adoniram,* who was in charge of the labor force, to restore order, but the people of Israel stoned him to death. When this news reached King Rehoboam, he quickly jumped into his chariot and fled to Jerusalem. ¹⁹And to this day the northern tribes of Israel have refused to be ruled by a descendant of David.

12:18 As in some Greek manuscripts and Syriac version (see also 4:6; 5:14); Hebrew reads *Adoram.*

Rehoboam talked to older people and to younger people. The younger people advised Rehoboam to be tough on the people he ruled over. But the younger people didn't understand what it took to be a good king. The older people had seen how other kings ruled, so their experience helped them know what was best. Since Rehoboam followed the wrong advice, he lost most of his kingdom. Sometimes our friends give us advice that's not the best for us to follow. Take time to check out their advice with older, more experienced people. You'll be glad you did!

My son, obey your father's commands, and don't neglect your mother's instruction. Keep their words always in your heart. Tie them around your neck. When you walk, their counsel will lead you. When you sleep, they will protect you. When you wake up, they will advise you. PROVERBS 6:20-22

APRIL 18

RaVENS FEED Elijah

God sent a famine to Israel. There was no rain, so no food crops could grow. How would God's prophet Elijah find anything to eat?

1 Kings 17:1-16

Now Elijah, who was from Tishbe in Gilead, told King Ahab, "As surely as the LORD, the God of Israel, lives—the God I serve—there will be no dew or rain during the next few years until I give the word!"

²Then the LORD said to Elijah, ³"Go to the east and hide by Kerith Brook, near where it enters the Jordan River. ⁴Drink from the brook and eat what the ravens bring you, for I have commanded them to bring you food."

⁵So Elijah did as the LORD told him and camped beside Kerith Brook, east of the Jordan. ⁶The ravens brought him bread and meat each morning and evening, and he drank from the brook. ⁷But after a while the brook dried up, for there was no rainfall anywhere in the land.

⁸Then the LORD said to Elijah, ⁹"Go and live in the village of Zarephath, near the city of Sidon. I have instructed a widow there to feed you."

¹⁰So he went to Zarephath. As he arrived at the gates of the village, he saw a widow gathering sticks, and he asked her, "Would you please bring me a little water in a cup?" ¹¹As she was going to get it, he called to her, "Bring me a bite of bread, too."

¹²But she said, "I swear by the LORD your God that I don't have a single piece of bread in the house. And I have only a handful of flour left in the jar and a little cooking oil in the bottom of the jug. I was just gathering a few sticks to cook this last meal, and then my son and I will die."

¹³But Elijah said to her, "Don't be afraid! Go ahead and do just what you've said, but make a little bread for me first. Then use what's left to prepare a meal for yourself and your son. ¹⁴For this is what the LORD, the God of Israel, says: There will always be flour and olive oil left in your containers until the time when the LORD sends rain and the crops grow again!"

¹⁵So she did as Elijah said, and she and Elijah and her son continued to eat for many days. ¹⁶There was always enough flour and olive oil left in the containers, just as the LORD had promised through Elijah.

Meals delivered by birds? Food provided by a poor widow who was down to her last meal? God provided for Elijah in ways the prophet never could have expected. God is like that. He has ways of helping us and guiding us that we never would have thought about. When you are in what seems to be a hopeless situation, remember Elijah. Look for God's caring touch to come in unexpected ways!

Don't be concerned about what to eat and what to drink. Don't worry about such things. . . . Seek the Kingdom of God above all else, and [God] will give you everything you need. LUKE 12:29, 31

APRIL 19

God and Baal

The Israelites were supposed to be God's chosen people, but they were worshiping other gods. Elijah set up a contest between the false god Baal and the Lord. Read about what happened.

1 Kings 18:20-39

Ahab summoned all the people of Israel and the prophets to Mount Carmel. [21]Then Elijah stood in front of them and said, "How much longer will you waver, hobbling between two opinions? If the LORD is God, follow him! But if Baal is God, then follow him!" But the people were completely silent.

[22]Then Elijah said to them, "I am the only prophet of the LORD who is left, but Baal has 450 prophets. [23]Now bring two bulls. The prophets of Baal may choose whichever one they wish and cut it into pieces and lay it on the wood of their altar, but without setting fire to it. I will prepare the other bull and lay it on the wood on the altar, but not set fire to it. [24]Then call on the name of your god, and I will call on the name of the LORD. The god who answers by setting fire to the wood is the true God!" And all the people agreed.

[25]Then Elijah said to the prophets of Baal, "You go first, for there are many of you. Choose one of the bulls, and prepare it and call on the name of your god. But do not set fire to the wood."

[26]So they prepared one of the bulls and placed it on the altar. Then they called on the name of Baal from morning until noontime, shouting, "O Baal, answer us!" But there was no reply of any kind. Then they danced, hobbling around the altar they had made.

[27]About noontime Elijah began mocking them. "You'll have to shout louder," he scoffed, "for surely he is a god! Perhaps he is daydreaming, or is relieving himself.* Or maybe he is away on a trip, or is asleep and needs to be wakened!"

[28]So they shouted louder, and following their normal custom, they cut themselves with knives and swords until the blood gushed out. [29]They raved all afternoon until the time of the evening sacrifice, but still there was no sound, no reply, no response.

[30]Then Elijah called to the people, "Come over here!" They all crowded around him as he repaired the altar of the LORD that had been torn down. [31]He took twelve stones, one to represent each of the tribes of Israel,* [32]and he used the stones to rebuild the altar in the name of the LORD. Then he dug a trench around the altar large enough to hold about three gallons.* [33]He piled wood on the altar, cut the bull into pieces, and laid the pieces on the wood.

Then he said, "Fill four large jars with water, and pour the water over the offering and the wood."

³⁴After they had done this, he said, "Do the same thing again!" And when they were finished, he said, "Now do it a third time!" So they did as he said, ³⁵and the water ran around the altar and even filled the trench.

³⁶At the usual time for offering the evening sacrifice, Elijah the prophet walked up to the altar and prayed, "O LORD, God of Abraham, Isaac, and Jacob,* prove today that you are God in Israel and that I am your servant. Prove that I have done all this at your command. ³⁷O LORD, answer me! Answer me so these people will know that you, O LORD, are God and that you have brought them back to yourself."

³⁸Immediately the fire of the LORD flashed down from heaven and burned up the young bull, the wood, the stones, and the dust. It even licked up all the water in the trench! ³⁹And when all the people saw it, they fell face down on the ground and cried out, "The LORD—he is God! Yes, the LORD is God!"

18:27 Or *is busy somewhere else,* or *is engaged in business.* 18:31 Hebrew *each of the tribes of the sons of Jacob to whom the Lord had said, "Your name will be Israel."* 18:32 Hebrew *2 seahs* [12 liters] *of seed.* 18:36 Hebrew *and Israel.* The names "Jacob" and "Israel" are often interchanged throughout the Old Testament, referring sometimes to the individual patriarch and sometimes to the nation.

God had already done so much for the Israelites. They shouldn't have needed more proof that he was the real God. But when Elijah asked, God showed his power in an amazing way. If you start to wonder about God's power, remember this story. Even if you never see God send fire from heaven, you can see his power in nature, like in a thunderstorm or in the chiseling of deep canyons and majestic mountains. Where have you seen God's power lately?

God made the earth by his power, and he preserves it by his wisdom. With his own understanding he stretched out the heavens. JEREMIAH 10:12

APRIL 20

anqel's food

Elijah was in big trouble and he didn't know what to do. Look how God helped him.

1 Kings 19:1-8

When Ahab got home, he told Jezebel everything Elijah had done, including the way he had killed all the prophets of Baal. ²So Jezebel sent this message to Elijah: "May the gods strike me and even kill me if by this time tomorrow I have not killed you just as you killed them."

³Elijah was afraid and fled for his life. He went to Beersheba, a town in Judah, and he left his servant there. ⁴Then he went on alone into the wilderness, traveling all day.

He sat down under a solitary broom tree and prayed that he might die. "I have had enough, LORD," he said. "Take my life, for I am no better than my ancestors who have already died."

⁵Then he lay down and slept under the broom tree. But as he was sleeping, an angel touched him and told him, "Get up and eat!" ⁶He looked around and there beside his head was some bread baked on hot stones and a jar of water! So he ate and drank and lay down again.

⁷Then the angel of the LORD came again and touched him and said, "Get up and eat some more, or the journey ahead will be too much for you."

⁸So he got up and ate and drank, and the food gave him enough strength to travel forty days and forty nights to Mount Sinai,* the mountain of God.

19:8 Hebrew to Horeb, another name for Sinai.

Elijah was tired and he was scared. He just wanted to quit. But God helped him so that the prophet was able to continue his work. When have you felt like quitting? Giving up is easy to do when we are tired or when we face difficulties. But God can encourage us in those times. He promises to give us strength and never leave us. The next time you feel like quitting, ask God to help you. His power is enough to make you strong no matter what happens.

I can do everything through Christ,* who gives me strength. PHILIPPIANS 4:13
4:13 Greek through the one.

APRIL 21

in a whisper

Elijah was discouraged. He felt like the last of God's prophets on earth. But God had a special message for Elijah. See how God spoke to Elijah.

1 Kings 19:9-21

[Elijah] came to a cave, where he spent the night.

But the LORD said to him, "What are you doing here, Elijah?"

¹⁰Elijah replied, "I have zealously served the LORD God Almighty. But the people of Israel have broken their covenant with you, torn down your altars, and killed every one of your prophets. I am the only one left, and now they are trying to kill me, too."

¹¹"Go out and stand before me on the mountain," the LORD told him. And as Elijah stood there, the LORD passed by, and a mighty windstorm hit the mountain. It was such a terrible blast that the rocks were torn loose, but the LORD was not in the wind. After the wind there was an earthquake, but the LORD was not in the earthquake. ¹²And after the earthquake there was a fire, but the LORD was not in the fire. And after the fire there was the sound of a gentle whisper. ¹³When Elijah heard it, he wrapped his face in his cloak and went out and stood at the entrance of the cave.

And a voice said, "What are you doing here, Elijah?"

¹⁴He replied again, "I have zealously served the LORD God Almighty. But the people of Israel have broken their covenant with you, torn down your altars, and killed every one of your prophets. I am the only one left, and now they are trying to kill me, too."

¹⁵Then the LORD told him, "Go back the same way you came, and travel to the wilderness of Damascus. When you arrive there, anoint Hazael to be king of Aram. ¹⁶Then anoint Jehu son of Nimshi to be king of Israel, and anoint Elisha son of Shaphat from the town of Abel-meholah to replace you as my prophet. ¹⁷Anyone who escapes from Hazael will be killed by Jehu, and those who escape Jehu will be killed by Elisha! ¹⁸Yet I will preserve 7,000 others in Israel who have never bowed down to Baal or kissed him!"

¹⁹So Elijah went and found Elisha son of Shaphat plowing a field. There were twelve teams of oxen in the field, and Elisha was plowing with the twelfth team. Elijah went over to him and threw his cloak across his shoulders and then walked away. ²⁰Elisha left the oxen standing there, ran after Elijah, and said to him, "First let me go and kiss my father and mother good-bye, and then I will go with you!"

Elijah replied, "Go on back, but think about what I have done to you."

²¹So Elisha returned to his oxen and slaughtered them. He used the wood from the plow to build a fire to roast their flesh. He passed around the meat to the townspeople, and they all ate. Then he went with Elijah as his assistant.

God didn't speak to Elijah in the windstorm or the earthquake, or even the roar of a fire—all signs of God's mighty power. Instead, God spoke to Elijah in a gentle whisper. God doesn't always reveal himself in powerful, miraculous ways. Sometimes we think God will speak only in something "big"—like a youth rally or a big concert or a worship service. Sometimes he does. But listen for God's voice in the quiet, too. You may hear him when you least expect it!

Be still, and know that I am God! I will be honored by every nation. I will be honored throughout the world. PSALM 46:10

APRIL 22

naboth's vineyard

King Ahab really wanted Naboth's vineyard. And he thought that since he was the king, he should be able to have whatever he wanted. What would he do to get it?

1 Kings 21:1-19

Now there was a man named Naboth, from Jezreel, who owned a vineyard in Jezreel beside the palace of King Ahab of Samaria. ²One day Ahab said to Naboth, "Since your vineyard is so convenient to my palace, I would like to buy it to use as a vegetable garden. I will give you a better vineyard in exchange, or if you prefer, I will pay you for it."

³But Naboth replied, "The LORD forbid that I should give you the inheritance that was passed down by my ancestors."

⁴So Ahab went home angry and sullen because of Naboth's answer. The king went to bed with his face to the wall and refused to eat!

⁵"What's the matter?" his wife Jezebel asked him. "What's made you so upset that you're not eating?"

⁶"I asked Naboth to sell me his vineyard or trade it, but he refused!" Ahab told her.

⁷"Are you the king of Israel or not?" Jezebel demanded. "Get up and eat something, and don't worry about it. I'll get you Naboth's vineyard!"

⁸So she wrote letters in Ahab's name, sealed them with his seal, and sent them to the elders and other leaders of the town where Naboth lived. ⁹In her letters she commanded: "Call the citizens together for fasting and prayer, and give Naboth a place

21:17 Hebrew *Elijah the Tishbite.*

of honor. ¹⁰And then seat two scoundrels across from him who will accuse him of cursing God and the king. Then take him out and stone him to death."

¹¹So the elders and other town leaders followed the instructions Jezebel had written in the letters. ¹²They called for a fast and put Naboth at a prominent place before the people. ¹³Then the two scoundrels came and sat down across from him. And they accused Naboth before all the people, saying, "He cursed God and the king." So he was dragged outside the town and stoned to death. ¹⁴The town leaders then sent word to Jezebel, "Naboth has been stoned to death."

¹⁵When Jezebel heard the news, she said to Ahab, "You know the vineyard Naboth wouldn't sell you? Well, you can have it now! He's dead!" ¹⁶So Ahab immediately went down to the vineyard of Naboth to claim it.

¹⁷But the LORD said to Elijah,* ¹⁸"Go down to meet King Ahab of Israel, who rules in Samaria. He will be at Naboth's vineyard in Jezreel, claiming it for himself. ¹⁹Give him this message: 'This is what the LORD says: Wasn't it enough that you killed Naboth? Must you rob him, too? Because you have done this, dogs will lick your blood at the very place where they licked the blood of Naboth!'"

King Ahab was horribly selfish in this story. He let his desire to have Naboth's vineyard get out of control. Ahab didn't care how he got it—even if it meant having Naboth killed. We all have strong desires and want things. That's when we need to be careful that our desires don't control us. The best way to fight those desires is to talk to God about them. Let God help you keep things under control.

Let the Holy Spirit guide your lives. Then you won't be doing what your sinful nature craves. The sinful nature wants to do evil, which is just the opposite of what the Spirit wants. And the Spirit gives us desires that are the opposite of what the sinful nature desires. These two forces are constantly fighting each other, so you are not free to carry out your good intentions.
GALATIANS 5:16-17

APRIL 23

fiery chariots

Before Elijah went to heaven, Elisha had one big favor to ask him. What did Elisha ask for?

2 Kings 2:1-15

When the LORD was about to take Elijah up to heaven in a whirlwind, Elijah and Elisha were traveling from Gilgal. ²And Elijah said to Elisha, "Stay here, for the LORD has told me to go to Bethel."

But Elisha replied, "As surely as the LORD lives and you yourself live, I will never leave you!" So they went down together to Bethel.

³The group of prophets from Bethel came to Elisha and asked him, "Did you know that the LORD is going to take your master away from you today?"

"Of course I know," Elisha answered. "But be quiet about it."

⁴Then Elijah said to Elisha, "Stay here, for the LORD has told me to go to Jericho."

But Elisha replied again, "As surely as the LORD lives and you yourself live, I will never leave you." So they went on together to Jericho.

⁵Then the group of prophets from Jericho came to Elisha and asked him, "Did you know that the LORD is going to take your master away from you today?"

"Of course I know," Elisha answered. "But be quiet about it."

⁶Then Elijah said to Elisha, "Stay here, for the LORD has told me to go to the Jordan River."

But again Elisha replied, "As surely as the LORD lives and you yourself live, I will never leave you." So they went on together.

⁷Fifty men from the group of prophets also went and watched from a distance as

Elijah and Elisha stopped beside the Jordan River. ⁸Then Elijah folded his cloak together and struck the water with it. The river divided, and the two of them went across on dry ground!

⁹When they came to the other side, Elijah said to Elisha, "Tell me what I can do for you before I am taken away."

And Elisha replied, "Please let me inherit a double share of your spirit and become your successor."

¹⁰"You have asked a difficult thing," Elijah replied. "If you see me when I am taken from you, then you will get your request. But if not, then you won't."

¹¹As they were walking along and talking, suddenly a chariot of fire appeared, drawn by horses of fire. It drove between the two men, separating them, and Elijah was carried by a whirlwind into heaven. ¹²Elisha saw it and cried out, "My father! My father! I see the chariots and charioteers of Israel!" And as they disappeared from sight, Elisha tore his clothes in distress.

¹³Elisha picked up Elijah's cloak, which had fallen when he was taken up. Then Elisha returned to the bank of the Jordan River. ¹⁴He struck the water with Elijah's cloak and cried out, "Where is the LORD, the God of Elijah?" Then the river divided, and Elisha went across.

¹⁵When the group of prophets from Jericho saw from a distance what happened, they exclaimed, "Elijah's spirit rests upon Elisha!" And they went to meet him and bowed to the ground before him.

Elisha's request was big. He wanted to be the next prophet in Israel—just like Elijah. Only God could grant that request. God gave Elisha what he wanted, because God knew that this man was not interested in fame or power. Rather, Elisha wanted to do more for God! When you request something from God, you need to ask yourself: *Do I want this for me or for God's purposes?* When your request is in tune with God's plan, you too can accomplish more for God.

We are confident that [Jesus] hears us whenever we ask for anything that pleases him. And since we know he hears us when we make our requests, we also know that he will give us what we ask for. I JOHN 5:14-15

APRIL 24

The widow's oil

A widow had lots of bills to pay, but she didn't have any money. How would God help her?

2 Kings 4:1-7

One day the widow of a member of the group of prophets came to Elisha and cried out, "My husband who served you is dead, and you know how he feared the LORD. But now a creditor has come, threatening to take my two sons as slaves."

²"What can I do to help you?" Elisha

asked. "Tell me, what do you have in the house?"

"Nothing at all, except a flask of olive oil," she replied.

³And Elisha said, "Borrow as many empty jars as you can from your friends and neighbors. ⁴Then go into your house with your sons and shut the door behind you. Pour olive oil from your flask into the jars, setting each one aside when it is filled."

⁵So she did as she was told. Her sons kept bringing jars to her, and she filled one after another. ⁶Soon every container was full to the brim!

"Bring me another jar," she said to one of her sons.

"There aren't any more!" he told her. And then the olive oil stopped flowing.

⁷When she told the man of God what had happened, he said to her, "Now sell the olive oil and pay your debts, and you and your sons can live on what is left over."

God provided money for this woman in a very unusual way. God filled the woman's olive oil jars with enough oil to sell and pay all her bills. God knew exactly how much the woman needed—and he provided not only that amount, but enough additional money to continue supporting the woman and her sons! God knows exactly what you need too. God is loving and generous and will provide for all your needs—and more.

Look at the birds. They don't plant or harvest or store food in barns, for your heavenly Father feeds them. And aren't you far more valuable to him than they are? MATTHEW 6:26

APRIL 25

The Healing of Naaman

Naaman had never heard of the one true God. But an Israelite girl told him that God could heal him of his skin disease. Would Naaman give it a try?

2 Kings 5:1-14

The king of Aram had great admiration for Naaman, the commander of his army, because through him the LORD had given Aram great victories. But though Naaman was a mighty warrior, he suffered from leprosy.*

²At this time Aramean raiders had invaded the land of Israel, and among their captives was a young girl who had been given to Naaman's wife as a maid. ³One day the girl said to her mistress, "I wish my master would go to see the prophet in Samaria. He would heal him of his leprosy."

⁴So Naaman told the king what the young girl from Israel had said. ⁵"Go and visit the prophet," the king of Aram told him. "I will send a letter of introduction for you to take to the king of Israel." So

Naaman started out, carrying as gifts 750 pounds of silver, 150 pounds of gold,* and ten sets of clothing. ⁶The letter to the king of Israel said: "With this letter I present my servant Naaman. I want you to heal him of his leprosy."

⁷When the king of Israel read the letter, he tore his clothes in dismay and said, "This man sends me a leper to heal! Am I God, that I can give life and take it away? I can see that he's just trying to pick a fight with me."

⁸But when Elisha, the man of God, heard that the king of Israel had torn his clothes in dismay, he sent this message to him: "Why are you so upset? Send Naaman to me, and he will learn that there is a true prophet here in Israel."

⁹So Naaman went with his horses and chariots and waited at the door of Elisha's house. ¹⁰But Elisha sent a messenger out to him with this message: "Go and wash yourself seven times in the Jordan River. Then your skin will be restored, and you will be healed of your leprosy."

¹¹But Naaman became angry and stalked away. "I thought he would certainly come out to meet me!" he said. "I expected him to wave his hand over the leprosy and call on the name of the LORD his God and heal me! ¹²Aren't the rivers of Damascus, the Abana and the Pharpar, better than any of the rivers of Israel? Why shouldn't I wash in them and be healed?" So Naaman turned and went away in a rage.

¹³But his officers tried to reason with him and said, "Sir,* if the prophet had told you to do something very difficult, wouldn't you have done it? So you should certainly obey him when he says simply, 'Go and wash and be cured!' " ¹⁴So Naaman went down to the Jordan River and dipped himself seven times, as the man of God had instructed him. And his skin became as healthy as the skin of a young child's, and he was healed!

5:1 Or *from a contagious skin disease.* The Hebrew word used here and throughout this passage can describe various skin diseases.   5:5 Hebrew *10 talents* [340 kilograms] *of silver, 6,000 shekels* [68 kilograms] *of gold.*   5:13 Hebrew *My father.*

Naaman wanted to see if the power of God could heal him. But when Elisha told him to wash in the Jordan River, Naaman didn't want to do it. Then he humbled himself and obeyed, and he was healed! Obeying others isn't always fun. But obeying, even when we don't want to, can bring us good things. Try it and see!

[Jesus said,] "Those who accept my commandments and obey them are the ones who love me. And because they love me, my Father will love them. And I will love them and reveal myself to each of them." JOHN 14:21

APRIL 26

THE BOY KING

Athaliah, the king's mother, tried to kill all her grandchildren so she could be queen. But her grandson Joash escaped. What would happen to him?

2 Kings 11:1-8, 12-21

When Athaliah, the mother of King Ahaziah of Judah, learned that her son was dead, she began to destroy the rest of the royal family. ²But Ahaziah's sister Jehosheba, the daughter of King Jehoram,* took Ahaziah's infant son, Joash, and stole him away from among the rest of the king's children, who were about to be killed. She put Joash and his nurse in a bedroom to hide him from Athaliah, so the child was not murdered. ³Joash remained hidden in the Temple of the LORD for six years while Athaliah ruled over the land.

⁴In the seventh year of Athaliah's reign, Jehoiada the priest summoned the commanders, the Carite mercenaries, and the palace guards to come to the Temple of the LORD. He made a solemn pact with them and made them swear an oath of loyalty there in the LORD's Temple; then he showed them the king's son.

⁵Jehoiada told them, "This is what you must do. A third of you who are on duty on the Sabbath are to guard the royal palace itself. ⁶Another third of you are to stand guard at the Sur Gate. And the final third must stand guard behind the palace guard. These three groups will all guard the palace. ⁷The other two units who are off duty on the Sabbath must stand guard for the king at the LORD's Temple. ⁸Form a bodyguard around the king and keep your weapons in hand. Kill anyone who tries to break through. Stay with the king wherever he goes."

¹²Then Jehoiada brought out Joash, the king's son, placed the crown on his head, and presented him with a copy of God's laws.* They anointed him and proclaimed him king, and everyone clapped their hands and shouted, "Long live the king!"

¹³When Athaliah heard all the noise made by the palace guards and the people, she hurried to the LORD's Temple to see what was happening. ¹⁴When she arrived, she saw the newly crowned king standing in his place of authority by the pillar, as was the custom at times of coronation. The commanders and trumpeters were surrounding him, and people from all over the land were rejoicing and blowing trumpets. When Athaliah saw all this, she tore her clothes in despair and shouted, "Treason! Treason!"

¹⁵Then Jehoiada the priest ordered the commanders who were in charge of the troops, "Take her to the soldiers in front of the Temple,* and kill anyone who tries to rescue her." For the priest had said, "She must not be killed in the Temple of the LORD." ¹⁶So they seized her and led her out to the gate where horses enter the palace grounds, and she was killed there.

¹⁷Then Jehoiada made a covenant

between the LORD and the king and the people that they would be the LORD's people. He also made a covenant between the king and the people. [18]And all the people of the land went over to the temple of Baal and tore it down. They demolished the altars and smashed the idols to pieces, and they killed Mattan the priest of Baal in front of the altars.

Jehoiada the priest stationed guards at the Temple of the LORD. [19]Then the commanders, the Carite mercenaries, the palace guards, and all the people of the land escorted the king from the Temple of the LORD. They went through the gate of the guards and into the palace, and the king took his seat on the royal throne. [20]So all the people of the land rejoiced, and the city was peaceful because Athaliah had been killed at the king's palace.

[21]*Joash* was seven years old when he became king.

11:2 Hebrew *Joram*, a variant spelling of Jehoram. 11:12 Or *a copy of the covenant*. 11:15 Or *Bring her out from between the ranks*; or *Take her out of the Temple precincts*. The meaning of the Hebrew is uncertain. 11:21a Verse 11:21 is numbered 12:1 in Hebrew text. 11:21b Hebrew *Jehoash*, a variant spelling of Joash.

God protected Joash from Athaliah's horrible plans to take over the kingdom. When you are in danger, God is able to protect you, too. When you feel afraid, ask God to take care of you. His power is stronger than anyone who might try to harm you.

[Jesus prayed,] "I'm not asking you to take them out of the world, but to keep them safe from the evil one." JOHN 17:15

APRIL 27
Lost and Found

It had been years since anyone had read God's Word. No one even remembered where it was. Look what happened when Hilkiah found the Book of the Law in the Temple.

2 Chronicles 34:14-33

While they were bringing out the money collected at the LORD's Temple, Hilkiah the priest found the Book of the Law of the LORD that was written by Moses. [15]Hilkiah said to Shaphan the court secretary, "I have found the Book of the Law in the LORD's Temple!" Then Hilkiah gave the scroll to Shaphan.

[16]Shaphan took the scroll to the king and reported, "Your officials are doing everything they were assigned to do. [17]The money that was collected at the Temple of the LORD has been turned over to the supervisors and workmen." [18]Shaphan also told the king, "Hilkiah the priest has given me a scroll." So Shaphan read it to the king.

[19]When the king heard what was written in the Law, he tore his clothes in despair. [20]Then he gave these orders to Hilkiah, Ahikam son of Shaphan, Acbor son of Micaiah,* Shaphan the court secretary, and

Asaiah the king's personal adviser: [21]"Go to the Temple and speak to the LORD for me and for all the remnant of Israel and Judah. Inquire about the words written in the scroll that has been found. For the LORD's great anger has been poured out on us because our ancestors have not obeyed the word of the LORD. We have not been doing everything this scroll says we must do."

[22]So Hilkiah and the other men went to the New Quarter* of Jerusalem to consult with the prophet Huldah. She was the wife of Shallum son of Tikvah, son of Harhas,* the keeper of the Temple wardrobe.

[23]She said to them, "The LORD, the God of Israel, has spoken! Go back and tell the man who sent you, [24]'This is what the LORD says: I am going to bring disaster on this city* and its people. All the curses written in the scroll that was read to the king of Judah will come true. [25]For my people have abandoned me and offered sacrifices to pagan gods, and I am very angry with them for everything they have done. My anger will be poured out on this place, and it will not be quenched.'

[26]"But go to the king of Judah who sent you to seek the LORD and tell him: 'This is what the LORD, the God of Israel, says concerning the message you have just heard: [27]You were sorry and humbled yourself before God when you heard his words against this city and its people. You humbled yourself and tore your clothing in despair and wept before me in repen-tance. And I have indeed heard you, says the LORD. [28]So I will not send the promised disaster until after you have died and been buried in peace. You yourself will not see the disaster I am going to bring on this city and its people.'"

So they took her message back to the king.

[29]Then the king summoned all the elders of Judah and Jerusalem. [30]And the king went up to the Temple of the LORD with all the people of Judah and Jerusalem, along with the priests and the Levites—all the people from the greatest to the least. There the king read to them the entire Book of the Covenant that had been found in the LORD's Temple. [31]The king took his place of authority beside the pillar and renewed the covenant in the LORD's presence. He pledged to obey the LORD by keeping all his commands, laws, and decrees with all his heart and soul. He promised to obey all the terms of the covenant that were written in the scroll. [32]And he required everyone in Jerusalem and the people of Benjamin to make a similar pledge. The people of Jerusalem did so, renewing their covenant with God, the God of their ancestors.

[33]So Josiah removed all detestable idols from the entire land of Israel and required everyone to worship the LORD their God. And throughout the rest of his lifetime, they did not turn away from the LORD, the God of their ancestors.

34:20 As in parallel text at 2 Kgs 22:12; Hebrew reads *Abdon son of Micah.*   34:22a Or *the Second Quarter,* a newer section of Jerusalem. Hebrew reads *the Mishneh.*   34:22b As in parallel text at 2 Kgs 22:14; Hebrew reads *son of Tokhath, son of Hasrah.*   34:24 Hebrew *this place;* also in 34:27, 28.

When King Josiah read God's Word, he felt awful about the way God's people had been acting. The people had disobeyed God's rules for a long time because they didn't know them! Josiah immediately told God how sorry he was. Sometimes we do something wrong without knowing. When we find out, we need to take action like Josiah and the Israelites did. We need to tell God we are sorry and stop doing it!

I confess my sins; I am deeply sorry for what I have done. PSALM 38:18

APRIL 28

Rebuilding the Temple

After many years of living as prisoners in a foreign country, God's people finally returned to Jerusalem. The first thing they did was to rebuild the Temple. Read about how happy they were to have the Temple again.

Ezra 3:7-13

Then the people hired masons and carpenters and bought cedar logs from the people of Tyre and Sidon, paying them with food, wine, and olive oil. The logs were brought down from the Lebanon mountains and floated along the coast of the Mediterranean Sea* to Joppa, for King Cyrus had given permission for this.

⁸The construction of the Temple of God began in midspring,* during the second year after they arrived in Jerusalem. The work force was made up of everyone who had returned from exile, including Zerubbabel son of Shealtiel, Jeshua son of Jehozadak and his fellow priests, and all the Levites. The Levites who were twenty years old or older were put in charge of rebuilding the LORD's Temple. ⁹The workers at the Temple of God were supervised by Jeshua with his sons and relatives, and Kadmiel and his sons, all descendants of Hodaviah.* They were helped in this task by the Levites of the family of Henadad.

¹⁰When the builders completed the foundation of the LORD's Temple, the priests put on their robes and took their places to blow their trumpets. And the Levites, descendants of Asaph, clashed their cymbals to praise the LORD, just as King David had prescribed. ¹¹With praise and thanks, they sang this song to the LORD:

"He is so good!
His faithful love for Israel endures forever!"

Then all the people gave a great shout, praising the LORD because the foundation of the LORD's Temple had been laid.

[12]But many of the older priests, Levites, and other leaders who had seen the first Temple wept aloud when they saw the new Temple's foundation. The others, however, were shouting for joy. [13]The joyful shouting and weeping mingled together in a loud noise that could be heard far in the distance.

3:7 Hebrew *the sea.*   3:8 Hebrew *in the second month.* This month in the ancient Hebrew lunar calendar occurred within the months of April and May 536 B.C.   3:9 Hebrew *sons of Judah* (i.e., *bene Yehudah*). *Bene* might also be read here as the proper name Binnui; *Yehudah* is probably another name for Hodaviah. Compare 2:40; Neh 7:43; 1 Esdras 5:58.

When the Temple's foundation was completed, the people celebrated. The Israelites praised God and thanked him for his goodness to them. Can you think of five things that you can thank God for right now? God loves to give gifts to his kids, but he also likes to hear "Thank you"!

Be thankful in all circumstances, for this is God's will for you who belong to Christ Jesus. | THESSALONIANS 5:18

APRIL 29

Rebuilding Jerusalem

As Nehemiah and the Israelites were rebuilding the city walls around Jerusalem, they met opposition from their enemies. How did Nehemiah respond?

Nehemiah 4:1-21

Sanballat was very angry when he learned that we were rebuilding the wall. He flew into a rage and mocked the Jews, [2]saying in front of his friends and the Samarian army officers, "What does this bunch of poor, feeble Jews think they're doing? Do they think they can build the wall in a single day by just offering a few sacrifices? Do they actually think they can make something of stones from a rubbish heap—and charred ones at that?"

[3]Tobiah the Ammonite, who was standing beside him, remarked, "That stone wall would collapse if even a fox walked along the top of it!"

[4]Then I prayed, "Hear us, our God, for we are being mocked. May their scoffing fall back on their own heads, and may they themselves become captives in a foreign land! [5]Do not ignore their guilt. Do not blot out their sins, for they have provoked you to anger here in front of* the builders."

[6]At last the wall was completed to half its height around the entire city, for the people had worked with enthusiasm.

[7]*But when Sanballat and Tobiah and the Arabs, Ammonites, and Ashdodites heard that the work was going ahead and that the gaps in the wall of Jerusalem were being repaired, they were furious. [8]They all made plans to come and fight against Jerusalem and throw us into confusion. [9]But we

prayed to our God and guarded the city day and night to protect ourselves.

[10]Then the people of Judah began to complain, "The workers are getting tired, and there is so much rubble to be moved. We will never be able to build the wall by ourselves."

[11]Meanwhile, our enemies were saying, "Before they know what's happening, we will swoop down on them and kill them and end their work."

[12]The Jews who lived near the enemy came and told us again and again, "They will come from all directions and attack us!"* [13]So I placed armed guards behind the lowest parts of the wall in the exposed areas. I stationed the people to stand guard by families, armed with swords, spears, and bows.

[14]Then as I looked over the situation, I called together the nobles and the rest of the people and said to them, "Don't be afraid of the enemy! Remember the Lord, who is great and glorious, and fight for your brothers, your sons, your daughters, your wives, and your homes!"

[15]When our enemies heard that we knew of their plans and that God had frustrated them, we all returned to our work on the wall. [16]But from then on, only half my men worked while the other half stood guard with spears, shields, bows, and coats of mail. The leaders stationed themselves behind the people of Judah [17]who were building the wall. The laborers carried on their work with one hand supporting their load and one hand holding a weapon. [18]All the builders had a sword belted to their side. The trumpeter stayed with me to sound the alarm.

[19]Then I explained to the nobles and officials and all the people, "The work is very spread out, and we are widely separated from each other along the wall. [20]When you hear the blast of the trumpet, rush to wherever it is sounding. Then our God will fight for us!"

[21]We worked early and late, from sunrise to sunset. And half the men were always on guard.

4:1 Verses 4:1-6 are numbered 3:33-38 in Hebrew text.   4:2 The meaning of the Hebrew is uncertain.   4:5 Or *for they have thrown insults in the face of.*   4:7 Verses 4:7-23 are numbered 4:1-17 in Hebrew text.   4:12 The meaning of the Hebrew is uncertain.

The enemies' insults and threats were meant to discourage and stop the Israelites from rebuilding the walls. But that plan backfired. Nehemiah refused to get distracted by the enemies' actions. Instead, he prayed to God and concentrated on leading the Israelites to complete the project. We all will face opposition from time to time. People will try to discourage us. Don't get sidetracked by insults, threats, or mocking. Be like Nehemiah and pray for your enemies.

See that no one pays back evil for evil, but always try to do good to each other and to all people. I THESSALONIANS 5:15

APRIL 30

concern for the poor

Some of the Israelites were very poor. Would their friends and neighbors help them?

Nehemiah 5:1-11

About this time some of the men and their wives raised a cry of protest against their fellow Jews. ²They were saying, "We have such large families. We need more food to survive."

³Others said, "We have mortgaged our fields, vineyards, and homes to get food during the famine."

⁴And others said, "We have had to borrow money on our fields and vineyards to pay our taxes. ⁵We belong to the same family as those who are wealthy, and our children are just like theirs. Yet we must sell our children into slavery just to get enough money to live. We have already sold some of our daughters, and we are helpless to do anything about it, for our fields and vineyards are already mortgaged to others."

⁶When I [Nehemiah] heard their complaints, I was very angry. ⁷After thinking it over, I spoke out against these nobles and officials. I told them, "You are hurting your own relatives by charging interest when they borrow money!" Then I called a public meeting to deal with the problem.

⁸At the meeting I said to them, "We are doing all we can to redeem our Jewish relatives who have had to sell themselves to pagan foreigners, but you are selling them back into slavery again. How often must we redeem them?" And they had nothing to say in their defense.

⁹Then I pressed further, "What you are doing is not right! Should you not walk in the fear of our God in order to avoid being mocked by enemy nations? ¹⁰I myself, as well as my brothers and my workers, have been lending the people money and grain, but now let us stop this business of charging interest. ¹¹You must restore their fields, vineyards, olive groves, and homes to them this very day. And repay the interest you charged when you lent them money, grain, new wine, and olive oil."

Instead of helping their poor neighbors, the Jewish leaders were trying to make money from them. They made the poor people pay back more money than they had borrowed. That's no way for God's people to act. Nehemiah took immediate action to help the poor. When we see people who are in need, we should do what we can to help them—without expecting anything in return. Who can you unselfishly help today?

Whoever gives to the poor will lack nothing, but those who close their eyes to poverty will be cursed. PROVERBS 28:27

APRIL CHALLENGE
Great job!

You're really springing ahead now—you have just finished the month of April. It's time to challenge yourself to make it to the top. Need some help to keep going? Talk to God about it. If you have a friend who is taking the challenge with you, encourage each other. And don't forget to use your favorite marker or highlighter to fill in the number of levels you've completed so far.

You have been reading a lot of stories about what happened to God's people. Remember what you read this month? What was one of your favorite stories? Tell the story to someone in your family, and talk about why it was a favorite.

IMPORTANT STUFF TO REMEMBER FROM APRIL

❑ God wants his people to obey him.

❑ God gives his people wisdom.

❑ God can do amazing miracles to help his people.

God gave Solomon a chance to ask for whatever he wanted. Do you remember what he asked for? In the puzzle below, cross out all the Z's to find out what he said to God. (Check your answer in the reading for April 14.)

```
Z G Z Z I V Z E M Z E A Z N U N Z D E

Z R S T Z A N D Z I Z N G Z H E A Z R

T Z S Z O Z T H Z A Z T I Z C A Z N Z

G O Z V Z E Z R N Y Z O Z U Z R Z P E

O Z P Z L Z E W E Z Z Z L L Z A N Z D

Z K Z N O W Z T H Z E Z D Z I Z F F Z

E R Z E Z N Z Z C E Z B Z E T Z W E E

Z N R I Z G Z H T A Z N Z D W Z R O Z

N Z G Z F Z O Z R W Z H O B Z Y Z H I

Z M Z S E Z L F Z I Z S A Z B Z L E Z

T Z O Z G O Z V Z E R Z N Z T H Z I S

Z G Z R E Z A Z T Z P E Z O Z P L Z E

Z O F Z Y O Z U Z R S?
```

MAY 1

Reading and Weeping

Ezra read God's Word to the Israelites and taught them what it meant. Read how the Israelites responded to hearing the Word.

Nehemiah 8:2-6, 8-12

So on October 8* Ezra the priest brought the Book of the Law before the assembly, which included the men and women and all the children old enough to understand. [3] He faced the square just inside the Water Gate from early morning until noon and read aloud to everyone who could understand. All the people listened closely to the Book of the Law.

[4] Ezra the scribe stood on a high wooden platform that had been made for the occasion. To his right stood Mattithiah, Shema, Anaiah, Uriah, Hilkiah, and Maaseiah. To his left stood Pedaiah, Mishael, Malkijah, Hashum, Hashbaddanah, Zechariah, and Meshullam. [5] Ezra stood on the platform in full view of all the people. When they saw him open the book, they all rose to their feet.

[6] Then Ezra praised the LORD, the great God, and all the people chanted, "Amen! Amen!" as they lifted their hands. Then they bowed down and worshiped the LORD with their faces to the ground.

[8] They read from the Book of the Law of God and clearly explained the meaning of what was being read, helping the people understand each passage.

[9] Then Nehemiah the governor, Ezra the priest and scribe, and the Levites who were interpreting for the people said to them, "Don't mourn or weep on such a day as this! For today is a sacred day before the LORD your God." For the people had all been weeping as they listened to the words of the Law.

[10] And Nehemiah* continued, "Go and celebrate with a feast of rich foods and sweet drinks, and share gifts of food with people who have nothing prepared. This is a sacred day before our Lord. Don't be dejected and sad, for the joy of the LORD is your strength!"

[11] And the Levites, too, quieted the people, telling them, "Hush! Don't weep! For this is a sacred day." [12] So the people went away to eat and drink at a festive meal, to share gifts of food, and to celebrate with great joy because they had heard God's words and understood them.

8:2 Hebrew *on the first day of the seventh month,* of the ancient Hebrew lunar calendar. This day was October 8, 445 B.C.
8:10 Hebrew *he.*

When the Israelites heard the Word of God, they realized that their actions had not been pleasing to God. Because of what they heard, they were very sad and told God that they wanted to change. God's Word, the Bible, is very powerful. It shows us clearly when we are doing wrong and what we need to do to change. The Bible encourages us to serve God with our whole lives. As you read the Bible, think about what God is telling you.

All Scripture is inspired by God and is useful to teach us what is true and to make us realize what is wrong in our lives. It corrects us when we are wrong and teaches us to do what is right. 2 TIMOTHY 3:16

MAY 2

esther meets the King

Esther was going to meet the king for the first time. Her cousin Mordecai and others gave her instructions about how to act around him. See what happened!

Esther 2:5-11, 15-20

At that time there was a Jewish man in the fortress of Susa whose name was Mordecai son of Jair. He was from the tribe of Benjamin and was a descendant of Kish and Shimei. ⁶His family* had been among those who, with King Jehoiachin* of Judah, had been exiled from Jerusalem to Babylon by King Nebuchadnezzar. ⁷This man had a very beautiful and lovely young cousin, Hadassah, who was also called Esther. When her father and mother died, Mordecai adopted her into his family and raised her as his own daughter.

⁸As a result of the king's decree, Esther, along with many other young women, was brought to the king's harem at the fortress of Susa and placed in Hegai's care. ⁹Hegai was very impressed with Esther and treated her kindly. He quickly ordered a special menu for her and provided her with beauty treatments. He also assigned her seven maids specially chosen from the king's palace, and he moved her and her maids into the best place in the harem.

¹⁰Esther had not told anyone of her nationality and family background, because Mordecai had directed her not to do so. ¹¹Every day Mordecai would take a walk near the courtyard of the harem to find out about Esther and what was happening to her.

¹⁵Esther was the daughter of Abihail, who was Mordecai's uncle. (Mordecai had adopted his younger cousin Esther.) When it was Esther's turn to go to the king, she accepted the advice of Hegai, the eunuch in charge of the harem. She asked for

nothing except what he suggested, and she was admired by everyone who saw her.

¹⁶Esther was taken to King Xerxes at the royal palace in early winter* of the seventh year of his reign. ¹⁷And the king loved Esther more than any of the other young women. He was so delighted with her that he set the royal crown on her head and declared her queen instead of Vashti. ¹⁸To celebrate the occasion, he gave a great banquet in Esther's honor for all his nobles and officials, declaring a public holiday for the provinces and giving generous gifts to everyone.

¹⁹Even after all the young women had been transferred to the second harem* and Mordecai had become a palace official,* ²⁰Esther continued to keep her family background and nationality a secret. She was still following Mordecai's directions, just as she did when she lived in his home.

2:6a Hebrew *He.* 2:6b Hebrew *Jeconiah,* a variant spelling of Jehoiachin. 2:16 Hebrew *in the tenth month, the month of Tebeth.* A number of dates in the book of Esther can be cross-checked with dates in surviving Persian records and related accurately to our modern calendar. This month of the ancient Hebrew lunar calendar occurred within the months of December 479 B.C. and January 478 B.C. 2:19a The meaning of the Hebrew is uncertain. 2:19b Hebrew *and Mordecai was sitting in the gate of the king.*

Esther listened to the instructions Mordecai and others gave her. When she met the king, her actions were humble and she simply listened. As a result, the king was very impressed and declared Esther the new queen. First impressions are important! But no matter whether you are meeting someone for the first time or the twentieth time, if your actions are humble and you're willing to listen like Esther, you will make a good impression.

Even children are known by the way they act, whether their conduct is pure, and whether it is right. PROVERBS 20:11

MAY 3

Haman and Mordecai

Haman, one of the king's officials, thought he was really important. The king had ordered that everyone bow down to Haman. Would Mordecai bow down to him?

Esther 3:2-14

All the king's officials would bow down before Haman to show him respect whenever he passed by, for so the king had commanded. But Mordecai refused to bow down or show him respect.

³Then the palace officials at the king's gate asked Mordecai, "Why are you disobeying the king's command?" ⁴They spoke to him day after day, but still he refused to comply with the order. So they spoke to Haman about this to see if he would tolerate Mordecai's conduct, since Mordecai had told them he was a Jew.

⁵When Haman saw that Mordecai would not bow down or show him respect, he was

filled with rage. [6]He had learned of Mordecai's nationality, so he decided it was not enough to lay hands on Mordecai alone. Instead, he looked for a way to destroy all the Jews throughout the entire empire of Xerxes.

[7]So in the month of April,* during the twelfth year of King Xerxes' reign, lots were cast in Haman's presence (the lots were called *purim*) to determine the best day and month to take action. And the day selected was March 7, nearly a year later.*

[8]Then Haman approached King Xerxes and said, "There is a certain race of people scattered through all the provinces of your empire who keep themselves separate from everyone else. Their laws are different from those of any other people, and they refuse to obey the laws of the king. So it is not in the king's interest to let them live. [9]If it please the king, issue a decree that they be destroyed, and I will give 10,000 large sacks* of silver to the government administrators to be deposited in the royal treasury."

[10]The king agreed, confirming his decision by removing his signet ring from his finger and giving it to Haman son of Hammedatha the Agagite, the enemy of the Jews. [11]The king said, "The money and the people are both yours to do with as you see fit."

[12]So on April 17* the king's secretaries were summoned, and a decree was written exactly as Haman dictated. It was sent to the king's highest officers, the governors of the respective provinces, and the nobles of each province in their own scripts and languages. The decree was written in the name of King Xerxes and sealed with the king's signet ring. [13]Dispatches were sent by swift messengers into all the provinces of the empire, giving the order that all Jews—young and old, including women and children—must be killed, slaughtered, and annihilated on a single day. This was scheduled to happen on March 7 of the next year.* The property of the Jews would be given to those who killed them.

[14]A copy of this decree was to be issued as law in every province and proclaimed to all peoples, so that they would be ready to do their duty on the appointed day.

3:7a Hebrew *in the first month, the month of Nisan.* This month of the ancient Hebrew lunar calendar occurred within the months of April and May 474 B.C.; also see note on 2:16.   3:7b As in Greek version, which reads *the thirteenth day of the twelfth month, the month of Adar* (see also 3:13). Hebrew reads *in the twelfth month,* of the ancient Hebrew lunar calendar. The date selected was March 7, 473 B.C.; also see note on 2:16.   3:9 Hebrew *10,000 talents,* about 375 tons or 340 metric tons in weight. 3:12 Hebrew *On the thirteenth day of the first month,* of the ancient Hebrew lunar calendar. This day was April 17, 474 B.C.; also see note on 2:16.   3:13 Hebrew *on the thirteenth day of the twelfth month, the month of Adar,* of the ancient Hebrew lunar calendar. The date selected was March 7, 473 B.C.; also see note on 2:16.

Mordecai, Esther's cousin, knew it was wrong to bow down before anyone except God. So he refused to go along with the king's orders to bow down to Haman—even though Mordecai knew he could get into big trouble for disobeying. He made the right choice. If he obeyed Haman, Mordecai would have been disobeying God. And God is more powerful—and important— than any person. When you feel pressured to do something wrong, remember who it is you should obey!

Don't copy the behavior and customs of this world, but let God transform you into a new person by changing the way you think. Then you will learn to know God's will for you, which is good and pleasing and perfect. ROMANS 12:2

MAY 4

ESTHER RISKS HER LIFE

The king was planning to kill all of the Jewish people. Esther was the only one who could save her people. Would she take the risk?

Esther 4:1–5:2

When Mordecai learned about all that had been done, he tore his clothes, put on burlap and ashes, and went out into the city, crying with a loud and bitter wail. ²He went as far as the gate of the palace, for no one was allowed to enter the palace gate while wearing clothes of mourning. ³And as news of the king's decree reached all the provinces, there was great mourning among the Jews. They fasted, wept, and wailed, and many people lay in burlap and ashes.

⁴When Queen Esther's maids and eunuchs came and told her about Mordecai, she was deeply distressed. She sent clothing to him to replace the burlap, but he refused it. ⁵Then Esther sent for Hathach, one of the king's eunuchs who had been appointed as her attendant. She ordered him to go to Mordecai and find out what was troubling him and why he was in mourning. ⁶So Hathach went out to Mordecai in the square in front of the palace gate.

⁷Mordecai told him the whole story, including the exact amount of money Haman had promised to pay into the royal treasury for the destruction of the Jews. ⁸Mordecai gave Hathach a copy of the decree issued in Susa that called for the death of all Jews. He asked Hathach to show it to Esther and explain the situation to her. He also asked Hathach to direct her to go to the king to beg for mercy and plead for her people. ⁹So Hathach returned to Esther with Mordecai's message.

¹⁰Then Esther told Hathach to go back and relay this message to Mordecai: ¹¹"All the king's officials and even the people in the provinces know that anyone who appears before the king in his inner court without being invited is doomed to die unless the king holds out his gold scepter. And the king has not called for me to come to him for thirty days." ¹²So Hathach* gave Esther's message to Mordecai.

¹³Mordecai sent this reply to Esther: "Don't think for a moment that because you're in the palace you will escape when all other Jews are killed. ¹⁴If you keep quiet at a time like this, deliverance and relief for the Jews will arise from some other place, but you and your relatives will die. Who knows if perhaps you were made queen for just such a time as this?"

¹⁵Then Esther sent this reply to Mordecai: ¹⁶"Go and gather together all the Jews of Susa and fast for me. Do not eat or drink for three days, night or day. My maids and I will do the same. And then, though it is against the law, I will go in to see the king. If I must die, I must die." ¹⁷So Mordecai went away and did everything as Esther had ordered him.

⁵:¹On the third day of the fast, Esther put on her royal robes and entered the inner court of the palace, just across from the king's hall. The king was sitting on his

royal throne, facing the entrance. ²When he saw Queen Esther standing there in the inner court, he welcomed her and held out the gold scepter to her. So Esther approached and touched the end of the scepter.

4:12 As in Greek version; Hebrew reads *they*.

It was extremely dangerous for Esther to approach the king without being summoned. She could have been killed. But Esther was willing to take the risk, because she knew God had appointed her to this task. Sometimes God gives us tasks or jobs that seem scary. But if we are doing what God wants, we can be sure that God is with us and that he will guide us and help us.

If you try to hang on to your life, you will lose it. But if you give up your life for [Jesus'] sake and for the sake of the Good News, you will save it. MARK 8:35

MAY 5

Haman Humiliated

Haman was very proud of himself. He told all his friends about the special way the king was treating him. Look what happened to him after all his bragging.

Esther 5:9–6:13

Haman was a happy man as he left the banquet! But when he saw Mordecai sitting at the palace gate, not standing up or trembling nervously before him, Haman became furious. ¹⁰However, he restrained himself and went on home.

Then Haman gathered together his friends and Zeresh, his wife, ¹¹and boasted to them about his great wealth and his many children. He bragged about the honors the king had given him and how he had been promoted over all the other nobles and officials.

¹²Then Haman added, "And that's not all! Queen Esther invited only me and the king himself to the banquet she prepared for us. And she has invited me to dine with her and the king again tomorrow!" ¹³Then he added, "But this is all worth nothing as long as I see Mordecai the Jew just sitting there at the palace gate."

¹⁴So Haman's wife, Zeresh, and all his friends suggested, "Set up a sharpened pole that stands seventy-five feet* tall, and in the morning ask the king to impale Mordecai on it. When this is done, you can go on your merry way to the banquet with the king." This pleased Haman, and he ordered the pole set up.

⁶:¹That night the king had trouble sleeping, so he ordered an attendant to bring the book of the history of his reign so it could be read to him. ²In those records he discovered an account of how Mordecai had exposed the plot of Bigthana and Teresh, two of the eunuchs who guarded the door to the king's private quarters.

They had plotted to assassinate King Xerxes.

³"What reward or recognition did we ever give Mordecai for this?" the king asked.

His attendants replied, "Nothing has been done for him."

⁴"Who is that in the outer court?" the king inquired. As it happened, Haman had just arrived in the outer court of the palace to ask the king to impale Mordecai on the pole he had prepared.

⁵So the attendants replied to the king, "Haman is out in the court."

"Bring him in," the king ordered. ⁶So Haman came in, and the king said, "What should I do to honor a man who truly pleases me?"

Haman thought to himself, "Whom would the king wish to honor more than me?" ⁷So he replied, "If the king wishes to honor someone, ⁸he should bring out one of the king's own royal robes, as well as a horse that the king himself has ridden—one with a royal emblem on its head. ⁹Let the robes and the horse be handed over to one of the king's most noble officials.

5:14 Hebrew *50 cubits* [22.5 meters].

And let him see that the man whom the king wishes to honor is dressed in the king's robes and led through the city square on the king's horse. Have the official shout as they go, 'This is what the king does for someone he wishes to honor!'"

¹⁰"Excellent!" the king said to Haman. "Quick! Take the robes and my horse, and do just as you have said for Mordecai the Jew, who sits at the gate of the palace. Leave out nothing you have suggested!"

¹¹So Haman took the robes and put them on Mordecai, placed him on the king's own horse, and led him through the city square, shouting, "This is what the king does for someone he wishes to honor!" ¹²Afterward Mordecai returned to the palace gate, but Haman hurried home dejected and completely humiliated.

¹³When Haman told his wife, Zeresh, and all his friends what had happened, his wise advisers and his wife said, "Since Mordecai—this man who has humiliated you—is of Jewish birth, you will never succeed in your plans against him. It will be fatal to continue opposing him."

Haman thought he was really great. And he made sure everyone knew how great he was. So when Haman discovered that the king wanted to honor Mordecai instead of himself, Haman was humiliated. Haman's experience shows us how dangerous it can be to boast. Be careful not to fall into the "Haman trap." Instead of boasting about what *you* can do, tell someone about how great *God* is and what great things *he* has done.

As for me, may I never boast about anything except the cross of our Lord Jesus Christ. Because of that cross,* my interest in this world has been crucified, and the world's interest in me has also died. GALATIANS 6:14

6:14 Or *Because of him.*

MAY 6

The Jewish People Are Saved

Esther risked her life so the king would listen to her. Now it was time to ask him to save her people. Would the king listen to her?

Esther 7:1-10

So the king and Haman went to Queen Esther's banquet. ²On this second occasion, while they were drinking wine, the king again said to Esther, "Tell me what you want, Queen Esther. What is your request? I will give it to you, even if it is half the kingdom!"

³Queen Esther replied, "If I have found favor with the king, and if it pleases the king to grant my request, I ask that my life and the lives of my people will be spared. ⁴For my people and I have been sold to those who would kill, slaughter, and annihilate us. If we had merely been sold as slaves, I could remain quiet, for that would be too trivial a matter to warrant disturbing the king."

⁵"Who would do such a thing?" King Xerxes demanded. "Who would be so presumptuous as to touch you?"

⁶Esther replied, "This wicked Haman is our adversary and our enemy." Haman grew pale with fright before the king and

7:9 Hebrew *50 cubits* [22.5 meters].

queen. ⁷Then the king jumped to his feet in a rage and went out into the palace garden.

Haman, however, stayed behind to plead for his life with Queen Esther, for he knew that the king intended to kill him. ⁸In despair he fell on the couch where Queen Esther was reclining, just as the king was returning from the palace garden.

The king exclaimed, "Will he even assault the queen right here in the palace, before my very eyes?" And as soon as the king spoke, his attendants covered Haman's face, signaling his doom.

⁹Then Harbona, one of the king's eunuchs, said, "Haman has set up a sharpened pole that stands seventy-five feet* tall in his own courtyard. He intended to use it to impale Mordecai, the man who saved the king from assassination."

"Then impale Haman on it!" the king ordered. ¹⁰So they impaled Haman on the pole he had set up for Mordecai, and the king's anger subsided.

Even though Esther was afraid to approach the king, she was the one person the king would listen to. And he had the power to act on her behalf. Through Esther, God protected the Jewish people from certain death. Esther's story is a wonderful picture of how God helps his people. God's name is never mentioned in the book, but his work is evident in all that happens. God has ultimate power over all kings, governments, and presidents. We can trust him to raise up people who will influence those in authority for good.

Everyone must submit to governing authorities. For all authority comes from God, and those in positions of authority have been placed there by God. ROMANS 13:1

MAY 7

JOB'S TROUBLES

Job was a good person who loved God. But he had never experienced any major problems in his life. How would he react when trouble—big trouble—hit?

Job 1:6-22

One day the members of the heavenly court* came to present themselves before the LORD, and the Accuser, Satan,* came with them. 7"Where have you come from?" the LORD asked Satan.

Satan answered the LORD, "I have been patrolling the earth, watching everything that's going on."

8Then the LORD asked Satan, "Have you noticed my servant Job? He is the finest man in all the earth. He is blameless—a man of complete integrity. He fears God and stays away from evil."

9Satan replied to the LORD, "Yes, but Job has good reason to fear God. 10You have always put a wall of protection around him and his home and his property. You have made him prosper in everything he does. Look how rich he is! 11But reach out and take away everything he has, and he will surely curse you to your face!"

12"All right, you may test him," the LORD said to Satan. "Do whatever you want with everything he possesses, but don't harm him physically." So Satan left the LORD's presence.

13One day when Job's sons and daughters were feasting at the oldest brother's house, 14a messenger arrived at Job's home with this news: "Your oxen were plowing, with the donkeys feeding beside them, 15when the Sabeans raided us. They stole all the animals and killed all the farmhands. I am the only one who escaped to tell you."

16While he was still speaking, another messenger arrived with this news: "The fire of God has fallen from heaven and burned up your sheep and all the shepherds. I am the only one who escaped to tell you."

17While he was still speaking, a third messenger arrived with this news: "Three bands of Chaldean raiders have stolen your camels and killed your servants. I am the only one who escaped to tell you."

18While he was still speaking, another messenger arrived with this news: "Your sons and daughters were feasting in their oldest brother's home. 19Suddenly, a powerful wind swept in from the wilderness and hit the house on all sides. The house collapsed, and all your children are dead. I am the only one who escaped to tell you."

20Job stood up and tore his robe in grief. Then he shaved his head and fell to the ground to worship. 21He said,

"I came naked from my mother's
    womb,
    and I will be naked when I leave.
The LORD gave me what I had,
    and the LORD has taken it away.
Praise the name of the LORD!"

22In all of this, Job did not sin by blaming God.

1:6a Hebrew *the sons of God.* 1:6b Hebrew *and the satan;* similarly throughout this chapter.

In one day, Job lost all of his children and all of his possessions. Yet he didn't get angry with God. He grieved, but he praised God even when everything was going wrong. When bad things happen to us, we need to keep our faith like Job did. During difficult times, turn to God, not away from him. Remember, God loves you and will give you the strength to get through hard times.

Dear brothers and sisters,* when troubles come your way, consider it an opportunity for great joy. For you know that when your faith is tested, your endurance has a chance to grow. JAMES 1:2-3

1:2 Greek *brothers.*

MAY 8

JOB IN ASHES

Satan was determined to make Job angry with God. See what Job did when Satan made him sick.

Job 2:1-10

One day the members of the heavenly court* came again to present themselves before the LORD, and the Accuser, Satan,* came with them. ²"Where have you come from?" the LORD asked Satan.

Satan answered the LORD, "I have been patrolling the earth, watching everything that's going on."

³Then the LORD asked Satan, "Have you noticed my servant Job? He is the finest man in all the earth. He is blameless—a man of complete integrity. He fears God and stays away from evil. And he has maintained his integrity, even though you urged me to harm him without cause."

⁴Satan replied to the LORD, "Skin for skin! A man will give up everything he has to save his life. ⁵But reach out and take away his health, and he will surely curse you to your face!"

⁶"All right, do with him as you please," the LORD said to Satan. "But spare his life."

⁷So Satan left the LORD's presence, and he struck Job with terrible boils from head to foot.

⁸Job scraped his skin with a piece of broken pottery as he sat among the ashes. ⁹His wife said to him, "Are you still trying to maintain your integrity? Curse God and die."

¹⁰But Job replied, "You talk like a foolish woman. Should we accept only good things from the hand of God and never anything bad?" So in all this, Job said nothing wrong.

2:1a Hebrew *the sons of God.* 2:1b Hebrew *and the satan;* similarly throughout this chapter.

Job's problems continued. Now he was covered with horrible skin infections. Still, he did not blame God. Job understood that God sometimes allows bad things to happen. Through those difficulties, God can still be trusted. Is there something bad happening to you right now? Cling to God through the good times and the bad times. He will not leave you.

Can anything ever separate us from Christ's love? Does it mean he no longer loves us if we have trouble or calamity, or are persecuted, or hungry, or destitute, or in danger, or threatened with death? . . . No, despite all these things, overwhelming victory is ours through Christ, who loved us. ROMANS 8:35, 37

MAY 9

Job's Friends

Three of Job's friends came to visit him. Find out what they did.

Job 2:11–3:7

When three of Job's friends heard of the tragedy he had suffered, they got together and traveled from their homes to comfort and console him. Their names were Eliphaz the Temanite, Bildad the Shuhite, and Zophar the Naamathite. ¹²When they saw Job from a distance, they scarcely recognized him. Wailing loudly, they tore their robes and threw dust into the air over their heads to show their grief. ¹³Then they sat on the ground with him for seven days and nights. No one said a word to Job, for they saw that his suffering was too great for words.

³·¹At last Job spoke, and he cursed the day of his birth. ²He said:

³"Let the day of my birth be erased,
    and the night I was conceived.
⁴Let that day be turned to darkness.
    Let it be lost even to God on high,
    and let no light shine on it.
⁵Let the darkness and utter gloom claim
        that day for its own.
    Let a black cloud overshadow it,
    and let the darkness terrify it.
⁶Let that night be blotted off the
        calendar,
    never again to be counted among the
        days of the year,
    never again to appear among the
        months.
⁷Let that night be childless.
    Let it have no joy."

When people go through hard times, having friends who care can make all the difference. Job's friends acted just right around Job at this point. They cried with him; they listened to him; they sat with him in silence. Sometimes just spending time with friends who are sad can be better than giving them advice. When you have a friend who is in trouble, show him or her you care by being there.

I hurt with the hurt of my people. I mourn and am overcome with grief.
JEREMIAH 8:21

MAY 10

God Speaks

Job had been going through much pain and sadness without hearing from God. When God finally did speak, look how he answered all Job's questions.

Job 38:1-18; 40:1-5

Then the LORD answered Job from the whirlwind:

²"Who is this that questions my wisdom
    with such ignorant words?
³Brace yourself like a man,
    because I have some questions
      for you,
    and you must answer them.

⁴"Where were you when I laid the
    foundations of the earth?
    Tell me, if you know so much.
⁵Who determined its dimensions
    and stretched out the surveying
      line?
⁶What supports its foundations,
    and who laid its cornerstone
⁷as the morning stars sang together
    and all the angels* shouted
      for joy?

⁸"Who kept the sea inside its boundaries
    as it burst from the womb,
⁹and as I clothed it with clouds
    and wrapped it in thick darkness?
¹⁰For I locked it behind barred gates,
    limiting its shores.
¹¹I said, 'This far and no farther will you
      come.
    Here your proud waves must stop!'

¹²"Have you ever commanded the
      morning to appear
    and caused the dawn to rise in the
      east?
¹³Have you made daylight spread to the
      ends of the earth,
    to bring an end to the night's
      wickedness?
¹⁴As the light approaches,
    the earth takes shape like clay
      pressed beneath a seal;
    it is robed in brilliant colors.*

¹⁵The light disturbs the wicked
and stops the arm that is raised in violence.

¹⁶"Have you explored the springs from which the seas come?
Have you explored their depths?
¹⁷Do you know where the gates of death are located?
Have you seen the gates of utter gloom?
¹⁸Do you realize the extent of the earth?
Tell me about it if you know!"

38:7 Hebrew *the sons of God.*   38:14 Or *its features stand out like folds in a robe.*

⊙

^{40:1}Then the LORD said to Job,

²"Do you still want to argue with the Almighty?
You are God's critic, but do you have the answers?"

³Then Job replied to the LORD,

⁴"I am nothing—how could I ever find the answers?
I will cover my mouth with my hand.
⁵I have said too much already.
I have nothing more to say."

Sometimes when we look at our world, it can seem as if life is unfair. God's answer to Job is a good reminder that we can't understand everything that happens. God is the one who made the whole world. He is the one in control. Since we know that God is good, we can trust that what seems unfair now will be set right someday. God deserves our love and trust even when we don't understand our circumstances.

Humble yourselves before the Lord, and he will lift you up in honor. JAMES 4:10

MAY 11

JOB'S REPLY TO GOD

When Job heard all God had to say, he realized that he had been wrong to question God. Wait till you see how Job's life turned out!

Job 42:1-17
Then Job replied to the LORD:

²"I know that you can do anything,
and no one can stop you.
³You asked, 'Who is this that questions my wisdom with such ignorance?'
It is I—and I was talking about things I knew nothing about,
things far too wonderful for me.
⁴You said, 'Listen and I will speak!
I have some questions for you,
and you must answer them.'
⁵I had only heard about you before,
but now I have seen you with my own eyes.
⁶I take back everything I said,
and I sit in dust and ashes to show my repentance."

⁷After the LORD had finished speaking to Job, he said to Eliphaz the Temanite: "I am angry with you and your two friends, for

you have not spoken accurately about me, as my servant Job has. [8]So take seven bulls and seven rams and go to my servant Job and offer a burnt offering for yourselves. My servant Job will pray for you, and I will accept his prayer on your behalf. I will not treat you as you deserve, for you have not spoken accurately about me, as my servant Job has." [9]So Eliphaz the Temanite, Bildad the Shuhite, and Zophar the Naamathite did as the LORD commanded them, and the LORD accepted Job's prayer.

[10]When Job prayed for his friends, the LORD restored his fortunes. In fact, the LORD gave him twice as much as before! [11]Then all his brothers, sisters, and former friends came and feasted with him in his home. And they consoled him and comforted him because of all the trials the LORD had brought against him. And each of them brought him a gift of money* and a gold ring.

[12]So the LORD blessed Job in the second half of his life even more than in the beginning. For now he had 14,000 sheep, 6,000 camels, 1,000 teams of oxen, and 1,000 female donkeys. [13]He also gave Job seven more sons and three more daughters. [14]He named his first daughter Jemimah, the second Keziah, and the third Keren-happuch. [15]In all the land no women were as lovely as the daughters of Job. And their father put them into his will along with their brothers.

[16]Job lived 140 years after that, living to see four generations of his children and grandchildren. [17]Then he died, an old man who had lived a long, full life.

42:11 Hebrew *a kesitah;* the value or weight of the kesitah is no longer known.

At the end of Job's troubles—during the second half of his life—God blessed him and gave him even more than he had in the first place. We can experience some really tough situations. But then God often gives us wonderful blessings when we aren't expecting them. Look for those unexpected blessings—like a smile from a friend or a compliment from a teacher—that help you through the hard times.

Weeping may last through the night, but joy comes with the morning. PSALM 30:5

MAY 12

The Right Way and the Wrong Way

Read this psalm and find out about two different types of people: those who love God and those who love evil.

Psalm 1:1-6
Oh, the joys of those who do not
    follow the advice of the wicked,
    or stand around with sinners,
    or join in with mockers.

[2]But they delight in the law of the LORD,
    meditating on it day and night.
[3]They are like trees planted along the
    riverbank,
    bearing fruit each season.

Their leaves never wither,
and they prosper in all they do.

⁴But not the wicked!
They are like worthless chaff,
scattered by the wind.
⁵They will be condemned at the time
of judgment.

Sinners will have no place among the
godly.
⁶For the LORD watches over the path
of the godly,
but the path of the wicked leads to
destruction.

Everybody has a choice. We can choose to follow God and be like the
strong, healthy trees. Or we can choose to disobey God and become like
dead, dirty dust that is blown away by the wind. One path leads to life and
success, the other to destruction and judgment. Which path will you
choose?

*You can make this choice by loving the LORD your God, obeying him, and
committing yourself firmly to him. This* is the key to your life. And if you love
and obey the LORD, you will live long in the land the LORD swore to give your
ancestors Abraham, Isaac, and Jacob.* DEUTERONOMY 30:20
30:20 Or *He.*

MAY 13

The Work of God's Fingers

**As you read this psalm, you can make it your own prayer of praise
to God for creation. Notice what the psalm writer had to say
about people.**

Psalm 8:1-9

O LORD, our Lord, your majestic name
fills the earth!
Your glory is higher than the
heavens.
²You have taught children and infants
to tell of your strength,*
silencing your enemies
and all who oppose you.

³When I look at the night sky and see
the work of your fingers—
the moon and the stars you set
in place—

⁴what are people that you should think
about them,
mere mortals that you should
care for them?*
⁵Yet you made them only a little lower
than God*
and crowned them* with glory
and honor.
⁶You gave them charge of everything
you made,
putting all things under their authority—
⁷the flocks and the herds
and all the wild animals,
⁸the birds in the sky, the fish in the sea,

and everything that swims the ocean
currents.

⁹O LORD, our Lord, your majestic name
fills the earth!

Look around you. God has created an incredibly beautiful and complex world. The variety of animals, the diversity of plants, the vastness of our universe—God created it all. Yet his most treasured and valued creation is us, his people. See how much he loves and cares for us by placing us in authority over his creation. Our lives are valuable because God loves us. That fact alone is a good reason for praising God today.

We are God's masterpiece. He has created us anew in Christ Jesus, so we can do the good things he planned for us long ago. EPHESIANS 2:10

MAY 14

The Good Shepherd

What do you know about shepherds and sheep? While you read this psalm, think about how God is like a shepherd to you.

Psalm 23:1-6
The LORD is my shepherd;
  I have all that I need.
²He lets me rest in green meadows;
  he leads me beside peaceful streams.
³He renews my strength.
He guides me along right paths,
  bringing honor to his name.
⁴Even when I walk
  through the darkest valley,*
I will not be afraid,
  for you are close beside me.

23:4 Or *the dark valley of death.*

Your rod and your staff
  protect and comfort me.
⁵You prepare a feast for me
  in the presence of my enemies.
You honor me by anointing my head
  with oil.
My cup overflows with blessings.
⁶Surely your goodness and unfailing love
  will pursue me
all the days of my life,
and I will live in the house of the LORD
  forever.

This psalm tells us the many ways God takes care of us. He protects us when we are in trouble. He provides for our needs by giving us food, rest, and love. He guides us through life and then welcomes us into his home. Like David, we have a good shepherd too. His name is Jesus. He not only takes care of us, but he died to show us the way to heaven. Just follow Jesus.

[Jesus said,] "I am the good shepherd; I know my own sheep, and they know me, just as my Father knows me and I know the Father. So I sacrifice my life for the sheep." JOHN 10:14-15

MAY 15

wash me

David wrote this psalm when he was feeling very sorry about the sinful things he had done. Look what he asked God to do.

Psalm 51:1-17

Have mercy on me, O God,
    because of your unfailing love.
Because of your great compassion,
    blot out the stain of my sins.
²Wash me clean from my guilt.
    Purify me from my sin.
³For I recognize my rebellion;
    it haunts me day and night.
⁴Against you, and you alone, have
    I sinned;
    I have done what is evil in your sight.
You will be proved right in what you say,
    and your judgment against me
      is just.*
⁵For I was born a sinner—
    yes, from the moment my mother
      conceived me.
⁶But you desire honesty from the
    womb,*
    teaching me wisdom even there.

⁷Purify me from my sins,* and I will
    be clean;

wash me, and I will be whiter
    than snow.
⁸Oh, give me back my joy again;
    you have broken me—
    now let me rejoice.
⁹Don't keep looking at my sins.
    Remove the stain of my guilt.
¹⁰Create in me a clean heart, O God.
    Renew a loyal spirit within me.
¹¹Do not banish me from your
    presence,
    and don't take your Holy Spirit*
    from me.

¹²Restore to me the joy of your
    salvation,
    and make me willing to obey you.
¹³Then I will teach your ways to rebels,
    and they will return to you.
¹⁴Forgive me for shedding blood, O God
    who saves;
    then I will joyfully sing of your
      forgiveness.
¹⁵Unseal my lips, O Lord,
    that my mouth may praise you.

¹⁶You do not desire a sacrifice, or I would offer one.
You do not want a burnt offering.

¹⁷The sacrifice you desire is a broken spirit.
You will not reject a broken and repentant heart, O God.

51:4 Greek version reads *and you will win your case in court.* Compare Rom 3:4. **51:6** Or *from the heart;* Hebrew reads *in the inward parts.* **51:7** Hebrew *Purify me with the hyssop branch.* **51:11** Or *your spirit of holiness.*

Sin can make us feel dirty and awful. But when God forgives us, we feel like we've taken a bath after falling in the mud. We are completely clean! God can wash away our guilt and help us not to sin next time. Whenever you know you have sinned, tell God that you are sorry. He will remove your sin from you and give you a "clean heart." Take time right now to come clean before God.

If we confess our sins to [God], he is faithful and just to forgive us our sins and to cleanse us from all wickedness. I JOHN 1:9

MAY 16

AS HIGH AS THE HEAVENS

This psalm writer praised God for being strong enough and loving enough to help us when we are sinful and weak.

Psalm 103:1-22

Let all that I am praise the LORD;
   with my whole heart, I will praise
      his holy name.
²Let all that I am praise the LORD;
   may I never forget the good things
      he does for me.
³He forgives all my sins
   and heals all my diseases.
⁴He redeems me from death
   and crowns me with love and tender
      mercies.
⁵He fills my life with good things.
   My youth is renewed like the
      eagle's!

⁶The LORD gives righteousness
   and justice to all who are treated
      unfairly.

⁷He revealed his character to Moses
   and his deeds to the people of Israel.
⁸The LORD is compassionate and
      merciful,
   slow to get angry and filled with
      unfailing love.
⁹He will not constantly accuse us,
   nor remain angry forever.
¹⁰He does not punish us for all our sins;
   he does not deal harshly with us,
      as we deserve.
¹¹For his unfailing love toward those
      who fear him
   is as great as the height of the
      heavens above the earth.
¹²He has removed our sins as far from us
   as the east is from the west.
¹³The LORD is like a father to his children,

tender and compassionate to those
who fear him.
¹⁴For he knows how weak we are;
he remembers we are only dust.
¹⁵Our days on earth are like grass;
like wildflowers, we bloom
and die.
¹⁶The wind blows, and we are
gone—
as though we had never been here.
¹⁷But the love of the LORD remains
forever
with those who fear him.
His salvation extends to the children's
children
¹⁸of those who are faithful to his
covenant,
of those who obey his
commandments!
¹⁹The LORD has made the heavens
his throne;
from there he rules over everything.
²⁰Praise the LORD, you angels,
you mighty ones who carry out
his plans,
listening for each of his commands.
²¹Yes, praise the LORD, you armies of
angels
who serve him and do his will!
²²Praise the LORD, everything he has
created,
everything in all his kingdom.
Let all that I am praise the LORD.

What a wonderful word picture of God's love for us! He forgives us. He heals us. He gives us good things, like parents, food, and clothing. God doesn't punish us as we deserve. He cares deeply about us. He knows all our weaknesses, yet he loves us anyway. Whenever you are feeling that no one cares, read this psalm. Know that you are forgiven, cared for, provided for, and above all else, loved.

We know how much God loves us, and we have put our trust in his love. God is love, and all who live in love live in God, and God lives in them. I JOHN 4:16

MAY 17

A Lamp for my feet

How much do you love God's Word? This psalm helps us to be thankful for the way the Word helps us every day.

Psalm 119:97-106
Oh, how I love your instructions!
I think about them all day long.
⁹⁸Your commands make me wiser than
my enemies,
for they are my constant guide.
⁹⁹Yes, I have more insight than my
teachers,
for I am always thinking of your
laws.
¹⁰⁰I am even wiser than my elders,
for I have kept your commandments.

¹⁰¹I have refused to walk on any evil
path,
so that I may remain obedient
to your word.
¹⁰²I haven't turned away from your
regulations,
for you have taught me well.
¹⁰³How sweet your words taste
to me;
they are sweeter than honey.

¹⁰⁴Your commandments give me
understanding;
no wonder I hate every false way
of life.
¹⁰⁵Your word is a lamp to guide my feet
and a light for my path.
¹⁰⁶I've promised it once, and I'll promise
it again:
I will obey your righteous
regulations.

The writer of this psalm loved reading God's Word. And because he spent time daily reading God's Word, the psalm writer was able to grow closer to God. He was able to gain great wisdom and knowledge. Today, we can follow the writer's example. We can spend time each day reading the Bible. It tells us the right way to go and how to live a life that is pleasing to God.

[Jesus prayed,] "Make them holy by your truth; teach them your word, which is truth." JOHN 17:17

MAY 18

God Knows You

Who knows you really well? Is there anyone who knows absolutely everything about you? God does! Read and see.

Psalm 139:1-18
O LORD, you have examined my heart
and know everything about me.
²You know when I sit down or stand up.
You know my thoughts even when
I'm far away.
³You see me when I travel
and when I rest at home.
You know everything I do.
⁴You know what I am going to say
even before I say it, LORD.
⁵You go before me and follow me.
You place your hand of blessing
on my head.

⁶Such knowledge is too wonderful
for me,
too great for me to understand!
⁷I can never escape from your Spirit!
I can never get away from your
presence!
⁸If I go up to heaven, you are there;
if I go down to the grave,* you
are there.
⁹If I ride the wings of the morning,
if I dwell by the farthest oceans,
¹⁰even there your hand will guide me,
and your strength will support me.
¹¹I could ask the darkness to hide me

and the light around me to become night—
¹²but even in darkness I cannot hide from you.
To you the night shines as bright as day.
Darkness and light are the same to you.

¹³You made all the delicate, inner parts of my body
and knit me together in my mother's womb.
¹⁴Thank you for making me so wonderfully complex!
Your workmanship is marvelous— how well I know it.

¹⁵You watched me as I was being formed in utter seclusion,
as I was woven together in the dark of the womb.
¹⁶You saw me before I was born.
Every day of my life was recorded in your book.
Every moment was laid out before a single day had passed.

¹⁷How precious are your thoughts about me,* O God.
They cannot be numbered!
¹⁸I can't even count them;
they outnumber the grains of sand!
And when I wake up,
you are still with me!

139:8 Hebrew *to Sheol.*   139:17 Or *How precious to me are your thoughts.*

God has known everything about you since before you were born. He always knows where you are and what you are thinking about. God knows what your whole life will be like. God knows you even better than you know yourself, so he truly knows what's best for you. That's why you can trust him completely with everything. And he will always be with you!

Your Father knows exactly what you need even before you ask him! MATTHEW 6:8

MAY 19

GOD IS GREAT!

When we really like something, we can't wait to tell people about it. Look for all the ways people in this psalm are telling others how good God is.

Psalm 145:1-21
I will exalt you, my God and King,
and praise your name forever and ever.
²I will praise you every day;
yes, I will praise you forever.

³Great is the LORD! He is most worthy of praise!
No one can measure his greatness.

⁴Let each generation tell its children of your mighty acts;
let them proclaim your power.

⁵I will meditate* on your majestic,
   glorious splendor
and your wonderful miracles.
⁶Your awe-inspiring deeds will be on
   every tongue;
   I will proclaim your greatness.
⁷Everyone will share the story of your
   wonderful goodness;
   they will sing with joy about your
   righteousness.

⁸The Lord is merciful and
   compassionate,
   slow to get angry and filled with
   unfailing love.
⁹The Lord is good to everyone.
   He showers compassion on all
   his creation.
¹⁰All of your works will thank you, Lord,
   and your faithful followers will
   praise you.
¹¹They will speak of the glory of your
   kingdom;
   they will give examples of your
   power.
¹²They will tell about your mighty
   deeds
   and about the majesty and glory
   of your reign.
¹³For your kingdom is an everlasting
   kingdom.

You rule throughout all
   generations.

The Lord always keeps his promises;
   he is gracious in all he does.*
¹⁴The Lord helps the fallen
   and lifts those bent beneath their
   loads.
¹⁵The eyes of all look to you in hope;
   you give them their food as they
   need it.
¹⁶When you open your hand,
   you satisfy the hunger and thirst
   of every living thing.
¹⁷The Lord is righteous in everything
   he does;
   he is filled with kindness.
¹⁸The Lord is close to all who call
   on him,
   yes, to all who call on him in truth.
¹⁹He grants the desires of those who
   fear him;
   he hears their cries for help and
   rescues them.
²⁰The Lord protects all those who love
   him,
   but he destroys the wicked.

²¹I will praise the Lord,
   and may everyone on earth bless his
   holy name
   forever and ever.

145:5 Some manuscripts read *They will speak.*   145:13 The last two lines of 145:13 are not found in many of the ancient manuscripts.

There are so many reasons for praising our God. This psalm writer lists a few of them: God is good and fair; he does miracles; he is kind and merciful; he keeps his promises; and he helps people who are in trouble. What do you love most about God? Tell someone today about the wonderful God you serve.

We cannot stop telling about everything we have seen and heard. ACTS 4:20

MAY 20

WISE WORDS

King Solomon wrote these wise sayings called proverbs. Look what he had to say about wisdom.

Proverbs 4:1-27

My children,* listen when your father corrects you.
    Pay attention and learn good judgment,
²for I am giving you good guidance.
    Don't turn away from my instructions.
³For I, too, was once my father's son, tenderly loved as my mother's only child.

⁴My father taught me,
    "Take my words to heart.
    Follow my commands, and you will live.
⁵Get wisdom; develop good judgment.
    Don't forget my words or turn away from them.
⁶Don't turn your back on wisdom, for she will protect you.
    Love her, and she will guard you.
⁷Getting wisdom is the wisest thing you can do!
    And whatever else you do, develop good judgment.
⁸If you prize wisdom, she will make you great.
    Embrace her, and she will honor you.
⁹She will place a lovely wreath on your head;
    she will present you with a beautiful crown."

¹⁰My child,* listen to me and do as I say,
    and you will have a long, good life.

¹¹I will teach you wisdom's ways
    and lead you in straight paths.
¹²When you walk, you won't be held back;
    when you run, you won't stumble.
¹³Take hold of my instructions; don't let them go.
    Guard them, for they are the key to life.

¹⁴Don't do as the wicked do,
    and don't follow the path of evildoers.
¹⁵Don't even think about it; don't go that way.
    Turn away and keep moving.
¹⁶For evil people can't sleep until they've done their evil deed for the day.
    They can't rest until they've caused someone to stumble.
¹⁷They eat the food of wickedness
    and drink the wine of violence!

¹⁸The way of the righteous is like the first gleam of dawn,
    which shines ever brighter until the full light of day.
¹⁹But the way of the wicked is like total darkness.
    They have no idea what they are stumbling over.

²⁰My child, pay attention to what I say.
    Listen carefully to my words.
²¹Don't lose sight of them.
    Let them penetrate deep into your heart,

²²for they bring life to those who find them,
and healing to their whole body.

²³Guard your heart above all else,
for it determines the course
of your life.

²⁴Avoid all perverse talk;
stay away from corrupt speech.

²⁵Look straight ahead,
and fix your eyes on what lies
before you.
²⁶Mark out a straight path for your feet;
stay on the safe path.
²⁷Don't get sidetracked;
keep your feet from following
evil.

4:1 Hebrew *My sons*. 4:10 Hebrew *My son*; also in 4:20.

King Solomon said that wisdom is the most important thing to have if you want to live the right way. Wisdom helps you know right from wrong and helps you make good choices. Living without wisdom is like trying to walk around in the dark without a flashlight. One of the best ways to get wisdom is to listen to godly people who want to teach you. What have you learned from your parents or teachers lately that made you wiser?

If you need wisdom, ask our generous God, and he will give it to you. He will not rebuke you for asking. JAMES 1:5

MAY 21

REMEMBER GOD

This advice came from a wise teacher who wanted to help young people live the right way. What does he say is the most important thing to remember in life?

Ecclesiastes 11:7–12:2, 9-14

Light is sweet; how pleasant to see a new day dawning.

⁸When people live to be very old, let them rejoice in every day of life. But let them also remember there will be many dark days. Everything still to come is meaningless.

⁹Young people,* it's wonderful to be young! Enjoy every minute of it. Do everything you want to do; take it all in. But remember that you must give an account to God for everything you do. ¹⁰So refuse to worry, and keep your body healthy. But remember that youth, with a whole life before you, is meaningless.

¹²:¹Don't let the excitement of youth cause you to forget your Creator. Honor him in your youth before you grow old and say, "Life is not pleasant anymore." ²Remember him before the light of the sun, moon, and stars is dim to your old eyes, and rain clouds continually darken your sky.

⁹Keep this in mind: The Teacher was considered wise, and he taught the people

everything he knew. He listened carefully to many proverbs, studying and classifying them. [10]The Teacher sought to find just the right words to express truths clearly.*

[11]The words of the wise are like cattle prods—painful but helpful. Their collected sayings are like a nail-studded stick with which a shepherd* drives the sheep.

[12]But, my child,* let me give you some further advice: Be careful, for writing books is endless, and much study wears you out.

[13]That's the whole story. Here now is my final conclusion: Fear God and obey his commands, for this is everyone's duty. [14]God will judge us for everything we do, including every secret thing, whether good or bad.

11:9 Hebrew *Young man.*   12:10 Or *sought to write what was upright and true.*   12:11 Or *one shepherd.*   12:12 Hebrew *my son.*

Solomon had some good advice for young people. First, Solomon advised young people to enjoy this time of their lives. Look what he said: *Enjoy every minute of it. Take it all in.* But, he admonished, don't forget about God while you're doing that! Serve and obey God now while you are young. Then you will have a life that is filled with meaning and purpose not only now, but as you grow older.

Don't let anyone think less of you because you are young. Be an example to all believers in what you say, in the way you live, in your love, your faith, and your purity. I TIMOTHY 4:12

MAY 22
GOD'S THRONE

God allowed Isaiah to see what his throne looks like. Notice how Isaiah felt when he saw how holy God is.

Isaiah 6:1-8

It was in the year King Uzziah died* that I saw the Lord. He was sitting on a lofty throne, and the train of his robe filled the Temple. [2]Attending him were mighty seraphim, each having six wings. With two wings they covered their faces, with two they covered their feet, and with two they flew. [3]They were calling out to each other,

"Holy, holy, holy is the LORD of Heaven's Armies!
The whole earth is filled with his glory!"

[4]Their voices shook the Temple to its foundations, and the entire building was filled with smoke.

[5]Then I said, "It's all over! I am doomed, for I am a sinful man. I have filthy lips, and I live among a people with filthy lips. Yet I

have seen the King, the LORD of Heaven's Armies."

⁶Then one of the seraphim flew to me with a burning coal he had taken from the altar with a pair of tongs. ⁷He touched my lips with it and said, "See, this coal

6:1 King Uzziah died in 740 B.C.

has touched your lips. Now your guilt is removed, and your sins are forgiven."

⁸Then I heard the Lord asking, "Whom should I send as a messenger to this people? Who will go for us?"

I said, "Here I am. Send me."

Seeing God was almost too much for Isaiah. God is perfect and wonderful, but that makes people afraid to see him. When humans see God, they realize how sinful and dirty they are. But God makes us clean when we come before him, sorry for our sins. God took away Isaiah's sin and even gave him a special job to do. God wants to do the same for you.

Humble yourselves under the mighty power of God, and at the right time he will lift you up in honor. I PETER 5:6

MAY 23

THE MAN OF SORROWS

Isaiah told us what God's Son, Jesus, would be like hundreds of years before Jesus was born. Would he have an easy life, filled with fun?

Isaiah 53:1-12

Who has believed our message?
  To whom has the LORD revealed his
    powerful arm?
²My servant grew up in the LORD's
    presence like a tender green shoot,
    like a root in dry ground.
There was nothing beautiful or majestic
    about his appearance,
  nothing to attract us to him.
³He was despised and rejected—
  a man of sorrows, acquainted with
    deepest grief.
We turned our backs on him and looked
    the other way.
  He was despised, and we did
    not care.

⁴Yet it was our weaknesses he carried;
  it was our sorrows* that weighed
    him down.
And we thought his troubles were a
    punishment from God,
  a punishment for his own sins!
⁵But he was pierced for our rebellion,
  crushed for our sins.
He was beaten so we could be whole.
  He was whipped so we could be
    healed.
⁶All of us, like sheep, have strayed
    away.
  We have left God's paths to follow
    our own.
Yet the LORD laid on him
  the sins of us all.

7He was oppressed and treated harshly,
  yet he never said a word.
He was led like a lamb to the slaughter.
  And as a sheep is silent before the
    shearers,
  he did not open his mouth.
8Unjustly condemned,
  he was led away.*
No one cared that he died without
    descendants,
  that his life was cut short in
    midstream.*
But he was struck down
  for the rebellion of my people.
9He had done no wrong
  and had never deceived anyone.
But he was buried like a criminal;
  he was put in a rich man's
    grave.

10But it was the LORD's good plan
  to crush him

and cause him grief.
Yet when his life is made an offering
    for sin,
  he will have many descendants.
He will enjoy a long life,
  and the LORD's good plan will prosper
    in his hands.
11When he sees all that is accomplished
    by his anguish,
  he will be satisfied.
And because of his experience,
  my righteous servant will make
    it possible
for many to be counted righteous,
  for he will bear all their sins.
12I will give him the honors of a victorious
    soldier,
  because he exposed himself
    to death.
He was counted among the rebels.
  He bore the sins of many and
    interceded for rebels.

53:4 Or Yet it was our sicknesses he carried; / it was our diseases.   **53:8a** Greek version reads He was humiliated and received no justice. Compare Acts 8:33.   **53:8b** Or As for his contemporaries, / who cared that his life was cut short in midstream? Greek version reads Who can speak of his descendants? / For his life was taken from the earth. Compare Acts 8:33.

God showed Isaiah that Jesus' life would be filled with suffering. But because of Jesus' suffering, amazing things would happen. Jesus took the punishment that we all deserved so that we could be saved. If Jesus had not suffered and died, there would be no way for God to forgive our sins. But when Jesus died and rose again, he made a way for all people to be forgiven and live forever in heaven. That is wonderful news for sinners like us.

[Christ] personally carried our sins in his body on the cross so that we can be dead to sin and live for what is right. By his wounds you are healed. Once you were like sheep who wandered away. But now you have turned to your Shepherd, the Guardian of your souls. I PETER 2:24-25

MAY 24

Jeremiah's Calling

God called Jeremiah to be a prophet and give messages from God to the Israelites. Look at the great promises God gave to Jeremiah.

Jeremiah 1:4-12, 17-19

The LORD gave me this message:

5"I knew you before I formed you in your
mother's womb.
Before you were born I set you apart
and appointed you as my prophet to
the nations."

6"O Sovereign LORD," I said, "I can't
speak for you! I'm too young!"

7The LORD replied, "Don't say, 'I'm too
young,' for you must go wherever I send
you and say whatever I tell you. 8And don't
be afraid of the people, for I will be with
you and will protect you. I, the LORD, have
spoken!" 9Then the LORD reached out and
touched my mouth and said,

"Look, I have put my words in your
mouth!
10Today I appoint you to stand up
against nations and kingdoms.
Some you must uproot and tear down,
destroy and overthrow.
Others you must build up
and plant."

11Then the LORD said to me, "Look, Jeremiah! What do you see?"

And I replied, "I see a branch from an almond tree."

12And the LORD said, "That's right, and it means that I am watching,* and I will certainly carry out all my plans."

17"Get up and prepare for action.
Go out and tell them everything I tell
you to say.
Do not be afraid of them,
or I will make you look foolish in
front of them.
18For see, today I have made you strong
like a fortified city that cannot be
captured,
like an iron pillar or a bronze wall.
You will stand against the whole land—
the kings, officials, priests, and
people of Judah.
19They will fight you, but they will fail.
For I am with you, and I will take care
of you.
I, the LORD, have spoken!"

1:12 The Hebrew word for "watching" (*shoqed*) sounds like the word for "almond tree" (*shaqed*).

Being God's prophet was difficult, and Jeremiah wasn't sure he was up to the task. But God wouldn't accept Jeremiah's excuses. What God did give him was his promise to be with Jeremiah and help him as long as he obeyed. Jeremiah learned that he should be more afraid of disobeying God than of being a prophet. If God wants you to do something you think is scary, remember that he will be with you. What's really scary is disobeying God's commands.

One night the Lord spoke to Paul in a vision and told him, "Don't be afraid! Speak out! Don't be silent! For I am with you, and no one will attack and harm you, for many people in this city belong to me." ACTS 18:9-10

MAY 25

A Book Burning

God gave Jeremiah a message to write down for everyone to read. A lot of people didn't like what the message said. Would they listen to God or would they ignore the message?

Jeremiah 36:1-4, 21-31
During the fourth year that Jehoiakim son of Josiah was king in Judah,* the LORD gave this message to Jeremiah: ²"Get a scroll, and write down all my messages against Israel, Judah, and the other nations. Begin with the first message back in the days of Josiah, and write down every message, right up to the present time. ³Perhaps the people of Judah will repent when they hear again all the terrible things I have planned for them. Then I will be able to forgive their sins and wrongdoings."

⁴So Jeremiah sent for Baruch son of Neriah, and as Jeremiah dictated all the prophecies that the LORD had given him, Baruch wrote them on a scroll.

◉

²¹The king sent Jehudi to get the scroll. Jehudi brought it from Elishama's room and read it to the king as all his officials stood by. ²²It was late autumn, and the king was in a winterized part of the palace, sitting in front of a fire to keep warm. ²³Each time Jehudi finished reading three or four columns, the king took a knife and cut off that section of the scroll. He then threw it into the fire, section by section, until the whole scroll was burned up. ²⁴Neither the king nor his attendants showed any signs of fear or repentance at what they heard. ²⁵Even when Elnathan, Delaiah, and Gemariah begged the king not to burn the scroll, he wouldn't listen.

²⁶Then the king commanded his son Jerahmeel, Seraiah son of Azriel, and Shelemiah son of Abdeel to arrest Baruch and Jeremiah. But the LORD had hidden them.

²⁷After the king had burned the scroll on which Baruch had written Jeremiah's words, the LORD gave Jeremiah another

message. He said, ²⁸"Get another scroll, and write everything again just as you did on the scroll King Jehoiakim burned. ²⁹Then say to the king, 'This is what the LORD says: You burned the scroll because it said the king of Babylon would destroy this land and empty it of people and animals. ³⁰Now this is what the LORD says about King Jehoiakim of Judah: He will have no heirs to sit on the throne of David. His dead body will be thrown out to lie unburied—exposed to the heat of the day and the frost of the night. ³¹I will punish him and his family and his attendants for their sins. I will pour out on them and on all the people of Jerusalem and Judah all the disasters I promised, for they would not listen to my warnings.'"

36:1 The fourth year of Jehoiakim's reign was 605 B.C.

King Jehoiakim didn't like what he heard: *Stop sinning or God will punish you.* So the king cut up God's message and threw the scroll into the fire. But destroying the message didn't make it go away. God would still punish the king for his sins. Sometimes we pretend we can't hear or don't understand when we are warned about doing something wrong. We can choose to ignore it, like the king, but eventually we will have to face the consequences. The best course of action is to listen and obey.

[God's] voice from the cloud said, "This is my Son, my Chosen One.* Listen to him." LUKE 9:35

9:35 Some manuscripts read *This is my dearly loved Son.*

MAY 26

DrY BONES LIVE

God gave Ezekiel a message of hope by showing him a really strange sight. How would you have reacted to Ezekiel's vision?

Ezekiel 37:1-14

The LORD took hold of me, and I was carried away by the Spirit of the LORD to a valley filled with bones. ²He led me all around among the bones that covered the valley floor. They were scattered everywhere across the ground and were completely dried out. ³Then he asked me, "Son of man, can these bones become living people again?"

"O Sovereign LORD," I replied, "you alone know the answer to that."

⁴Then he said to me, "Speak a prophetic message to these bones and say, 'Dry bones, listen to the word of the LORD! ⁵This is what the Sovereign LORD says: Look! I am going to put breath into you and make you live again! ⁶I will put flesh and muscles on you and cover you with skin. I will put breath into you, and you will come to life. Then you will know that I am the LORD.'"

⁷So I spoke this message, just as he told me. Suddenly as I spoke, there was a rattling noise all across the valley. The bones of each body came together and attached themselves as complete skeletons. ⁸Then

as I watched, muscles and flesh formed over the bones. Then skin formed to cover their bodies, but they still had no breath in them.

⁹Then he said to me, "Speak a prophetic message to the winds, son of man. Speak a prophetic message and say, 'This is what the Sovereign LORD says: Come, O breath, from the four winds! Breathe into these dead bodies so they may live again.'"

¹⁰So I spoke the message as he commanded me, and breath came into their bodies. They all came to life and stood up on their feet—a great army.

¹¹Then he said to me, "Son of man, these bones represent the people of Israel. They are saying, 'We have become old, dry bones—all hope is gone. Our nation is finished.' ¹²Therefore, prophesy to them and say, 'This is what the Sovereign LORD says: O my people, I will open your graves of exile and cause you to rise again. Then I will bring you back to the land of Israel. ¹³When this happens, O my people, you will know that I am the LORD. ¹⁴I will put my Spirit in you, and you will live again and return home to your own land. Then you will know that I, the LORD, have spoken, and I have done what I said. Yes, the LORD has spoken!'"

Ezekiel's vision showed that God can restore dead things to life. That's good news for us! Since we all sin, eventually we will die. But God has the power to take dead things and give them new life. That's exactly what happens when we believe in Jesus and he gives us the Holy Spirit. If God gives us new life through the Holy Spirit, death can't hurt us. Isn't that great news?

Even though we were dead because of our sins, [God] gave us life when he raised Christ from the dead. (It is only by God's grace that you have been saved!)
EPHESIANS 2:5

MAY 27

steak or vegetables?

Daniel and his friends had been chosen by the king of Babylon to get the best treatment available, including rich and delicious food. But there was a problem. God had commanded his people not to eat the kind of food the king was serving. What would they do?

Daniel 1:3-5, 8-17
Then the king ordered Ashpenaz, his chief of staff, to bring to the palace some of the young men of Judah's royal family and other noble families, who had been brought to Babylon as captives. ⁴"Select only strong, healthy, and good-looking young men," he said. "Make sure they are well versed in every branch of learning, are gifted with knowledge and good judgment, and are suited to serve in the royal palace. Train these young men in the language and

literature of Babylon.*" ⁵The king assigned them a daily ration of food and wine from his own kitchens. They were to be trained for three years, and then they would enter the royal service.

⁸But Daniel was determined not to defile himself by eating the food and wine given to them by the king. He asked the chief of staff for permission not to eat these unacceptable foods. ⁹Now God had given the chief of staff both respect and affection for Daniel. ¹⁰But he responded, "I am afraid of my lord the king, who has ordered that you eat this food and wine. If you become pale and thin compared to the other youths your age, I am afraid the king will have me beheaded."

¹¹Daniel spoke with the attendant who had been appointed by the chief of staff to look after Daniel, Hananiah, Mishael, and Azariah. ¹²"Please test us for ten days on a diet of vegetables and water," Daniel said. ¹³"At the end of the ten days, see how we look compared to the other young men who are eating the king's food. Then make your decision in light of what you see." ¹⁴The attendant agreed to Daniel's suggestion and tested them for ten days.

¹⁵At the end of the ten days, Daniel and his three friends looked healthier and better nourished than the young men who had been eating the food assigned by the king. ¹⁶So after that, the attendant fed them only vegetables instead of the food and wine provided for the others.

¹⁷God gave these four young men an unusual aptitude for understanding every aspect of literature and wisdom. And God gave Daniel the special ability to interpret the meanings of visions and dreams.

1:4 Or *of the Chaldeans.*

The palace food probably looked really good. But Daniel was determined to obey God by doing the right thing. God was happy with Daniel's choice and blessed him by making him strong, healthy, and smart. Sometimes you might have to give up something that looks good because you know God doesn't want you to have it. But when you obey God, better things will be waiting for you. Just wait and see what God will do when you obey him.

If you look carefully into the perfect law that sets you free, and if you do what it says and don't forget what you heard, then God will bless you for doing it.
JAMES 1:25

MAY 28

Guessing the King's Dream

King Nebuchadnezzar recalled a dream that was really bothering him. He was so desperate to know what it meant that he was ready to start killing people. Would Daniel be able to help?

Daniel 2:1-19

One night during the second year of his reign,* Nebuchadnezzar had such disturbing dreams that he couldn't sleep. ²He called in his magicians, enchanters, sorcerers, and astrologers,* and he demanded that they tell him what he had dreamed. As they stood before the king, ³he said, "I have had a dream that deeply troubles me, and I must know what it means."

⁴Then the astrologers answered the king in Aramaic,* "Long live the king! Tell us the dream, and we will tell you what it means."

⁵But the king said to the astrologers, "I am serious about this. If you don't tell me what my dream was and what it means, you will be torn limb from limb, and your houses will be turned into heaps of rubble! ⁶But if you tell me what I dreamed and what the dream means, I will give you many wonderful gifts and honors. Just tell me the dream and what it means!"

⁷They said again, "Please, Your Majesty. Tell us the dream, and we will tell you what it means."

⁸The king replied, "I know what you are doing! You're stalling for time because you know I am serious when I say, ⁹'If you don't tell me the dream, you are doomed.' So you have conspired to tell me lies, hoping I will change my mind. But tell me the dream, and then I'll know that you can tell me what it means."

¹⁰The astrologers replied to the king, "No one on earth can tell the king his dream! And no king, however great and powerful, has ever asked such a thing of any magician, enchanter, or astrologer! ¹¹The king's demand is impossible. No one except the gods can tell you your dream, and they do not live here among people."

¹²The king was furious when he heard this, and he ordered that all the wise men of Babylon be executed. ¹³And because of the king's decree, men were sent to find and kill Daniel and his friends.

¹⁴When Arioch, the commander of the king's guard, came to kill them, Daniel handled the situation with wisdom and discretion. ¹⁵He asked Arioch, "Why has the king issued such a harsh decree?" So Arioch told him all that had happened. ¹⁶Daniel went at once to see the king and requested more time to tell the king what the dream meant.

¹⁷Then Daniel went home and told his friends Hananiah, Mishael, and Azariah what had happened. ¹⁸He urged them to ask the God of heaven to show them his mercy by telling them the secret, so they would not be executed along with the other wise men of Babylon. ¹⁹That night the secret was revealed to Daniel in a vision. Then Daniel praised the God of heaven.

2:1 The second year of Nebuchadnezzar's reign was 603 B.C.   2:2 Or *Chaldeans;* also in 2:4, 5, 10.   2:4 The original text from this point through chapter 7 is in Aramaic.

King Nebuchadnezzar was serious about killing his wise men if they couldn't tell him about his dream. Daniel knew that the only solution to this problem was prayer. There was no way Daniel (or any of the other wise men) could find out the king's dream and its meaning. But God could. When Daniel asked for God's help, God revealed to him the dream and its meaning. When you have to do something that seems impossible, remember to ask for God's help. He can do things that no one else can.

Keep on asking, and you will receive what you ask for. Keep on seeking, and you will find. Keep on knocking, and the door will be opened to you. MATTHEW 7:7

MAY 29

The Big Gold Statue

King Nebuchadnezzar had made a huge golden statue, and he wanted everyone in his empire to worship it. But Shadrach, Meshach, and Abednego knew that it was wrong to worship anyone but God. What would they do?

Daniel 3:1-18

King Nebuchadnezzar made a gold statue ninety feet tall and nine feet wide* and set it up on the plain of Dura in the province of Babylon. ²Then he sent messages to the high officers, officials, governors, advisers, treasurers, judges, magistrates, and all the provincial officials to come to the dedication of the statue he had set up. ³So all these officials* came and stood before the statue King Nebuchadnezzar had set up.

⁴Then a herald shouted out, "People of all races and nations and languages, listen to the king's command! ⁵When you hear the sound of the horn, flute, zither, lyre, harp, pipes, and other musical instruments,* bow to the ground to worship King Nebuchadnezzar's gold statue. ⁶Anyone who refuses to obey will immediately be thrown into a blazing furnace."

⁷So at the sound of the musical instruments,* all the people, whatever their race or nation or language, bowed to the ground and worshiped the gold statue that King Nebuchadnezzar had set up.

⁸But some of the astrologers* went to the king and informed on the Jews. ⁹They said to King Nebuchadnezzar, "Long live the king! ¹⁰You issued a decree requiring all the people to bow down and worship the gold statue when they hear the sound of the horn, flute, zither, lyre, harp, pipes, and other musical instruments. ¹¹That decree also states that those who refuse to obey must be thrown into a blazing furnace. ¹²But there are some Jews—Shadrach, Meshach, and Abednego—whom you have put in charge of the province of Babylon. They pay no attention to you, Your Majesty. They refuse to serve your gods

196

and do not worship the gold statue you have set up."

[13]Then Nebuchadnezzar flew into a rage and ordered that Shadrach, Meshach, and Abednego be brought before him. When they were brought in, [14]Nebuchadnezzar said to them, "Is it true, Shadrach, Meshach, and Abednego, that you refuse to serve my gods or to worship the gold statue I have set up? [15]I will give you one more chance to bow down and worship the statue I have made when you hear the sound of the musical instruments.* But if you refuse, you will be thrown immediately into the blazing furnace. And then what god will be able to rescue you from my power?"

[16]Shadrach, Meshach, and Abednego replied, "O Nebuchadnezzar, we do not need to defend ourselves before you. [17]If we are thrown into the blazing furnace, the God whom we serve is able to save us. He will rescue us from your power, Your Majesty. [18]But even if he doesn't, we want to make it clear to you, Your Majesty, that we will never serve your gods or worship the gold statue you have set up."

3:1 Aramaic *60 cubits* [27 meters] *tall and 6 cubits* [2.7 meters] *wide.*   3:3 Aramaic *the high officers, officials, governors, advisers, treasurers, judges, magistrates, and all the provincial officials.*   3:5 The identification of some of these musical instruments is uncertain.   3:7 Aramaic *the horn, flute, zither, lyre, harp, and other musical instruments.*   3:8 Aramaic *Chaldeans.*   3:15 Aramaic *the horn, flute, zither, lyre, harp, pipes, and other musical instruments.*

Shadrach, Meshach, and Abednego worshiped only the one true God. They refused to worship the statue, even though they could be killed. Today, there aren't many authorities who would *force* us to worship people or things other than God. But there are many things in our world that we sometimes worship without realizing it—movie stars, sports stars, money, possessions. Putting anything or anyone ahead of God is wrong. Follow the example of Shadrach, Meshach, and Abednego. Worship the one true God.

You must not have any other god but me. You must not make for yourself an idol of any kind or an image of anything in the heavens or on the earth or in the sea. You must not bow down to them or worship them, for I, the LORD your God, am a jealous God who will not tolerate your affection for any other gods. I lay the sins of the parents upon their children; the entire family is affected—even children in the third and fourth generations of those who reject me.
EXODUS 20:3-5

MAY 30

The Burning Furnace

Nebuchadnezzar was serious about throwing Shadrach, Meshach, and Abednego into the fire. Wait till you see what happened to them!

Daniel 3:19-28

Nebuchadnezzar was so furious with Shadrach, Meshach, and Abednego that his face became distorted with rage. He commanded that the furnace be heated seven times hotter than usual. [20]Then he ordered some of the strongest men of his army to bind Shadrach, Meshach, and Abednego and throw them into the blazing furnace. [21]So they tied them up and threw them into the furnace, fully dressed in their pants, turbans, robes, and other garments. [22]And because the king, in his anger, had demanded such a hot fire in the furnace, the flames killed the soldiers as they threw the three men in. [23]So Shadrach, Meshach, and Abednego, securely tied, fell into the roaring flames.

[24]But suddenly, Nebuchadnezzar jumped up in amazement and exclaimed to his advisers, "Didn't we tie up three men and throw them into the furnace?"

"Yes, Your Majesty, we certainly did," they replied.

3:25 Aramaic *like a son of the gods.*

[25]"Look!" Nebuchadnezzar shouted. "I see four men, unbound, walking around in the fire unharmed! And the fourth looks like a god*!"

[26]Then Nebuchadnezzar came as close as he could to the door of the flaming furnace and shouted: "Shadrach, Meshach, and Abednego, servants of the Most High God, come out! Come here!"

So Shadrach, Meshach, and Abednego stepped out of the fire. [27]Then the high officers, officials, governors, and advisers crowded around them and saw that the fire had not touched them. Not a hair on their heads was singed, and their clothing was not scorched. They didn't even smell of smoke!

[28]Then Nebuchadnezzar said, "Praise to the God of Shadrach, Meshach, and Abednego! He sent his angel to rescue his servants who trusted in him. They defied the king's command and were willing to die rather than serve or worship any god except their own God."

For Shadrach, Meshach, and Abednego the decision was easy. They trusted God completely with their lives—furnace or no furnace. God rewarded their trust by protecting them in the raging blaze. Is there a situation in which you need to trust God completely? You may never get thrown into a blazing furnace, but God is still there for you. He cares about you and will not abandon you. Ever.

[Jesus said,] "Don't let your hearts be troubled. Trust in God, and trust also in me."
JOHN 14:1

MAY 31

A King Eats Grass

King Nebuchadnezzar was so proud of himself that he thought he didn't have to honor God. Then God taught him to be humble in an unexpected way.

Daniel 4:29-37

Twelve months later [King Nebuchadnezzar] was taking a walk on the flat roof of the royal palace in Babylon. ³⁰As he looked out across the city, he said, "Look at this great city of Babylon! By my own mighty power, I have built this beautiful city as my royal residence to display my majestic splendor."

³¹While these words were still in his mouth, a voice called down from heaven, "O King Nebuchadnezzar, this message is for you! You are no longer ruler of this kingdom. ³²You will be driven from human society. You will live in the fields with the wild animals, and you will eat grass like a cow. Seven periods of time will pass while you live this way, until you learn that the Most High rules over the kingdoms of the world and gives them to anyone he chooses."

³³That same hour the judgment was fulfilled, and Nebuchadnezzar was driven from human society. He ate grass like a cow, and he was drenched with the dew of heaven. He lived this way until his hair was as long as eagles' feathers and his nails were like birds' claws.

³⁴After this time had passed, I, Nebuchadnezzar, looked up to heaven. My sanity returned, and I praised and worshiped the Most High and honored the one who lives forever.

His rule is everlasting,
and his kingdom is eternal.
³⁵All the people of the earth
are nothing compared to
him.
He does as he pleases
among the angels of heaven
and among the people of the earth.
No one can stop him or say to him,
"What do you mean by doing these
things?"

³⁶When my sanity returned to me, so did my honor and glory and kingdom. My advisers and nobles sought me out, and I was restored as head of my kingdom, with even greater honor than before.

³⁷Now I, Nebuchadnezzar, praise and glorify and honor the King of heaven. All his acts are just and true, and he is able to humble the proud.

God showed Nebuchadnezzar that without God's help, the king was no better than an animal. Everything we have and everything we can do are gifts from God. It's silly to brag about what God has given us. Besides, he can find unexpected ways to humble us, too. The best thing we can do is thank him for his gifts. What are you thankful for?

Those who exalt themselves will be humbled, and those who humble themselves will be exalted. MATTHEW 23:12

MAY CHALLENGE
way to go!

This month is a time for picnics and parades, so strike up the band for the great job you are doing! To show that you've finished the May readings, find a marker or highlighter in a spring color and fill in the level you reached this month.

You have been reading many of the psalms, which are like songs and prayers. Go back and find a psalm for a happy day. Find another psalm for a down day. Then read a favorite one to a younger brother or sister. Or read one as a prayer to God.

IMPORTANT STUFF TO REMEMBER FROM MAY

☐ God loves it when his people praise him.

☐ God is perfect and holy.

☐ God wants us to be wise—to understand what's right so we can please him by the way we live.

☐ God helps us do what he wants us to do.

Time for some word fun!

During this month, you read about Esther, a brave young Jewish woman who became the queen of a foreign kingdom and risked her life to save her people. Unscramble the words below to remember who Esther was and how she became queen. (Look at the passage for May 2 to check your answers.)

1. All the beautiful young girls of the kingdom were brought to

__ __ __ __ __ __' palace in __ __ __ __.
S X R E X E   U S A S

2. Esther's Jewish name was __ __ __ __ __ __ __ __, and her cousin's name was
           S H D A H A S A

__ __ __ __ __ __ __ __. They were from the tribe of __ __ __ __ __ __ __ __.
D A O M C E R I   J I N B M E A N

3. After being chosen by the king, Esther received twelve months of

__ __ __ __ __ __ treatments and a special __ __ __ __ .
U A Y T E B   U M N E

4. Esther was so beautiful, the king gave her the __ __ __ __ __ __ __ __ __ __ and
           Y L O A R   N R O C W

made her queen instead of __ __ __ __ __ __.
        T V A I H S

5. After becoming queen, Esther kept her __ __ __ __ __ __ __ __ __ __ a secret.
        K R U D A C O G N B

JUNE 1

writing on the wall

King Belshazzar didn't pay any attention to the lesson his father Nebuchadnezzar had learned about honoring God. God sent a message in a way that really got Belshazzar's attention!

Daniel 5:1-6, 13-30

Many years later King Belshazzar gave a great feast for 1,000 of his nobles, and he drank wine with them. ²While Belshazzar was drinking the wine, he gave orders to bring in the gold and silver cups that his predecessor,* Nebuchadnezzar, had taken from the Temple in Jerusalem. He wanted to drink from them with his nobles, his wives, and his concubines. ³So they brought these gold cups taken from the Temple, the house of God in Jerusalem, and the king and his nobles, his wives, and his concubines drank from them. ⁴While they drank from them they praised their idols made of gold, silver, bronze, iron, wood, and stone.

⁵Suddenly, they saw the fingers of a human hand writing on the plaster wall of the king's palace, near the lampstand. The king himself saw the hand as it wrote, ⁶and his face turned pale with fright. His knees knocked together in fear and his legs gave way beneath him.

⊙

¹³So Daniel was brought in before the king. The king asked him, "Are you Dan-iel, one of the exiles brought from Judah by my predecessor, King Nebuchadnezzar? ¹⁴I have heard that you have the spirit of the gods within you and that you are filled with insight, understanding, and wisdom. ¹⁵My wise men and enchanters have tried to read the words on the wall and tell me their meaning, but they cannot do it. ¹⁶I am told that you can give interpretations and solve difficult problems. If you can read these words and tell me their meaning, you will be clothed in purple robes of royal honor, and you will have a gold chain placed around your neck. You will become the third highest ruler in the kingdom."

¹⁷Daniel answered the king, "Keep your gifts or give them to someone else, but I will tell you what the writing means. ¹⁸Your Majesty, the Most High God gave sovereignty, majesty, glory, and honor to your predecessor, Nebuchadnezzar. ¹⁹He made him so great that people of all races and nations and languages trembled before him in fear. He killed those he wanted to kill and spared those he wanted to spare. He honored those he wanted to honor and

disgraced those he wanted to disgrace. [20]But when his heart and mind were puffed up with arrogance, he was brought down from his royal throne and stripped of his glory. [21]He was driven from human society. He was given the mind of a wild animal, and he lived among the wild donkeys. He ate grass like a cow, and he was drenched with the dew of heaven, until he learned that the Most High God rules over the kingdoms of the world and appoints anyone he desires to rule over them.

[22]"You are his successor,* O Belshazzar, and you knew all this, yet you have not humbled yourself. [23]For you have proudly defied the Lord of heaven and have had these cups from his Temple brought before you. You and your nobles and your wives and concubines have been drinking wine from them while praising gods of silver, gold, bronze, iron, wood, and stone—gods that neither see nor hear nor know anything at all. But you have not honored the God who gives you the breath of life and controls your destiny! [24]So God has sent this hand to write this message.

[25]"This is the message that was written: Mene, Mene, Tekel, and Parsin. [26]This is what these words mean:

Mene means 'numbered'—God has numbered the days of your reign and has brought it to an end.

[27]Tekel means 'weighed'—you have been weighed on the balances and have not measured up.

[28]Parsin* means 'divided'—your kingdom has been divided and given to the Medes and Persians."

[29]Then at Belshazzar's command, Daniel was dressed in purple robes, a gold chain was hung around his neck, and he was proclaimed the third highest ruler in the kingdom.

[30]That very night Belshazzar, the Babylonian* king, was killed.*

5:2 Aramaic *father;* also in 5:13, 18.   5:22 Aramaic *son.*   5:28 Aramaic *Peres,* the singular of *Parsin.*   5:30a Or *Chaldean.*
5:30b The Persians and Medes conquered Babylon in October 539 B.C.

God had a message for Belshazzar—time's up! The king had refused to honor God, so God decided to take away Belshazzar's kingdom. The message is clear for us as well. God opposes those who choose to ignore and defy him. But God will guide and support all who honor him. Choose to honor God today with your worship and your obedience.

All praise to God, the Father of our Lord Jesus Christ. It is by his great mercy that we have been born again, because God raised Jesus Christ from the dead.
1 Peter 1:3

204

JUNE 2

fault finders

God made Daniel very good at his job. King Darius was so pleased with Daniel that he wanted to put him in charge of the whole empire. But some people were jealous of Daniel. Would they find a way to get him in trouble?

Daniel 6:1-10

*Darius the Mede decided to divide the kingdom into 120 provinces, and he appointed a high officer to rule over each province. ²The king also chose Daniel and two others as administrators to supervise the high officers and protect the king's interests. ³Daniel soon proved himself more capable than all the other administrators and high officers. Because of Daniel's great ability, the king made plans to place him over the entire empire.

⁴Then the other administrators and high officers began searching for some fault in the way Daniel was handling government affairs, but they couldn't find anything to criticize or condemn. He was faithful, always responsible, and completely trustworthy. ⁵So they concluded, "Our only chance of finding grounds for accusing Daniel will be in connection with the rules of his religion."

6:1 Verses 6:1-28 are numbered 6:2-29 in Aramaic text.

⁶So the administrators and high officers went to the king and said, "Long live King Darius! ⁷We are all in agreement— we administrators, officials, high officers, advisers, and governors—that the king should make a law that will be strictly enforced. Give orders that for the next thirty days any person who prays to anyone, divine or human—except to you, Your Majesty—will be thrown into the den of lions. ⁸And now, Your Majesty, issue and sign this law so it cannot be changed, an official law of the Medes and Persians that cannot be revoked." ⁹So King Darius signed the law.

¹⁰But when Daniel learned that the law had been signed, he went home and knelt down as usual in his upstairs room, with its windows open toward Jerusalem. He prayed three times a day, just as he had always done, giving thanks to his God.

Daniel's enemies knew they couldn't find fault in his work or behavior. So they attacked his faith. They convinced the king to pass a law that banned praying to anyone but the king. But that didn't stop Daniel from doing what he knew was right—praying to God. Others may try to prevent us from doing what is right. Like Daniel, we need to follow God and his ways—no matter what the cost.

Live clean, innocent lives as children of God, shining like bright lights in a world full of crooked and perverse people. PHILIPPIANS 2:15

JUNE 3

HUNGRY LIONS

Daniel was arrested and thrown into the lions' den for praying to God. Would he survive the night?

Daniel 6:11-27

Then the officials went together to Daniel's house and found him praying and asking for God's help. [12]So they went straight to the king and reminded him about his law. "Did you not sign a law that for the next thirty days any person who prays to anyone, divine or human—except to you, Your Majesty—will be thrown into the den of lions?"

"Yes," the king replied, "that decision stands; it is an official law of the Medes and Persians that cannot be revoked."

[13]Then they told the king, "That man Daniel, one of the captives from Judah, is ignoring you and your law. He still prays to his God three times a day."

[14]Hearing this, the king was deeply troubled, and he tried to think of a way to save Daniel. He spent the rest of the day looking for a way to get Daniel out of this predicament.

[15]In the evening the men went together to the king and said, "Your Majesty, you know that according to the law of the Medes and the Persians, no law that the king signs can be changed."

[16]So at last the king gave orders for Daniel to be arrested and thrown into the den of lions. The king said to him, "May your God, whom you serve so faithfully, rescue you."

[17]A stone was brought and placed over the mouth of the den. The king sealed the stone with his own royal seal and the seals of his nobles, so that no one could rescue Daniel. [18]Then the king returned to his palace and spent the night fasting. He refused his usual entertainment and couldn't sleep at all that night.

[19]Very early the next morning, the king got up and hurried out to the lions' den. [20]When he got there, he called out in anguish, "Daniel, servant of the living God!

Was your God, whom you serve so faithfully, able to rescue you from the lions?"

²¹Daniel answered, "Long live the king! ²²My God sent his angel to shut the lions' mouths so that they would not hurt me, for I have been found innocent in his sight. And I have not wronged you, Your Majesty."

²³The king was overjoyed and ordered that Daniel be lifted from the den. Not a scratch was found on him, for he had trusted in his God.

²⁴Then the king gave orders to arrest the men who had maliciously accused Daniel. He had them thrown into the lions' den, along with their wives and children. The lions leaped on them and tore them apart before they even hit the floor of the den.

²⁵Then King Darius sent this message to the people of every race and nation and language throughout the world:

"Peace and prosperity to you!
    ²⁶"I decree that everyone throughout my kingdom should tremble with fear before the God of Daniel.

For he is the living God,
    and he will endure forever.
His kingdom will never be
    destroyed,
    and his rule will never end.
²⁷He rescues and saves his people;
    he performs miraculous signs
    and wonders
    in the heavens and on earth.
He has rescued Daniel
    from the power of the lions."

Because Daniel trusted God, he was kept safe from the hungry lions. And when the king saw that Daniel was okay, he praised God too. When you trust and obey God, he will take care of you. And other people will learn to praise God also. Thank God for the way he protects you.

The Lord will deliver me from every evil attack and will bring me safely into his heavenly Kingdom. All glory to God forever and ever! Amen. 2 TIMOTHY 4:18

JUNE 4

on the run

God wanted Jonah to go to Nineveh and tell the people to repent. But Jonah didn't want to go. Do you think he was able to run away from God?

Jonah 1:1-15

The LORD gave this message to Jonah son of Amittai: ²"Get up and go to the great city of Nineveh. Announce my judgment against it because I have seen how wicked its people are."

³But Jonah got up and went in the oppo-site direction to get away from the LORD. He went down to the port of Joppa, where he found a ship leaving for Tarshish. He bought a ticket and went on board, hoping to escape from the LORD by sailing to Tarshish.

⁴But the LORD hurled a powerful wind

207

over the sea, causing a violent storm that threatened to break the ship apart. ⁵Fearing for their lives, the desperate sailors shouted to their gods for help and threw the cargo overboard to lighten the ship.

But all this time Jonah was sound asleep down in the hold. ⁶So the captain went down after him. "How can you sleep at a time like this?" he shouted. "Get up and pray to your god! Maybe he will pay attention to us and spare our lives."

⁷Then the crew cast lots to see which of them had offended the gods and caused the terrible storm. When they did this, the lots identified Jonah as the culprit. ⁸"Why has this awful storm come down on us?" they demanded. "Who are you? What is your line of work? What country are you from? What is your nationality?"

⁹Jonah answered, "I am a Hebrew, and I worship the LORD, the God of heaven, who made the sea and the land."

¹⁰The sailors were terrified when they heard this, for he had already told them he was running away from the LORD. "Oh, why did you do it?" they groaned. ¹¹And since the storm was getting worse all the time, they asked him, "What should we do to you to stop this storm?"

¹²"Throw me into the sea," Jonah said, "and it will become calm again. I know that this terrible storm is all my fault."

¹³Instead, the sailors rowed even harder to get the ship to the land. But the stormy sea was too violent for them, and they couldn't make it. ¹⁴Then they cried out to the LORD, Jonah's God. "O LORD," they pleaded, "don't make us die for this man's sin. And don't hold us responsible for his death. O LORD, you have sent this storm upon him for your own good reasons."

¹⁵Then the sailors picked Jonah up and threw him into the raging sea, and the storm stopped at once!

Jonah tried to run from God. But he didn't get very far. After experiencing a terrible storm at sea and being thrown overboard, Jonah learned that running from God only got him into more trouble. Next time you're thinking about disobeying God, remember Jonah. Running *from* God means running *toward* trouble.

Be careful then, dear brothers and sisters. Make sure that your own hearts are not evil and unbelieving, turning you away from the living God.* HEBREWS 3:12

3:12 Greek *brothers.*

JUNE 5

A Fish Full

After Jonah was thrown out of the boat, a huge fish swallowed him. How do you think it felt to be inside a fish's belly?

Jonah 1:17–2:10

*Now the LORD had arranged for a great fish to swallow Jonah. And Jonah was inside the fish for three days and three nights. 2:1*Then Jonah prayed to the LORD his God from inside the fish. 2He said,

"I cried out to the LORD in my great
  trouble,
  and he answered me.
I called to you from the land of the dead,*
  and LORD, you heard me!
3You threw me into the ocean depths,
  and I sank down to the heart
    of the sea.
The mighty waters engulfed me;
  I was buried beneath your wild and
    stormy waves.
4Then I said, 'O LORD, you have driven
  me from your presence.
  Yet I will look once more toward your
    holy Temple.'
5"I sank beneath the waves,
  and the waters closed over me.

Seaweed wrapped itself around
  my head.
6I sank down to the very roots of the
  mountains.
I was imprisoned in the earth,
  whose gates lock shut forever.
But you, O LORD my God,
  snatched me from the jaws
    of death!
7As my life was slipping away,
  I remembered the LORD.
And my earnest prayer went out to you
  in your holy Temple.
8Those who worship false gods
  turn their backs on all God's
    mercies.
9But I will offer sacrifices to you with
  songs of praise,
  and I will fulfill all my vows.
  For my salvation comes from the
    LORD alone."

10Then the LORD ordered the fish to spit Jonah out onto the beach.

1:17 Verse 1:17 is numbered 2:1 in Hebrew text.   **2:1** Verses 2:1-10 are numbered 2:2-11 in Hebrew text.   **2:2** Hebrew *from Sheol.*

Jonah was not too comfortable. He was inside a fish! Jonah thought he was as good as dead. But then he prayed to God. God heard his prayer and rescued him from the fish. When you are in trouble, pray to God. He is powerful enough to save you from any bad situation.

Pray in the Spirit at all times and on every occasion. Stay alert and be persistent in your prayers for all believers everywhere. EPHESIANS 6:18

JUNE 6

news for nineveh

For the second time, God told Jonah to go to Nineveh. Would he listen now?

Jonah 3:1-10

Then the LORD spoke to Jonah a second time: ²"Get up and go to the great city of Nineveh, and deliver the message I have given you."

³This time Jonah obeyed the LORD's command and went to Nineveh, a city so large that it took three days to see it all.* ⁴On the day Jonah entered the city, he shouted to the crowds: "Forty days from now Nineveh will be destroyed!" ⁵The people of Nineveh believed God's message, and from the greatest to the least, they declared a fast and put on burlap to show their sorrow.

⁶When the king of Nineveh heard what Jonah was saying, he stepped down from his throne and took off his royal robes. He dressed himself in burlap and sat on a heap of ashes. ⁷Then the king and his nobles sent this decree throughout the city:

"No one, not even the animals from your herds and flocks, may eat or drink anything at all. ⁸People and animals alike must wear garments of mourning, and everyone must pray earnestly to God. They must turn from their evil ways and stop all their violence. ⁹Who can tell? Perhaps even yet God will change his mind and hold back his fierce anger from destroying us."

¹⁰When God saw what they had done and how they had put a stop to their evil ways, he changed his mind and did not carry out the destruction he had threatened.

3:3 Hebrew *a great city to God, of three days' journey.*

Jonah finally learned his lesson after his adventure with the storm and the big fish. This time when God said "Go," Jonah obeyed and went to Nineveh. The people of Nineveh listened to Jonah's message and turned away from their sin. So God forgave them instead of punishing them. We can help others too by telling them about God's great love and forgiveness. Is there someone you can share God's forgiveness with today?

The Lord isn't really being slow about his promise, as some people think. No, he is being patient for your sake. He does not want anyone to be destroyed, but wants everyone to repent. 2 PETER 3:9

JUNE 7

A Hungry Worm

When the Ninevites repented, Jonah wasn't happy. He wanted God to destroy the city the way he had threatened to do. But God taught Jonah an important lesson. Read and see.

Jonah 4:1-11

This change of plans greatly upset Jonah, and he became very angry. ²So he complained to the LORD about it: "Didn't I say before I left home that you would do this, LORD? That is why I ran away to Tarshish! I knew that you are a merciful and compassionate God, slow to get angry and filled with unfailing love. You are eager to turn back from destroying people. ³Just kill me now, LORD! I'd rather be dead than alive if what I predicted will not happen."

⁴The LORD replied, "Is it right for you to be angry about this?"

⁵Then Jonah went out to the east side of the city and made a shelter to sit under as he waited to see what would happen to the city. ⁶And the LORD God arranged for a leafy plant to grow there, and soon it spread its broad leaves over Jonah's head, shading him from the sun. This eased his discomfort, and Jonah was very grateful for the plant.

⁷But God also arranged for a worm! The next morning at dawn the worm ate through the stem of the plant so that it withered away. ⁸And as the sun grew hot, God arranged for a scorching east wind to blow on Jonah. The sun beat down on his head until he grew faint and wished to die. "Death is certainly better than living like this!" he exclaimed.

⁹Then God said to Jonah, "Is it right for you to be angry because the plant died?"

"Yes," Jonah retorted, "even angry enough to die!"

¹⁰Then the LORD said, "You feel sorry about the plant, though you did nothing to put it there. It came quickly and died quickly. ¹¹But Nineveh has more than 120,000 people living in spiritual darkness,* not to mention all the animals. Shouldn't I feel sorry for such a great city?"

4:11 Hebrew *people who don't know their right hand from their left.*

Jonah was very upset when God forgave the people of Nineveh. He was even more upset when the plant God gave to shelter him died. But God used the plant to teach Jonah what was most valuable—people! Sometimes we're like Jonah. We're concerned about our stuff or our reputation or our comfort rather than the people around us. God loves and cares about all people. He wants us to do the same.

We know what real love is because Jesus gave up his life for us. So we also ought to give up our lives for our brothers and sisters. I JOHN 3:16

JUNE 8

The Angel and Zechariah

While Zechariah was working in the Temple, an angel appeared and gave him a message from God. Would Zechariah believe what the angel said?

Luke 1:11-25

While Zechariah was in the sanctuary, an angel of the Lord appeared to him, standing to the right of the incense altar. ¹²Zechariah was shaken and overwhelmed with fear when he saw him. ¹³But the angel said, "Don't be afraid, Zechariah! God has heard your prayer. Your wife, Elizabeth, will give you a son, and you are to name him John. ¹⁴You will have great joy and gladness, and many will rejoice at his birth, ¹⁵for he will be great in the eyes of the Lord. He must never touch wine or other alcoholic drinks. He will be filled with the Holy Spirit, even before his birth.* ¹⁶And he will turn many Israelites to the Lord their God. ¹⁷He will be a man with the spirit and power of Elijah. He will prepare the people for the coming of the Lord. He will turn the hearts of the fathers to their children,* and he will cause those who are rebellious to accept the wisdom of the godly."

¹⁸Zechariah said to the angel, "How can I be sure this will happen? I'm an old man now, and my wife is also well along in years."

¹⁹Then the angel said, "I am Gabriel! I stand in the very presence of God. It was he who sent me to bring you this good news! ²⁰But now, since you didn't believe what I said, you will be silent and unable to speak until the child is born. For my words will certainly be fulfilled at the proper time."

²¹Meanwhile, the people were waiting for Zechariah to come out of the sanctuary, wondering why he was taking so long. ²²When he finally did come out, he couldn't speak to them. Then they realized from his gestures and his silence that he must have seen a vision in the sanctuary.

²³When Zechariah's week of service in the Temple was over, he returned home. ²⁴Soon afterward his wife, Elizabeth, became pregnant and went into seclusion for five months. ²⁵"How kind the Lord is!" she exclaimed. "He has taken away my disgrace of having no children."

1:15 Or *even from birth.* 1:17 See Mal 4:5-6.

Zechariah was amazed. He couldn't believe that God would bless him and his wife with a child in their old age. But this priest learned the hard way that nothing is impossible with God. Because of his unbelief, Zechariah couldn't speak until after his child was born. We can learn from Zechariah's experience. When God says he will do something, believe it! God is able to do what he says.

I am the LORD, the God of all the peoples of the world. Is anything too hard for me? JEREMIAH 32:27

JUNE 9

The Angel and Mary

The angel Gabriel appeared to Mary with some amazing news. Would she believe his message?

Luke 1:26-38

In the sixth month of Elizabeth's pregnancy, God sent the angel Gabriel to Nazareth, a village in Galilee, 27to a virgin named Mary. She was engaged to be married to a man named Joseph, a descendant of King David. 28Gabriel appeared to her and said, "Greetings, favored woman! The Lord is with you!*"

29Confused and disturbed, Mary tried to think what the angel could mean. 30"Don't be afraid, Mary," the angel told her, "for you have found favor with God! 31You will conceive and give birth to a son, and you will name him Jesus. 32He will be very great and will be called the Son of the Most High. The Lord God will give him the throne of his ancestor David. 33And he will reign over Israel* forever; his Kingdom will never end!"

34Mary asked the angel, "But how can this happen? I am a virgin."

35The angel replied, "The Holy Spirit will come upon you, and the power of the Most High will overshadow you. So the baby to be born will be holy, and he will be called the Son of God. 36What's more, your relative Elizabeth has become pregnant in her old age! People used to say she was barren, but she's now in her sixth month. 37For nothing is impossible with God.*"

38Mary responded, "I am the Lord's servant. May everything you have said about me come true." And then the angel left her.

1:28 Some manuscripts add *Blessed are you among women.* 1:33 Greek *over the house of Jacob.* 1:37 Some manuscripts read *For the word of God will never fail.*

What a difference between Zechariah's and Mary's responses! When the angel spoke to Mary, she believed him right away and made herself available for God to use. God wants to use all his followers for his service. But he never forces anyone to serve him. The choice is ours. Mary chose to serve God and was greatly blessed for it. You can serve God too. He wants to bless you.

Serve only the LORD your God and fear him alone. Obey his commands, listen to his voice, and cling to him. DEUTERONOMY 13:4

JUNE 10

John's Birth

God's promise came true, and Elizabeth and Zechariah had a son. How did Zechariah respond to God's gift?

Luke 1:57-68

When it was time for Elizabeth's baby to be born, she gave birth to a son. ⁵⁸And when her neighbors and relatives heard that the Lord had been very merciful to her, everyone rejoiced with her.

⁵⁹When the baby was eight days old, they all came for the circumcision ceremony. They wanted to name him Zechariah, after his father. ⁶⁰But Elizabeth said, "No! His name is John!"

⁶¹"What?" they exclaimed. "There is no one in all your family by that name." ⁶²So they used gestures to ask the baby's father what he wanted to name him. ⁶³He motioned for a writing tablet, and to everyone's surprise he wrote, "His name is John." ⁶⁴Instantly Zechariah could speak again, and he began praising God.

⁶⁵Awe fell upon the whole neighborhood, and the news of what had happened spread throughout the Judean hills. ⁶⁶Everyone who heard about it reflected on these events and asked, "What will this child turn out to be?" For the hand of the Lord was surely upon him in a special way.

⁶⁷Then his father, Zechariah, was filled with the Holy Spirit and gave this prophecy:

⁶⁸"Praise the Lord, the God of Israel,
because he has visited and redeemed his people."

Zechariah thanked God for giving him a son. In fact, the first words out of Zechariah's mouth after his son was born were words of praise. What has God given you? You can thank him for everything—from the food on your plate to the clothes you wear. Like Zechariah, tell God thank you today for what he has given you.

Give thanks to the LORD, for he is good! His faithful love endures forever.
PSALM 118:29

JUNE 11

An Angel and Joseph

An angel had an important message for Joseph. What did the angel tell him?

Matthew 1:18-25

This is how Jesus the Messiah was born. His mother, Mary, was engaged to be married to Joseph. But before the marriage took place, while she was still a virgin, she became pregnant through the power of the Holy Spirit. ¹⁹Joseph, her fiancé, was a good man and did not want to disgrace her publicly, so he decided to break the engagement* quietly.

²⁰As he considered this, an angel of the Lord appeared to him in a dream. "Joseph, son of David," the angel said, "do not be afraid to take Mary as your wife. For the child within her was conceived by the Holy Spirit. ²¹And she will have a son, and you are to name him Jesus,* for he will save his people from their sins."

²²All of this occurred to fulfill the Lord's message through his prophet:

²³"Look! The virgin will conceive a child!
    She will give birth to a son,
and they will call him Immanuel,*
    which means 'God is with us.'"

²⁴When Joseph woke up, he did as the angel of the Lord commanded and took Mary as his wife. ²⁵But he did not have sexual relations with her until her son was born. And Joseph named him Jesus.

1:19 Greek *to divorce her.*   1:21 *Jesus* means "The LORD saves."   1:23 Isa 7:14; 8:8, 10 (Greek version).

Joseph did not want Mary to be his wife after he found out she was pregnant. He didn't know that God was doing something huge and amazing. After the angel told him what was happening, things started to make more sense for Joseph and he did what God said. Sometimes we don't understand why things in life seem to go wrong. But God may be doing something wonderful that we just don't know about yet. We need to be ready to hear from God and obey him.

I listen carefully to what God the LORD is saying, for he speaks peace to his faithful people. But let them not return to their foolish ways. PSALM 85:8

JUNE 12

JESUS IS BORN

On the night Jesus was born, some special and unusual things happened. Who were the first people to worship Jesus?

Luke 2:4-20

And because Joseph was a descendant of King David, he had to go to Bethlehem in Judea, David's ancient home. He traveled there from the village of Nazareth in Galilee. ⁵He took with him Mary, his fiancée, who was now obviously pregnant.

⁶And while they were there, the time came for her baby to be born. ⁷She gave birth to her first child, a son. She wrapped him snugly in strips of cloth and laid him in a manger, because there was no lodging available for them.

⁸That night there were shepherds staying in the fields nearby, guarding their flocks of sheep. ⁹Suddenly, an angel of the Lord appeared among them, and the radiance of the Lord's glory surrounded them. They were terrified, ¹⁰but the angel reassured them. "Don't be afraid!" he said. "I bring you good news that will bring great joy to all people. ¹¹The Savior—yes, the Messiah, the Lord—has been born today in Bethlehem, the city of David! ¹²And you will recognize him by this sign: You will find a baby wrapped snugly in strips of cloth, lying in a manger."

¹³Suddenly, the angel was joined by a vast host of others—the armies of heaven—praising God and saying,

¹⁴"Glory to God in highest heaven,
    and peace on earth to those with
        whom God is pleased."

¹⁵When the angels had returned to heaven, the shepherds said to each other, "Let's go to Bethlehem! Let's see this thing that has happened, which the Lord has told us about."

¹⁶They hurried to the village and found Mary and Joseph. And there was the baby, lying in the manger. ¹⁷After seeing him, the

shepherds told everyone what had happened and what the angel had said to them about this child. [18]All who heard the shepherds' story were astonished, [19]but Mary kept all these things in her heart and thought about them often. [20]The shepherds went back to their flocks, glorifying and praising God for all they had heard and seen. It was just as the angel had told them.

When the shepherds heard the angels' amazing announcement, they immediately went to find Jesus. After they had found him, the shepherds told everyone they met about what they had heard and seen. Then they went back to the fields, praising God. How have you responded to Jesus' birth? Who have you told about Jesus? When have you thanked God for his Son? Don't wait for Christmas. Take time to celebrate Jesus' birth today!

Praise the Lord; praise God our savior! For each day he carries us in his arms.
PSALM 68:19

JUNE 13

A Long Wait

Simeon had waited a long time to see Jesus, the promised Savior. Look what Simeon said when he finally saw Jesus.

Luke 2:21-35

Eight days later, when the baby was circumcised, he was named Jesus, the name given him by the angel even before he was conceived.

[22]Then it was time for their purification offering, as required by the law of Moses after the birth of a child; so his parents took him to Jerusalem to present him to the Lord. [23]The law of the Lord says, "If a woman's first child is a boy, he must be dedicated to the LORD."* [24]So they offered the sacrifice required in the law of the Lord—"either a pair of turtledoves or two young pigeons."*

[25]At that time there was a man in Jerusalem named Simeon. He was righteous and devout and was eagerly waiting for the Messiah to come and rescue Israel. The Holy Spirit was upon him [26]and had revealed to him that he would not die until he had seen the Lord's Messiah. [27]That day the Spirit led him to the Temple. So when Mary and Joseph came to present the baby Jesus to the Lord as the law required, [28]Simeon was there. He took the child in his arms and praised God, saying,

[29]"Sovereign Lord, now let your servant
     die in peace,
   as you have promised.
[30]I have seen your salvation,
     [31]which you have prepared for all
       people.
[32]He is a light to reveal God to the nations,
     and he is the glory of your people
       Israel!"

³³Jesus' parents were amazed at what was being said about him. ³⁴Then Simeon blessed them, and he said to Mary, the baby's mother, "This child is destined to cause many in Israel to fall, but he will be a joy to many others. He has been sent as a sign from God, but many will oppose him. ³⁵As a result, the deepest thoughts of many hearts will be revealed. And a sword will pierce your very soul."

2:23 Exod 13:2. 2:24 Lev 12:8.

Simeon was very happy that God's promise to him was finally coming true. And he was overjoyed that God's Savior had come. He praised God that Jesus would save people from their sins. Isn't it wonderful that God kept his promise and sent us a Savior? You can praise God for Jesus just as Simeon did!

I thank you for answering my prayer and giving me victory! PSALM 118:21

JUNE 14

THE WISE MEN

Wise men came from far away to worship Jesus. See how happy they were when they finally found him.

Matthew 2:1-12

Jesus was born in Bethlehem in Judea, during the reign of King Herod. About that time some wise men* from eastern lands arrived in Jerusalem, asking, ²"Where is the newborn king of the Jews? We saw his star as it rose,* and we have come to worship him."

³King Herod was deeply disturbed when he heard this, as was everyone in Jerusalem. ⁴He called a meeting of the leading priests and teachers of religious law and asked, "Where is the Messiah supposed to be born?"

⁵"In Bethlehem in Judea," they said, "for this is what the prophet wrote:

⁶'And you, O Bethlehem in the land of Judah,
    are not least among the ruling cities* of Judah,

for a ruler will come from you
    who will be the shepherd for my people Israel.'*"

⁷Then Herod called for a private meeting with the wise men, and he learned from them the time when the star first appeared. ⁸Then he told them, "Go to Bethlehem and search carefully for the child. And when you find him, come back and tell me so that I can go and worship him, too!"

⁹After this interview the wise men went their way. And the star they had seen in the east guided them to Bethlehem. It went ahead of them and stopped over the place where the child was. ¹⁰When they saw the star, they were filled with joy! ¹¹They entered the house and saw the child with his mother, Mary, and they bowed down and worshiped him. Then they opened their

218

treasure chests and gave him gifts of gold, frankincense, and myrrh.

¹²When it was time to leave, they returned to their own country by another route, for God had warned them in a dream not to return to Herod.

2:1 Or *royal astrologers;* Greek reads *magi;* also in 2:7.   2:2 Or *star in the east.*   2:6a Greek *the rulers.*   2:6b Mic 5:2; 2 Sam 5:2.

The wise men had traveled far. They were determined to find the newborn king and worship him. When they saw Jesus, they bowed before him and gave him gifts chosen for him as king. How do you worship Jesus? Follow the wise men's example and give Jesus gifts that are good enough for the King of kings—your obedience and your love!

Come, let us worship and bow down. Let us kneel before the LORD our maker.
PSALM 95:6

JUNE 15

escape to egypt

Herod said he wanted to worship Jesus, but that wasn't what he really wanted to do. How would Mary and Joseph protect their son from Herod's plan to kill him?

Matthew 2:13-23

After the wise men were gone, an angel of the Lord appeared to Joseph in a dream. "Get up! Flee to Egypt with the child and his mother," the angel said. "Stay there until I tell you to return, because Herod is going to search for the child to kill him."

¹⁴That night Joseph left for Egypt with the child and Mary, his mother, ¹⁵and they stayed there until Herod's death. This fulfilled what the Lord had spoken through the prophet: "I called my Son out of Egypt."*

¹⁶Herod was furious when he realized that the wise men had outwitted him. He sent soldiers to kill all the boys in and around Bethlehem who were two years old and under, based on the wise men's report of the star's first appearance. ¹⁷Herod's brutal action fulfilled what God had spoken through the prophet Jeremiah:

¹⁸"A cry was heard in Ramah—
    weeping and great mourning.
Rachel weeps for her children,
    refusing to be comforted,
    for they are dead."*

¹⁹When Herod died, an angel of the Lord appeared in a dream to Joseph in Egypt. ²⁰"Get up!" the angel said. "Take the child and his mother back to the land of Israel, because those who were trying to kill the child are dead."

²¹So Joseph got up and returned to the land of Israel with Jesus and his mother. ²²But when he learned that the new ruler of Judea was Herod's son Archelaus, he

was afraid to go there. Then, after being warned in a dream, he left for the region of Galilee. ²³So the family went and lived in a town called Nazareth. This fulfilled what the prophets had said: "He will be called a Nazarene."

2:15 Hos 11:1.   2:18 Jer 31:15.

God sent an angel to warn Joseph. Through this warning, God rescued Jesus and his family from danger. Today's world is still filled with harmful situations and people. But God rescues his people. Rely on him. God will watch over you.

The LORD says, "I will rescue those who love me. I will protect those who trust in my name." PSALM 91:14

JUNE 16

Jesus at the Temple

When Jesus was twelve, he went to Jerusalem for Passover with his family. But when his parents were going home, they couldn't find Jesus. Where do you think he was?

Luke 2:41-52

Every year Jesus' parents went to Jerusalem for the Passover festival. ⁴²When Jesus was twelve years old, they attended the festival as usual. ⁴³After the celebration was over, they started home to Nazareth, but Jesus stayed behind in Jerusalem. His parents didn't miss him at first, ⁴⁴because they assumed he was among the other travelers. But when he didn't show up that evening, they started looking for him among their relatives and friends.

⁴⁵When they couldn't find him, they went back to Jerusalem to search for him there. ⁴⁶Three days later they finally discovered him in the Temple, sitting among the religious teachers, listening to them and asking questions. ⁴⁷All who heard him were amazed at his understanding and his answers.

⁴⁸His parents didn't know what to think. "Son," his mother said to him, "why have you done this to us? Your father and I have been frantic, searching for you everywhere."

⁴⁹"But why did you need to search?" he asked. "Didn't you know that I must be in my Father's house?"* ⁵⁰But they didn't understand what he meant.

⁵¹Then he returned to Nazareth with them and was obedient to them. And his mother stored all these things in her heart.

⁵²Jesus grew in wisdom and in stature and in favor with God and all the people.

2:49 Or *"Didn't you realize that I should be involved with my Father's affairs?"*

Even as a young boy, Jesus was very wise. Adults at the Temple marveled at his wisdom and understanding. How can we follow Jesus' example and be wise? Above all, we need to fear God. To fear God means to realize who God is, to love him, and to obey him.

Fear of the LORD is the foundation of wisdom. Knowledge of the Holy One results in good judgment. PROVERBS 9:10

JUNE 17

A DESERT HERMIT'S MESSAGE

John the Baptist lived out in the desert and ate locusts and honey. Many people came to hear him preach. What was his message to the people?

Matthew 3:1-17

In those days John the Baptist came to the Judean wilderness and began preaching. His message was, ²"Repent of your sins and turn to God, for the Kingdom of Heaven is near.*" ³The prophet Isaiah was speaking about John when he said,

"He is a voice shouting in the wilderness,
'Prepare the way for the LORD's coming!
    Clear the road for him!'"*

⁴John's clothes were woven from coarse camel hair, and he wore a leather belt around his waist. For food he ate locusts and wild honey. ⁵People from Jerusalem and from all of Judea and all over the Jordan Valley went out to see and hear John. ⁶And when they confessed their sins, he baptized them in the Jordan River.

⁷But when he saw many Pharisees and Sadducees coming to watch him baptize,* he denounced them. "You brood of snakes!" he exclaimed. "Who warned you to flee God's coming wrath? ⁸Prove by the way you live that you have repented of your sins and turned to God. ⁹Don't just say to each other, 'We're safe, for we are descendants of Abraham.' That means nothing, for I tell you, God can create children of Abraham from these very stones. ¹⁰Even now the ax of God's judgment is poised, ready to sever the roots of the trees. Yes, every tree that does not produce good fruit will be chopped down and thrown into the fire.

¹¹"I baptize with* water those who repent of their sins and turn to God. But someone is coming soon who is greater than I am—so much greater that I'm not worthy even to be his slave and carry his sandals. He will baptize you with the Holy Spirit and with fire.* ¹²He is ready to separate the chaff from the wheat with his winnowing fork. Then he will clean up the threshing area, gathering the wheat into his barn but burning the chaff with never-ending fire."

¹³Then Jesus went from Galilee to the

Jordan River to be baptized by John. [14]But John tried to talk him out of it. "I am the one who needs to be baptized by you," he said, "so why are you coming to me?"

[15]But Jesus said, "It should be done, for we must carry out all that God requires.*" So John agreed to baptize him.

[16]After his baptism, as Jesus came up out of the water, the heavens were opened* and he saw the Spirit of God descending like a dove and settling on him. [17]And a voice from heaven said, "This is my dearly loved Son, who brings me great joy."

3:2 Or *has come*, or *is coming soon.*   3:3 Isa 40:3 (Greek version).   3:7 Or *coming to be baptized.*   3:11a Or *in.*   3:11b Or *in the Holy Spirit and in fire.*   3:15 Or *for we must fulfill all righteousness.*   3:16 Some manuscripts read *opened to him.*

John the Baptist's message was simple and straightforward: Change your ways and stop sinning. That was the only way to prepare for Jesus' coming. That still is the way to prepare for Jesus. Jesus promised that he will return someday, so we need to be ready. What do you need to do to get ready for Jesus? Don't wait. Believe in the one who died for your sins, and live according to his Word.

I will judge each of you, O people of Israel, according to your actions, says the Sovereign LORD. Repent, and turn from your sins. Don't let them destroy you!
EZEKIEL 18:30

JUNE 18

Jesus and the Devil

The devil tempted Jesus when he was hungry and tired. How did Jesus keep from sinning?

Matthew 4:1-11
Then Jesus was led by the Spirit into the wilderness to be tempted there by the devil. [2]For forty days and forty nights he fasted and became very hungry.

[3]During that time the devil* came and said to him, "If you are the Son of God, tell these stones to become loaves of bread."

[4]But Jesus told him, "No! The Scriptures say,

'People do not live by bread alone,
	but by every word that comes from
		the mouth of God.'*"

[5]Then the devil took him to the holy city, Jerusalem, to the highest point of the Temple, [6]and said, "If you are the Son of God, jump off! For the Scriptures say,

'He will order his angels to protect you.
And they will hold you up with their hands
	so you won't even hurt your foot on a
		stone.'*"

[7]Jesus responded, "The Scriptures also say, 'You must not test the LORD your God.'*"

[8]Next the devil took him to the peak of a very high mountain and showed him the

kingdoms of the world and all their glory. ⁹"I will give it all to you," he said, "if you will kneel down and worship me."

¹⁰"Get out of here, Satan," Jesus told him. "For the Scriptures say,

'You must worship the LORD your God and serve only him.'*"

¹¹Then the devil went away, and angels came and took care of Jesus.

4:3 Greek *the tempter.* **4:4** Deut 8:3. **4:6** Ps 91:11-12. **4:7** Deut 6:16. **4:10** Deut 6:13.

Every time the devil tried to make Jesus do something wrong, Jesus used God's Word to fight off temptation. What a great example for us! The Bible is a powerful weapon to use in resisting temptation. Memorize Bible verses and use them when you are tempted to do something you know is wrong.

I have hidden your [God's] word in my heart, that I might not sin against you.
PSALM 119:11

JUNE 19

FOLLOW ME

Jesus called Andrew, Peter, Philip, and Nathanael to follow him. Would they leave everything and go?

John 1:35-51

The following day John was again standing with two of his disciples. ³⁶As Jesus walked by, John looked at him and declared, "Look! There is the Lamb of God!" ³⁷When John's two disciples heard this, they followed Jesus.

³⁸Jesus looked around and saw them following. "What do you want?" he asked them.

They replied, "Rabbi" (which means "Teacher"), "where are you staying?"

³⁹"Come and see," he said. It was about four o'clock in the afternoon when they went with him to the place where he was staying, and they remained with him the rest of the day.

⁴⁰Andrew, Simon Peter's brother, was one of these men who heard what John said and then followed Jesus. ⁴¹Andrew went to find his brother, Simon, and told him, "We have found the Messiah" (which means "Christ"*).

⁴²Then Andrew brought Simon to meet Jesus. Looking intently at Simon, Jesus said, "Your name is Simon, son of John—but you will be called Cephas" (which means "Peter"*).

⁴³The next day Jesus decided to go to Galilee. He found Philip and said to him, "Come, follow me." ⁴⁴Philip was from Bethsaida, Andrew and Peter's hometown.

⁴⁵Philip went to look for Nathanael and told him, "We have found the very person Moses* and the prophets wrote about! His name is Jesus, the son of Joseph from Nazareth."

⁴⁶"Nazareth!" exclaimed Nathanael. "Can anything good come from Nazareth?"

"Come and see for yourself," Philip replied.

[47]As they approached, Jesus said, "Now here is a genuine son of Israel—a man of complete integrity."

[48]"How do you know about me?" Nathanael asked.

Jesus replied, "I could see you under the fig tree before Philip found you."

[49]Then Nathanael exclaimed, "Rabbi, you are the Son of God—the King of Israel!"

[50]Jesus asked him, "Do you believe this just because I told you I had seen you under the fig tree? You will see greater things than this." [51]Then he said, "I tell you the truth, you will all see heaven open and the angels of God going up and down on the Son of Man, the one who is the stairway between heaven and earth.*"

1:41 *Messiah* (a Hebrew term) and *Christ* (a Greek term) both mean "the anointed one." 1:42 The names *Cephas* (from Aramaic) and *Peter* (from Greek) both mean "rock." 1:45 Greek *Moses in the law.* 1:51 Greek *going up and down on the Son of Man;* see Gen 28:10-17. "Son of Man" is a title Jesus used for himself.

When Jesus called these disciples, they followed. They left everything behind—jobs, families, homes—to get to know Jesus. Nothing in the world is worth more than knowing Jesus as your Savior, Lord, and friend. Jesus calls you to follow him too. Don't let anything stop you from knowing him.

[Jesus said,] "I assure you that everyone who has given up house or wife or brothers or parents or children, for the sake of the Kingdom of God, will be repaid many times over in this life, and will have eternal life in the world to come."
LUKE 18:29-30

JUNE 20

JESUS IS ANGRY

Jesus went to the Temple to worship God. What do you think people were doing in the Temple?

John 2:13-23

It was nearly time for the Jewish Passover celebration, so Jesus went to Jerusalem. [14]In the Temple area he saw merchants selling cattle, sheep, and doves for sacrifices; he also saw dealers at tables exchanging foreign money. [15]Jesus made a whip from some ropes and chased them all out of the Temple. He drove out the sheep and cattle, scattered the money changers' coins over the floor, and turned over their tables. [16]Then, going over to the people who sold doves, he told them, "Get these things out of here. Stop turning my Father's house into a marketplace!"

[17]Then his disciples remembered this prophecy from the Scriptures: "Passion for God's house will consume me."*

[18]But the Jewish leaders demanded, "What are you doing? If God gave you authority to do this, show us a miraculous sign to prove it."

¹⁹"All right," Jesus replied. "Destroy this temple, and in three days I will raise it up."

²⁰"What!" they exclaimed. "It has taken forty-six years to build this Temple, and you can rebuild it in three days?" ²¹But when Jesus said "this temple," he meant his own body. ²²After he was raised from the dead, his disciples remembered he had said this, and they believed both the Scriptures and what Jesus had said.

²³Because of the miraculous signs Jesus did in Jerusalem at the Passover celebration, many began to trust in him.

2:17 Or *"Concern for God's house will be my undoing."* Ps 69:9.

Jesus wanted to find people worshiping God at the Temple. Instead he found people trying to make money by selling sheep, cattle, and doves. These people were distracting others from worshiping God. Jesus got angry and drove the sellers from his Father's house. As Jesus' actions show us, worshiping God is important. We shouldn't let anything or anyone distract us from honoring God.

O God, we meditate on your unfailing love as we worship in your Temple.
PSALM 48:9

JUNE 21

JESUS and nicodemus

Under the cover of night, Nicodemus, a Jewish religious leader, went to talk to Jesus about the Kingdom of God. What would Jesus tell him?

John 3:1-21

There was a man named Nicodemus, a Jewish religious leader who was a Pharisee. ²After dark one evening, he came to speak with Jesus. "Rabbi," he said, "we all know that God has sent you to teach us. Your miraculous signs are evidence that God is with you."

³Jesus replied, "I tell you the truth, unless you are born again,* you cannot see the Kingdom of God."

⁴"What do you mean?" exclaimed Nicodemus. "How can an old man go back into his mother's womb and be born again?"

⁵Jesus replied, "I assure you, no one can enter the Kingdom of God without being born of water and the Spirit.* ⁶Humans can reproduce only human life, but the Holy Spirit gives birth to spiritual life.* ⁷So don't be surprised when I say, 'You* must be born again.' ⁸The wind blows wherever it wants. Just as you can hear the wind but can't tell where it comes from or where it is going, so you can't explain how people are born of the Spirit."

⁹"How are these things possible?" Nicodemus asked.

¹⁰Jesus replied, "You are a respected Jewish teacher, and yet you don't

understand these things? ¹¹I assure you, we tell you what we know and have seen, and yet you won't believe our testimony. ¹²But if you don't believe me when I tell you about earthly things, how can you possibly believe if I tell you about heavenly things? ¹³No one has ever gone to heaven and returned. But the Son of Man* has come down from heaven. ¹⁴And as Moses lifted up the bronze snake on a pole in the wilderness, so the Son of Man must be lifted up, ¹⁵so that everyone who believes in him will have eternal life.*

¹⁶"For God loved the world so much that he gave his one and only Son, so that everyone who believes in him will not perish but

have eternal life. ¹⁷God sent his Son into the world not to judge the world, but to save the world through him.

¹⁸"There is no judgment against anyone who believes in him. But anyone who does not believe in him has already been judged for not believing in God's one and only Son. ¹⁹And the judgment is based on this fact: God's light came into the world, but people loved the darkness more than the light, for their actions were evil. ²⁰All who do evil hate the light and refuse to go near it for fear their sins will be exposed. ²¹But those who do what is right come to the light so others can see that they are doing what God wants.*"

3:3 Or *born from above;* also in 3:7. **3:5** Or *and spirit.* The Greek word for *Spirit* can also be translated *wind;* see 3:8.
3:6 Greek *what is born of the Spirit is spirit.* **3:7** The Greek word for *you* is plural; also in 3:12. **3:13** Some manuscripts add *who lives in heaven.* "Son of Man" is a title Jesus used for himself. **3:15** Or *everyone who believes will have eternal life in him.*
3:21 Or *can see God at work in what he is doing.*

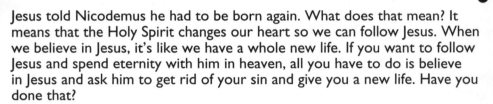

Jesus told Nicodemus he had to be born again. What does that mean? It means that the Holy Spirit changes our heart so we can follow Jesus. When we believe in Jesus, it's like we have a whole new life. If you want to follow Jesus and spend eternity with him in heaven, all you have to do is believe in Jesus and ask him to get rid of your sin and give you a new life. Have you done that?

Believe in the Lord Jesus and you will be saved, along with everyone in your household. ACTS 16:31

JUNE 22

JESUS' Ministry Grows

Many of John the Baptist's followers were starting to follow Jesus. Would John be angry that his followers were leaving?

John 3:22-36

Then Jesus and his disciples left Jerusalem and went into the Judean countryside. Jesus spent some time with them there, baptizing people.

²³At this time John the Baptist was bap-

tizing at Aenon, near Salim, because there was plenty of water there; and people kept coming to him for baptism. ²⁴(This was before John was thrown into prison.) ²⁵A debate broke out between John's disciples and a certain Jew* over ceremonial cleansing. [26]So John's disciples came to him and said, "Rabbi, the man you met on the other side of the Jordan River, the one you identified as the Messiah, is also baptizing people. And everybody is going to him instead of coming to us."

[27]John replied, "No one can receive anything unless God gives it from heaven. [28]You yourselves know how plainly I told you, 'I am not the Messiah. I am only here to prepare the way for him.' [29]It is the bridegroom who marries the bride, and the best man is simply glad to stand with him and hear his vows. Therefore, I am filled with joy at his success. [30]He must become greater and greater, and I must become less and less.

[31]"He has come from above and is greater than anyone else. We are of the earth, and we speak of earthly things, but he has come from heaven and is greater than anyone else.* [32]He testifies about what he has seen and heard, but how few believe what he tells them! [33]Anyone who accepts his testimony can affirm that God is true. [34]For he is sent by God. He speaks God's words, for God gives him the Spirit without limit. [35]The Father loves his Son and has put everything into his hands. [36]And anyone who believes in God's Son has eternal life. Anyone who doesn't obey the Son will never experience eternal life but remains under God's angry judgment."

3:25 Some manuscripts read *some Jews.*   3:31 Some manuscripts omit *and is greater than anyone else.*

John's disciples were upset that more people were now following Jesus. But John was happy. The whole reason John was preaching was so people would be ready to believe and follow Jesus! That was God's plan, and John was fitting into it. What a great example to follow. Everything we do should help people believe in Jesus. What can you do to point people to Jesus?

You are the light of the world—like a city on a hilltop that cannot be hidden.
MATTHEW 5:14

JUNE 23

food for Thought

Jesus hadn't eaten in a while, and the disciples thought he must be getting hungry. But what kind of food was important to him?

John 4:27-42

His disciples came back. They were shocked to find [Jesus] talking to a woman, but none of them had the nerve to ask, "What do you want with her?" or "Why are you talking to her?" [28]The woman left her water jar beside the well and ran back to the village, telling everyone, [29]"Come and see a man who told me everything I ever did! Could he possibly be the Messiah?" [30]So the people came streaming from the village to see him.

[31]Meanwhile, the disciples were urging Jesus, "Rabbi, eat something."

³²But Jesus replied, "I have a kind of food you know nothing about."

³³"Did someone bring him food while we were gone?" the disciples asked each other.

³⁴Then Jesus explained: "My nourishment comes from doing the will of God, who sent me, and from finishing his work. ³⁵You know the saying, 'Four months between planting and harvest.' But I say, wake up and look around. The fields are already ripe* for harvest. ³⁶The harvesters are paid good wages, and the fruit they harvest is people brought to eternal life. What joy awaits both the planter and the harvester alike! ³⁷You know the saying, 'One plants

4:35 Greek *white*.

and another harvests.' And it's true. ³⁸I sent you to harvest where you didn't plant; others had already done the work, and now you will get to gather the harvest."

³⁹Many Samaritans from the village believed in Jesus because the woman had said, "He told me everything I ever did!" ⁴⁰When they came out to see him, they begged him to stay in their village. So he stayed for two days, ⁴¹long enough for many more to hear his message and believe. ⁴²Then they said to the woman, "Now we believe, not just because of what you told us, but because we have heard him ourselves. Now we know that he is indeed the Savior of the world."

When Jesus was talking about food, he wasn't referring to the kind we eat. Instead, Jesus was talking about spiritual food. What kind of food is that? For Jesus, it meant doing God's will. As humans, we need food to feed our bodies. But we also need spiritual food to grow as Christians. We feed our soul as we obey God, read his Word, and spend time in prayer. Have you fed your soul today?

[God] humbled you by letting you go hungry and then feeding you with manna, a food previously unknown to you and your ancestors. He did it to teach you that people do not live by bread alone; rather, we live by every word that comes from the mouth of the LORD. DEUTERONOMY 8:3

JUNE 24

A Sick Son

A man's son was very sick. How would the man try to help his son?

John 4:46-54

As [Jesus] traveled through Galilee, he came to Cana, where he had turned the water into wine. There was a government official in nearby Capernaum whose son was very sick. ⁴⁷When he heard that Jesus

had come from Judea to Galilee, he went and begged Jesus to come to Capernaum to heal his son, who was about to die.

⁴⁸Jesus asked, "Will you never believe in me unless you see miraculous signs and wonders?"

⁴⁹The official pleaded, "Lord, please come now before my little boy dies."

⁵⁰Then Jesus told him, "Go back home. Your son will live!" And the man believed what Jesus said and started home.

⁵¹While the man was on his way, some of his servants met him with the news that his son was alive and well. ⁵²He asked them when the boy had begun to get better, and they replied, "Yesterday afternoon at one o'clock his fever suddenly disappeared!" ⁵³Then the father realized that that was the very time Jesus had told him, "Your son will live." And he and his entire household believed in Jesus. ⁵⁴This was the second miraculous sign Jesus did in Galilee after coming from Judea.

This man believed enough in Jesus to walk twenty miles to ask Jesus to heal his son. Then the man believed Jesus' promise that his son would live, and he acted on that belief by returning home. When the man saw his son healed, he and his whole household believed in Jesus. Faith is a gift that grows! As you live *and* act in faith, your faith will grow stronger and deeper each day.

I pray that your love will overflow more and more, and that you will keep on growing in knowledge and understanding. For I want you to understand what really matters, so that you may live pure and blameless lives until the day of Christ's return. PHILIPPIANS 1:9-10

JUNE 25

HOMETOWN BOY

Jesus went back to Nazareth, the town where he grew up. Do you think his old neighbors would listen to what he wanted to teach them?

Luke 4:16-30

When he came to the village of Nazareth, his boyhood home, he went as usual to the synagogue on the Sabbath and stood up to read the Scriptures. ¹⁷The scroll of Isaiah the prophet was handed to him. He unrolled the scroll and found the place where this was written:

¹⁸"The Spirit of the LORD is upon me,
> for he has anointed me to bring Good News to the poor.
He has sent me to proclaim that captives will be released,
> that the blind will see,
that the oppressed will be
> set free,
¹⁹and that the time of the LORD's favor has come.*"

²⁰He rolled up the scroll, handed it back to the attendant, and sat down. All eyes in the synagogue looked at him intently. ²¹Then he began to speak to them. "The Scripture you've just heard has been fulfilled this very day!"

²²Everyone spoke well of him and was amazed by the gracious words that came

from his lips. "How can this be?" they asked. "Isn't this Joseph's son?"

²³Then he said, "You will undoubtedly quote me this proverb: 'Physician, heal yourself'—meaning, 'Do miracles here in your hometown like those you did in Capernaum.' ²⁴But I tell you the truth, no prophet is accepted in his own hometown.

²⁵"Certainly there were many needy widows in Israel in Elijah's time, when the heavens were closed for three and a half years, and a severe famine devastated the land. ²⁶Yet Elijah was not sent to any of them. He was sent instead to a foreigner—a widow of Zarephath in the land of Sidon. ²⁷And there were many lepers in Israel in the time of the prophet Elisha, but the only one healed was Naaman, a Syrian."

²⁸When they heard this, the people in the synagogue were furious. ²⁹Jumping up, they mobbed him and forced him to the edge of the hill on which the town was built. They intended to push him over the cliff, ³⁰but he passed right through the crowd and went on his way.

4:18-19 Or *and to proclaim the acceptable year of the Lord.* Isa 61:1-2 (Greek version); 58:6.

The people who lived in Nazareth couldn't believe Jesus was anyone special. Since they had known him when he was a little boy, they thought there was no way Jesus could possibly be a prophet . . . let alone the Son of God. They made up their mind about Jesus without listening to what God might want to tell them. God does things in ways that we can't even imagine. We should try not to let our own ideas keep us from believing in what God is doing.

"My thoughts are nothing like your thoughts," says the LORD. "And my ways are far beyond anything you could imagine. For just as the heavens are higher than the earth, so my ways are higher than your ways and my thoughts higher than your thoughts." ISAIAH 55:8-9

JUNE 26
fishermen's catch

Some fishermen weren't catching any fish. Jesus gave them advice on where to put down their nets. Would his advice help?

Luke 5:1-11

One day as Jesus was preaching on the shore of the Sea of Galilee,* great crowds pressed in on him to listen to the word of God. ²He noticed two empty boats at the water's edge, for the fishermen had left them and were washing their nets. ³Stepping into one of the boats, Jesus asked Simon,* its owner, to push it out into the water. So he sat in the boat and taught the crowds from there.

⁴When he had finished speaking, he said to Simon, "Now go out where it is deeper, and let down your nets to catch some fish."

⁵"Master," Simon replied, "we worked

hard all last night and didn't catch a thing. But if you say so, I'll let the nets down again." ⁶And this time their nets were so full of fish they began to tear! ⁷A shout for help brought their partners in the other boat, and soon both boats were filled with fish and on the verge of sinking.

⁸When Simon Peter realized what had happened, he fell to his knees before Jesus and said, "Oh, Lord, please leave me—I'm too much of a sinner to be around you." ⁹For he was awestruck by the number of fish they had caught, as were the others with him. ¹⁰His partners, James and John, the sons of Zebedee, were also amazed.

Jesus replied to Simon, "Don't be afraid! From now on you'll be fishing for people!" ¹¹And as soon as they landed, they left everything and followed Jesus.

5:1 Greek *Lake Gennesaret*, another name for the Sea of Galilee.   5:3 *Simon* is called "Peter" in 6:14 and thereafter.

The three fishermen were amazed at how many fish they caught after following Jesus' advice. When they came ashore, they dropped everything and followed Jesus. We also may have to leave something we love to follow Jesus. But Jesus promises us so much more when we follow him with our whole heart—eternal life with him. Are you ready to follow?

[Jesus said,] "I give them eternal life, and they will never perish. No one can snatch them away from me." JOHN 10:28

JUNE 27
GOD'S SON

How do you think the Jewish leaders reacted when Jesus healed a man who couldn't walk?

John 5:1-18

Afterward Jesus returned to Jerusalem for one of the Jewish holy days. ²Inside the city, near the Sheep Gate, was the pool of Bethesda,* with five covered porches. ³Crowds of sick people—blind, lame, or paralyzed—lay on the porches.* ⁵One of the men lying there had been sick for thirty-eight years. ⁶When Jesus saw him and knew he had been ill for a long time, he asked him, "Would you like to get well?"

⁷"I can't, sir," the sick man said, "for I have no one to put me into the pool when the water bubbles up. Someone else always gets there ahead of me."

⁸Jesus told him, "Stand up, pick up your mat, and walk!"

⁹Instantly, the man was healed! He rolled up his sleeping mat and began walking! But this miracle happened on the Sabbath, ¹⁰so the Jewish leaders objected. They said to the man who was cured, "You can't work on the Sabbath! The law doesn't allow you to carry that sleeping mat!"

¹¹But he replied, "The man who healed me told me, 'Pick up your mat and walk.'"

¹²"Who said such a thing as that?" they demanded.

¹³The man didn't know, for Jesus had disappeared into the crowd. ¹⁴But afterward Jesus found him in the Temple and told him, "Now you are well; so stop sinning, or something even worse may happen to you." ¹⁵Then the man went and told the Jewish leaders that it was Jesus who had healed him.

¹⁶So the Jewish leaders began harassing* Jesus for breaking the Sabbath rules. ¹⁷But Jesus replied, "My Father is always working, and so am I." ¹⁸So the Jewish leaders tried all the harder to find a way to kill him. For he not only broke the Sabbath, he called God his Father, thereby making himself equal with God.

5:2 Other manuscripts read *Beth-zatha;* still others read *Bethsaida.* 5:3 Some manuscripts add *waiting for a certain movement of the water,* ⁴*for an angel of the Lord came from time to time and stirred up the water. And the first person to step in after the water was stirred was healed of whatever disease he had.* 5:16 Or *persecuting.*

Jesus asked the man if he wanted to be healed. The man said yes, but he couldn't get into the water when it was stirred up. The man had put his hope in the water. But Jesus had compassion on him and healed him. Sometimes we act like that man when we put our hope in people or things, rather than in Jesus. Only Jesus has what we really need. Put your hope in him today. You won't be disappointed.

Blessed are those who trust in the LORD and have made the LORD their hope and confidence. JEREMIAH 17:7

JUNE 28

A HOLE IN THE ROOF

Jesus was teaching in a house when all of a sudden some people broke through the roof and lowered a man down to him. What was going on?

Mark 2:1-12

When Jesus returned to Capernaum several days later, the news spread quickly that he was back home. ²Soon the house where he was staying was so packed with visitors that there was no more room, even outside the door. While he was preaching God's word to them, ³four men arrived carrying a paralyzed man on a mat. ⁴They couldn't bring him to Jesus because of the crowd, so they dug a hole through the roof above his head. Then they lowered the man on his mat, right down in front of Jesus. ⁵Seeing their faith, Jesus said to the paralyzed man, "My child, your sins are forgiven."

⁶But some of the teachers of religious law who were sitting there thought to themselves, ⁷"What is he saying? This is blasphemy! Only God can forgive sins!"

8Jesus knew immediately what they were thinking, so he asked them, "Why do you question this in your hearts? 9Is it easier to say to the paralyzed man 'Your sins are forgiven,' or 'Stand up, pick up your mat, and walk'? 10So I will prove to you that the Son of Man* has the authority on earth to forgive sins." Then Jesus turned to the paralyzed man and said, 11"Stand up, pick up your mat, and go home!"

12And the man jumped up, grabbed his mat, and walked out through the stunned onlookers. They were all amazed and praised God, exclaiming, "We've never seen anything like this before!"

2:10 "Son of Man" is a title Jesus used for himself.

These men knew Jesus could heal their friend, so they were willing to do whatever they had to do to bring their friend to Jesus. When Jesus saw their faith, he did so much more for the man—he forgave the man's sins and healed him! Jesus still offers healing and forgiveness to whoever comes to him in faith. If you or a friend needs healing or forgiveness today, just ask Jesus. You can have faith that he will do it.

Let all that I am praise the LORD; may I never forget the good things he does for me. He forgives all my sins and heals all my diseases. PSALM 103:2-3

JUNE 29

Happiness is . . .

Jesus told his followers what kinds of people are blessed by God. Who do you think are the people God blesses?

Matthew 5:1-12

One day as he saw the crowds gathering, Jesus went up on the mountainside and sat down. His disciples gathered around him, 2and he began to teach them.

3"God blesses those who are poor and realize their need for him,*
for the Kingdom of Heaven is theirs.
4God blesses those who mourn,
for they will be comforted.
5God blesses those who are humble,
for they will inherit the whole earth.
6God blesses those who hunger and thirst for justice,*
for they will be satisfied.

7God blesses those who are merciful,
for they will be shown mercy.
8God blesses those whose hearts are pure,
for they will see God.
9God blesses those who work for peace,
for they will be called the children of God.
10God blesses those who are persecuted for doing right,
for the Kingdom of Heaven is theirs.

11"God blesses you when people mock you and persecute you and lie about you* and say all sorts of evil things against you because you are my followers. 12Be happy

233

about it! Be very glad! For a great reward awaits you in heaven. And remember, the ancient prophets were persecuted in the same way."

5:3 Greek *poor in spirit.*   5:6 Or *for righteousness.*   5:11 Some manuscripts omit *and lie about you.*

A lot of people think they'll be happy if they have lots of money. Others think they'll be happy if they have lots of friends. Still others say happiness comes with fame. But Jesus says we find true happiness when we live God's way. God blesses people who know they need him, who are sad and need comfort, who are gentle, and who are fair, merciful, and peaceful. Do any of those words describe you?

The humble will see their God at work and be glad. Let all who seek God's help be encouraged. PSALM 69:32

JUNE 30

Good and Angry

Jesus was teaching his disciples about the Kingdom of Heaven. Do you think it's okay to be angry with someone in the Kingdom of Heaven?

Matthew 5:17-26

[Jesus said,] "Don't misunderstand why I have come. I did not come to abolish the law of Moses or the writings of the prophets. No, I came to accomplish their purpose. [18]I tell you the truth, until heaven and earth disappear, not even the smallest detail of God's law will disappear until its purpose is achieved. [19]So if you ignore the least commandment and teach others to do the same, you will be called the least in the Kingdom of Heaven. But anyone who obeys God's laws and teaches them will be called great in the Kingdom of Heaven.

[20]"But I warn you—unless your righteousness is better than the righteousness of the teachers of religious law and the Pharisees, you will never enter the Kingdom of Heaven!

[21]"You have heard that our ancestors were told, 'You must not murder. If you commit murder, you are subject to judgment.'* [22]But I say, if you are even angry with someone,* you are subject to judgment! If you call someone an idiot,* you are in danger of being brought before the court. And if you curse someone,* you are in danger of the fires of hell.*

[23]"So if you are presenting a sacrifice at the altar in the Temple and you suddenly remember that someone has something against you, [24]leave your sacrifice there at the altar. Go and be reconciled to that person. Then come and offer your sacrifice to God.

[25]"When you are on the way to court with your adversary, settle your differences quickly. Otherwise, your accuser may hand you over to the judge, who will

hand you over to an officer, and you will be thrown into prison. ²⁶And if that happens, you surely won't be free again until you have paid the last penny.*"

5:21 Exod 20:13; Deut 5:17.   5:22a Some manuscripts add *without cause.*   5:22b Greek uses an Aramaic term of contempt: *If you say to your brother, 'Raca.'*   5:22c Greek *if you say, 'You fool.'*   5:22d Greek *Gehenna.*   5:26 Greek *the last kodrantes* [i.e., quadrans].

Jesus told his disciples that being angry with someone is just as bad as murdering the person. Rather than being angry, Jesus said people should forgive and love others. Are you angry with anyone? If so, forgive that person and ask him or her to forgive you for being angry.

Do not seek revenge or bear a grudge against a fellow Israelite, but love your neighbor as yourself. I am the LORD. LEVITICUS 19:18

outstanding!

Time to celebrate! Summer is here *and* you made it to the New Testament! To show that you've finished the June readings, find a marker or highlighter in a bright summer color, and fill in the level you reached this month. If you started reading in January, you're halfway through your Bible readings for the year!

In the New Testament we hear about when Jesus came to earth and how he saves us. What new info did you learn about Jesus this month? Maybe you and your family would like to put on a neighborhood play about one of the stories.

....

....

....

....

....

....

IMPORTANT STUFF TO REMEMBER FROM JUNE

❏ Angels are God's messengers.

❏ Jesus calls people to leave everything and follow him.

❏ Jesus does amazing miracles.

TimE For SomE Word Fun!

You read this month about John the Baptist, his birth, and his mission. Fill in the missing words by finding the correct word in the Word Bank. You can check your answers by looking at the Bible readings for June 8 and June 17.

1. John's birth was announced by an _____.
   (Luke 1:13)

2. John was never to drink any _____.
   (Luke 1:15)

3. John would preach in the power of _____.
   (Luke 1:17)

4. John began preaching in the _____.
   (Matthew 3:1)

5. John's clothes were made of _____ _____.
   (Matthew 3:4)

6. John ate _____ and wild honey.
   (Matthew 3:4)

WORD BANK

ANGEL   WILDERNESS   LOCUSTS

CAMEL HAIR   ELIJAH   WINE

JULY 1

friends and enemies

Jesus taught his disciples how to treat their enemies. What was unusual about his teaching?

Matthew 5:38-48

"You have heard the law that says the punishment must match the injury: 'An eye for an eye, and a tooth for a tooth.'* ³⁹But I say, do not resist an evil person! If someone slaps you on the right cheek, offer the other cheek also. ⁴⁰If you are sued in court and your shirt is taken from you, give your coat, too. ⁴¹If a soldier demands that you carry his gear for a mile,* carry it two miles. ⁴²Give to those who ask, and don't turn away from those who want to borrow.

⁴³"You have heard the law that says, 'Love your neighbor'* and hate your enemy. ⁴⁴But I say, love your enemies!* Pray for those who persecute you! ⁴⁵In that way, you will be acting as true children of your Father in heaven. For he gives his sunlight to both the evil and the good, and he sends rain on the just and the unjust alike. ⁴⁶If you love only those who love you, what reward is there for that? Even corrupt tax collectors do that much. ⁴⁷If you are kind only to your friends,* how are you different from anyone else? Even pagans do that. ⁴⁸But you are to be perfect, even as your Father in heaven is perfect."

5:38 Greek *the law that says: 'An eye for an eye and a tooth for a tooth.'* Exod 21:24; Lev 24:20; Deut 19:21.   **5:41** Greek *milion* [4,854 feet or 1,478 meters].   **5:43** Lev 19:18.   **5:44** Some manuscripts add *Bless those who curse you. Do good to those who hate you.* Compare Luke 6:27-28.   **5:47** Greek *your brothers.*

When someone does something to hurt you, you probably don't feel like being nice to that person. But that's exactly what Jesus wants us to do. Jesus wants his followers to be different from everyone else. He wants us to act like God. Since God loves and takes care of all of us even when our actions are bad, we should treat others the way he does—even when they are mean to us. How can you show love to somebody who acts like your enemy?

If your enemies are hungry, give them food to eat. If they are thirsty, give them water to drink. PROVERBS 25:21

JULY 2

The model prayer

When Jesus taught his followers how to pray, he gave them a prayer to use as an example. When you read what he said, see what you can learn about how we should pray.

Matthew 6:5-18

"When you pray, don't be like the hypocrites who love to pray publicly on street corners and in the synagogues where everyone can see them. I tell you the truth, that is all the reward they will ever get. ⁶But when you pray, go away by yourself, shut the door behind you, and pray to your Father in private. Then your Father, who sees everything, will reward you.

⁷"When you pray, don't babble on and on as people of other religions do. They think their prayers are answered merely by repeating their words again and again. ⁸Don't be like them, for your Father knows exactly what you need even before you ask him! ⁹Pray like this:

Our Father in heaven,
  may your name be kept holy.
¹⁰May your Kingdom come
  soon.
May your will be done on earth,
as it is in heaven.
¹¹Give us today the food we need,*
¹²and forgive us our sins,
  as we have forgiven those who sin
  against us.
¹³And don't let us yield to temptation,*
  but rescue us from the evil one.*

¹⁴"If you forgive those who sin against you, your heavenly Father will forgive you. ¹⁵But if you refuse to forgive others, your Father will not forgive your sins.

¹⁶"And when you fast, don't make it obvious, as the hypocrites do, for they try to look miserable and disheveled so people will admire them for their fasting. I tell you the truth, that is the only reward they will ever get. ¹⁷But when you fast, comb your hair and wash your face. ¹⁸Then no one will notice that you are fasting, except your Father, who knows what you do in private. And your Father, who sees everything, will reward you."

6:11 Or *Give us today our food for the day;* or *Give us today our food for tomorrow.* 6:13a Or *And keep us from being tested.* 6:13b Or *from evil.* Some manuscripts add *For yours is the kingdom and the power and the glory forever. Amen.*

When we pray, Jesus wants us to be more concerned about the one we are speaking to than about the words we are saying. Jesus doesn't want us to show off by using fancy words, because our focus shouldn't be on impressing other people. Instead, Jesus tells us to keep our focus on God when we pray. We should praise God, ask him for forgiveness, seek his protection, and request what we need. Try to follow Jesus' directions when you pray.

The LORD is close to all who call on him, yes, to all who call on him in truth.
PSALM 145:18

JULY 3

Birds and Lilies

Jesus taught people a great way to keep from worrying. What should you remember when you are worried?

Matthew 6:19-34

"Don't store up treasures here on earth, where moths eat them and rust destroys them, and where thieves break in and steal. ²⁰Store your treasures in heaven, where moths and rust cannot destroy, and thieves do not break in and steal. ²¹Wherever your treasure is, there the desires of your heart will also be.

²²"Your eye is a lamp that provides light for your body. When your eye is good, your whole body is filled with light. ²³But when your eye is bad, your whole body is filled with darkness. And if the light you think you have is actually darkness, how deep that darkness is!

²⁴"No one can serve two masters. For you will hate one and love the other; you will be devoted to one and despise the other. You cannot serve both God and money.

²⁵"That is why I tell you not to worry about everyday life—whether you have enough food and drink, or enough clothes to wear. Isn't life more than food, and your body more than clothing? ²⁶Look at the birds. They don't plant or harvest or store food in barns, for your heavenly Father feeds them. And aren't you far more valuable to him than they are? ²⁷Can all your worries add a single moment to your life?

²⁸"And why worry about your clothing? Look at the lilies of the field and how they grow. They don't work or make their clothing, ²⁹yet Solomon in all his glory was not dressed as beautifully as they are. ³⁰And if God cares so wonderfully for wildflowers that are here today and thrown into the fire tomorrow, he will certainly care for you. Why do you have so little faith?

³¹"So don't worry about these things, saying, 'What will we eat? What will we drink? What will we wear?' ³²These things dominate the thoughts of unbelievers, but your heavenly Father already knows all your needs. ³³Seek the Kingdom of God* above all else, and live righteously, and he will give you everything you need.

³⁴"So don't worry about tomorrow, for tomorrow will bring its own worries. Today's trouble is enough for today."

6:33 Some manuscripts do not include *of God*.

We worry about lots of stuff—grades, our future, what we will eat, or what we will wear. But Jesus teaches us in this passage that we shouldn't worry about these things. Our God cares for all his creatures—even the birds and the flowers. Since he loves us much more than a bird or a flower, we can trust him to take care of us, too! Remember that truth the next time worries begin creeping into your thoughts.

This same God who takes care of me will supply all your needs from his glorious riches, which have been given to us in Christ Jesus. PHILIPPIANS 4:19

JULY 4

The Golden Rule

Jesus taught his disciples how to treat other people. He said one rule sums up all of the others. See if you can find it.

Matthew 7:1-12

"Do not judge others, and you will not be judged. ²For you will be treated as you treat others.* The standard you use in judging is the standard by which you will be judged.*

³"And why worry about a speck in your friend's eye* when you have a log in your own? ⁴How can you think of saying to your friend,* 'Let me help you get rid of that speck in your eye,' when you can't see past the log in your own eye? ⁵Hypocrite! First get rid of the log in your own eye; then you will see well enough to deal with the speck in your friend's eye.

⁶"Don't waste what is holy on people who are unholy.* Don't throw your pearls to pigs! They will trample the pearls, then turn and attack you.

⁷"Keep on asking, and you will receive what you ask for. Keep on seeking, and you will find. Keep on knocking, and the door will be opened to you. ⁸For everyone who asks, receives. Everyone who seeks, finds. And to everyone who knocks, the door will be opened.

⁹"You parents—if your children ask for a loaf of bread, do you give them a stone instead? ¹⁰Or if they ask for a fish, do you give them a snake? Of course not! ¹¹So if you sinful people know how to give good gifts to your children, how much more will your heavenly Father give good gifts to those who ask him.

¹²"Do to others whatever you would like them to do to you. This is the essence of all that is taught in the law and the prophets."

7:2a Or *For God will judge you as you judge others.*   7:2b Or *The measure you give will be the measure you get back.*
7:3 Greek *your brother's eye;* also in 7:5.   7:4 Greek *your brother.*   7:6 Greek *Don't give the sacred to dogs.*

There are lots of rules for getting along with others—don't talk behind someone's back; don't call each other names; say please and thank you. You probably know some others. But all those rules can be summed up in one thought—treat others the way you want to be treated. Follow that Golden Rule and you will get along with others. Try it today with your friends and family.

Owe nothing to anyone—except for your obligation to love one another. If you love your neighbor, you will fulfill the requirements of God's law. ROMANS 13:8

JULY 5

ROCK SOLID

Do you think it's a big deal whether or not you obey Jesus' teachings? Read what Jesus said about how important it is to follow his instructions.

Matthew 7:13-27

"You can enter God's Kingdom only through the narrow gate. The highway to hell* is broad, and its gate is wide for the many who choose that way. ¹⁴But the gateway to life is very narrow and the road is difficult, and only a few ever find it.

¹⁵"Beware of false prophets who come disguised as harmless sheep but are really vicious wolves. ¹⁶You can identify them by their fruit, that is, by the way they act. Can you pick grapes from thornbushes, or figs from thistles? ¹⁷A good tree produces good fruit, and a bad tree produces bad fruit. ¹⁸A good tree can't produce bad fruit, and a bad tree can't produce good fruit. ¹⁹So every tree that does not produce good fruit is chopped down and thrown into the fire. ²⁰Yes, just as you can identify a tree by its fruit, so you can identify people by their actions.

²¹"Not everyone who calls out to me, 'Lord! Lord!' will enter the Kingdom of Heaven. Only those who actually do the will of my Father in heaven will enter. ²²On judgment day many will say to me, 'Lord! Lord! We prophesied in your name and cast out demons in your name and performed many miracles in your name.' ²³But I will reply, 'I never knew you. Get away from me, you who break God's laws.'

²⁴"Anyone who listens to my teaching and follows it is wise, like a person who builds a house on solid rock. ²⁵Though the rain comes in torrents and the floodwaters rise and the winds beat against that house, it won't collapse because it is built on bedrock. ²⁶But anyone who hears my teaching and ignores it is foolish, like a person who builds a house on sand. ²⁷When the rains and floods come and the winds beat against that house, it will collapse with a mighty crash."

7:13 Greek *The road that leads to destruction.*

Jesus compared the life of a person who obeys his teachings to a house that is built on a rock. When the storms come, the house survives because it's built on a solid foundation. The same is true for a person who chooses to build his or her life on Jesus' teachings. That person will be able to survive the tough times and problems in life because Jesus is there to help. What are you building your life on? Choose Jesus, our rock-solid foundation!

This is how I spend my life: obeying your commandments. PSALM 119:56

JULY 6

Jesus and a Roman Officer

Jesus has amazing power to heal people. Look what he did to help a slave and a widow's son.

Luke 7:1-17

When Jesus had finished saying all this to the people, he returned to Capernaum. ²At that time the highly valued slave of a Roman officer* was sick and near death. ³When the officer heard about Jesus, he sent some respected Jewish elders to ask him to come and heal his slave. ⁴So they earnestly begged Jesus to help the man. "If anyone deserves your help, he does," they said, ⁵"for he loves the Jewish people and even built a synagogue for us."

⁶So Jesus went with them. But just before they arrived at the house, the officer sent some friends to say, "Lord, don't trouble yourself by coming to my home, for I am not worthy of such an honor. ⁷I am not even worthy to come and meet you. Just say the word from where you are, and my servant will be healed. ⁸I know this because I am under the authority of my superior officers, and I have authority over my soldiers. I only need to say, 'Go,' and they go, or 'Come,' and they come. And if I say to my slaves, 'Do this,' they do it."

⁹When Jesus heard this, he was amazed. Turning to the crowd that was following him, he said, "I tell you, I haven't seen faith like this in all Israel!" ¹⁰And when the officer's friends returned to his house, they found the slave completely healed.

¹¹Soon afterward Jesus went with his disciples to the village of Nain, and a large crowd followed him. ¹²A funeral procession was coming out as he approached the village gate. The young man who had died was a widow's only son, and a large crowd from the village was with her. ¹³When the Lord saw her, his heart overflowed with compassion. "Don't cry!" he said. ¹⁴Then he walked over to the coffin and touched it, and the bearers stopped. "Young man," he said, "I tell you, get up." ¹⁵Then the dead boy sat up and began to talk! And Jesus gave him back to his mother.

¹⁶Great fear swept the crowd, and they praised God, saying, "A mighty prophet has risen among us," and "God has visited his people today." ¹⁷And the news about Jesus spread throughout Judea and the surrounding countryside.

Jesus healed many people while he was teaching. That was one reason why people learned to know and believe he was God's Son. God still shows his power by healing people. If you or someone you know is sick, ask Jesus to bring comfort, strength, and healing to that person. Whenever God's healing touch is needed, just ask him for it. Then trust him to know the best thing to do and the best time to do it!

Let all that I am praise the LORD; may I never forget the good things he does for me. He forgives all my sins and heals all my diseases. PSALM 103:2-3

JULY 7

John's Question

John the Baptist wanted Jesus to say clearly whether or not he was the Messiah. What did Jesus say?

Matthew 11:1-19

When Jesus had finished giving these instructions to his twelve disciples, he went out to teach and preach in towns throughout the region.

²John the Baptist, who was in prison, heard about all the things the Messiah was doing. So he sent his disciples to ask Jesus, ³"Are you the Messiah we've been expecting,* or should we keep looking for someone else?"

⁴Jesus told them, "Go back to John and tell him what you have heard and seen— ⁵the blind see, the lame walk, the lepers are cured, the deaf hear, the dead are raised to life, and the Good News is being preached to the poor. ⁶And tell him, 'God blesses those who do not turn away because of me.*'"

⁷As John's disciples were leaving, Jesus began talking about him to the crowds. "What kind of man did you go into the wilderness to see? Was he a weak reed, swayed by every breath of wind? ⁸Or were you expecting to see a man dressed in expensive clothes? No, people with expensive clothes live in palaces. ⁹Were you looking for a prophet? Yes, and he is more than a prophet. ¹⁰John is the man to whom the Scriptures refer when they say,

'Look, I am sending my messenger
    ahead of you,
    and he will prepare your way
    before you.'*

¹¹"I tell you the truth, of all who have ever lived, none is greater than John the Baptist. Yet even the least person in the Kingdom of Heaven is greater than he is! ¹²And from the time John the Baptist

began preaching until now, the Kingdom of Heaven has been forcefully advancing, and violent people are attacking it.* ¹³For before John came, all the prophets and the law of Moses looked forward to this present time. ¹⁴And if you are willing to accept what I say, he is Elijah, the one the prophets said would come.* ¹⁵Anyone with ears to hear should listen and understand!

¹⁶"To what can I compare this generation? It is like children playing a game in the public square. They complain to their friends,

¹⁷'We played wedding songs,
 and you didn't dance,
so we played funeral songs,
 and you didn't mourn.'

¹⁸For John didn't spend his time eating and drinking, and you say, 'He's possessed by a demon.' ¹⁹The Son of Man,* on the other hand, feasts and drinks, and you say, 'He's a glutton and a drunkard, and a friend of tax collectors and other sinners!' But wisdom is shown to be right by its results."

11:3 Greek *Are you the one who is coming?*   11:6 Or *who are not offended by me.*   11:10 Mal 3:1.   11:12 Or *until now, eager multitudes have been pressing into the Kingdom of Heaven.*   11:14 See Mal 4:5.   11:19 "Son of Man" is a title Jesus used for himself.

When John had his followers ask Jesus to declare whether or not he was the Messiah, Jesus said that John should pay attention to what was happening. The lame could walk. The blind could see again. Lepers were cured, and the poor heard the Good News. The Old Testament prophets had said that the Messiah would do all of these things. Jesus alone fulfilled all those prophecies. He is the promised Savior. Believe!

Say to those with fearful hearts, "Be strong, and do not fear, for your God is coming to destroy your enemies. He is coming to save you." And when he comes, he will open the eyes of the blind and unplug the ears of the deaf. ISAIAH 35:4-5

JULY 8

PErfUME for JESUS

A proud Pharisee and a sinful woman treated Jesus very differently. How did Jesus react?

Luke 7:36-50

One of the Pharisees asked Jesus to have dinner with him, so Jesus went to his home and sat down to eat.* ³⁷When a certain immoral woman from that city heard he was eating there, she brought a beautiful alabaster jar filled with expensive perfume.

³⁸Then she knelt behind him at his feet, weeping. Her tears fell on his feet, and she wiped them off with her hair. Then she kept kissing his feet and putting perfume on them.

³⁹When the Pharisee who had invited him saw this, he said to himself, "If this man

were a prophet, he would know what kind of woman is touching him. She's a sinner!"

⁴⁰Then Jesus answered his thoughts. "Simon," he said to the Pharisee, "I have something to say to you."

"Go ahead, Teacher," Simon replied.

⁴¹Then Jesus told him this story: "A man loaned money to two people—500 pieces of silver* to one and 50 pieces to the other. ⁴²But neither of them could repay him, so he kindly forgave them both, canceling their debts. Who do you suppose loved him more after that?"

⁴³Simon answered, "I suppose the one for whom he canceled the larger debt."

"That's right," Jesus said. ⁴⁴Then he turned to the woman and said to Simon, "Look at this woman kneeling here. When I entered your home, you didn't offer me water to wash the dust from my feet, but she has washed them with her tears and wiped them with her hair. ⁴⁵You didn't greet me with a kiss, but from the time I first came in, she has not stopped kissing my feet. ⁴⁶You neglected the courtesy of olive oil to anoint my head, but she has anointed my feet with rare perfume.

⁴⁷"I tell you, her sins—and they are many—have been forgiven, so she has shown me much love. But a person who is forgiven little shows only little love." ⁴⁸Then Jesus said to the woman, "Your sins are forgiven."

⁴⁹The men at the table said among themselves, "Who is this man, that he goes around forgiving sins?"

⁵⁰And Jesus said to the woman, "Your faith has saved you; go in peace."

7:36 Or *and reclined.*   7:41 Greek *500 denarii.* A denarius was equivalent to a laborer's full day's wage.

Jesus forgave the sinful woman because she was sorry for her sins. Although Simon, a Pharisee, was also a sinner, he wasn't sorry for his sins. There are many people like Simon in the world. But you don't have to be one of them. You can be like the woman and come to Jesus, humble and sorry for your sins. As you pray, you can thank Jesus for his wonderful love and the forgiveness he offers you.

Thank God for this gift too wonderful for words!* 2 CORINTHIANS 9:15

9:15 Greek *his gift.*

JULY 9

JESUS' FAMILY

The Pharisees said Jesus was getting his power from Satan. Read what Jesus had to say about knowing whether someone is on God's side or on Satan's side.

Matthew 12:22-37, 46-50

Then a demon-possessed man, who was blind and couldn't speak, was brought to Jesus. He healed the man so that he could both speak and see. ²³The crowd was amazed and asked, "Could it be that Jesus is the Son of David, the Messiah?"

²⁴But when the Pharisees heard about

the miracle, they said, "No wonder he can cast out demons. He gets his power from Satan,* the prince of demons."

²⁵Jesus knew their thoughts and replied, "Any kingdom divided by civil war is doomed. A town or family splintered by feuding will fall apart. ²⁶And if Satan is casting out Satan, he is divided and fighting against himself. His own kingdom will not survive. ²⁷And if I am empowered by Satan, what about your own exorcists? They cast out demons, too, so they will condemn you for what you have said. ²⁸But if I am casting out demons by the Spirit of God, then the Kingdom of God has arrived among you. ²⁹For who is powerful enough to enter the house of a strong man like Satan and plunder his goods? Only someone even stronger—someone who could tie him up and then plunder his house.

³⁰"Anyone who isn't with me opposes me, and anyone who isn't working with me is actually working against me.

³¹"Every sin and blasphemy can be forgiven—except blasphemy against the Holy Spirit, which will never be forgiven. ³²Anyone who speaks against the Son of Man can be forgiven, but anyone who speaks against the Holy Spirit will never be for-given, either in this world or in the world to come.

³³"A tree is identified by its fruit. If a tree is good, its fruit will be good. If a tree is bad, its fruit will be bad. ³⁴You brood of snakes! How could evil men like you speak what is good and right? For whatever is in your heart determines what you say. ³⁵A good person produces good things from the treasury of a good heart, and an evil person produces evil things from the treasury of an evil heart. ³⁶And I tell you this, you must give an account on judgment day for every idle word you speak. ³⁷The words you say will either acquit you or condemn you."

⁴⁶As Jesus was speaking to the crowd, his mother and brothers stood outside, asking to speak to him. ⁴⁷Someone told Jesus, "Your mother and your brothers are outside, and they want to speak to you."*

⁴⁸Jesus asked, "Who is my mother? Who are my brothers?" ⁴⁹Then he pointed to his disciples and said, "Look, these are my mother and brothers. ⁵⁰Anyone who does the will of my Father in heaven is my brother and sister and mother!"

12:24 Greek *Beelzeboul;* also in 12:27. Other manuscripts read *Beezeboul;* Latin version reads *Beelzebub.* 12:47 Some manuscripts do not include verse 47. Compare Mark 3:32 and Luke 8:20.

Jesus had some tough words about who are his followers—and who are not. In Jesus' words, there is no middle ground. Anyone who is not actively following Jesus has actually chosen to reject him. We are either with Jesus or we are not. If we refuse to follow Jesus, we're choosing to be on Satan's side. Make sure you are on the right team—follow Jesus with all your heart!

Oh, the joys of those who do not follow the advice of the wicked, or stand around with sinners, or join in with mockers. But they delight in the law of the LORD, meditating on it day and night. PSALM 1:1-2

JULY 10

soil and Toil

Jesus told his disciples a story with a hidden message. See if you can figure out what his story means.

Mark 4:1-20

Once again Jesus began teaching by the lakeshore. A very large crowd soon gathered around him, so he got into a boat. Then he sat in the boat while all the people remained on the shore. ²He taught them by telling many stories in the form of parables, such as this one:

³"Listen! A farmer went out to plant some seed. ⁴As he scattered it across his field, some of the seed fell on a footpath, and the birds came and ate it. ⁵Other seed fell on shallow soil with underlying rock. The seed sprouted quickly because the soil was shallow. ⁶But the plant soon wilted under the hot sun, and since it didn't have deep roots, it died. ⁷Other seed fell among thorns that grew up and choked out the tender plants so they produced no grain. ⁸Still other seeds fell on fertile soil, and they sprouted, grew, and produced a crop that was thirty, sixty, and even a hundred times as much as had been planted!" ⁹Then he said, "Anyone with ears to hear should listen and understand."

¹⁰Later, when Jesus was alone with the twelve disciples and with the others who were gathered around, they asked him what the parables meant.

¹¹He replied, "You are permitted to understand the secret* of the Kingdom of God. But I use parables for everything I say

4:11 Greek *mystery.*   4:12 Isa 6:9-10 (Greek version).

to outsiders, ¹²so that the Scriptures might be fulfilled:

'When they see what I do,
     they will learn nothing.
When they hear what I say,
     they will not understand.
Otherwise, they will turn to me
     and be forgiven.'*"

¹³Then Jesus said to them, "If you can't understand the meaning of this parable, how will you understand all the other parables? ¹⁴The farmer plants seed by taking God's word to others. ¹⁵The seed that fell on the footpath represents those who hear the message, only to have Satan come at once and take it away. ¹⁶The seed on the rocky soil represents those who hear the message and immediately receive it with joy. ¹⁷But since they don't have deep roots, they don't last long. They fall away as soon as they have problems or are persecuted for believing God's word. ¹⁸The seed that fell among the thorns represents others who hear God's word, ¹⁹but all too quickly the message is crowded out by the worries of this life, the lure of wealth, and the desire for other things, so no fruit is produced. ²⁰And the seed that fell on good soil represents those who hear and accept God's word and produce a harvest of thirty, sixty, or even a hundred times as much as had been planted!"

249

The seed represents God's Word. The good soil represents the lives of people who hear God's Word and put it into practice. Their lives are filled with good works that please God. They don't let worries distract them from serving him. Is your life like the good soil, where God's Word can be sown and grow? If not, ask God to help change you. Don't let the troubles, worries, and distractions of this world prevent you from growing in your understanding of God's Word and your obedience to it.

Merely listening to the law doesn't make us right with God. It is obeying the law that makes us right in his sight. ROMANS 2:13

JULY 11

seeds and weeds

In this passage, Jesus describes God's kingdom as a wheat field. What happens to the weeds? What happens to the wheat?

Matthew 13:24-32, 36-43

Here is another story Jesus told: "The Kingdom of Heaven is like a farmer who planted good seed in his field. 25But that night as the workers slept, his enemy came and planted weeds among the wheat, then slipped away. 26When the crop began to grow and produce grain, the weeds also grew.

27"The farmer's workers went to him and said, 'Sir, the field where you planted that good seed is full of weeds! Where did they come from?'

28"'An enemy has done this!' the farmer exclaimed.

"'Should we pull out the weeds?' they asked.

29"'No,' he replied, 'you'll uproot the wheat if you do. 30Let both grow together until the harvest. Then I will tell the harvesters to sort out the weeds, tie them into bundles, and burn them, and to put the wheat in the barn.'"

31Here is another illustration Jesus used: "The Kingdom of Heaven is like a mustard seed planted in a field. 32It is the smallest of all seeds, but it becomes the largest of garden plants; it grows into a tree, and birds come and make nests in its branches."

36Then, leaving the crowds outside, Jesus went into the house. His disciples said, "Please explain to us the story of the weeds in the field."

37Jesus replied, "The Son of Man* is the farmer who plants the good seed. 38The field is the world, and the good seed represents the people of the Kingdom. The weeds are the people who belong to the evil one. 39The enemy who planted the weeds

250

among the wheat is the devil. The harvest is the end of the world,* and the harvesters are the angels.

⁴⁰"Just as the weeds are sorted out and burned in the fire, so it will be at the end of the world. ⁴¹The Son of Man will send his angels, and they will remove from his King-dom everything that causes sin and all who do evil. ⁴²And the angels will throw them into the fiery furnace, where there will be weeping and gnashing of teeth. ⁴³Then the righteous will shine like the sun in their Fa-ther's Kingdom. Anyone with ears to hear should listen and understand!"

13:37 "Son of Man" is a title Jesus used for himself.   13:39 Or *the age;* also in 13:40.

The wheat planted in this field represents God's people. The weeds represent those who choose not to believe in Jesus. When Jesus returns, he will separate those who believe in him from those who don't. All the believers will go to heaven, but those who reject Jesus will be punished and thrown into hell. Not a pleasant thought, is it? The good news is that we have a choice about whose side we are on. Choose Jesus and choose life.

Today I [the Lord] have given you the choice between life and death, between blessings and curses. Now I call on heaven and earth to witness the choice you make. Oh, that you would choose life, so that you and your descendants might live! DEUTERONOMY 30:19

JULY 12
wild and crazy

Jesus freed a man from a lot of demons that had been controlling him. Once the man was free, he wanted to go with Jesus. Did Jesus let him come along?

Luke 8:26-39

[Jesus and the disciples] arrived in the re-gion of the Gerasenes,* across the lake from Galilee. ²⁷As Jesus was climbing out of the boat, a man who was possessed by demons came out to meet him. For a long time he had been homeless and naked, liv-ing in a cemetery outside the town.

²⁸As soon as he saw Jesus, he shrieked and fell down in front of him. Then he screamed, "Why are you interfering with me, Jesus, Son of the Most High God? Please, I beg you, don't torture me!" ²⁹For Jesus had already commanded the evil* spirit to come out of him. This spirit had often taken control of the man. Even when he was placed under guard and put in chains and shackles, he simply broke them and rushed out into the wilderness, com-pletely under the demon's power.

³⁰Jesus demanded, "What is your name?"

"Legion," he replied, for he was filled with many demons. ³¹The demons kept begging Jesus not to send them into the bottomless pit.*

³²There happened to be a large herd of pigs feeding on the hillside nearby, and the demons begged him to let them enter into the pigs.

So Jesus gave them permission. ³³Then the demons came out of the man and entered the pigs, and the entire herd plunged down the steep hillside into the lake and drowned.

³⁴When the herdsmen saw it, they fled to the nearby town and the surrounding countryside, spreading the news as they ran. ³⁵People rushed out to see what had happened. A crowd soon gathered around Jesus, and they saw the man who had been freed from the demons. He was sitting at Jesus' feet, fully clothed and perfectly sane, and they were all afraid. ³⁶Then those who had seen what happened told the others how the demon-possessed man had been healed. ³⁷And all the people in the region of the Gerasenes begged Jesus to go away and leave them alone, for a great wave of fear swept over them.

So Jesus returned to the boat and left, crossing back to the other side of the lake. ³⁸The man who had been freed from the demons begged to go with him. But Jesus sent him home, saying, ³⁹"No, go back to your family, and tell them everything God has done for you." So he went all through the town proclaiming the great things Jesus had done for him.

8:26 Other manuscripts read *Gadarenes;* still others read *Gergesenes;* also in 8:37. See Matt 8:28; Mark 5:1.   8:29 Greek *unclean.*   8:31 Or *the abyss,* or *the underworld.*

Jesus had completely changed this man's life. The man wanted to go with Jesus. But Jesus told the man to go back and tell his family all that God had done for him. If we accept Jesus as our Savior, he changes our life too. Then we can be like that man and go tell everyone we know what God has done for us. Who can you tell today about what Jesus has done for you?

Come and listen, all you who fear God, and I will tell you what he did for me.
PSALM 66:16

JULY 13

sheep without a shepherd

People were always crowding around Jesus to ask him for help. Do you think he ever got annoyed by all the people?

Matthew 9:27-38

Two blind men followed along behind [Jesus], shouting, "Son of David, have mercy on us!"

²⁸They went right into the house where he was staying, and Jesus asked them, "Do you believe I can make you see?"

"Yes, Lord," they told him, "we do."

²⁹Then he touched their eyes and said, "Because of your faith, it will happen." ³⁰Then their eyes were opened, and they could see! Jesus sternly warned them, "Don't tell anyone about this." ³¹But instead, they went out and spread his fame all over the region.

³²When they left, a demon-possessed man who couldn't speak was brought to Jesus. ³³So Jesus cast out the demon, and then the man began to speak. The crowds were amazed. "Nothing like this has ever happened in Israel!" they exclaimed.

³⁴But the Pharisees said, "He can cast out demons because he is empowered by the prince of demons."

³⁵Jesus traveled through all the towns and villages of that area, teaching in the synagogues and announcing the Good News about the Kingdom. And he healed every kind of disease and illness. ³⁶When he saw the crowds, he had compassion on them because they were confused and helpless, like sheep without a shepherd. ³⁷He said to his disciples, "The harvest is great, but the workers are few. ³⁸So pray to the Lord who is in charge of the harvest; ask him to send more workers into his fields."

Jesus' heart went out to all the people who needed his help. He wanted to protect them and guide them. He wants to be everyone's shepherd, for all people are like sheep. When you're in trouble or don't know what to do, remember that Jesus loves you and wants to help you. He especially cares about you when you feel like a lost sheep. Ask for his help with a problem you're having right now.

He will feed his flock like a shepherd. He will carry the lambs in his arms, holding them close to his heart. He will gently lead the mother sheep with their young.
ISAIAH 40:11

JULY 14

Preach It

Jesus visited his hometown of Nazareth. What kind of a welcome do you think he received?

Mark 6:1-13

Jesus left that part of the country and returned with his disciples to Nazareth, his hometown. ²The next Sabbath he began teaching in the synagogue, and many who heard him were amazed. They asked, "Where did he get all this wisdom and the power to perform such miracles?" ³Then they scoffed, "He's just a carpenter, the son of Mary* and the brother of James, Joseph,* Judas, and Simon. And his sisters live right here among us." They were deeply offended and refused to believe in him.

⁴Then Jesus told them, "A prophet is honored everywhere except in his own hometown and among his relatives and his

own family." [5]And because of their unbelief, he couldn't do any mighty miracles among them except to place his hands on a few sick people and heal them. [6]And he was amazed at their unbelief.

Then Jesus went from village to village, teaching the people. [7]And he called his twelve disciples together and began sending them out two by two, giving them authority to cast out evil* spirits. [8]He told them to take nothing for their journey except a walking stick—no food, no traveler's bag, no money.* [9]He allowed them to wear sandals but not to take a change of clothes.

[10]"Wherever you go," he said, "stay in the same house until you leave town. [11]But if any place refuses to welcome you or listen to you, shake its dust from your feet as you leave to show that you have abandoned those people to their fate."

[12]So the disciples went out, telling everyone they met to repent of their sins and turn to God. [13]And they cast out many demons and healed many sick people, anointing them with olive oil.

6:3a Some manuscripts read *He's just the son of the carpenter and of Mary.*   6:3b Most manuscripts read *Joses;* see Matt 13:55.   6:7 Greek *unclean.*   6:8 Greek *no copper coins in their money belts.*

The people in Jesus' hometown did not believe in him. They thought they knew him—the carpenter's son, the boy down the street. How could he possibly be God's Son? Because of their unbelief, Jesus did not perform any major miracles among them. We, too, can limit Jesus' miracles in our life when we lack faith. Do you believe Jesus has the power to change you?

"But you are my witnesses, O Israel!" says the LORD. "You are my servant. You have been chosen to know me, believe in me, and understand that I alone am God. There is no other God—there never has been, and there never will be."
ISAIAH 43:10

JULY 15
sheep among wolves
Jesus warned his disciples that it would be difficult to follow him. How would they be able to make it?

Matthew 10:16-39
[Jesus said,] "Look, I am sending you out as sheep among wolves. So be as shrewd as snakes and harmless as doves. [17]But beware! For you will be handed over to the courts and will be flogged with whips in the synagogues. [18]You will stand trial before governors and kings because you are my followers. But this will be your opportunity to tell the rulers and other unbelievers about me.* [19]When you are arrested, don't worry about how to respond or what to say. God will give you the right words at the right time. [20]For it is not you who will be speaking—it will be the Spirit of your Father speaking through you.

254

21"A brother will betray his brother to death, a father will betray his own child, and children will rebel against their parents and cause them to be killed. 22And all nations will hate you because you are my followers.* But everyone who endures to the end will be saved. 23When you are persecuted in one town, flee to the next. I tell you the truth, the Son of Man* will return before you have reached all the towns of Israel.

24"Students* are not greater than their teacher, and slaves are not greater than their master. 25Students are to be like their teacher, and slaves are to be like their master. And since I, the master of the household, have been called the prince of demons,* the members of my household will be called by even worse names!

26"But don't be afraid of those who threaten you. For the time is coming when everything that is covered will be revealed, and all that is secret will be made known to all. 27What I tell you now in the darkness, shout abroad when daybreak comes. What I whisper in your ear, shout from the housetops for all to hear!

28"Don't be afraid of those who want to kill your body; they cannot touch your soul. Fear only God, who can destroy both soul and body in hell.* 29What is the price of two sparrows—one copper coin*? But not a single sparrow can fall to the ground without your Father knowing it. 30And the very hairs on your head are all numbered. 31So don't be afraid; you are more valuable to God than a whole flock of sparrows.

32"Everyone who acknowledges me publicly here on earth, I will also acknowledge before my Father in heaven. 33But everyone who denies me here on earth, I will also deny before my Father in heaven.

34"Don't imagine that I came to bring peace to the earth! I came not to bring peace, but a sword.

35"I have come to set a man against his
father,
a daughter against her mother,
and a daughter-in-law against her
mother-in-law.
36'Your enemies will be right in your
own household!'*

37"If you love your father or mother more than you love me, you are not worthy of being mine; or if you love your son or daughter more than me, you are not worthy of being mine. 38If you refuse to take up your cross and follow me, you are not worthy of being mine. 39If you cling to your life, you will lose it; but if you give up your life for me, you will find it."

10:18 Or *But this will be your testimony against the rulers and other unbelievers.*   **10:22** Greek *on account of my name.*   **10:23** "Son of Man" is a title Jesus used for himself.   **10:24** Or *Disciples.*   **10:25** Greek *Beelzeboul;* other manuscripts read *Beezeboul;* Latin version reads *Beelzebub.*   **10:28** Greek *Gehenna.*   **10:29** Greek *one assarion* [i.e., one "as," a Roman coin equal to 1/16 of a denarius].   **10:35-36** Mic 7:6.

Jesus did not try to sugarcoat what it would mean to follow him. He told his followers that they would be beaten, betrayed, and forced to stand trial because of their faith. But Jesus also told them that God's Spirit would be with them, comforting them and guiding them. The same is true today: people who don't know Jesus may give us trouble because of our faith. But be encouraged! God will comfort us and give us the strength to withstand our troubles.

All praise to God, the Father of our Lord Jesus Christ. God is our merciful Father and the source of all comfort. 2 CORINTHIANS 1:3

255

JULY 16

feeding five Thousand

Jesus was teaching more than five thousand people. Everyone was getting hungry, but there wasn't any food around. Would everyone have to go home?

Mark 6:30-44

The apostles returned to Jesus from their ministry tour and told him all they had done and taught. [31]Then Jesus said, "Let's go off by ourselves to a quiet place and rest awhile." He said this because there were so many people coming and going that Jesus and his apostles didn't even have time to eat.

[32]So they left by boat for a quiet place, where they could be alone. [33]But many people recognized them and saw them leaving, and people from many towns ran ahead along the shore and got there ahead of them. [34]Jesus saw the huge crowd as he stepped from the boat, and he had compassion on them because they were like sheep without a shepherd. So he began teaching them many things.

[35]Late in the afternoon his disciples came to him and said, "This is a remote place, and it's already getting late. [36]Send the crowds away so they can go to the nearby farms and villages and buy something to eat."

[37]But Jesus said, "You feed them."

"With what?" they asked. "We'd have to work for months to earn enough money* to buy food for all these people!"

[38]"How much bread do you have?" he asked. "Go and find out."

They came back and reported, "We have five loaves of bread and two fish."

[39]Then Jesus told the disciples to have the people sit down in groups on the green grass. [40]So they sat down in groups of fifty or a hundred.

[41]Jesus took the five loaves and two fish, looked up toward heaven, and blessed them. Then, breaking the loaves into pieces, he kept giving the bread to the disciples so they could distribute it to the people. He also divided the fish for everyone to share. [42]They all ate as much as they wanted, [43]and afterward, the disciples picked up twelve baskets of leftover bread and fish. [44]A total of 5,000 men and their families were fed from those loaves!

6:37 Greek *It would take 200 denarii.* A denarius was equivalent to a laborer's full day's wage.

Jesus performed an amazing miracle. Not only did he keep the people from being hungry, but he showed them that he had God's power. Jesus took care of his followers in the same way that God provided manna for the Israelites in the desert. Jesus, the Son, has the same power as God, the Father, to take care of his followers. Trust him with your needs today. And read God's Word to get your spiritual vitamins.

[God] humbled you by letting you go hungry and then feeding you with manna, a food previously unknown to you and your ancestors. He did it to teach you that people do not live by bread alone; rather, we live by every word that comes from the mouth of the LORD. DEUTERONOMY **8:3**

JULY 17

Jesus Walks on Water

Out on a dark and stormy sea, the disciples thought they saw a ghost. Fear gripped them. What (or who) did they see?

Mark 6:45-56

Immediately after this, Jesus insisted that his disciples get back into the boat and head across the lake to Bethsaida, while he sent the people home. ⁴⁶After telling everyone good-bye, he went up into the hills by himself to pray.

⁴⁷Late that night, the disciples were in their boat in the middle of the lake, and Jesus was alone on land. ⁴⁸He saw that they were in serious trouble, rowing hard and struggling against the wind and waves. About three o'clock in the morning* Jesus came toward them, walking on the water. He intended to go past them, ⁴⁹but when they saw him walking on the water, they cried out in terror, thinking he was a ghost. ⁵⁰They were all terrified when they saw him.

But Jesus spoke to them at once. "Don't be afraid," he said. "Take courage! I am here!*" ⁵¹Then he climbed into the boat, and the wind stopped. They were totally amazed, ⁵²for they still didn't understand the significance of the miracle of the loaves. Their hearts were too hard to take it in.

⁵³After they had crossed the lake, they landed at Gennesaret. They brought the boat to shore ⁵⁴and climbed out. The people recognized Jesus at once, ⁵⁵and they ran throughout the whole area, carrying sick people on mats to wherever they heard he was. ⁵⁶Wherever he went—in villages, cities, or the countryside—they brought the sick out to the marketplaces. They begged him to let the sick touch at least the fringe of his robe, and all who touched him were healed.

6:48 Greek *About the fourth watch of the night.* **6:50** Or *The 'I AM' is here;* Greek reads *I am.* See Exod 3:14.

The disciples were terrified. The last thing they expected in the middle of a storm on a lake was to see someone walking toward them! But Jesus quickly calmed their fears, reassuring them that it was he. What are your darkest fears? Jesus wants to let you know that he is always with you. Listen to his voice: *It's all right. I am here! Don't be afraid.*

Be strong and courageous! Do not be afraid and do not panic before them. For the LORD your God will personally go ahead of you. He will neither fail you nor abandon you. DEUTERONOMY 31:6

JULY 18

The Bread of Life

People had heard that Jesus could miraculously provide bread. But would Jesus give people all the free food they wanted?

John 6:22-40

The next day the crowd that had stayed on the far shore saw that the disciples had taken the only boat, and they realized Jesus had not gone with them. ²³Several boats from Tiberias landed near the place where the Lord had blessed the bread and the people had eaten. ²⁴So when the crowd saw that neither Jesus nor his disciples were there, they got into the boats and went across to Capernaum to look for him. ²⁵They found him on the other side of the lake and asked, "Rabbi, when did you get here?"

²⁶Jesus replied, "I tell you the truth, you want to be with me because I fed you, not because you understood the miraculous signs. ²⁷But don't be so concerned about perishable things like food. Spend your energy seeking the eternal life that the Son of Man* can give you. For God the Father has given me the seal of his approval."

²⁸They replied, "We want to perform God's works, too. What should we do?"

²⁹Jesus told them, "This is the only work God wants from you: Believe in the one he has sent."

³⁰They answered, "Show us a miraculous sign if you want us to believe in you. What can you do? ³¹After all, our ancestors ate manna while they journeyed through the wilderness! The Scriptures say, 'Moses gave them bread from heaven to eat.'*"

³²Jesus said, "I tell you the truth, Moses didn't give you bread from heaven. My Father did. And now he offers you the true bread from heaven. ³³The true bread of God is the one who comes down from heaven and gives life to the world."

³⁴"Sir," they said, "give us that bread every day."

³⁵Jesus replied, "I am the bread of life. Whoever comes to me will never be hungry again. Whoever believes in me will never be thirsty. ³⁶But you haven't believed in me even though you have seen me. ³⁷However those the Father has given me will come to

me, and I will never reject them. ³⁸For I have come down from heaven to do the will of God who sent me, not to do my own will. ³⁹And this is the will of God, that I should not lose even one of all those he has given me, but that I should raise them up at the last day. ⁴⁰For it is my Father's will that all who see his Son and believe in him should have eternal life. I will raise them up at the last day."

6:27 "Son of Man" is a title Jesus used for himself.   6:31 Exod 16:4; Ps 78:24.

The crowd was looking for Jesus for the wrong reason. They wanted free food. But Jesus wanted to give them so much more, something lasting. He wanted to give them eternal life. Sometimes we look to Jesus only because we need a quick fix or we're in a jam. But Jesus wants to give us so much more than that. He wants to give us a brand-new life that will last forever! Will you take the gift of a new life, or are you just looking for a little bit of help? Don't settle for anything less than what Jesus wants to give you.

Now all glory to God, who is able, through his mighty power at work within us, to accomplish infinitely more than we might ask or think. EPHESIANS 3:20

JULY 19

JESUS REJECTED

Many people thought some of Jesus' teachings were too hard. Would his disciples stay with him?

John 6:41-71

Then the people* began to murmur in disagreement because [Jesus] had said, "I am the bread that came down from heaven." ⁴²They said, "Isn't this Jesus, the son of Joseph? We know his father and mother. How can he say, 'I came down from heaven'?"

⁴³But Jesus replied, "Stop complaining about what I said. ⁴⁴For no one can come to me unless the Father who sent me draws them to me, and at the last day I will raise them up. ⁴⁵As it is written in the Scriptures,* 'They will all be taught by God.' Everyone who listens to the Father and learns from him comes to me. ⁴⁶(Not that anyone has ever seen the Father; only I, who was sent from God, have seen him.)

⁴⁷"I tell you the truth, anyone who believes has eternal life. ⁴⁸Yes, I am the bread of life! ⁴⁹Your ancestors ate manna in the wilderness, but they all died. ⁵⁰Anyone who eats the bread from heaven, however, will never die. ⁵¹I am the living bread that came down from heaven. Anyone who eats this bread will live forever; and this bread, which I will offer so the world may live, is my flesh."

⁵²Then the people began arguing with each other about what he meant. "How can this man give us his flesh to eat?" they asked.

⁵³So Jesus said again, "I tell you the truth, unless you eat the flesh of the Son of Man and drink his blood, you cannot have

eternal life within you. ⁵⁴But anyone who eats my flesh and drinks my blood has eternal life, and I will raise that person at the last day. ⁵⁵For my flesh is true food, and my blood is true drink. ⁵⁶Anyone who eats my flesh and drinks my blood remains in me, and I in him. ⁵⁷I live because of the living Father who sent me; in the same way, anyone who feeds on me will live because of me. ⁵⁸I am the true bread that came down from heaven. Anyone who eats this bread will not die as your ancestors did (even though they ate the manna) but will live forever."

⁵⁹He said these things while he was teaching in the synagogue in Capernaum.

⁶⁰Many of his disciples said, "This is very hard to understand. How can anyone accept it?"

⁶¹Jesus was aware that his disciples were complaining, so he said to them, "Does this offend you? ⁶²Then what will you think if you see the Son of Man ascend to heaven again? ⁶³The Spirit alone gives eternal life. Human effort accomplishes nothing. And the very words I have spoken to you are spirit and life. ⁶⁴But some of you do not believe me." (For Jesus knew from the beginning which ones didn't believe, and he knew who would betray him.) ⁶⁵Then he said, "That is why I said that people can't come to me unless the Father gives them to me."

⁶⁶At this point many of his disciples turned away and deserted him. ⁶⁷Then Jesus turned to the Twelve and asked, "Are you also going to leave?"

⁶⁸Simon Peter replied, "Lord, to whom would we go? You have the words that give eternal life. ⁶⁹We believe, and we know you are the Holy One of God.*"

⁷⁰Then Jesus said, "I chose the twelve of you, but one is a devil." ⁷¹He was speaking of Judas, son of Simon Iscariot, one of the Twelve, who would later betray him.

6:41 Greek *Jewish people;* also in 6:52.   6:45 Greek *in the prophets.* Isa 54:13.   6:69 Other manuscripts read *you are the Christ, the Holy One of God;* still others read *you are the Christ, the Son of God;* and still others read *you are the Christ, the Son of the living God.*

Even though some things Jesus said were hard to understand and obey, Peter knew that Jesus was the true God. No matter how hard his teachings were, Jesus was the only one who could give eternal life. Peter made the right choice. Are you willing to stick with Jesus no matter how hard it gets? Ask him to help you. It will be worth it!

[Jesus said,] "I am the way, the truth, and the life. No one can come to the Father except through me." JOHN 14:6

JULY 20
A Clean Heart

The Pharisees were upset with Jesus because he wasn't following one of their traditions. How did Jesus answer them?

Mark 7:1-23

One day some Pharisees and teachers of religious law arrived from Jerusalem to see Jesus. ²They noticed that some of his disciples failed to follow the Jewish ritual of hand washing before eating. ³(The Jews, especially the Pharisees, do not eat until they have poured water over their cupped hands,* as required by their ancient traditions. ⁴Similarly, they don't eat anything from the market until they immerse their hands* in water. This is but one of many traditions they have clung to—such as their ceremonial washing of cups, pitchers, and kettles.*)

⁵So the Pharisees and teachers of religious law asked him, "Why don't your disciples follow our age-old tradition? They eat without first performing the hand-washing ceremony."

⁶Jesus replied, "You hypocrites! Isaiah was right when he prophesied about you, for he wrote,

'These people honor me with their lips,
  but their hearts are far from me.
⁷Their worship is a farce,
  for they teach man-made ideas as
    commands from God.'*

⁸For you ignore God's law and substitute your own tradition."

⁹Then he said, "You skillfully sidestep God's law in order to hold on to your own tradition. ¹⁰For instance, Moses gave you this law from God: 'Honor your father and mother,'* and 'Anyone who speaks disrespectfully of father or mother must be put to death.'* ¹¹But you say it is all right for people to say to their parents, 'Sorry, I can't help you. For I have vowed to give to God what I would have given to you.'* ¹²In this way, you let them disregard their needy parents. ¹³And so you cancel the word of God in order to hand down your own tradition. And this is only one example among many others."

¹⁴Then Jesus called to the crowd to come and hear. "All of you listen," he said, "and try to understand. ¹⁵It's not what goes into your body that defiles you; you are defiled by what comes from your heart.*"

¹⁷Then Jesus went into a house to get away from the crowd, and his disciples asked him what he meant by the parable he had just used. ¹⁸"Don't you understand either?" he asked. "Can't you see that the food you put into your body cannot defile you? ¹⁹Food doesn't go into your heart, but only passes through the stomach and then goes into the sewer." (By saying this, he declared that every kind of food is acceptable in God's eyes.)

²⁰And then he added, "It is what comes from inside that defiles you. ²¹For from within, out of a person's heart, come evil thoughts, sexual immorality, theft, murder, ²²adultery, greed, wickedness,

deceit, lustful desires, envy, slander, pride, and foolishness. ²³All these vile things come from within; they are what defile you."

7:3 Greek *have washed with the fist.* 7:4a Some manuscripts read *sprinkle themselves.* 7:4b Some manuscripts add *and dining couches.* 7:7 Isa 29:13 (Greek version). 7:10a Exod 20:12; Deut 5:16. 7:10b Exod 21:17 (Greek version); Lev 20:9 (Greek version). 7:11 Greek *'What I would have given to you is Corban'* (that is, a gift). 7:15 Some manuscripts add verse 16, *Anyone with ears to hear should listen and understand.* Compare 4:9, 23.

The Pharisees were very good at keeping rules made by people, like washing their hands before they ate. So when they complained to Jesus that his disciples weren't obeying the rules, Jesus told them that God cares more about people than rituals. God is far more concerned that we have a clean heart than clean hands. A clean heart is free from hatred and pride. It is full of love for others and for God. A clean heart is what God desires. Give your heart to God. He will make it clean.

I [God] will give you a new heart, and I will put a new spirit in you. I will take out your stony, stubborn heart and give you a tender, responsive heart.* And I will put my Spirit in you so that you will follow my decrees and be careful to obey my regulations. EZEKIEL 36:26-27

36:26 Hebrew *a heart of flesh.*

JULY 21

Jesus and the Pharisees

The disciples still were focused on the wrong thing—physical needs instead of spiritual ones. Read what Jesus had to say to them.

Matthew 16:1-12

One day the Pharisees and Sadducees came to test Jesus, demanding that he show them a miraculous sign from heaven to prove his authority.

²He replied, "You know the saying, 'Red sky at night means fair weather tomorrow; ³red sky in the morning means foul weather all day.' You know how to interpret the weather signs in the sky, but you don't know how to interpret the signs of the times!* ⁴Only an evil, adulterous generation would demand a miraculous sign, but the only sign I will give them is the sign of the prophet Jonah.*" Then Jesus left them and went away.

⁵Later, after they crossed to the other side of the lake, the disciples discovered they had forgotten to bring any bread. ⁶"Watch out!" Jesus warned them. "Beware of the yeast of the Pharisees and Sadducees."

⁷At this they began to argue with each other because they hadn't brought any bread. ⁸Jesus knew what they were saying, so he said, "You have so little faith! Why are you arguing with each other about having no bread? ⁹Don't you understand even yet? Don't you remember the 5,000 I fed with five loaves, and the baskets of leftovers you picked up? ¹⁰Or the 4,000 I fed with seven loaves, and the large baskets of

leftovers you picked up? [11]Why can't you understand that I'm not talking about bread? So again I say, 'Beware of the yeast of the Pharisees and Sadducees.'"

[12]Then at last they understood that he wasn't speaking about the yeast in bread, but about the deceptive teaching of the Pharisees and Sadducees.

16:2-3 Several manuscripts do not include any of the words in 16:2-3 after *He replied.*   16:4 Greek *the sign of Jonah.*

While the disciples were thinking about lack of food, Jesus was warning them of a greater danger—false teachers. The Pharisees and Sadducees were leading people away from God with their teachings. Jesus wanted his disciples to be aware of these false teachers. Today there still are leaders who teach things that are against God's laws. We need to be careful not to listen to them. Make sure you are listening to those who teach what the Bible says.

This is what the LORD of Heaven's Armies says to his people: "Do not listen to these prophets when they prophesy to you, filling you with futile hopes. They are making up everything they say. They do not speak for the LORD!" JEREMIAH 23:16

JULY 22

peter takes a stand

People had all kinds of ideas about who Jesus was. But Jesus wanted to know what his disciples thought. What did they say?

Luke 9:18-27

One day Jesus left the crowds to pray alone. Only his disciples were with him, and he asked them, "Who do people say I am?"

[19]"Well," they replied, "some say John the Baptist, some say Elijah, and others say you are one of the other ancient prophets risen from the dead."

[20]Then he asked them, "But who do you say I am?"

Peter replied, "You are the Messiah* sent from God!"

[21]Jesus warned his disciples not to tell anyone who he was. [22]"The Son of Man* must suffer many terrible things," he said.

"He will be rejected by the elders, the leading priests, and the teachers of religious law. He will be killed, but on the third day he will be raised from the dead."

[23]Then he said to the crowd, "If any of you wants to be my follower, you must turn from your selfish ways, take up your cross daily, and follow me. [24]If you try to hang on to your life, you will lose it. But if you give up your life for my sake, you will save it. [25]And what do you benefit if you gain the whole world but are yourself lost or destroyed? [26]If anyone is ashamed of me and my message, the Son of Man will be ashamed of that person when he returns in his glory and in the glory of the

Father and the holy angels. [27]I tell you the truth, some standing here right now will not die before they see the Kingdom of God."

9.20 Or *the Christ. Messiah* (a Hebrew term) and *Christ* (a Greek term) both mean "the anointed one."   9.22 "Son of Man" is a title Jesus used for himself.

God had shown Peter that Jesus was God's own Son. And Peter wasn't afraid to say it. Jesus told his followers not to be ashamed to say that they had faith in him. We shouldn't be either. Instead of worrying about what others will think of us, we should be willing to share our faith with everyone. After all, we wouldn't want Jesus to be ashamed of us! Don't be afraid to tell others what you believe.

*I am not ashamed of this Good News about Christ. It is the power of God at work, saving everyone who believes—the Jew first and also the Gentile.**
ROMANS 1:16

1:16 Greek *also the Greek.*

JULY 23

Dumbfounded Disciples

Jesus took three of his disciples up to the top of a mountain. Wait till you find out what happened there!

Matthew 17:1-13

Six days later Jesus took Peter and the two brothers, James and John, and led them up a high mountain to be alone. [2]As the men watched, Jesus' appearance was transformed so that his face shone like the sun, and his clothes became as white as light. [3]Suddenly, Moses and Elijah appeared and began talking with Jesus.

[4]Peter blurted out, "Lord, it's wonderful for us to be here! If you want, I'll make three shelters as memorials*—one for you, one for Moses, and one for Elijah."

[5]But even as he spoke, a bright cloud came over them, and a voice from the cloud said, "This is my dearly loved Son, who brings me great joy. Listen to him." [6]The disciples were terrified and fell face down on the ground.

[7]Then Jesus came over and touched them. "Get up," he said. "Don't be afraid." [8]And when they looked, they saw only Jesus.

[9]As they went back down the mountain, Jesus commanded them, "Don't tell anyone what you have seen until the Son of Man* has been raised from the dead."

[10]Then his disciples asked him, "Why do the teachers of religious law insist that Elijah must return before the Messiah comes?*"

[11]Jesus replied, "Elijah is indeed coming first to get everything ready for the Messiah. [12]But I tell you, Elijah has already come, but he wasn't recognized, and they chose to abuse him. And in the same way they will also make the Son of Man suffer." [13]Then the disciples realized he was talking about John the Baptist.

17:4 Greek *three tabernacles.*   17:9 "Son of Man" is a title Jesus used for himself.   17:10 Greek *that Elijah must come first?*

God gave these three men a very special privilege. They got to see Jesus as he really is—in all his glory—and to hear the voice of God. It's not likely that anyone alive today will get to see Jesus this way on earth. But one day, when Jesus comes back, everyone will see his glory and worship him. Just imagine! We can think about that wonderful day whenever we worship Jesus.

Then the glory of the LORD will be revealed, and all people will see it together. The LORD has spoken! ISAIAH **40:5**

JULY 24

THE Greatest

The disciples asked Jesus which one of them would be the greatest in heaven. What did Jesus tell them about greatness?

Matthew 18:1-9

The disciples came to Jesus and asked, "Who is greatest in the Kingdom of Heaven?"

²Jesus called a little child to him and put the child among them. ³Then he said, "I tell you the truth, unless you turn from your sins and become like little children, you will never get into the Kingdom of Heaven. ⁴So anyone who becomes as humble as this little child is the greatest in the Kingdom of Heaven.

⁵"And anyone who welcomes a little child like this on my behalf* is welcoming me. ⁶But if you cause one of these little ones who trusts in me to fall into sin, it would be better for you to have a large millstone tied around your neck and be drowned in the depths of the sea.

⁷"What sorrow awaits the world, because it tempts people to sin. Temptations are inevitable, but what sorrow awaits the person who does the tempting. ⁸So if your hand or foot causes you to sin, cut it off and throw it away. It's better to enter eternal life with only one hand or one foot than to be thrown into eternal fire with both of your hands and feet. ⁹And if your eye causes you to sin, gouge it out and throw it away. It's better to enter eternal life with only one eye than to have two eyes and be thrown into the fire of hell.*"

18:5 Greek *in my name.* **18:9** Greek *the Gehenna of fire.*

Jesus told his disciples that you get to be the best in the Kingdom of God by being humble, like a little child. A child is completely dependent on adults to provide his or her basic needs, like food, a home, and clothing. In the same way, we as Jesus' followers need to be completely dependent on him to forgive us and save us. There is nothing that we can do to save ourselves.

The LORD delights in his people; he crowns the humble with victory. PSALM 149:4

JULY 25

Lost Sheep

Jesus told his followers a story to show them how much God cares for his people.

Matthew 18:12-20

[Jesus said,] "If a man has a hundred sheep and one of them wanders away, what will he do? Won't he leave the ninety-nine others on the hills and go out to search for the one that is lost? ¹³And if he finds it, I tell you the truth, he will rejoice over it more than over the ninety-nine that didn't wander away! ¹⁴In the same way, it is not my heavenly Father's will that even one of these little ones should perish.

¹⁵"If another believer* sins against you,* go privately and point out the offense. If the other person listens and confesses it, you have won that person back. ¹⁶But if you are unsuccessful, take one or two others with you and go back again, so that everything you say may be confirmed by two or three witnesses. ¹⁷If the person still refuses to listen, take your case to the church. Then if he or she won't accept the church's decision, treat that person as a pagan or a corrupt tax collector.

¹⁸"I tell you the truth, whatever you forbid* on earth will be forbidden in heaven, and whatever you permit* on earth will be permitted in heaven.

¹⁹"I also tell you this: If two of you agree here on earth concerning anything you ask, my Father in heaven will do it for you. ²⁰For where two or three gather together as my followers,* I am there among them."

18:15a Greek *If your brother.* **18:15b** Some manuscripts do not include *against you.* **18:18a** Or *bind,* or *lock.* **18:18b** Or *loose,* or *open.* **18:20** Greek *gather together in my name.*

If you ever had a pet run away, you know how worried you were until that pet was found. God feels that way about lost people. A lost person is someone who has strayed away from God and is headed in the wrong direction. God loves people so much that he sent his only Son, Jesus, to seek and save lost people everywhere. Whenever a lost person is found and saved, all of heaven rejoices with God.

Acknowledge that the LORD is God! He made us, and we are his. We are his people, the sheep of his pasture. PSALM 100:3

JULY 26

from Your Heart

Peter wanted to know how many times he should forgive someone who sins against him. What do you think Jesus told him?

Matthew 18:21-35

Then Peter came to him and asked, "Lord, how often should I forgive someone* who sins against me? Seven times?"

²²"No, not seven times," Jesus replied, "but seventy times seven!*

²³"Therefore, the Kingdom of Heaven can be compared to a king who decided to bring his accounts up to date with servants who had borrowed money from him. ²⁴In the process, one of his debtors was brought in who owed him millions of dollars.* ²⁵He couldn't pay, so his master ordered that he be sold—along with his wife, his children, and everything he owned—to pay the debt.

²⁶"But the man fell down before his master and begged him, 'Please, be patient with me, and I will pay it all.' ²⁷Then his master was filled with pity for him, and he released him and forgave his debt.

²⁸"But when the man left the king, he went to a fellow servant who owed him a few thousand dollars.* He grabbed him by the throat and demanded instant payment.

²⁹"His fellow servant fell down before him and begged for a little more time. 'Be patient with me, and I will pay it,' he pleaded. ³⁰But his creditor wouldn't wait. He had the man arrested and put in prison until the debt could be paid in full.

³¹"When some of the other servants saw this, they were very upset. They went to the king and told him everything that had happened. ³²Then the king called in the man he had forgiven and said, 'You evil servant! I forgave you that tremendous debt because you pleaded with me. ³³Shouldn't you have mercy on your fellow servant, just as I had mercy on you?' ³⁴Then the angry king sent the man to prison to be tortured until he had paid his entire debt.

³⁵"That's what my heavenly Father will do to you if you refuse to forgive your brothers and sisters* from your heart."

18:21 Greek *my brother.* 18:22 Or *seventy-seven times.* 18:24 Greek *10,000 talents* [375 tons or 340 metric tons of silver].
18:28 Greek *100 denarii.* A denarius was equivalent to a laborer's full day's wage. 18:35 Greek *your brother.*

How many times should we forgive someone who sins against us? The same number of times that God forgives us! God's love and forgiveness have no limits. He will always forgive us! So we should not put a limit on the number of times we'll forgive other people. Every time you need to forgive someone, just remember how much God has forgiven you. Show God's love by forgiving that person over and over.

Oh, what joy for those whose disobedience is forgiven, whose sin is put out of sight! PSALM 32:1

JULY 27

critics and Believers

People didn't know what to think of Jesus. Look how much confusion there was about him in this story.

John 7:10-31

After his brothers left for the festival, Jesus also went, though secretly, staying out of public view. [11]The Jewish leaders tried to find him at the festival and kept asking if anyone had seen him. [12]There was a lot of grumbling about him among the crowds. Some argued, "He's a good man," but others said, "He's nothing but a fraud who deceives the people." [13]But no one had the courage to speak favorably about him in public, for they were afraid of getting in trouble with the Jewish leaders.

[14]Then, midway through the festival, Jesus went up to the Temple and began to teach. [15]The people* were surprised when they heard him. "How does he know so much when he hasn't been trained?" they asked.

[16]So Jesus told them, "My message is not my own; it comes from God who sent me. [17]Anyone who wants to do the will of God will know whether my teaching is from God or is merely my own. [18]Those who speak for themselves want glory only for themselves, but a person who seeks to honor the one who sent him speaks truth, not lies. [19]Moses gave you the law, but none of you obeys it! In fact, you are trying to kill me."

[20]The crowd replied, "You're demon possessed! Who's trying to kill you?"

[21]Jesus replied, "I did one miracle on the Sabbath, and you were amazed. [22]But you work on the Sabbath, too, when you obey Moses' law of circumcision. (Actually, this tradition of circumcision began with the patriarchs, long before the law of Moses.) [23]For if the correct time for circumcising your son falls on the Sabbath, you go ahead and do it so as not to break the law of Moses. So why should you be angry with me for healing a man on the Sabbath? [24]Look beneath the surface so you can judge correctly."

²⁵Some of the people who lived in Jerusalem started to ask each other, "Isn't this the man they are trying to kill? ²⁶But here he is, speaking in public, and they say nothing to him. Could our leaders possibly believe that he is the Messiah? ²⁷But how could he be? For we know where this man comes from. When the Messiah comes, he will simply appear; no one will know where he comes from."

²⁸While Jesus was teaching in the Temple, he called out, "Yes, you know me, and you know where I come from. But I'm not here on my own. The one who sent me is true, and you don't know him. ²⁹But I know him because I come from him, and he sent me to you." ³⁰Then the leaders tried to arrest him; but no one laid a hand on him, because his time* had not yet come.

³¹Many among the crowds at the Temple believed in him. "After all," they said, "would you expect the Messiah to do more miraculous signs than this man has done?"

7:15 Greek *Jewish people.*   7:30 Greek *his hour.*

Jesus said that people would understand that he was from God if they *really* wanted to do the will of God. Many people today like to argue about Jesus. Some people like to talk as if they know all about him. But those who actually obey God are the ones who truly know who Jesus is. Do you want to know Jesus? Then obey God and do his will.

This is what the LORD of Heaven's Armies, the God of Israel, says . . . "Obey me, and I will be your God, and you will be my people. Do everything as I say, and all will be well!" JEREMIAH 7:21, 23

JULY 28

An Attempted Arrest
The Pharisees wanted to arrest Jesus. But the guards they sent to arrest Jesus didn't do it. Why not?

John 7:32-52
When the Pharisees heard that the crowds were whispering such things, they and the leading priests sent Temple guards to arrest Jesus. ³³But Jesus told them, "I will be with you only a little longer. Then I will return to the one who sent me. ³⁴You will search for me but not find me. And you cannot go where I am going."

³⁵The Jewish leaders were puzzled by this statement. "Where is he planning to go?" they asked. "Is he thinking of leaving the country and going to the Jews in other lands?* Maybe he will even teach the Greeks! ³⁶What does he mean when he says, 'You will search for me but not find me,' and 'You cannot go where I am going'?"

³⁷On the last day, the climax of the festival, Jesus stood and shouted to the crowds, "Anyone who is thirsty may come to me! ³⁸Anyone who believes in me may

269

come and drink! For the Scriptures declare, 'Rivers of living water will flow from his heart.' "* 39(When he said "living water," he was speaking of the Spirit, who would be given to everyone believing in him. But the Spirit had not yet been given,* because Jesus had not yet entered into his glory.)

40When the crowds heard him say this, some of them declared, "Surely this man is the Prophet we've been expecting."* 41Others said, "He is the Messiah." Still others said, "But he can't be! Will the Messiah come from Galilee? 42For the Scriptures clearly state that the Messiah will be born of the royal line of David, in Bethlehem, the village where King David was born."* 43So the crowd was divided about him. 44Some even wanted him arrested, but no one laid a hand on him.

45When the Temple guards returned without having arrested Jesus, the leading priests and Pharisees demanded, "Why didn't you bring him in?"

46"We have never heard anyone speak like this!" the guards responded.

47"Have you been led astray, too?" the Pharisees mocked. 48"Is there a single one of us rulers or Pharisees who believes in him? 49This foolish crowd follows him, but they are ignorant of the law. God's curse is on them!"

50Then Nicodemus, the leader who had met with Jesus earlier, spoke up. 51"Is it legal to convict a man before he is given a hearing?" he asked.

52They replied, "Are you from Galilee, too? Search the Scriptures and see for yourself—no prophet ever comes* from Galilee!"

7:35 Or *the Jews who live among the Greeks?* 7:37-38 Or *"Let anyone who is thirsty come to me and drink.* 38*For the Scriptures declare, 'Rivers of living water will flow from the heart of anyone who believes in me.'"* 7:39 Some manuscripts read *But as yet there was no (Holy) Spirit.* 7:40 See Deut 18:15, 18; Mal 4:5-6. 7:42 See Mic 5:2. 7:52 Some manuscripts read *the prophet does not come.*

The guards were amazed by what Jesus said, so they didn't arrest him! When people see Jesus for who he really is and when they listen to what he has to say, amazing things happen. People often do something completely different from what they had planned (like the guards did). Maybe they even change their entire life because of Jesus! Have you really listened to what Jesus says? Is there anything in your life that you need to change based on his words?

Anyone who belongs to Christ has become a new person. The old life is gone; a new life has begun! 2 CORINTHIANS 5:17

JULY 29

A forgiven woman

The Pharisees brought a woman to Jesus because they wanted to see if he would get her in big trouble for sinning. What did Jesus say to her?

John 8:1-11

Jesus returned to the Mount of Olives, ²but early the next morning he was back again at the Temple. A crowd soon gathered, and he sat down and taught them. ³As he was speaking, the teachers of religious law and the Pharisees brought a woman who had been caught in the act of adultery. They put her in front of the crowd.

⁴"Teacher," they said to Jesus, "this woman was caught in the act of adultery. ⁵The law of Moses says to stone her. What do you say?"

⁶They were trying to trap him into saying something they could use against him, but Jesus stooped down and wrote in the dust with his finger. ⁷They kept demanding an answer, so he stood up again and said, "All right, but let the one who has never sinned throw the first stone!" ⁸Then he stooped down again and wrote in the dust.

⁹When the accusers heard this, they slipped away one by one, beginning with the oldest, until only Jesus was left in the middle of the crowd with the woman. ¹⁰Then Jesus stood up again and said to the woman, "Where are your accusers? Didn't even one of them condemn you?"

¹¹"No, Lord," she said.

And Jesus said, "Neither do I. Go and sin no more."

Instead of punishing the woman, Jesus asked the people there to look at their own life. It's easy to see others' sins but often hard to recognize our own wrongdoings. When we are willing to think about our own sins, it makes us less ready to point a finger and blame others. Everyone sins. Instead of focusing on other people, we should pay attention to our own life. Ask God today to forgive the sin in your life.

Help us, O God of our salvation! Help us for the glory of your name. Save us and forgive our sins for the honor of your name. PSALM 79:9

JULY 30

The Light of Life

The Pharisees still didn't believe in Jesus. What did Jesus say that they needed to do?

John 8:12-30

Jesus spoke to the people once more and said, "I am the light of the world. If you follow me, you won't have to walk in darkness, because you will have the light that leads to life."

[13]The Pharisees replied, "You are making those claims about yourself! Such testimony is not valid."

[14]Jesus told them, "These claims are valid even though I make them about myself. For I know where I came from and where I am going, but you don't know this about me. [15]You judge me by human standards, but I do not judge anyone. [16]And if I did, my judgment would be correct in every respect because I am not alone. The Father* who sent me is with me. [17]Your own law says that if two people agree about something, their witness is accepted as fact.* [18]I am one witness, and my Father who sent me is the other."

[19]"Where is your father?" they asked.

Jesus answered, "Since you don't know who I am, you don't know who my Father is. If you knew me, you would also know my Father." [20]Jesus made these statements while he was teaching in the section of the Temple known as the Treasury. But he was not arrested, because his time* had not yet come.

[21]Later Jesus said to them again, "I am going away. You will search for me but will die in your sin. You cannot come where I am going."

[22]The people* asked, "Is he planning to commit suicide? What does he mean, 'You cannot come where I am going'?"

[23]Jesus continued, "You are from below; I am from above. You belong to this world; I do not. [24]That is why I said that you will die in your sins; for unless you believe that I AM who I claim to be,* you will die in your sins."

[25]"Who are you?" they demanded.

Jesus replied, "The one I have always claimed to be.* [26]I have much to say about you and much to condemn, but I won't. For I say only what I have heard from the one who sent me, and he is completely truthful." [27]But they still didn't understand that he was talking about his Father.

[28]So Jesus said, "When you have lifted up the Son of Man on the cross, then you will understand that I AM he.* I do nothing on my own but say only what the Father taught me. [29]And the one who sent me is with me—he has not deserted me. For I always do what pleases him." [30]Then many who heard him say these things believed in him.

8:16 Some manuscripts read *The One*.   **8:17** See Deut 19:15.   **8:20** Greek *his hour*.   **8:22** Greek *Jewish people*.   **8:24** Greek *unless you believe that I am*. See Exod 3:14.   **8:25** Or *Why do I speak to you at all?*   **8:28** Greek *When you have lifted up the Son of Man, then you will know that I am*. "Son of Man" is a title Jesus used for himself.

Jesus said that he is the Light of the World. When we believe in him, we are able to see and understand what he says. Jesus lights the way for us and shows us how to live. But when people won't listen or believe in him, it's like they are in the darkness. They are unable to understand him. As Jesus' followers, we are to point others to Jesus' light so they no longer will be left in the dark. Who can you show Jesus' light to today?

You light a lamp for me. The LORD, my God, lights up my darkness. PSALM 18:28

JULY 31

TWO by TWO

Jesus sent out his followers to preach. What if people wouldn't listen to them?

Luke 10:1-24

The Lord now chose seventy-two* other disciples and sent them ahead in pairs to all the towns and places he planned to visit. ²These were his instructions to them: "The harvest is great, but the workers are few. So pray to the Lord who is in charge of the harvest; ask him to send more workers into his fields. ³Now go, and remember that I am sending you out as lambs among wolves. ⁴Don't take any money with you, nor a traveler's bag, nor an extra pair of sandals. And don't stop to greet anyone on the road.

⁵"Whenever you enter someone's home, first say, 'May God's peace be on this house.' ⁶If those who live there are peaceful, the blessing will stand; if they are not, the blessing will return to you. ⁷Don't move around from home to home. Stay in one place, eating and drinking what they provide. Don't hesitate to accept hospitality, because those who work deserve their pay.

⁸"If you enter a town and it welcomes you, eat whatever is set before you. ⁹Heal the sick, and tell them, 'The Kingdom of God is near you now.' ¹⁰But if a town refuses to welcome you, go out into its streets and say, ¹¹'We wipe even the dust of your town from our feet to show that we have abandoned you to your fate. And know this—the Kingdom of God is near!' ¹²I assure you, even wicked Sodom will be better off than such a town on judgment day.

¹³"What sorrow awaits you, Korazin and Bethsaida! For if the miracles I did in you had been done in wicked Tyre and Sidon, their people would have repented of their sins long ago, clothing themselves in burlap and throwing ashes on their heads to show their remorse. ¹⁴Yes, Tyre and Sidon will be better off on judgment day than you. ¹⁵And you people of Capernaum, will you be honored in heaven? No, you will go down to the place of the dead.*"

273

¹⁶Then he said to the disciples, "Anyone who accepts your message is also accepting me. And anyone who rejects you is rejecting me. And anyone who rejects me is rejecting God, who sent me."

¹⁷When the seventy-two disciples returned, they joyfully reported to him, "Lord, even the demons obey us when we use your name!"

¹⁸"Yes," he told them, "I saw Satan fall from heaven like lightning! ¹⁹Look, I have given you authority over all the power of the enemy, and you can walk among snakes and scorpions and crush them. Nothing will injure you. ²⁰But don't rejoice because evil spirits obey you; rejoice because your names are registered in heaven."

²¹At that same time Jesus was filled with the joy of the Holy Spirit, and he said, "O Father, Lord of heaven and earth, thank you for hiding these things from those who think themselves wise and clever, and for revealing them to the childlike. Yes, Father, it pleased you to do it this way.

²²"My Father has entrusted everything to me. No one truly knows the Son except the Father, and no one truly knows the Father except the Son and those to whom the Son chooses to reveal him."

²³Then when they were alone, he turned to the disciples and said, "Blessed are the eyes that see what you have seen. ²⁴I tell you, many prophets and kings longed to see what you see, but they didn't see it. And they longed to hear what you hear, but they didn't hear it."

10:1 Some manuscripts read *seventy;* also in 10:17.   10:15 Greek *to Hades.*

Jesus' followers were going from town to town. Those who rejected the message would be judged by God. But those who listened would receive God's reward. We need to listen to God's messengers too. Who in your life tells you about Jesus? Make sure you are listening!

[The Lord said,] "I will raise up a prophet like you from among their fellow Israelites. I will put my words in his mouth, and he will tell the people everything I command him. I will personally deal with anyone who will not listen to the messages the prophet proclaims on my behalf." DEUTERONOMY 18:18-19

JULY CHALLENGE
Hooray For You!

Time for some fireworks! You've earned it. You are more than halfway through the Bible if you started reading at the beginning of the year! Way to go. You're doing great, but maybe it seems as if you still have a long way to go. Did you ever hear someone say that things worth doing are never easy? Think about it. Is it easy to become a good soccer player or a great guitar player? No, it takes work! Reading through the whole Bible takes work too. But just keep doing it, and someday you'll look back and say it really was worth it. Really!

To show that you've finished the July readings, use a marker or highlighter to fill in the level you reached this month.

What is your favorite story about Jesus from this month's readings? Think of a way to remember the details of the story. Maybe you'd like to retell it in your own words. Or you might want to draw a favorite scene from the story. Read it again to be sure that you show exactly what happened.

IMPORTANT STUFF TO REMEMBER FROM JULY

❏ God wants us to believe in Jesus.

❏ One day we will be judged on whether or not we believe in Jesus.

❏ God wants us to serve him with our heart and actions, not just our words.

Time for some word fun!

In this month's readings, Jesus told the people how to treat one another. Find out what Jesus had to say by using the words below to make a sentence. The first and last words have been filled in to give you a head start. (Check your answer by looking at the reading for July 4. The answer is in Matthew 7:12.)

WORD BANK

you	whatever	to	to
like	them	others	you
to	Do	do	would

Do ____ _____ _____ _____

_____ _____ _____ ___ ___ ____ you.

Below, make a list of things you'd like others to do to you. Sign your name if you're going to try to do these things to others.

_____

_____

_____

_____

_____

_____

_____

Signature

276

AUGUST 1

The Good Neighbor

Jesus said that we need to love our neighbors. But would he expect us to love some person we don't even know or like?

Luke 10:25-37

One day an expert in religious law stood up to test Jesus by asking him this question: "Teacher, what should I do to inherit eternal life?"

²⁶Jesus replied, "What does the law of Moses say? How do you read it?"

²⁷The man answered, " 'You must love the LORD your God with all your heart, all your soul, all your strength, and all your mind.' And, 'Love your neighbor as yourself.'"*

²⁸"Right!" Jesus told him. "Do this and you will live!"

²⁹The man wanted to justify his actions, so he asked Jesus, "And who is my neighbor?"

³⁰Jesus replied with a story: "A Jewish man was traveling on a trip from Jerusalem to Jericho, and he was attacked by bandits. They stripped him of his clothes, beat him up, and left him half dead beside the road.

³¹"By chance a priest came along. But when he saw the man lying there, he crossed to the other side of the road and passed him by. ³²A Temple assistant* walked over and looked at him lying there, but he also passed by on the other side.

³³"Then a despised Samaritan came along, and when he saw the man, he felt compassion for him. ³⁴Going over to him, the Samaritan soothed his wounds with olive oil and wine and bandaged them. Then he put the man on his own donkey and took him to an inn, where he took care of him. ³⁵The next day he handed the innkeeper two silver coins,* telling him, 'Take care of this man. If his bill runs higher than this, I'll pay you the next time I'm here.'

³⁶"Now which of these three would you say was a neighbor to the man who was attacked by bandits?" Jesus asked.

³⁷The man replied, "The one who showed him mercy."

Then Jesus said, "Yes, now go and do the same."

10:27 Deut 6:5; Lev 19:18.   **10:32** Greek *A Levite*.   **10:35** Greek *two denarii*. A denarius was equivalent to a laborer's full day's wage.

Through this story, Jesus taught a startling lesson: Our "neighbors" include our enemies! This means that in order to obey God's command to love our neighbors, we need to love our enemies as well. Jesus wants us to love all people, whether we know and like them or not. Is there someone in your life who is difficult to love? Keep in mind the Good Samaritan's example. Love those you don't get along with. Then you will be keeping God's command to love your neighbor as yourself.

Do not seek revenge or bear a grudge against a fellow Israelite, but love your neighbor as yourself. LEVITICUS 19:18

AUGUST 2
Asking and Seeking

Jesus' disciples wanted to know how to pray. Look what Jesus told them about how to talk to God.

Luke 11:1-13

Once Jesus was in a certain place praying. As he finished, one of his disciples came to him and said, "Lord, teach us to pray, just as John taught his disciples."

²Jesus said, "This is how you should pray:*

"Father, may your name be kept holy.
    May your Kingdom come soon.
³Give us each day the food we need,*
    ⁴and forgive us our sins,
    as we forgive those who sin
        against us.
And don't let us yield to temptation.*"

⁵Then, teaching them more about prayer, he used this story: "Suppose you went to a friend's house at midnight, wanting to borrow three loaves of bread. You say to him, ⁶'A friend of mine has just arrived for a visit, and I have nothing for him to eat.' ⁷And suppose he calls out from his bedroom, 'Don't bother me. The door is locked for the night, and my family and I are all in bed. I can't help you.' ⁸But I tell you this—though he won't do it for friendship's sake, if you keep knocking long enough, he will get up and give you whatever you need because of your shameless persistence.*

⁹"And so I tell you, keep on asking, and you will receive what you ask for. Keep on seeking, and you will find. Keep on knocking, and the door will be opened to you. ¹⁰For everyone who asks, receives. Everyone who seeks, finds. And to everyone who knocks, the door will be opened.

¹¹"You fathers—if your children ask* for a fish, do you give them a snake instead? ¹²Or if they ask for an egg, do you give them a scorpion? Of course not! ¹³So if

you sinful people know how to give good gifts to your children, how much more will your heavenly Father give the Holy Spirit to those who ask him."

11:2 Some manuscripts add additional phrases from the Lord's Prayer as it reads in Matt 6:9-13.   11:3 Or *Give us each day our food for the day;* or *Give us each day our food for tomorrow.*   11:4 Or *And keep us from being tested.*   11:8 Or *in order to avoid shame,* or *so his reputation won't be damaged.*   11:11 Some manuscripts add *for bread, do you give them a stone? Or if they ask.*

Jesus told his disciples that God gives to those who ask. He also encouraged them to keep asking God for good things. Don't be afraid to ask God for what you need. He likes to give his children good gifts. But God will always give you what he knows is best. Sometimes God will say no, and sometimes he will have you wait. But you can be assured that God will always give you what is best!

*Whatever is good and perfect comes down to us from God our Father, who created all the lights in the heavens.** JAMES 1:17

1:17a Greek *from above, from the Father of lights.*

AUGUST 3

Testing Jesus

A woman in the crowd said Jesus' mother, Mary, was blessed. What did Jesus have to say about that?

Luke 11:14-28

One day Jesus cast out a demon from a man who couldn't speak, and when the demon was gone, the man began to speak. The crowds were amazed, [15]but some of them said, "No wonder he can cast out demons. He gets his power from Satan,* the prince of demons." [16]Others, trying to test Jesus, demanded that he show them a miraculous sign from heaven to prove his authority.

[17]He knew their thoughts, so he said, "Any kingdom divided by civil war is doomed. A family splintered by feuding will fall apart. [18]You say I am empowered by Satan. But if Satan is divided and fighting against himself, how can his kingdom survive? [19]And if I am empowered by Satan, what about your own exorcists? They

cast out demons, too, so they will condemn you for what you have said. [20]But if I am casting out demons by the power of God,* then the Kingdom of God has arrived among you. [21]For when a strong man like Satan is fully armed and guards his palace, his possessions are safe—[22]until someone even stronger attacks and overpowers him, strips him of his weapons, and carries off his belongings.

[23]"Anyone who isn't with me opposes me, and anyone who isn't working with me is actually working against me.

[24]"When an evil* spirit leaves a person, it goes into the desert, searching for rest. But when it finds none, it says, 'I will return to the person I came from.' [25]So it returns and finds that its former home is all swept and in order. [26]Then the spirit finds seven

other spirits more evil than itself, and they all enter the person and live there. And so that person is worse off than before."

²⁷As he was speaking, a woman in the crowd called out, "God bless your mother— the womb from which you came, and the breasts that nursed you!"

²⁸Jesus replied, "But even more blessed are all who hear the word of God and put it into practice."

11:15 Greek *Beelzeboul;* also in 11:18, 19. Other manuscripts read *Beezeboul;* Latin version reads *Beelzebub.* 11:20 Greek *by the finger of God.* 11:24 Greek *unclean.*

In Jesus' time, a woman's value—or blessings—came from the sons she raised. A man's blessings came from his family line—those who came before him. But Jesus' response to the woman meant that a person's obedience to God is more important than their place in the family. Obeying God is more important than the honor of bearing a respected son—even the Son of God! Don't miss out on God's very important blessings for you. Read his Word daily and obey it. God will honor and bless you as he did Mary.

Oh, how I love [God's] instructions! I think about them all day long. PSALM 119:97

AUGUST 4

Foolish Pharisees

A Pharisee criticized Jesus for not washing his hands according to tradition. Look what Jesus had to say in reply.

Luke 11:37-54

As Jesus was speaking, one of the Pharisees invited him home for a meal. So he went in and took his place at the table.* ³⁸His host was amazed to see that he sat down to eat without first performing the hand-washing ceremony required by Jewish custom. ³⁹Then the Lord said to him, "You Pharisees are so careful to clean the outside of the cup and the dish, but inside you are filthy—full of greed and wickedness! ⁴⁰Fools! Didn't God make the inside as well as the outside? ⁴¹So clean the inside by giving gifts to the poor, and you will be clean all over.

⁴²"What sorrow awaits you Pharisees! For you are careful to tithe even the tiniest income from your herb gardens,* but you ignore justice and the love of God. You should tithe, yes, but do not neglect the more important things.

⁴³"What sorrow awaits you Pharisees! For you love to sit in the seats of honor in the synagogues and receive respectful greetings as you walk in the marketplaces. ⁴⁴Yes, what sorrow awaits you! For you are like hidden graves in a field. People walk over them without knowing the corruption they are stepping on."

⁴⁵"Teacher," said an expert in religious law, "you have insulted us, too, in what you just said."

⁴⁶"Yes," said Jesus, "what sorrow also awaits you experts in religious law! For you

crush people with impossible religious demands, and you never lift a finger to ease the burden. ⁴⁷What sorrow awaits you! For you build monuments for the prophets your own ancestors killed long ago. ⁴⁸But in fact, you stand as witnesses who agree with what your ancestors did. They killed the prophets, and you join in their crime by building the monuments! ⁴⁹This is what God in his wisdom said about you:* 'I will send prophets and apostles to them, but they will kill some and persecute the others.'

⁵⁰"As a result, this generation will be held responsible for the murder of all God's prophets from the creation of the world—⁵¹from the murder of Abel to the murder of Zechariah, who was killed between the altar and the sanctuary. Yes, it will certainly be charged against this generation.

⁵²"What sorrow awaits you experts in religious law! For you remove the key to knowledge from the people. You don't enter the Kingdom yourselves, and you prevent others from entering."

⁵³As Jesus was leaving, the teachers of religious law and the Pharisees became hostile and tried to provoke him with many questions. ⁵⁴They wanted to trap him into saying something they could use against him.

11:37 Or *and reclined.*   11:42 Greek *tithe the mint, the rue, and every herb.*   11:49 Greek *Therefore, the wisdom of God said.*

The Pharisees were so concerned about looking good on the outside that they completely missed the importance of keeping clean on the inside! Although they had clean hands, their hearts were filled with greed and hatred. They missed the main point of a relationship with God—repentance and a new, clean heart. How clean is your heart? Take Jesus' warnings to the Pharisees seriously.

Who may climb the mountain of the LORD? Who may stand in his holy place? Only those whose hands and hearts are pure, who do not worship idols and never tell lies. PSALM 24:3-4

AUGUST 5

A Rich Fool

Jesus told this story to show why we shouldn't worry too much about money and our possessions.

Luke 12:13-21
Someone called from the crowd, "Teacher, please tell my brother to divide our father's estate with me."

¹⁴Jesus replied, "Friend, who made me a judge over you to decide such things as that?" ¹⁵Then he said, "Beware! Guard against every kind of greed. Life is not measured by how much you own."

¹⁶Then he told them a story: "A rich man

had a fertile farm that produced fine crops. ¹⁷He said to himself, 'What should I do? I don't have room for all my crops.' ¹⁸Then he said, 'I know! I'll tear down my barns and build bigger ones. Then I'll have room enough to store all my wheat and other goods. ¹⁹And I'll sit back and say to myself, "My friend, you have enough stored away for years to come. Now take it easy! Eat, drink, and be merry!"'

²⁰"But God said to him, 'You fool! You will die this very night. Then who will get everything you worked for?'

²¹"Yes, a person is a fool to store up earthly wealth but not have a rich relationship with God."

The rich man in this story was proud of all his money and the things he owned. But as he found out when it was time for him to die, all his wealth and possessions would be useless to him after he was dead. New clothes, new shoes, or the latest computer game cannot make us truly happy. They can't last. Place your trust in things that do last, like the Kingdom of God.

Greed causes fighting; trusting the LORD leads to prosperity. PROVERBS 28:25

AUGUST 6
Don't Worry

Jesus told his disciples not to worry about food and clothing. Why shouldn't we worry? Read and see.

Luke 12:22-34

Turning to his disciples, Jesus said, "That is why I tell you not to worry about everyday life—whether you have enough food to eat or enough clothes to wear. ²³For life is more than food, and your body more than clothing. ²⁴Look at the ravens. They don't plant or harvest or store food in barns, for God feeds them. And you are far more valuable to him than any birds! ²⁵Can all your worries add a single moment to your life? ²⁶And if worry can't accomplish a little thing like that, what's the use of worrying over bigger things?

²⁷"Look at the lilies and how they grow. They don't work or make their clothing, yet Solomon in all his glory was not dressed as beautifully as they are. ²⁸And if God cares so wonderfully for flowers that are here today and thrown into the fire tomorrow, he will certainly care for you. Why do you have so little faith?

²⁹"And don't be concerned about what to eat and what to drink. Don't worry about such things. ³⁰These things dominate the thoughts of unbelievers all over the world, but your Father already knows your needs. ³¹Seek the Kingdom of God above all else, and he will give you everything you need.

³²"So don't be afraid, little flock. For it gives your Father great happiness to give you the Kingdom.

³³"Sell your possessions and give to those in need. This will store up treasure

for you in heaven! And the purses of heaven never get old or develop holes. Your treasure will be safe; no thief can steal it and no moth can destroy it. ³⁴Wherever your treasure is, there the desires of your heart will also be."

Jesus told his disciples not to worry about food or clothes. Why? Because their worries would distract them from more important concerns, such as building God's kingdom. God knows what we need and he is able to provide for us. Rather than worrying about those things, spend your time and energy telling others about Jesus. Trust God to take care of you as you work to expand his kingdom here on earth.

[God] gives food to those who fear him; he always remembers his covenant.
PSALM 111:5

AUGUST 7

A Faithful Servant

Jesus told his disciples to be ready. What were they to be ready for?

Luke 12:35-48

[Jesus said,] "Be dressed for service and keep your lamps burning, ³⁶as though you were waiting for your master to return from the wedding feast. Then you will be ready to open the door and let him in the moment he arrives and knocks. ³⁷The servants who are ready and waiting for his return will be rewarded. I tell you the truth, he himself will seat them, put on an apron, and serve them as they sit and eat! ³⁸He may come in the middle of the night or just before dawn.* But whenever he comes, he will reward the servants who are ready.

³⁹"Understand this: If a homeowner knew exactly when a burglar was coming, he would not permit his house to be broken into. ⁴⁰You also must be ready all the time, for the Son of Man will come when least expected."

⁴¹Peter asked, "Lord, is that illustration just for us or for everyone?"

⁴²And the Lord replied, "A faithful, sensible servant is one to whom the master can give the responsibility of managing his other household servants and feeding them. ⁴³If the master returns and finds that the servant has done a good job, there will be a reward. ⁴⁴I tell you the truth, the master will put that servant in charge of all he owns. ⁴⁵But what if the servant thinks, 'My master won't be back for a while,' and he begins beating the other servants, partying, and getting drunk? ⁴⁶The master will return unannounced and unexpected, and he will cut the servant in pieces and banish him with the unfaithful.

⁴⁷"And a servant who knows what the master wants, but isn't prepared and doesn't carry out those instructions, will be severely punished. ⁴⁸But someone who

does not know, and then does something wrong, will be punished only lightly. When someone has been given much, much will be required in return; and when someone has been entrusted with much, even more will be required."

Jesus' disciples were to be ready for his return. Jesus told them that he would be coming again soon. But no one would know when. So they would have to be ready at all times. Being ready means obeying Jesus' commands and serving him daily by helping and loving others. Everyone needs to be ready. Continue to obey and serve him. If you do, when Jesus comes, you'll be ready!

[Jesus] will come as unexpectedly as a thief! Blessed are all who are watching for [him], who keep their clothing ready so they will not have to walk around naked and ashamed. REVELATION 16:15

AUGUST 8

Life and Freedom

Why do bad things happen? Jesus told the disciples how to react to catastrophes.

Luke 13:1-17

Jesus was informed that Pilate had murdered some people from Galilee as they were offering sacrifices at the Temple. 2"Do you think those Galileans were worse sinners than all the other people from Galilee?" Jesus asked. "Is that why they suffered? 3Not at all! And you will perish, too, unless you repent of your sins and turn to God. 4And what about the eighteen people who died when the tower in Siloam fell on them? Were they the worst sinners in Jerusalem? 5No, and I tell you again that unless you repent, you will perish, too."

6Then Jesus told this story: "A man planted a fig tree in his garden and came again and again to see if there was any fruit on it, but he was always disappointed. 7Finally, he said to his gardener, 'I've waited three years, and there hasn't been a single fig! Cut it down. It's just taking up space in the garden.'

8"The gardener answered, 'Sir, give it one more chance. Leave it another year, and I'll give it special attention and plenty of fertilizer. 9If we get figs next year, fine. If not, then you can cut it down.'"

10One Sabbath day as Jesus was teaching in a synagogue, 11he saw a woman who had been crippled by an evil spirit. She had been bent double for eighteen years and was unable to stand up straight. 12When Jesus saw her, he called her over and said, "Dear woman, you are healed of your sickness!" 13Then he touched her, and instantly she could stand straight. How she praised God!

14But the leader in charge of the synagogue was indignant that Jesus had healed her on the Sabbath day. "There are six days of the week for working," he said to the crowd. "Come on those days to be healed, not on the Sabbath."

¹⁵But the Lord replied, "You hypocrites! Each of you works on the Sabbath day! Don't you untie your ox or your donkey from its stall on the Sabbath and lead it out for water? ¹⁶This dear woman, a daughter of Abraham, has been held in bondage by Satan for eighteen years. Isn't it right that she be released, even on the Sabbath?"

¹⁷This shamed his enemies, but all the people rejoiced at the wonderful things he did.

A commonly held belief in Jesus' day was that those who suffered were bad people. But Jesus said that wasn't true then, so it's not true today either. When tragedy strikes, it should remind us that we all need to turn from our sins and accept Jesus as our Savior before it is too late.

I don't want you to die, says the Sovereign LORD. Turn back and live!
EZEKIEL 18:32

AUGUST 9

A Blind man sees

Jesus met a man who was born blind. How would Jesus react?

John 9:1-17

As Jesus was walking along, he saw a man who had been blind from birth. ²"Rabbi," his disciples asked him, "why was this man born blind? Was it because of his own sins or his parents' sins?"

³"It was not because of his sins or his parents' sins," Jesus answered. "This happened so the power of God could be seen in him. ⁴We must quickly carry out the tasks assigned us by the one who sent us.* The night is coming, and then no one can work. ⁵But while I am here in the world, I am the light of the world."

⁶Then he spit on the ground, made mud with the saliva, and spread the mud over the blind man's eyes. ⁷He told him, "Go wash yourself in the pool of Siloam" (Siloam means "sent"). So the man went and washed and came back seeing!

⁸His neighbors and others who knew him as a blind beggar asked each other, "Isn't this the man who used to sit and beg?" ⁹Some said he was, and others said, "No, he just looks like him!"

But the beggar kept saying, "Yes, I am the same one!"

¹⁰They asked, "Who healed you? What happened?"

¹¹He told them, "The man they call Jesus made mud and spread it over my eyes and told me, 'Go to the pool of Siloam and wash yourself.' So I went and washed, and now I can see!"

¹²"Where is he now?" they asked.

"I don't know," he replied.

[13]Then they took the man who had been blind to the Pharisees, [14]because it was on the Sabbath that Jesus had made the mud and healed him. [15]The Pharisees asked the man all about it. So he told them, "He put the mud over my eyes, and when I washed it away, I could see!"

[16]Some of the Pharisees said, "This man Jesus is not from God, for he is working on the Sabbath." Others said, "But how could an ordinary sinner do such miraculous signs?" So there was a deep division of opinion among them.

[17]Then the Pharisees again questioned the man who had been blind and demanded, "What's your opinion about this man who healed you?"

The man replied, "I think he must be a prophet."

9:4 Other manuscripts read *I must quickly carry out the tasks assigned me by the one who sent me;* still others read *We must quickly carry out the tasks assigned us by the one who sent me.*

Jesus demonstrated God's glory by healing this man and giving him sight. Many of the other people who saw this weren't sure what had happened and didn't believe that Jesus could have the power of God. However, the man who had been healed knew without a doubt that Jesus was from God. When we see Jesus at work in our life, our doubts about him will disappear also. Ask Jesus to open your eyes of faith.

The LORD says, "Now I will show them my power; now I will show them my might. At last they will know and understand that I am the LORD." JEREMIAH 16:21

AUGUST 10
They Couldn't See
The Pharisees wanted to know who had healed the blind man. What did they find out?

John 9:18-41

The Jewish leaders still refused to believe the man had been blind and could now see, so they called in his parents. [19]They asked them, "Is this your son? Was he born blind? If so, how can he now see?"

[20]His parents replied, "We know this is our son and that he was born blind, [21]but we don't know how he can see or who healed him. Ask him. He is old enough to speak for himself." [22]His parents said this because they were afraid of the Jewish leaders, who had announced that anyone saying Jesus was the Messiah would be expelled from the synagogue. [23]That's why they said, "He is old enough. Ask him."

[24]So for the second time they called in the man who had been blind and told him, "God should get the glory for this,* because we know this man Jesus is a sinner."

[25]"I don't know whether he is a sinner," the man replied. "But I know this: I was blind, and now I can see!"

[26]"But what did he do?" they asked.

"How did he heal you?"

²⁷"Look!" the man exclaimed. "I told you once. Didn't you listen? Why do you want to hear it again? Do you want to become his disciples, too?"

²⁸Then they cursed him and said, "You are his disciple, but we are disciples of Moses! ²⁹We know God spoke to Moses, but we don't even know where this man comes from."

³⁰"Why, that's very strange!" the man replied. "He healed my eyes, and yet you don't know where he comes from? ³¹We know that God doesn't listen to sinners, but he is ready to hear those who worship him and do his will. ³²Ever since the world began, no one has been able to open the eyes of someone born blind. ³³If this man were not from God, he couldn't have done it."

³⁴"You were born a total sinner!" they answered. "Are you trying to teach us?" And they threw him out of the synagogue.

³⁵When Jesus heard what had happened, he found the man and asked, "Do you believe in the Son of Man?*"

³⁶The man answered, "Who is he, sir? I want to believe in him."

³⁷"You have seen him," Jesus said, "and he is speaking to you!"

³⁸"Yes, Lord, I believe!" the man said. And he worshiped Jesus.

³⁹Then Jesus told him,* "I entered this world to render judgment—to give sight to the blind and to show those who think they see* that they are blind."

⁴⁰Some Pharisees who were standing nearby heard him and asked, "Are you saying we're blind?"

⁴¹"If you were blind, you wouldn't be guilty," Jesus replied. "But you remain guilty because you claim you can see."

9:24 Or *Give glory to God, not to Jesus;* Greek reads *Give glory to God.* **9:35** Some manuscripts read *the Son of God?* "Son of Man" is a title Jesus used for himself. **9:38-39a** Some manuscripts do not include "*Yes, Lord, I believe!" the man said. And he worshiped Jesus. Then Jesus told him.* **9:39b** Greek *those who see.*

Rather than rejoicing in the miracle of the man's restored sight, the Pharisees were intent on discrediting Jesus. They thought Jesus was a sinner because he had healed the man on the Sabbath. They even kicked the healed man out of the synagogue when he defended Jesus. It was the Pharisees who were blind, because they were unable to see that Jesus really is the Son of God. Make sure your eyes aren't shut like the Pharisees' were. See for yourself that Jesus is the Son of God!

Listen, you who are deaf! Look and see, you blind! Who is as blind as my own people, my servant? Who is as deaf as my messenger? Who is as blind as my chosen people, the servant of the LORD? ISAIAH 42:18-19

AUGUST 11

The Good Shepherd

Jesus told his disciples that he was like a good shepherd. What do you think he meant by that? Read and see.

John 10:1-18

[Jesus said,] "I tell you the truth, anyone who sneaks over the wall of a sheepfold, rather than going through the gate, must surely be a thief and a robber! ²But the one who enters through the gate is the shepherd of the sheep. ³The gatekeeper opens the gate for him, and the sheep recognize his voice and come to him. He calls his own sheep by name and leads them out. ⁴After he has gathered his own flock, he walks ahead of them, and they follow him because they know his voice. ⁵They won't follow a stranger; they will run from him because they don't know his voice."

⁶Those who heard Jesus use this illustration didn't understand what he meant, ⁷so he explained it to them: "I tell you the truth, I am the gate for the sheep. ⁸All who came before me* were thieves and robbers. But the true sheep did not listen to them. ⁹Yes, I am the gate. Those who come in through me will be saved.* They will come and go freely and will find good pastures. ¹⁰The thief's purpose is to steal and kill and destroy. My purpose is to give them a rich and satisfying life.

¹¹"I am the good shepherd. The good shepherd sacrifices his life for the sheep. ¹²A hired hand will run when he sees a wolf coming. He will abandon the sheep because they don't belong to him and he isn't their shepherd. And so the wolf attacks them and scatters the flock. ¹³The hired hand runs away because he's working only for the money and doesn't really care about the sheep.

¹⁴"I am the good shepherd; I know my own sheep, and they know me, ¹⁵just as my Father knows me and I know the Father. So I sacrifice my life for the sheep. ¹⁶I have other sheep, too, that are not in this sheepfold. I must bring them also. They will listen to my voice, and there will be one flock with one shepherd.

¹⁷"The Father loves me because I sacrifice my life so I may take it back again. ¹⁸No one can take my life from me. I sacrifice it voluntarily. For I have the authority to lay it down when I want to and also to take it up again. For this is what my Father has commanded."

10:8 Some manuscripts do not include *before me*.   10:9 Or *will find safety*.

A good shepherd takes care of his sheep, keeps them safe, and is even willing to give his own life for his sheep. That's exactly what Jesus does for us. He leads us to heaven, and he has given his life so we can get there safely. Will you follow Jesus as one of his much-loved sheep? Trust him to do whatever it takes to get you to heaven safely.

The LORD is my shepherd; I have all that I need. He lets me rest in green meadows; he leads me beside peaceful streams. PSALM 23:1-2

AUGUST 12

watch where you sit

Jesus scolded the Pharisees for trying to sit in the best places at the table. What did he tell them to do instead?

Luke 14:1-14

One Sabbath day Jesus went to eat dinner in the home of a leader of the Pharisees, and the people were watching him closely. ²There was a man there whose arms and legs were swollen.* ³Jesus asked the Pharisees and experts in religious law, "Is it permitted in the law to heal people on the Sabbath day, or not?" ⁴When they refused to answer, Jesus touched the sick man and healed him and sent him away. ⁵Then he turned to them and said, "Which of you doesn't work on the Sabbath? If your son* or your cow falls into a pit, don't you rush to get him out?" ⁶Again they could not answer.

⁷When Jesus noticed that all who had come to the dinner were trying to sit in the seats of honor near the head of the table, he gave them this advice: ⁸"When you are invited to a wedding feast, don't sit in the seat of honor. What if someone who is more distinguished than you has also been invited? ⁹The host will come and say, 'Give this person your seat.' Then you will be embarrassed, and you will have to take whatever seat is left at the foot of the table! ¹⁰"Instead, take the lowest place at the foot of the table. Then when your host sees you, he will come and say, 'Friend, we have a better place for you!' Then you will be honored in front of all the other guests. ¹¹For those who exalt themselves will be humbled, and those who humble themselves will be exalted."

¹²Then he turned to his host. "When you put on a luncheon or a banquet," he said, "don't invite your friends, brothers, relatives, and rich neighbors. For they will invite you back, and that will be your only reward. ¹³Instead, invite the poor, the crippled, the lame, and the blind. ¹⁴Then at the resurrection of the righteous, God will reward you for inviting those who could not repay you."

14:2 Or *who had dropsy.* 14:5 Some manuscripts read *donkey.*

Some people spend a great deal of time trying to make themselves look popular and important. But that's not what Jesus wants his followers to do. Jesus wants us to be humble and reach out to those who are rejected by everyone else. Do you know people like that? Try talking to them in the hall or sit with them at lunch. When we humble ourselves and try to respect and honor others, God will honor us as well.

All of you, serve each other in humility, for "God opposes the proud but favors the humble." I PETER 5:5
5:5 Prov 3:34 (Greek version).

AUGUST 13
Following Jesus
Jesus told his disciples that following him would not be easy. Why did he say that?

Luke 14:15-35
A man sitting at the table with Jesus exclaimed, "What a blessing it will be to attend a banquet* in the Kingdom of God!"

[16]Jesus replied with this story: "A man prepared a great feast and sent out many invitations. [17]When the banquet was ready, he sent his servant to tell the guests, 'Come, the banquet is ready.' [18]But they all began making excuses. One said, 'I have just bought a field and must inspect it. Please excuse me.' [19]Another said, 'I have just bought five pairs of oxen, and I want to try them out. Please excuse me.' [20]Another said, 'I now have a wife, so I can't come.'

[21]"The servant returned and told his master what they had said. His master was furious and said, 'Go quickly into the streets and alleys of the town and invite the poor, the crippled, the blind, and the lame.' [22]After the servant had done this, he reported, 'There is still room for more.'

[23]So his master said, 'Go out into the country lanes and behind the hedges and urge anyone you find to come, so that the house will be full. [24]For none of those I first invited will get even the smallest taste of my banquet.'"

[25]A large crowd was following Jesus. He turned around and said to them, [26]"If you want to be my disciple, you must hate everyone else by comparison—your father and mother, wife and children, brothers and sisters—yes, even your own life. Otherwise, you cannot be my disciple. [27]And if you do not carry your own cross and follow me, you cannot be my disciple.

[28]"But don't begin until you count the cost. For who would begin construction of a building without first calculating the cost to see if there is enough money to finish it? [29]Otherwise, you might complete only the foundation before running out of money, and then everyone would laugh at

you. ³⁰They would say, 'There's the person who started that building and couldn't afford to finish it!'

³¹"Or what king would go to war against another king without first sitting down with his counselors to discuss whether his army of 10,000 could defeat the 20,000 soldiers marching against him? ³²And if he can't, he will send a delegation to discuss

14:15 Greek *to eat bread.*

terms of peace while the enemy is still far away. ³³So you cannot become my disciple without giving up everything you own.

³⁴"Salt is good for seasoning. But if it loses its flavor, how do you make it salty again? ³⁵Flavorless salt is good neither for the soil nor for the manure pile. It is thrown away. Anyone with ears to hear should listen and understand!"

Jesus wanted committed followers. He did not want people to follow him and then decide that it was too hard. Even though following Jesus is not easy, it is worth the cost. Jesus has promised that if you give up some things to follow him, you will be rewarded with much better treasures, such as love, peace, and joy. Decide to follow Jesus no matter what the cost.

The eyes of the LORD search the whole earth in order to strengthen those whose hearts are fully committed to him. 2 CHRONICLES 16:9

AUGUST 14

Love the sinner

The Pharisees complained about the kinds of people Jesus taught. How did Jesus respond?

Luke 15:1-10

Tax collectors and other notorious sinners often came to listen to Jesus teach. ²This made the Pharisees and teachers of religious law complain that he was associating with such sinful people—even eating with them!

³So Jesus told them this story: ⁴"If a man has a hundred sheep and one of them gets lost, what will he do? Won't he leave the ninety-nine others in the wilderness and go to search for the one that is lost until he finds it? ⁵And when he has found it, he will joyfully carry it home on his shoulders. ⁶When he arrives, he will call together his friends and neighbors,

saying, 'Rejoice with me because I have found my lost sheep.' ⁷In the same way, there is more joy in heaven over one lost sinner who repents and returns to God than over ninety-nine others who are righteous and haven't strayed away!

⁸"Or suppose a woman has ten silver coins* and loses one. Won't she light a lamp and sweep the entire house and search carefully until she finds it? ⁹And when she finds it, she will call in her friends and neighbors and say, 'Rejoice with me because I have found my lost coin.' ¹⁰In the same way, there is joy in the presence of God's angels when even one sinner repents."

15:8 Greek *ten drachmas.* A drachma was the equivalent of a full day's wage.

Jesus knew that the Pharisees didn't care for the sinners who came to hear him preach. So Jesus told these stories about the lost coin and the lost sheep to show the Pharisees how much God loves sinners. What's your attitude toward those who have a bad reputation at school or in your neighborhood? Remember that God loves them, too. Instead of acting unkind to them and gossiping about them, pray for them and do what you can to make them aware of God's love for them.

God showed his great love for us by sending Christ to die for us while we were still sinners. ROMANS 5:8

AUGUST 15

A Runaway Son

Jesus told a story about a son who did some awful things that hurt his family and messed up his life. Would the boy's father be able to forgive him?

Luke 15:11-32

Jesus told them this story: "A man had two sons. [12]The younger son told his father, 'I want my share of your estate now before you die.' So his father agreed to divide his wealth between his sons.

[13]"A few days later this younger son packed all his belongings and moved to a distant land, and there he wasted all his money in wild living. [14]About the time his money ran out, a great famine swept over the land, and he began to starve. [15]He persuaded a local farmer to hire him, and the man sent him into his fields to feed the pigs. [16]The young man became so hungry that even the pods he was feeding the pigs looked good to him. But no one gave him anything.

[17]"When he finally came to his senses, he said to himself, 'At home even the hired servants have food enough to spare, and here I am dying of hunger! [18]I will go home to my father and say, "Father, I have sinned against both heaven and you, [19]and I am no longer worthy of being called your son. Please take me on as a hired servant."'

[20]"So he returned home to his father. And while he was still a long way off, his father saw him coming. Filled with love and compassion, he ran to his son, embraced him, and kissed him. [21]His son said to him, 'Father, I have sinned against both heaven and you, and I am no longer worthy of being called your son.*'

[22]"But his father said to the servants, 'Quick! Bring the finest robe in the house and put it on him. Get a ring for his finger and sandals for his feet. [23]And kill the calf we have been fattening. We must celebrate with a feast, [24]for this son of mine

was dead and has now returned to life. He was lost, but now he is found.' So the party began.

²⁵"Meanwhile, the older son was in the fields working. When he returned home, he heard music and dancing in the house, ²⁶and he asked one of the servants what was going on. ²⁷'Your brother is back,' he was told, 'and your father has killed the fattened calf. We are celebrating because of his safe return.'

²⁸"The older brother was angry and wouldn't go in. His father came out and begged him, ²⁹but he replied, 'All these years I've slaved for you and never once refused to do a single thing you told me to. And in all that time you never gave me even one young goat for a feast with my friends. ³⁰Yet when this son of yours comes back after squandering your money on prostitutes, you celebrate by killing the fattened calf!'

³¹"His father said to him, 'Look, dear son, you have always stayed by me, and everything I have is yours. ³²We had to celebrate this happy day. For your brother was dead and has come back to life! He was lost, but now he is found!'"

15:21 Some manuscripts add *Please take me on as a hired servant.*

The runaway son thought there was no way his dad would want him to come back home. But before the son even got to the front door, his dad came running out to hug and welcome him! Sometimes it may feel like you have done something so bad that God could never forgive you. But he can't wait for you to come back home to him. Don't be afraid to confess your sins to God. He is just waiting for you to come to him.

The LORD is like a father to his children, tender and compassionate to those who fear him. PSALM 103:13

AUGUST 16

God or money

Jesus taught many lessons about money. What did he teach about giving money away?

Luke 16:1-15

Jesus told this story to his disciples: "There was a certain rich man who had a manager handling his affairs. One day a report came that the manager was wasting his employer's money. ²So the employer called him in and said, 'What's this I hear about you? Get your report in order, because you are going to be fired.'

³"The manager thought to himself, 'Now what? My boss has fired me. I don't have the strength to dig ditches, and I'm too proud to beg. ⁴Ah, I know how to ensure that I'll have plenty of friends who will give me a home when I am fired.'

⁵"So he invited each person who owed money to his employer to come and discuss the situation. He asked the first one, 'How much do you owe him?' ⁶The man replied, 'I

owe him 800 gallons of olive oil.' So the manager told him, 'Take the bill and quickly change it to 400 gallons.*'

7"'And how much do you owe my employer?' he asked the next man. 'I owe him 1,000 bushels of wheat,' was the reply. 'Here,' the manager said, 'take the bill and change it to 800 bushels.*'

8"The rich man had to admire the dishonest rascal for being so shrewd. And it is true that the children of this world are more shrewd in dealing with the world around them than are the children of the light. 9Here's the lesson: Use your worldly resources to benefit others and make friends. Then, when your earthly possessions are gone, they will welcome you to an eternal home.*

10"If you are faithful in little things, you will be faithful in large ones. But if you are dishonest in little things, you won't be honest with greater responsibilities. 11And if you are untrustworthy about worldly wealth, who will trust you with the true riches of heaven? 12And if you are not faithful with other people's things, why should you be trusted with things of your own?

13"No one can serve two masters. For you will hate one and love the other; you will be devoted to one and despise the other. You cannot serve both God and money."

14The Pharisees, who dearly loved their money, heard all this and scoffed at him. 15Then he said to them, "You like to appear righteous in public, but God knows your hearts. What this world honors is detestable in the sight of God."

16:6 Greek *100 baths . . . 50 [baths].*   16:7 Greek *100 korous . . . 80 [korous].*   16:9 Or *you will be welcomed into eternal homes.*

Jesus taught his disciples to use their money to help others. Doing this would not only help people who needed it here on earth, but it would also store up rewards in heaven for the giver. Rather than always buying new things for yourself, look for ways to give to others. You will benefit more from giving some of your money away than from keeping it all to yourself.

Those who love money will never have enough. How meaningless to think that wealth brings true happiness! ECCLESIASTES 5:10

AUGUST 17

A Great Question

Jesus' disciples wanted to be honored in heaven. Wait till you see what Jesus told them about how to achieve greatness in God's kingdom.

Mark 10:35-45

James and John, the sons of Zebedee, came over and spoke to him. "Teacher," they said, "we want you to do us a favor."

36"What is your request?" he asked.

37They replied, "When you sit on your glorious throne, we want to sit in places of honor next to you, one on your right and the other on your left."

38But Jesus said to them, "You don't know what you are asking! Are you able to drink from the bitter cup of suffering I am about to drink? Are you able to be baptized with the baptism of suffering I must be baptized with?"

39"Oh yes," they replied, "we are able!"

Then Jesus told them, "You will indeed drink from my bitter cup and be baptized with my baptism of suffering. 40But I have no right to say who will sit on my right or my left. God has prepared those places for the ones he has chosen."

41When the ten other disciples heard what James and John had asked, they were indignant. 42So Jesus called them together and said, "You know that the rulers in this world lord it over their people, and officials flaunt their authority over those under them. 43But among you it will be different. Whoever wants to be a leader among you must be your servant, 44and whoever wants to be first among you must be the slave of everyone else. 45For even the Son of Man came not to be served but to serve others and to give his life as a ransom for many."

Jesus said those who serve others by helping them are the ones who are truly great in God's kingdom. Jesus is the King of heaven, but his mission on earth was to serve others. Those who are closest to him now will be most like him in heaven. Would you like to be great in the Kingdom of Heaven? Look around you. Find someone you can serve. Remember, when you serve others, you are serving God. Who can you help today?

You have been called to live in freedom, my brothers and sisters. But don't use your freedom to satisfy your sinful nature. Instead, use your freedom to serve one another in love. GALATIANS 5:13

AUGUST 18

Lazarus Dies

Jesus' friend Lazarus had died. Read about what happened when Jesus went to visit Lazarus's sisters.

John 11:17-36

When Jesus arrived at Bethany, he was told that Lazarus had already been in his grave for four days. [18]Bethany was only a few miles* down the road from Jerusalem, [19]and many of the people had come to console Martha and Mary in their loss. [20]When Martha got word that Jesus was coming, she went to meet him. But Mary stayed in the house. [21]Martha said to Jesus, "Lord, if only you had been here, my brother would not have died. [22]But even now I know that God will give you whatever you ask."

[23]Jesus told her, "Your brother will rise again."

[24]"Yes," Martha said, "he will rise when everyone else rises, at the last day."

[25]Jesus told her, "I am the resurrection and the life.* Anyone who believes in me will live, even after dying. [26]Everyone who lives in me and believes in me will never ever die. Do you believe this, Martha?"

[27]"Yes, Lord," she told him. "I have always believed you are the Messiah, the Son of God, the one who has come into the world from God." [28]Then she returned to Mary. She called Mary aside from the mourners and told her, "The Teacher is here and wants to see you." [29]So Mary immediately went to him.

[30]Jesus had stayed outside the village, at the place where Martha met him. [31]When the people who were at the house consoling Mary saw her leave so hastily, they assumed she was going to Lazarus's grave to weep. So they followed her there. [32]When Mary arrived and saw Jesus, she fell at his feet and said, "Lord, if only you had been here, my brother would not have died."

[33]When Jesus saw her weeping and saw the other people wailing with her, a deep anger welled up within him,* and he was deeply troubled. [34]"Where have you put him?" he asked them.

They told him, "Lord, come and see." [35]Then Jesus wept. [36]The people who were standing nearby said, "See how much he loved him!"

11:18 Greek *was about 15 stadia* [about 2.8 kilometers]. 11:25 Some manuscripts do not include *and the life.* 11:33 Or *he was angry in his spirit.*

Jesus cared deeply about his friends Lazarus, Mary, and Martha. When Jesus met Martha after Lazarus died, he comforted her with God's truth. Then he cried with Mary. Jesus cares deeply about you, too. If troubles surround you or if you are sad or feeling alone, come to Jesus. He understands your problems and your feelings. He wants to comfort you with his love and compassion.

I have seen what they do, but I will heal them anyway! I will lead them. I will comfort those who mourn. ISAIAH 57:18

AUGUST 19

Lazarus Lives

Lazarus had been dead for four days. But look what happened when Jesus told him to come out of the grave!

John 11:38-52

Jesus was still angry as he arrived at [Lazarus's] tomb, a cave with a stone rolled across its entrance. ³⁹"Roll the stone aside," Jesus told them.

But Martha, the dead man's sister, protested, "Lord, he has been dead for four days. The smell will be terrible."

⁴⁰Jesus responded, "Didn't I tell you that you would see God's glory if you believe?" ⁴¹So they rolled the stone aside. Then Jesus looked up to heaven and said, "Father, thank you for hearing me. ⁴²You always hear me, but I said it out loud for the sake of all these people standing here, so that they will believe you sent me." ⁴³Then Jesus shouted, "Lazarus, come out!" ⁴⁴And the dead man came out, his hands and feet bound in graveclothes, his face wrapped in a headcloth. Jesus told them, "Unwrap him and let him go!"

⁴⁵Many of the people who were with Mary believed in Jesus when they saw this happen. ⁴⁶But some went to the Pharisees and told them what Jesus had done. ⁴⁷Then the leading priests and Pharisees called the high council* together. "What are we going to do?" they asked each other. "This man certainly performs many miraculous signs. ⁴⁸If we allow him to go on like this, soon everyone will believe in him. Then the Roman army will come and destroy both our Temple* and our nation."

⁴⁹Caiaphas, who was high priest at that time,* said, "You don't know what you're talking about! ⁵⁰You don't realize that it's better for you that one man should die for the people than for the whole nation to be destroyed."

⁵¹He did not say this on his own; as high priest at that time he was led to prophesy that Jesus would die for the entire nation. ⁵²And not only for that nation, but to bring together and unite all the children of God scattered around the world.

11:47 Greek *the Sanhedrin.* 11:48 Or *our position;* Greek reads *our place.* 11:49 Greek *that year;* also in 11:51.

wheat is planted in the soil and dies, it remains alone. But its death will produce many new kernels—a plentiful harvest of new lives. ²⁵Those who love their life in this world will lose it. Those who care nothing for their life in this world will keep it for eternity. ²⁶Anyone who wants to be my disciple must follow me, because my servants must be where I am. And the Father will honor anyone who serves me.

²⁷"Now my soul is deeply troubled. Should I pray, 'Father, save me from this hour'? But this is the very reason I came! ²⁸Father, bring glory to your name."

Then a voice spoke from heaven, saying, "I have already brought glory to my name, and I will do so again." ²⁹When the crowd heard the voice, some thought it was thunder, while others declared an angel had spoken to him.

³⁰Then Jesus told them, "The voice was for your benefit, not mine. ³¹The time for judging this world has come, when Satan, the ruler of this world, will be cast out. ³²And when I am lifted up from the earth, I will draw everyone to myself." ³³He said this to indicate how he was going to die.

³⁴The crowd responded, "We understood from Scripture* that the Messiah would live forever. How can you say the Son of Man will die? Just who is this Son of Man, anyway?"

³⁵Jesus replied, "My light will shine for you just a little longer. Walk in the light while you can, so the darkness will not overtake you. Those who walk in the darkness cannot see where they are going. ³⁶Put your trust in the light while there is still time; then you will become children of the light."

After saying these things, Jesus went away and was hidden from them.

12:23 "Son of Man" is a title Jesus used for himself.   12:34 Greek *from the law.*

The crowd was confused. They thought that Jesus was the Messiah, Israel's future king, and that he would live forever. They were right in thinking that Jesus was the Messiah. But they didn't understand that Jesus had to die in order to pay the penalty for our sins. They didn't understand that Jesus would not remain dead but would rise from the dead three days later. Because of his death and resurrection, all who believe in him will live forever with him in heaven. That is wonderful news!

We apostles are witnesses of all he did throughout Judea and in Jerusalem. They put him to death by hanging him on a cross,* but God raised him to life on the third day. Then God allowed him to appear, not to the general public,* but to us whom God had chosen in advance to be his witnesses. We were those who ate and drank with him after he rose from the dead. ACTS 10:39-41

10:39 Greek *on a tree.*   10:41 Greek *the people.*

AUGUST 29

JESUS' MESSAGE

Even though Jesus had done many miracles, most people still wouldn't believe in him. See what Jesus said about people who reject him.

John 12:37-50

Despite all the miraculous signs Jesus had done, most of the people still did not believe in him. ³⁸This is exactly what Isaiah the prophet had predicted:

"LORD, who has believed our message?
    To whom has the LORD revealed his
        powerful arm?"*

³⁹But the people couldn't believe, for as Isaiah also said,

⁴⁰"The Lord has blinded their eyes
    and hardened their hearts—
so that their eyes cannot see,
    and their hearts cannot understand,
and they cannot turn to me
    and have me heal them."*

⁴¹Isaiah was referring to Jesus when he said this, because he saw the future and spoke of the Messiah's glory. ⁴²Many people did believe in him, however, including some of the Jewish leaders. But they wouldn't admit it for fear that the Pharisees would expel them from the synagogue. ⁴³For they loved human praise more than the praise of God.

⁴⁴Jesus shouted to the crowds, "If you trust me, you are trusting not only me, but also God who sent me. ⁴⁵For when you see me, you are seeing the one who sent me. ⁴⁶I have come as a light to shine in this dark world, so that all who put their trust in me will no longer remain in the dark. ⁴⁷I will not judge those who hear me but don't obey me, for I have come to save the world and not to judge it. ⁴⁸But all who reject me and my message will be judged on the day of judgment by the truth I have spoken. ⁴⁹I don't speak on my own authority. The Father who sent me has commanded me what to say and how to say it. ⁵⁰And I know his commands lead to eternal life; so I say whatever the Father tells me to say."

12:38 Isa 53:1.   12:40 Isa 6:10.

Jesus made it clear that he had come into the world for one reason—to save it. If people rejected him and his message, those people were really rejecting God. They will be judged by the truth of Jesus' words on the final judgment day. The choice is clear-cut: life or death; heaven or hell. Choose to spend eternity with Jesus. Take him at his word.

This one [Jesus] who is life itself was revealed to us, and we have seen him. And now we testify and proclaim to you that he is the one who is eternal life. He was with the Father, and then he was revealed to us. 1 JOHN 1:2

AUGUST 30

TWO SONS

Jesus told a story to show the religious leaders the difference between saying you will obey and actually obeying.

Matthew 21:23-32

When Jesus returned to the Temple and began teaching, the leading priests and elders came up to him. They demanded, "By what authority are you doing all these things? Who gave you the right?"

²⁴"I'll tell you by what authority I do these things if you answer one question," Jesus replied. ²⁵"Did John's authority to baptize come from heaven, or was it merely human?"

They talked it over among themselves. "If we say it was from heaven, he will ask us why we didn't believe John. ²⁶But if we say it was merely human, we'll be mobbed because the people believe John was a prophet." ²⁷So they finally replied, "We don't know."

And Jesus responded, "Then I won't tell you by what authority I do these things.

²⁸"But what do you think about this? A man with two sons told the older boy, 'Son, go out and work in the vineyard today.' ²⁹The son answered, 'No, I won't go,' but later he changed his mind and went anyway. ³⁰Then the father told the other son, 'You go,' and he said, 'Yes, sir, I will.' But he didn't go.

³¹"Which of the two obeyed his father?"

They replied, "The first."*

Then Jesus explained his meaning: "I tell you the truth, corrupt tax collectors and prostitutes will get into the Kingdom of God before you do. ³²For John the Baptist came and showed you the right way to live, but you didn't believe him, while tax collectors and prostitutes did. And even when you saw this happening, you refused to believe him and repent of your sins."

21:29-31 Other manuscripts read *"The second."* In still other manuscripts the first son says "Yes" but does nothing, the second son says "No" but then repents and goes, and the answer to Jesus' question is that the second son obeyed his father.

Jesus told this story to show people that God is not impressed by a "religious show." Instead, he wants our obedience. In this passage, the "sinners" were the ones who would enter God's kingdom because they had decided to obey God. The religious leaders acted like they were obeying God, but their obedience was just a show. God doesn't want lip service from people who simply say they follow him. If you say you will obey God, then do it. God wants your obedience, not just your talk.

What good is it, dear brothers and sisters, if you say you have faith but don't show it by your actions? Can that kind of faith save anyone? JAMES 2:14

AUGUST 31

A Hostile Takeover

Jesus told a story about vineyard workers. He was showing the reason why some people reject him. Can you tell what it is?

Matthew 21:33-46

[Jesus said,] "Now listen to another story. A certain landowner planted a vineyard, built a wall around it, dug a pit for pressing out the grape juice, and built a lookout tower. Then he leased the vineyard to tenant farmers and moved to another country. 34At the time of the grape harvest, he sent his servants to collect his share of the crop. 35But the farmers grabbed his servants, beat one, killed one, and stoned another. 36So the landowner sent a larger group of his servants to collect for him, but the results were the same.

37"Finally, the owner sent his son, thinking, 'Surely they will respect my son.'

38"But when the tenant farmers saw his son coming, they said to one another, 'Here comes the heir to this estate. Come on, let's kill him and get the estate for ourselves!' 39So they grabbed him, dragged him out of the vineyard, and murdered him.

40"When the owner of the vineyard returns," Jesus asked, "what do you think he will do to those farmers?"

41The religious leaders replied, "He will put the wicked men to a horrible death and lease the vineyard to others who will give him his share of the crop after each harvest."

42Then Jesus asked them, "Didn't you ever read this in the Scriptures?

'The stone that the builders rejected
　　has now become the cornerstone.
This is the Lord's doing,
　　and it is wonderful to see.'*

43I tell you, the Kingdom of God will be taken away from you and given to a nation that will produce the proper fruit. 44Anyone who stumbles over that stone will be broken to pieces, and it will crush anyone it falls on.*"

45When the leading priests and Pharisees heard this parable, they realized he was telling the story against them—they were the wicked farmers. 46They wanted to arrest him, but they were afraid of the crowds, who considered Jesus to be a prophet.

21:42 Ps 118:22-23.　21:44 This verse is omitted in some early manuscripts. Compare Luke 20:18.

The farmers in this story killed the messengers and the son because they didn't want to listen to them. They wanted to be the bosses. Sometimes people reject Jesus because they want to be their own boss and follow their own rules. The problem with being your own boss is that one day God, who is the *real* boss, will judge us on whether we have listened to his Son. How about you? Do you listen to Jesus or try to be your own boss?

I [God] will personally deal with anyone who will not listen to the messages the prophet proclaims on my behalf. DEUTERONOMY 18:19

AUGUST CHALLENGE
All right!

The weather is heating up, and so are you. One more month down! If you began reading in January, you are two-thirds of the way through the year. That's a great accomplishment. Keep it up!

To show that you've finished the August readings, use a marker or highlighter to fill in the level you reached this month.

What's the most exciting thing you learned about Jesus this month? What's the saddest thing? Pretend Jesus is coming to your town and there is going to be a parade. How will you get ready for the event? Will you try to get close to Jesus? What will you say to him? Perhaps you'd like to make a banner to wave as Jesus rides by.

....

....

....

....

....

IMPORTANT STUFF TO REMEMBER FROM AUGUST

❏ Jesus has power over life and death.

❏ Jesus heals people.

❏ Jesus takes care of his followers like a good shepherd takes care of his sheep.

❏ God has mercy on people even when they don't deserve it.

Time for some number fun!

When Jesus raised Lazarus from the dead, he told Martha something very unusual to comfort her. Do you remember what he said? Use the number code below to find out. (See the reading for August 18. The answer is in John 11:25.)

A	B	C	D	E	F	G	H	I	J	K	L	M
1	2	3	4	5	6	7	8	9	10	11	12	13

N	O	P	Q	R	S	T	U	V	W	X	Y	Z
14	15	16	17	18	19	20	21	22	23	24	25	26

 __   __ __   __ __ __   __ __ __ __ __ __ __ __ __ __ __ __ __
 9   1 13   20 8 5   18 5 19 21 18 18 5 3 20 9 15 14

 __ __ __   __ __ __   __ __ __ __ .   __ __ __ __ __ __ __   __ __ __
 1 14 4   20 8 5   12 9 6 5   1 14 25 15 14 5   23 8 15

 __ __ __ __ __ __ __ __ __   __ __   __ __   __ __ __ __   __ __ __ __ ,
 2 5 12 9 5 22 5 19   9 14   13 5   23 9 12 12   12 9 22 5

 __ __ __ __   __ __ __ __ __ __   __ __ __ __ __ __ .
 5 22 5 14   1 6 20 5 18   4 25 9 14 7

313

SEPTEMBER 1

The Wedding Feast

Jesus told a story about a wedding feast. Read to find out who was invited to the feast.

Matthew 22:1-14

Jesus also told them other parables. He said, ²"The Kingdom of Heaven can be illustrated by the story of a king who prepared a great wedding feast for his son. ³When the banquet was ready, he sent his servants to notify those who were invited. But they all refused to come!

⁴"So he sent other servants to tell them, 'The feast has been prepared. The bulls and fattened cattle have been killed, and everything is ready. Come to the banquet!' ⁵But the guests he had invited ignored them and went their own way, one to his farm, another to his business. ⁶Others seized his messengers and insulted them and killed them.

⁷"The king was furious, and he sent out his army to destroy the murderers and burn their town. ⁸And he said to his servants, 'The wedding feast is ready, and the guests I invited aren't worthy of the honor. ⁹Now go out to the street corners and invite everyone you see.' ¹⁰So the servants brought in everyone they could find, good and bad alike, and the banquet hall was filled with guests.

¹¹"But when the king came in to meet the guests, he noticed a man who wasn't wearing the proper clothes for a wedding. ¹²'Friend,' he asked, 'how is it that you are here without wedding clothes?' But the man had no reply. ¹³Then the king said to his aides, 'Bind his hands and feet and throw him into the outer darkness, where there will be weeping and gnashing of teeth.'

¹⁴"For many are called, but few are chosen."

Many people were invited to the feast. But a lot of them refused to come. The wedding feast in the story represents eternal life with Christ. Those who turn down the invitation know about Jesus but refuse to believe in him. You also have received an invitation to the wedding feast. Will you go? You don't want to miss out on the greatest celebration ever!

Enter [the Lord's] gates with thanksgiving; go into his courts with praise. Give thanks to him and praise his name. PSALM 100:4

SEPTEMBER 2

Trick Questions

The Pharisees tried to trap Jesus. But Jesus answered wisely. How did Jesus teach the Pharisees a lesson?

Luke 20:20-40

Watching for their opportunity, the leaders sent spies pretending to be honest men. They tried to get Jesus to say something that could be reported to the Roman governor so he would arrest Jesus. ²¹"Teacher," they said, "we know that you speak and teach what is right and are not influenced by what others think. You teach the way of God truthfully. ²²Now tell us—is it right for us to pay taxes to Caesar or not?"

²³He saw through their trickery and said, ²⁴"Show me a Roman coin.* Whose picture and title are stamped on it?"

"Caesar's," they replied.

²⁵"Well then," he said, "give to Caesar what belongs to Caesar, and give to God what belongs to God."

²⁶So they failed to trap him by what he said in front of the people. Instead, they were amazed by his answer, and they became silent.

²⁷Then Jesus was approached by some Sadducees—religious leaders who say there is no resurrection from the dead. ²⁸They posed this question: "Teacher, Moses gave us a law that if a man dies, leaving a wife but no children, his brother should marry the widow and have a child who will carry on the brother's name.* ²⁹Well, suppose there were seven brothers. The oldest one married and then died without children. ³⁰So the second brother married the widow, but he also died. ³¹Then the third brother married her. This continued with all seven of them, who died without children. ³²Finally, the woman also died. ³³So tell us, whose wife will she be in the resurrection? For all seven were married to her!"

³⁴Jesus replied, "Marriage is for people here on earth. ³⁵But in the age to come, those worthy of being raised from the dead will neither marry nor be given in marriage. ³⁶And they will never die again. In this respect they will be like angels. They are children of God and children of the resurrection.

³⁷"But now, as to whether the dead will be raised—even Moses proved this when he wrote about the burning bush. Long after Abraham, Isaac, and Jacob had died, he referred to the Lord* as 'the God of Abraham, the God of Isaac, and the God of Jacob.'* ³⁸So he is the God of the living, not the dead, for they are all alive to him."

³⁹"Well said, Teacher!" remarked some of the teachers of religious law who were standing there. ⁴⁰And then no one dared to ask him any more questions.

20:24 Greek *a denarius.* 20:28 See Deut 25:5-6. 20:37a Greek *when he wrote about the bush. He referred to the Lord.* 20:37b Exod 3:6.

Jesus knew that the Pharisees didn't really want an answer to their questions; they just wanted to get Jesus in trouble. Jesus showed them how wise he was by avoiding their traps. Sometimes others will try to get you to say or do something that will get you in trouble. How can you avoid these traps? Ask Jesus to show you the way out. Trust Jesus—he has been there.

The temptations in your life are no different from what others experience. And God is faithful. He will not allow the temptation to be more than you can stand. When you are tempted, he will show you a way out so that you can endure.
I CORINTHIANS 10:13

SEPTEMBER 3
The Greatest command
A religious leader asked Jesus which was the most important command. What did Jesus tell him?

Mark 12:28-37

One of the teachers of religious law was standing there listening to the debate. He realized that Jesus had answered well, so he asked, "Of all the commandments, which is the most important?"

29Jesus replied, "The most important commandment is this: 'Listen, O Israel! The LORD our God is the one and only LORD. 30And you must love the LORD your God with all your heart, all your soul, all your mind, and all your strength.'* 31The second is equally important: 'Love your neighbor as yourself.'* No other commandment is greater than these."

32The teacher of religious law replied, "Well said, Teacher. You have spoken the truth by saying that there is only one God and no other. 33And I know it is important to love him with all my heart and all my understanding and all my strength, and to love my neighbor as myself. This is more

important than to offer all of the burnt offerings and sacrifices required in the law."

34Realizing how much the man understood, Jesus said to him, "You are not far from the Kingdom of God." And after that, no one dared to ask him any more questions.

35Later, as Jesus was teaching the people in the Temple, he asked, "Why do the teachers of religious law claim that the Messiah is the son of David? 36For David himself, speaking under the inspiration of the Holy Spirit, said,

'The LORD said to my Lord,
Sit in the place of honor at my right hand
until I humble your enemies beneath your feet.'*

37Since David himself called the Messiah 'my Lord,' how can the Messiah be his son?" The large crowd listened to him with great delight.

12:29-30 Deut 6:4-5.   12:31 Lev 19:18.   12:36 Ps 110:1.

317

Jesus told the religious leader that the most important commandment is to love God with all your heart, soul, mind, and strength. How can we live by this command? We can start showing our love for God by obeying his commands found in his Word, the Bible. We can spend time getting to know and love God in prayer and worship. And we can ask God to show us if our wants, dreams, and goals are part of his plan for our life.

You must love the LORD your God with all your heart, all your soul, and all your strength. DEUTERONOMY 6:5

SEPTEMBER 4

Dirty on the Inside

Jesus scolded the Pharisees for their actions. What were they doing that made Jesus angry?

Matthew 23:1-26

Jesus said to the crowds and to his disciples, 2"The teachers of religious law and the Pharisees are the official interpreters of the law of Moses.* 3So practice and obey whatever they tell you, but don't follow their example. For they don't practice what they teach. 4They crush people with impossible religious demands and never lift a finger to ease the burden.

5"Everything they do is for show. On their arms they wear extra wide prayer boxes with Scripture verses inside, and they wear robes with extra long tassels.* 6And they love to sit at the head table at banquets and in the seats of honor in the synagogues. 7They love to receive respectful greetings as they walk in the marketplaces, and to be called 'Rabbi.'*

8"Don't let anyone call you 'Rabbi,' for you have only one teacher, and all of you are equal as brothers and sisters.* 9And don't address anyone here on earth as 'Father,' for only God in heaven is your spiritual Father. 10And don't let anyone call you 'Teacher,' for you have only one teacher, the Messiah. 11The greatest among you must be a servant. 12But those who exalt themselves will be humbled, and those who humble themselves will be exalted.

13"What sorrow awaits you teachers of religious law and you Pharisees. Hypocrites! For you shut the door of the Kingdom of Heaven in people's faces. You won't go in yourselves, and you don't let others enter either.*

15"What sorrow awaits you teachers of religious law and you Pharisees. Hypocrites! For you cross land and sea to make one convert, and then you turn that person into twice the child of hell* you yourselves are!

16"Blind guides! What sorrow awaits you! For you say that it means nothing to swear 'by God's Temple,' but that it is binding to swear 'by the gold in the Temple.' ¹⁷Blind fools! Which is more important—the gold or the Temple that makes the gold sacred? ¹⁸And you say that to swear 'by the altar' is not binding, but to swear 'by the gifts on the altar' is binding. ¹⁹How blind! For which is more important—the gift on the altar or the altar that makes the gift sacred? ²⁰When you swear 'by the altar,' you are swearing by it and by everything on it. ²¹And when you swear 'by the Temple,' you are swearing by it and by God, who lives in it. ²²And when you swear 'by heaven,' you are swearing by the throne of God and by God, who sits on the throne.

²³"What sorrow awaits you teachers of religious law and you Pharisees. Hypocrites! For you are careful to tithe even the tiniest income from your herb gardens,* but you ignore the more important aspects of the law—justice, mercy, and faith. You should tithe, yes, but do not neglect the more important things. ²⁴Blind guides! You strain your water so you won't accidentally swallow a gnat, but you swallow a camel!*

²⁵"What sorrow awaits you teachers of religious law and you Pharisees. Hypocrites! For you are so careful to clean the outside of the cup and the dish, but inside you are filthy—full of greed and self-indulgence! ²⁶You blind Pharisee! First wash the inside of the cup and the dish,* and then the outside will become clean, too."

23:2 Greek *and the Pharisees sit in the seat of Moses.*   23:5 Greek *They enlarge their phylacteries and lengthen their tassels.* 23:7 *Rabbi*, from Aramaic, means "master" or "teacher."   23:8 Greek *brothers.*   23:13 Some manuscripts add verse 14, *What sorrow awaits you teachers of religious law and you Pharisees. Hypocrites! You shamelessly cheat widows out of their property and then pretend to be pious by making long prayers in public. Because of this, you will be severely punished.* Compare Mark 12:40 and Luke 20:47.   23:15 Greek *of Gehenna.*   23:23 Greek *tithe the mint, the dill, and the cumin.*   23:24 See Lev 11:4, 23, where gnats and camels are both forbidden as food.   23:26 Some manuscripts do not include *and the dish.*

The Pharisees didn't obey God's commands. Instead, they made up their own rules to live by and then insisted that others live by their rules too. As a result, the Pharisees' lives were full of sin. Just as living by rules that people had made up didn't work for the Pharisees, it won't work for us either. Jesus said that God is our ultimate authority and that we should live by his rules. Studying the Bible helps us know what God's rules are so we can live in a way that pleases him.

I have hidden your [God's] word in my heart, that I might not sin against you.
PSALM 119:11

SEPTEMBER 5

The Future

Jesus told his disciples some bad news about the future. How did he comfort them?

Luke 21:5-19

Some of [Jesus'] disciples began talking about the majestic stonework of the Temple and the memorial decorations on the walls. But Jesus said, ⁶"The time is coming when all these things will be completely demolished. Not one stone will be left on top of another!"

⁷"Teacher," they asked, "when will all this happen? What sign will show us that these things are about to take place?"

⁸He replied, "Don't let anyone mislead you, for many will come in my name, claiming, 'I am the Messiah,'* and saying, 'The time has come!' But don't believe them. ⁹And when you hear of wars and insurrections, don't panic. Yes, these things must take place first, but the end won't follow immediately." ¹⁰Then he added, "Nation will go to war against nation, and kingdom against kingdom. ¹¹There will be great earthquakes, and there will be famines and plagues in many lands, and there will be terrifying things and great miraculous signs from heaven.

¹²"But before all this occurs, there will be a time of great persecution. You will be dragged into synagogues and prisons, and you will stand trial before kings and governors because you are my followers. ¹³But this will be your opportunity to tell them about me.* ¹⁴So don't worry in advance about how to answer the charges against you, ¹⁵for I will give you the right words and such wisdom that none of your opponents will be able to reply or refute you! ¹⁶Even those closest to you—your parents, brothers, relatives, and friends—will betray you. They will even kill some of you. ¹⁷And everyone will hate you because you are my followers.* ¹⁸But not a hair of your head will perish! ¹⁹By standing firm, you will win your souls."

21:8 Greek claiming, 'I am.' 21:13 Or This will be your testimony against them. 21:17 Greek on account of my name.

Jesus told his disciples that hard times were ahead of them. But he also said that he would give them the wisdom and the words they needed when they were questioned about their faith. This promise is true for us, too, if we live as Jesus' followers. We can stand firm in our faith no matter what our circumstances, because we know that God is with us. He will give us strength and wisdom in difficult times.

The Lord knows how to rescue godly people from their trials, even while keeping the wicked under punishment until the day of final judgment. 2 PETER 2:9

SEPTEMBER 6

watch and pray

What did Jesus tell his disciples to do to prepare for the end of the world?

Luke 21:25-36

[Jesus said,] "There will be strange signs in the sun, moon, and stars. And here on earth the nations will be in turmoil, perplexed by the roaring seas and strange tides. ²⁶People will be terrified at what they see coming upon the earth, for the powers in the heavens will be shaken. ²⁷Then everyone will see the Son of Man* coming on a cloud with power and great glory.* ²⁸So when all these things begin to happen, stand and look up, for your salvation is near!"

²⁹Then he gave them this illustration: "Notice the fig tree, or any other tree. ³⁰When the leaves come out, you know without being told that summer is near.

³¹In the same way, when you see all these things taking place, you can know that the Kingdom of God is near. ³²I tell you the truth, this generation will not pass from the scene until all these things have taken place. ³³Heaven and earth will disappear, but my words will never disappear.

³⁴"Watch out! Don't let your hearts be dulled by carousing and drunkenness, and by the worries of this life. Don't let that day catch you unaware, ³⁵like a trap. For that day will come upon everyone living on the earth. ³⁶Keep alert at all times. And pray that you might be strong enough to escape these coming horrors and stand before the Son of Man."

21:27a "Son of Man" is a title Jesus used for himself.   21:27b See Dan 7:13.

Jesus told his disciples to be ready for his return. He warned them to watch for the signs of his return, to pray, and to not live carelessly. As followers of Jesus, we need to pay attention to this warning as well. We can make ourselves ready for Jesus' return by reading and obeying God's Word and by spending time in prayer. We can also look for ways to show God's love and to help others know about Jesus as we watch for his return. Are you ready?

Devote yourselves to prayer with an alert mind and a thankful heart.
COLOSSIANS 4:2

SEPTEMBER 7

Ready and waiting

In this parable, Jesus is represented by the bridegroom. What happened to the bridesmaids who were not ready for the bridegroom's coming?

Matthew 25:1-13

[Jesus said,] "The Kingdom of Heaven can be illustrated by the story of ten brides-maids* who took their lamps and went to meet the bridegroom. ²Five of them were foolish, and five were wise. ³The five who were foolish didn't take enough olive oil for their lamps, ⁴but the other five were wise enough to take along extra oil. ⁵When the bridegroom was delayed, they all became drowsy and fell asleep.

⁶"At midnight they were roused by the shout, 'Look, the bridegroom is coming! Come out and meet him!'

⁷"All the bridesmaids got up and prepared their lamps. ⁸Then the five foolish ones asked the others, 'Please give us some of your oil because our lamps are going out.'

⁹"But the others replied, 'We don't have enough for all of us. Go to a shop and buy some for yourselves.'

¹⁰"But while they were gone to buy oil, the bridegroom came. Then those who were ready went in with him to the marriage feast, and the door was locked. ¹¹Later, when the other five bridesmaids returned, they stood outside, calling, 'Lord! Lord! Open the door for us!'

¹²"But he called back, 'Believe me, I don't know you!'

¹³"So you, too, must keep watch! For you do not know the day or hour of my return."

25:1 Or *virgins;* also in 25:7, 11.

Jesus told this story to prepare the disciples for his return. In the story, five of the ten bridesmaids were not ready when the bridegroom returned. They lost out and did not get in to the marriage feast. Like the bridegroom in the story, Jesus will return. Our job is to be ready so we won't miss out on all God has planned for us. Be prepared for Jesus' return. Live each day as if he might come at any moment.

You, too, must keep watch! For you don't know what day your Lord is coming.
MATTHEW 24:42

SEPTEMBER 8

The Three Servants

Jesus told the story of a master who left three of his servants in charge of some money. What was Jesus teaching about in this story?

Matthew 25:14-30

[Jesus said,] "The Kingdom of Heaven can be illustrated by the story of a man going on a long trip. He called together his servants and entrusted his money to them while he was gone. ¹⁵He gave five bags of silver* to one, two bags of silver to another, and one bag of silver to the last—dividing it in proportion to their abilities. He then left on his trip.

¹⁶"The servant who received the five bags of silver began to invest the money and earned five more. ¹⁷The servant with two bags of silver also went to work and earned two more. ¹⁸But the servant who received the one bag of silver dug a hole in the ground and hid the master's money.

¹⁹"After a long time their master returned from his trip and called them to give an account of how they had used his money. ²⁰The servant to whom he had entrusted the five bags of silver came forward with five more and said, 'Master, you gave me five bags of silver to invest, and I have earned five more.'

²¹"The master was full of praise. 'Well done, my good and faithful servant. You have been faithful in handling this small amount, so now I will give you many more responsibilities. Let's celebrate together!*'

²²"The servant who had received the two bags of silver came forward and said, 'Master, you gave me two bags of silver to invest, and I have earned two more.'

²³"The master said, 'Well done, my good and faithful servant. You have been faithful in handling this small amount, so now I will give you many more responsibilities. Let's celebrate together!'

²⁴"Then the servant with the one bag of silver came and said, 'Master, I knew you were a harsh man, harvesting crops you didn't plant and gathering crops you didn't cultivate. ²⁵I was afraid I would lose your money, so I hid it in the earth. Look, here is your money back.'

²⁶"But the master replied, 'You wicked and lazy servant! If you knew I harvested crops I didn't plant and gathered crops I didn't cultivate, ²⁷why didn't you deposit my money in the bank? At least I could have gotten some interest on it.'

²⁸"Then he ordered, 'Take the money from this servant, and give it to the one with the ten bags of silver. ²⁹To those who use well what they are given, even more will be given, and they will have an abundance. But from those who do nothing, even what little they have will be taken away. ³⁰Now throw this useless servant into outer darkness, where there will be weeping and gnashing of teeth.'"

25:15 Greek *talents;* also throughout the story. A talent is equal to 75 pounds or 34 kilograms.   25:21 Greek *Enter into the joy of your master* [or *your Lord*]; also in 25:23.

Jesus used this story to teach about stewardship—the responsible use of all that God has given us, whether it's our time, money, or talents. Two of the servants were good stewards, managing well what the master had given. The third servant didn't use what he had been given at all and was punished for being a poor steward. The lesson for us is clear: God has given each of us gifts, abilities, time, and possessions to manage. We are to use them to serve him and others. What has God given to you? Are you using what he has given in ways that please him?

In his grace, God has given us different gifts for doing certain things well.
ROMANS 12:6

SEPTEMBER 9
The Sheep and the Goats
Jesus described how he will judge us at the end of the world. Who gets to enter God's kingdom?

Matthew 25:31-46

[Jesus said,] "When the Son of Man* comes in his glory, and all the angels with him, then he will sit upon his glorious throne. ³²All the nations* will be gathered in his presence, and he will separate the people as a shepherd separates the sheep from the goats. ³³He will place the sheep at his right hand and the goats at his left.

³⁴"Then the King will say to those on his right, 'Come, you who are blessed by my Father, inherit the Kingdom prepared for you from the creation of the world. ³⁵For I was hungry, and you fed me. I was thirsty, and you gave me a drink. I was a stranger, and you invited me into your home. ³⁶I was naked, and you gave me clothing. I was sick, and you cared for me. I was in prison, and you visited me.'

³⁷"Then these righteous ones will reply, 'Lord, when did we ever see you hungry and feed you? Or thirsty and give you something to drink? ³⁸Or a stranger and show you hospitality? Or naked and give you clothing? ³⁹When did we ever see you sick or in prison and visit you?'

⁴⁰"And the King will say, 'I tell you the truth, when you did it to one of the least of these my brothers and sisters,* you were doing it to me!'

⁴¹"Then the King will turn to those on the left and say, 'Away with you, you cursed ones, into the eternal fire prepared for the devil and his demons.* ⁴²For I was hungry, and you didn't feed me. I was thirsty, and you didn't give me a drink. ⁴³I was a stranger, and you didn't invite me into your home. I was naked, and you didn't give me clothing. I was sick and in prison, and you didn't visit me.'

⁴⁴"Then they will reply, 'Lord, when did

we ever see you hungry or thirsty or a stranger or naked or sick or in prison, and not help you?'

⁴⁵"And he will answer, 'I tell you the truth, when you refused to help the least of these my brothers and sisters, you were refusing to help me.'

⁴⁶"And they will go away into eternal punishment, but the righteous will go into eternal life."

25:31 "Son of Man" is a title Jesus used for himself. 25:32 Or *peoples.* 25:40 Greek *my brothers.* 25:41 Greek *his angels.*

Some people in this story gave food and clothes to the poor. They helped care for the sick and those in need. These people were called sheep. They followed the example of their Shepherd, Jesus, by loving and caring for others. And they were rewarded for their faith and obedience by being allowed to enter God's kingdom. Jesus said that anyone who helps the poor and needy will enter this kingdom. We need to follow Jesus' example and the example of the sheep in the story by caring for others. Who can you help today?

There will always be some in the land who are poor. That is why I [God] am commanding you to share freely with the poor and with other Israelites in need.
DEUTERONOMY 15:11

SEPTEMBER 10

Preparing the Last Supper

The time of Jesus' death was near. How did he spend his last evening with his disciples?

Luke 22:1-20

The Festival of Unleavened Bread, which is also called Passover, was approaching. ²The leading priests and teachers of religious law were plotting how to kill Jesus, but they were afraid of the people's reaction.

³Then Satan entered into Judas Iscariot, who was one of the twelve disciples, ⁴and he went to the leading priests and captains of the Temple guard to discuss the best way to betray Jesus to them. ⁵They were delighted, and they promised to give him money. ⁶So he agreed and began looking for an opportunity to betray Jesus so they could arrest him when the crowds weren't around.

⁷Now the Festival of Unleavened Bread arrived, when the Passover lamb is sacrificed. ⁸Jesus sent Peter and John ahead and said, "Go and prepare the Passover meal, so we can eat it together."

⁹"Where do you want us to prepare it?" they asked him.

¹⁰He replied, "As soon as you enter Jerusalem, a man carrying a pitcher of water will meet you. Follow him. At the house he enters, ¹¹say to the owner, 'The Teacher asks: Where is the guest room where I can eat the Passover meal with my disciples?'

¹²He will take you upstairs to a large room that is already set up. That is where you should prepare our meal." ¹³They went off to the city and found everything just as Jesus had said, and they prepared the Passover meal there.

¹⁴When the time came, Jesus and the apostles sat down together at the table.* ¹⁵Jesus said, "I have been very eager to eat this Passover meal with you before my suffering begins. ¹⁶For I tell you now that I won't eat this meal again until its meaning is fulfilled in the Kingdom of God."

¹⁷Then he took a cup of wine and gave thanks to God for it. Then he said, "Take this and share it among yourselves. ¹⁸For I will not drink wine again until the Kingdom of God has come."

¹⁹He took some bread and gave thanks to God for it. Then he broke it in pieces and gave it to the disciples, saying, "This is my body, which is given for you. Do this to remember me."

²⁰After supper he took another cup of wine and said, "This cup is the new covenant between God and his people—an agreement confirmed with my blood, which is poured out as a sacrifice for you.*"

22:14 Or *reclined together.* 22:19-20 Some manuscripts omit 22:19b-20, *which is given for you . . . which is poured out as a sacrifice for you.*

Jesus celebrated the Passover meal with his disciples. At their meal, he began the tradition called Communion. When we celebrate Communion, we remember Jesus' death for sinners. It is also a celebration of the new agreement that God made with people through Jesus' death. If you follow Jesus, you are invited to participate in this special time of remembering what Jesus did when he died for you.

Every time you eat this bread and drink this cup, you are announcing the Lord's death until he comes again. I CORINTHIANS 11:26

SEPTEMBER 11

washing feet

After Jesus washed his disciples' feet, what did he tell the disciples to do?

John 13:1-17

Before the Passover celebration, Jesus knew that his hour had come to leave this world and return to his Father. He had loved his disciples during his ministry on earth, and now he loved them to the very end.* ²It was time for supper, and the devil had already prompted Judas,* son of Simon Iscariot, to betray Jesus. ³Jesus knew that the Father had given him authority over everything and that he had come from God and would return to God. ⁴So he got up from the table, took off his robe, wrapped a towel around his waist, ⁵and poured water into a basin. Then he began to wash the disciples' feet, drying them with the towel he had around him.

⁶When Jesus came to Simon Peter, Peter

said to him, "Lord, are you going to wash my feet?"

[7]Jesus replied, "You don't understand now what I am doing, but someday you will."

[8]"No," Peter protested, "you will never ever wash my feet!"

Jesus replied, "Unless I wash you, you won't belong to me."

[9]Simon Peter exclaimed, "Then wash my hands and head as well, Lord, not just my feet!"

[10]Jesus replied, "A person who has bathed all over does not need to wash, except for the feet,* to be entirely clean. And you disciples are clean, but not all of you." [11]For Jesus knew who would betray him. That is what he meant when he said, "Not all of you are clean."

[12]After washing their feet, he put on his robe again and sat down and asked, "Do you understand what I was doing? [13]You call me 'Teacher' and 'Lord,' and you are right, because that's what I am. [14]And since I, your Lord and Teacher, have washed your feet, you ought to wash each other's feet. [15]I have given you an example to follow. Do as I have done to you. [16]I tell you the truth, slaves are not greater than their master. Nor is the messenger more important than the one who sends the message. [17]Now that you know these things, God will bless you for doing them."

13:1 Or *he showed them the full extent of his love.*   13:2 Or *the devil had already intended for Judas.*   13:10 Some manuscripts do not include *except for the feet.*

As the King of heaven and earth, no one was above Jesus in power or authority. Yet he became like the lowest of servants and washed his disciples' dirty feet. He served the very people who should have been serving him! Jesus wants you to be like him. Humble yourself and be willing to serve others. Who can you serve today?

All of you, serve each other in humility, for "God opposes the proud but favors the humble." | PETER 5:5

5:5 Prov 3:34 (Greek version).

SEPTEMBER 12
A New Command
Jesus gave a new command. What was it?

John 13:21-38

Now Jesus was deeply troubled,* and he exclaimed, "I tell you the truth, one of you will betray me!"

[22]The disciples looked at each other, wondering whom he could mean. [23]The disciple Jesus loved was sitting next to Jesus at the table.* [24]Simon Peter motioned to him to ask, "Who's he talking about?" [25]So that disciple leaned over to Jesus and asked, "Lord, who is it?"

[26]Jesus responded, "It is the one to whom I give the bread I dip in the bowl." And when he had dipped it, he gave it to Judas, son of Simon Iscariot. [27]When Judas had eaten the bread, Satan entered into

him. Then Jesus told him, "Hurry and do what you're going to do." ²⁸None of the others at the table knew what Jesus meant. ²⁹Since Judas was their treasurer, some thought Jesus was telling him to go and pay for the food or to give some money to the poor. ³⁰So Judas left at once, going out into the night.

³¹As soon as Judas left the room, Jesus said, "The time has come for the Son of Man* to enter into his glory, and God will be glorified because of him. ³²And since God receives glory because of the Son,* he will soon give glory to the Son. ³³Dear children, I will be with you only a little longer. And as I told the Jewish leaders, you will search for me, but you can't come where I am going. ³⁴So now I am giving you a new commandment: Love each other. Just as I have loved you, you should love each other. ³⁵Your love for one another will prove to the world that you are my disciples."

³⁶Simon Peter asked, "Lord, where are you going?"

And Jesus replied, "You can't go with me now, but you will follow me later."

³⁷"But why can't I come now, Lord?" he asked. "I'm ready to die for you."

³⁸Jesus answered, "Die for me? I tell you the truth, Peter—before the rooster crows tomorrow morning, you will deny three times that you even know me."

13:21 Greek *was troubled in his spirit.* 13:23 Greek *was reclining on Jesus' bosom.* The "disciple Jesus loved" was probably John. 13:31 "Son of Man" is a title Jesus used for himself. 13:32 Some manuscripts omit *And since God receives glory because of the Son.*

The new command Jesus gave was for his followers to love one another as he loves us. Jesus said that when we do this, the world will know we are his followers. Loving others the way Jesus does is hard. It requires putting another person's needs ahead of our own. In a selfish world, that kind of love stands out. Love others just as Jesus does. Then the world will know who you belong to.

Do not seek revenge or bear a grudge against a fellow Israelite, but love your neighbor as yourself. LEVITICUS 19:18

SEPTEMBER 13

The only way

Jesus declared that he is the only way to God. How could he make this claim?

John 14:1-14

[Jesus said,] "Don't let your hearts be troubled. Trust in God, and trust also in me. ²There is more than enough room in my Father's home.* If this were not so, would I have told you that I am going to prepare a place for you?* ³When everything is ready, I will come and get you, so that you will always be with me where I am. ⁴And you know the way to where I am going."

⁵"No, we don't know, Lord," Thomas said. "We have no idea where you are going, so how can we know the way?"

⁶Jesus told him, "I am the way, the truth, and the life. No one can come to the Father except through me. ⁷If you had really known me, you would know who my Father is.* From now on, you do know him and have seen him!"

⁸Philip said, "Lord, show us the Father, and we will be satisfied."

⁹Jesus replied, "Have I been with you all this time, Philip, and yet you still don't know who I am? Anyone who has seen me has seen the Father! So why are you asking me to show him to you? ¹⁰Don't you believe that I am in the Father and the Father is in me? The words I speak are not my own, but my Father who lives in me does his work through me. ¹¹Just believe that I am in the Father and the Father is in me. Or at least believe because of the work you have seen me do.

¹²"I tell you the truth, anyone who believes in me will do the same works I have done, and even greater works, because I am going to be with the Father. ¹³You can ask for anything in my name, and I will do it, so that the Son can bring glory to the Father. ¹⁴Yes, ask me for anything in my name, and I will do it!"

14:2a Or *There are many rooms in my Father's house.* 14:2b Or *If this were not so, I would have told you that I am going to prepare a place for you.* Some manuscripts read *If this were not so, I would have told you. I am going to prepare a place for you.* 14:7 Some manuscripts read *If you have really known me, you will know who my Father is.*

Jesus could say he is the only way to God because he is God's only Son. As his Son, Jesus not only knew God's plan for saving people from their sins, but he also *is* the way that God saves people. There is no other way for a person to be saved from the punishment he or she deserves for sin. That is why Jesus said he is "the way, the truth, and the life." Believe it!

There is salvation in no one else! God has given no other name under heaven by which we must be saved. ACTS 4:12

SEPTEMBER 14
The Spirit of Truth

It was time for Jesus to leave his disciples and return to heaven. Whom did he promise to send to help them?

John 14:15-31

[Jesus said,] "If you love me, obey* my commandments. ¹⁶And I will ask the Father, and he will give you another Advocate,* who will never leave you. ¹⁷He is the Holy Spirit, who leads into all truth. The world cannot receive him, because it isn't looking for him and doesn't recognize him. But you know him, because he lives with you now and later will be in you.* ¹⁸No, I will not abandon you as orphans—I will come to you. ¹⁹Soon the world will no longer see me, but you will see me. Since I live, you also will live. ²⁰When I am raised to life again, you will know that I am in my Father, and you are in me, and I am in you. [21]Those who accept my commandments and obey them are the ones who love me. And because they love me, my Father will love them. And I will love them and reveal myself to each of them."

[22]Judas (not Judas Iscariot, but the other disciple with that name) said to him, "Lord, why are you going to reveal yourself only to us and not to the world at large?"

[23]Jesus replied, "All who love me will do what I say. My Father will love them, and we will come and make our home with each of them. [24]Anyone who doesn't love me will not obey me. And remember, my words are not my own. What I am telling you is from the Father who sent me. [25]I am telling you these things now while I am still with you. [26]But when the Father sends the Advocate as my representative—that is, the Holy Spirit—he will teach you everything and will remind you of everything I have told you.

[27]"I am leaving you with a gift—peace of mind and heart. And the peace I give is a gift the world cannot give. So don't be troubled or afraid. [28]Remember what I told you: I am going away, but I will come back to you again. If you really loved me, you would be happy that I am going to the Father, who is greater than I am. [29]I have told you these things before they happen so that when they do happen, you will believe.

[30]"I don't have much more time to talk to you, because the ruler of this world approaches. He has no power over me, [31]but I will do what the Father requires of me, so that the world will know that I love the Father. Come, let's be going."

14:15 Other manuscripts read *you will obey;* still others read *you should obey.* 14:16 Or *Comforter,* or *Encourager,* or *Counselor.* Greek reads *Paraclete;* also in 14:26. 14:17 Some manuscripts read *and is in you.*

Jesus promised to send the Holy Spirit, who would live in all Christians. The Holy Spirit teaches us and reminds us of God's truth. As our advocate, he gives us his support and counsel. He also gives us peace and comfort when we go through hard times.

I [the Lord] will give them singleness of heart and put a new spirit within them. I will take away their stony, stubborn heart and give them a tender, responsive heart,* so they will obey my decrees and regulations. Then they will truly be my people, and I will be their God. EZEKIEL 11:19-20

11:19 Hebrew *a heart of flesh.*

SEPTEMBER 15

The Vine and the Branches
Jesus said that he was the vine. Who are the branches?

John 15:1-16
[Jesus said,] "I am the true grapevine, and my Father is the gardener. [2]He cuts off every branch of mine that doesn't produce fruit, and he prunes the branches that do bear fruit so they will produce even more.

³You have already been pruned and purified by the message I have given you. ⁴Remain in me, and I will remain in you. For a branch cannot produce fruit if it is severed from the vine, and you cannot be fruitful unless you remain in me.

⁵"Yes, I am the vine; you are the branches. Those who remain in me, and I in them, will produce much fruit. For apart from me you can do nothing. ⁶Anyone who does not remain in me is thrown away like a useless branch and withers. Such branches are gathered into a pile to be burned. ⁷But if you remain in me and my words remain in you, you may ask for anything you want, and it will be granted! ⁸When you produce much fruit, you are my true disciples. This brings great glory to my Father.

⁹"I have loved you even as the Father has loved me. Remain in my love. ¹⁰When you obey my commandments, you remain in my love, just as I obey my Father's commandments and remain in his love. ¹¹I have told you these things so that you will be filled with my joy. Yes, your joy will overflow! ¹²This is my commandment: Love each other in the same way I have loved you. ¹³There is no greater love than to lay down one's life for one's friends. ¹⁴You are my friends if you do what I command. ¹⁵I no longer call you slaves, because a master doesn't confide in his slaves. Now you are my friends, since I have told you everything the Father told me. ¹⁶You didn't choose me. I chose you. I appointed you to go and produce lasting fruit, so that the Father will give you whatever you ask for, using my name."

Jesus used this example of a vine and branches to show his followers how much they needed to stay connected to him. When a branch falls off a vine, it turns brown and dies. In the same way, our spirit will begin to wither and die if we do not stay connected to Jesus. This means that we need to read God's Word, spend time talking to him in prayer, and worship with other Christians.

Whoever has the Son has life; whoever does not have God's Son does not have life. I JOHN 5:12

SEPTEMBER 16

Troubles Just for a While

Jesus talked about leaving his disciples. How did he comfort them?

John 16:16-33

"In a little while you won't see me [Jesus] anymore. But a little while after that, you will see me again."

¹⁷Some of the disciples asked each other, "What does he mean when he says, 'In a little while you won't see me, but then you will see me,' and 'I am going to the Father'? ¹⁸And what does he mean by 'a little while'? We don't understand."

[19]Jesus realized they wanted to ask him about it, so he said, "Are you asking yourselves what I meant? I said in a little while you won't see me, but a little while after that you will see me again. [20]I tell you the truth, you will weep and mourn over what is going to happen to me, but the world will rejoice. You will grieve, but your grief will suddenly turn to wonderful joy. [21]It will be like a woman suffering the pains of labor. When her child is born, her anguish gives way to joy because she has brought a new baby into the world. [22]So you have sorrow now, but I will see you again; then you will rejoice, and no one can rob you of that joy. [23]At that time you won't need to ask me for anything. I tell you the truth, you will ask the Father directly, and he will grant your request because you use my name. [24]You haven't done this before. Ask, using my name, and you will receive, and you will have abundant joy.

[25]"I have spoken of these matters in figures of speech, but soon I will stop speaking figuratively and will tell you plainly all about the Father. [26]Then you will ask in my name. I'm not saying I will ask the Father on your behalf, [27]for the Father himself loves you dearly because you love me and believe that I came from God. [28]Yes, I came from the Father into the world, and now I will leave the world and return to the Father."

[29]Then his disciples said, "At last you are speaking plainly and not figuratively. [30]Now we understand that you know everything, and there's no need to question you. From this we believe that you came from God."

[31]Jesus asked, "Do you finally believe? [32]But the time is coming—indeed it's here now—when you will be scattered, each one going his own way, leaving me alone. Yet I am not alone because the Father is with me. [33]I have told you all this so that you may have peace in me. Here on earth you will have many trials and sorrows. But take heart, because I have overcome the world."

Even though Jesus had to return to God, he promised that he would see his disciples again. He told them that there would be hard things to endure in life, but they could trust God to answer their prayers. Jesus' resurrection brought hope to the disciples, and it can bring us hope too. Knowing that we are saved from our sins and that Jesus is alive and will come back for us gives us the hope we need to live through hard times.

All praise to God, the Father of our Lord Jesus Christ. It is by his great mercy that we have been born again, because God raised Jesus Christ from the dead. Now we live with great expectation. I PETER 1:3

SEPTEMBER 17

JESUS PRAYS FOR US

Jesus knew he would die soon. He prayed for his disciples and for those who would believe him in the future—including you! What did Jesus pray for you?

John 17:1-26

After saying all these things, Jesus looked up to heaven and said, "Father, the hour has come. Glorify your Son so he can give glory back to you. ²For you have given him authority over everyone. He gives eternal life to each one you have given him. ³And this is the way to have eternal life—to know you, the only true God, and Jesus Christ, the one you sent to earth. ⁴I brought glory to you here on earth by completing the work you gave me to do. ⁵Now, Father, bring me into the glory we shared before the world began.

⁶"I have revealed you* to the ones you gave me from this world. They were always yours. You gave them to me, and they have kept your word. ⁷Now they know that everything I have is a gift from you, ⁸for I have passed on to them the message you gave me. They accepted it and know that I came from you, and they believe you sent me.

⁹"My prayer is not for the world, but for those you have given me, because they belong to you. ¹⁰All who are mine belong to you, and you have given them to me, so they bring me glory. ¹¹Now I am departing from the world; they are staying in this world, but I am coming to you. Holy Father, you have given me your name;* now protect them by the power of your name so that they will be united just as we are. ¹²During my time here, I protected them by the power of the name you gave me.* I

guarded them so that not one was lost, except the one headed for destruction, as the Scriptures foretold.

¹³"Now I am coming to you. I told them many things while I was with them in this world so they would be filled with my joy. ¹⁴I have given them your word. And the world hates them because they do not belong to the world, just as I do not belong to the world. ¹⁵I'm not asking you to take them out of the world, but to keep them safe from the evil one. ¹⁶They do not belong to this world any more than I do. ¹⁷Make them holy by your truth; teach them your word, which is truth. ¹⁸Just as you sent me into the world, I am sending them into the world. ¹⁹And I give myself as a holy sacrifice for them so they can be made holy by your truth.

²⁰"I am praying not only for these disciples but also for all who will ever believe in me through their message. ²¹I pray that they will all be one, just as you and I are one—as you are in me, Father, and I am in you. And may they be in us so that the world will believe you sent me.

²²"I have given them the glory you gave me, so they may be one as we are one. ²³I am in them and you are in me. May they experience such perfect unity that the world will know that you sent me and that you love them as much as you love me. ²⁴Father, I want these whom you have given me to be with me where I am. Then they can see all

the glory you gave me because you loved me even before the world began!

²⁵"O righteous Father, the world doesn't know you, but I do; and these disciples know you sent me. ²⁶I have revealed you to them, and I will continue to do so. Then your love for me will be in them, and I will be in them."

17:6 Greek *have revealed your name;* also in 17:26.   17:11 Some manuscripts read *you have given me these [disciples].* 17:12 Some manuscripts read *I protected those you gave me, by the power of your name.*

Jesus prayed that God would take care of his disciples after he left this world. That prayer wasn't only for the disciples who were following him at that time. Jesus' prayer was also for us. God has protected you and will continue to do so. Think of all the ways God has protected you in the last week. Thank him for the care he gives you each day.

*The Lord is faithful; he will strengthen you and guard you from the evil one.**
2 THESSALONIANS 3:3

3:3 Or *from evil.*

SEPTEMBER 18
A Painful Prayer
Just before his arrest, Jesus prayed to God. What did he pray?

Mark 14:32-42

They went to the olive grove called Gethsemane, and Jesus said, "Sit here while I go and pray." ³³He took Peter, James, and John with him, and he became deeply troubled and distressed. ³⁴He told them, "My soul is crushed with grief to the point of death. Stay here and keep watch with me."

³⁵He went on a little farther and fell to the ground. He prayed that, if it were possible, the awful hour awaiting him might pass him by. ³⁶"Abba, Father,"* he cried out, "everything is possible for you. Please take this cup of suffering away from me. Yet I want your will to be done, not mine."

³⁷Then he returned and found the disciples asleep. He said to Peter, "Simon, are you asleep? Couldn't you watch with me even one hour? ³⁸Keep watch and pray, so that you will not give in to temptation. For the spirit is willing, but the body is weak."

³⁹Then Jesus left them again and prayed the same prayer as before. ⁴⁰When he returned to them again, he found them sleeping, for they couldn't keep their eyes open. And they didn't know what to say.

⁴¹When he returned to them the third time, he said, "Go ahead and sleep. Have your rest. But no—the time has come. The Son of Man is betrayed into the hands of sinners. ⁴²Up, let's be going. Look, my betrayer is here!"

14:36 *Abba* is an Aramaic term for "father."

Jesus did not want to face the hardships of torture and death that lay ahead of him. What did he do? He prayed. He asked God to help him. At the same time, Jesus was willing to obey God's plan. Jesus' example is an excellent one to follow when we face problems or tough times. We can pray to God, asking for him to help. We should also be obedient to him and trust him to bring us through the hard times.

I take joy in doing your will, my God, for your instructions are written on my heart.
PSALM 40:8

SEPTEMBER 19

Betrayed!

Judas led a group of soldiers to arrest Jesus. How did the soldiers react when Jesus told them who he was?

John 18:1-24

After saying these things, Jesus crossed the Kidron Valley with his disciples and entered a grove of olive trees. ²Judas, the betrayer, knew this place, because Jesus had often gone there with his disciples. ³The leading priests and Pharisees had given Judas a contingent of Roman soldiers and Temple guards to accompany him. Now with blazing torches, lanterns, and weapons, they arrived at the olive grove.

⁴Jesus fully realized all that was going to happen to him, so he stepped forward to meet them. "Who are you looking for?" he asked.

⁵"Jesus the Nazarene,"* they replied.

"I AM he,"* Jesus said. (Judas, who betrayed him, was standing with them.) ⁶As Jesus said "I AM he," they all drew back and fell to the ground! ⁷Once more he asked them, "Who are you looking for?"

And again they replied, "Jesus the Nazarene."

⁸"I told you that I AM he," Jesus said. "And since I am the one you want, let these others go." ⁹He did this to fulfill his own statement: "I did not lose a single one of those you have given me."*

¹⁰Then Simon Peter drew a sword and slashed off the right ear of Malchus, the high priest's slave. ¹¹But Jesus said to Peter, "Put your sword back into its sheath. Shall I not drink from the cup of suffering the Father has given me?"

¹²So the soldiers, their commanding officer, and the Temple guards arrested Jesus and tied him up. ¹³First they took him to Annas, the father-in-law of Caiaphas, the high priest at that time.* ¹⁴Caiaphas was the one who had told the other Jewish leaders, "It's better that one man should die for the people."

¹⁵Simon Peter followed Jesus, as did another of the disciples. That other disciple was acquainted with the high priest, so he was allowed to enter the high priest's

335

courtyard with Jesus. ¹⁶Peter had to stay outside the gate. Then the disciple who knew the high priest spoke to the woman watching at the gate, and she let Peter in. ¹⁷The woman asked Peter, "You're not one of that man's disciples, are you?"

"No," he said, "I am not."

¹⁸Because it was cold, the household servants and the guards had made a charcoal fire. They stood around it, warming themselves, and Peter stood with them, warming himself.

¹⁹Inside, the high priest began asking Jesus about his followers and what he had been teaching them. ²⁰Jesus replied, "Every- one knows what I teach. I have preached regularly in the synagogues and the Temple, where the people* gather. I have not spoken in secret. ²¹Why are you asking me this question? Ask those who heard me. They know what I said."

²²Then one of the Temple guards standing nearby slapped Jesus across the face. "Is that the way to answer the high priest?" he demanded.

²³Jesus replied, "If I said anything wrong, you must prove it. But if I'm speaking the truth, why are you beating me?"

²⁴Then Annas bound Jesus and sent him to Caiaphas, the high priest.

18:5a Or *Jesus of Nazareth;* also in 18:7. **18:5b** Or *"The 'I AM' is here";* or *"I am the Lord";* Greek reads *I am;* also in 18:6, 8. See Exod 3:14. **18:9** See John 6:39 and 17:12. **18:13** Greek *that year.* **18:20** Greek *Jewish people;* also in 18:38.

When Jesus identified himself, the soldiers were frightened and fell to the ground. Jesus was so powerful that he had to willingly give himself up before the soldiers could arrest him. What an encouragement for those who follow Jesus! No one is more powerful than he is. It is clear that Jesus can easily defeat those who do evil. Trust Jesus to handle these people in the world.

The Lord knows how to rescue godly people from their trials, even while keeping the wicked under punishment until the day of final judgment. 2 PETER 2:9

SEPTEMBER 20
Jesus on Trial

The high priest questioned Jesus. What did Jesus say that made the high priest angry?

Matthew 26:57-68

Then the people who had arrested Jesus led him to the home of Caiaphas, the high priest, where the teachers of religious law and the elders had gathered. ⁵⁸Meanwhile, Peter followed him at a distance and came to the high priest's courtyard. He went in and sat with the guards and waited to see how it would all end.

⁵⁹Inside, the leading priests and the entire high council* were trying to find witnesses who would lie about Jesus, so they could put him to death. ⁶⁰But even though they found many who agreed to give false

336

witness, they could not use anyone's testimony. Finally, two men came forward [61]who declared, "This man said, 'I am able to destroy the Temple of God and rebuild it in three days.'"

[62]Then the high priest stood up and said to Jesus, "Well, aren't you going to answer these charges? What do you have to say for yourself?" [63]But Jesus remained silent. Then the high priest said to him, "I demand in the name of the living God—tell us if you are the Messiah, the Son of God."

[64]Jesus replied, "You have said it. And in the future you will see the Son of Man seated in the place of power at God's right hand* and coming on the clouds of heaven."*

[65]Then the high priest tore his clothing to show his horror and said, "Blasphemy! Why do we need other witnesses? You have all heard his blasphemy. [66]What is your verdict?"

"Guilty!" they shouted. "He deserves to die!"

[67]Then they began to spit in Jesus' face and beat him with their fists. And some slapped him, [68]jeering, "Prophesy to us, you Messiah! Who hit you that time?"

26:59 Greek *the Sanhedrin.*   26:64a Greek *seated at the right hand of the power.* See Ps 110:1.   26:64b See Dan 7:13.

Jesus said that he was God's Son. The high priest refused to believe him and accused Jesus of lying about something very serious. He considered what Jesus said blasphemy. Claiming to be God, if that's not who he was, would have been an insult to God. But Jesus wasn't lying. God's Word, the Bible, tells us that he was—and is—God's Son. God said so himself.

[God's] voice from the cloud said, "This is my Son, my Chosen One. Listen to him."* LUKE 9:35

9:35 Some manuscripts read *This is my dearly loved Son.*

SEPTEMBER 21

Peter's Denial

Peter denied even knowing Jesus. How did he feel after he did this?

Matthew 26:69-75

Meanwhile, Peter was sitting outside in the courtyard. A servant girl came over and said to him, "You were one of those with Jesus the Galilean."

[70]But Peter denied it in front of everyone. "I don't know what you're talking about," he said.

[71]Later, out by the gate, another servant girl noticed him and said to those standing around, "This man was with Jesus of Nazareth.*"

[72]Again Peter denied it, this time with an oath. "I don't even know the man," he said.

[73]A little later some of the other bystanders came over to Peter and said, "You must be one of them; we can tell by your Galilean accent."

[74]Peter swore, "A curse on me if I'm

337

lying—I don't know the man!" And immediately the rooster crowed.

⁷⁵Suddenly, Jesus' words flashed through Peter's mind: "Before the rooster crows, you will deny three times that you even know me." And he went away, weeping bitterly.

26:71 Or *Jesus the Nazarene.*

When Peter realized what he had done, he was truly sorry. He wept because he was sad and ashamed to have denied knowing Jesus. There may be times when we sin and feel bad about it. We may be ashamed of our actions or thoughts. We may even cry like Peter did. But despite our sins and shameful behavior, God will forgive us when we're sorry and confess what we have done. We can be very thankful for that.

If we confess our sins to [God], he is faithful and just to forgive us our sins and to cleanse us from all wickedness. I JOHN 1:9

SEPTEMBER 22

Herod Questions Jesus

Jesus was brought before Herod. How did Jesus respond to Herod's questions?

Luke 23:1-12

Then the entire council took Jesus to Pilate, the Roman governor. ²They began to state their case: "This man has been leading our people astray by telling them not to pay their taxes to the Roman government and by claiming he is the Messiah, a king."

³So Pilate asked him, "Are you the king of the Jews?"

Jesus replied, "You have said it."

⁴Pilate turned to the leading priests and to the crowd and said, "I find nothing wrong with this man!"

⁵Then they became insistent. "But he is causing riots by his teaching wherever he goes—all over Judea, from Galilee to Jerusalem!"

⁶"Oh, is he a Galilean?" Pilate asked.

⁷When they said that he was, Pilate sent him to Herod Antipas, because Galilee was under Herod's jurisdiction, and Herod happened to be in Jerusalem at the time.

⁸Herod was delighted at the opportunity to see Jesus, because he had heard about him and had been hoping for a long time to see him perform a miracle. ⁹He asked Jesus question after question, but Jesus refused to answer. ¹⁰Meanwhile, the leading priests and the teachers of religious law stood there shouting their accusations. ¹¹Then Herod and his soldiers began mocking and ridiculing Jesus. Finally, they put a royal robe on him and sent him back to Pilate. ¹²(Herod and Pilate, who had been enemies before, became friends that day.)

Jesus was silent. He did not answer Herod's questions because this ruler only wanted to make fun of the truth. Sometimes people are like Herod—they ask questions, but they don't really want to know the truth. They only want to mock our faith. In those situations, it is better not to say anything. Like Jesus, we need to know when people are interested in the truth and when they only want to make fun of it. Ask God to help you know when it is better just to be silent and when it's important to speak the truth.

Oh, the joys of those who do not follow the advice of the wicked, or stand around with sinners, or join in with mockers. PSALM 1:1

SEPTEMBER 23
sentenced to Death

Pilate gave in to the demands of the crowd. What did they want him to do?

Mark 15:6-24

Now it was the governor's custom each year during the Passover celebration to release one prisoner—anyone the people requested. [7]One of the prisoners at that time was Barabbas, a revolutionary who had committed murder in an uprising. [8]The crowd went to Pilate and asked him to release a prisoner as usual.

[9]"Would you like me to release this 'King of the Jews'?" Pilate asked. [10](For he realized by now that the leading priests had arrested Jesus out of envy.) [11]But at this point the leading priests stirred up the crowd to demand the release of Barabbas instead of Jesus. [12]Pilate asked them, "Then what should I do with this man you call the king of the Jews?"

[13]They shouted back, "Crucify him!"

[14]"Why?" Pilate demanded. "What crime has he committed?"

But the mob roared even louder, "Crucify him!"

[15]So to pacify the crowd, Pilate released Barabbas to them. He ordered Jesus flogged with a lead-tipped whip, then turned him over to the Roman soldiers to be crucified.

[16]The soldiers took Jesus into the courtyard of the governor's headquarters (called the Praetorium) and called out the entire regiment. [17]They dressed him in a purple robe, and they wove thorn branches into a crown and put it on his head. [18]Then they saluted him and taunted, "Hail! King of the Jews!" [19]And they struck him on the head with a reed stick, spit on him, and dropped to their knees in mock worship. [20]When they were finally tired of mocking him, they took off the purple robe and put his own clothes on him again. Then they led him away to be crucified.

²¹A passerby named Simon, who was from Cyrene,* was coming in from the countryside just then, and the soldiers forced him to carry Jesus' cross. (Simon was the father of Alexander and Rufus.) ²²And they brought Jesus to a place called Golgotha (which means "Place of the Skull"). ²³They offered him wine drugged with myrrh, but he refused it.

²⁴Then the soldiers nailed him to the cross. They divided his clothes and threw dice* to decide who would get each piece.

15:21 *Cyrene* was a city in northern Africa.   15:24 Greek *cast lots.* See Ps 22:18.

Pilate knew that Jesus was innocent. Yet he gave in to the crowd's demands. Do not give in to those who urge you to do wrong. Find friends who will encourage you to do what's right.

You must not follow the crowd in doing wrong. When you are called to testify in a dispute, do not be swayed by the crowd to twist justice. EXODUS 23:2

SEPTEMBER 24

Jesus Crucified

Jesus hung on the cross between two criminals. What did the criminals say about Jesus when he was dying?

Luke 23:32-49

Two others, both criminals, were led out to be executed with [Jesus]. ³³When they came to a place called The Skull,* they nailed him to the cross. And the criminals were also crucified—one on his right and one on his left.

³⁴Jesus said, "Father, forgive them, for they don't know what they are doing."* And the soldiers gambled for his clothes by throwing dice.*

³⁵The crowd watched and the leaders scoffed. "He saved others," they said, "let him save himself if he is really God's Messiah, the Chosen One." ³⁶The soldiers mocked him, too, by offering him a drink of sour wine. ³⁷They called out to him, "If you are the King of the Jews, save yourself!" ³⁸A sign was fastened to the cross above him with these words: "This is the King of the Jews."

³⁹One of the criminals hanging beside him scoffed, "So you're the Messiah, are you? Prove it by saving yourself—and us, too, while you're at it!"

⁴⁰But the other criminal protested, "Don't you fear God even when you have been sentenced to die? ⁴¹We deserve to die for our crimes, but this man hasn't done anything wrong." ⁴²Then he said, "Jesus, remember me when you come into your Kingdom."

⁴³And Jesus replied, "I assure you, today you will be with me in paradise."

⁴⁴By this time it was noon, and darkness fell across the whole land until three o'clock. ⁴⁵The light from the sun was gone. And suddenly, the curtain in the

sanctuary of the Temple was torn down the middle. ⁴⁶Then Jesus shouted, "Father, I entrust my spirit into your hands!"* And with those words he breathed his last.

⁴⁷When the Roman officer* overseeing the execution saw what had happened, he worshiped God and said, "Surely this man was innocent.*" ⁴⁸And when all the crowd that came to see the crucifixion saw what had happened, they went home in deep sorrow.* ⁴⁹But Jesus' friends, including the women who had followed him from Galilee, stood at a distance watching.

23:33 Sometimes rendered *Calvary*, which comes from the Latin word for "skull." 23:34a This sentence is not included in many ancient manuscripts. 23:34b Greek *by casting lots*. See Ps 22:18. 23:46 Ps 31:5. 23:47a Greek *the centurion*. 23:47b Or *righteous*. 23:48 Greek *went home beating their breasts*.

One criminal mocked Jesus, but the other one repented of his sins and asked Jesus to remember him in heaven. Jesus told the repentant criminal he would be in heaven that same day. It is almost never too late to believe in Jesus. The only time it is too late is after you die. While you are living, believe in Jesus as your Savior. He offers forgiveness and eternal life to all who call on him.

For God loved the world so much that he gave his one and only Son, so that everyone who believes in him will not perish but have eternal life. JOHN 3:16

SEPTEMBER 25

In the Tomb

Joseph of Arimathea risked his life by burying Jesus. Read about his loyalty to Jesus.

Matthew 27:57-66

As evening approached, Joseph, a rich man from Arimathea who had become a follower of Jesus, ⁵⁸went to Pilate and asked for Jesus' body. And Pilate issued an order to release it to him. ⁵⁹Joseph took the body and wrapped it in a long sheet of clean linen cloth. ⁶⁰He placed it in his own new tomb, which had been carved out of the rock. Then he rolled a great stone across the entrance and left. ⁶¹Both Mary Magdalene and the other Mary were sitting across from the tomb and watching.

⁶²The next day, on the Sabbath,* the leading priests and Pharisees went to see Pilate. ⁶³They told him, "Sir, we remember what that deceiver once said while he was still alive: 'After three days I will rise from the dead.' ⁶⁴So we request that you seal the tomb until the third day. This will prevent his disciples from coming and stealing his body and then telling everyone he was raised from the dead! If that happens, we'll be worse off than we were at first."

⁶⁵Pilate replied, "Take guards and secure it the best you can." ⁶⁶So they sealed the tomb and posted guards to protect it.

27:62 Or *On the next day, which is after the Preparation*.

Joseph of Arimathea took a big risk when he placed Jesus in his own grave. The religious leaders could have punished him for his loyalty to Jesus. But Joseph was willing to take that risk. He was not ashamed of his belief in Jesus. Like Joseph, we should not be ashamed to identify ourselves as a follower of Jesus. After all, he is our King and our God. Let people know who you serve.

Nebuchadnezzar said, "Praise to the God of Shadrach, Meshach, and Abednego! He sent his angel to rescue his servants who trusted in him. They defied the king's command and were willing to die rather than serve or worship any god except their own God." DANIEL 3:28

SEPTEMBER 26

JESUS IS ALIVE!

The stone to Jesus' tomb had been rolled away. What did Mary Magdalene find inside?

John 20:1-18

Early on Sunday morning,* while it was still dark, Mary Magdalene came to the tomb and found that the stone had been rolled away from the entrance. ²She ran and found Simon Peter and the other disciple, the one whom Jesus loved. She said, "They have taken the Lord's body out of the tomb, and we don't know where they have put him!"

³Peter and the other disciple started out for the tomb. ⁴They were both running, but the other disciple outran Peter and reached the tomb first. ⁵He stooped and looked in and saw the linen wrappings lying there, but he didn't go in. ⁶Then Simon Peter arrived and went inside. He also noticed the linen wrappings lying there, ⁷while the cloth that had cov-

ered Jesus' head was folded up and lying apart from the other wrappings. ⁸Then the disciple who had reached the tomb first also went in, and he saw and believed—⁹for until then they still hadn't understood the Scriptures that said Jesus must rise from the dead. ¹⁰Then they went home.

¹¹Mary was standing outside the tomb crying, and as she wept, she stooped and looked in. ¹²She saw two white-robed angels, one sitting at the head and the other at the foot of the place where the body of Jesus had been lying. ¹³"Dear woman, why are you crying?" the angels asked her.

"Because they have taken away my Lord," she replied, "and I don't know where they have put him."

¹⁴She turned to leave and saw someone

standing there. It was Jesus, but she didn't recognize him. [15]"Dear woman, why are you crying?" Jesus asked her. "Who are you looking for?"

She thought he was the gardener. "Sir," she said, "if you have taken him away, tell me where you have put him, and I will go and get him."

[16]"Mary!" Jesus said.

She turned to him and cried out,

"Rabboni!" (which is Hebrew for "Teacher").

[17]"Don't cling to me," Jesus said, "for I haven't yet ascended to the Father. But go find my brothers and tell them that I am ascending to my Father and your Father, to my God and your God."

[18]Mary Magdalene found the disciples and told them, "I have seen the Lord!" Then she gave them his message.

Jesus lives! Death could not hold him back. He appeared to Mary, to Peter and John, and to all the disciples. Jesus lives today. That means we can believe in the living Jesus. Because he lives, we know that one day we will live with him. Jesus alone is worthy of your belief and trust.

Jesus [said], "I am the resurrection and the life.* Anyone who believes in me will live, even after dying." JOHN 11:25

SEPTEMBER 27

Raised from the Dead

Jesus was alive, and the religious leaders wanted to cover up the truth. What did they try to do to keep people from believing in Jesus?

Matthew 28:1-17

Early on Sunday morning,* as the new day was dawning, Mary Magdalene and the other Mary went out to visit the tomb.

[2]Suddenly there was a great earthquake! For an angel of the Lord came down from heaven, rolled aside the stone, and sat on it. [3]His face shone like lightning, and his clothing was as white as snow. [4]The guards shook with fear when they saw him, and they fell into a dead faint.

[5]Then the angel spoke to the women. "Don't be afraid!" he said. "I know you are looking for Jesus, who was crucified. [6]He

isn't here! He is risen from the dead, just as he said would happen. Come, see where his body was lying. [7]And now, go quickly and tell his disciples that he has risen from the dead, and he is going ahead of you to Galilee. You will see him there. Remember what I have told you."

[8]The women ran quickly from the tomb. They were very frightened but also filled with great joy, and they rushed to give the disciples the angel's message. [9]And as they went, Jesus met them and greeted them. And they ran to him, grasped his feet, and worshiped him. [10]Then Jesus said to them,

343

"Don't be afraid! Go tell my brothers to leave for Galilee, and they will see me there."

¹¹As the women were on their way, some of the guards went into the city and told the leading priests what had happened. ¹²A meeting with the elders was called, and they decided to give the soldiers a large bribe. ¹³They told the soldiers, "You must say, 'Jesus' disciples came during the night while we were sleeping, and they stole his body.' ¹⁴If the governor hears about it, we'll stand up for you so you won't get in trouble." ¹⁵So the guards accepted the bribe and said what they were told to say. Their story spread widely among the Jews, and they still tell it today.

¹⁶Then the eleven disciples left for Galilee, going to the mountain where Jesus had told them to go. ¹⁷When they saw him, they worshiped him—but some of them doubted!

28:1 Greek *After the Sabbath, on the first day of the week.*

The religious leaders came up with a lie and paid the guards to spread it. They wouldn't accept the truth about Jesus, even though the guards were eyewitnesses to the greatest miracle ever. There are still people today who refuse to believe that Jesus is God's Son. Some of these people spread lies about Jesus like the religious leaders did right after the Resurrection. As Christians, we need to recognize the lies and believe only what the Bible says is true.

There were also false prophets in Israel, just as there will be false teachers among you. They will cleverly teach destructive heresies and even deny the Master who bought them. In this way, they will bring sudden destruction on themselves.
2 PETER 2:1

SEPTEMBER 28

JESUS ON THE ROAD

Jesus appeared to two of his followers walking down a road. What did his followers have difficulty understanding?

Luke 24:13-35

That same day two of Jesus' followers were walking to the village of Emmaus, seven miles* from Jerusalem. ¹⁴As they walked along they were talking about everything that had happened. ¹⁵As they talked and discussed these things, Jesus himself suddenly came and began walking with them. ¹⁶But God kept them from recognizing him.

¹⁷He asked them, "What are you discussing so intently as you walk along?"

They stopped short, sadness written across their faces. ¹⁸Then one of them, Cleopas, replied, "You must be the only person in Jerusalem who hasn't heard about all the things that have happened there the last few days."

¹⁹"What things?" Jesus asked.

"The things that happened to Jesus, the man from Nazareth," they said. "He was a prophet who did powerful miracles, and he was a mighty teacher in the eyes of God and all the people. [20]But our leading priests and other religious leaders handed him over to be condemned to death, and they crucified him. [21]We had hoped he was the Messiah who had come to rescue Israel. This all happened three days ago.

[22]"Then some women from our group of his followers were at his tomb early this morning, and they came back with an amazing report. [23]They said his body was missing, and they had seen angels who told them Jesus is alive! [24]Some of our men ran out to see, and sure enough, his body was gone, just as the women had said."

[25]Then Jesus said to them, "You foolish people! You find it so hard to believe all that the prophets wrote in the Scriptures. [26]Wasn't it clearly predicted that the Messiah would have to suffer all these things before entering his glory?" [27]Then Jesus took them through the writings of Moses and all the prophets, explaining from all the Scriptures the things concerning himself.

[28]By this time they were nearing Emmaus and the end of their journey. Jesus acted as if he were going on, [29]but they begged him, "Stay the night with us, since it is getting late." So he went home with them. [30]As they sat down to eat,* he took the bread and blessed it. Then he broke it and gave it to them. [31]Suddenly, their eyes were opened, and they recognized him. And at that moment he disappeared!

[32]They said to each other, "Didn't our hearts burn within us as he talked with us on the road and explained the Scriptures to us?" [33]And within the hour they were on their way back to Jerusalem. There they found the eleven disciples and the others who had gathered with them, [34]who said, "The Lord has really risen! He appeared to Peter.*"

[35]Then the two from Emmaus told their story of how Jesus had appeared to them as they were walking along the road, and how they had recognized him as he was breaking the bread.

24:13 Greek 60 stadia [11.1 kilometers].   24:30 Or As they reclined.   24:34 Greek Simon.

Jesus' followers had a hard time understanding why he had come to earth. They even began to doubt that Jesus was God's Son. So he used God's Word to show his disciples that he really was God's Son. Today we have the same Scriptures to teach us these same truths. The Bible can help you learn more about Jesus. Read your Bible every day. Get to know Jesus personally!

He was oppressed and treated harshly, yet he never said a word. He was led like a lamb to the slaughter. And as a sheep is silent before the shearers, he did not open his mouth. Unjustly condemned, he was led away.* . . . He had done no wrong and had never deceived anyone. But he was buried like a criminal; he was put in a rich man's grave. ISAIAH 53:7-9

53:8a Greek version reads He was humiliated and received no justice. Compare Acts 8:33.

SEPTEMBER 29

I Doubt It

Thomas didn't believe that Jesus was alive. What changed his mind?

John 20:19-31

That Sunday evening* the disciples were meeting behind locked doors because they were afraid of the Jewish leaders. Suddenly, Jesus was standing there among them! "Peace be with you," he said. ²⁰As he spoke, he showed them the wounds in his hands and his side. They were filled with joy when they saw the Lord! ²¹Again he said, "Peace be with you. As the Father has sent me, so I am sending you." ²²Then he breathed on them and said, "Receive the Holy Spirit. ²³If you forgive anyone's sins, they are forgiven. If you do not forgive them, they are not forgiven."

²⁴One of the disciples, Thomas (nicknamed the Twin),* was not with the others when Jesus came. ²⁵They told him, "We have seen the Lord!"

But he replied, "I won't believe it unless I see the nail wounds in his hands, put my fingers into them, and place my hand into the wound in his side."

²⁶Eight days later the disciples were together again, and this time Thomas was with them. The doors were locked; but suddenly, as before, Jesus was standing among them. "Peace be with you," he said. ²⁷Then he said to Thomas, "Put your finger here, and look at my hands. Put your hand into the wound in my side. Don't be faithless any longer. Believe!"

²⁸"My Lord and my God!" Thomas exclaimed.

²⁹Then Jesus told him, "You believe because you have seen me. Blessed are those who believe without seeing me."

³⁰The disciples saw Jesus do many other miraculous signs in addition to the ones recorded in this book. ³¹But these are written so that you may continue to believe* that Jesus is the Messiah, the Son of God, and that by believing in him you will have life by the power of his name.

20:19 Greek *In the evening of that day, the first day of the week.*   20:24 Greek *Thomas, who was called Didymus.*
20:31 Some manuscripts read *that you may believe.*

When Thomas doubted, Jesus showed him the wounds in his hands and side to prove that he really was Jesus, risen from the dead. After this, Thomas believed that Jesus was telling the truth about who he was. Many people are like Thomas. They want to see Jesus with their own eyes before they will believe in him. But Jesus said that he is pleased with those people who believe in him even though they haven't seen him. Do you believe in Jesus? If so, your faith pleases him. Keep believing even when others doubt.

The LORD said to Moses, "How long will these people treat me with contempt? Will they never believe me, even after all the miraculous signs I have done among them?" NUMBERS 14:11

SEPTEMBER 30

DO YOU LOVE ME?

Jesus asked Peter some questions that upset the disciple. Why did Jesus keep asking Peter the same thing over and over?

John 21:15-25

After breakfast Jesus asked Simon Peter, "Simon son of John, do you love me more than these?*"

"Yes, Lord," Peter replied, "you know I love you."

"Then feed my lambs," Jesus told him.

[16]Jesus repeated the question: "Simon son of John, do you love me?"

"Yes, Lord," Peter said, "you know I love you."

"Then take care of my sheep," Jesus said.

[17]A third time he asked him, "Simon son of John, do you love me?"

Peter was hurt that Jesus asked the question a third time. He said, "Lord, you know everything. You know that I love you."

Jesus said, "Then feed my sheep.

[18]"I tell you the truth, when you were young, you were able to do as you liked; you dressed yourself and went wherever you wanted to go. But when you are old, you will stretch out your hands, and others* will dress you and take you where you don't want to go." [19]Jesus said this to let him know by what kind of death he would glorify God. Then Jesus told him, "Follow me."

[20]Peter turned around and saw behind them the disciple Jesus loved—the one who had leaned over to Jesus during supper and asked, "Lord, who will betray you?" [21]Peter asked Jesus, "What about him, Lord?"

[22]Jesus replied, "If I want him to remain alive until I return, what is that to you? As for you, follow me." [23]So the rumor spread among the community of believers* that this disciple wouldn't die. But that isn't what Jesus said at all. He only said, "If I want him to remain alive until I return, what is that to you?"

[24]This disciple is the one who testifies to these events and has recorded them here. And we know that his account of these things is accurate.

[25]Jesus also did many other things. If they were all written down, I suppose the whole world could not contain the books that would be written.

21:15 Or *more than these others do?* 21:18 Some manuscripts read *and another one.* 21:23 Greek *the brothers.*

Jesus asked Peter three times if he really loved him. Jesus wanted Peter to think about whether he truly loved Jesus more than anything else. Jesus' question shows us how important it is to love him with our whole heart. Loving Jesus means putting him ahead of every person and thing in your life. Are you willing to do this?

What does the LORD your God require of you? He requires only that you fear the LORD your God, and live in a way that pleases him, and love him and serve him with all your heart and soul. DEUTERONOMY 10:12

SEPTEMBER CHALLENGE
nice work!

You just finished another month of reading the Bible every day. That's awesome! If you started reading in January, you've been reading God's Word for nine months. Did you think at one time that you wouldn't be able to make it to the end of the year? No need to worry about that anymore. You now have only three months to go!

To show that you've finished the September readings, use a marker or highlighter to fill in the level you reached this month.

You've been reading about the most important events that ever happened in human history—Jesus' death and resurrection. What does Jesus' resurrection mean to you? Find a CD or DVD with a song that expresses how you feel about Jesus' death on the cross for you or what his resurrection means to you.

IMPORTANT STUFF TO REMEMBER FROM SEPTEMBER

☐ Jesus loves us enough that he died for us.

☐ Jesus took the punishment for all of our sins even though he never sinned himself.

☐ Jesus rose from the dead because death has no power over him.

Time for some "a-maze-ing" fun!

After Jesus rose from the dead, some of his friends went to the empty tomb to see what had happened. Help Peter and John find their way to the tomb.

OCTOBER 1

A mission

Jesus gave his disciples a mission to accomplish. What did he tell them to do?

Matthew 28:8-10, 16-20

The women ran quickly from the tomb. They were very frightened but also filled with great joy, and they rushed to give the disciples the angel's message. ⁹And as they went, Jesus met them and greeted them. And they ran to him, grasped his feet, and worshiped him. ¹⁰Then Jesus said to them, "Don't be afraid! Go tell my brothers to leave for Galilee, and they will see me there."

◉

28:19 Or *all peoples.*

¹⁶Then the eleven disciples left for Galilee, going to the mountain where Jesus had told them to go. ¹⁷When they saw him, they worshiped him—but some of them doubted! ¹⁸Jesus came and told his disciples, "I have been given all authority in heaven and on earth. ¹⁹Therefore, go and make disciples of all the nations,* baptizing them in the name of the Father and the Son and the Holy Spirit. ²⁰Teach these new disciples to obey all the commands I have given you. And be sure of this: I am with you always, even to the end of the age."

Jesus told his disciples to go and tell others about him. This mission also applies to all those today who trust in Jesus as their Savior. If Jesus is your Savior, this means *you!* You can obey his command by telling your friends about Jesus' love for them.

You must also testify about me [Jesus] because you have been with me from the beginning of my ministry. JOHN 15:27

OCTOBER 2

In the clouds

Jesus was about to disappear into a cloud. What did he say to his disciples just before he returned to heaven?

Acts 1:1-11

In my first book* I told you, Theophilus, about everything Jesus began to do and teach ²until the day he was taken up to heaven after giving his chosen apostles further instructions through the Holy Spirit. ³During the forty days after his crucifixion, he appeared to the apostles from time to time, and he proved to them in many ways that he was actually alive. And he talked to them about the Kingdom of God.

⁴Once when he was eating with them, he commanded them, "Do not leave Jerusalem until the Father sends you the gift he promised, as I told you before. ⁵John baptized with* water, but in just a few days you will be baptized with the Holy Spirit."

⁶So when the apostles were with Jesus, they kept asking him, "Lord, has the time come for you to free Israel and restore our kingdom?"

⁷He replied, "The Father alone has the authority to set those dates and times, and they are not for you to know. ⁸But you will receive power when the Holy Spirit comes upon you. And you will be my witnesses, telling people about me everywhere—in Jerusalem, throughout Judea, in Samaria, and to the ends of the earth."

⁹After saying this, he was taken up into a cloud while they were watching, and they could no longer see him. ¹⁰As they strained to see him rising into heaven, two white-robed men suddenly stood among them. ¹¹"Men of Galilee," they said, "why are you standing here staring into heaven? Jesus has been taken from you into heaven, but someday he will return from heaven in the same way you saw him go!"

1:1 The reference is to the Gospel of Luke.   1:5 Or *in;* also in 1:5b.

Jesus promised to send the Holy Spirit to help his followers. The disciples needed the Holy Spirit to help them tell others about Jesus. If you are one of Jesus' followers, the Holy Spirit will help you, too. He will give you courage whenever you ask him to help you share your love for Jesus with someone else.

We have received God's Spirit (not the world's spirit), so we can know the wonderful things God has freely given us. I CORINTHIANS 2:12

OCTOBER 3

TONGUES OF FIRE

Something exciting happened while the disciples were meeting together one day. Read on to find out what it was.

Acts 2:1-12

On the day of Pentecost* all the believers were meeting together in one place. ²Suddenly, there was a sound from heaven like the roaring of a mighty windstorm, and it filled the house where they were sitting. ³Then, what looked like flames or tongues of fire appeared and settled on each of them. ⁴And everyone present was filled with the Holy Spirit and began speaking in other languages,* as the Holy Spirit gave them this ability.

⁵At that time there were devout Jews from every nation living in Jerusalem. ⁶When they heard the loud noise, everyone came running, and they were bewildered to hear their own languages being spoken by the believers.

⁷They were completely amazed. "How can this be?" they exclaimed. "These people are all from Galilee, ⁸and yet we hear them speaking in our own native languages! ⁹Here we are—Parthians, Medes, Elamites, people from Mesopotamia, Judea, Cappadocia, Pontus, the province of Asia, ¹⁰Phrygia, Pamphylia, Egypt, and the areas of Libya around Cyrene, visitors from Rome (both Jews and converts to Judaism), ¹¹Cretans, and Arabs. And we all hear these people speaking in our own languages about the wonderful things God has done!" ¹²They stood there amazed and perplexed. "What can this mean?" they asked each other.

2:1 The Festival of Pentecost came 50 days after Passover (when Jesus was crucified). 2:4 Or *in other tongues*.

When Jesus' disciples were filled with the Holy Spirit, they were able to speak about Jesus in languages they had never learned. God's Spirit worked in an amazing way that day so many more people from many different places would hear the Good News about Jesus. God's Spirit still works in some amazing ways today. But to see his mighty work, we need to be willing to obey God, put his will ahead of our own, and believe he is able to do all that we cannot.

In those days I [God] will pour out my Spirit even on servants—men and women alike. JOEL 2:29

OCTOBER 4

Peter Preaches

Some people thought Jesus' followers were drunk. Why did they think this?

Acts 2:13-38

Others in the crowd ridiculed them, saying, "They're just drunk, that's all!"

¹⁴Then Peter stepped forward with the eleven other apostles and shouted to the crowd, "Listen carefully, all of you, fellow Jews and residents of Jerusalem! Make no mistake about this. ¹⁵These people are not drunk, as some of you are assuming. Nine o'clock in the morning is much too early for that. ¹⁶No, what you see was predicted long ago by the prophet Joel:

¹⁷"'In the last days,' God says,
    'I will pour out my Spirit upon all
        people.
Your sons and daughters will prophesy.
    Your young men will see visions,
    and your old men will dream
        dreams.
¹⁸In those days I will pour out my Spirit
    even on my servants—men and
        women alike—
    and they will prophesy.
¹⁹And I will cause wonders in the heavens
        above
    and signs on the earth below—
    blood and fire and clouds of smoke.
²⁰The sun will become dark,
    and the moon will turn blood red
    before that great and glorious day of
        the LORD arrives.
²¹But everyone who calls on the name of
        the LORD
    will be saved.'*

²²"People of Israel, listen! God publicly endorsed Jesus the Nazarene* by doing powerful miracles, wonders, and signs through him, as you well know. ²³But God knew what would happen, and his pre-arranged plan was carried out when Jesus was betrayed. With the help of lawless Gentiles, you nailed him to a cross and killed him. ²⁴But God released him from the horrors of death and raised him back to life, for death could not keep him in its grip. ²⁵King David said this about him:

'I see that the LORD is always with me.
    I will not be shaken, for he is right
        beside me.
²⁶No wonder my heart is glad,
    and my tongue shouts his praises!
    My body rests in hope.
²⁷For you will not leave my soul among
        the dead*
    or allow your Holy One to rot in the
        grave.
²⁸You have shown me the way of life,
    and you will fill me with the joy of
        your presence.'*

²⁹"Dear brothers, think about this! You can be sure that the patriarch David wasn't referring to himself, for he died and was buried, and his tomb is still here among us. ³⁰But he was a prophet, and he knew God had promised with an oath that one of David's own descendants would sit on his throne. ³¹David was looking into the future and speaking of the Messiah's resurrec-

tion. He was saying that God would not leave him among the dead or allow his body to rot in the grave.

[32]"God raised Jesus from the dead, and we are all witnesses of this. [33]Now he is exalted to the place of highest honor in heaven, at God's right hand. And the Father, as he had promised, gave him the Holy Spirit to pour out upon us, just as you see and hear today. [34]For David himself never ascended into heaven, yet he said,

'The Lord said to my Lord,

"Sit in the place of honor at my right hand

[35]until I humble your enemies,

making them a footstool under your feet."'*

[36]"So let everyone in Israel know for certain that God has made this Jesus, whom you crucified, to be both Lord and Messiah!"

[37]Peter's words pierced their hearts, and they said to him and to the other apostles, "Brothers, what should we do?"

[38]Peter replied, "Each of you must repent of your sins, turn to God, and be baptized in the name of Jesus Christ to show that you have received forgiveness for your sins. Then you will receive the gift of the Holy Spirit."

2:17-21 Joel 2:28-32.   2:22 Or *Jesus of Nazareth.*   2:27 Greek *in Hades;* also in 2:31.   2:25-28 Ps 16:8-11 (Greek version). 2:34-35 Ps 110:1.

The power of the Holy Spirit was so amazing to the people that at first they didn't believe it was real. They thought Peter and his disciples were acting crazy and were drunk. Peter was bold and told the crowd the truth about what had happened. Whenever you have the chance to tell someone about Jesus, remember Peter's example and be strong.

Never be ashamed to tell others about our Lord. And don't be ashamed of me [Paul], either, even though I'm in prison for him. With the strength God gives you, be ready to suffer with me for the sake of the Good News. 2 TIMOTHY 1:8

OCTOBER 5
Begging to Believe
A beggar was asking for money. What did Peter and John do in this situation?

Acts 2:41–3:11
Those who believed what Peter said were baptized and added to the church that day—about 3,000 in all.

[42]All the believers devoted themselves to the apostles' teaching, and to fellowship, and to sharing in meals (including the Lord's Supper*), and to prayer.

[43]A deep sense of awe came over them all, and the apostles performed many miraculous signs and wonders. [44]And all the believers met together in one place and

shared everything they had. 45They sold their property and possessions and shared the money with those in need. 46They worshiped together at the Temple each day, met in homes for the Lord's Supper, and shared their meals with great joy and generosity*—47all the while praising God and enjoying the goodwill of all the people. And each day the Lord added to their fellowship those who were being saved.

3:1Peter and John went to the Temple one afternoon to take part in the three o'clock prayer service. 2As they approached the Temple, a man lame from birth was being carried in. Each day he was put beside the Temple gate, the one called the Beautiful Gate, so he could beg from the people going into the Temple. 3When he saw Peter and John about to enter, he asked them for some money.

4Peter and John looked at him intently, and Peter said, "Look at us!" 5The lame man looked at them eagerly, expecting some money. 6But Peter said, "I don't have any silver or gold for you. But I'll give you what I have. In the name of Jesus Christ the Nazarene,* get up and walk!"

7Then Peter took the lame man by the right hand and helped him up. And as he did, the man's feet and ankles were instantly healed and strengthened. 8He jumped up, stood on his feet, and began to walk! Then, walking, leaping, and praising God, he went into the Temple with them.

9All the people saw him walking and heard him praising God. 10When they realized he was the lame beggar they had seen so often at the Beautiful Gate, they were absolutely astounded! 11They all rushed out in amazement to Solomon's Colonnade, where the man was holding tightly to Peter and John.

2:42 Greek *the breaking of bread;* also in 2:46.   2:46 Or *and sincere hearts.*   3:6 Or *Jesus Christ of Nazareth.*

Instead of giving the beggar money, Peter healed him so he could walk again. The beggar was so amazed by his healing that he began leaping around and praising God. We may or may not experience miracles like this, but we can always praise God for everything he has done for us. Praise him today for his power and for sending Jesus to save us from our sins. That is a miracle beyond all others!

Sing to the LORD; praise his name. Each day proclaim the good news that he saves. PSALM 96:2

OCTOBER 6

In Jesus' name!

The people were amazed when they saw Peter heal the beggar. How did Peter react to the crowd?

Acts 3:12-26

Peter saw his opportunity and addressed the crowd. "People of Israel," he said, "what is so surprising about this? And why stare at us as though we had made this man walk by our own power or godliness?

¹³For it is the God of Abraham, Isaac, and Jacob—the God of all our ancestors—who has brought glory to his servant Jesus by doing this. This is the same Jesus whom you handed over and rejected before Pilate, despite Pilate's decision to release him. ¹⁴You rejected this holy, righteous one and instead demanded the release of a murderer. ¹⁵You killed the author of life, but God raised him from the dead. And we are witnesses of this fact!

¹⁶"Through faith in the name of Jesus, this man was healed—and you know how crippled he was before. Faith in Jesus' name has healed him before your very eyes.

¹⁷"Friends,* I realize that what you and your leaders did to Jesus was done in ignorance. ¹⁸But God was fulfilling what all the prophets had foretold about the Messiah—that he must suffer these things. ¹⁹Now repent of your sins and turn to God, so that your sins may be wiped away. ²⁰Then times of refreshment will come from the presence of the Lord, and he will again send you Jesus, your appointed Messiah. ²¹For he must remain in heaven until the time for the final restoration of all things, as God promised long ago through his holy prophets. ²²Moses said, 'The Lord your God will raise up for you a Prophet like me from among your own people. Listen carefully to everything he tells you.'* ²³Then Moses said, 'Anyone who will not listen to that Prophet will be completely cut off from God's people.'*

²⁴"Starting with Samuel, every prophet spoke about what is happening today. ²⁵You are the children of those prophets, and you are included in the covenant God promised to your ancestors. For God said to Abraham, 'Through your descendants all the families on earth will be blessed.'* ²⁶When God raised up his servant, Jesus, he sent him first to you people of Israel, to bless you by turning each of you back from your sinful ways."

3:17 Greek Brothers.   3:22 Deut 18:15.   3:23 Deut 18:19; Lev 23:29.   3:25 Gen 12:3; 22:18.

The crowd was really impressed by Peter. It would have been easy for him to take credit for this miraculous healing. Instead of doing this, Peter was humble and gave all the credit to God. He used the opportunity to teach the people about Jesus. God is very pleased when we are humble. Remember Peter's example and be humble the next time you are praised for something you do. Give credit where it is due—to God!

The LORD delights in his people; he crowns the humble with victory. PSALM 149:4

OCTOBER 7

Peter and John

The Jewish council ordered Peter and John to stop speaking about Jesus. What did Peter and John tell the council?

Acts 4:5-22

The next day the council of all the rulers and elders and teachers of religious law met in Jerusalem. ⁶Annas the high priest was there, along with Caiaphas, John, Alexander, and other relatives of the high priest. ⁷They brought in the two disciples and demanded, "By what power, or in whose name, have you done this?"

⁸Then Peter, filled with the Holy Spirit, said to them, "Rulers and elders of our people, ⁹are we being questioned today because we've done a good deed for a crippled man? Do you want to know how he was healed? ¹⁰Let me clearly state to all of you and to all the people of Israel that he was healed by the powerful name of Jesus Christ the Nazarene,* the man you crucified but whom God raised from the dead. ¹¹For Jesus is the one referred to in the Scriptures, where it says,

'The stone that you builders
    rejected
    has now become the cornerstone.'*

¹²There is salvation in no one else! God has given no other name under heaven by which we must be saved."

¹³The members of the council were amazed when they saw the boldness of Peter and John, for they could see that they were ordinary men with no special training in the Scriptures. They also recognized them as men who had been with Jesus. ¹⁴But since they could see the man who had been healed standing right there among them, there was nothing the council could say. ¹⁵So they ordered Peter and John out of the council chamber* and conferred among themselves.

¹⁶"What should we do with these men?" they asked each other. "We can't deny that they have performed a miraculous sign, and everybody in Jerusalem knows about it. ¹⁷But to keep them from spreading their propaganda any further we must warn them not to speak to anyone in Jesus' name again." ¹⁸So they called the apostles back in and commanded them never again to speak or teach in the name of Jesus.

¹⁹But Peter and John replied, "Do you think God wants us to obey you rather than him? ²⁰We cannot stop telling about everything we have seen and heard."

²¹The council then threatened them further, but they finally let them go because they didn't know how to punish them without starting a riot. For everyone was praising God ²²for this miraculous sign—the healing of a man who had been lame for more than forty years.

4:10 Or *Jesus Christ of Nazareth.*   **4:11** Ps 118:22.   **4:15** Greek *the Sanhedrin.*

Peter and John asked the council a simple question: Should we obey you or God? Then they told the council that they wouldn't stop telling others about what they had seen. There may be times in your life when someone orders you to do something that's wrong. If you find yourself in that situation, remember what Peter and John did. Just as they chose to obey God, you too must choose to obey him.

Serve only the LORD your God and fear him alone. Obey his commands, listen to his voice, and cling to him. DEUTERONOMY 13:4

OCTOBER 8

Bold Prayer

The believers prayed together. What did they ask God?

Acts 4:23-31

As soon as they were freed, Peter and John returned to the other believers and told them what the leading priests and elders had said. ²⁴When they heard the report, all the believers lifted their voices together in prayer to God: "O Sovereign Lord, Creator of heaven and earth, the sea, and everything in them—²⁵you spoke long ago by the Holy Spirit through our ancestor David, your servant, saying,

'Why were the nations so
　　angry?
　Why did they waste their time
　　with futile plans?
²⁶The kings of the earth prepared for
　　battle;
　the rulers gathered together

4:25-26 Or *his anointed one;* or *his Christ.* Ps 2:1-2.

against the LORD
　　and against his Messiah.'*

²⁷"In fact, this has happened here in this very city! For Herod Antipas, Pontius Pilate the governor, the Gentiles, and the people of Israel were all united against Jesus, your holy servant, whom you anointed. ²⁸But everything they did was determined beforehand according to your will. ²⁹And now, O Lord, hear their threats, and give us, your servants, great boldness in preaching your word. ³⁰Stretch out your hand with healing power; may miraculous signs and wonders be done through the name of your holy servant Jesus."

³¹After this prayer, the meeting place shook, and they were all filled with the Holy Spirit. Then they preached the word of God with boldness.

The believers prayed for boldness. They did not want the high priests' threats to stop them from talking about Jesus. God wants us, like those first believers, to speak boldly about Jesus. You can ask God to give you courage whenever you are afraid or threatened by peer pressure. Pray for boldness to speak out no matter what may happen.

I have not kept the good news of your justice hidden in my heart; I have talked about your faithfulness and saving power. I have told everyone in the great assembly of your unfailing love and faithfulness. PSALM 40:10

OCTOBER 9

Dishonest Dealings

Ananias and Sapphira lied about how much money they were giving. What was the consequence of their lie?

Acts 4:34-35; 5:1-11

There were no needy people among them, because those who owned land or houses would sell them ³⁵and bring the money to the apostles to give to those in need.

^{5:1}But there was a certain man named Ananias who, with his wife, Sapphira, sold some property. ²He brought part of the money to the apostles, claiming it was the full amount. With his wife's consent, he kept the rest.

³Then Peter said, "Ananias, why have you let Satan fill your heart? You lied to the Holy Spirit, and you kept some of the money for yourself. ⁴The property was yours to sell or not sell, as you wished. And after selling it, the money was also yours to give away. How could you do a thing like this? You weren't lying to us but to God!"

⁵As soon as Ananias heard these words, he fell to the floor and died. Everyone who heard about it was terrified. ⁶Then some young men got up, wrapped him in a sheet, and took him out and buried him.

⁷About three hours later his wife came in, not knowing what had happened. ⁸Peter asked her, "Was this the price you and your husband received for your land?"

"Yes," she replied, "that was the price."

⁹And Peter said, "How could the two of you even think of conspiring to test the Spirit of the Lord like this? The young men who buried your husband are just outside the door, and they will carry you out, too."

¹⁰Instantly, she fell to the floor and died. When the young men came in and saw that she was dead, they carried her out and buried her beside her husband. ¹¹Great fear gripped the entire church and everyone else who heard what had happened.

It wasn't wrong that Ananias and Sapphira gave only part of their money to the church. What was wrong was saying that they had given the full price for the land. Ananias and Sapphira thought they could get away with lying and still look good in the eyes of the people. But they couldn't fool the Holy Spirit, and both of them died for lying. This story shows how much God values the truth. Lying is a very serious offense to the Lord. God has commanded us to tell the truth—and we should take his commands seriously.

Do not steal. Do not deceive or cheat one another. LEVITICUS 19:11

OCTOBER 10

An Arresting Thought

The high priest and the Jewish council were jealous of the apostles, so they had them arrested. What did Gamaliel say about the apostles' actions?

Acts 5:12, 16-39

The apostles were performing many miraculous signs and wonders among the people. And all the believers were meeting regularly at the Temple in the area known as Solomon's Colonnade.

[16]Crowds came from the villages around Jerusalem, bringing their sick and those possessed by evil* spirits, and they were all healed.

[17]The high priest and his officials, who were Sadducees, were filled with jealousy. [18]They arrested the apostles and put them in the public jail. [19]But an angel of the Lord came at night, opened the gates of the jail, and brought them out. Then he told them, [20]"Go to the Temple and give the people this message of life!"

[21]So at daybreak the apostles entered the Temple, as they were told, and immediately began teaching.

When the high priest and his officials arrived, they convened the high council*— the full assembly of the elders of Israel. Then they sent for the apostles to be brought from the jail for trial. [22]But when the Temple guards went to the jail, the men were gone. So they returned to the council and reported, [23]"The jail was securely locked, with the guards standing outside, but when we opened the gates, no one was there!"

[24]When the captain of the Temple guard and the leading priests heard this, they were perplexed, wondering where it would all end. [25]Then someone arrived with startling news: "The men you put in jail are standing in the Temple, teaching the people!"

[26]The captain went with his Temple

361

guards and arrested the apostles, but without violence, for they were afraid the people would stone them. ²⁷Then they brought the apostles before the high council, where the high priest confronted them. ²⁸"Didn't we tell you never again to teach in this man's name?" he demanded. "Instead, you have filled all Jerusalem with your teaching about him, and you want to make us responsible for his death!"

²⁹But Peter and the apostles replied, "We must obey God rather than any human authority. ³⁰The God of our ancestors raised Jesus from the dead after you killed him by hanging him on a cross.* ³¹Then God put him in the place of honor at his right hand as Prince and Savior. He did this so the people of Israel would repent of their sins and be forgiven. ³²We are witnesses of these things and so is the Holy Spirit, who is given by God to those who obey him."

³³When they heard this, the high council was furious and decided to kill them.

³⁴But one member, a Pharisee named Gamaliel, who was an expert in religious law and respected by all the people, stood up and ordered that the men be sent outside the council chamber for a while. ³⁵Then he said to his colleagues, "Men of Israel, take care what you are planning to do to these men! ³⁶Some time ago there was that fellow Theudas, who pretended to be someone great. About 400 others joined him, but he was killed, and all his followers went their various ways. The whole movement came to nothing. ³⁷After him, at the time of the census, there was Judas of Galilee. He got people to follow him, but he was killed, too, and all his followers were scattered.

³⁸"So my advice is, leave these men alone. Let them go. If they are planning and doing these things merely on their own, it will soon be overthrown. ³⁹But if it is from God, you will not be able to overthrow them. You may even find yourselves fighting against God!"

5:16 Greek *unclean.* 5:21 Greek *Sanhedrin;* also in 5:27. 5:30 Greek *on a tree.*

Gamaliel understood that if the apostles were acting on their own, their works would soon come to an end. But if the apostles were acting on God's commands, then there was nothing the high priest and the Jewish council could do to stop them. Gamaliel understood God's power and knew it was useless to fight against God. You probably don't fight against God by opposing those who speak out for Jesus. But you may fight against God by disobeying his Word or refusing to speak out yourself. Make sure you are fighting *for* God—not *against* him.

The LORD is a jealous God, filled with vengeance and wrath. He takes revenge on all who oppose him and continues to rage against his enemies! NAHUM 1:2

OCTOBER 11

stephen is seized

Some men made up lies about Stephen. What happened to Stephen when they said these things about him?

Acts 6:8-15

Stephen, a man full of God's grace and power, performed amazing miracles and signs among the people. ⁹But one day some men from the Synagogue of Freed Slaves, as it was called, started to debate with him. They were Jews from Cyrene, Alexandria, Cilicia, and the province of Asia. ¹⁰None of them could stand against the wisdom and the Spirit with which Stephen spoke.

¹¹So they persuaded some men to lie about Stephen, saying, "We heard him blaspheme Moses, and even God." ¹²This roused the people, the elders, and the teachers of religious law. So they arrested Stephen and brought him before the high council.*

¹³The lying witnesses said, "This man is always speaking against the holy Temple and against the law of Moses. ¹⁴We have heard him say that this Jesus of Nazareth* will destroy the Temple and change the customs Moses handed down to us."

¹⁵At this point everyone in the high council stared at Stephen, because his face became as bright as an angel's.

6:12 Greek *Sanhedrin;* also in 6:15.   6:14 Or *Jesus the Nazarene.*

The men became very angry when they couldn't win their arguments with Stephen. He said things they didn't like. As a way of getting back at him, these men began spreading lies so that Stephen would get in trouble. Have you ever spread a lie about someone you don't like? That's not how God wants us to treat others.

Do to others whatever you would like them to do to you. This is the essence of all that is taught in the law and the prophets. MATTHEW 7:12

OCTOBER 12

stephen speaks

The high priest asked Stephen if what people were saying about him was true. How did Stephen defend himself?

Acts 7:37-53

[Stephen said,] "Moses himself told the people of Israel, 'God will raise up for you a Prophet like me from among your own people.'* [38]Moses was with our ancestors, the assembly of God's people in the wilderness, when the angel spoke to him at Mount Sinai. And there Moses received life-giving words to pass on to us.*

[39]"But our ancestors refused to listen to Moses. They rejected him and wanted to return to Egypt. [40]They told Aaron, 'Make us some gods who can lead us, for we don't know what has become of this Moses, who brought us out of Egypt.' [41]So they made an idol shaped like a calf, and they sacrificed to it and celebrated over this thing they had made. [42]Then God turned away from them and abandoned them to serve the stars of heaven as their gods! In the book of the prophets it is written,

'Was it to me you were bringing
　　sacrifices and offerings
　during those forty years in the
　　wilderness, Israel?
[43]No, you carried your pagan gods—
　　the shrine of Molech,
　the star of your god Rephan,
　and the images you made to worship
　　them.
So I will send you into exile
　　as far away as Babylon.'*

[44]"Our ancestors carried the Tabernacle* with them through the wilderness. It was constructed according to the plan Go[d] had shown to Moses. [45]Years later, whe[n] Joshua led our ancestors in battle again[st] the nations that God drove out of this land[,] the Tabernacle was taken with them int[o] their new territory. And it stayed there un[til the time of King David.

[46]"David found favor with God an[d] asked for the privilege of building a per[manent Temple for the God of Jacob. [47]But it was Solomon who actually built i[t]. [48]However, the Most High doesn't live i[n] temples made by human hands. As th[e] prophet says,

[49]'Heaven is my throne,
　　and the earth is my footstool.
Could you build me a temple as good
　　as that?'
　asks the LORD.
'Could you build me such a resting
　　place?
[50]Didn't my hands make both heaven
　　and earth?'*

[51]"You stubborn people! You are heathen[?] at heart and deaf to the truth. Must yo[u] forever resist the Holy Spirit? That's wh[at] your ancestors did, and so do you! [52]Nam[e] one prophet your ancestors didn't persecut[e]! They even killed the ones who predicted th[e] coming of the Righteous One—the Messia[h], whom you betrayed and murdered. [53]Yo[u] deliberately disobeyed God's law, eve[n] though you received it from the hands o[f] angels."

7:37 Deut 18:15.　7:38 Some manuscripts read *to you*.　7:42-43 Amos 5:25-27 (Greek version).　7:44 Greek *the tent of witness*.　7:46 Some manuscripts read *the house of Jacob*.　7:49-50 Isa 66:1-2.　7:51 Greek *uncircumcised*.

Stephen used stories from the Israelites' past to show the people how they were disobeying God. People still disobey God just like the Israelites did. God wants us to obey his commands because he loves us. He gave us the commands in his Word because he knew that obeying them would keep us from getting in trouble and having to endure the consequences.

[God's] laws are wonderful. No wonder I obey them! PSALM 119:129

OCTOBER 13

Stephen Dies

Stephen's preaching made the Jewish leaders really mad. What did they do to him?

Acts 7:54-60

The Jewish leaders were infuriated by Stephen's accusation, and they shook their fists at him in rage.* ⁵⁵But Stephen, full of the Holy Spirit, gazed steadily into heaven and saw the glory of God, and he saw Jesus standing in the place of honor at God's right hand. ⁵⁶And he told them, "Look, I see the heavens opened and the Son of Man standing in the place of honor at God's right hand!"

⁵⁷Then they put their hands over their ears and began shouting. They rushed at him ⁵⁸and dragged him out of the city and began to stone him. His accusers took off their coats and laid them at the feet of a young man named Saul.*

⁵⁹As they stoned him, Stephen prayed, "Lord Jesus, receive my spirit." ⁶⁰He fell to his knees, shouting, "Lord, don't charge them with this sin!" And with that, he died.

7:54 Greek *they were grinding their teeth against him.* **7:58** *Saul* is later called Paul; see 13:9.

Even while the Jewish leaders were murdering Stephen, he prayed that God would forgive them. Stephen followed Jesus' example by forgiving those who were hurting him. Jesus died for us so that we could be forgiven for all the ways we've sinned and hurt God. Next time someone does something that hurts you, remember how Jesus forgave you and how Stephen forgave those Jewish leaders.

God showed his great love for us by sending Christ to die for us while we were still sinners. ROMANS 5:8

OCTOBER 14

money can't Buy it

Simon tried to buy the Holy Spirit. Why did Peter scold him?

Acts 8:1-25

Saul was one of the witnesses, and he agreed completely with the killing of Stephen.

A great wave of persecution began that day, sweeping over the church in Jerusalem; and all the believers except the apostles were scattered through the regions of Judea and Samaria. ²(Some devout men came and buried Stephen with great mourning.) ³But Saul was going everywhere to destroy the church. He went from house to house, dragging out both men and women to throw them into prison.

⁴But the believers who were scattered preached the Good News about Jesus wherever they went. ⁵Philip, for example, went to the city of Samaria and told the people there about the Messiah. ⁶Crowds listened intently to Philip because they were eager to hear his message and see the miraculous signs he did. ⁷Many evil* spirits were cast out, screaming as they left their victims. And many who had been paralyzed or lame were healed. ⁸So there was great joy in that city.

⁹A man named Simon had been a sorcerer there for many years, amazing the people of Samaria and claiming to be someone great. ¹⁰Everyone, from the least to the greatest, often spoke of him as "the Great One—the Power of God." ¹¹They listened closely to him because for a long time he had astounded them with his magic.

¹²But now the people believed Philip's message of Good News concerning the Kingdom of God and the name of Jesus Christ. As a result, many men and women were baptized. ¹³Then Simon himself believed and was baptized. He began following Philip wherever he went, and he was amazed by the signs and great miracles Philip performed.

¹⁴When the apostles in Jerusalem heard that the people of Samaria had accepted God's message, they sent Peter and John there. ¹⁵As soon as they arrived, they prayed for these new believers to receive the Holy Spirit. ¹⁶The Holy Spirit had not yet come upon any of them, for they had only been baptized in the name of the Lord Jesus. ¹⁷Then Peter and John laid their hands upon these believers, and they received the Holy Spirit.

¹⁸When Simon saw that the Spirit was given when the apostles laid their hands on people, he offered them money to buy this power. ¹⁹"Let me have this power, too," he exclaimed, "so that when I lay my hands on people, they will receive the Holy Spirit!"

²⁰But Peter replied, "May your money be destroyed with you for thinking God's gift can be bought! ²¹You can have no part in this, for your heart is not right with God. ²²Repent of your wickedness and pray to the Lord. Perhaps he will forgive your evil thoughts, ²³for I can see that you are full of bitter jealousy and are held captive by sin."

²⁴"Pray to the Lord for me," Simon exclaimed, "that these terrible things you've said won't happen to me!"

²⁵After testifying and preaching the

word of the Lord in Samaria, Peter and John returned to Jerusalem. And they

8:7 Greek *unclean.*

stopped in many Samaritan villages along the way to preach the Good News.

Simon wanted the power of the Holy Spirit for making money. But the Holy Spirit cannot be bought. Only true followers of Jesus can receive the Holy Spirit in their life. To use God's power for your own profit is an insult to God. Enjoy God's gift of the Holy Spirit, letting him help you as he chooses instead of trying to tell him what to do.

Do not bring sorrow to God's Holy Spirit by the way you live. Remember, he has identified you as his own,* guaranteeing that you will be saved on the day of redemption. EPHESIANS 4:30

4:30 Or *has put his seal on you.*

OCTOBER 15

unexpected appointment

An angel guided Philip to an Ethiopian who needed to hear about Jesus. What did the Ethiopian ask Philip to do for him?

Acts 8:26-39

As for Philip, an angel of the Lord said to him, "Go south* down the desert road that runs from Jerusalem to Gaza." ²⁷So he started out, and he met the treasurer of Ethiopia, a eunuch of great authority under the Kandake, the queen of Ethiopia. The eunuch had gone to Jerusalem to worship, ²⁸and he was now returning. Seated in his carriage, he was reading aloud from the book of the prophet Isaiah.

²⁹The Holy Spirit said to Philip, "Go over and walk along beside the carriage."

³⁰Philip ran over and heard the man reading from the prophet Isaiah. Philip asked, "Do you understand what you are reading?"

³¹The man replied, "How can I, unless someone instructs me?" And he urged Philip to come up into the carriage and sit with him.

³²The passage of Scripture he had been reading was this:

"He was led like a sheep to the slaughter.
    And as a lamb is silent before the
        shearers,
    he did not open his mouth.
³³He was humiliated and received no
        justice.
    Who can speak of his descendants?
    For his life was taken from the
        earth."*

³⁴The eunuch asked Philip, "Tell me, was the prophet talking about himself or someone else?" ³⁵So beginning with this same Scripture, Philip told him the Good News about Jesus.

³⁶As they rode along, they came to some water, and the eunuch said, "Look! There's some water! Why can't I be baptized?"* ³⁸He ordered the carriage to stop, and they

went down into the water, and Philip baptized him.

³⁹When they came up out of the water, the Spirit of the Lord snatched Philip away. The eunuch never saw him again but went on his way rejoicing.

8:26 Or *Go at noon.* 8:32-33 Isa 53:7-8 (Greek version). 8:36 Some manuscripts add verse 37, *"You can,"* Philip answered, *"if you believe with all your heart." And the eunuch replied, "I believe that Jesus Christ is the Son of God."*

When Philip told him the Good News, the Ethiopian believed it and asked Philip to baptize him immediately. Philip had this opportunity to tell the Ethiopian about Jesus because Philip listened to the Holy Spirit and obeyed his leading. We can do the same if we pay attention to the opportunities the Holy Spirit gives us to tell others about Jesus. Ask the Holy Spirit to give you openings to share the Good News, and be thinking about what you might say to someone who doesn't know Jesus.

Let the whole earth sing to the LORD! Each day proclaim the good news that he saves. I CHRONICLES 16:23

OCTOBER 16

Blindsided

Saul wanted to put Christians in prison, but God had other plans for Saul. What did God do to change Saul's mind?

Acts 9:1-18

Saul was uttering threats with every breath and was eager to kill the Lord's followers.* So he went to the high priest. ²He requested letters addressed to the synagogues in Damascus, asking for their cooperation in the arrest of any followers of the Way he found there. He wanted to bring them—both men and women—back to Jerusalem in chains.

³As he was approaching Damascus on this mission, a light from heaven suddenly shone down around him. ⁴He fell to the ground and heard a voice saying to him, "Saul! Saul! Why are you persecuting me?"

⁵"Who are you, lord?" Saul asked.

And the voice replied, "I am Jesus, the one you are persecuting! ⁶Now get up and go into the city, and you will be told what you must do."

⁷The men with Saul stood speechless, for they heard the sound of someone's voice but saw no one! ⁸Saul picked himself up off the ground, but when he opened his eyes he was blind. So his companions led him by the hand to Damascus. ⁹He remained there blind for three days and did not eat or drink.

¹⁰Now there was a believer* in Damascus named Ananias. The Lord spoke to him in a vision, calling, "Ananias!"

"Yes, Lord!" he replied.

¹¹The Lord said, "Go over to Straight Street, to the house of Judas. When you get there, ask for a man from Tarsus named Saul. He is praying to me right now. ¹²I

have shown him a vision of a man named Ananias coming in and laying hands on him so he can see again."

¹³"But Lord," exclaimed Ananias, "I've heard many people talk about the terrible things this man has done to the believers in Jerusalem! ¹⁴And he is authorized by the leading priests to arrest everyone who calls upon your name."

¹⁵But the Lord said, "Go, for Saul is my chosen instrument to take my message to the Gentiles and to kings, as well as to the people of Israel. ¹⁶And I will show him how much he must suffer for my name's sake."

¹⁷So Ananias went and found Saul. He laid his hands on him and said, "Brother Saul, the Lord Jesus, who appeared to you on the road, has sent me so that you might regain your sight and be filled with the Holy Spirit." ¹⁸Instantly something like scales fell from Saul's eyes, and he regained his sight. Then he got up and was baptized.

9:1 Greek *disciples.*   9:10 Greek *disciple.*

Saul's life was changed for good that day he went to Damascus. God had chosen to use him to teach many people about Jesus. When you become a Christian, everything about your life and what you believe changes. The Bible says that you become a new person. This is exactly what happened to Saul. How has your life changed since you began following Jesus?

Anyone who belongs to Christ has become a new person. The old life is gone; a new life has begun! 2 CORINTHIANS 5:17

OCTOBER 17

A changed man

After Saul became a Christian, he started preaching to people about Jesus. How did the people respond to his preaching?

Acts 9:20-31

[Saul] began preaching about Jesus in the synagogues, saying, "He is indeed the Son of God!"

²¹All who heard him were amazed. "Isn't this the same man who caused such devastation among Jesus' followers in Jerusalem?" they asked. "And didn't he come here to arrest them and take them in chains to the leading priests?"

²²Saul's preaching became more and more powerful, and the Jews in Damascus couldn't refute his proofs that Jesus was indeed the Messiah. ²³After a while some of the Jews plotted together to kill him. ²⁴They were watching for him day and night at the city gate so they could murder him, but Saul was told about their plot. ²⁵So during the night, some of the other believers* lowered him in a large basket through an opening in the city wall.

²⁶When Saul arrived in Jerusalem, he tried to meet with the believers, but they were all afraid of him. They did not believe he had truly become a believer! ²⁷Then Barnabas brought him to the apostles and

told them how Saul had seen the Lord on the way to Damascus and how the Lord had spoken to Saul. He also told them that Saul had preached boldly in the name of Jesus in Damascus.

²⁸So Saul stayed with the apostles and went all around Jerusalem with them, preaching boldly in the name of the Lord. ²⁹He debated with some Greek-speaking Jews, but they tried to murder him. ³⁰When the believers* heard about this, they took him down to Caesarea and sent him away to Tarsus, his hometown.

³¹The church then had peace throughout Judea, Galilee, and Samaria, and it became stronger as the believers lived in the fear of the Lord. And with the encouragement of the Holy Spirit, it also grew in numbers.

9:25 Greek *his disciples.*   9:30 Greek *brothers.*

For Saul, becoming a Christian meant putting his life in danger. People were not happy about the message he was preaching. The believers were afraid of him, and the Jewish leaders didn't like his powerful teaching. Even though Saul was in danger, God was always with him. When we give our life to God, we can be confident that he cares about what happens to us and will help us.

Rescue me from my enemies, LORD; I run to you to hide me. PSALM 143:9

OCTOBER 18

It's a miracle!

God used Peter to heal others. How did the people who saw these miracles react?

Acts 9:32-42

Meanwhile, Peter traveled from place to place, and he came down to visit the believers in the town of Lydda. ³³There he met a man named Aeneas, who had been paralyzed and bedridden for eight years. ³⁴Peter said to him, "Aeneas, Jesus Christ heals you! Get up, and roll up your sleeping mat!" And he was healed instantly. ³⁵Then the whole population of Lydda and Sharon saw Aeneas walking around, and they turned to the Lord.

³⁶There was a believer in Joppa named Tabitha (which in Greek is Dorcas*). She was always doing kind things for others and helping the poor. ³⁷About this time she became ill and died. Her body was washed for burial and laid in an upstairs room. ³⁸But the believers had heard that Peter was nearby at Lydda, so they sent two men to beg him, "Please come as soon as possible!"

³⁹So Peter returned with them; and as soon as he arrived, they took him to the upstairs room. The room was filled with widows who were weeping and showing him the coats and other clothes Dorcas had made for them. ⁴⁰But Peter asked them all to leave the room; then he knelt and prayed. Turning to the body he said, "Get up, Tabitha." And she opened her eyes! When she saw Peter, she sat up! ⁴¹He gave her his hand and helped her up. Then he

called in the widows and all the believers, and he presented her to them alive. ⁴²The news spread through the whole town, and many believed in the Lord.

Peter had the power of the Holy Spirit. This power caused many people to believe in Jesus because they saw the miracles he was doing. God wants everyone to believe in his Son, and he will do whatever it takes to convince people. But you don't have to wait for a miracle to believe. God wants you to believe in his Son today!

There is salvation in no one else! God has given no other name under heaven by which we must be saved. ACTS 4:12

OCTOBER 19
An Angel Visits Cornelius

A Roman officer named Cornelius had a vision. What can you learn from his life?

Acts 10:1-23

In Caesarea there lived a Roman army officer* named Cornelius, who was a captain of the Italian Regiment. ²He was a devout, God-fearing man, as was everyone in his household. He gave generously to the poor and prayed regularly to God. ³One afternoon about three o'clock, he had a vision in which he saw an angel of God coming toward him. "Cornelius!" the angel said.

⁴Cornelius stared at him in terror. "What is it, sir?" he asked the angel.

And the angel replied, "Your prayers and gifts to the poor have been received by God as an offering! ⁵Now send some men to Joppa, and summon a man named Simon Peter. ⁶He is staying with Simon, a tanner who lives near the seashore."

⁷As soon as the angel was gone, Cornelius called two of his household servants and a devout soldier, one of his personal attendants. ⁸He told them what had happened and sent them off to Joppa.

⁹The next day as Cornelius's messengers were nearing the town, Peter went up on the flat roof to pray. It was about noon, ¹⁰and he was hungry. But while a meal was being prepared, he fell into a trance. ¹¹He saw the sky open, and something like a large sheet was let down by its four corners. ¹²In the sheet were all sorts of animals, reptiles, and birds. ¹³Then a voice said to him, "Get up, Peter; kill and eat them."

¹⁴"No, Lord," Peter declared. "I have never eaten anything that our Jewish laws have declared impure and unclean.*"

¹⁵But the voice spoke again: "Do not call something unclean if God has made it clean." ¹⁶The same vision was repeated three times. Then the sheet was suddenly pulled up to heaven.

¹⁷Peter was very perplexed. What could

the vision mean? Just then the men sent by Cornelius found Simon's house. Standing outside the gate, ¹⁸they asked if a man named Simon Peter was staying there.

¹⁹Meanwhile, as Peter was puzzling over the vision, the Holy Spirit said to him, "Three men have come looking for you. ²⁰Get up, go downstairs, and go with them without hesitation. Don't worry, for I have sent them."

²¹So Peter went down and said, "I'm the man you are looking for. Why have you come?"

²²They said, "We were sent by Cornelius, a Roman officer. He is a devout and God-fearing man, well respected by all the Jews. A holy angel instructed him to summon you to his house so that he can hear your message." ²³So Peter invited the men to stay for the night. The next day he went with them, accompanied by some of the brothers from Joppa.

10:1 Greek *a centurion;* similarly in 10:22. 10:14 Greek *anything common and unclean.*

God was pleased with Cornelius because he prayed regularly and gave money to the poor. We can learn from Cornelius about how to please the Lord. When we spend time talking to God in prayer and helping those in need around us, we show God how much we love him. And we become more aware of God's love for us.

The eyes of the LORD search the whole earth in order to strengthen those whose hearts are fully committed to him. 2 CHRONICLES 16:9

OCTOBER 20
PETER VISITS CORNELIUS
Peter went to Cornelius's house. What did Peter learn about God while he was there?

Acts 10:24-48

They arrived in Caesarea the following day. Cornelius was waiting for them and had called together his relatives and close friends. ²⁵As Peter entered his home, Cornelius fell at his feet and worshiped him. ²⁶But Peter pulled him up and said, "Stand up! I'm a human being just like you!" ²⁷So they talked together and went inside, where many others were assembled.

²⁸Peter told them, "You know it is against our laws for a Jewish man to enter a Gentile home like this or to associate with you. But God has shown me that I should no longer think of anyone as impure or unclean. ²⁹So I came without objection as soon as I was sent for. Now tell me why you sent for me."

³⁰Cornelius replied, "Four days ago I was praying in my house about this same time, three o'clock in the afternoon. Suddenly, a man in dazzling clothes was standing in front of me. ³¹He told me, 'Cornelius, your prayer has been heard, and your gifts to the poor have been noticed by God! ³²Now

send messengers to Joppa, and summon a man named Simon Peter. He is staying in the home of Simon, a tanner who lives near the seashore.' ³³So I sent for you at once, and it was good of you to come. Now we are all here, waiting before God to hear the message the Lord has given you."

³⁴Then Peter replied, "I see very clearly that God shows no favoritism. ³⁵In every nation he accepts those who fear him and do what is right. ³⁶This is the message of Good News for the people of Israel—that there is peace with God through Jesus Christ, who is Lord of all. ³⁷You know what happened throughout Judea, beginning in Galilee, after John began preaching his message of baptism. ³⁸And you know that God anointed Jesus of Nazareth with the Holy Spirit and with power. Then Jesus went around doing good and healing all who were oppressed by the devil, for God was with him.

³⁹"And we apostles are witnesses of all he did throughout Judea and in Jerusalem. They put him to death by hanging him on a cross,* ⁴⁰but God raised him to life on the third day. Then God allowed him to appear, ⁴¹not to the general public,* but to us whom God had chosen in advance to be his witnesses. We were those who ate and drank with him after he rose from the dead. ⁴²And he ordered us to preach everywhere and to testify that Jesus is the one appointed by God to be the judge of all— the living and the dead. ⁴³He is the one all the prophets testified about, saying that everyone who believes in him will have their sins forgiven through his name."

⁴⁴Even as Peter was saying these things, the Holy Spirit fell upon all who were listening to the message. ⁴⁵The Jewish believers* who came with Peter were amazed that the gift of the Holy Spirit had been poured out on the Gentiles, too. ⁴⁶For they heard them speaking in tongues and praising God.

Then Peter asked, ⁴⁷"Can anyone object to their being baptized, now that they have received the Holy Spirit just as we did?" ⁴⁸So he gave orders for them to be baptized in the name of Jesus Christ. Afterward Cornelius asked him to stay with them for several days.

10:39 Greek *on a tree.*   **10:41** Greek *the people.*   **10:45** Greek *The faithful ones of the circumcision.*

Peter learned that God does not play favorites. God loves everyone and wants all to come to him. You can benefit from the lesson Peter learned. Don't show favoritism to people because of their age, race, gender, or religion. Instead, show love to everyone.

The LORD is good to everyone. He showers compassion on all his creation.
PSALM 145:9

OCTOBER 21

food Drive

A famine was coming. How did the church in Antioch prepare for it?

Acts 11:19-30

The believers who had been scattered during the persecution after Stephen's death traveled as far as Phoenicia, Cyprus, and Antioch of Syria. They preached the word of God, but only to Jews. ²⁰However, some of the believers who went to Antioch from Cyprus and Cyrene began preaching to the Gentiles* about the Lord Jesus. ²¹The power of the Lord was with them, and a large number of these Gentiles believed and turned to the Lord.

²²When the church at Jerusalem heard what had happened, they sent Barnabas to Antioch. ²³When he arrived and saw this evidence of God's blessing, he was filled with joy, and he encouraged the believers to stay true to the Lord. ²⁴Barnabas was a good man, full of the Holy Spirit and strong in faith. And many people were brought to the Lord.

²⁵Then Barnabas went on to Tarsus to look for Saul. ²⁶When he found him, he brought him back to Antioch. Both of them stayed there with the church for a full year, teaching large crowds of people. (It was at Antioch that the believers* were first called Christians.)

²⁷During this time some prophets traveled from Jerusalem to Antioch. ²⁸One of them named Agabus stood up in one of the meetings and predicted by the Spirit that a great famine was coming upon the entire Roman world. (This was fulfilled during the reign of Claudius.) ²⁹So the believers in Antioch decided to send relief to the brothers and sisters* in Judea, everyone giving as much as they could. ³⁰This they did, entrusting their gifts to Barnabas and Saul to take to the elders of the church in Jerusalem.

11:20 Greek *the Hellenists* (i.e., those who speak Greek); other manuscripts read *the Greeks.* **11:26** Greek *disciples;* also in 11:29. **11:29** Greek *the brothers.*

The church in Antioch decided to send relief to the believers in Judea. They gave as much as they could and trusted Saul and Barnabas to deliver their gift to the church in Jerusalem. In the same way, we should help those around us who are in need. When you see someone in need, think of what you can do to help.

Those who oppress the poor insult their Maker, but helping the poor honors him.
PROVERBS 14:31

374

OCTOBER 22

Jailbreak

Herod had Peter arrested and put into jail. What happened when the angel appeared?

Acts 12:1-19

About that time King Herod Agrippa* began to persecute some believers in the church. ²He had the apostle James (John's brother) killed with a sword. ³When Herod saw how much this pleased the Jewish people, he also arrested Peter. (This took place during the Passover celebration.*) ⁴Then he imprisoned him, placing him under the guard of four squads of four soldiers each. Herod intended to bring Peter out for public trial after the Passover. ⁵But while Peter was in prison, the church prayed very earnestly for him.

⁶The night before Peter was to be placed on trial, he was asleep, fastened with two chains between two soldiers. Others stood guard at the prison gate. ⁷Suddenly, there was a bright light in the cell, and an angel of the Lord stood before Peter. The angel struck him on the side to awaken him and said, "Quick! Get up!" And the chains fell off his wrists. ⁸Then the angel told him, "Get dressed and put on your sandals." And he did. "Now put on your coat and follow me," the angel ordered.

⁹So Peter left the cell, following the angel. But all the time he thought it was a vision. He didn't realize it was actually happening. ¹⁰They passed the first and second guard posts and came to the iron gate leading to the city, and this opened for them all by itself. So they passed through and started walking down the street, and then the angel suddenly left him.

¹¹Peter finally came to his senses. "It's really true!" he said. "The Lord has sent his angel and saved me from Herod and from what the Jewish leaders* had planned to do to me!"

¹²When he realized this, he went to the home of Mary, the mother of John Mark, where many were gathered for prayer. ¹³He knocked at the door in the gate, and a servant girl named Rhoda came to open it. ¹⁴When she recognized Peter's voice, she was so overjoyed that, instead of opening the door, she ran back inside and told everyone, "Peter is standing at the door!"

¹⁵"You're out of your mind!" they said. When she insisted, they decided, "It must be his angel."

¹⁶Meanwhile, Peter continued knocking. When they finally opened the door and saw him, they were amazed. ¹⁷He motioned for them to quiet down and told them how the Lord had led him out of prison. "Tell James and the other brothers what happened," he said. And then he went to another place.

¹⁸At dawn there was a great commotion among the soldiers about what had happened to Peter. ¹⁹Herod Agrippa ordered a thorough search for him. When he couldn't be found, Herod interrogated the guards and sentenced them to death. Afterward Herod left Judea to stay in Caesarea for a while.

12:1 Greek *Herod the king*. He was the nephew of Herod Antipas and a grandson of Herod the Great.   12:3 Greek *the days of unleavened bread*.   12:11 Or *the Jewish people*.

When the believers prayed for Peter, God heard their prayer and sent an angel to free Peter. When you or people you know have problems, ask God for help. You can also ask others to pray for you. Remember that our God is powerful. He can rescue you or your friends and provide the strength to endure. Just ask him!

God is our refuge and strength, always ready to help in times of trouble.
PSALM 46:1

OCTOBER 23

unstoppable

Elymas tried to stop Paul and Barnabas from spreading the Word of God. What happened to him?

Acts 13:2-12

One day as these men were worshiping the Lord and fasting, the Holy Spirit said, "Dedicate Barnabas and Saul for the special work to which I have called them." ³So after more fasting and prayer, the men laid their hands on them and sent them on their way.

⁴So Barnabas and Saul were sent out by the Holy Spirit. They went down to the seaport of Seleucia and then sailed for the island of Cyprus. ⁵There, in the town of Salamis, they went to the Jewish synagogues and preached the word of God. John Mark went with them as their assistant.

⁶Afterward they traveled from town to town across the entire island until finally they reached Paphos, where they met a Jewish sorcerer, a false prophet named Bar-Jesus. ⁷He had attached himself to the governor, Sergius Paulus, who was an intelligent man. The governor invited Barnabas and Saul to visit him, for he wanted to hear the word of God. ⁸But Elymas, the sorcerer (as his name means in Greek), interfered and urged the governor to pay no attention to what Barnabas and Saul said. He was trying to keep the governor from believing.

⁹Saul, also known as Paul, was filled with the Holy Spirit, and he looked the sorcerer in the eye. ¹⁰Then he said, "You son of the devil, full of every sort of deceit and fraud, and enemy of all that is good! Will you never stop perverting the true ways of the Lord? ¹¹Watch now, for the Lord has laid his hand of punishment upon you, and you will be struck blind. You will not see the sunlight for some time." Instantly mist and darkness came over the man's eyes, and he began groping around begging for someone to take his hand and lead him.

¹²When the governor saw what had happened, he became a believer, for he was astonished at the teaching about the Lord.

Elymas thought he could stop Paul and Barnabas from sharing the Good News. Elymas was wrong, and God blinded him for his actions. Some people today try to stop Christians from sharing their faith. In fact, someone might have tried to stop *you* from sharing your faith. Although it may appear at times that these people are winning, they will never succeed. God is much more powerful. Remember that God is always on your side, and he will defeat anyone who opposes him. Your job is to keep sharing the Good News no matter what!

What shall we say about such wonderful things as these? If God is for us, who can ever be against us? ROMANS 8:31

OCTOBER 24

mistaken identity

The crowd thought Paul and Barnabas were gods. Why were Paul and Barnabas so upset to learn that the people thought this?

Acts 14:8-20

While they were at Lystra, Paul and Barnabas came upon a man with crippled feet. He had been that way from birth, so he had never walked. He was sitting [9]and listening as Paul preached. Looking straight at him, Paul realized he had faith to be healed. [10]So Paul called to him in a loud voice, "Stand up!" And the man jumped to his feet and started walking.

[11]When the crowd saw what Paul had done, they shouted in their local dialect, "These men are gods in human form!" [12]They decided that Barnabas was the Greek god Zeus and that Paul was Hermes, since he was the chief speaker. [13]Now the temple of Zeus was located just outside the town. So the priest of the temple and the crowd brought bulls and wreaths of flowers to the town gates, and they prepared to offer sacrifices to the apostles.

[14]But when Barnabas and Paul heard what was happening, they tore their clothing in dismay and ran out among the people, shouting, [15]"Friends,* why are you doing this? We are merely human beings—just like you! We have come to bring you the Good News that you should turn from these worthless things and turn to the living God, who made heaven and earth, the sea, and everything in them. [16]In the past he permitted all the nations to go their own ways, [17]but he never left them without evidence of himself and his goodness. For instance, he sends you rain and good crops and gives you food and joyful hearts." [18]But even with these words, Paul and Barnabas could scarcely restrain the people from sacrificing to them.

[19]Then some Jews arrived from Antioch and Iconium and won the crowds to their side. They stoned Paul and dragged him

out of town, thinking he was dead. [20]But as the believers* gathered around him, he got up and went back into the town. The next day he left with Barnabas for Derbe.

14:15 Greek *Men.* 14:20 Greek *disciples.*

Paul and Barnabas were upset about the crowd's reaction because they wanted everyone to know and worship the one true God, Jesus Christ. They didn't want people to worship them. Their desire for everyone to know and worship Jesus showed that they were more interested in serving others than in receiving praise. Do you have a humble attitude when people start to praise you?

You must worship no other gods, for the LORD, whose very name is Jealous, is a God who is jealous about his relationship with you. EXODUS 34:14

OCTOBER 25

An Important Meeting

The Jewish Christians were upset that the Gentiles weren't following the same laws and practices as the Jews. What did the apostles say to settle the matter?

Acts 15:1-12

While Paul and Barnabas were at Antioch of Syria, some men from Judea arrived and began to teach the believers*: "Unless you are circumcised as required by the law of Moses, you cannot be saved." [2]Paul and Barnabas disagreed with them, arguing vehemently. Finally, the church decided to send Paul and Barnabas to Jerusalem, accompanied by some local believers, to talk to the apostles and elders about this question. [3]The church sent the delegates to Jerusalem, and they stopped along the way in Phoenicia and Samaria to visit the believers. They told them— much to everyone's joy—that the Gentiles, too, were being converted.

[4]When they arrived in Jerusalem, Barnabas and Paul were welcomed by the whole church, including the apostles and elders. They reported everything God had done through them. [5]But then some of the believers who belonged to the sect of the Pharisees stood up and insisted, "The Gentile converts must be circumcised and required to follow the law of Moses."

[6]So the apostles and elders met together to resolve this issue. [7]At the meeting, after a long discussion, Peter stood and addressed them as follows: "Brothers, you all know that God chose me from among you some time ago to preach to the Gentiles so that they could hear the Good News and believe. [8]God knows people's hearts, and he confirmed that he accepts Gentiles by giving them the Holy Spirit, just as he did to us. [9]He

made no distinction between us and them, for he cleansed their hearts through faith. [10]So why are you now challenging God by burdening the Gentile believers* with a yoke that neither we nor our ancestors were able to bear? [11]We believe that we are all saved the same way, by the undeserved grace of the Lord Jesus."

[12]Everyone listened quietly as Barnabas and Paul told about the miraculous signs and wonders God had done through them among the Gentiles.

15:1 Greek *brothers;* also in 15:3.   15:10 Greek *disciples.*

Like the Jewish Christians back in Paul's day, some people today think that being a Christian is about following a list of dos and don'ts. But living as a Christian is not about a bunch of rules—it is all about a relationship with Jesus. Your relationship with Jesus should affect your attitude and behavior so that you *want* to do things that please him. That's better than simply checking off a list of things you think you *have* to do. Are you a rule-follower or a Jesus-follower?

O people, the LORD has told you what is good, and this is what he requires of you: to do what is right, to love mercy, and to walk humbly with your God. MICAH 6:8

OCTOBER 26

An Important Letter

Paul and Barnabas disagreed about whether they should take John Mark along on their journey. What did they do about this problem?

Acts 15:22-41

The apostles and elders together with the whole church in Jerusalem chose delegates, and they sent them to Antioch of Syria with Paul and Barnabas to report on this decision. The men chosen were two of the church leaders*—Judas (also called Barsabbas) and Silas. [23]This is the letter they took with them:

"This letter is from the apostles and elders, your brothers in Jerusalem. It is written to the Gentile believers in Antioch, Syria, and Cilicia. Greetings!

[24]"We understand that some men from here have troubled you and upset you with their teaching, but we did not send them! [25]So we decided, having come to complete agreement, to send you official representatives, along with our beloved Barnabas and Paul, [26]who have risked their lives for the name of our Lord Jesus Christ. [27]We are sending Judas and Silas to confirm what we have decided concerning your question.

[28]"For it seemed good to the Holy Spirit and to us to lay no greater burden on you than these few requirements: [29]You must abstain from eating

food offered to idols, from consuming blood or the meat of strangled animals, and from sexual immorality. If you do this, you will do well. Farewell."

[30]The messengers went at once to Antioch, where they called a general meeting of the believers and delivered the letter. [31]And there was great joy throughout the church that day as they read this encouraging message.

[32]Then Judas and Silas, both being prophets, spoke at length to the believers, encouraging and strengthening their faith. [33]They stayed for a while, and then the believers sent them back to the church in Jerusalem with a blessing of peace.* [35]Paul and Barnabas stayed in Antioch. They and

many others taught and preached the word of the Lord there.

[36]After some time Paul said to Barnabas, "Let's go back and visit each city where we previously preached the word of the Lord, to see how the new believers are doing." [37]Barnabas agreed and wanted to take along John Mark. [38]But Paul disagreed strongly, since John Mark had deserted them in Pamphylia and had not continued with them in their work. [39]Their disagreement was so sharp that they separated. Barnabas took John Mark with him and sailed for Cyprus. [40]Paul chose Silas, and as he left, the believers entrusted him to the Lord's gracious care. [41]Then he traveled throughout Syria and Cilicia, strengthening the churches there.

15:22 Greek *were leaders among the brothers.*   15:33 Some manuscripts add verse 34, *But Silas decided to stay there.*

Since Paul and Barnabas couldn't agree on whether or not John Mark should go along, they decided to separate. People disagree with each other all the time. You probably have disagreed at times with your parents, your brother or sister, and your friends. When we disagree with others, we need to be careful that it doesn't cause a broken relationship or hurt feelings. Remember that God wants us to love the people around us, even if we sometimes disagree with them.

Don't get involved in foolish, ignorant arguments that only start fights.
2 TIMOTHY 2:23

OCTOBER 27
A NEW DIRECTION
Paul tried to enter a part of Asia Minor, but the Holy Spirit stopped him from going there. Where did God want Paul to go?

Acts 16:1-15
Paul went first to Derbe and then to Lystra, where there was a young disciple named

Timothy. His mother was a Jewish believer, but his father was a Greek. [2]Timothy was well thought of by the believers* in Lystra and Iconium, [3]so Paul wanted him to join them on their journey. In deference to the Jews of the area, he arranged for Timothy to be circumcised before they left, for everyone knew that his father was a Greek. [4]Then they went from town to town, instructing the believers to follow the decisions made by the apostles and elders in Jerusalem. [5]So the churches were strengthened in their faith and grew larger every day.

[6]Next Paul and Silas traveled through the area of Phrygia and Galatia, because the Holy Spirit had prevented them from preaching the word in the province of Asia at that time. [7]Then coming to the borders of Mysia, they headed north for the province of Bithynia,* but again the Spirit of Jesus did not allow them to go there. [8]So instead, they went on through Mysia to the seaport of Troas.

[9]That night Paul had a vision: A man from Macedonia in northern Greece was standing there, pleading with him, "Come over to Macedonia and help us!" [10]So we* decided to leave for Macedonia at once, having concluded that God was calling us to preach the Good News there.

[11]We boarded a boat at Troas and sailed straight across to the island of Samothrace, and the next day we landed at Neapolis. [12]From there we reached Philippi, a major city of that district of Macedonia and a Roman colony. And we stayed there several days.

[13]On the Sabbath we went a little way outside the city to a riverbank, where we thought people would be meeting for prayer, and we sat down to speak with some women who had gathered there. [14]One of them was Lydia from Thyatira, a merchant of expensive purple cloth, who worshiped God. As she listened to us, the Lord opened her heart, and she accepted what Paul was saying. [15]She was baptized along with other members of her household, and she asked us to be her guests. "If you agree that I am a true believer in the Lord," she said, "come and stay at my home." And she urged us until we agreed.

16:2 Greek *brothers*.   16:6-7 *Phrygia, Galatia, Asia, Mysia,* and *Bithynia* were all districts in what is now Turkey.   16:10 Luke, the writer of this book, here joined Paul and accompanied him on his journey.

God instructed Paul through a vision to go to Macedonia. Paul was obedient to the Holy Spirit's direction, and more people learned about Jesus because of his obedience. The Holy Spirit leads in different ways—sometimes through what we read in the Bible, sometimes through the wisdom of people we trust, and sometimes through our circumstances. Ask God to help you know when the Holy Spirit is leading you to do something. If you follow the Holy Spirit's guidance, amazing things can happen!

When the Spirit of truth comes, he will guide you into all truth. He will not speak on his own but will tell you what he has heard. He will tell you about the future.
JOHN 16:13

OCTOBER 28

Paul and Silas in Jail

Paul and Silas were arrested and thrown into jail. What happened when a sudden earthquake shook open all the prison doors?

Acts 16:16-34

One day as we [Paul and Silas] were going down to the place of prayer, we met a demon-possessed slave girl. She was a fortune-teller who earned a lot of money for her masters. [17]She followed Paul and the rest of us, shouting, "These men are servants of the Most High God, and they have come to tell you how to be saved."

[18]This went on day after day until Paul got so exasperated that he turned and said to the demon within her, "I command you in the name of Jesus Christ to come out of her." And instantly it left her.

[19]Her masters' hopes of wealth were now shattered, so they grabbed Paul and Silas and dragged them before the authorities at the marketplace. [20]"The whole city is in an uproar because of these Jews!" they shouted to the city officials. [21]"They are teaching customs that are illegal for us Romans to practice."

[22]A mob quickly formed against Paul and Silas, and the city officials ordered them stripped and beaten with wooden rods. [23]They were severely beaten, and then they were thrown into prison. The jailer was ordered to make sure they didn't escape. [24]So the jailer put them into the inner dungeon and clamped their feet in the stocks.

[25]Around midnight Paul and Silas were praying and singing hymns to God, and the other prisoners were listening. [26]Suddenly, there was a massive earthquake, and the prison was shaken to its foundations. All the doors immediately flew open, and the chains of every prisoner fell off! [27]The jailer woke up to see the prison doors wide open. He assumed the prisoners had escaped, so he drew his sword to kill himself. [28]But Paul shouted to him, "Stop! Don't kill yourself! We are all here!"

[29]The jailer called for lights and ran to the dungeon and fell down trembling before Paul and Silas. [30]Then he brought them out and asked, "Sirs, what must I do to be saved?"

[31]They replied, "Believe in the Lord Jesus and you will be saved, along with everyone in your household." [32]And they shared the word of the Lord with him and with all who lived in his household. [33]Even at that hour of the night, the jailer cared for them and washed their wounds. Then he and everyone in his household were immediately baptized. [34]He brought them into his house and set a meal before them, and he and his entire household rejoiced because they all believed in God.

God used Paul and Silas to save the jailer's life and tell him about Jesus. Because they willingly shared their faith, the jailer's entire family accepted Jesus as Savior. God took the negative situation in which Paul and Silas found themselves and used it for something good. Bad circumstances aren't always bad experiences. God can, and does, work miracles through hard times. Even when your situation looks really awful, trust that God will use it for good somehow.

Dear brothers and sisters,* when troubles come your way, consider it an opportunity for great joy. For you know that when your faith is tested, your endurance has a chance to grow. JAMES 1:2-3
1:2 Greek *brothers;* also in 1:16, 19.

OCTOBER 29

Paul in Athens

Paul noticed that the people of Athens had an altar with the inscription "To an Unknown God." What did Paul have to say about the God those people didn't know?

Acts 17:16-34

While Paul was waiting for them in Athens, he was deeply troubled by all the idols he saw everywhere in the city. 17He went to the synagogue to reason with the Jews and the God-fearing Gentiles, and he spoke daily in the public square to all who happened to be there.

18He also had a debate with some of the Epicurean and Stoic philosophers. When he told them about Jesus and his resurrection, they said, "What's this babbler trying to say with these strange ideas he's picked up?" Others said, "He seems to be preaching about some foreign gods."

19Then they took him to the high council of the city.* "Come and tell us about this new teaching," they said. 20"You are saying some rather strange things, and we want to know what it's all about." 21(It

should be explained that all the Athenians as well as the foreigners in Athens seemed to spend all their time discussing the latest ideas.)

22So Paul, standing before the council,* addressed them as follows: "Men of Athens, I notice that you are very religious in every way, 23for as I was walking along I saw your many shrines. And one of your altars had this inscription on it: 'To an Unknown God.' This God, whom you worship without knowing, is the one I'm telling you about.

24"He is the God who made the world and everything in it. Since he is Lord of heaven and earth, he doesn't live in man-made temples, 25and human hands can't serve his needs—for he has no needs. He himself gives life and breath to everything, and he satisfies every need. 26From one man* he created all the nations through-out the whole earth. He decided before-hand when they should rise and fall, and he determined their boundaries.

²⁷"His purpose was for the nations to seek after God and perhaps feel their way toward him and find him—though he is not far from any one of us. ²⁸For in him we live and move and exist. As some of your* own poets have said, 'We are his offspring.' ²⁹And since this is true, we shouldn't think of God as an idol designed by craftsmen from gold or silver or stone.

³⁰"God overlooked people's ignorance about these things in earlier times, but now he commands everyone everywhere to repent of their sins and turn to him. ³¹For he has set a day for judging the world with justice by the man he has appointed, and he proved to everyone who this is by raising him from the dead."

³²When they heard Paul speak about the resurrection of the dead, some laughed in contempt, but others said, "We want to hear more about this later." ³³That ended Paul's discussion with them, ³⁴but some joined him and became believers. Among them were Dionysius, a member of the council,* a woman named Damaris, and others with them.

17:19 Or *the most learned society of philosophers in the city.* Greek reads *the Areopagus.*   17:22 Traditionally rendered *standing in the middle of Mars Hill;* Greek reads *standing in the middle of the Areopagus.*   17:26 Greek *From one;* other manuscripts read *From one blood.*   17:28 Some manuscripts read *our.*   17:34 Greek *an Areopagite.*

Paul said that the "unknown God" was the one true God. Then he told the people of Athens about Jesus, God's Son. There are still many people today who do not know who God is because they don't believe in his Son, Jesus. God wants us to do what Paul did and tell people about Jesus whenever we have the opportunity.

Go and make disciples of all the nations, baptizing them in the name of the Father and the Son and the Holy Spirit.* MATTHEW 28:19
28:19 Or *all peoples.*

OCTOBER 30
Paul in Corinth
The Jews wouldn't listen to Paul when he preached to them about Jesus. What did God tell Paul to do?

Acts 18:1-11
Then Paul left Athens and went to Corinth.* ²There he became acquainted with a Jew named Aquila, born in Pontus, who had recently arrived from Italy with his wife, Priscilla. They had left Italy when Claudius Caesar deported all Jews from Rome. ³Paul lived and worked with them, for they were tentmakers* just as he was.

⁴Each Sabbath found Paul at the synagogue, trying to convince the Jews and Greeks alike. ⁵And after Silas and Timothy came down from Macedonia, Paul spent all his time preaching the word. He testi-

fied to the Jews that Jesus was the Messiah. ⁶But when they opposed and insulted him, Paul shook the dust from his clothes and said, "Your blood is upon your own heads— I am innocent. From now on I will go preach to the Gentiles."

⁷Then he left and went to the home of Titius Justus, a Gentile who worshiped God and lived next door to the synagogue. ⁸Crispus, the leader of the synagogue, and everyone in his household believed in the Lord. Many others in Corinth also heard Paul, became believers, and were baptized.

⁹One night the Lord spoke to Paul in a vision and told him, "Don't be afraid! Speak out! Don't be silent! ¹⁰For I am with you, and no one will attack and harm you, for many people in this city belong to me." ¹¹So Paul stayed there for the next year and a half, teaching the word of God.

18:1 *Athens* and *Corinth* were major cities in Achaia, the region in the southern portion of the Greek peninsula. 18:3 Or *leatherworkers.*

God told Paul to keep preaching about Jesus. He comforted Paul and told him not to be afraid. It is easy to be scared when other people insult you and tell you you're wrong about what you believe. If this happens to you, remember the words God spoke to Paul. Because God has promised to watch over you, there is no need to be afraid to tell other people about Jesus.

When I am afraid, I will put my trust in [God]. PSALM 56:3

OCTOBER 31

Paul in Ephesus

Paul performed miracles in Ephesus. The people confessed their sins. What did they do to show that they were truly sorry for their sins?

Acts 19:1-20

While Apollos was in Corinth, Paul traveled through the interior regions until he reached Ephesus, on the coast, where he found several believers.* ²"Did you receive the Holy Spirit when you believed?" he asked them.

"No," they replied, "we haven't even heard that there is a Holy Spirit."

³"Then what baptism did you experience?" he asked.

And they replied, "The baptism of John."

⁴Paul said, "John's baptism called for repentance from sin. But John himself told the people to believe in the one who would come later, meaning Jesus."

⁵As soon as they heard this, they were baptized in the name of the Lord Jesus. ⁶Then when Paul laid his hands on them, the Holy Spirit came on them, and they spoke in other tongues and prophesied. ⁷There were about twelve men in all.

⁸Then Paul went to the synagogue and preached boldly for the next three months, arguing persuasively about the Kingdom of God. ⁹But some became stubborn,

rejecting his message and publicly speaking against the Way. So Paul left the synagogue and took the believers with him. Then he held daily discussions at the lecture hall of Tyrannus. [10]This went on for the next two years, so that people throughout the province of Asia—both Jews and Greeks—heard the word of the Lord.

[11]God gave Paul the power to perform unusual miracles. [12]When handkerchiefs or aprons that had merely touched his skin were placed on sick people, they were healed of their diseases, and evil spirits were expelled.

[13]A group of Jews was traveling from town to town casting out evil spirits. They tried to use the name of the Lord Jesus in their incantation, saying, "I command you in the name of Jesus, whom Paul preaches, to come out!" [14]Seven sons of Sceva, a lead- ing priest, were doing this. [15]But one time when they tried it, the evil spirit replied, "I know Jesus, and I know Paul, but who are you?" [16]Then the man with the evil spirit leaped on them, overpowered them, and attacked them with such violence that they fled from the house, naked and battered.

[17]The story of what happened spread quickly all through Ephesus, to Jews and Greeks alike. A solemn fear descended on the city, and the name of the Lord Jesus was greatly honored. [18]Many who became believers confessed their sinful practices. [19]A number of them who had been practicing sorcery brought their incantation books and burned them at a public bonfire. The value of the books was several million dollars.* [20]So the message about the Lord spread widely and had a powerful effect.

19:1 Greek *disciples;* also in 19:9.   19:19 Greek *50,000 pieces of silver,* each of which was the equivalent of a day's wage.

The people burned the books that had led them away from God. If something causes us to sin, we should get rid of it. This demonstrates that we are serious about turning from the sin in our life. It also shows that we really love God. Is there something in your life that you need to turn from today?

I confess my sins; I am deeply sorry for what I have done. PSALM 38:18

OCTOBER CHALLENGE
Fantastic!

You are nearing the goal line! Ten months down and only two to go if you started reading in January. You are almost there! Just keep up a steady, even pace, and you'll be sure to get to the top of Challenge Mountain. It won't be hard. After all the practice you've had with daily Bible readings, the final two months will be a breeze!

To show that you've finished the October readings, use a fall-color marker or highlighter to fill in the level you have reached.

This month you learned a lot about the beginnings of the Christian faith. What was the most interesting fact you learned about the early Christians?

. . . .

. . . .

. . . .

. . . .

. . . .

. . . .

IMPORTANT STUFF TO REMEMBER FROM OCTOBER

❑ The Holy Spirit helps the church grow.

❑ Followers of Jesus will face trouble in their life.

❑ Anyone can be a Christian, no matter what his or her background is.

TiME FOR SOME PUZZLE FUN!

Fill in the word stack puzzle below with the names of these people from the book of Acts.

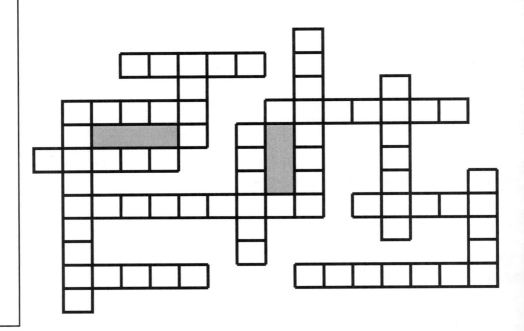

WORD BANK

Ananias (Acts 9)   Jason (Acts 17)   Peter (Acts 2)   Silas (Acts 15)

Barnabas (Acts 11)   Julius (Acts 27)   Priscilla (Acts 18)   Stephen (Acts 6–7)

Cornelius (Acts 10)   Lydia (Acts 16)   Rhoda (Acts 12)   Timothy (Acts 16)

James (Acts 15)   Mark (Acts 13)

NOVEMBER 1

A Riot

Some Ephesian silversmiths were worried that their idol-making business would slow down. Who did they blame?

Acts 19:23-41

Serious trouble developed in Ephesus concerning the Way. ²⁴It began with Demetrius, a silversmith who had a large business manufacturing silver shrines of the Greek goddess Artemis.* He kept many craftsmen busy. ²⁵He called them together, along with others employed in similar trades, and addressed them as follows:

"Gentlemen, you know that our wealth comes from this business. ²⁶But as you have seen and heard, this man Paul has persuaded many people that handmade gods aren't really gods at all. And he's done this not only here in Ephesus but throughout the entire province! ²⁷Of course, I'm not just talking about the loss of public respect for our business. I'm also concerned that the temple of the great goddess Artemis will lose its influence and that Artemis—this magnificent goddess worshiped throughout the province of Asia and all around the world—will be robbed of her great prestige!"

²⁸At this their anger boiled, and they began shouting, "Great is Artemis of the Ephesians!" ²⁹Soon the whole city was filled with confusion. Everyone rushed to the amphitheater, dragging along Gaius and Aristarchus, who were Paul's traveling companions from Macedonia. ³⁰Paul wanted to go in, too, but the believers wouldn't let him. ³¹Some of the officials of the province, friends of Paul, also sent a message to him, begging him not to risk his life by entering the amphitheater.

³²Inside, the people were all shouting, some one thing and some another. Everything was in confusion. In fact, most of them didn't even know why they were there. ³³The Jews in the crowd pushed Alexander forward and told him to explain the situation. He motioned for silence and tried to speak. ³⁴But when the crowd realized he was a Jew, they started shouting again and kept it up for two hours: "Great is Artemis of the Ephesians! Great is Artemis of the Ephesians!"

³⁵At last the mayor was able to quiet them down enough to speak. "Citizens of Ephesus," he said. "Everyone knows that Ephesus is the official guardian of the temple of the great Artemis, whose image fell down to us from heaven. ³⁶Since this is

389

an undeniable fact, you should stay calm and not do anything rash. [37]You have brought these men here, but they have stolen nothing from the temple and have not spoken against our goddess.

[38]"If Demetrius and the craftsmen have a case against them, the courts are in session and the officials can hear the case at once. Let them make formal charges.

[39]And if there are complaints about other matters, they can be settled in a legal assembly. [40]I am afraid we are in danger of being charged with rioting by the Roman government, since there is no cause for all this commotion. And if Rome demands an explanation, we won't know what to say." [41]Then he dismissed them, and they dispersed.

19:24 *Artemis* is otherwise known as Diana.

The silversmiths blamed Paul because as more people believed in what he was saying, they had little need for silver idols anymore. Although Christians today don't bow down and worship idols, they often put things before their relationship with Jesus. When this happens, they really are setting up idols in their heart. Is there anything or anyone you value more than Jesus? If so, begin putting Jesus first in your life. That's the place he deserves.

At the name of Jesus every knee should bow, in heaven and on earth and under the earth, and every tongue confess that Jesus Christ is Lord, to the glory of God the Father. PHILIPPIANS 2:10-11

NOVEMBER 2

Paul Says Good-bye

Paul knew that he would face trouble in the future. What did he decide to do?

Acts 20:17-38

But when we landed at Miletus, [Paul] sent a message to the elders of the church at Ephesus, asking them to come and meet him.

[18]When they arrived he declared, "You know that from the day I set foot in the province of Asia until now [19]I have done the Lord's work humbly and with many tears. I have endured the trials that came to me from the plots of the Jews. [20]I never shrank back from telling you what you needed to hear, either publicly or in your homes. [21]I have had one message for Jews and Greeks alike—the necessity of repenting from sin and turning to God, and of having faith in our Lord Jesus.

[22]"And now I am bound by the Spirit* to go to Jerusalem. I don't know what awaits me, [23]except that the Holy Spirit tells me in city after city that jail and suffering lie ahead. [24]But my life is worth nothing to me unless I use it for finishing the work assigned me by the Lord Jesus—the work of telling others the Good News about the wonderful grace of God.

²⁵"And now I know that none of you to whom I have preached the Kingdom will ever see me again. ²⁶I declare today that I have been faithful. If anyone suffers eternal death, it's not my fault,* ²⁷for I didn't shrink from declaring all that God wants you to know.

²⁸"So guard yourselves and God's people. Feed and shepherd God's flock—his church, purchased with his own blood*—over which the Holy Spirit has appointed you as elders.* ²⁹I know that false teachers, like vicious wolves, will come in among you after I leave, not sparing the flock. ³⁰Even some men from your own group will rise up and distort the truth in order to draw a following. ³¹Watch out! Remember the three years I was with you—my constant watch and care over you night and day, and my many tears for you.

³²"And now I entrust you to God and the message of his grace that is able to build you up and give you an inheritance with all those he has set apart for himself.

³³"I have never coveted anyone's silver or gold or fine clothes. ³⁴You know that these hands of mine have worked to supply my own needs and even the needs of those who were with me. ³⁵And I have been a constant example of how you can help those in need by working hard. You should remember the words of the Lord Jesus: 'It is more blessed to give than to receive.'"

³⁶When he had finished speaking, he knelt and prayed with them. ³⁷They all cried as they embraced and kissed him good-bye. ³⁸They were sad most of all because he had said that they would never see him again. Then they escorted him down to the ship.

20:22 Or by my spirit, or by an inner compulsion; Greek reads by the spirit.   20:26 Greek I am innocent of the blood of all.   20:28a Or with the blood of his own [Son].   20:28b Greek overseers.

Even during times of trouble, Paul was determined to serve God. He was willing to give up everything—even his life—for his Lord and Savior, Jesus. Today, Jesus demands no less of us. To be true disciples, we must be willing to dedicate everything we have and everything we are to Jesus' service. How can you serve God today?

If you try to hang on to your life, you will lose it. But if you give up your life for [Jesus'] sake, you will save it. LUKE 9:24

NOVEMBER 3

A DIFFICULT JOURNEY

On his way to Jerusalem, many people warned Paul that there would be hard times ahead. How did Paul respond?

Acts 21:1-17

After saying farewell to the Ephesian elders, we sailed straight to the island of Cos. The next day we reached Rhodes and then went to Patara. ²There we boarded a ship sailing for Phoenicia. ³We sighted the island of Cyprus, passed it on our left, and landed at the harbor of Tyre, in Syria, where the ship was to unload its cargo.

⁴We went ashore, found the local believers,* and stayed with them a week. These believers prophesied through the Holy Spirit that Paul should not go on to Jerusalem. ⁵When we returned to the ship at the end of the week, the entire congregation, including wives and children, left the city and came down to the shore with us. There we knelt, prayed, ⁶and said our farewells. Then we went aboard, and they returned home.

⁷The next stop after leaving Tyre was Ptolemais, where we greeted the brothers and sisters* and stayed for one day. ⁸The next day we went on to Caesarea and stayed at the home of Philip the Evangelist, one of the seven men who had been chosen to distribute food. ⁹He had four unmarried daughters who had the gift of prophecy.

¹⁰Several days later a man named Aga-bus, who also had the gift of prophecy, arrived from Judea. ¹¹He came over, took Paul's belt, and bound his own feet and hands with it. Then he said, "The Holy Spirit declares, 'So shall the owner of this belt be bound by the Jewish leaders in Jerusalem and turned over to the Gentiles.'" ¹²When we heard this, we and the local believers all begged Paul not to go on to Jerusalem.

¹³But he said, "Why all this weeping? You are breaking my heart! I am ready not only to be jailed at Jerusalem but even to die for the sake of the Lord Jesus." ¹⁴When it was clear that we couldn't persuade him, we gave up and said, "The Lord's will be done."

¹⁵After this we packed our things and left for Jerusalem. ¹⁶Some believers from Caesarea accompanied us, and they took us to the home of Mnason, a man originally from Cyprus and one of the early believers. ¹⁷When we arrived, the brothers and sisters in Jerusalem welcomed us warmly.

21:4 Greek *disciples;* also in 21:16.   21:7 Greek *brothers;* also in 21:17.

Paul was touched by his friends' concern for him. But he was determined to continue on to Jerusalem. Before leaving the island of Cyprus, Paul had taken time to pray with the church family there. Those prayers helped him know the right thing to do. Follow Paul's example. When you face something you can't handle, ask someone to pray with you. God will use other believers to encourage you. What do you need prayer for today? Ask someone to pray with you about it.

As soon as I pray, you [God] answer me; you encourage me by giving me strength.
PSALM 138:3

NOVEMBER 4

Paul is Arrested

Paul was in the Temple at Jerusalem when he got into big trouble. Read what happened when an angry mob tried to kill him.

Acts 21:26-40

So Paul went to the Temple the next day with the other men. They had already started the purification ritual, so he publicly announced the date when their vows would end and sacrifices would be offered for each of them.

[27]The seven days were almost ended when some Jews from the province of Asia saw Paul in the Temple and roused a mob against him. They grabbed him, [28]yelling, "Men of Israel, help us! This is the man who preaches against our people everywhere and tells everybody to disobey the Jewish laws. He speaks against the Temple—and even defiles this holy place by bringing in Gentiles.*" [29](For earlier that day they had seen him in the city with Trophimus, a Gentile from Ephesus,* and they assumed Paul had taken him into the Temple.)

[30]The whole city was rocked by these accusations, and a great riot followed. Paul was grabbed and dragged out of the Temple, and immediately the gates were closed behind him. [31]As they were trying to kill him, word reached the commander of the Roman regiment that all Jerusalem was in an uproar. [32]He immediately called out his soldiers and officers* and ran down among the crowd. When the mob saw the commander and the troops coming, they stopped beating Paul.

[33]Then the commander arrested him and ordered him bound with two chains. He asked the crowd who he was and what he had done. [34]Some shouted one thing and some another. Since he couldn't find out the truth in all the uproar and confusion, he ordered that Paul be taken to the fortress. [35]As Paul reached the stairs, the mob grew so violent the soldiers had to lift him to their shoulders to protect him. [36]And the crowd followed behind, shouting, "Kill him, kill him!"

[37]As Paul was about to be taken inside, he said to the commander, "May I have a word with you?"

"Do you know Greek?" the commander asked, surprised. [38]"Aren't you the Egyptian who led a rebellion some time ago and took 4,000 members of the Assassins out into the desert?"

[39]"No," Paul replied, "I am a Jew and a citizen of Tarsus in Cilicia, which is an important city. Please, let me talk to these people." [40]The commander agreed, so Paul stood on the stairs and motioned to the people to be quiet. Soon a deep silence enveloped the crowd, and he addressed them in their own language, Aramaic.*

21:28 Greek *Greeks.* 21:29 Greek *Trophimus, the Ephesian.* 21:32 Greek *centurions.* 21:40 Or *Hebrew.*

This crowd of people had been trying to kill Paul. He narrowly escaped with his life. But as soon as he had the chance, Paul wanted to speak to the people. Instead of being afraid of the angry crowd, Paul just kept trying to obey God. Would you be able to stay calm and trust God under so much pressure? It would be hard! But God always gives us the strength we need to do whatever he wants us to do.

The LORD is my strength and shield. I trust him with all my heart. He helps me, and my heart is filled with joy. I burst out in songs of thanksgiving. PSALM 28:7

NOVEMBER 5

Paul's story

Beaten and bruised, Paul told his life story and how he came to know Jesus. How did the crowd respond?

Acts 22:1-24

"Brothers and esteemed fathers," Paul said, "listen to me as I offer my defense." ²When they heard him speaking in their own language,* the silence was even greater.

³Then Paul said, "I am a Jew, born in Tarsus, a city in Cilicia, and I was brought up and educated here in Jerusalem under Gamaliel. As his student, I was carefully trained in our Jewish laws and customs. I became very zealous to honor God in everything I did, just like all of you today. ⁴And I persecuted the followers of the Way, hounding some to death, arresting both men and women and throwing them in prison. ⁵The high priest and the whole council of elders can testify that this is so. For I received letters from them to our Jewish brothers in Damascus, authorizing me to bring the Christians from there to Jerusalem, in chains, to be punished.

⁶"As I was on the road, approaching Damascus about noon, a very bright light from heaven suddenly shone down around me. ⁷I fell to the ground and heard a voice saying to me, 'Saul, Saul, why are you persecuting me?'

⁸"'Who are you, lord?' I asked.

"And the voice replied, 'I am Jesus the Nazarene,* the one you are persecuting.' ⁹The people with me saw the light but didn't understand the voice speaking to me.

¹⁰"I asked, 'What should I do, Lord?'

"And the Lord told me, 'Get up and go into Damascus, and there you will be told everything you are to do.'

¹¹"I was blinded by the intense light and had to be led by the hand to Damascus by my companions. ¹²A man named Ananias lived there. He was a godly man, deeply devoted to the law, and well regarded by all the Jews of Damascus. ¹³He came and

stood beside me and said, 'Brother Saul, regain your sight.' And that very moment I could see him!

¹⁴"Then he told me, 'The God of our ancestors has chosen you to know his will and to see the Righteous One and hear him speak. ¹⁵For you are to be his witness, telling everyone what you have seen and heard. ¹⁶What are you waiting for? Get up and be baptized. Have your sins washed away by calling on the name of the Lord.'

¹⁷"After I returned to Jerusalem, I was praying in the Temple and fell into a trance. ¹⁸I saw a vision of Jesus* saying to me, 'Hurry! Leave Jerusalem, for the people here won't accept your testimony about me.'

¹⁹" 'But Lord,' I argued, 'they certainly know that in every synagogue I imprisoned and beat those who believed in you. ²⁰And I was in complete agreement when your witness Stephen was killed. I stood by and kept the coats they took off when they stoned him.'

²¹"But the Lord said to me, 'Go, for I will send you far away to the Gentiles!'"

²²The crowd listened until Paul said that word. Then they all began to shout, "Away with such a fellow! He isn't fit to live!" ²³They yelled, threw off their coats, and tossed handfuls of dust into the air.

²⁴The commander brought Paul inside and ordered him lashed with whips to make him confess his crime. He wanted to find out why the crowd had become so furious.

22:2 Greek *in Aramaic,* or *in Hebrew.*   22:8 Or *Jesus of Nazareth.*   22:18 Greek *him.*

At first the crowd listened to Paul. But when Paul mentioned preaching to the Gentiles (people who were not Jewish), the crowd went crazy. The Jewish people believed that God had chosen them and that Gentiles were not worthy to enter God's kingdom. But the gospel says that anyone who confesses his or her sins and believes in Jesus will be saved. Have you ever thought that someone is too bad to be saved? Nobody is! God can save any person. Don't ever give up because you think that somebody is beyond God's reach.

This is a trustworthy saying, and everyone should accept it: "Christ Jesus came into the world to save sinners"—and I am the worst of them all. I TIMOTHY 1:15

November 6

A murder plot

Some religious leaders plotted to kill Paul. Would Paul be able to escape from their plan?

Acts 23:6-24

Paul realized that some members of the high council were Sadducees and some were Pharisees, so he shouted, "Brothers, I am a Pharisee, as were my ancestors! And I am on trial because my hope is in the resurrection of the dead!"

7This divided the council—the Pharisees against the Sadducees—8for the Sadducees say there is no resurrection or angels or spirits, but the Pharisees believe in all of these. 9So there was a great uproar. Some of the teachers of religious law who were Pharisees jumped up and began to argue forcefully. "We see nothing wrong with him," they shouted. "Perhaps a spirit or an angel spoke to him." 10As the conflict grew more violent, the commander was afraid they would tear Paul apart. So he ordered his soldiers to go and rescue him by force and take him back to the fortress.

11That night the Lord appeared to Paul and said, "Be encouraged, Paul. Just as you have been a witness to me here in Jerusalem, you must preach the Good News in Rome as well."

12The next morning a group of Jews* got together and bound themselves with an oath not to eat or drink until they had killed Paul. 13There were more than forty of them in the conspiracy. 14They went to the leading priests and elders and told them, "We have bound ourselves with an oath to eat nothing until we have killed Paul. 15So you and the high council should ask the com-

mander to bring Paul back to the counc[il] again. Pretend you want to examine his cas[e] more fully. We will kill him on the way."

16But Paul's nephew—his sister's son— heard of their plan and went to the for[-] tress and told Paul. 17Paul called for on[e] of the Roman officers* and said, "Tak[e] this young man to the commander. H[e] has something important to tell him."

18So the officer did, explaining, "Pau[l] the prisoner, called me over and asked m[e] to bring this young man to you because h[e] has something to tell you."

19The commander took his hand, le[d] him aside, and asked, "What is it you wan[t] to tell me?"

20Paul's nephew told him, "Some Jew[s] are going to ask you to bring Paul befor[e] the high council tomorrow, pretendin[g] they want to get some more informatio[n.] 21But don't do it! There are more tha[n] forty men hiding along the way ready t[o] ambush him. They have vowed not to ea[t] or drink anything until they have kille[d] him. They are ready now, just waiting fo[r] your consent."

22"Don't let anyone know you told m[e] this," the commander warned the youn[g] man.

23Then the commander called two of hi[s] officers and ordered, "Get 200 soldiers read[y] to leave for Caesarea at nine o'clock tonigh[t.] Also take 200 spearmen and 70 mounte[d] troops. 24Provide horses for Paul to rid[e] and get him safely to Governor Felix."

23:12 Greek *the Jews*. 23:17 Greek *centurions;* also in 23:23.

God kept Paul safe by allowing Paul's nephew to find out about the men's plans. Since God knows everything, he is able to protect us even when we don't realize we are in danger. If you follow God and do what he wants you to do, you can trust that he will take care of you. Thank God today for his constant protection.

[God] did rescue us from mortal danger, and he will rescue us again. We have placed our confidence in him, and he will continue to rescue us.
2 CORINTHIANS 1:10

NOVEMBER 7

paul speaks to felix

Paul was on trial before Felix, the governor. What did Felix think of Paul's message?

Acts 24:10-25

The governor then motioned for Paul to speak. Paul said, "I know, sir, that you have been a judge of Jewish affairs for many years, so I gladly present my defense before you. [11]You can quickly discover that I arrived in Jerusalem no more than twelve days ago to worship at the Temple. [12]My accusers never found me arguing with anyone in the Temple, nor stirring up a riot in any synagogue or on the streets of the city. [13]These men cannot prove the things they accuse me of doing.

[14]"But I admit that I follow the Way, which they call a cult. I worship the God of our ancestors, and I firmly believe the Jewish law and everything written in the prophets. [15]I have the same hope in God that these men have, that he will raise both the righteous and the unrighteous. [16]Because of this, I always try to maintain a clear conscience before God and all people.

[17]"After several years away, I returned to Jerusalem with money to aid my people and to offer sacrifices to God. [18]My accusers saw me in the Temple as I was completing a purification ceremony. There was no crowd around me and no rioting. [19]But some Jews from the province of Asia were there—and they ought to be here to bring charges if they have anything against me! [20]Ask these men here what crime the Jewish high council* found me guilty of, [21]except for the one time I shouted out, 'I am on trial before you today because I believe in the resurrection of the dead!'"

[22]At that point Felix, who was quite familiar with the Way, adjourned the hearing and said, "Wait until Lysias, the garrison commander, arrives. Then I will decide the case." [23]He ordered an officer* to keep Paul in custody but to give him some freedom and allow his friends to visit him and take care of his needs.

[24]A few days later Felix came back with

his wife, Drusilla, who was Jewish. Sending for Paul, they listened as he told them about faith in Christ Jesus. ²⁵As he reasoned with them about righteousness and self-control and the coming day of judgment, Felix became frightened. "Go away for now," he replied. "When it is more convenient, I'll call for you again."

24:20 Greek *Sanhedrin*.   24:23 Greek *a centurion*.

When Paul spoke about Jesus, Felix became afraid. Felix must have realized that Paul was telling the truth and that he needed to be forgiven for his sins. But since he didn't want to accept Jesus, Felix just wanted Paul to stop talking. We might not like it when God shows us that we need to confess our sins and ask for forgiveness. But when he does, we need to listen. What is God telling you right now?

I confessed all my sins to you and stopped trying to hide my guilt. I said to myself, "I will confess my rebellion to the LORD." And you forgave me! All my guilt is gone. PSALM 32:5

NOVEMBER 8

Paul speaks to Agrippa

Paul spoke to King Agrippa about what Jesus had done for him. See if Paul acted afraid to tell this powerful man about Jesus.

Acts 26:1-3, 9-29
Then Agrippa said to Paul, "You may speak in your defense."

So Paul, gesturing with his hand, started his defense: ²"I am fortunate, King Agrippa, that you are the one hearing my defense today against all these accusations made by the Jewish leaders, ³for I know you are an expert on all Jewish customs and controversies. Now please listen to me patiently!

⁹"I used to believe that I ought to do everything I could to oppose the very name of Jesus the Nazarene.* ¹⁰Indeed, I did just that in Jerusalem. Authorized by the leading priests, I caused many believers there to be sent to prison. And I cast my vote against them when they were condemned to death. ¹¹Many times I had them punished in the synagogues to get them to curse Jesus.* I was so violently opposed to them that I even chased them down in foreign cities.

¹²"One day I was on such a mission to Damascus, armed with the authority and commission of the leading priests. ¹³About noon, Your Majesty, as I was on the road, a light from heaven brighter than the sun shone down on me and my companions. ¹⁴We all fell down, and I heard a voice saying to me in Aramaic,* 'Saul, Saul, why are you persecuting me? It is useless for you to fight against my will.*'

¹⁵"'Who are you, lord?' I asked.

"And the Lord replied, 'I am Jesus, the one you are persecuting. ¹⁶Now get to your feet! For I have appeared to you to appoint you as my servant and witness. You are to tell the world what you have seen and what I will show you in the future. ¹⁷And I will rescue you from both your own people and the Gentiles. Yes, I am sending you to the Gentiles ¹⁸to open their eyes, so they may turn from darkness to light and from the power of Satan to God. Then they will receive forgiveness for their sins and be given a place among God's people, who are set apart by faith in me.'

¹⁹"And so, King Agrippa, I obeyed that vision from heaven. ²⁰I preached first to those in Damascus, then in Jerusalem and throughout all Judea, and also to the Gentiles, that all must repent of their sins and turn to God—and prove they have changed by the good things they do. ²¹Some Jews arrested me in the Temple for preaching this, and they tried to kill me. ²²But God has protected me right up to this present time so I can testify to everyone, from the least to the greatest. I teach nothing except what the prophets and Moses said would happen—²³that the Messiah would suffer and be the first to rise from the dead, and in this way announce God's light to Jews and Gentiles alike."

²⁴Suddenly, Festus shouted, "Paul, you are insane. Too much study has made you crazy!"

²⁵But Paul replied, "I am not insane, Most Excellent Festus. What I am saying is the sober truth. ²⁶And King Agrippa knows about these things. I speak boldly, for I am sure these events are all familiar to him, for they were not done in a corner! ²⁷King Agrippa, do you believe the prophets? I know you do—"

²⁸Agrippa interrupted him. "Do you think you can persuade me to become a Christian so quickly?"*

²⁹Paul replied, "Whether quickly or not, I pray to God that both you and everyone here in this audience might become the same as I am, except for these chains."

26:9 Or *Jesus of Nazareth.*   26:11 Greek *to blaspheme.*   26:14a Or *Hebrew.*   26:14b Greek *It is hard for you to kick against the oxgoads.*   26:28 Or *"A little more, and your arguments would make me a Christian."*

As he stood before King Agrippa, Paul's main concern was that his audience hear about Jesus and believe. Unfortunately, Agrippa and the rest of Paul's audience were not interested in knowing Jesus as their Savior. If you are faithful in telling others about Jesus, you may get the same reaction as Paul did. Not everyone you meet will be interested in Jesus. But don't give up! God wants you to be faithful in sharing your faith—he will take care of the rest.

I have told all your people about your justice. I have not been afraid to speak out, as you, O LORD, well know. I have not kept the good news of your justice hidden in my heart; I have talked about your faithfulness and saving power. I have told everyone in the great assembly of your unfailing love and faithfulness.
PSALM 40:9-10

NOVEMBER 9

caught in a storm

Paul was a prisoner on a ship at sea when a terrible storm came up. How did he react?

Acts 27:13-26

When a light wind began blowing from the south, the sailors thought they could make it. So they pulled up anchor and sailed close to the shore of Crete. [14]But the weather changed abruptly, and a wind of typhoon strength (called a "northeaster") caught the ship and blew it out to sea. [15]They couldn't turn the ship into the wind, so they gave up and let it run before the gale.

[16]We sailed along the sheltered side of a small island named Cauda,* where with great difficulty we hoisted aboard the lifeboat being towed behind us. [17]Then the sailors bound ropes around the hull of the ship to strengthen it. They were afraid of being driven across to the sandbars of Syrtis off the African coast, so they lowered the sea anchor to slow the ship and were driven before the wind.

[18]The next day, as gale-force winds continued to batter the ship, the crew began throwing the cargo overboard. [19]The following day they even took some of the ship's gear and threw it overboard. [20]The terrible storm raged for many days, blotting out the sun and the stars, until at last all hope was gone.

[21]No one had eaten for a long time. Finally, Paul called the crew together and said, "Men, you should have listened to me in the first place and not left Crete. You would have avoided all this damage and loss. [22]But take courage! None of you will lose your lives, even though the ship will go down. [23]For last night an angel of the God to whom I belong and whom I serve stood beside me, [24]and he said, 'Don't be afraid, Paul, for you will surely stand trial before Caesar! What's more, God in his goodness has granted safety to everyone sailing with you.' [25]So take courage! For I believe God. It will be just as he said. [26]But we will be shipwrecked on an island."

27:16 Some manuscripts read *Clauda*.

Paul didn't stop trusting God when the storm came up. He knew that the same God who had saved him in all kinds of situations before would protect him from the storm, too. When our circumstances look scary, it can be hard to remember God's power to save us. But our situation—no matter how difficult—doesn't change who God is. No matter what's happening to you, remember to trust God like Paul did!

I am suffering and in pain. Rescue me, O God, by your saving power. PSALM **69:29**

NOVEMBER 10

Shipwreck!

When the ship that was on its way to Rome was about to run aground and break to bits, what did Paul do?

Acts 27:27-44

About midnight on the fourteenth night of the storm, as we were being driven across the Sea of Adria,* the sailors sensed land was near. ²⁸They dropped a weighted line and found that the water was 120 feet deep. But a little later they measured again and found it was only 90 feet deep.* ²⁹At this rate they were afraid we would soon be driven against the rocks along the shore, so they threw out four anchors from the back of the ship and prayed for daylight.

³⁰Then the sailors tried to abandon the ship; they lowered the lifeboat as though they were going to put out anchors from the front of the ship. ³¹But Paul said to the commanding officer and the soldiers, "You will all die unless the sailors stay aboard." ³²So the soldiers cut the ropes to the lifeboat and let it drift away.

³³Just as day was dawning, Paul urged everyone to eat. "You have been so worried that you haven't touched food for two weeks," he said. ³⁴"Please eat something now for your own good. For not a hair of your heads will perish." ³⁵Then he took some bread, gave thanks to God before them all, and broke off a piece and ate it. ³⁶Then everyone was encouraged and began to eat—³⁷all 276 of us who were on board. ³⁸After eating, the crew lightened the ship further by throwing the cargo of wheat overboard.

³⁹When morning dawned, they didn't recognize the coastline, but they saw a bay with a beach and wondered if they could get to shore by running the ship aground. ⁴⁰So they cut off the anchors and left them in the sea. Then they lowered the rudders, raised the foresail, and headed toward shore. ⁴¹But they hit a shoal and ran the ship aground too soon. The bow of the ship stuck fast, while the stern was repeatedly smashed by the force of the waves and began to break apart.

⁴²The soldiers wanted to kill the prisoners to make sure they didn't swim ashore and escape. ⁴³But the commanding officer wanted to spare Paul, so he didn't let them carry out their plan. Then he ordered all who could swim to jump overboard first and make for land. ⁴⁴The others held onto planks or debris from the broken ship.* So everyone escaped safely to shore.

27:27 The *Sea of Adria* includes the central portion of the Mediterranean. 27:28 Greek *20 fathoms . . . 15 fathoms* [37 meters . . . 27 meters]. 27:44 Or *or were helped by members of the ship's crew.*

In a time of crisis, Paul clearly demonstrated his trust in God by taking positive action and encouraging the sailors. When you face a time of crisis, remember to ask God for strength and comfort. Then encourage others with the strength and comfort that God gives to you.

All praise to God, the Father of our Lord Jesus Christ. God is our merciful Father and the source of all comfort. He comforts us in all our troubles so that we can comfort others. When they are troubled, we will be able to give them the same comfort God has given us. 2 CORINTHIANS 1:3-4

NOVEMBER 11

Paul in Chains

While under house arrest in Rome, Paul continued to preach boldly. Look how he used his situation to tell more people about Jesus.

Acts 28:16-31

When we arrived in Rome, Paul was permitted to have his own private lodging, though he was guarded by a soldier.

¹⁷Three days after Paul's arrival, he called together the local Jewish leaders. He said to them, "Brothers, I was arrested in Jerusalem and handed over to the Roman government, even though I had done nothing against our people or the customs of our ancestors. ¹⁸The Romans tried me and wanted to release me, because they found no cause for the death sentence. ¹⁹But when the Jewish leaders protested the decision, I felt it necessary to appeal to Caesar, even though I had no desire to press charges against my own people. ²⁰I asked you to come here today so we could get acquainted and so I could explain to you that I am bound with this chain because I believe that the hope of Israel—the Messiah—has already come."

²¹They replied, "We have had no letters from Judea or reports against you from anyone who has come here. ²²But we want to hear what you believe, for the only thing we know about this movement is that it is denounced everywhere."

²³So a time was set, and on that day a large number of people came to Paul's lodging. He explained and testified about the Kingdom of God and tried to persuade them about Jesus from the Scriptures. Using the law of Moses and the books of the prophets, he spoke to them from morning until evening. ²⁴Some were persuaded by the things he said, but others did not believe. ²⁵And after they had argued back and forth among themselves, they left with this final word from Paul:

"The Holy Spirit was right when he said to your ancestors through Isaiah the prophet,

'Go and say to this people:
When you hear what I say,
    you will not understand.
When you see what I do,
    you will not comprehend.
27For the hearts of these people are
    hardened,
    and their ears cannot hear,
    and they have closed their
        eyes—
so their eyes cannot see,

and their ears cannot hear,
    and their hearts cannot understand,
and they cannot turn to me
    and let me heal them.'*

28So I want you to know that this salvation from God has also been offered to the Gentiles, and they will accept it."*

30For the next two years, Paul lived in Rome at his own expense.* He welcomed all who visited him, 31boldly proclaiming the Kingdom of God and teaching about the Lord Jesus Christ. And no one tried to stop him.

28:26-27 Isa 6:9-10 (Greek version). 28:28 Some manuscripts add verse 29, *And when he had said these words, the Jews departed, greatly disagreeing with each other.* 28:30 Or *in his own rented quarters.*

Paul boldly told others about Jesus, even with guards watching and listening. He didn't let anyone keep him from preaching the Good News. If you are serious about following Jesus, don't let anyone scare you into not speaking up for him. Live boldly for Jesus, no matter who is around.

Pray for us, too, that God will give us many opportunities to speak about his mysterious plan concerning Christ. That is why I [Paul] am here in chains.
COLOSSIANS 4:3

NOVEMBER 12

NO ONE IS GOOD

In his letter to the Romans, Paul asked if Jews are better than others. What answer did he give for this question?

Romans 3:9-26

Well then, should we conclude that we Jews are better than others? No, not at all, for we have already shown that all people, whether Jews or Gentiles,* are under the power of sin. 10As the Scriptures say,

"No one is righteous—
    not even one.
11No one is truly wise;

    no one is seeking God.
12All have turned away;
    all have become useless.
No one does good,
    not a single one."*
13"Their talk is foul, like the stench from
        an open grave.
    Their tongues are filled
        with lies."
"Snake venom drips from their lips."*

¹⁴"Their mouths are full of cursing and bitterness."*
¹⁵"They rush to commit murder.
¹⁶Destruction and misery always follow them.
¹⁷They don't know where to find peace."*
¹⁸"They have no fear of God at all."*

¹⁹Obviously, the law applies to those to whom it was given, for its purpose is to keep people from having excuses, and to show that the entire world is guilty before God. ²⁰For no one can ever be made right with God by doing what the law commands. The law simply shows us how sinful we are.

²¹But now God has shown us a way to be made right with him without keeping the requirements of the law, as was promised in the writings of Moses* and the prophets long ago. ²²We are made right with God by placing our faith in Jesus Christ. And th is true for everyone who believes, no ma ter who we are.

²³For everyone has sinned; we all fa short of God's glorious standard. ²⁴Y God, with undeserved kindness, declar that we are righteous. He did this throug Christ Jesus when he freed us from th penalty for our sins. ²⁵For God presente Jesus as the sacrifice for sin. People a made right with God when they believ that Jesus sacrificed his life, shedding h blood. This sacrifice shows that God w being fair when he held back and did n punish those who sinned in times pa ²⁶for he was looking ahead and includir them in what he would do in this preser time. God did this to demonstrate h righteousness, for he himself is fair ar just, and he declares sinners to be right his sight when they believe in Jesus.

3:9 Greek *or Greeks.* **3:10-12** Pss 14:1-3; 53:1-3 (Greek version). **3:13** Pss 5:9 (Greek version); 140:3. **3:14** Ps 10:7 (Greek version). **3:15-17** Isa 59:7-8. **3:18** Ps 36:1. **3:21** Greek *in the law.*

People are always saying, "Well, nobody's perfect." And that's true! This passage says that not a single person, other than Jesus, has ever lived without sinning. No one is good. But because Jesus died and rose from the dead, God will forgive us for our sins if we believe in Jesus. Do you believe in Jesus? If you do, thank God for forgiving you and for seeing only Jesus' goodness in you!

All have turned away; all have become corrupt. No one does good, not a single one!* PSALM 14:3

14:3 Greek version reads *have become useless.* Compare Rom 3:12.

NOVEMBER 13

GOD'S LOVE

Paul wrote that it wasn't likely that someone would die even for a good person. What made Jesus' death so amazing?

Romans 5:1-11

Therefore, since we have been made right in God's sight by faith, we have peace with God because of what Jesus Christ our Lord has done for us. ²Because of our faith, Christ has brought us into this place of undeserved privilege where we now stand, and we confidently and joyfully look forward to sharing God's glory.

³We can rejoice, too, when we run into problems and trials, for we know that they help us develop endurance. ⁴And endurance develops strength of character, and character strengthens our confident hope of salvation. ⁵And this hope will not lead to disappointment. For we know how dearly God loves us, because he has given us the Holy Spirit to fill our hearts with his love.

⁶When we were utterly helpless, Christ came at just the right time and died for us sinners. ⁷Now, most people would not be willing to die for an upright person, though someone might perhaps be willing to die for a person who is especially good. ⁸But God showed his great love for us by sending Christ to die for us while we were still sinners. ⁹And since we have been made right in God's sight by the blood of Christ, he will certainly save us from God's condemnation. ¹⁰For since our friendship with God was restored by the death of his Son while we were still his enemies, we will certainly be saved through the life of his Son. ¹¹So now we can rejoice in our wonderful new relationship with God because our Lord Jesus Christ has made us friends of God.

Jesus' death was amazing because he died for sinners. He died for those who loved God and for those who hated God. In his death, we see God's incredible love for us. God gave up his own Son to die on the cross so that we might be able to live with him forever. And Jesus was willing to do it. Think about it. Could you give up your life for one of your enemies? Or even for one of your friends? That is what Jesus did for you.

O Lord, you are so good, so ready to forgive, so full of unfailing love for all who ask for your help. PSALM **86:5**

NOVEMBER 14

FREE FROM SIN

Before people become Christians, they are slaves to sin. What sets a person free from sin?

Romans 6:6-23

We know that our old sinful selves were crucified with Christ so that sin might lose its power in our lives. We are no longer slaves to sin. [7]For when we died with Christ we were set free from the power of sin. [8]And since we died with Christ, we know we will also live with him. [9]We are sure of this because Christ was raised from the dead, and he will never die again. Death no longer has any power over him. [10]When he died, he died once to break the power of sin. But now that he lives, he lives for the glory of God. [11]So you also should consider yourselves to be dead to the power of sin and alive to God through Christ Jesus.

[12]Do not let sin control the way you live;* do not give in to sinful desires. [13]Do not let any part of your body become an instrument of evil to serve sin. Instead, give yourselves completely to God, for you were dead, but now you have new life. So use your whole body as an instrument to do what is right for the glory of God. [14]Sin is no longer your master, for you no longer live under the requirements of the law. Instead, you live under the freedom of God's grace.

[15]Well then, since God's grace has set us free from the law, does that mean we can go on sinning? Of course not! [16]Don't you realize that you become the slave of whatever you choose to obey? You can be a slave to sin, which leads to death, or you can choose to obey God, which leads to righteous living. [17]Thank God! Once you were slaves of sin, but now you wholeheartedly obey this teaching we have given you. [18]Now you are free from your slavery to sin, and you have become slaves to righteous living.

[19]Because of the weakness of your human nature, I am using the illustration of slavery to help you understand all this. Previously, you let yourselves be slaves to impurity and lawlessness, which led ever deeper into sin. Now you must give yourselves to be slaves to righteous living so that you will become holy.

[20]When you were slaves to sin, you were free from the obligation to do right. [21]And what was the result? You are now ashamed of the things you used to do, things that end in eternal doom. [22]But now you are free from the power of sin and have become slaves of God. Now you do those things that lead to holiness and result in eternal life. [23]For the wages of sin is death, but the free gift of God is eternal life through Christ Jesus our Lord.

6:12 Or *Do not let sin reign in your body, which is subject to death.*

God's grace sets a person free from sin. His grace refers to his kindness and love. It means that God gave his Son, Jesus, to pay the penalty for everyone's sin. He did it because he loves us, not because we deserve his kindness. Those who accept Jesus' payment by believing in him are set free from the power that sin has over their life. If you believe that Jesus died for you and took your punishment for sin, then you have been set free from sin. If you've never thought about doing that before, you can believe in Jesus as your Savior today. He will set you free!

You will know the truth, and the truth will set you free. JOHN 8:32

NOVEMBER 15

God, our Father

Since Christians are controlled by the Spirit of God, they are God's children. What do you think it means to be God's child?

Romans 8:1-17

Now there is no condemnation for those who belong to Christ Jesus. ²And because you belong to him, the power* of the life-giving Spirit has freed you* from the power of sin that leads to death. ³The law of Moses was unable to save us because of the weakness of our sinful nature.* So God did what the law could not do. He sent his own Son in a body like the bodies we sinners have. And in that body God declared an end to sin's control over us by giving his Son as a sacrifice for our sins. ⁴He did this so that the just requirement of the law would be fully satisfied for us, who no longer follow our sinful nature but instead follow the Spirit.

⁵Those who are dominated by the sinful nature think about sinful things, but those who are controlled by the Holy Spirit think about things that please the Spirit. ⁶So letting your sinful nature control your mind leads to death. But letting the Spirit control your mind leads to life and peace. ⁷For the sinful nature is always hostile to God. It never did obey God's laws, and it never will. ⁸That's why those who are still under the control of their sinful nature can never please God.

⁹But you are not controlled by your sinful nature. You are controlled by the Spirit if you have the Spirit of God living in you. (And remember that those who do not have the Spirit of Christ living in them do not belong to him at all.) ¹⁰And Christ lives within you, so even though your body will die because of sin, the Spirit gives you life* because you have been made right with God. ¹¹The Spirit of God, who raised Jesus from the dead, lives in you. And just as God raised Christ Jesus from the dead, he will give life to your mortal bodies by this same Spirit living within you.

¹²Therefore, dear brothers and sisters,*

you have no obligation to do what your sinful nature urges you to do. ¹³For if you live by its dictates, you will die. But if through the power of the Spirit you put to death the deeds of your sinful nature,* you will live. ¹⁴For all who are led by the Spirit of God are children* of God.

¹⁵So you have not received a spirit that makes you fearful slaves. Instead, you received God's Spirit when he adopted you as his own children.* Now we call him, "Abba, Father."* ¹⁶For his Spirit joins with our spirit to affirm that we are God's children. ¹⁷And since we are his children, we are his heirs. In fact, together with Christ we are heirs of God's glory. But if we are to share his glory, we must also share his suffering.

8:2a Greek *the law;* also in 8:2b. 8:2b Some manuscripts read *me.* 8:3 Greek *our flesh;* similarly in 8:4, 5, 6, 7, 8, 9, 12. 8:10 Or *your spirit is alive.* 8:12 Greek *brothers.* 8:13 Greek *deeds of the body.* 8:14 Greek *sons.* 8:15a Greek *you received a spirit of sonship.* 8:15b *Abba* is an Aramaic term for "father."

If you believe in Jesus, you are God's child! You have God's Spirit within you as a sign that you are in his family. Paul says that children of God don't have to be afraid of God's punishment. Instead, we can call him our Father, and we can look forward to sharing his treasures in heaven. As God's child, you're one of the family. Do you enjoy the privileges and share in the responsibilities?

Christ, as the Son, is in charge of God's entire house. And we are God's house, if we keep our courage and remain confident in our hope in Christ. HEBREWS 3:6
3:6 Some manuscripts add *to the end.*

NOVEMBER 16

VICTORY IS OURS

When we become a Christian, we aren't guaranteed that our life will be easy. But look what Paul says about why we can be happy and hopeful even when everything is going wrong.

Romans 8:28-39

We know that God causes everything to work together* for the good of those who love God and are called according to his purpose for them. ²⁹For God knew his people in advance, and he chose them to become like his Son, so that his Son would be the firstborn among many brothers and sisters. ³⁰And having chosen them, he called them to come to him. And having called them, he gave them right standing with himself. And having given them right standing, he gave them his glory.

³¹What shall we say about such wonderful things as these? If God is for us, who can ever be against us? ³²Since he did not spare even his own Son but gave him up for us all, won't he also give us everything else? ³³Who dares accuse us whom God has chosen for his own? No one—for God himself has given us right standing

with himself. ³⁴Who then will condemn us? No one—for Christ Jesus died for us and was raised to life for us, and he is sitting in the place of honor at God's right hand, pleading for us.

³⁵Can anything ever separate us from Christ's love? Does it mean he no longer loves us if we have trouble or calamity, or are persecuted, or hungry, or destitute, or in danger, or threatened with death? ³⁶(As the Scriptures say, "For your sake we are killed every day; we are being slaughtered like sheep."*) ³⁷No, despite all these things,

overwhelming victory is ours through Christ, who loved us.

³⁸And I am convinced that nothing can ever separate us from God's love. Neither death nor life, neither angels nor demons,* neither our fears for today nor our worries about tomorrow—not even the powers of hell can separate us from God's love. ³⁹No power in the sky above or in the earth below—indeed, nothing in all creation will ever be able to separate us from the love of God that is revealed in Christ Jesus our Lord.

8:28 Some manuscripts read *And we know that everything works together.*   **8:36** Ps 44:22.   **8:38** Greek *nor rulers.*

God is always with his children, even when they suffer. There isn't any trial or problem or trouble that can separate us from God. He will never abandon us. If you are one of God's followers, you will never be separated from his love. No trouble is so great that it can totally defeat you. Take hope! You have the victory!

We know how much God loves us, and we have put our trust in his love. God is love, and all who live in love live in God, and God lives in them. I JOHN 4:16

NOVEMBER 17

overcoming evil

Paul wrote that Christians shouldn't seek revenge. How did he say Christians should treat their enemies?

Romans 12:1-21
Dear brothers and sisters,* I plead with you to give your bodies to God because of all he has done for you. Let them be a living and holy sacrifice—the kind he will find acceptable. This is truly the way to worship him.* ²Don't copy the behavior and customs of this world, but let God transform you into a new person by changing the way you think. Then you will learn to

know God's will for you, which is good and pleasing and perfect.

³Because of the privilege and authority* God has given me, I give each of you this warning: Don't think you are better than you really are. Be honest in your evaluation of yourselves, measuring yourselves by the faith God has given us.* ⁴Just as our bodies have many parts and each part has a special function, ⁵so it is with Christ's body.

We are many parts of one body, and we all belong to each other.

⁶In his grace, God has given us different gifts for doing certain things well. So if God has given you the ability to prophesy, speak out with as much faith as God has given you. ⁷If your gift is serving others, serve them well. If you are a teacher, teach well. ⁸If your gift is to encourage others, be encouraging. If it is giving, give generously. If God has given you leadership ability, take the responsibility seriously. And if you have a gift for showing kindness to others, do it gladly.

⁹Don't just pretend to love others. Really love them. Hate what is wrong. Hold tightly to what is good. ¹⁰Love each other with genuine affection,* and take delight in honoring each other. ¹¹Never be lazy, but work hard and serve the Lord enthusiastically.* ¹²Rejoice in our confident hope. Be patient in trouble, and keep on praying. ¹³When God's people are in need, be ready to help them. Always be eager to practice hospitality.

¹⁴Bless those who persecute you. Don't curse them; pray that God will bless them.

¹⁵Be happy with those who are happy, and weep with those who weep. ¹⁶Live in harmony with each other. Don't be too proud to enjoy the company of ordinary people. And don't think you know it all!

¹⁷Never pay back evil with more evil. Do things in such a way that everyone can see you are honorable. ¹⁸Do all that you can to live in peace with everyone.

¹⁹Dear friends, never take revenge. Leave that to the righteous anger of God. For the Scriptures say,

"I will take revenge;
   I will pay them back,"*
   says the LORD.

²⁰Instead,

"If your enemies are hungry, feed them.
   If they are thirsty, give them
     something to drink.
In doing this, you will heap
   burning coals of shame on their
     heads."*

²¹Don't let evil conquer you, but conquer evil by doing good.

12:1a Greek *brothers.*   12:1b Or *This is your spiritual worship;* or *This is your reasonable service.*   12:3a Or *Because of the grace;* compare 1:5.   12:3b Or *by the faith God has given you;* or *by the standard of our God-given faith.*   12:10 Greek *with brotherly love.*   12:11 Or *but serve the Lord with a zealous spirit;* or *but let the Spirit excite you as you serve the Lord.*   12:19 Deut 32:35.   12:20 Prov 25:21-22.

Christians should show love to their enemies. For Jesus' followers, this command replaced the belief that people should get revenge by hurting others in the same way they were injured. The new command was a way of showing God's love for people. How can you love your enemies? How about saying a kind word to those who insult you and praying for those who wrong you?

[Saul] said to David, "You are a better man than I am, for you have repaid me good for evil." I SAMUEL 24:17

Our Leaders

In Paul's day, people in authority sometimes treated those under them unkindly. Why did Paul tell Christians to obey those in authority?

Romans 13:1-10

Everyone must submit to governing authorities. For all authority comes from God, and those in positions of authority have been placed there by God. ²So anyone who rebels against authority is rebelling against what God has instituted, and they will be punished. ³For the authorities do not strike fear in people who are doing right, but in those who are doing wrong. Would you like to live without fear of the authorities? Do what is right, and they will honor you. ⁴The authorities are God's servants, sent for your good. But if you are doing wrong, of course you should be afraid, for they have the power to punish you. They are God's servants, sent for the very purpose of punishing those who do what is wrong. ⁵So you must submit to them, not only to avoid punishment, but also to keep a clear conscience.

⁶Pay your taxes, too, for these same reasons. For government workers need to be paid. They are serving God in what they do. ⁷Give to everyone what you owe them: Pay your taxes and government fees to those who collect them, and give respect and honor to those who are in authority.

⁸Owe nothing to anyone—except for your obligation to love one another. If you love your neighbor, you will fulfill the requirements of God's law. ⁹For the commandments say, "You must not commit adultery. You must not murder. You must not steal. You must not covet."* These—and other such commandments—are summed up in this one commandment: "Love your neighbor as yourself."* ¹⁰Love does no wrong to others, so love fulfills the requirements of God's law.

13:9a Exod 20:13-15, 17.   **13:9b** Lev 19:18.

Paul wrote that those in authority have been placed in their position by God. Because God has put them in power, Christians should respect those people by obeying them. Who is in authority over you? Your parents? Your teachers? The police? Show your love for God by obeying those people he has placed in authority.

You also are complete through your union with Christ, who is the head over every ruler and authority. COLOSSIANS 2:10

NOVEMBER 19

The Greatest

Paul wanted his readers to know that just about everything they do i useless if it is missing one thing. What is that one thing?

1 Corinthians 13:1-13

If I could speak all the languages of earth and of angels, but didn't love others, I would only be a noisy gong or a clanging cymbal. ²If I had the gift of prophecy, and if I understood all of God's secret plans and possessed all knowledge, and if I had such faith that I could move mountains, but didn't love others, I would be nothing. ³If I gave everything I have to the poor and even sacrificed my body, I could boast about it;* but if I didn't love others, I would have gained nothing.

⁴Love is patient and kind. Love is not jealous or boastful or proud ⁵or rude. It does not demand its own way. It is not irritable, and it keeps no record of being wronged. ⁶It does not rejoice about injustice but rejoices whenever the truth wins out. ⁷Love never gives up, never loses faith, is always hopeful, and endures through every circumstance.

⁸Prophecy and speaking in unknow languages* and special knowledge w become useless. But love will last foreve ⁹Now our knowledge is partial and i complete, and even the gift prophecy reveals only part of the who picture! ¹⁰But when full understandi comes, these partial things will becon useless.

¹¹When I was a child, I spoke an thought and reasoned as a child. B when I grew up, I put away childi things. ¹²Now we see things imperfect as in a cloudy mirror, but then we w see everything with perfect clarity.* that I know now is partial and incor plete, but then I will know everythi completely, just as God now knows n completely.

¹³Three things will last forever—fai hope, and love—and the greatest of the is love.

13:3 Some manuscripts read *sacrificed my body to be burned.*   13:8 Or *in tongues.*   13:12 Greek *see face to face.*

Love is the one thing that gives meaning to everything we do. That's becaus God has commanded us to love him and to love others. Without love, all that we do is meaningless. So how can we show love to others? We can be patient with them when they annoy us. We can be kind to them when they don't deserve it. We can do what is best for others rather than what is bes for ourselves. How can you show love to someone close to you today?

[Jesus said,] "I am giving you a new commandment: Love each other. Just as I ha loved you, you should love each other. Your love for one another will prove to the world that you are my disciples." JOHN 13:34-35

NOVEMBER 20

our Hope in Christ

Some believers had a few questions about the resurrection of believers. How did Paul answer their questions?

1 Corinthians 15:35-58

Someone may ask, "How will the dead be raised? What kind of bodies will they have?" ³⁶What a foolish question! When you put a seed into the ground, it doesn't grow into a plant unless it dies first. ³⁷And what you put in the ground is not the plant that will grow, but only a bare seed of wheat or whatever you are planting. ³⁸Then God gives it the new body he wants it to have. A different plant grows from each kind of seed. ³⁹Similarly there are different kinds of flesh—one kind for humans, another for animals, another for birds, and another for fish.

⁴⁰There are also bodies in the heavens and bodies on the earth. The glory of the heavenly bodies is different from the glory of the earthly bodies. ⁴¹The sun has one kind of glory, while the moon and stars each have another kind. And even the stars differ from each other in their glory.

⁴²It is the same way with the resurrection of the dead. Our earthly bodies are planted in the ground when we die, but they will be raised to live forever. ⁴³Our bodies are buried in brokenness, but they will be raised in glory. They are buried in weakness, but they will be raised in strength. ⁴⁴They are buried as natural human bodies, but they will be raised as spiritual bodies. For just as there are natural bodies, there are also spiritual bodies.

⁴⁵The Scriptures tell us, "The first man, Adam, became a living person."* But the last Adam—that is, Christ—is a life-giving Spirit. ⁴⁶What comes first is the natural body, then the spiritual body comes later. ⁴⁷Adam, the first man, was made from the dust of the earth, while Christ, the second man, came from heaven. ⁴⁸Earthly people are like the earthly man, and heavenly people are like the heavenly man. ⁴⁹Just as we are now like the earthly man, we will someday be like* the heavenly man.

⁵⁰What I am saying, dear brothers and sisters, is that our physical bodies cannot inherit the Kingdom of God. These dying bodies cannot inherit what will last forever.

⁵¹But let me reveal to you a wonderful secret. We will not all die, but we will all be transformed! ⁵²It will happen in a moment, in the blink of an eye, when the last trumpet is blown. For when the trumpet sounds, those who have died will be raised to live forever. And we who are living will also be transformed. ⁵³For our dying bodies must be transformed into bodies that will never die; our mortal bodies must be transformed into immortal bodies.

⁵⁴Then, when our dying bodies have been transformed into bodies that will never die,* this Scripture will be fulfilled:

"Death is swallowed up in victory.*
⁵⁵O death, where is your victory?
O death, where is your sting?*"

413

⁵⁶For sin is the sting that results in death, and the law gives sin its power. ⁵⁷But thank God! He gives us victory over sin and death through our Lord Jesus Christ.

⁵⁸So, my dear brothers and sisters, be strong and immovable. Always work enthusiastically for the Lord, for you know that nothing you do for the Lord is ever useless.

15:45 Gen 2:7.   15:49 Some manuscripts read *let us be like.*   15:54a Some manuscripts add *and our mortal bodies have been transformed into immortal bodies.*   15:54b Isa 25:8.   15:55 Hos 13:14 (Greek version).

Paul said that when believers are raised from the dead, they will have new bodies. These bodies will be even better than the ones they had on earth. If you are a follower of Jesus, this is good news. Your new body will never get sick, never hurt, never feel pain, and never get tired. Because Jesus died and rose again, all who believe in him will live with Jesus forever in heaven. Our new body will never die!

I [John] heard a loud shout from the throne, saying, "Look, God's home is now among his people! He will live with them, and they will be his people. God himself will be with them. He will wipe every tear from their eyes, and there will be no more death or sorrow or crying or pain. All these things are gone forever."*

REVELATION 21:3-4

21:3 Some manuscripts read *God himself will be with them, their God.*

NOVEMBER 21

Power for Pain

Paul had faced a lot of trouble. He was even beaten and thrown into jail because he believed in Jesus. Read what he had to say about dealing with suffering.

2 Corinthians 4:7-18

We now have this light shining in our hearts, but we ourselves are like fragile clay jars containing this great treasure.* This makes it clear that our great power is from God, not from ourselves.

⁸We are pressed on every side by troubles, but we are not crushed. We are perplexed, but not driven to despair. ⁹We are hunted down, but never abandoned by God. We get knocked down, but we are not destroyed. ¹⁰Through suffering, our bodies continue to share in the death of Jesus so that the life of Jesus may also be seen in our bodies.

¹¹Yes, we live under constant danger of death because we serve Jesus, so that the life of Jesus will be evident in our dying bodies. ¹²So we live in the face of death, but this has resulted in eternal life for you.

¹³But we continue to preach because we have the same kind of faith the psalmist had when he said, "I believed in God, so I spoke."* ¹⁴We know that God, who raised the Lord Jesus,* will also raise us with Jesus

and present us to himself together with you. ¹⁵All of this is for your benefit. And as God's grace reaches more and more people, there will be great thanksgiving, and God will receive more and more glory.

¹⁶That is why we never give up. Though our bodies are dying, our spirits are* being renewed every day. ¹⁷For our present troubles are small and won't last very long. Yet they produce for us a glory that vastly outweighs them and will last forever! ¹⁸So we don't look at the troubles we can see now; rather, we fix our gaze on things that cannot be seen. For the things we see now will soon be gone, but the things we cannot see will last forever.

4:7 Greek *We now have this treasure in clay jars.*   4:13 Ps 116:10.   4:14 Some manuscripts read *who raised Jesus.*
4:16 Greek *our inner being is.*

Paul saw the big picture. He understood that every trouble he had on earth would soon be over. Paul understood that the joy he would experience one day in heaven would last forever. In Paul's view, the pain he suffered would be a small price to pay for the joy he would have in heaven. When you face problems, try to see your situation from Jesus' point of view. Your joy in his kingdom will be much greater than your present sorrows. Learn what you can from your difficulties. Soon your pain will be turned into joy.

Since we are his children, we are his heirs. In fact, together with Christ we are heirs of God's glory. But if we are to share his glory, we must also share his suffering.
ROMANS 8:17

NOVEMBER 22
cheerful Giver
Paul wrote to the Christians in Corinth about how good it is to be generous.

2 Corinthians 9:6-15
Remember this—a farmer who plants only a few seeds will get a small crop. But the one who plants generously will get a generous crop. ⁷You must each decide in your heart how much to give. And don't give reluctantly or in response to pressure. "For God loves a person who gives cheerfully."* ⁸And God will generously provide all you need. Then you will always have everything you need and plenty left over to share with others. ⁹As the Scriptures say,

"They share freely and give generously
   to the poor.
Their good deeds will be
   remembered forever."*

¹⁰For God is the one who provides seed for the farmer and then bread to eat. In the same way, he will provide and increase your resources and then produce a great harvest of generosity* in you.

¹¹Yes, you will be enriched in every way so that you can always be generous. And

when we take your gifts to those who need them, they will thank God. [12]So two good things will result from this ministry of giving—the needs of the believers in Jerusalem will be met, and they will joyfully express their thanks to God.

[13]As a result of your ministry, they will give glory to God. For your generosity to them and to all believers will prove that you are obedient to the Good News of Christ. [14]And they will pray for you with deep affection because of the overflowing grace God has given to you. [15]Thank God for this gift* too wonderful for words!

9:7 See footnote on Prov 22:8.   9:9 Ps 112:9.   9:10 Greek *righteousness.*   9:15 Greek *his gift.*

Giving to other people is a great way to show God that you are thankful for what he has given to you. Think about the gifts you have received from God. He has given you food, clothes, a place to live, and a family. Thank God for the gifts he has given—and continues to give. Then think of how you can share these gifts with others. God loves it when we give to others cheerfully!

Generous people plan to do what is generous, and they stand firm in their generosity. ISAIAH 32:8

NOVEMBER 23

Life in Christ

Paul was telling the Christians in Galatia what it's like to live under the Holy Spirit's control. Look for what kinds of activities identify a non-Christian and a Christian.

Galatians 5:13-26

For you have been called to live in freedom, my brothers and sisters. But don't use your freedom to satisfy your sinful nature. Instead, use your freedom to serve one another in love. [14]For the whole law can be summed up in this one command: "Love your neighbor as yourself."* [15]But if you are always biting and devouring one another, watch out! Beware of destroying one another.

[16]So I say, let the Holy Spirit guide your lives. Then you won't be doing what your sinful nature craves. [17]The sinful nature wants to do evil, which is just the opposite of what the Spirit wants. And the Spirit gives us desires that are the opposite of what the sinful nature desires. These two forces are constantly fighting each other, so you are not free to carry out your good intentions. [18]But when you are directed by the Spirit, you are not under obligation to the law of Moses.

[19]When you follow the desires of your sinful nature, the results are very clear: sexual immorality, impurity, lustful pleasures,

²⁰idolatry, sorcery, hostility, quarreling, jealousy, outbursts of anger, selfish ambition, dissension, division, ²¹envy, drunkenness, wild parties, and other sins like these. Let me tell you again, as I have before, that anyone living that sort of life will not inherit the Kingdom of God.

²²But the Holy Spirit produces this kind of fruit in our lives: love, joy, peace, patience, kindness, goodness, faithfulness, ²³gentleness, and self-control. There is no law against these things!

²⁴Those who belong to Christ Jesus have nailed the passions and desires of their sinful nature to his cross and crucified them there. ²⁵Since we are living by the Spirit, let us follow the Spirit's leading in every part of our lives. ²⁶Let us not become conceited, or provoke one another, or be jealous of one another.

5:14 Lev 19:18.

What a person's life is like says a lot about whether the person is a Christian or not. Since Christians are under the Holy Spirit's control, they shouldn't get involved in sinful activities or behaviors. Instead, their lives display the fruit of the Spirit. Do you see love, joy, peace, patience, kindness, goodness, faithfulness, gentleness, and self-control in your own life? Ask the Holy Spirit to control your life so you'll be able to exhibit these fruits.

I [God] will give you a new heart, and I will put a new spirit in you. I will take out your stony, stubborn heart and give you a tender, responsive heart. * EZEKIEL 36:26
36:26 Hebrew *a heart of flesh.*

NOVEMBER 24

Paul's Prayers

Paul prayed for his friends in Ephesus all the time. What did he pray for?

Ephesians 1:15-23

Ever since I first heard of your strong faith in the Lord Jesus and your love for God's people everywhere,* ¹⁶I have not stopped thanking God for you. I pray for you constantly, ¹⁷asking God, the glorious Father of our Lord Jesus Christ, to give you spiritual wisdom* and insight so that you might grow in your knowledge of God. ¹⁸I pray that your hearts will be flooded with light so that you can understand the confident hope he has given to those he called—his holy people who are his rich and glorious inheritance.*

¹⁹I also pray that you will understand the incredible greatness of God's power for us who believe him. This is the same mighty power ²⁰that raised Christ from the dead and seated him in the place of honor at God's right hand in the heavenly realms. ²¹Now he is far above any ruler or authority or power or leader or anything

else—not only in this world but also in the world to come. [22]God has put all things under the authority of Christ and has made him head over all things for the benefit of the church. [23]And the church is his body; it is made full and complete by Christ, who fills all things everywhere with himself.

1:15 Some manuscripts read *your faithfulness to the Lord Jesus and to God's people everywhere.* 1:17 Or *to give you the Spirit of wisdom.* 1:18 Or *called, and the rich and glorious inheritance he has given to his holy people.*

Paul asked God to give his friends wisdom and greater knowledge so they would grow in their faith. He also prayed that they would understand the wonderful future that God planned for them. Then Paul prayed that his friends would realize God's power was at work and available to them. What do you pray for your friends and family? Follow Paul's example and pray that your family and friends will grow in faith and wisdom so they will recognize God's power in their life. Who can you pray for today?

I pray that your love will overflow more and more, and that you will keep on growing in knowledge and understanding. PHILIPPIANS 1:9

NOVEMBER 25

alive in JESUS

Paul wrote about God's riches. How is God rich?

Ephesians 2:1-10

Once you were dead because of your disobedience and your many sins. [2]You used to live in sin, just like the rest of the world, obeying the devil—the commander of the powers in the unseen world.* He is the spirit at work in the hearts of those who refuse to obey God. [3]All of us used to live that way, following the passionate desires and inclinations of our sinful nature. By our very nature we were subject to God's anger, just like everyone else.

[4]But God is so rich in mercy, and he loved us so much, [5]that even though we were dead because of our sins, he gave us life when he raised Christ from the dead. (It is only by God's grace that you have

2:2 Greek *obeying the commander of the power of the air.*

been saved!) [6]For he raised us from the dead along with Christ and seated us with him in the heavenly realms because we are united with Christ Jesus. [7]So God can point to us in all future ages as examples of the incredible wealth of his grace and kindness toward us, as shown in all he has done for us who are united with Christ Jesus.

[8]God saved you by his grace when you believed. And you can't take credit for this; it is a gift from God. [9]Salvation is not a reward for the good things we have done, so none of us can boast about it. [10]For we are God's masterpiece. He has created us anew in Christ Jesus, so we can do the good things he planned for us long ago.

God is rich in mercy and love. He showed his mercy (undeserved favor) by not destroying us because of our sin. He showed his love for us by sending his perfect Son, Jesus, to pay the penalty for our sin. And he showers us with that love and mercy each day! Thank God right now for the love and mercy he has shown you.

God showed his great love for us by sending Christ to die for us while we were still sinners. ROMANS 5:8

NOVEMBER 26

Brand-new

Paul described the way non-Christians act. Instead of acting like people who don't believe in God, who should Christians act like?

Ephesians 4:17–5:2

With the Lord's authority I say this: Live no longer as the Gentiles do, for they are hopelessly confused. 18Their minds are full of darkness; they wander far from the life God gives because they have closed their minds and hardened their hearts against him. 19They have no sense of shame. They live for lustful pleasure and eagerly practice every kind of impurity.

20But that isn't what you learned about Christ. 21Since you have heard about Jesus and have learned the truth that comes from him, 22throw off your old sinful nature and your former way of life, which is corrupted by lust and deception. 23Instead, let the Spirit renew your thoughts and attitudes. 24Put on your new nature, created to be like God—truly righteous and holy.

25So stop telling lies. Let us tell our neighbors the truth, for we are all parts of the same body. 26And "don't sin by letting anger control you."* Don't let the sun go down while you are still angry, 27for anger gives a foothold to the devil.

28If you are a thief, quit stealing. Instead, use your hands for good hard work, and then give generously to others in need. 29Don't use foul or abusive language. Let everything you say be good and helpful, so that your words will be an encouragement to those who hear them.

30And do not bring sorrow to God's Holy Spirit by the way you live. Remember, he has identified you as his own,* guaranteeing that you will be saved on the day of redemption.

31Get rid of all bitterness, rage, anger, harsh words, and slander, as well as all types of evil behavior. 32Instead, be kind to each other, tenderhearted, forgiving one another, just as God through Christ has forgiven you.

5:1Imitate God, therefore, in everything you do, because you are his dear children.

²Live a life filled with love, following the example of Christ. He loved us* and offered himself as a sacrifice for us, a pleasing aroma to God.

Sometimes when we are around people who don't know anything about God, it can be tempting to talk and act like they do. But Christians shouldn't act like people who don't know God! Once we have been saved, our life should be totally different. Instead of following the example of non-Christians, we should follow the example of Jesus. What can you do to be like Jesus today?

The LORD also said to Moses, "Give the following instructions to the entire community of Israel. You must be holy because I, the LORD your God, am holy." LEVITICUS 19:1-2

NOVEMBER 27

Parents

Paul wrote to tell us how to treat the people who have authority over us.

Ephesians 6:1-9

Children, obey your parents because you belong to the Lord,* for this is the right thing to do. ²"Honor your father and mother." This is the first commandment with a promise: ³If you honor your father and mother, "things will go well for you, and you will have a long life on the earth."*

⁴Fathers, do not provoke your children to anger by the way you treat them. Rather, bring them up with the discipline and instruction that comes from the Lord.

⁵Slaves, obey your earthly masters with deep respect and fear. Serve them sincerely as you would serve Christ. ⁶Try to please them all the time, not just when they are watching you. As slaves of Christ, do the will of God with all your heart. ⁷Work with enthusiasm, as though you were working for the Lord rather than for people. ⁸Remember that the Lord will reward each one of us for the good we do, whether we are slaves or free.

⁹Masters, treat your slaves in the same way. Don't threaten them; remember, you both have the same Master in heaven, and he has no favorites.

In this passage Paul reminds us how important it is to obey parents and other authority figures. Are you good at obeying your parents and teachers? Even though we sometimes don't like to be told what to do, it's important to respect those in authority. When we obey our parents, our teachers, and others, it's like we are obeying Jesus.

My child,* listen when your father corrects you. Don't neglect your mother's instruction. What you learn from them will crown you with grace and be a chain of honor around your neck. PROVERBS 1:8-9

1:8 Hebrew *My son.*

NOVEMBER 28

Heavy-Duty Armor

Paul tells us how to be ready to fight spiritual battles. What kinds of weapons do you think we need for spiritual warfare?

Ephesians 6:10-20

A final word: Be strong in the Lord and in his mighty power. ¹¹Put on all of God's armor so that you will be able to stand firm against all strategies of the devil. ¹²For we* are not fighting against flesh-and-blood enemies, but against evil rulers and authorities of the unseen world, against mighty powers in this dark world, and against evil spirits in the heavenly places.

¹³Therefore, put on every piece of God's armor so you will be able to resist the enemy in the time of evil. Then after the battle you will still be standing firm. ¹⁴Stand your ground, putting on the belt of truth and the body armor of God's righteousness. ¹⁵For shoes, put on the peace that comes from the Good News so that you will be fully prepared.* ¹⁶In addition to all of these, hold up the shield of faith to stop the fiery arrows of the devil.* ¹⁷Put on salvation as your helmet, and take the sword of the Spirit, which is the word of God.

¹⁸Pray in the Spirit at all times and on every occasion. Stay alert and be persistent in your prayers for all believers everywhere.

¹⁹And pray for me, too. Ask God to give me the right words so I can boldly explain God's mysterious plan that the Good News is for Jews and Gentiles alike.* ²⁰I am in chains now, still preaching this message as God's ambassador. So pray that I will keep on speaking boldly for him, as I should.

6:12 Some manuscripts read *you.*   6:15 Or *For shoes, put on the readiness to preach the Good News of peace with God.*
6:16 Greek *the evil one.*   6:19 Greek *explain the mystery of the Good News;* some manuscripts read simply *explain the mystery.*

Christians can put on God's armor to defend themselves in spiritual battles. God's armor isn't made of metal. Rather, it's made of truth, righteousness, peace, faith, salvation, and God's Word. We can put on this armor only by staying connected to God. To do that, we need to read his Word and pray daily. Are you wearing God's armor today?

The night is almost gone; the day of salvation will soon be here. So remove your dark deeds like dirty clothes, and put on the shining armor of right living.
ROMANS 13:12

NOVEMBER 29

Jesus' Attitude

When Jesus came to earth, he gave up his rights as God. Why did he do this?

Philippians 2:1-15

Is there any encouragement from belonging to Christ? Any comfort from his love? Any fellowship together in the Spirit? Are your hearts tender and compassionate? ²Then make me truly happy by agreeing wholeheartedly with each other, loving one another, and working together with one mind and purpose.

³Don't be selfish; don't try to impress others. Be humble, thinking of others as better than yourselves. ⁴Don't look out only for your own interests, but take an interest in others, too.

⁵You must have the same attitude that Christ Jesus had.

⁶Though he was God,*
he did not think of equality
with God
as something to cling to.
⁷Instead, he gave up his divine
privileges*;

he took the humble position
of a slave*
and was born as a human being.
When he appeared in human form,*
⁸he humbled himself in obedience
to God
and died a criminal's death on a
cross.
⁹Therefore, God elevated him to the place
of highest honor
and gave him the name above all
other names,
¹⁰that at the name of Jesus every knee
should bow,
in heaven and on earth and under
the earth,
¹¹and every tongue confess that Jesus
Christ is Lord,
to the glory of God the Father.

¹²Dear friends, you always followed my instructions when I was with you. And now that I am away, it is even more impor-

tant. Work hard to show the results of your salvation, obeying God with deep reverence and fear. [13]For God is working in you, giving you the desire and the power to do what pleases him.

[14]Do everything without complaining and arguing, [15]so that no one can criticize you. Live clean, innocent lives as children of God, shining like bright lights in a world full of crooked and perverse people.

2:6 Or *Being in the form of God.* 2:7a Greek *he emptied himself.* 2:7b Or *the form of a slave.* 2:7c Some English translations put this phrase in verse 8.

Jesus came to serve God and people, not to be served by them. Even though he is God, he humbled himself and became a servant. Christians should follow Jesus' example. We need to have a humble attitude like his. We shouldn't think too highly of ourselves. Instead, we should see ourselves as God's servants and be willing to do what he asks.

[The Lord] leads the humble in doing right, teaching them his way. PSALM 25:9

NOVEMBER 30

REJOICE

Paul encouraged the Christians at Philippi to grow in their faith. What would help them grow?

Philippians 3:12–4:9

I don't mean to say that I have already achieved these things or that I have already reached perfection. But I press on to possess that perfection for which Christ Jesus first possessed me. [13]No, dear brothers and sisters, I have not achieved it,* but I focus on this one thing: Forgetting the past and looking forward to what lies ahead, [14]I press on to reach the end of the race and receive the heavenly prize for which God, through Christ Jesus, is calling us.

[15]Let all who are spiritually mature agree on these things. If you disagree on some point, I believe God will make it plain to you. [16]But we must hold on to the progress we have already made.

[17]Dear brothers and sisters, pattern your lives after mine, and learn from those who follow our example. [18]For I have told you often before, and I say it again with tears in my eyes, that there are many whose conduct shows they are really enemies of the cross of Christ. [19]They are headed for destruction. Their god is their appetite, they brag about shameful things, and they think only about this life here on earth. [20]But we are citizens of heaven, where the Lord Jesus Christ lives. And we are eagerly waiting for him to return as our Savior. [21]He will take our weak mortal bodies and change them into glorious bodies like his own, using the same power with which he will bring everything under his control.

[4:1]Therefore, my dear brothers and sisters,* stay true to the Lord. I love you and long to see you, dear friends, for you are my joy and the crown I receive for my work.

423

²Now I appeal to Euodia and Syntyche. Please, because you belong to the Lord, settle your disagreement. ³And I ask you, my true partner,* to help these two women, for they worked hard with me in telling others the Good News. They worked along with Clement and the rest of my co-workers, whose names are written in the Book of Life.

⁴Always be full of joy in the Lord. I say it again—rejoice! ⁵Let everyone see that you are considerate in all you do. Remember, the Lord is coming soon.

⁶Don't worry about anything; instead, pray about everything. Tell God what you need, and thank him for all he has done. ⁷Then you will experience God's peace, which exceeds anything we can understand. His peace will guard your hearts and minds as you live in Christ Jesus.

⁸And now, dear brothers and sisters, one final thing. Fix your thoughts on what is true, and honorable, and right, and pure, and lovely, and admirable. Think about things that are excellent and worthy of praise. ⁹Keep putting into practice all you learned and received from me—everything you heard from me and saw me doing. Then the God of peace will be with you.

3:13 Some manuscripts read *not yet achieved it.*   4:1 Greek *brothers;* also in 4:8.   4:3 Or *loyal Syzygus.*

Paul encouraged the believers to grow in their faith by not worrying, but instead being joyful and praying about everything! Being joyful gives us the right point of view. When we are joyful, we can thank God for his goodness no matter what our situation. Not worrying about our problems keeps our focus on Jesus and gives us peace. Praying about everything helps us depend on God to take care of us. How is your faith growing?

You [the Lord] will keep in perfect peace all who trust in you, all whose thoughts are fixed on you! ISAIAH 26:3

NOVEMBER CHALLENGE
incredible!

Wow! You're almost there. Did you start reading in January? Then you've finished eleven months of reading the Bible every day. You can't give up now! It's time to use that final burst of energy so you're sure to make it to the end of the year. You can enjoy all of the holiday activities during December and still continue the habit of daily Bible reading. It takes just a few minutes each day, and by now you've most likely discovered that reading about what your Creator wants you to know is definitely worth the effort.

To show that you've finished the November readings, use a marker or highlighter to fill in the level you reached this month.

Take a few minutes to thank God for his Word. What makes you thankful for it? How has it helped you? What have you learned about God? What have you learned about yourself? You may want to write a Thanksgiving note to God, thanking him for the most challenging lesson you learned from your Bible readings this month.

IMPORTANT STUFF TO REMEMBER FROM NOVEMBER

☐ To be saved, you need to repent of your sins and believe in Jesus.

☐ If you believe in Jesus, your old sinful self is dead and the Holy Spirit is making you a new person.

☐ Unless you love people, you can't do anything really good for them.

Time for some Word fun!

You've read a lot of Paul's advice for Christians. In the puzzle below, unscramble the words that God had Paul write to explain what love is and what it isn't. You'll find the answers in the reading for November 19 in 1 Corinthians 13:4-6.

NIATEPT	URODP	CEDROR
IDKN	EDUR	GEWRNDO
ASOJLEU	NDAEMD	EJIRCOE
TOLAFBUS	BRLIRATIE	HUTRT

Love is (1) __ __ __ __ __ __ __ and (2) __ __ __ __.

Love is not (3) __ __ __ __ __ __ __ or (4) __ __ __ __ __ __ __ __

or (5) __ __ __ __ __ __ or (6) __ __ __ __ __. It does not (7) __ __ __ __ __ __ its own way.

It is not (8) __ __ __ __ __ __ __ __ __ __, and it keeps no (9) __ __ __ __ __ __ of being

(10) __ __ __ __ __ __ __. It does not (11) __ __ __ __ __ __ __ about injustice

but rejoices whenever the (12) __ __ __ __ __ wins out.

DECEMBER 1

Roots

Growing in faith is important for all Christians. Read what Paul says about how to grow in Christ.

Colossians 1:28–2:15

So we tell others about Christ, warning everyone and teaching everyone with all the wisdom God has given us. We want to present them to God, perfect* in their relationship to Christ. ²⁹That's why I work and struggle so hard, depending on Christ's mighty power that works within me.

²:¹I want you to know how much I have agonized for you and for the church at Laodicea, and for many other believers who have never met me personally. ²I want them to be encouraged and knit together by strong ties of love. I want them to have complete confidence that they understand God's mysterious plan, which is Christ himself. ³In him lie hidden all the treasures of wisdom and knowledge.

⁴I am telling you this so no one will deceive you with well-crafted arguments. ⁵For though I am far away from you, my heart is with you. And I rejoice that you are living as you should and that your faith in Christ is strong.

⁶And now, just as you accepted Christ Jesus as your Lord, you must continue to follow him. ⁷Let your roots grow down into him, and let your lives be built on him. Then your faith will grow strong in the truth you were taught, and you will overflow with thankfulness.

⁸Don't let anyone capture you with empty philosophies and high-sounding nonsense that come from human thinking and from the spiritual powers* of this world, rather than from Christ. ⁹For in Christ lives all the fullness of God in a human body.* ¹⁰So you also are complete through your union with Christ, who is the head over every ruler and authority.

¹¹When you came to Christ, you were "circumcised," but not by a physical procedure. Christ performed a spiritual circumcision—the cutting away of your sinful nature.* ¹²For you were buried with Christ when you were baptized. And with him you were raised to new life because you trusted the mighty power of God, who raised Christ from the dead.

¹³You were dead because of your sins and because your sinful nature was not yet cut away. Then God made you alive with Christ, for he forgave all our sins. ¹⁴He

canceled the record of the charges against us and took it away by nailing it to the cross. ¹⁵In this way, he disarmed* the spiri-tual rulers and authorities. He shamed them publicly by his victory over them on the cross.

1:28 Or *mature*.   2:8 Or *the spiritual principles*.   2:9 Or *in him dwells all the completeness of the Godhead bodily*.   2:11 Greek *the cutting away of the body of the flesh*.   2:15 Or *he stripped off*.

Paul wrote that Christians should let the roots of their faith grow deep into Jesus. Roots do two things. First, they allow a plant to soak up food and water from the soil. Second, they keep the plant from falling over. The same is true of your faith in Jesus. Through faith, you receive love, forgiveness, and everything you need from Jesus for each day. Faith also keeps you connected to Jesus so you are able to stand firm against trials and temptations. Follow Paul's advice, and let your roots grow deep.

[Jesus said,] "I am the vine; you are the branches. Those who remain in me, and I in them, will produce much fruit. For apart from me you can do nothing."
JOHN 15:5

DECEMBER 2

Get Dressed

Paul talked about the godlike attitudes we should put on every day, just as we put on our clothes. What attitudes should Christians put on?

Colossians 3:1-17

Since you have been raised to new life with Christ, set your sights on the realities of heaven, where Christ sits in the place of honor at God's right hand. ²Think about the things of heaven, not the things of earth. ³For you died to this life, and your real life is hidden with Christ in God. ⁴And when Christ, who is your* life, is revealed to the whole world, you will share in all his glory.

⁵So put to death the sinful, earthly things lurking within you. Have nothing to do with sexual immorality, impurity, lust, and evil desires. Don't be greedy, for a greedy person is an idolater, worshiping the things of this world. ⁶Because of these sins, the anger of God is coming.* ⁷You used to do these things when your life was still part of this world. ⁸But now is the time to get rid of anger, rage, malicious behav-ior, slander, and dirty language. ⁹Don't lie to each other, for you have stripped off your old sinful nature and all its wicked deeds. ¹⁰Put on your new nature, and be re-newed as you learn to know your Creator and become like him. ¹¹In this new life, it doesn't matter if you are a Jew or a Gen-tile,* circumcised or uncircumcised, bar-baric, uncivilized,* slave, or free. Christ is all that matters, and he lives in all of us.

¹²Since God chose you to be the holy peo-

428

ple he loves, you must clothe yourselves with tenderhearted mercy, kindness, humility, gentleness, and patience. ¹³Make allowance for each other's faults, and forgive anyone who offends you. Remember, the Lord forgave you, so you must forgive others. ¹⁴Above all, clothe yourselves with love, which binds us all together in perfect harmony. ¹⁵And let the peace that comes from Christ rule in your hearts. For as members of one body you are called to live in peace. And always be thankful.

¹⁶Let the message about Christ, in all its richness, fill your lives. Teach and counsel each other with all the wisdom he gives. Sing psalms and hymns and spiritual songs to God with thankful hearts. ¹⁷And whatever you do or say, do it as a representative of the Lord Jesus, giving thanks through him to God the Father.

3:4 Some manuscripts read *our*.   3:6 Some manuscripts read *is coming on all who disobey him*.   3:11a Greek *a Greek*.
3:11b Greek *Barbarian, Scythian*.

Christians should put on the attitudes of mercy, kindness, humility, gentleness, and patience. These attitudes help us love others. Before you leave your house in the morning, be sure to clothe yourself with these godlike attitudes for the day! Then you know you will be living and behaving as a follower of Jesus.

Don't copy the behavior and customs of this world, but let God transform you into a new person by changing the way you think. Then you will learn to know God's will for you, which is good and pleasing and perfect. ROMANS 12:2

DECEMBER 3

A Good Example

The gospel had changed the lives of the Thessalonians, and everyone was talking about it. Read about what a good example these people were to other Christians.

1 Thessalonians 1:1-10

This letter is from Paul, Silas,* and Timothy.

We are writing to the church in Thessalonica, to you who belong to God the Father and the Lord Jesus Christ.

May God give you grace and peace.

²We always thank God for all of you and pray for you constantly. ³As we pray to our God and Father about you, we think of your faithful work, your loving deeds, and the enduring hope you have because of our Lord Jesus Christ.

⁴We know, dear brothers and sisters,* that God loves you and has chosen you to be his own people. ⁵For when we brought you the Good News, it was not only with words but also with power, for the Holy Spirit gave you full assurance* that what we said was true. And you know of our concern for you from the way we lived when we were with you. ⁶So you received

the message with joy from the Holy Spirit in spite of the severe suffering it brought you. In this way, you imitated both us and the Lord. ⁷As a result, you have become an example to all the believers in Greece— throughout both Macedonia and Achaia.*

⁸And now the word of the Lord is ringing out from you to people everywhere, even beyond Macedonia and Achaia, for wherever we go we find people telling us about your faith in God. We don't need to tell them about it, ⁹for they keep talking about the wonderful welcome you gave us and how you turned away from idols to serve the living and true God. ¹⁰And they speak of how you are looking forward to the coming of God's Son from heaven— Jesus, whom God raised from the dead. He is the one who has rescued us from the terrors of the coming judgment.

1:1 Greek *Silvanus*, the Greek form of the name.   1:4 Greek *brothers*.   1:5 Or *with the power of the Holy Spirit, so you can have full assurance*.   1:7 *Macedonia* and *Achaia* were the northern and southern regions of Greece.

It can really help to know someone who has already done something you are trying to do. The way the Thessalonians were following Jesus inspired other people to be like them. Do you know anyone who can be an example for you by the way they love Jesus? Try to copy that person's faith. Before you know it, you will be an example to others too!

You yourself must be an example to them by doing good works of every kind. Let everything you do reflect the integrity and seriousness of your teaching. TITUS 2:7

DECEMBER 4

stay awake

Paul warned the readers of this letter to stay alert. Why did he do that?

1 Thessalonians 5:5-24

You are all children of the light and of the day; we don't belong to darkness and night. ⁶So be on your guard, not asleep like the others. Stay alert and be clearheaded. ⁷Night is the time when people sleep and drinkers get drunk. ⁸But let us who live in the light be clearheaded, protected by the armor of faith and love, and wearing as our helmet the confidence of our salvation.

⁹For God chose to save us through our Lord Jesus Christ, not to pour out his anger on us. ¹⁰Christ died for us so that, whether we are dead or alive when he returns, we can live with him forever. ¹¹So encourage each other and build each other up, just as you are already doing.

¹²Dear brothers and sisters, honor those who are your leaders in the Lord's work. They work hard among you and give you spiritual guidance. ¹³Show them great respect and wholehearted love because of their work. And live peacefully with each other.

¹⁴Brothers and sisters, we urge you to

warn those who are lazy. Encourage those who are timid. Take tender care of those who are weak. Be patient with everyone.

¹⁵See that no one pays back evil for evil, but always try to do good to each other and to all people.

¹⁶Always be joyful. ¹⁷Never stop praying. ¹⁸Be thankful in all circumstances, for this is God's will for you who belong to Christ Jesus.

¹⁹Do not stifle the Holy Spirit. ²⁰Do not scoff at prophecies, ²¹but test everything that is said. Hold on to what is good. ²²Stay away from every kind of evil.

²³Now may the God of peace make you holy in every way, and may your whole spirit and soul and body be kept blameless until our Lord Jesus Christ comes again. ²⁴God will make this happen, for he who calls you is faithful.

Paul wanted the people who read this letter to know that Jesus could come back at any time. He urged Christians to be ready for Jesus' return. Paul's message still applies to us today. We need to be ready for Jesus to come back. What does that mean? It means we must live a life that pleases God— by obeying his commands and helping others. Are you ready for Jesus' return?

Since you don't know when that time will come, be on guard! Stay alert!*
MARK 13:33
13:33 Some manuscripts add *and pray*.

DECEMBER 5
endurance
The Thessalonians were being treated badly because of their faith in Jesus. What could they look forward to during their trials?

2 Thessalonians 1:1-12
This letter is from Paul, Silas,* and Timothy.

We are writing to the church in Thessalonica, to you who belong to God our Father and the Lord Jesus Christ.

²May God our Father* and the Lord Jesus Christ give you grace and peace.

³Dear brothers and sisters,* we can't help but thank God for you, because your faith is flourishing and your love for one another is growing. ⁴We proudly tell God's other churches about your endur-ance and faithfulness in all the persecu-tions and hardships you are suffering. ⁵And God will use this persecution to show his justice and to make you worthy of his Kingdom, for which you are suffer-ing. ⁶In his justice he will pay back those who persecute you.

⁷And God will provide rest for you who are being persecuted and also for us when the Lord Jesus appears from heaven. He will come with his mighty angels, ⁸in flam-ing fire, bringing judgment on those who don't know God and on those who refuse

to obey the Good News of our Lord Jesus. ⁹They will be punished with eternal destruction, forever separated from the Lord and from his glorious power. ¹⁰When he comes on that day, he will receive glory from his holy people—praise from all who believe. And this includes you, for you believed what we told you about him.

¹¹So we keep on praying for you, asking our God to enable you to live a life worthy of his call. May he give you the power to accomplish all the good things your faith prompts you to do. ¹²Then the name of our Lord Jesus will be honored because of the way you live, and you will be honored along with him. This is all made possible because of the grace of our God and our Lord Jesus Christ.*

1:1 Greek *Silvanus*, the Greek form of the name.   1:2 Some manuscripts read *God the Father*.   1:3 Greek *Brothers*.   1:12 Or *of our God and Lord, Jesus Christ*.

These believers trusted God to one day judge those who were hurting them. They knew that God saw how badly they were being treated by evil people. Like these believers, we can trust God to deal with people in our own life who hurt us. So don't be discouraged. When Jesus comes back, he will defeat those people who do evil, and he will bring us into the safety of his presence.

[God] will judge the world with justice and rule the nations with fairness. PSALM 9:8

DECEMBER 6
Get to work!
Paul told us how important it is to work. Read why.

2 Thessalonians 3:1-18

Finally, dear brothers and sisters,* we ask you to pray for us. Pray that the Lord's message will spread rapidly and be honored wherever it goes, just as when it came to you. ²Pray, too, that we will be rescued from wicked and evil people, for not everyone is a believer. ³But the Lord is faithful; he will strengthen you and guard you from the evil one.* ⁴And we are confident in the Lord that you are doing and will continue to do the things we commanded you. ⁵May the Lord lead your hearts into a full understanding and expression of the love of God and the patient endurance that comes from Christ.

⁶And now, dear brothers and sisters, we give you this command in the name of our Lord Jesus Christ: Stay away from all believers* who live idle lives and don't follow the tradition they received* from us. ⁷For you know that you ought to imitate us. We were not idle when we were with you. ⁸We never accepted food from anyone without paying for it. We worked hard day and night so we would not be a burden to any of you. ⁹We certainly had the right to ask you to feed us, but we wanted to give you an example to

follow. ¹⁰Even while we were with you, we gave you this command: "Those unwilling to work will not get to eat."

¹¹Yet we hear that some of you are living idle lives, refusing to work and meddling in other people's business. ¹²We command such people and urge them in the name of the Lord Jesus Christ to settle down and work to earn their own living. ¹³As for the rest of you, dear brothers and sisters, never get tired of doing good. ¹⁴Take note of those who refuse to obey what we say in this letter. Stay away from them so they will be ashamed. ¹⁵Don't think of them as enemies, but warn them as you would a brother or sister.*

¹⁶Now may the Lord of peace himself give you his peace at all times and in every situation. The Lord be with you all.

¹⁷Here is my greeting in my own handwriting—Paul. I do this in all my letters to prove they are from me.

¹⁸May the grace of our Lord Jesus Christ be with you all.

3:1 Greek *brothers;* also in 3:6, 13.   3:3 Or *from evil.*   3:6a Greek *from every brother.*   3:6b Some manuscripts read *you received.*   3:15 Greek *as a brother.*

Are you a hard worker? It's important for Christians not to be lazy. Paul told the Thessalonians to keep busy because idleness can lead to trouble. Rather than sitting around doing nothing, find a way to help out a family member or friend. Working hard pleases God, and he will reward you for your work.

Work brings profit, but mere talk leads to poverty! PROVERBS 14:23

DECEMBER 7

spiritual Training

Paul encouraged Timothy to train himself to do the right things. What could Timothy do to train?

1 Timothy 4:4-16

Since everything God created is good, we should not reject any of it but receive it with thanks. ⁵For we know it is made acceptable* by the word of God and prayer.

⁶If you explain these things to the brothers and sisters,* Timothy, you will be a worthy servant of Christ Jesus, one who is nourished by the message of faith and the good teaching you have followed. ⁷Do not waste time arguing over godless ideas and old wives' tales. Instead, train yourself to be godly. ⁸"Physical training is good, but training for godliness is much better, promising benefits in this life and in the life to come." ⁹This is a trustworthy saying, and everyone should accept it. ¹⁰This is why we work hard and continue to struggle,* for our hope is in the living God, who is the Savior of all people and particularly of all believers.

¹¹Teach these things and insist that everyone learn them. ¹²Don't let anyone think less of you because you are young. Be an example to all believers in what you say, in the way you live, in your love, your faith,

and your purity. ¹³Until I get there, focus on reading the Scriptures to the church, encouraging the believers, and teaching them.

¹⁴Do not neglect the spiritual gift you received through the prophecy spoken over you when the elders of the church laid their hands on you. ¹⁵Give your complete attention to these matters. Throw yourself into your tasks so that everyone will see your progress. ¹⁶Keep a close watch on how you live and on your teaching. Stay true to what is right for the sake of your own salvation and the salvation of those who hear you.

4:5 Or *made holy.* 4:6 Greek *brothers.* 4:10 Some manuscripts read *continue to suffer.*

Maybe you have practiced hard to make a sports team or to get ready for a music recital. You know it required a lot of discipline and persistence. Just like with music and sports, growing in your faith takes practice. Take time to read the Bible and pray. Treat other people right. What are some other ways you can stay spiritually fit?

Study this Book of Instruction continually. Meditate on it day and night so you will be sure to obey everything written in it. Only then will you prosper and succeed in all you do. JOSHUA 1:8

DECEMBER 8

money

How much money do you think it would take to make you really happy?

1 Timothy 6:6-21

True godliness with contentment is itself great wealth. ⁷After all, we brought nothing with us when we came into the world, and we can't take anything with us when we leave it. ⁸So if we have enough food and clothing, let us be content.

⁹But people who long to be rich fall into temptation and are trapped by many foolish and harmful desires that plunge them into ruin and destruction. ¹⁰For the love of money is the root of all kinds of evil. And some people, craving money, have wandered from the true faith and pierced themselves with many sorrows.

¹¹But you, Timothy, are a man of God; so run from all these evil things. Pursue righteousness and a godly life, along with faith, love, perseverance, and gentleness. ¹²Fight the good fight for the true faith. Hold tightly to the eternal life to which God has called you, which you have confessed so well before many witnesses. ¹³And I charge you before God, who gives life to all, and before Christ Jesus, who gave a good testimony before Pontius Pilate, ¹⁴that you obey this command without wavering. Then no one can find fault with you from now until our Lord Jesus Christ comes again. ¹⁵For at just the right time Christ will be revealed from heaven by the blessed and only almighty God, the King of all kings and Lord

of all lords. ¹⁶He alone can never die, and he lives in light so brilliant that no human can approach him. No human eye has ever seen him, nor ever will. All honor and power to him forever! Amen.

¹⁷Teach those who are rich in this world not to be proud and not to trust in their money, which is so unreliable. Their trust should be in God, who richly gives us all we need for our enjoyment. ¹⁸Tell them to use their money to do good. They should be rich in good works and generous to those in need, always being ready to share with others. ¹⁹By doing this they will be storing up their treasure as a good foundation for the future so that they may experience true life.

²⁰Timothy, guard what God has entrusted to you. Avoid godless, foolish discussions with those who oppose you with their so-called knowledge. ²¹Some people have wandered from the faith by following such foolishness.

May God's grace be with you all.

Sometimes it seems like if we could just have enough money to get whatever we wanted, we would be really happy. But the truth is that no matter how much we have, we'll always want more. To be truly happy, you have to be content with what you already have. If you're not good at being happy without a lot of money, you'll never be happy with it either.

I know how to live on almost nothing or with everything. I have learned the secret of living in every situation, whether it is with a full stomach or empty, with plenty or little. For I can do everything through Christ,* who gives me strength.
PHILIPPIANS 4:12-13

4:13 Greek *through the one.*

DECEMBER 9
A Hard Worker
Paul told Timothy to work hard as a servant of God. What kinds of things was Timothy to do?

2 Timothy 2:1-24

Timothy, my dear son, be strong through the grace that God gives you in Christ Jesus. ²You have heard me teach things that have been confirmed by many reliable witnesses. Now teach these truths to other trustworthy people who will be able to pass them on to others.

³Endure suffering along with me, as a good soldier of Christ Jesus. ⁴Soldiers don't get tied up in the affairs of civilian life, for then they cannot please the officer who enlisted them. ⁵And athletes cannot win the prize unless they follow the rules. ⁶And hardworking farmers should be the first to enjoy the fruit of their labor. ⁷Think about what I am saying. The Lord will help you understand all these things.

⁸Always remember that Jesus Christ, a descendant of King David, was raised from

the dead. This is the Good News I preach. [9]And because I preach this Good News, I am suffering and have been chained like a criminal. But the word of God cannot be chained. [10]So I am willing to endure anything if it will bring salvation and eternal glory in Christ Jesus to those God has chosen.

[11]This is a trustworthy saying:

If we die with him,
   we will also live with him.
[12]If we endure hardship,
   we will reign with him.
If we deny him,
   he will deny us.
[13]If we are unfaithful,
   he remains faithful,
   for he cannot deny who
     he is.

[14]Remind everyone about these things, and command them in God's presence to stop fighting over words. Such arguments are useless, and they can ruin those who hear them.

[15]Work hard so you can present yourself to God and receive his approval. Be a good worker, one who does not need to be ashamed and who correctly explains the word of truth. [16]Avoid worthless, foolish talk that only leads to more godless behavior. [17]This kind of talk spreads like cancer, as in the case of Hymenaeus and Philetus. [18]They have left the path of truth, claiming that the resurrection of the dead has already occurred; in this way, they have turned some people away from the faith.

[19]But God's truth stands firm like a foundation stone with this inscription: "The LORD knows those who are his,"* and "All who belong to the LORD must turn away from evil."*

[20]In a wealthy home some utensils are made of gold and silver, and some are made of wood and clay. The expensive utensils are used for special occasions, and the cheap ones are for everyday use. [21]If you keep yourself pure, you will be a special utensil for honorable use. Your life will be clean, and you will be ready for the Master to use you for every good work.

[22]Run from anything that stimulates youthful lusts. Instead, pursue righteous living, faithfulness, love, and peace. Enjoy the companionship of those who call on the Lord with pure hearts.

[23]Again I say, don't get involved in foolish, ignorant arguments that only start fights. [24]A servant of the Lord must not quarrel but must be kind to everyone, be able to teach, and be patient with difficult people.

2:19a Num 16:5.   2:19b See Isa 52:11.

Serving God should be the most important activity for a believer. That means we should be careful not to get caught up in things that distract us and make us forget about serving God. That could be TV shows, video games, or even hanging out with certain friends. Make sure that whatever you do helps you get closer to Christ. Is anything distracting you from serving Jesus?

Teach me your decrees, O LORD; I will keep them to the end. PSALM 119:33

DECEMBER 10

The Bible

Paul wanted to be sure Timothy knew what to teach the people in his church. Where did he tell him to look for the truth?

2 Timothy 3:10–4:5

You, Timothy, certainly know what I teach, and how I live, and what my purpose in life is. You know my faith, my patience, my love, and my endurance. ¹¹You know how much persecution and suffering I have endured. You know all about how I was persecuted in Antioch, Iconium, and Lystra—but the Lord rescued me from all of it. ¹²Yes, and everyone who wants to live a godly life in Christ Jesus will suffer persecution. ¹³But evil people and impostors will flourish. They will deceive others and will themselves be deceived.

¹⁴But you must remain faithful to the things you have been taught. You know they are true, for you know you can trust those who taught you. ¹⁵You have been taught the holy Scriptures from childhood, and they have given you the wisdom to receive the salvation that comes by trusting in Christ Jesus. ¹⁶All Scripture is inspired by God and is useful to teach us what is true and to make us realize what is wrong in our lives. It corrects us when we are wrong and teaches us to do what is right. ¹⁷God uses it to prepare and equip his people to do every good work.

⁴:¹I solemnly urge you in the presence of God and Christ Jesus, who will someday judge the living and the dead when he appears to set up his Kingdom: ²Preach the word of God. Be prepared, whether the time is favorable or not. Patiently correct, rebuke, and encourage your people with good teaching.

³For a time is coming when people will no longer listen to sound and wholesome teaching. They will follow their own desires and will look for teachers who will tell them whatever their itching ears want to hear. ⁴They will reject the truth and chase after myths.

⁵But you should keep a clear mind in every situation. Don't be afraid of suffering for the Lord. Work at telling others the Good News, and fully carry out the ministry God has given you.

The Bible is like a road map. It shows us what to do and where to go in life. We can be sure that the Bible will always tell us the truth and help us know whether things are good or bad. If you are wondering about God or about what is right, the Bible is the place to look! The more you study the Bible, the more prepared you will be for life.

How can a young person stay pure? By obeying [God's] word. PSALM 119:9

DECEMBER 11

Live Right

The way a Christian lives is important. Read what Paul wrote to Titus about how people of all different ages should live.

Titus 2:1-15

As for you, Titus, promote the kind of living that reflects wholesome teaching. ²Teach the older men to exercise self-control, to be worthy of respect, and to live wisely. They must have sound faith and be filled with love and patience.

³Similarly, teach the older women to live in a way that honors God. They must not slander others or be heavy drinkers.* Instead, they should teach others what is good. ⁴These older women must train the younger women to love their husbands and their children, ⁵to live wisely and be pure, to work in their homes,* to do good, and to be submissive to their husbands. Then they will not bring shame on the word of God.

⁶In the same way, encourage the young men to live wisely. ⁷And you yourself must be an example to them by doing good works of every kind. Let everything you do reflect the integrity and seriousness of your teaching. ⁸Teach the truth so that your teaching can't be criticized. Then those who oppose us will be ashamed and have nothing bad to say about us.

⁹Slaves must always obey their masters and do their best to please them. They must not talk back ¹⁰or steal, but must show themselves to be entirely trustworthy and good. Then they will make the teaching about God our Savior attractive in every way.

¹¹For the grace of God has been revealed, bringing salvation to all people. ¹²And we are instructed to turn from godless living and sinful pleasures. We should live in this evil world with wisdom, righteousness, and devotion to God, ¹³while we look forward with hope to that wonderful day when the glory of our great God and Savior, Jesus Christ, will be revealed. ¹⁴He gave his life to free us from every kind of sin, to cleanse us, and to make us his very own people, totally committed to doing good deeds.

¹⁵You must teach these things and encourage the believers to do them. You have the authority to correct them when necessary, so don't let anyone disregard what you say.

2:3 Greek *be enslaved to much wine.*   2:5 Some manuscripts read *to care for their homes.*

It's important for everyone who is a Christian to live in a way that pleases God and brings him honor. When that happens, even people who don't believe in Jesus notice. Living right is a way to tell people how wonderful God is without saying a word. What does your life say about God?

If you look carefully into the perfect law that sets you free, and if you do what it says and don't forget what you heard, then God will bless you for doing it.
JAMES 1:25

438

DECEMBER 12

Doing Good

In this letter, Paul told Titus about why God saved us. Do people deserve to be saved by God?

Titus 3:1-11

Remind the believers to submit to the government and its officers. They should be obedient, always ready to do what is good. They must not slander anyone and must avoid quarreling. Instead, they should be gentle and show true humility to everyone.

³Once we, too, were foolish and disobedient. We were misled and became slaves to many lusts and pleasures. Our lives were full of evil and envy, and we hated each other.

⁴But—"When God our Savior revealed his kindness and love, ⁵he saved us, not because of the righteous things we had done, but because of his mercy. He washed away our sins, giving us a new birth and new life through the Holy Spirit.* ⁶He generously poured out the Spirit upon us through Jesus Christ our Savior. ⁷Because of his grace he declared us righteous and gave us confidence that we will inherit eternal life." ⁸This is a trustworthy saying, and I want you to insist on these teachings so that all who trust in God will devote themselves to doing good. These teachings are good and beneficial for everyone.

⁹Do not get involved in foolish discussions about spiritual pedigrees* or in quarrels and fights about obedience to Jewish laws. These things are useless and a waste of time. ¹⁰If people are causing divisions among you, give a first and second warning. After that, have nothing more to do with them. ¹¹For people like that have turned away from the truth, and their own sins condemn them.

3:5 Greek *He saved us through the washing of regeneration and renewing of the Holy Spirit.* 3:9 Or *spiritual genealogies.*

God saves sinful people just because he loves them. Even though we don't deserve his love, he gives it to us for free because he is so good and loving. But once we've been saved, God wants us to stop sinning and do what's right instead. Ask God to help you live in a way that makes him happy.

The LORD approves of those who are good, but he condemns those who plan wickedness. PROVERBS 12:2

DECEMBER 13

Jesus understands

Jesus is God. But at the same time, he came to earth as a person. Why do you think it was important for Jesus to experience what it's like to be human?

Hebrews 4:12–5:9

For the word of God is alive and powerful. It is sharper than the sharpest two-edged sword, cutting between soul and spirit, between joint and marrow. It exposes our innermost thoughts and desires. ¹³Nothing in all creation is hidden from God. Everything is naked and exposed before his eyes, and he is the one to whom we are accountable.

¹⁴So then, since we have a great High Priest who has entered heaven, Jesus the Son of God, let us hold firmly to what we believe. ¹⁵This High Priest of ours understands our weaknesses, for he faced all of the same testings we do, yet he did not sin. ¹⁶So let us come boldly to the throne of our gracious God. There we will receive his mercy, and we will find grace to help us when we need it most.

^{5:1}Every high priest is a man chosen to represent other people in their dealings with God. He presents their gifts to God and offers sacrifices for their sins. ²And he is able to deal gently with ignorant and wayward people because he himself is subject to the same weaknesses. ³That is why he must offer sacrifices for his own sins as well as theirs.

⁴And no one can become a high priest simply because he wants such an honor. He must be called by God for this work, just as Aaron was. ⁵That is why Christ did not honor himself by assuming he could become High Priest. No, he was chosen by God, who said to him,

"You are my Son.
   Today I have become your Father.*"

⁶And in another passage God said to him,

"You are a priest forever in the order of
   Melchizedek."*

⁷While Jesus was here on earth, he offered prayers and pleadings, with a loud cry and tears, to the one who could rescue him from death. And God heard his prayers because of his deep reverence for God. ⁸Even though Jesus was God's Son, he learned obedience from the things he suffered. ⁹In this way, God qualified him as a perfect High Priest, and he became the source of eternal salvation for all those who obey him.

5:5 Or *Today I reveal you as my Son.* Ps 2:7.   5:6 Ps 110:4.

440

Since Jesus lived on earth for more than thirty years as a real person, he understands what it's like to be tempted. All people are tempted to do things that they shouldn't do. But Jesus is the only person who never gave in to temptation. Since he knows how to beat temptation, he can help us beat it too. When you feel tempted to do something you shouldn't do, ask Jesus to help you!

From the depths of despair, O LORD, I call for your help. Hear my cry, O Lord. Pay attention to my prayer. PSALM 130:1-2

DECEMBER 14

Real Heroes

People can show that they have faith in God by what they do and how they act. Read about ways that some of the characters from the Old Testament showed their trust in God.

Hebrews 11:1-16

Faith is the confidence that what we hope for will actually happen; it gives us assurance about things we cannot see. ²Through their faith, the people in days of old earned a good reputation.

³By faith we understand that the entire universe was formed at God's command, that what we now see did not come from anything that can be seen.

⁴It was by faith that Abel brought a more acceptable offering to God than Cain did. Abel's offering gave evidence that he was a righteous man, and God showed his approval of his gifts. Although Abel is long dead, he still speaks to us by his example of faith.

⁵It was by faith that Enoch was taken up to heaven without dying—"he disappeared, because God took him."* For before he was taken up, he was known as a person who pleased God. ⁶And it is impossible to please God without faith. Anyone who wants to come to him must believe that God exists and that he rewards those who sincerely seek him.

⁷It was by faith that Noah built a large boat to save his family from the flood. He obeyed God, who warned him about things that had never happened before. By his faith Noah condemned the rest of the world, and he received the righteousness that comes by faith.

⁸It was by faith that Abraham obeyed when God called him to leave home and go to another land that God would give him as his inheritance. He went without knowing where he was going. ⁹And even when he reached the land God promised him, he lived there by faith—for he was like a foreigner, living in tents. And so did Isaac and Jacob, who inherited the same promise.

[10]Abraham was confidently looking forward to a city with eternal foundations, a city designed and built by God.

[11]It was by faith that even Sarah was able to have a child, though she was barren and was too old. She believed* that God would keep his promise. [12]And so a whole nation came from this one man who was as good as dead—a nation with so many people that, like the stars in the sky and the sand on the seashore, there is no way to count them.

[13]All these people died still believing what God had promised them. They did not receive what was promised, but they saw it all from a distance and welcomed it. They agreed that they were foreigners and nomads here on earth. [14]Obviously people who say such things are looking forward to a country they can call their own. [15]If they had longed for the country they came from, they could have gone back. [16]But they were looking for a better place, a heavenly homeland. That is why God is not ashamed to be called their God, for he has prepared a city for them.

11:5 Gen 5:24.   11:11 Or It was by faith that he [Abraham] was able to have a child, even though Sarah was barren and he was too old. He believed.

Faith is trusting God to keep his promises even when you can't see what is happening or what is going to happen. The people whose lives are discussed in this passage trusted God even when they didn't know how or when his promises would come true. But God didn't fail any of them. He always does what he says he will do. Do you ever have a hard time believing God? Remember the way these people trusted him, and follow their example.

Trust in the LORD with all your heart; do not depend on your own understanding. Seek his will in all you do, and he will show you which path to take.
PROVERBS 3:5-6

DECEMBER 15

Run the Race

Following Jesus can be like running in a race. Think about how those two activities are alike as you read.

Hebrews 12:1-13

Therefore, since we are surrounded by such a huge crowd of witnesses to the life of faith, let us strip off every weight that slows us down, especially the sin that so easily trips us up. And let us run with endurance the race God has set before us.

[2]We do this by keeping our eyes on Jesus, the champion who initiates and perfects our faith.* Because of the joy* awaiting him, he endured the cross, disregarding its shame. Now he is seated in the place of honor beside God's throne. [3]Think of all the hostility he endured from sinful peo-

ple;* then you won't become weary and give up. [4]After all, you have not yet given your lives in your struggle against sin.

[5]And have you forgotten the encouraging words God spoke to you as his children?* He said,

"My child,* don't make light of the
Lord's discipline,
and don't give up when he corrects
you.
[6]For the Lord disciplines those he
loves,
and he punishes each one he accepts
as his child."*

[7]As you endure this divine discipline, remember that God is treating you as his own children. Who ever heard of a child who is never disciplined by its father? [8]If God doesn't discipline you as he does all of his children, it means that you are illegitimate and are not really his children at all. [9]Since we respected our earthly fathers who disciplined us, shouldn't we submit even more to the discipline of the Father of our spirits, and live forever?*

[10]For our earthly fathers disciplined us for a few years, doing the best they knew how. But God's discipline is always good for us, so that we might share in his holiness. [11]No discipline is enjoyable while it is happening—it's painful! But afterward there will be a peaceful harvest of right living for those who are trained in this way.

[12]So take a new grip with your tired hands and strengthen your weak knees. [13]Mark out a straight path for your feet so that those who are weak and lame will not fall but become strong.

12:2a Or *Jesus, the originator and perfecter of our faith.*   **12:2b** Or *Instead of the joy.*   **12:3** Some manuscripts read *Think of how people hurt themselves by opposing him.*   **12:5a** Greek *sons;* also in 12:7, 8.   **12:5b** Greek *son;* also in 12:6, 7. **12:5-6** Prov 3:11-12 (Greek version).   **12:9** Or *and really live?*

When you run in a race, you have to work hard to finish well. It's important to keep your eyes on the finish line, to avoid distractions, and to remember how badly you want to win. As Christians, we also should always think about where we are going. Heaven is so important that nothing should distract us. Keeping focused on Jesus and listening to the people who are cheering us on will help us. Ask God to give you the strength and determination to stay strong in your faith and finish well.

God arms me with strength, and he makes my way perfect. He makes me as surefooted as a deer, enabling me to stand on mountain heights. PSALM 18:32-33

DECEMBER 16

Rock Solid

Do you think that God is kind and loving? Or is he powerful and scary? Read and see what this passage says.

Hebrews 12:14-29

Work at living in peace with everyone, and work at living a holy life, for those who are not holy will not see the Lord. [15]Look after each other so that none of you fails to receive the grace of God. Watch out that no poisonous root of bitterness grows up to trouble you, corrupting many. [16]Make sure that no one is immoral or godless like Esau, who traded his birthright as the firstborn son for a single meal. [17]You know that afterward, when he wanted his father's blessing, he was rejected. It was too late for repentance, even though he begged with bitter tears.

[18]You have not come to a physical mountain,* to a place of flaming fire, darkness, gloom, and whirlwind, as the Israelites did at Mount Sinai. [19]For they heard an awesome trumpet blast and a voice so terrible that they begged God to stop speaking. [20]They staggered back under God's command: "If even an animal touches the mountain, it must be stoned to death."* [21]Moses himself was so frightened at the sight that he said, "I am terrified and trembling."*

[22]No, you have come to Mount Zion, to the city of the living God, the heavenly Jerusalem, and to countless thousands of angels in a joyful gathering. [23]You have come to the assembly of God's firstborn children, whose names are written in heaven. You have come to God himself, who is the judge over all things. You have come to the spirits of the righteous ones in heaven who have now been made perfect. [24]You have come to Jesus, the one who mediates the new covenant between God and people, and to the sprinkled blood, which speaks of forgiveness instead of crying out for vengeance like the blood of Abel.

[25]Be careful that you do not refuse to listen to the One who is speaking. For if the people of Israel did not escape when they refused to listen to Moses, the earthly messenger, we will certainly not escape if we reject the One who speaks to us from heaven! [26]When God spoke from Mount Sinai his voice shook the earth, but now he makes another promise: "Once again I will shake not only the earth but the heavens also."* [27]This means that all of creation will be shaken and removed, so that only unshakable things will remain.

[28]Since we are receiving a Kingdom that is unshakable, let us be thankful and please God by worshiping him with holy fear and awe. [29]For our God is a devouring fire.

12:18 Greek *to something that can be touched.*   12:20 Exod 19:13.   12:21 Deut 9:19.   12:26 Hag 2:6.

God is both loving and powerful. He loves his people so much. But he also becomes angry when we deliberately ignore him and choose to go our own way. It's important to remember how strong and mighty God is so we show him the respect and honor he deserves. It's even more amazing that such a powerful God is willing to forgive us and keep loving us. Thank God that even though he is incredibly powerful, he really loves you!

How great is our Lord! His power is absolute! His understanding is beyond comprehension! PSALM 147:5

DECEMBER 17

unchanging God

Jesus never changes. He is always the same. Why is this important to know?

Hebrews 13:1-21

Keep on loving each other as brothers and sisters.* ²Don't forget to show hospitality to strangers, for some who have done this have entertained angels without realizing it! ³Remember those in prison, as if you were there yourself. Remember also those being mistreated, as if you felt their pain in your own bodies.

⁴Give honor to marriage, and remain faithful to one another in marriage. God will surely judge people who are immoral and those who commit adultery.

⁵Don't love money; be satisfied with what you have. For God has said,

"I will never fail you.
    I will never abandon you."*

⁶So we can say with confidence,

"The LORD is my helper,
    so I will have no fear.

What can mere people do
    to me?"*

⁷Remember your leaders who taught you the word of God. Think of all the good that has come from their lives, and follow the example of their faith.

⁸Jesus Christ is the same yesterday, today, and forever. ⁹So do not be attracted by strange, new ideas. Your strength comes from God's grace, not from rules about food, which don't help those who follow them.

¹⁰We have an altar from which the priests in the Tabernacle* have no right to eat. ¹¹Under the old system, the high priest brought the blood of animals into the Holy Place as a sacrifice for sin, and the bodies of the animals were burned outside the camp. ¹²So also Jesus suffered and died outside the city gates to make his people holy by means of his own blood. ¹³So let us go out to him, outside the camp, and bear

the disgrace he bore. [14]For this world is not our permanent home; we are looking forward to a home yet to come.

[15]Therefore, let us offer through Jesus a continual sacrifice of praise to God, proclaiming our allegiance to his name. [16]And don't forget to do good and to share with those in need. These are the sacrifices that please God.

[17]Obey your spiritual leaders, and do what they say. Their work is to watch over your souls, and they are accountable to God. Give them reason to do this with joy and not with sorrow. That would certainly not be for your benefit.

[18]Pray for us, for our conscience is clear and we want to live honorably in everything we do. [19]And especially pray that I will be able to come back to you soon.

[20]Now may the God of peace—
who brought up from the dead our
Lord Jesus,
the great Shepherd of the sheep,
and ratified an eternal covenant with
his blood—
[21]may he equip you with all you need
for doing his will.
May he produce in you,*
through the power of Jesus Christ,
every good thing that is pleasing
to him.
All glory to him forever and ever!
Amen.

13:1 Greek *Continue in brotherly love.*   13:5 Deut 31:6, 8.   13:6 Ps 118:6.   13:10 Or *tent.*   13:21 Some manuscripts read *in us.*

Jesus is perfect and has no need to change. This is important to know because many people try to twist the truth about who Jesus is and what he has done. But we can be sure that any teaching about Jesus that isn't based on what's in the Bible is a lie. All we need to know about Jesus is found in God's Word. Want to know Jesus better? Read your Bible every day.

You happily put up with whatever anyone tells you, even if they preach a different Jesus than the one we preach, or a different kind of Spirit than the one you received, or a different kind of gospel than the one you believed.
2 CORINTHIANS 11:4

DECEMBER 18

Tough Times

James wrote about how we should think about troubles and temptations. See if you think about your problems in this way.

James 1:2-18

Dear brothers and sisters,* when troubles come your way, consider it an opportunity for great joy. [3]For you know that when your faith is tested, your endurance has a chance to grow. [4]So let it grow, for when your endurance is fully developed, you will be perfect and complete, needing nothing.

[5]If you need wisdom, ask our generous God, and he will give it to you. He will not rebuke you for asking. [6]But when you ask him, be sure that your faith is in God alone. Do not waver, for a person with divided loyalty is as unsettled as a wave of the sea that is blown and tossed by the wind. [7]Such people should not expect to receive anything from the Lord. [8]Their loyalty is divided between God and the world, and they are unstable in everything they do.

[9]Believers who are* poor have something to boast about, for God has honored them. [10]And those who are rich should boast that God has humbled them. They will fade away like a little flower in the field. [11]The hot sun rises and the grass withers; the little flower droops and falls, and its beauty fades away. In the same way, the rich will fade away with all of their achievements.

[12]God blesses those who patiently endure testing and temptation. Afterward they will receive the crown of life that God has promised to those who love him. [13]And remember, when you are being tempted, do not say, "God is tempting me." God is never tempted to do wrong,* and he never tempts anyone else. [14]Temptation comes from our own desires, which entice us and drag us away. [15]These desires give birth to sinful actions. And when sin is allowed to grow, it gives birth to death.

[16]So don't be misled, my dear brothers and sisters. [17]Whatever is good and perfect comes down to us from God our Father, who created all the lights in the heavens.* He never changes or casts a shifting shadow.* [18]He chose to give birth to us by giving us his true word. And we, out of all creation, became his prized possession.*

1:2 Greek *brothers;* also in 1:16.   1:9 Greek *The brother who is.*   1:13 Or *God should not be put to a test by evil people.* 1:17a Greek *from above, from the Father of lights.*   1:17b Some manuscripts read *He never changes, as a shifting shadow does.* 1:18 Greek *we became a kind of firstfruit of his creatures.*

Troubles help us trust God more completely. They help us to learn patience and love. We should always trust in God, but in difficult times it's especially important to turn to God and depend on him. When you are facing trouble or temptation, pray for God to give you strength. Is there anything you need his help with today?

The LORD hears his people when they call to him for help. He rescues them from all their troubles. PSALM 34:17

DECEMBER 19

Playing Favorites

Some Christians were giving special treatment to rich people. What did James say about that?

James 2:1-17

My dear brothers and sisters,* how can you claim to have faith in our glorious Lord Jesus Christ if you favor some people over others?

²For example, suppose someone comes into your meeting* dressed in fancy clothes and expensive jewelry, and another comes in who is poor and dressed in dirty clothes. ³If you give special attention and a good seat to the rich person, but you say to the poor one, "You can stand over there, or else sit on the floor"—well, ⁴doesn't this discrimination show that your judgments are guided by evil motives?

⁵Listen to me, dear brothers and sisters. Hasn't God chosen the poor in this world to be rich in faith? Aren't they the ones who will inherit the Kingdom he promised to those who love him? ⁶But you dishonor the poor! Isn't it the rich who oppress you and drag you into court? ⁷Aren't they the ones who slander Jesus Christ, whose noble name* you bear?

⁸Yes indeed, it is good when you obey the royal law as found in the Scriptures: "Love your neighbor as yourself."* ⁹But if you favor some people over others, you are committing a sin. You are guilty of breaking the law.

¹⁰For the person who keeps all of the laws except one is as guilty as a person who has broken all of God's laws. ¹¹For the same God who said, "You must not commit adultery," also said, "You must not murder."* So if you murder someone but do not commit adultery, you have still broken the law.

¹²So whatever you say or whatever you do, remember that you will be judged by the law that sets you free. ¹³There will be no mercy for those who have not shown mercy to others. But if you have been merciful, God will be merciful when he judges you.

¹⁴What good is it, dear brothers and sisters, if you say you have faith but don't show it by your actions? Can that kind of faith save anyone? ¹⁵Suppose you see a brother or sister who has no food or clothing, ¹⁶and you say, "Good-bye and have a good day; stay warm and eat well"—but then you don't give that person any food or clothing. What good does that do?

¹⁷So you see, faith by itself isn't enough. Unless it produces good deeds, it is dead and useless.

2:1 Greek *brothers;* also in 2:5, 14.   **2:2** Greek *your synagogue.*   **2:7** Greek *slander the noble name.*   **2:8** Lev 19:18.
2:11 Exod 20:13-14; Deut 5:17-18.

Christians should live differently from the way the rest of the world lives. Instead of showing favoritism to some people, Christians should show love to all people. James said that loving others, no matter if they are rich or poor, and showing it by our actions indicates that our faith is strong. If we have real faith, we will put it into practice. What do your actions say about your love for others and about your faith?

It is a sin to belittle one's neighbor; blessed are those who help the poor.
PROVERBS 14:21

DECEMBER 20
THE TONGUE

James wrote about the most powerful muscle in our body. What do you think he was talking about?

James 3:1-18

Dear brothers and sisters,* not many of you should become teachers in the church, for we who teach will be judged more strictly. ²Indeed, we all make many mistakes. For if we could control our tongues, we would be perfect and could also control ourselves in every other way.

³We can make a large horse go wherever we want by means of a small bit in its mouth. ⁴And a small rudder makes a huge ship turn wherever the pilot chooses to go, even though the winds are strong. ⁵In the same way, the tongue is a small thing that makes grand speeches.

But a tiny spark can set a great forest on fire. ⁶And the tongue is a flame of fire. It is a whole world of wickedness, corrupting your entire body. It can set your whole life on fire, for it is set on fire by hell itself.*

⁷People can tame all kinds of animals, birds, reptiles, and fish, ⁸but no one can tame the tongue. It is restless and evil, full of deadly poison. ⁹Sometimes it praises our Lord and Father, and sometimes it curses those who have been made in the image of God. ¹⁰And so blessing and cursing come pouring out of the same mouth. Surely, my brothers and sisters, this is not right! ¹¹Does a spring of water bubble out with both fresh water and bitter water? ¹²Does a fig tree produce olives, or a grapevine produce figs? No, and you can't draw fresh water from a salty spring.*

¹³If you are wise and understand God's ways, prove it by living an honorable life, doing good works with the humility that comes from wisdom. ¹⁴But if you are bitterly jealous and there is selfish ambition in your heart, don't cover up the truth with boasting and lying. ¹⁵For jealousy and selfishness are not God's kind of wisdom. Such things are earthly, unspiritual, and demonic. ¹⁶For wherever there is jealousy and selfish ambition, there you will find disorder and evil of every kind.

¹⁷But the wisdom from above is first of all pure. It is also peace loving, gentle at all times, and willing to yield to others. It is full of mercy and good deeds. It shows no favoritism and is always sincere. ¹⁸And those who are peacemakers will plant seeds of peace and reap a harvest of righteousness.*

Our tongue is pretty small compared to the rest of our body. But James says that the tongue has the most power to hurt people. The words people form with their tongue can be helpful and kind, or they can be harmful and cruel. The things we say can change the way people think about us. We need God's wisdom to say words that please him and that hurt other people. Remember to think before you speak and be careful what you say to others.

The crooked heart will not prosper; the lying tongue tumbles into trouble.
PROVERBS 17:20

DECEMBER 21
FREE TO SERVE

All Christians are servants of God. Their work is to do good. What example did Jesus leave for all Christians to follow?

1 Peter 2:13-25

For the Lord's sake, respect all human authority—whether the king as head of state, ¹⁴or the officials he has appointed. For the king has sent them to punish those who do wrong and to honor those who do right.

¹⁵It is God's will that your honorable lives should silence those ignorant people who make foolish accusations against you. ¹⁶For you are free, yet you are God's slaves, so don't use your freedom as an excuse to do evil. ¹⁷Respect everyone, and love your Christian brothers and sisters.* Fear God, and respect the king.

¹⁸You who are slaves must accept the authority of your masters with all respect.* Do what they tell you—not only if they are kind and reasonable, but even if they are cruel. ¹⁹For God is pleased with you when you do what you know is right and patiently endure unfair treatment. ²⁰Of course, you get no credit for being patient if you are beaten for doing wrong. But if you suffer for doing good and endure it patiently, God is pleased with you.

²¹For God called you to do good, even if it means suffering, just as Christ suffered* for you. He is your example, and you must follow in his steps.

²²He never sinned,
nor ever deceived anyone.*
²³He did not retaliate when he was insulted,
nor threaten revenge when he suffered.

He left his case in the hands
of God,
who always judges fairly.
²⁴He personally carried our sins
in his body on the cross
so that we can be dead to sin
and live for what is right.

By his wounds
you are healed.
²⁵Once you were like sheep
who wandered away.
But now you have turned to your
Shepherd,
the Guardian of your souls.

2:17 Greek *love the brotherhood.* 2:18 Or *because you fear God.* 2:21 Some manuscripts read *died.* 2:22 Isa 53:9.

Jesus left the perfect example for all Christians to follow. He served others, and he suffered at the hands of the authorities without making any attempt to get even. Has anyone ever hurt you unfairly? How did you respond? If you want to be like Jesus, you shouldn't try to get even. Instead, follow Jesus' example and trust God to deal with that person.

Dear friends, never take revenge. Leave that to the righteous anger of God. For the Scriptures say, "I will take revenge; I will pay them back," says the LORD.*
ROMANS 12:19

12:19 Deut 32:35.

DECEMBER 22

A Giving God

God gives all his followers gifts. What kinds of gifts does God give?

1 Peter 4:7-19

The end of the world is coming soon. Therefore, be earnest and disciplined in your prayers. ⁸Most important of all, continue to show deep love for each other, for love covers a multitude of sins. ⁹Cheerfully share your home with those who need a meal or a place to stay.

¹⁰God has given each of you a gift from his great variety of spiritual gifts. Use them well to serve one another. ¹¹Do you have the gift of speaking? Then speak as though God himself were speaking through you. Do you have the gift of helping others? Do it with all the strength and energy that God supplies. Then every-

thing you do will bring glory to God through Jesus Christ. All glory and power to him forever and ever! Amen.

¹²Dear friends, don't be surprised at the fiery trials you are going through, as if something strange were happening to you. ¹³Instead, be very glad—for these trials make you partners with Christ in his suffering, so that you will have the wonderful joy of seeing his glory when it is revealed to all the world.

¹⁴So be happy when you are insulted for being a Christian,* for then the glorious Spirit of God* rests upon you.* ¹⁵If you suffer, however, it must not be for murder, stealing, making trouble, or prying into

other people's affairs. ¹⁶But it is no shame to suffer for being a Christian. Praise God for the privilege of being called by his name! ¹⁷For the time has come for judgment, and it must begin with God's household. And if judgment begins with us, what terrible fate awaits those who have never obeyed God's Good News? ¹⁸And also,

"If the righteous are barely saved,
what will happen to godless
sinners?"*

¹⁹So if you are suffering in a manner that pleases God, keep on doing what is right, and trust your lives to the God who created you, for he will never fail you.

4:14a Greek *for the name of Christ.* **4:14b** Or *for the glory of God, which is his Spirit.* **4:14c** Some manuscripts add *On their part he is blasphemed, but on your part he is glorified.* **4:18** Prov 11:31 (Greek version).

God gives his children spiritual gifts. These are gifts that we can use to serve him and help others. Peter listed two of the gifts in this passage: speaking and helping. What spiritual gift has God given you? If you don't know, ask a trusted friend, parent, or your pastor to help you recognize your gift. When you learn what your gift is, use it to serve God in the best way you can.

A spiritual gift is given to each of us so we can help each other.
I CORINTHIANS 12:7

DECEMBER 23

Knowing God

In his second letter, Peter told Christians that what he said about Jesus was absolutely true. How did they know that Peter wasn't lying?

2 Peter 1:2-21

May God give you more and more grace and peace as you grow in your knowledge of God and Jesus our Lord.

³By his divine power, God has given us everything we need for living a godly life. We have received all of this by coming to know him, the one who called us to himself by means of his marvelous glory and excellence. ⁴And because of his glory and excellence, he has given us great and precious promises. These are the promises that enable you to share his divine nature

and escape the world's corruption caused by human desires.

⁵In view of all this, make every effort to respond to God's promises. Supplement your faith with a generous provision of moral excellence, and moral excellence with knowledge, ⁶and knowledge with self-control, and self-control with patient endurance, and patient endurance with godliness, ⁷and godliness with brotherly affection, and brotherly affection with love for everyone.

⁸The more you grow like this, the more

452

productive and useful you will be in your knowledge of our Lord Jesus Christ. [9]But those who fail to develop in this way are shortsighted or blind, forgetting that they have been cleansed from their old sins.

[10]So, dear brothers and sisters,* work hard to prove that you really are among those God has called and chosen. Do these things, and you will never fall away. [11]Then God will give you a grand entrance into the eternal Kingdom of our Lord and Savior Jesus Christ.

[12]Therefore, I will always remind you about these things—even though you already know them and are standing firm in the truth you have been taught. [13]And it is only right that I should keep on reminding you as long as I live.* [14]For our Lord Jesus Christ has shown me that I must soon leave this earthly life,* [15]so I will work hard to make sure you always remember these things after I am gone.

[16]For we were not making up clever stories when we told you about the powerful coming of our Lord Jesus Christ. We saw his majestic splendor with our own eyes [17]when he received honor and glory from God the Father. The voice from the majestic glory of God said to him, "This is my dearly loved Son, who brings me great joy."* [18]We ourselves heard that voice from heaven when we were with him on the holy mountain.

[19]Because of that experience, we have even greater confidence in the message proclaimed by the prophets. You must pay close attention to what they wrote, for their words are like a lamp shining in a dark place—until the Day dawns, and Christ the Morning Star shines* in your hearts. [20]Above all, you must realize that no prophecy in Scripture ever came from the prophet's own understanding,* [21]or from human initiative. No, those prophets were moved by the Holy Spirit, and they spoke from God.

1:10 Greek *brothers.*   **1:13** Greek *as long as I am in this tent* [or *tabernacle*].   **1:14** Greek *I must soon put off my tent* [or *tabernacle*].   **1:17** Matt 17:5; Mark 9:7; Luke 9:35.   **1:19** Or *rises.*   **1:20** Or *is a matter of one's own interpretation.*

The Christians knew what Peter was saying about Jesus was true. He had been there and had seen and heard all the wonderful things Jesus did. He wanted the new Christians to be as certain about Jesus as he was. Having confidence in Jesus' teachings and promises helps us love him and want to obey his commands. Think about the incredible power Jesus has to save you and help you live a new life.

Oh, how I love [God's] instructions! I think about them all day long. Your commands make me wiser than my enemies, for they are my constant guide.
PSALM 119:97-98

DECEMBER 24

forgive and forget

John wrote to tell Christians what to do after they sinned.

1 John 1:1-10

We proclaim to you the one who existed from the beginning,* whom we have heard and seen. We saw him with our own eyes and touched him with our own hands. He is the Word of life. ²This one who is life itself was revealed to us, and we have seen him. And now we testify and proclaim to you that he is the one who is eternal life. He was with the Father, and then he was revealed to us. ³We proclaim to you what we ourselves have actually seen and heard so that you may have fellowship with us. And our fellowship is with the Father and with his Son, Jesus Christ. ⁴We are writing these things so that you may fully share our joy.* ⁵This is the message we heard from Jesus* and now declare to you: God is light, and there is no darkness in him at all. ⁶So we are lying if we say we have fellowship with God but go on living in spiritual darkness; we are not practicing the truth. ⁷But if we are living in the light, as God is in the light, then we have fellowship with each other, and the blood of Jesus, his Son, cleanses us from all sin.

⁸If we claim we have no sin, we are only fooling ourselves and not living in the truth. ⁹But if we confess our sins to him, he is faithful and just to forgive us our sins and to cleanse us from all wickedness. ¹⁰If we claim we have not sinned, we are calling God a liar and showing that his word has no place in our hearts.

1:1 Greek *What was from the beginning.* 1:4 Or *so that our joy may be complete;* some manuscripts read *your joy.* 1:5 Greek *from him.*

Jesus will forgive all people who confess their sins to him. He will also wash their sins away so they can live a clean life for him. Have you confessed your sins to Jesus today? Don't let sin stand in the way of enjoying a clear conscience and a close relationship with God.

Help us, O God of our salvation! Help us for the glory of your name. Save us and forgive our sins for the honor of your name. PSALM **79:9**

DECEMBER 25

GOD IS LOVE

John says there are two signs that a person is a real Christian. See if you can find them as you read.

1 John 3:1-18

See how very much our Father loves us, for he calls us his children, and that is what we are! But the people who belong to this world don't recognize that we are God's children because they don't know him. ²Dear friends, we are already God's children, but he has not yet shown us what we will be like when Christ appears. But we do know that we will be like him, for we will see him as he really is. ³And all who have this eager expectation will keep themselves pure, just as he is pure.

⁴Everyone who sins is breaking God's law, for all sin is contrary to the law of God. ⁵And you know that Jesus came to take away our sins, and there is no sin in him. ⁶Anyone who continues to live in him will not sin. But anyone who keeps on sinning does not know him or understand who he is.

⁷Dear children, don't let anyone deceive you about this: When people do what is right, it shows that they are righteous, even as Christ is righteous. ⁸But when people keep on sinning, it shows that they belong to the devil, who has been sinning since the beginning. But the Son of God came to destroy the works of the devil. ⁹Those who have been born into God's family do not make a practice of sinning, because God's life* is in them. So they can't keep on sin-

ning, because they are children of God. ¹⁰So now we can tell who are children of God and who are children of the devil. Anyone who does not live righteously and does not love other believers* does not belong to God.

¹¹This is the message you have heard from the beginning: We should love one another. ¹²We must not be like Cain, who belonged to the evil one and killed his brother. And why did he kill him? Because Cain had been doing what was evil, and his brother had been doing what was righteous. ¹³So don't be surprised, dear brothers and sisters,* if the world hates you.

¹⁴If we love our Christian brothers and sisters,* it proves that we have passed from death to life. But a person who has no love is still dead. ¹⁵Anyone who hates another brother or sister* is really a murderer at heart. And you know that murderers don't have eternal life within them.

¹⁶We know what real love is because Jesus gave up his life for us. So we also ought to give up our lives for our brothers and sisters. ¹⁷If someone has enough money to live well and sees a brother or sister* in need but shows no compassion— how can God's love be in that person?

¹⁸Dear children, let's not merely say that we love each other; let us show the truth by our actions.

3:9 Greek *because his seed.*   **3:10** Greek *does not love his brother.*   **3:13** Greek *brothers.*   **3:14** Greek *the brothers;* similarly in 3:16.   **3:15** Greek *hates his brother.*   **3:17** Greek *sees his brother.*

People who love Jesus and have accepted him as Savior (1) don't continue to live a sinful life, and (2) love other Christians. It's really important for your life to show that Christ has forgiven your sins. If you are Jesus' follower, you should notice that he is helping you not to sin and that he is giving you his love for other people. Is your life like that? If you aren't sure, tell Jesus that you believe in him and want him to save you. Then get ready for a new kind of life filled with God's love!

The second [commandment] is equally important: "Love your neighbor as yourself."* No other commandment is greater than these. MARK 12:31
12:31 Lev 19:18.

DECEMBER 26

God Hears

As Christians we can be sure that we have eternal life. We can also be sure that God is listening to our prayers. Read what John wrote about how we can know this.

1 John 5:1-15
Everyone who believes that Jesus is the Christ* has become a child of God. And everyone who loves the Father loves his children, too. ²We know we love God's children if we love God and obey his commandments. ³Loving God means keeping his commandments, and his commandments are not burdensome. ⁴For every child of God defeats this evil world, and we achieve this victory through our faith. ⁵And who can win this battle against the world? Only those who believe that Jesus is the Son of God.

⁶And Jesus Christ was revealed as God's Son by his baptism in water and by shedding his blood on the cross*—not by water only, but by water and blood. And the Spirit, who is truth, confirms it with his testimony. ⁷So we have these three witnesses*—⁸the Spirit, the water, and the blood—and all three agree. ⁹Since we believe human testimony, surely we can believe the greater testimony that comes from God. And God has testified about his Son. ¹⁰All who believe in the Son of God know in their hearts that this testimony is true. Those who don't believe this are actually calling God a liar because they don't believe what God has testified about his Son.

¹¹And this is what God has testified: He has given us eternal life, and this life is in his Son. ¹²Whoever has the Son has life; whoever does not have God's Son does not have life.

¹³I have written this to you who believe in the name of the Son of God, so that you

may know you have eternal life. ¹⁴And we are confident that he hears us whenever we ask for anything that pleases him.

¹⁵And since we know he hears us when we make our requests, we also know that he will give us what we ask for.

5:1 Or *the Messiah.*   5:6 Greek *This is he who came by water and blood.*   5:7 A few very late manuscripts add *in heaven—the Father, the Word, and the Holy Spirit, and these three are one. And we have three witnesses on earth.*

John said that the Holy Spirit helps us believe in Jesus. If we believe in Jesus, the Holy Spirit is in us, helping to make us sure we have eternal life. John also said that we can be confident God hears our prayers when they are in line with his will. As you learn to love Jesus more and more, the things you want to ask God for will be the things he wants you to have. What do you need to pray about today?

Listen to my cry for help, my King and my God, for I pray to no one but you.
PSALM 5:2

DECEMBER 27

walk in Love

John urged Christians to love others. Why did he do this?

2 John 1:1-11

This letter is from John, the elder.*

I am writing to the chosen lady and to her children,* whom I love in the truth—as does everyone else who knows the truth— ²because the truth lives in us and will be with us forever.

³Grace, mercy, and peace, which come from God the Father and from Jesus Christ—the Son of the Father—will continue to be with us who live in truth and love.

⁴How happy I was to meet some of your children and find them living according to the truth, just as the Father commanded. ⁵I am writing to remind you, dear friends,* that we should love one another. This is not a new commandment, but one we have had from the beginning. ⁶Love means doing what God has commanded us, and he has commanded us to love one another, just as you heard from the beginning.

⁷I say this because many deceivers have gone out into the world. They deny that Jesus Christ came* in a real body. Such a person is a deceiver and an antichrist. ⁸Watch out that you do not lose what we* have worked so hard to achieve. Be diligent so that you receive your full reward. ⁹Anyone who wanders away from this teaching has no relationship with God. But anyone who remains in the teaching of Christ has a relationship with both the Father and the Son.

¹⁰If anyone comes to your meeting and does not teach the truth about Christ,

don't invite that person into your home or give any kind of encouragement. ¹¹Anyone who encourages such people becomes a partner in their evil work.

1a Greek *From the elder*. 1b Or *the church God has chosen and its members*. 5 Greek *I urge you, lady*. 7 Or *will come*. 8 Some manuscripts read *you*.

John wrote that the most important commandment God has given us is to love one another. We show that we really are followers of God when we obey this commandment. Do you love the other Christians you know? Ask God to help you obey his commandment to love the people around you.

Pure and genuine religion in the sight of God the Father means caring for orphans and widows in their distress and refusing to let the world corrupt you.
JAMES 1:27

DECEMBER 28
Hang In There
Jude warned his readers about those who were trying to divide the church. What advice did he give them?

Jude 1:14-25

Enoch, who lived in the seventh generation after Adam, prophesied about these people. He said, "Listen! The Lord is coming with countless thousands of his holy ones ¹⁵to execute judgment on the people of the world. He will convict every person of all the ungodly things they have done and for all the insults that ungodly sinners have spoken against him."*

¹⁶These people are grumblers and complainers, living only to satisfy their desires. They brag loudly about themselves, and they flatter others to get what they want.

¹⁷But you, my dear friends, must remember what the apostles of our Lord Jesus Christ said. ¹⁸They told you that in the last times there would be scoffers whose purpose in life is to satisfy their ungodly desires. ¹⁹These people are the ones who are creating divisions among you. They follow their natural instincts because they do not have God's Spirit in them.

²⁰But you, dear friends, must build each other up in your most holy faith, pray in the power of the Holy Spirit,* ²¹and await the mercy of our Lord Jesus Christ, who will bring you eternal life. In this way, you will keep yourselves safe in God's love.

²²And you must show mercy to* those whose faith is wavering. ²³Rescue others by snatching them from the flames of judgment. Show mercy to still others,* but do so with great caution, hating the sins that contaminate their lives.*

²⁴Now all glory to God, who is able to keep you from falling away and will bring you with great joy into his glorious pres-

ence without a single fault. ²⁵All glory to him who alone is God, our Savior through Jesus Christ our Lord. All glory, majesty, power, and authority are his before all time, and in the present, and beyond all time! Amen.

14-15 The quotation comes from intertestamental literature: Enoch 1:9. **20** Greek *pray in the Holy Spirit.* **22** Some manuscripts read *must reprove.* **22-23a** Some manuscripts have only two categories of people: (1) those whose faith is wavering and therefore need to be snatched from the flames of judgment, and (2) those who need to be shown mercy. **23b** Greek *with fear, hating even the clothing stained by the flesh.*

Jude told believers to continue to live in a way that pleases God. What does that mean for you? It means obeying God's commands in the Bible. It means listening to the Holy Spirit as he leads you to pray about certain people and things. It means showing kindness to others and sharing your faith with them. Living a life like that pleases God.

You who love the LORD, hate evil! He protects the lives of his godly people and rescues them from the power of the wicked. PSALM 97:10

DECEMBER 29

AN AWESOME GOD

John saw a vision of Jesus in all his power and glory. How do you think John felt when he saw Jesus?

Revelation 1:1-19

This is a revelation from* Jesus Christ, which God gave him to show his servants the events that must soon* take place. He sent an angel to present this revelation to his servant John, ²who faithfully reported everything he saw. This is his report of the word of God and the testimony of Jesus Christ.

³God blesses the one who reads the words of this prophecy to the church, and he blesses all who listen to its message and obey what it says, for the time is near.

⁴This letter is from John to the seven churches in the province of Asia.* Grace and peace to you from the one who is, who always was, and who is still to come; from the sevenfold Spirit* before his throne; ⁵and from Jesus Christ. He is the faithful witness to these things, the first to rise from the dead, and the ruler of all the kings of the world.

All glory to him who loves us and has freed us from our sins by shedding his blood for us. ⁶He has made us a Kingdom of priests for God his Father. All glory and power to him forever and ever! Amen.

⁷Look! He comes with the clouds of heaven.
And everyone will see him—
even those who pierced him.
And all the nations of the world
will mourn for him.
Yes! Amen!

⁸"I am the Alpha and the Omega—the beginning and the end,"* says the Lord God. "I am the one who is, who always was,

and who is still to come—the Almighty One."

⁹I, John, am your brother and your partner in suffering and in God's Kingdom and in the patient endurance to which Jesus calls us. I was exiled to the island of Patmos for preaching the word of God and for my testimony about Jesus. ¹⁰It was the Lord's Day, and I was worshiping in the Spirit.* Suddenly, I heard behind me a loud voice like a trumpet blast. ¹¹It said, "Write in a book* everything you see, and send it to the seven churches in the cities of Ephesus, Smyrna, Pergamum, Thyatira, Sardis, Philadelphia, and Laodicea."

¹²When I turned to see who was speaking to me, I saw seven gold lampstands. ¹³And standing in the middle of the lampstands was someone like the Son of Man.* He was wearing a long robe with a gold sash across his chest. ¹⁴His head and his hair were white like wool, as white as snow. And his eyes were like flames of fire. ¹⁵His feet were like polished bronze refined in a furnace, and his voice thundered like mighty ocean waves. ¹⁶He held seven stars in his right hand, and a sharp two-edged sword came from his mouth. And his face was like the sun in all its brilliance.

¹⁷When I saw him, I fell at his feet as if I were dead. But he laid his right hand on me and said, "Don't be afraid! I am the First and the Last. ¹⁸I am the living one. I died, but look—I am alive forever and ever! And I hold the keys of death and the grave.*

¹⁹"Write down what you have seen—both the things that are now happening and the things that will happen.*'"

1:1a Or *of*.   1:1b Or *suddenly*, or *quickly*.   1:4a *Asia* was a Roman province in what is now western Turkey.   1:4b Greek *the seven spirits*.   1:8 Greek *I am the Alpha and the Omega*, referring to the first and last letters of the Greek alphabet.   1:10 Or *in spirit*.   1:11 Or *on a scroll*.   1:13 Or *like a son of man*. See Dan 7:13. "Son of Man" is a title Jesus used for himself.   1:18 Greek *and Hades*.   1:19 Or *what you have seen and what they mean—the things that have already begun to happen*.

We know that Jesus is the King over all kings. We know that he is the first and the last, the A and the Z, and that he is the holy and powerful Son of God. But we haven't actually seen Jesus in his glory the way John did. Jesus was so amazing that John was afraid. All he could do was fall down at Jesus' feet to worship him. When Jesus returns to earth, everyone will see him in all his glory and power, and we will respond like John, falling down to worship Jesus. Think about John's description and practice worshiping Jesus now.

The LORD's fame will be celebrated in Zion, his praises in Jerusalem, when multitudes gather together and kingdoms come to worship the LORD.
PSALM 102:21-22

DECEMBER 30

everything made new

When Jesus comes again, he will create a new heaven and a new earth. Read about what the new creation will be like.

Revelation 21:1-12, 22-27

Then I saw a new heaven and a new earth, for the old heaven and the old earth had disappeared. And the sea was also gone. ²And I saw the holy city, the new Jerusalem, coming down from God out of heaven like a bride beautifully dressed for her husband.

³I heard a loud shout from the throne, saying, "Look, God's home is now among his people! He will live with them, and they will be his people. God himself will be with them.* ⁴He will wipe every tear from their eyes, and there will be no more death or sorrow or crying or pain. All these things are gone forever."

⁵And the one sitting on the throne said, "Look, I am making everything new!" And then he said to me, "Write this down, for what I tell you is trustworthy and true." ⁶And he also said, "It is finished! I am the Alpha and the Omega—the Beginning and the End. To all who are thirsty I will give freely from the springs of the water of life. ⁷All who are victorious will inherit all these blessings, and I will be their God, and they will be my children.

⁸"But cowards, unbelievers, the corrupt, murderers, the immoral, those who practice witchcraft, idol worshipers, and all liars—their fate is in the fiery lake of burning sulfur. This is the second death."

⁹Then one of the seven angels who held the seven bowls containing the seven last plagues came and said to me, "Come with me! I will show you the bride, the wife of the Lamb."

¹⁰So he took me in the Spirit* to a great, high mountain, and he showed me the holy city, Jerusalem, descending out of heaven from God. ¹¹It shone with the glory of God and sparkled like a precious stone—like jasper as clear as crystal. ¹²The city wall was broad and high, with twelve gates guarded by twelve angels. And the names of the twelve tribes of Israel were written on the gates.

◉

²²I saw no temple in the city, for the Lord God Almighty and the Lamb are its temple. ²³And the city has no need of sun or moon, for the glory of God illuminates the city, and the Lamb is its light. ²⁴The nations will walk in its light, and the kings of the world will enter the city in all their glory. ²⁵Its gates will never be closed at the end of day because there is no night there. ²⁶And all the nations will bring their glory and honor into the city. ²⁷Nothing evil* will be allowed to enter, nor anyone who practices shameful idolatry and dishonesty—but only those whose names are written in the Lamb's Book of Life.

21:3 Some manuscripts read *God himself will be with them, their God.*   21:10 Or *in spirit.*   21:27 Or *ceremonially unclean.*

The new heaven and earth will be perfect! There won't be any darkness or sadness or pain or death. Those who believe in Jesus will live with him forever. When you feel overwhelmed by trouble in this life, think about what heaven will be like and have hope. One day Jesus will greatly reward his servants. Believe in Jesus and look forward to life in heaven with him.

Surely righteous people are praising [the Lord's] name; the godly will live in your presence. PSALM 140:13

DECEMBER 31
The words of God
Jesus told John to share with other people the message Jesus had given to him. What was Jesus' message?

Revelation 22:1-20
Then the angel showed me a river with the water of life, clear as crystal, flowing from the throne of God and of the Lamb. ²It flowed down the center of the main street. On each side of the river grew a tree of life, bearing twelve crops of fruit,* with a fresh crop each month. The leaves were used for medicine to heal the nations.

³No longer will there be a curse upon anything. For the throne of God and of the Lamb will be there, and his servants will worship him. ⁴And they will see his face, and his name will be written on their foreheads. ⁵And there will be no night there—no need for lamps or sun—for the Lord God will shine on them. And they will reign forever and ever.

⁶Then the angel said to me, "Everything you have heard and seen is trustworthy and true. The Lord God, who inspires his prophets,* has sent his angel to tell his servants what will happen soon.*"

⁷"Look, I am coming soon! Blessed are those who obey the words of prophecy written in this book.*"

⁸I, John, am the one who heard and saw all these things. And when I heard and saw them, I fell down to worship at the feet of the angel who showed them to me. ⁹But he said, "No, don't worship me. I am a servant of God, just like you and your brothers the prophets, as well as all who obey what is written in this book. Worship only God!"

¹⁰Then he instructed me, "Do not seal up the prophetic words in this book, for the time is near. ¹¹Let the one who is doing harm continue to do harm; let the one who is vile continue to be vile; let the one who is righteous continue to live righteously; let the one who is holy continue to be holy."

¹²"Look, I am coming soon, bringing my reward with me to repay all people according to their deeds. ¹³I am the Alpha and the Omega, the First and the Last, the Beginning and the End."

¹⁴Blessed are those who wash their robes. They will be permitted to enter through the gates of the city and eat the fruit from the tree of life. ¹⁵Outside the city are the dogs—the sorcerers, the sexually immoral, the murderers, the idol worshipers, and all who love to live a lie.

¹⁶"I, Jesus, have sent my angel to give you this message for the churches. I am both the source of David and the heir to his throne.* I am the bright morning star."

¹⁷The Spirit and the bride say, "Come." Let anyone who hears this say, "Come." Let anyone who is thirsty come. Let anyone who desires drink freely from the water of life. ¹⁸And I solemnly declare to everyone who hears the words of prophecy written in this book: If anyone adds anything to what is written here, God will add to that person the plagues described in this book. ¹⁹And if anyone removes any of the words from this book of prophecy, God will remove that person's share in the tree of life and in the holy city that are described in this book.

²⁰He who is the faithful witness to all these things says, "Yes, I am coming soon!"

Amen! Come, Lord Jesus!

22:2 Or *twelve kinds of fruit.* 22:6a Or *The Lord, the God of the spirits of the prophets.* 22:6b Or *suddenly,* or *quickly;* also in 22:7, 12, 20. 22:7 Or *scroll;* also in 22:9, 10, 18, 19. 22:16 Greek *I am the root and offspring of David.*

Jesus urged everyone to come to him for eternal life. Those who come to Jesus will live with him forever in a place of beauty and peace. Have you come to Jesus yet? Don't delay. Time is short.

Surely [God's] goodness and unfailing love will pursue me all the days of my life, and I will live in the house of the LORD forever. PSALM 23:6

DECEMBER CHALLENGE
you did it!

CONGRATULATIONS! You're all done! If you started reading in January, you've read all the way from Genesis to Revelation. Now that you've successfully met that challenge, how about looking for another one-year book of devotions? Reading God's Word is a habit you'll want to continue throughout your life.

If you started this book at another time of the year, you can go back to the beginning of this book on January 1 and keep going until you have finished all of the readings. Nothing is too hard to finish when you ask God to help you.

To show that you've finished the December readings, find a red, green, or gold marker, and fill in the level you completed.

You have learned so much about who God is and how you should live because of what you believe. What is the most important lesson you learned this month?

How about wrapping up a box in leftover Christmas paper and putting a gift card on it from God to you? Keep it in your room as a reminder of God's many gifts to you, including his gift of the Bible.

IMPORTANT STUFF TO REMEMBER FROM DECEMBER

☐ A Christian's life should show that he or she is a follower of Jesus.

☐ It's important to try to control the words you say.

☐ Jesus will come back someday soon to be the King of earth and heaven.

e very last book of the Bible is Revelation. In it, Jesus talks about the end of the
rld. In the puzzle below, cross out every third letter to see what he promises to his
owers. (The words are from Revelation 22:12, which you'll find in the December 31
ding.)

L O H O K R I A N M C B O M V I N Y G

S W O O A N B H R I T N G X I N R G M

K Y R L E W J A R C D W P I T F H M D

E T H O R U E P B A Y D A L F L P T E

O Q P L I E A N C C K O R G D I Z N G

L T O H T H Y E I J R D M E E F D S.

465

who is God?

God Is the Creator

He created everything—even you!

Come, let us worship and bow down. Let us kneel before the LORD our maker.
(Psalm 95:6)

The LORD is the everlasting God, the Creator of all the earth. (Isaiah 40:28)

God Is Father, Son, and Holy Spirit

God is one God, but three separate persons all at the same time.

God the Father is a loving dad who wants all of us to be part of his family.

You received God's Spirit when he adopted you as his own children. Now we call him,
"Abba, Father." (Romans 8:15)

God the Son—Jesus—came to earth to be our Savior. He saves everyone who asks
him for forgiveness. If you believe in Jesus and follow him, God will save you, and you
will live with him in heaven forever.

For God loved the world so much that he gave his one and only Son, so that everyone
who believes in him will not perish but have eternal life. (John 3:16)

God the Holy Spirit lives in us when we believe in Jesus. He helps us live for Jesus
and keeps us safe from all that is evil.

When you believed in Christ, he identified you as his own by giving you the Holy
Spirit, whom he promised long ago. (Ephesians 1:13)

God Is the Holy One

He is completely different from any person. He is perfect and does not sin.

Holy, holy, holy is the LORD of Heaven's Armies! The whole earth is filled with his
glory! (Isaiah 6:3)

Who will not fear you, Lord, and glorify your name? For you alone are holy. All
nations will come and worship before you. (Revelation 15:4)

God Is Powerful

He is stronger than any person or machine. He controls everything.

O LORD God of Heaven's Armies! Where is there anyone as mighty as you, O LORD?
(Psalm 89:8)

I am the LORD, the God of all the peoples of the world. Is anything too hard for me?
(Jeremiah 32:27)

467

God Is Everywhere

He has promised that he will never leave us.

The LORD your God is with you wherever you go. (Joshua 1:9)

God Knows Everything

He knows everything about you—the good and the bad. He is pleased with all that's good, but even the bad doesn't keep him from caring about you.

All that I know now is partial and incomplete, but then I will know everything completely, just as God now knows me completely. (1 Corinthians 13:12)

God Is Love

He loves you and cares for you so much that he will provide everything you need.

Look at the birds. They don't plant or harvest or store food in barns, for your heavenly Father feeds them. And aren't you far more valuable to him than they are? . . . And why worry about your clothing? Look at the lilies of the field and how they grow. They don't work or make their clothing, yet Solomon in all his glory was not dressed as beautifully as they are. And if God cares so wonderfully for wildflowers that are here today and thrown into the fire tomorrow, he will certainly care for you. (Matthew 6:26-30)

God Is Forgiving

God forgives you when you're sorry for the wrong things you've done—the "little sins," the "big sins," and everything in between. He is waiting patiently, giving everyone time to come to him for salvation before Jesus returns to earth.

The Lord isn't really being slow about his promise, as some people think. No, he is being patient for your sake. He does not want anyone to be destroyed, but wants everyone to repent. (2 Peter 3:9)

God Is the Fair Judge

God is just and fair. He doesn't play favorites, and he will do what's right when he judges everyone at the end of the world.

He will judge the world with justice and rule the nations with fairness. (Psalm 9:8)

The laws of the LORD are true; each one is fair. (Psalm 19:9)

God Is Kind

The Bible uses several different words to describe God's kindness.

God is gracious, offering us his kindness (or *grace*) even though we don't deserve it.

Oh, how generous and gracious our Lord was! He filled me with the faith and love that come from Christ Jesus. (1 Timothy 1:14)

God is merciful. That means he is kind even though he is more powerful than we are and wouldn't have to be kind.

The LORD your God is a merciful God; he will not abandon you. (Deuteronomy 4:31)

He saved us, not because of the righteous things we had done, but because of his mercy. (Titus 3:5)

God is also compassionate. That means he is sad when you're sad and hurts when you hurt. He is not only *able* to help you—he *wants* to do it!

The LORD is good to everyone. He showers compassion on all his creation. (Psalm 145:9)

who is jesus?

Jesus Is God

Jesus is the Son of God. He is completely God, but at the same time he became completely human. He came to help us know God the Father.

We know that the Son of God has come, and he has given us understanding so that we can know the true God. (1 John 5:20)

Jesus is the Messiah, the Christ. He is the one God promised to send to Israel.

The woman said, "I know the Messiah is coming—the one who is called Christ. When he comes, he will explain everything to us." Then Jesus told her, "I AM the Messiah!" (John 4:25-26)

Jesus is our Savior. He died on the cross to save us from our sins. Those who believe in him will have eternal life with him in heaven.

He personally carried our sins in his body on the cross so that we can be dead to sin and live for what is right. (1 Peter 2:24)

The Father sent his Son to be the Savior of the world. (1 John 4:14)

Jesus Lived on Earth

Jesus called people to turn away from their sins—to repent—and follow him.

I have come to call not those who think they are righteous, but those who know they are sinners and need to repent. (Luke 5:32)

Jesus taught people about the Kingdom of God.

The Kingdom of Heaven is like a treasure that a man discovered hidden in a field. In his excitement, he hid it again and sold everything he owned to get enough money to buy the field. (Matthew 13:44)

Jesus healed the sick.

In one of the villages, Jesus met a man with an advanced case of leprosy. When the man saw Jesus, he bowed with his face to the ground, begging to be healed. "Lord," he said, "if you are willing, you can heal me and make me clean." Jesus reached out and touched him. "I am willing," he said. "Be healed!" And instantly the leprosy disappeared. (Luke 5:12-13)

Jesus showed compassion to sinners.

Jesus saw the huge crowd as he stepped from the boat, and he had compassion on them because they were like sheep without a shepherd. So he began teaching them many things. (Mark 6:34)

Jesus Helps You Today

Jesus took the punishment for sin that we deserved.

Our old sinful selves were crucified with Christ so that sin might lose its power in our lives. We are no longer slaves to sin. For when we died with Christ we were set free from the power of sin. And since we died with Christ, we know we will also live with him. We are sure of this because Christ was raised from the dead, and he will never die again. Death no longer has any power over him. (Romans 6:6-9)

Jesus gives you the power to resist temptation.

We know that God's children do not make a practice of sinning, for God's Son holds them securely, and the evil one cannot touch them. (1 John 5:18)

Jesus forgives your sin.

If we confess our sins to him, he is faithful and just to forgive us our sins and to cleanse us from all wickedness. (1 John 1:9)

Jesus gives you the gift of eternal life. In the following prayer, Jesus talks to God about himself and the authority God has given him.

You have given him [Jesus] authority over everyone. He gives eternal life to each one you have given him. (John 17:2)

Jesus sends you the Holy Spirit as his representative to stand by you (be your Advocate) and live in you. The Holy Spirit shows you what is true.

When the Father sends the Advocate as my representative—that is, the Holy Spirit— he will teach you everything and will remind you of everything I have told you. (John 14:26)

when you are tempted

Everyone is tempted at some point—even Jesus was tempted. It is not a sin to be tempted, but it is wrong to give in to temptation. With God's help, we can resist when we're tempted and make the right decision, just like Jesus did. Here's how:

Pray. This is the most important thing you can do. Only God can provide the strength to resist temptation. God will show you a way out of the tough situation you're facing and help you make the right choice.

The temptations in your life are no different from what others experience. And God is faithful. He will not allow the temptation to be more than you can stand. When you are tempted, he will show you a way out so that you can endure. (1 Corinthians 10:13)

Say no! You can even say it out loud. Tell God you're going to listen to him, not to Satan. The things you've learned from God's Word will help you know what's best to do. In Luke 4:1-13 you can read how Jesus quoted Scripture when he was tempted.

Humble yourselves before God. Resist the devil, and he will flee from you. (James 4:7)

Run. Sometimes you might just need to get out of there! Ask God to help you leave tempting situations like Joseph did when he ran from Potiphar's wife.

Run from anything that stimulates youthful lusts. Instead, pursue righteous living, faithfulness, love, and peace. Enjoy the companionship of those who call on the Lord with pure hearts. (2 Timothy 2:22)

The Prayer Jesus Taught

In Matthew 6:9-13, Jesus gave all of his followers a model for their prayers. That model has four basic subjects to include:

1. Spend time praising and thanking God.

Praise God for who he is—tell him how awesome it is that he is so great, perfect, and loving. Then thank him for what he has done for you. You may want to start by thanking him for your home, family, food, clothing, and friends. (*Matthew 6:9-10*)

2. Ask God for what you need.

Ask God to give you everything you need each day, including friends who will encourage you to follow him. Remember that not everything you *want* is something you *need*. (*Matthew 6:11*)

3. Ask God for forgiveness.

Ask God to forgive all your sins—both the ones you know about and the ones you don't. Have you been trying to forget some of them? Ask God to show you if you need help remembering sometimes. (*Matthew 6:12*)

4. Ask God for protection.

Ask God to protect you from evil and to give you strength to resist temptation. Ask him for help to know what is right and for the power to do it. (*Matthew 6:13*)

Below is Jesus' prayer from the Bible. But remember that prayer is really just talking to God and listening to what he says. Your words don't need to sound exactly the same as these—you can use your own words. Jesus' prayer is simply an example of how to include all of the topics he wants you to pray about.

Our Father in heaven,
*   may your name be kept holy.*
May your Kingdom come soon.
May your will be done on earth,

as it is in heaven.
Give us today the food we need,
and forgive us our sins,
as we have forgiven those who sin against us.
And don't let us yield to temptation,
but rescue us from the evil one.

(Matthew 6:9-13)

God Promises . . .

Everyone knows what it's like to be let down by a friend or family member. Others may disappoint you, but God will never let you down. Look at what God has promised you!

God promises everlasting life to all who believe in Jesus:

I have written this to you who believe in the name of the Son of God, so that you may know you have eternal life. (1 John 5:13)

God promises to never leave those who believe in him:

My sheep listen to my voice; I know them, and they follow me. I give them eternal life, and they will never perish. No one can snatch them away from me. (John 10:27-28)

I am convinced that nothing can ever separate us from God's love. (Romans 8:38)

God promises to hear and answer your prayers:

If my people who are called by my name will humble themselves and pray and seek my face and turn from their wicked ways, I will hear from heaven and will forgive their sins and restore their land. (2 Chronicles 7:14)

We are confident that he hears us whenever we ask for anything that pleases him. And since we know he hears us when we make our requests, we also know that he will give us what we ask for. (1 John 5:14-15)

God promises to forgive your sins:

I will forgive their wickedness, and I will never again remember their sins. (Hebrews 8:12)

God promises to meet all your needs:

This same God who takes care of me will supply all your needs from his glorious riches, which have been given to us in Christ Jesus. (Philippians 4:19)

God promises to give you wisdom:

If you need wisdom, ask our generous God, and he will give it to you. He will not rebuke you for asking. (James 1:5)

God promises to give you strength and courage:

Don't be afraid, for I am with you. Don't be discouraged, for I am your God. I will strengthen you and help you. I will hold you up with my victorious right hand. (Isaiah 41:10)

God promises that he has a plan for you:

*"I know the plans I have for you," says the L*ORD*. "They are plans for good and not for disaster, to give you a future and a hope." (Jeremiah 29:11)*

when i've done something wrong

All of us do things that are wrong at one time or another. Sometimes we do things on purpose, like making fun of a younger brother. Other times it's not on purpose, like hurting a friend's feelings. But there's good news! In 1 John 1:9, God promises that if we confess what we've done wrong, he will forgive us. Forgiveness is kind of like washing away dirt. If a window in a house gets too dirty, the owner isn't pleased because the window isn't useful. No one can see through it until the owner gets a rag and cleans the dirt away. In the same way, God's forgiveness cleans away the dirt of our sins so we can please him and be useful to him.

Any time you find yourself getting dirty from sin and wondering how to make things right with God, you can follow these steps.

1. Tell God what you have done wrong. He already knows . . . and he wants you to turn to him, even when you sin.

God . . . commands everyone everywhere to repent of their sins and turn to him. (Acts 17:30)

2. Ask God to forgive you. He has promised to forgive those who turn away from what's wrong.

If we confess our sins to him, he is faithful and just to forgive us our sins and to cleanse us from all wickedness. (1 John 1:9)

3. Ask God to help you not to sin again. God's own Son, Jesus, was tempted, so he understands the temptations you face and can help you keep from sinning again and again.

All sin is contrary to the law of God. And you know that Jesus came to take away our sins, and there is no sin in him. Anyone who continues to live in him will not sin. (1 John 3:4-6)

4. Ask any person you may have wronged to forgive you. Jesus tells you not only to ask *God* for forgiveness, but to ask *others* for forgiveness too.

If you are presenting a sacrifice at the altar in the Temple and you suddenly remember that someone has something against you, leave your sacrifice there at the altar. Go and be reconciled to that person. Then come and offer your sacrifice to God. (Matthew 5:23-24)

Not sure where to start?

Here is a prayer you can pray after you have sinned:

Dear God,
    I have done something wrong.
    I'm sorry. Will you please forgive me?
    And help me not to do it again.
    Lord, thank you for forgiving me.
    And thanks for helping me choose to do what's right the next time I'm tempted.
In Jesus' name. Amen.

when everything is going wrong

Have you ever had a bad day—and then it got worse? Your sister tore up your homework. Then your best friend sat with someone else at lunch. And to top that off, the neighborhood bully stole your favorite hat on the way home from school. Everything went wrong! What do you do?

Remember:

God loves you.

This is real love—not that we loved God, but that he loved us and sent his Son as a sacrifice to take away our sins. (1 John 4:10)

God is in control of your situation and has a good plan for you—even if you don't see it.

God causes everything to work together for the good of those who love God and are called according to his purpose for them. (Romans 8:28)

God wants you to learn from tough situations.

These trials will show that your faith is genuine. It is being tested as fire tests and purifies gold—though your faith is far more precious than mere gold. (1 Peter 1:7)

God wants to help you.

God is our refuge and strength, always ready to help in times of trouble. (Psalm 46:1)

Pray:

Ask God to help you learn what he's teaching you.

Look, God is all-powerful. Who is a teacher like him? (Job 36:22)

Ask God to give you power and wisdom—you might need lots of patience with other people or lots of help making some important choices.

Seek his will in all you do, and he will show you which path to take. Don't be impressed with your own wisdom. Instead, fear the LORD and turn away from evil. (Proverbs 3:6-7)

Ask God to help you trust him—sometimes that's the hardest part. But God's ready to help you trust.

Trust in the LORD with all your heart; do not depend on your own understanding.
  (Proverbs 3:5)

Ask:

Don't be nervous about asking for help. Everyone has bad days.

Plans go wrong for lack of advice; many advisers bring success. (Proverbs 15:22)

You can ask for help from an older sister or brother, one of your parents, or even a teacher.

Two people are better off than one, for they can help each other succeed. If one person falls, the other can reach out and help. (Ecclesiastes 4:9-10)